Neil Gaiman is the author of over thirty accl
received many literary honours. Born and rai
England and dreams of endless libraries.

Praise for Neil Gaiman:

'A very fine and imaginative writer' *The Sunday Times*

'Both a pitch-perfect fantasy and a moving examination of childhood memories and their effects on our adult selves . . . superb' *The Times*

'In prose as delicate and diaphanous as a cobweb, and with a painstakingly precise use of symbolism, Gaiman traces one boy's journey from innocence, through fear and regret, to experience. In doing so, he traces all of our journeys, and beautifully' *Financial Times*

'Possibly Gaiman's most lyrical, scary and beautiful work yet. It's a tale about childhood for grown-ups, a fantasy rooted in the darkest corners of reality' *Independent on Sunday*

'Gaiman has written a book that reads like a half-remembered fairy-tale from childhood. It has the easy flow of a story already heard, deeply known, and slots perfectly into the canon of British magical fiction' *New Statesman*

'A hugely satisfying scary fantasy and a moving, subtle exploration of family, of what it's really like to be a child, and how the memories of childhood affect the adults we become. It's a wonderful book' *Irish Times*

'The most affecting book Gaiman has written, a novel whose intensity of real-world observation and feeling make its other-worldly episodes doubly startling and persuasive' *Daily Telegraph*

'Extraordinary, complicated, hilarious, melancholy and terrifying' *Independent*

'Bizarre, bonkers . . . rather brilliant' Ian Hislop

'In prose that dances and dazzles, Gaiman describes the indescribable: the eerie colours, ravishing scents and dangerous laughter of Faerie' Susanna Clarke

'Neil Gaiman is a star. He constructs stories like some demented cook might make a wedding cake, building layer upon layer, including all kinds of sweet and sour in the mix' Clive Barker

'Funny, scary and perverse by turns . . . a class act and a rich and exciting read' *Time Out*

'Dark, fun and nourishing to the soul' Michael Chabon

By Neil Gaiman

American Gods
&
Anansi Boys

Neil Gaiman

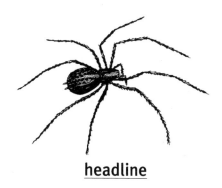

headline

American Gods first published in Great Britain in 2001 by HEADLINE BOOK PUBLISHING
Anansi Boys first published in Great Britain in 2005 by Headline Review
an imprint of HEADLINE BOOK PUBLISHING

First published in this omnibus edition in 2014 by HEADLINE PUBLISHING GROUP

1

We gratefully acknowledge the following for granting us permission to use their material in *American Gods*:

Excerpt from 'The Witch of Coos' from 'Two Witches' from *The Poetry of Robert
Frost*, edited by Edward Connery Latham, © 1951 Robert Frost, copyright 1923, 1969 by
Henry Holt and Co. Reprinted by permission of Henry Holt and Co., LLC. 'Tango Til
They're Sore' by Tom Waits. Copyright © 1985 Jalma Music. Used by permission. All
rights reserved. 'Old Friends' music and lyrics by Stephen Sondheim, © 1981 Rilting
Music, Inc. All rights reserved. Used by permission. Warner Bros. Publications US Inc.,
Miami, FL 33014. 'In the Dark With You' by Greg Brown. Copyright © 1985
Brown/Feldman Music, Hacklebarney Music/ASCAP. Used by permission. All rights
reserved. The lines from 'in Just—', copyright 1923, 1951, © 1991 Trustees for the
E. E. Cummings Trust. Copyright © 1976 George James Firmage, from *Complete Poems:
1904–1962* by E. E. Cummings, edited by George J. Firmage. Used by permission of
Liveright Publishing Corp. 'Don't let me be Misunderstood' by Bennie Benjamin, Sol
Marcus and Gloria Caldwell, © 1964 Bennie Benjamin Music Inc., © renewed, assigned
to WB Music Corp., Bennie Benjamin Music, Inc. and Chris-N-Jen Music. All rights o/b/o
Bennie Benjamin Music Inc. administered by Chappell & Co. All rights reserved. Used by
permission. Warner Bros. Publications US Inc., Miami, FL 33014. Excerpt from 'The
Second Coming' reprinted with the permission of Scribner, a division of Simon &
Schuster Inc., from *The Poems of W. B. Yeats: A New Edition*, edited by Richard J.
Finneran. Copyright © 1924 Macmillan Publishing Company; copyright renewed
© 1952 Bertha Georgie Yeats. (Every effort has been made to locate and contact
the copyright owners of material reproduced in this book. Omissions brought
to our attention will be corrected in subsequent editions.)

'Some of These Days' used in *Anansi Boys* by permission
Jerry Vogel Music Company Inc.

Cataloguing in Publication Data is available from the British Library

ISBN 978 1 4722 2020 2

Printed and bound in Great Britain by CPI Group (UK) Ltd, Croydon CR0 4YY

Headline's policy is to use papers that are natural, renewable and recyclable products and made from wood
grown in sustainable forests. The logging and manufacturing processes are expected to conform to the
environmental regulations of the country of origin.

HEADLINE PUBLISHING GROUP
An Hachette UK Company
338 Euston Road
London NW1 3BH

www.headline.co.uk
www.hachette.co.uk

American Gods

For absent friends – Kathy Acker and Roger Zelazny,
and all points between

Caveat, and Warning for Travellers

This is a work of fiction, not a guidebook. While the geography of the United States of America in this tale is not entirely imaginary – many of the landmarks in this book can be visited, paths can be followed, ways can be mapped – I have taken liberties. Fewer liberties than you might imagine, but liberties nonetheless.

Permission has neither been asked nor given for the use of real places in this story when they appear: I expect that the owners of Rock City or the House on the Rock, and the hunters who own the motel in the centre of America are as perplexed as anyone would be to find their properties here.

I have obscured the location of several of the places in this book: the town of Lakeside, for example, and the farm with the ash-tree an hour south of Blacksburg. You may look for them if you wish. You might even find them. Furthermore, it goes without saying that all of the people, living, dead and otherwise in this story are fictional or used in a fictional context. Only the gods are real.

One question that has always intrigued me is what happens to demonic beings when immigrants move from their homelands. Irish-Americans remember the fairies, Norwegian-Americans the *nisser*, Greek-Americans the *vrykólakas*, but only in relation to events remembered in the Old Country. When I once asked why such demons are not seen in America, my informants giggled confusedly and said, 'They're scared to pass the ocean, it's too far,' pointing out that Christ and the apostles never came to America.

Richard Dorson, 'A Theory For American Folklore', *American Folklore and the Historian*, (University of Chicago Press, 1971)

Part 1

Shadows

1

The boundaries of our country, sir? Why sir, on the north we are
bounded by the Aurora Borealis, on the east we are bounded by the
rising sun, on the south we are bounded by the procession of the
Equinoxes, and on the west by the Day of Judgment
– The American Joe Miller's Jest Book

Shadow had done three years in prison. He was big enough, and looked don't-fuck-with-me enough, that his biggest problem was killing time. So he kept himself in shape, and taught himself coin tricks, and thought a lot about how much he loved his wife.

The best thing – in Shadow's opinion, perhaps the only good thing – about being in prison, was a feeling of relief. The feeling that he'd plunged as low as he could plunge and he'd hit bottom. He didn't worry that the man was going to get him, because the man had got him. He was no longer scared of what tomorrow might bring, because yesterday had brought it.

It did not matter, Shadow decided, if you had done what you had been convicted of or not. In his experience everyone he met in prison was aggrieved about something: there was always something the authorities had got wrong, something they said you did when you didn't – or you didn't do quite like they said you did. What was important was that they had gotten you.

He had noticed it in the first few days, when everything, from the slang to the bad food, was new. Despite the misery and the utter skin-crawling horror of incarceration, he was breathing relief.

Shadow tried not to talk too much. Somewhere around the middle of year two he mentioned his theory to Low Key Lyesmith, his cell-mate.

Low Key, who was a grifter from Minnesota, smiled his scarred smile. 'Yeah,' he said. 'That's true. It's even better when you've been sentenced to death. That's when you remember the jokes about the guys who kicked their boots off as the noose flipped around their necks, because their friends always told them they'd die with their boots on.'

'Is that a joke?' asked Shadow.

'Damn right. Gallows humour. Best kind there is.'

'When did they last hang a man in this state?' asked Shadow.

'How the hell should I know?' Lyesmith kept his orange-blond hair pretty much shaved. You could see the lines of his skull. 'Tell you what, though. This country started going to hell when they stopped hanging folks. No gallows dirt. No gallows deals.'

Shadow shrugged. He could see nothing romantic in a death sentence.

If you didn't have a death sentence, he decided, then prison was, at best, only a temporary reprieve from life, for two reasons. First, life creeps back into prison. There are always places to go further down. Life goes on. And second, if you just hang in there, some day they're going to have to let you out.

In the beginning it was too far away for Shadow to focus on. Then it became a distant beam of hope, and he learned how to tell himself 'this too shall pass' when the prison shit went down, as prison shit always did. One day the magic door would open and he'd walk through it. So he marked off the days on his Songbirds of North America calendar, which was the only calendar they sold in the prison commissary, and the sun went down and he didn't see it and the sun came up and he didn't see it. He practised coin tricks from a book he found in the wasteland of the prison library, and he worked out, and he made lists in his head of what he'd do when he got out of prison.

Shadow's lists got shorter and shorter. After two years he had it down to three things.

First, he was going to take a bath. A real, long, serious soak, in a tub with bubbles in. Maybe read the paper, maybe not. Some days he thought one way, some days the other.

Second he was going to towel himself off, put on a robe. Maybe slippers. He liked the idea of slippers. If he smoked he would be smoking a pipe about now, but he didn't smoke. He would pick up his wife in his arms ('Puppy,' she would squeal in mock horror and real delight, 'what are you *doing*?'). He would carry her into the bedroom, and close the door. They'd call out for pizzas if they got hungry.

Third, after he and Laura had come out of the bedroom, maybe a couple of days later, he was going to keep his head down and stay out of trouble for the rest of his life.

'And then you'll be happy?' asked Low Key Lyesmith. That day they were working in the prison shop, assembling birdfeeders, which was barely more interesting than stamping out license plates.

'Call no man happy,' said Shadow, 'until he is dead.'

'Herodotus,' said Low Key. 'Hey. You're learning.'

'Who the fuck's Herodotus?' asked the Iceman, slotting together the sides of a birdfeeder, and passing it to Shadow, who bolted and screwed it tight.

'Dead Greek,' said Shadow.

'My last girlfriend was Greek,' said the Iceman. 'The shit her family ate. You would not believe. Like rice wrapped in leaves. Shit like that.'

The Iceman was the same size and shape as a Coke machine, with blue eyes and hair so blond it was almost white. He had beaten the crap out of some guy who had made the mistake of copping a feel off his girlfriend in the bar where she danced and the Iceman bounced. The guy's friends had called the police, who arrested the Iceman and ran a check on him which revealed that the Iceman had walked from a work-release program eighteen months earlier.

'So what was I supposed to do?' asked the Iceman, aggrieved, when he had told Shadow the whole sad tale. 'I'd told him she was my girlfriend. Was I supposed to let him disrespect me like that? Was I? I mean, he had his hands all over her.'

Shadow had said 'You tell 'em,' and left it at that. One thing he had learned early, you do your own time in prison. You don't do anyone else's time for them.

Keep your head down. Do your own time.

Lyesmith had loaned Shadow a battered paperback copy of

Herodotus's *Histories* several months earlier. 'It's not boring. It's cool,' he said, when Shadow protested that he didn't read books. 'Read it first, then tell me it's cool.'

Shadow had made a face, but he had started to read, and had found himself hooked against his will.

'Greeks,' said the Iceman, with disgust. 'And it ain't true what they say about them, neither. I tried giving it to my girlfriend in the ass, she almost clawed my eyes out.'

Lyesmith was transferred one day, without warning. He left Shadow his copy of Herodotus. There was a nickel hidden in the pages. Coins were contraband: you can sharpen the edges against a stone, slice open someone's face in a fight. Shadow didn't want a weapon; Shadow just wanted something to do with his hands.

Shadow was not superstitious. He did not believe in anything he could not see. Still, he could feel disaster hovering above the prison in those final weeks, just as he had felt it in the days before the robbery. There was a hollowness in the pit of his stomach which he told himself was simply a fear of going back to the world on the outside. But he could not be sure. He was more paranoid than usual, and in prison usual is very, and is a survival skill. Shadow became more quiet, more shadowy, than ever. He found himself watching the body language of the guards, of the other inmates, searching for a clue to the bad thing that was going to happen, as he was certain that it would.

A month before he was due to be released. Shadow sat in a chilly office, facing a short man with a port-wine birthmark on his forehead. They sat across a desk from each other; the man had Shadow's file open in front of him, and was holding a ballpoint pen. The end of the pen was badly chewed.

'You cold, Shadow?'

'Yes,' said Shadow. 'A little.'

The man shrugged. 'That's the system,' he said. 'Furnaces don't go on until December the first. Then they go off March the first. I don't make the rules.' He ran his forefinger down the sheet of paper stapled to the inside left of the folder. 'You're thirty-two years old?'

'Yes sir.'

'You look younger.'

'Clean living.'

'Says here you've been a model inmate.'

'I learned my lesson, sir.'

'Did you really?' He looked at Shadow intently, the birthmark on his forehead lowering. Shadow thought about telling the man some of his theories about prison, but he said nothing. He nodded, instead, and concentrated on appearing properly remorseful.

'Says here you've got a wife, Shadow.'

'Her name's Laura.'

'How's everything there?'

'Pretty good. She's come down to see me as much as she could – it's a long way to travel. We write and I call her when I can.'

'What does your wife do?'

'She's a travel agent. Sends people all over the world.'

'How'd you meet her?'

Shadow could not decide why the man was asking. He considered telling him it was none of his business, then said, 'She was my best buddy's wife's best friend. They set us up on a blind date. We hit it off.'

'And you've got a job waiting for you?'

'Yessir. My buddy, Robbie, the one I just told you about, he owns the Muscle Farm, the place I used to train. He says my old job is waiting for me.'

An eyebrow raised. 'Really?'

'Says he figures I'll be a big draw. Bring back some old timers, and pull in the tough crowd who want to be tougher.'

The man seemed satisfied. He chewed the end of his ballpoint pen, then turned over the sheet of paper.

'How do you feel about your offense?'

Shadow shrugged. 'I was stupid,' he said, and meant it.

The man with the birthmark sighed. He ticked off a number of items on a checklist. Then he riffled through the papers in Shadow's file. 'How're you getting home from here?' he asked. 'Greyhound?'

'Flying home. It's good to have a wife who's a travel agent.'

The man frowned, and the birthmark creased. 'She sent you a ticket?'

'Didn't need to. Just sent me a confirmation number. Electronic ticket. All I have to do is turn up at the airport in a month and show 'em my ID, and I'm outta here.'

The man nodded, scribbled one final note, then he closed the file and put down the ballpoint pen. Two pale hands rested on the grey desk like pink animals. He brought his hands close together, made a steeple of his forefingers, and stared at Shadow with watery hazel eyes.

'You're lucky,' he said. 'You have someone to go back to, you got a job waiting. You can put all this behind you. You got a second chance. Make the most of it.'

The man did not offer to shake Shadow's hand as he rose to leave, nor did Shadow expect him to.

The last week was the worst. In some ways it was worse than the whole three years put together. Shadow wondered if it was the weather: oppressive, still and cold. It felt as if a storm was on the way, but the storm never came. He had the jitters and the heebie-jeebies, a feeling deep in his stomach that something was entirely wrong. In the exercise yard the wind gusted. Shadow imagined that he could smell snow on the air.

He called his wife, collect. Shadow knew that the phone companies whacked a three dollar surcharge on every call made from a prison phone. That was why operators are always real polite to people calling from prisons, Shadow had decided: they knew that he paid their wages.

'Something feels weird,' he told Laura. That wasn't the first thing he said to her. The first thing was 'I love you,' because it's a good thing to say if you can mean it, and Shadow did.

'Hello,' said Laura. 'I love you too. What feels weird?'

'I don't know,' he said. 'Maybe the weather. It feels like if we could only get a storm, everything would be okay.'

'It's nice here,' she said. 'The last of the leaves haven't quite fallen. If we don't get a storm, you'll be able to see them when you get home.'

'Five days,' said Shadow.

'A hundred and twenty hours, and then you come home,' she said.

'Everything okay there? Nothing wrong?'

'Everything's fine. I'm seeing Robbie tonight. We're planning your surprise welcome-home party.'

'Surprise party?'

'Of course. You don't know anything about it, do you?'

'Not a thing.'

'That's my husband,' she said. Shadow realised that he was smiling. He had been inside for three years, but she could still make him smile.

'Love you babes,' said Shadow.

'Love you, puppy,' said Laura.

Shadow put down the phone.

When they got married Laura told Shadow that she wanted a puppy, but their landlord had pointed out they weren't allowed pets under the terms of their lease. 'Hey,' Shadow had said, 'I'll be your puppy. What do you want me to do? Chew your slippers? Piss on the kitchen floor? Lick your nose? Sniff your crotch? I bet there's nothing a puppy can do I can't do!' And he picked her up as if she weighed nothing at all, and began to lick her nose while she giggled and shrieked, and then he carried her to the bed.

In the food hall Sam Fetisher sidled over to Shadow and smiled, showing his old teeth. He sat down beside Shadow, and began to eat his macaroni and cheese.

'We got to talk,' said Sam Fetisher.

Sam Fetisher was one of the blackest men that Shadow had ever seen. He might have been sixty. He might have been eighty. Then again, Shadow had met thirty-year-old crackheads who looked older than Sam Fetisher.

'Mm?' said Shadow.

'Storm's on the way,' said Sam.

'Feels like it,' said Shadow, 'Maybe it'll snow soon.'

'Not that kind of storm. Bigger storms than that coming. I tell you, boy, you're better off in here than out on the street when the big storm comes.'

'Done my time,' said Shadow. 'Friday, I'm gone.'

Sam Fetisher stared at Shadow. 'Where you from?' he asked.

'Eagle Point. Indiana.'

'You're a lying fuck,' said Sam Fetisher. 'I mean originally. Where are your folks from?'

'Chicago,' said Shadow. His mother had lived in Chicago as a girl, and she had died there, half a lifetime ago.

'Like I said. Big storm coming. Keep your head down, Shadow-boy. It's like . . . what do they call those things continents ride around on? Some kind of plates?'

'Tectonic plates?' Shadow hazarded.

'That's it. Tectonic plates. It's like when they go riding, when North America goes skidding into South America, you don't want to be in the middle. You dig me?'

'Not even a little.'

One brown eye closed in a slow wink. 'Hell, don't say I didn't warn you,' said Sam Fetisher, and he spooned a trembling lump of orange Jell-O into his mouth.

'I won't.'

Shadow spent the night half-awake, drifting in and out of sleep, listening to his new cell-mate grunt and snore in the bunk below him. Several cells away a man whined and howled and sobbed like an animal, and from time to time someone would scream at him to shut the fuck up. Shadow tried not to hear. He let the empty minutes wash over him, lonely and slow.

Two days to go. Forty-eight hours, starting with oatmeal and prison coffee, and a guard named Wilson who tapped Shadow harder than he had to on the shoulder and said, 'Shadow? This way.'

Shadow checked his conscience. It was quiet, which did not, he had observed, in a prison, mean that he was not in deep shit. The two men walked more or less side by side, feet echoing on metal and concrete.

Shadow tasted fear in the back of his throat, bitter as old coffee. The bad thing was happening . . .

There was a voice in the back of his head whispering that they were going to slap another year onto his sentence, drop him into solitary, cut off his hands, cut off his head. He told himself he was being stupid, but his heart was pounding fit to burst out of his chest.

'I don't get you, Shadow,' said Wilson, as they walked.

'What's not to get, sir?'

'You. You're too fucking quiet. Too polite. You wait like the old guys, but you're what? Twenty-five? Twenty-eight?'

'Thirty-two, sir.'

'And what are you? A spic? A gypsy?'

'Not that I know of, sir. Maybe.'

'Maybe you got nigger blood in you. You got nigger blood in you, Shadow?'

'Could be, sir.' Shadow stood tall and looked straight ahead, and concentrated on not allowing himself to be riled by this man.

'Yeah? Well, all I know is, you fucking spook me.' Wilson had sandy blond hair and a sandy blond face and a sandy blond smile. 'You leaving us soon.'

'Hope so, sir.'

They walked through a couple of checkpoints. Wilson showed his ID each time. Up a set of stairs, and they were standing outside the prison warden's office. It had the prison warden's name – G. Patterson – on the door in black letters, and beside the door, a miniature traffic light.

The top light burned red.

Wilson pressed a button below the traffic light.

They stood there in silence for a couple of minutes. Shadow tried to tell himself that everything was all right, that on Friday morning he'd be on the plane up to Eagle Point, but he did not believe it himself.

The red light went out and the green light went on, and Wilson opened the door. They went inside.

Shadow had seen the warden a handful of times in the last three years. Once he had been showing a politician around. Once, during a lock-down, the warden had spoken to them in groups of a hundred, telling them that the prison was overcrowded, and that, since it would remain overcrowded, they had better get used to it.

Up close, Patterson looked worse. His face was oblong, with grey hair cut into a military bristle cut. He smelled of Old Spice. Behind him was a shelf of books, each with the word Prison in the title; his desk was perfectly clean, empty but for a telephone and a tear-off-the-pages *Far Side* calendar. He had a hearing aid in his right ear.

'Please, sit down.'

Shadow sat down. Wilson stood behind him.

The warden opened a desk-drawer and took out a file, placed it on his desk.

'Says here you were sentenced to six years for aggravated assault and battery. You've served three years. You were due to be released on Friday.'

Were? Shadow felt his stomach lurch inside him. He wondered how much longer he was going to have to serve – another year? Two years? All three? All he said was 'Yes, sir.'

The warden licked his lips. 'What did you say?'

'I said Yes, sir.'

'Shadow, we're going to be releasing you later this afternoon. You'll be getting out a couple of days early.' Shadow nodded, and he waited for the other shoe to drop. The warden looked down at the paper on his desk. 'This came from the Johnson Memorial Hospital in Eagle Point . . . Your wife. She died in the early hours of this morning. It was an automobile accident. I'm sorry.'

Shadow nodded once more.

Wilson walked him back to his cell, not saying anything. He unlocked the cell door and let Shadow in. Then he said, 'It's like one of them good news, bad news jokes, isn't it? Good news, we're letting you out early, bad news, your wife is dead.' He laughed, as if it were genuinely funny.

Shadow said nothing at all.

Numbly, he packed up his possessions, gave most of them away. He left behind Low Key's Herodotus, and the book of coin tricks and, with a momentary pang, he abandoned the blank metal disks he had smuggled out of the workshop which had served him for coins. There would be coins, real coins, on the outside. He shaved. He dressed in civilian clothes. He walked through door after door, knowing that he would never walk back through them again, feeling empty inside.

The rain had started to gust from the grey sky, a freezing rain. Pellets of ice stung Shadow's face, while the rain soaked the thin overcoat as they walked toward the yellow ex-school-bus that would take them to the nearest city.

By the time they got to the bus they were soaked. Eight of them were leaving. Fifteen hundred still inside. Shadow sat on the bus and shivered until the heaters started working, wondering what he was doing, where he would go now.

Ghost images filled his head, unbidden. In his imagination he was leaving another prison, long ago.

He had been imprisoned in a lightless room for far too long: his beard was wild and his hair was a tangle. The guards had walked him down a grey stone stairway and out into a plaza filled with brightly-coloured things, with people and with objects. It was a market day and he was dazzled by the noise and the colour, squinting at the sunlight that filled the square, smelling the salt-wet air and all the good things of the market, and on his left the sun glittered from the water . . .

The bus shuddered to a halt at a red light.

The wind howled about the bus, and the wipers *slooshed* heavily back and forth across the windshield, smearing the city into a red and yellow neon wetness. It was early afternoon, but it looked like night through the glass.

'Shit,' said the man in the seat behind Shadow, rubbing the condensation from the window with his hand, staring at a wet figure hurrying down the sidewalk. 'There's pussy out there.'

Shadow swallowed. It occurred to him that he had not cried yet – had in fact felt nothing at all. No tears. No sorrow. Nothing.

He found himself thinking about a guy named Johnnie Larch he'd shared a cell with when he'd first been put inside, who told Shadow how he'd once got out after five years behind bars, with $100 and a ticket to Seattle where his sister lived.

Johnnie Larch had got to the airport, and he handed his ticket to the woman on the counter, and she asked to see his driver's license.

He showed it to her. It had expired a couple of years earlier. She told him it was not valid as ID. He told her it might not be valid as a driver's license, but it sure as hell was fine identification, and damn it, who else did she think he was, if he wasn't him?

She said she'd thank him to keep his voice down.

He told her to give him a fucking boarding pass, or she was going to regret it, and that he wasn't going to be disrespected. You don't let people disrespect you in prison.

Then she pressed a button, and few moments later the airport security showed up, and they tried to persuade Johnnie Larch to leave the airport quietly, and he did not wish to leave, and there was something of an altercation.

The upshot of it all was that Johnnie Larch never actually made it to Seattle, and he spent the next couple of days in town in bars, and when his $100 was gone he held up a gas station with a toy gun for money to keep drinking, and the police finally picked him up for pissing in the street. Pretty soon he was back inside serving the rest of his sentence and a little extra for the gas station job.

And the moral of this story, according to Johnnie Larch, was this: don't piss off people who work in airports.

'Are you sure it's not something like "The kind of behavior that works in a specialised environment, such as a prison, can fail to work and in fact become harmful when used outside such an environment"?' said Shadow, when Johnnie Larch told him the story.

'No, listen to me, I'm *telling* you man,' said Johnnie Larch, 'don't piss off those bitches in airports.'

Shadow half-smiled at the memory. His own driver's license had several months still to go before it expired.

'Bus station! Everybody out!'

The building stank of piss and sour beer. Shadow climbed into a taxi and told the driver to take him to the airport. He told him that there was an extra five dollars if he could do it in silence. They made it in twenty minutes and the driver never said a word.

Then Shadow was stumbling through the brightly lit airport terminal. Shadow worried about the whole e-ticket business. He knew he had a ticket for a flight on Friday, but he didn't know if it would work today. Anything electronic seemed fundamentally magical to Shadow, and liable to evaporate at any moment.

Still, he had his wallet, back in his possession for the first time in three years, containing several expired credit cards and one Visa card which, he was pleasantly surprised to discover, didn't expire until the end of January. He had a reservation number. And, he realised, he had the certainty that once he got home everything would, somehow, be okay. Laura would be fine again. Maybe it was some kind of scam to spring him a few days early. Or perhaps it was a simple mix-up: some other Laura Moon's body had been dragged from the highway wreckage.

Lightning flickered outside the airport, through the windows-walls. Shadow realised he was holding his breath, waiting for something. A distant boom of thunder. He exhaled.

A tired white woman stared at him from behind the counter.

'Hello,' said Shadow. *You're the first strange woman I've spoken to, in the flesh, in three years.* 'I've got an e-ticket number. I was supposed to be travelling on Friday but I have to go today. There was a death in my family.'

'Mm. I'm sorry to hear that.' She tapped at the keyboard, stared at the screen, tapped again. 'No problem. I've put you on the 3:30. It may be delayed, because of the storm, so keep an eye on the screens. Checking any baggage?'

He held up a shoulder bag. 'I don't need to check this, do I?'

'No,' she said. 'It's fine. Do you have any picture ID?'

Shadow showed her his driver's license.

It was not a big airport, but the number of people wandering, just wandering, amazed him. He watched people put down bags casually, observed wallets stuffed into back pockets, saw purses put down, unwatched, under chairs. That was when he realised he was no longer in prison.

Thirty minutes to wait until boarding. Shadow bought a slice of pizza and burned his lip on the hot cheese. He took his change and went to the phones. Called Robbie at the Muscle Farm, but the machine picked up.

'Hey Robbie,' said Shadow. 'They tell me that Laura's dead. They let me out early. I'm coming home.'

Then, because people do make mistakes, he'd seen it happen, he called home, and listened to Laura's voice.

'Hi,' she said. 'I'm not here or I can't come to the phone. Leave a message and I'll get back to you. And have a *good* day.'

Shadow couldn't bring himself to leave a message.

He sat in a plastic chair by the gate, and held his bag so tight he hurt his hand.

He was thinking about the first time he had ever seen Laura. He hadn't even known her name then. She was Audrey Burton's friend. He had been sitting with Robbie in a booth at Chi-Chi's when Laura had walked in a pace or so behind Audrey, and Shadow had found himself staring. She had long, chestnut hair and eyes so blue Shadow mistakenly thought she was wearing tinted contact lenses. She had ordered a strawberry daiquiri, and insisted that Shadow taste it, and laughed delightedly when he did.

Laura loved people to taste what she tasted.

He had kissed her goodnight, that night, and she had tasted like strawberry daiquiris, and he had never wanted to kiss anyone else again.

A woman announced that his plane was boarding, and Shadow's row was the first to be called. He was in the very back, an empty seat beside him. The rain pattered continually against the side of the plane: he imagined small children tossing down dried peas by the handful from the skies.

As the plane took off he fell asleep.

Shadow was in a dark place, and the thing staring at him wore a buffalo's head, rank and furry with huge wet eyes. Its body was a man's body, oiled and slick.

'Changes are coming,' said the buffalo without moving its lips. 'There are certain decisions that will have to be made.'

Firelight flickered from wet cave walls.

'Where am I?' Shadow asked.

'In the Earth and under the Earth,' said the buffalo man. 'You are where the forgotten wait.' His eyes were liquid black marbles, and his voice was a rumble from beneath the world. He smelled like wet cow. 'Believe,' said the rumbling voice. 'If you are to survive, you must believe.'

'Believe what?' asked Shadow. 'What should I believe?'

He stared at Shadow, the buffalo man, and he drew himself up huge, and his eyes filled with fire. He opened his spit-flecked buffalo mouth and it was red inside with the flames that burned inside him, under the Earth.

'*Everything*,' roared the buffalo man.

The world tipped and spun, and Shadow was on the plane once more; but the tipping continued. In the front of the plane a woman screamed, half-heartedly.

Lightning burst in blinding flashes around the plane. The captain came on the intercom to tell them that he was going to try and gain some altitude, to get away from the storm.

The plane shook and shuddered, and Shadow wondered, coldly and idly, if he were going to die. It seemed possible, he decided, but unlikely. He stared out of the window and watched the lightning illuminate the horizon.

Then he dozed once more, and dreamed he was back in prison and that Low Key had whispered to him in the food line that someone had put out a contract on his life, but that Shadow could not find out who or why; and when he woke up they were coming in for a landing.

He stumbled off the plane, blinking into wakefulness.

All airports, he thought, look very much the same. It doesn't actually matter where you are, you are in an airport: tiles and walkways and restrooms, gates and newsstands and fluorescent lights. This airport looked like an airport. The trouble is, this wasn't the airport he was going to. This was a big airport, with way too many people, and way too many gates.

'Excuse me, ma'am?'

The woman looked at him over the clipboard. 'Yes?'

'What airport is this?'

She looked at him, puzzled, trying to decide whether or not he was joking, then she said, 'St. Louis.'

'I thought this was the plane to Eagle Point.'

'It was. They redirected it here because of the storms. Didn't they make an announcement?'

'Probably. I fell asleep.'

'You'll need to talk to that man over there, in the red coat.'

The man was almost as tall as Shadow: he looked like the father from a Seventies sitcom, and he tapped something in to a computer and told Shadow to run – *run!* – to a gate on the far side of the terminal.

Shadow ran through the airport, but the doors were already closed when he got to the gate. He watched the plane pull away from the gate, through the plate glass.

The woman at the passenger assistance desk (short and brown, with a mole on the side of her nose) consulted with another woman and made a phone call ('Nope, that one's out. They've just cancelled it.') then she printed out another boarding card. 'This will get you there,' she told him. 'We'll call ahead to the gate and tell them you're coming.'

Shadow felt like a pea being flicked between three cups, or a card being shuffled through a deck. Again he ran through the airport, ending up near where he had gotten off originally.

A small man at the gate took his boarding pass. 'We've been waiting for you,' he confided, tearing off the stub of the boarding pass, with Shadow's seat assignment – 17-D – on it. Shadow hurried onto the plane, and they closed the door behind him.

He walked through first class – there were only four first class seats, three of which were occupied. The bearded man in a pale suit seated next to the unoccupied seat at the very front grinned at Shadow as he got onto the plane, then raised his wrist and tapped his watch, as Shadow walked past.

Yeah, yeah, I'm making you late, thought Shadow. *Let that be the worst of your worries.*

The plane seemed pretty full, as he made his way down toward the back. Actually, Shadow found, it was completely full, and there was a middle-aged woman sitting in seat 17-D. Shadow showed her his boarding card stub, and she showed him hers: they matched.

'Can you take your seat, please?' asked the flight attendant.

'No,' he said, 'I'm afraid I can't.'

She clicked her tongue and checked their boarding cards, then she led him back up to the front of the plane, and pointed him to the empty seat in first class. 'Looks like it's your lucky day,' she told him. 'Can I bring you something to drink? We'll just have time before we take off. And I'm sure you need one after that.'

'I'd like a beer, please,' said Shadow. 'Whatever you've got.'

The flight attendant went away.

The man in the pale suit in the seat beside Shadow tapped his watch with his fingernail. It was a black Rolex. 'You're late,' said the man, and he grinned a huge grin with no warmth in it at all.

'Sorry?'

'I said, you're late.'

The flight attendant handed Shadow a glass of beer.

For one moment, he wondered if the man were crazy, and then he decided he must have been referring to the plane, waiting for one last passenger. 'Sorry if I held you up,' he said, politely. 'You in a hurry?'

The plane backed away from the gate. The flight attendant came back and took away Shadow's beer. The man in the pale suit grinned at her and said, 'Don't worry, I'll hold onto this tightly,' and she let him keep his glass of Jack Daniel's, while protesting, weakly, that it violated airline regulations. ('Let me be the judge of that, m'dear.')

'Time is certainly of the essence,' said the man. 'But no. I was merely concerned that you would not make the plane.'

'That was kind of you.'

The plane sat restlessly on the ground, engines throbbing, aching to be off.

'Kind my ass,' said the man in the pale suit. 'I've got a job for you, Shadow.'

A roar of engines. The little plane jerked forward, pushing Shadow back into his seat. Then they were airborne, and the airport lights were falling away below them. Shadow looked at the man in the seat next to him.

His hair was a reddish-grey; his beard, little more than stubble, was greyish-red. A craggy, square face with pale grey eyes. The suit looked expensive, and was the colour of melted vanilla ice-cream. His tie was dark grey silk, and the tie-pin was a tree, worked in silver: trunk, branches, and deep roots.

He held his glass of Jack Daniel's as they took off, and did not spill a drop.

'Aren't you going to ask me what kind of job?' he asked.

'How do you know who I am?'

The man chuckled. 'Oh, it's the easiest thing in the world to know what people call themselves. A little thought, a little luck, a little memory. Ask me what kind of job.'

'No,' said Shadow. The attendant brought him another glass of beer, and he sipped at it.

'Why not?'

'I'm going home. I've got a job waiting for me there. I don't want any other job.'

The man's craggy smile did not change, outwardly, but now he seemed, actually, amused. 'You don't have a job waiting for you at home,' he said. 'You have nothing waiting for you there. Meanwhile, I am offering you a perfectly legal job – good money, limited security, remarkable fringe benefits. Hell, if you live that long, I could throw in a pension plan. You think maybe you'd like one of them?'

Shadow said, 'You must have seen my name on the side of my bag.'

The man said nothing.

'Whoever you are,' said Shadow, 'you couldn't have known I was going to be on this plane. I didn't know I was going to be on this plane, and if my plane hadn't been diverted to St. Louis, I wouldn't have been. My guess is you're a practical joker. Maybe you're hustling something. But I think maybe we'll have a better time if we end this conversation here.'

The man shrugged.

Shadow picked up the in-flight magazine. The little plane jerked and bumped through the sky, making it harder to concentrate. The words floated through his mind like soap bubbles, there as he read them, gone completely a moment later.

The man sat quietly in the seat beside him, sipping his Jack Daniel's. His eyes were closed.

Shadow read the list of in-flight music channels available on transatlantic flights, and then he was looking at the map of the world with red lines on it that showed where the airline flew. Then he had finished reading the magazine, and, reluctantly, he closed the cover, and slipped it into the pocket.

The man opened his eyes. There was something strange about his eyes, Shadow thought. One of them was a darker grey than the other. He looked at Shadow. 'By the way,' he said, 'I was sorry to hear about your wife, Shadow. A great loss.'

Shadow nearly hit the man, then. Instead he took a deep breath. ('Like I said, don't piss off those bitches in airports,' said Johnnie Larch, in the back of his mind, 'or they'll haul your sorry ass back here before you can spit.') He counted to five.

'So was I,' he said.

The man shook his head. 'If it could but have been any other way,' he said, and sighed.

'She died in a car crash,' said Shadow. 'There are worse ways to die.'

The man shook his head, slowly. For a moment it seemed to Shadow as if the man was insubstantial; as if the plane had suddenly become more real, while his neighbour had become less so.

'Shadow,' he said. 'It's not a joke. It's not a trick. I can pay you better than any other job you'll find will pay you. You're an ex-con. There won't be a long line of people elbowing each other out of the way to hire you.'

'Mister whoever-the-fuck you are,' said Shadow, just loud enough to be heard over the din of the engines, 'there isn't enough money in the world.'

The grin got bigger. Shadow found himself remembering a PBS show about chimpanzees. The show claimed that when apes and chimps smile it's only to bare their teeth in a grimace of hate or aggression or terror. When a chimp grins, it's a threat.

'Work for me. There may be a little risk, of course, but if you survive you can have whatever your heart desires. You could be the next King of America. Now,' said the man, 'who else is going to pay you that well. Hmm?'

'Who are you?' asked Shadow.

'Ah, yes. The age of information – young lady, could you pour me another glass of Jack Daniel's? Easy on the ice, – not, of course, that there has ever been any other kind of age. Information and knowledge: a currency that has never gone out of style.'

'I said, who are you?'

'Let's see. Well, seeing that today certainly is my day – why don't you call me Wednesday? Mister Wednesday. Although given the weather, it might as well be Thursday, eh?'

'What's your real name?'

'Work for me long enough and well enough,' said the man in the pale suit, 'and I may even tell you that. There. Job offer. Think about it. No-one expects you to say yes immediately, not knowing whether you're leaping into a piranha tank or a pit of bears. Take your time.' He closed his eyes and leaned back in his seat.

'I don't think so,' said Shadow. 'I don't like you. I don't want to work with you.'

'Like I say,' said the man, without opening his eyes, 'don't rush into it. Take your time.'

The plane landed with a bump, and a few passengers got off. Shadow looked out of the window: it was a little airport in the middle of nowhere, and there were still two little airports to go before Eagle Point. Shadow transferred his glance to the man in the pale suit – Mr Wednesday? He seemed to be asleep.

Impulsively, Shadow stood up, grabbed his bag, and stepped off the plane, down the steps onto the slick wet tarmac, walking at an even pace toward the lights of the terminal. A light rain spattered his face.

Before he went inside the airport building, he stopped, and turned, and watched. No-one else got off the plane. The ground crew rolled the steps away, the door was closed, and it took off. Shadow walked inside and he rented what turned out, when he got to the parking lot, to be a small red Toyota.

Shadow unfolded the map they'd given him. He spread it out on the passenger's seat. Eagle Point was about two hundred and fifty miles away.

The storms had passed, if they had come this far. It was cold and clear. Clouds scudded in front of the moon, and for a moment Shadow could not be certain whether it was the clouds or the moon that were moving.

He drove north for an hour and a half.

It was getting late. He was hungry, and when he realised how hungry he really was, he pulled off at the next exit, and drove into the town of Nottamun (Pop. 1301). He filled the gas-tank at the Amoco, and asked the bored woman at the cash register where he could get something to eat.

'Jack's Crocodile Bar,' she told him. 'It's west on County Road N.'

'Crocodile Bar?'

'Yeah. Jack says they add character.' She drew him a map on the back of a mauve flyer, which advertised a chicken roast for the benefit of a young girl who needed a new kidney. 'He's got a couple of crocodiles, a snake, one a them big lizard things.'

'An iguana?'

'That's him.'

Through the town, over a bridge, on for a couple of miles, and he stopped at a low, rectangular building with an illuminated Pabst sign.

The parking lot was half empty.

Inside the air was thick with smoke and 'Walking After Midnight' was playing on the jukebox. Shadow looked around for the crocodiles, but could not see them. He wondered if the woman in the gas station had been pulling his leg.

'What'll it be?' asked the bartender.

'House beer, and a hamburger with all the trimmings. Fries.'

'Bowl of chili to start? Best chili in the state.'

'Sounds good,' said Shadow. 'Where's the rest room?'

The man pointed to a door in the corner of the bar. There was a stuffed alligator head mounted on the door. Shadow went through the door.

It was a clean, well-lit restroom. Shadow looked around the room first; force of habit. ('Remember, Shadow, you can't fight back when you're pissing,' Low Key said, low key as always, in the back of his head.) He took the urinal stall on the left. Then he unzipped his fly and pissed for an age, feeling relief. He read the yellowing press clipping framed at eye-level, with a photo of Jack and two alligators.

There was a polite grunt from the urinal immediately to his right, although he had heard nobody come in.

The man in the pale suit was bigger standing than he had seemed sitting on the plane beside Shadow. He was almost Shadow's height, and Shadow was a big man. He was staring ahead of him. He finished pissing, shook off the last few drops, and zipped himself up.

Then he grinned, like a fox eating shit from a barbed wire fence. 'So,' said Mr Wednesday, 'you've had time to think, Shadow. Do you want a job?'

Somewhere In America

Los Angeles. 11:26 p.m.

In a dark red room – the colour of the walls is close to that of raw liver – is a tall woman dressed cartoonishly in too-tight silk shorts, her breasts pulled up and pushed forward by the yellow blouse tied beneath them. Her black hair is piled high and knotted on top of her head. Standing beside her is a short man wearing an olive tee shirt and expensive blue jeans. He is holding, in his right hand, a wallet and a Nokia mobile phone with a red white and blue face-plate.

The red room contains a bed, upon which are white satin-style sheets and an ox-blood bedspread. At the foot of the bed is a small wooden table, upon which is a small, stone statue of a woman with enormous hips, and a candleholder.

The woman hands the man a small red candle. 'Here,' she says. 'Light it.'

'Me?'

'Yes,' she says, 'If you want to have me.'

'I shoulda just got you to suck me off in the car.'

'Perhaps,' she says. 'Don't you want me?' Her hand runs up her body from thigh to breast, a gesture of presentation, as if she were demonstrating a new product.

Red silk scarves over the lamp in the corner of the room make the light red.

The man looks at her hungrily, then he takes the candle from her and pushes it into the candleholder. 'You got a light?'

She passes him a book of matches. He tears off a match, lights the wick: it flickers and then burns with a steady flame, which gives the illusion of motion to the faceless statue beside it, all hips and breasts.

'Put the money beneath the statue.'

'Fifty bucks.'

'Yes,' she says. 'Now, come love me.'

He unbuttons his blue jeans, and removes his olive tee shirt. She massages his white shoulders with her brown fingers; then she turns him over, and begins to make love to him with her hands, and her fingers, and her tongue.

It seems to him that the lights in the red room have been dimmed, and the sole illumination comes from the candle, which burns with a bright flame.

'What's your name?' he asks her.

'Bilquis,' she tells him, raising her head. 'With a Q.'

'A what?'

'Never mind.'

He is gasping now. 'Let me fuck you,' he says. 'I have to fuck you.'

'Okay, hon,' she says. 'We'll do it. But will you do something for me, while you're doing it?'

'Hey,' he says, suddenly tetchy, '*I'm* paying *you*, you know.'

She straddles him, in one smooth movement, whispering, 'I know, honey, I know, you're paying me, and I mean, look at you, I should be paying you, I'm so lucky . . .'

He purses his lips, trying to show that her hooker talk is having no effect on him, he can't be taken; that she's a street whore for Chrissakes, while he's practically a *producer*, and he knows all about last-minute ripoffs, but she doesn't ask for money. Instead she says, 'Honey, while you're giving it to me, while you're pushing that big hard thing inside of me, will you *worship* me?'

'Will I what?'

She is rocking back and forth on him: the engorged head of his penis is being rubbed against the wet lips of her vulva.

'Will you call me goddess? Will you pray to me? Will you worship me with your body?'

He smiles. Is that all she wants? We've all got our kinks, at the end of the day. 'Sure,' he says. She reaches her hand between her legs and slips him inside her.

'Is that good, is it, goddess?' he asks, gasping.

'Worship me, honey,' says Bilquis, the hooker.

'Yes,' he says. 'I worship your breasts and your hair and your cunt. I worship your thighs and your eyes and your cherry-red lips . . .'

'Yes . . .' she croons, riding him.

'I worship your nipples, from which the milk of life flows. Your kiss is honey and your touch scorches like fire, and I worship it.' His words are becoming more rhythmic now, keeping pace with the thrust and roll of their bodies. 'Bring me your lust in the morning, and bring me relief and your blessing in the evening. Let me walk in dark places unharmed and let me come to you once more and sleep beside you and make love with you again. I worship you with everything that is within me, and everything inside my mind, with everywhere I've been and my dreams and my . . .' he breaks off, panting for breath, '. . . what are you *doing*? That feels a*maz*ing. So a*maz*ing . . .' and he looks down at his hips, at the place where the two of them conjoin, but her forefinger touches his chin and pushes his head back, so he is looking only at her face and at the ceiling once again.

'Keep talking honey,' she says. 'Don't stop. Doesn't it feel good?'

'It feels better than anything has ever felt,' he tells her, meaning it as he says it. 'Your eyes are stars, burning in the, shit, the firmament, and your lips are gentle waves that lick the sand, and I worship them,' and now he's thrusting deeper and deeper inside her: he feels electric, as if his whole lower body has become sexually charged: priapic, engorged, blissful.

'Bring me your gift,' he mutters, no longer knowing what he is saying, 'your one true gift, and make me always this . . . always so . . . I pray . . . I . . .'

And then the pleasure crests into orgasm, blasting his mind into void, his head and self and entire being a perfect blank as he thrusts deeper into her and deeper still . . .

Eyes closed, spasming, he luxuriates in the moment; and then he feels a lurch, and it seems to him that he is hanging, head-down, although the pleasure continues.

He opens his eyes.

He thinks, grasping for thought and reason again, of birth, and wonders, without fear, in a moment of perfect postcoital clarity, whether what he sees is some kind of illusion.

This is what he sees:

He is inside her to the chest, and as he stares at this in disbelief and wonder she rests both hands upon his shoulders and puts gentle pressure on his body.

He slipslides further inside her.

'How are you doing this to me?' he asks, or he thinks he asks, but perhaps it is only in his head.

'You're doing it, honey,' she whispers. He feels the lips of her vulva tight around his upper chest and back, constricting and enveloping him. He wonders what this would look like to some-body watching them. He wonders why he is not scared. And then he knows.

'I worship you with my body,' he whispers, as she pushes him inside her. Her labia pull slickly across his face, and his eyes slip into darkness.

She stretches on the bed, like a huge cat, and then she yawns. 'Yes,' she says, 'You do.'

The Nokia phone plays a high, electrical transposition of the Ode to Joy. She picks it up, and thumbs a key, and puts the telephone to her ear.

Her belly is flat, her labia small and closed. A sheen of sweat glistens on her forehead and on her upper lip.

'Yeah?' she says. And then she says, 'No, honey, he's not here. He's gone away.'

She turns the telephone off before she flops out on the bed in the dark red room, then she stretches once more, and she closes her eyes, and she sleeps.

2

They took her to the cemet'ry
In a big ol' Cadillac
They took her to the cemet'ry
But they did not bring her back.
– Old Song.

'I have taken the liberty,' said Mr Wednesday, washing his hands in the men's room of Jack's Crocodile Bar, 'of ordering food for myself, to be delivered to your table. We have much to discuss, after all.'

'I don't think so,' said Shadow. He dried his own hands on a paper towel and crumpled it, and dropped it into the bin.

'You need a job,' said Wednesday. 'People don't hire ex-cons. You folk make them uncomfortable.'

'I have a job waiting. A good job.'

'Would that be the job at the Muscle Farm?'

'Maybe,' said Shadow.

'Nope. You don't. Robbie Burton's dead. Without him the Muscle Farm's dead too.'

'You're a liar.'

'Of course. And a good one. The best you will ever meet. But, I'm afraid, I'm not lying to you about this.' He reached into his pocket, produced a folded newspaper, and handed it to Shadow. 'Page seven,' he said. 'Come on back to the bar. You can read it at the table.'

Shadow pushed open the door, back into the bar. The air was blue with smoke, and the Dixie Cups were on the juke box singing 'Iko Iko'. Shadow smiled, slightly, in recognition of the old children's song.

The barman pointed to a table in the corner. There was a bowl of chili and a burger at one side of the table, a rare steak and a bowl of fries laid in the place across from it.

Look at my King all dressed in red,
Iko Iko all day,
I bet you five dollars he'll kill you dead,
Jockamo-feena-nay

Shadow took his seat at the table. He put the newspaper down. 'This is my first meal as a free man. I'll wait until after I've eaten to read your page seven.'

Shadow ate his hamburger. It was better than prison hamburgers. The chili was good but, he decided, after a couple of mouthfuls, not the best in the state.

Laura made a great chili. She used lean meat, dark kidney beans, carrots cut small, a bottle or so of dark beer, and freshly sliced hot peppers. She would let the chili cook for a while, then add red wine, lemon juice and a pinch of fresh dill, and, finally, measure out and add her chili powders. On more than one occasion Shadow had tried to get her to show him how she made it: he would watch everything she did, from slicing the onions and dropping them into the olive oil at the bottom of the pot. He had even written down the recipe, ingredient by ingredient, and he had once made Laura's chili for himself on a weekend when she had been out of town. It had tasted okay – it was certainly edible, but it had not been Laura's chili.

The news item on page seven was the first account of his wife's death that Shadow had read. Laura Moon, whose age was given in the article as 27, and Robbie Burton, 39, were in Robbie's car on the interstate, when they swerved into the path of a thirty-two wheeler. The truck brushed Robbie's car and sent it spinning off the side of the road.

Rescue crews pulled Robbie and Laura from the wreckage. They were both dead by the time they arrived at the hospital.

Shadow folded the newspaper up once more, and slid it back across the table, toward Wednesday, who was gorging himself on a steak so bloody and so blue it might never have been introduced to a kitchen flame.

'Here. Take it back,' said Shadow.

Robbie had been driving. He must have been drunk, although the newspaper account said nothing about this. Shadow found himself imagining Laura's face when she realised that Robbie was too drunk to drive. The scenario unfolded in Shadow's mind, and there was nothing he could do to stop it: Laura shouting at Robbie – shouting at him to pull off the road, then the thud of car against truck, and the steering wheel wrenching over . . .

. . . the car on the side of the road, broken glass glittering like ice and diamonds in the headlights, blood pooling in rubies on the road beside them. Two bodies being carried from the wreck, or laid neatly by the side of the road.

'Well?' asked Mr Wednesday. He had finished his steak, devoured it like a starving man. Now he was munching the french fries, spearing them with his fork.

'You're right,' said Shadow. 'I don't have a job.'

Shadow took a quarter from his pocket, tails up. He flicked it up in the air, knocking it against his finger as it left his hand, giving it a wobble as if it were turning, caught it, slapped it down on the back of his hand.

'Call,' he said.

'Why?' asked Wednesday.

'I don't want to work for anyone with worse luck than me. Call.'

'Heads,' said Mr Wednesday.

'Sorry,' said Shadow, without even bothering to glance at the quarter. 'It was tails. I rigged the toss.'

'Rigged games are the easiest ones to beat,' said Wednesday, wagging a square finger at Shadow. 'Take another look at it.'

Shadow glanced down at it. The head was face up.

'I must have fumbled the toss,' he said, puzzled.

'You do yourself a disservice,' said Wednesday, and he grinned. 'I'm just a lucky, lucky guy.' Then he looked up. 'Well I never. Mad Sweeney. Will you have a drink with us?'

'Southern Comfort and Coke, straight up,' said a voice from behind Shadow.

'I'll go and talk to the barman,' said Wednesday. He stood up, and began to make his way toward the bar.

'Aren't you going to ask what I'm drinking?' called Shadow.

'I already know what you're drinking,' said Wednesday, and then he was standing by the bar. Patsy Cline started to sing 'Walking After Midnight' on the juke box again.

The Southern Comfort and Coke sat down beside Shadow. He had a short ginger beard. He wore a denim jacket covered with bright sew-on patches, and under the jacket a stained white tee shirt. On the tee shirt was printed:

IF YOU CAN'T EAT IT, DRINK IT, SMOKE IT OR SNORT IT . . .
THEN F*CK IT!

He wore a baseball cap, on which was printed:

THE ONLY WOMAN I HAVE EVER LOVED WAS ANOTHER
MAN'S WIFE . . . MY MOTHER!

He opened a soft pack of Lucky Strikes with a dirty thumbnail, took a cigarette, offered one to Shadow. Shadow was about to take one, automatically – he did not smoke, but a cigarette makes good barter material – when he realised that he was no longer inside. He shook his head.

'You working for our man then?' asked the bearded man. He was not sober, although he was not yet drunk.

'It looks that way,' said Shadow. 'What do you do?'

The bearded man lit his cigarette. 'I'm a leprechaun,' he said, with a grin.

Shadow did not smile. 'Really?' he said. 'Shouldn't you be drinking Guinness?'

'Stereotypes. You have to learn to think outside the box,' said the bearded man. 'There's a lot more to Ireland than Guinness.'

'You don't have an Irish accent.'

'I've been over here too fucken long.'

'So you *are* originally from Ireland?'

'I told you. I'm a leprechaun. We don't come from fucken Moscow.'

'I guess not.'

Wednesday returned to the table, three drinks held easily in his paw-like hands. 'Southern Comfort and Coke for you, Mad

Sweeney m'man, and a Jack Daniel's for me. And *this* is for you, Shadow.'

'What is it?'

'Taste it.'

The drink was a tawny golden colour. Shadow took a sip, tasting an odd blend of sour and sweet on his tongue. He could taste the alcohol underneath, and a strange blend of flavours. It reminded him a little of prison hooch, brewed in a garbage bag from rotten fruit and bread and sugar and water, but it was sweeter, and far stranger.

'Okay,' said Shadow. 'I tasted it. What was it?'

'Mead,' said Wednesday. 'Honey wine. The drink of heroes. The drink of the gods.'

Shadow took another tentative sip. Yes, he could taste the honey, he decided. That was one of the tastes. 'Tastes kinda like pickle juice,' he said. 'Sweet pickle juice wine.'

'Tastes like a drunken diabetic's piss,' agreed Wednesday. 'I hate the stuff.'

'Then why did you bring it for me?' asked Shadow, reasonably.

Wednesday stared at Shadow with his mismatched eyes. One of them, Shadow decided, was a glass eye, but he could not decide which one. 'I brought you mead to drink because it's traditional. And right now we need all the tradition we can get. It seals our bargain.'

'We haven't made a bargain.'

'Sure we have. You work for me, now. You protect me. You transport me from place to place. You run errands. In an emergency, but only in an emergency, you hurt people who need to be hurt. In the unlikely event of my death, you will hold my vigil. And in return I shall make sure that your needs are adequately taken care of.'

'He's hustling you,' said Mad Sweeney, rubbing his bristly ginger beard. 'He's a hustler.'

'Damn straight I'm a hustler,' said Wednesday. 'That's why I need someone to look out for my best interests.'

The song on the juke box ended, and for a moment the bar fell quiet, every conversation at a lull.

'Someone once told me that you only get those everybody-shuts-up-at-once moments at twenty past or twenty to the hour,' said Shadow.

Sweeney pointed to the clock above the bar, held in the massive and indifferent jaws of a stuffed alligator head. The time was 11:20.

'There,' said Shadow. 'Damned if I know why that happens.'

'I know why,' said Wednesday. 'Drink your mead.'

Shadow knocked the rest of the mead back in one long gulp. 'It might be better over ice,' he said.

'Or it might not,' said Wednesday. 'It's terrible stuff.'

'That it is,' agreed Mad Sweeney. 'You'll excuse me for a moment, gentlemen, but I find myself in deep and urgent need of a lengthy piss.' He stood up and walked away, an impossibly tall man. He had to be almost seven feet tall, decided Shadow.

A waitress wiped a cloth across the table and took their empty plates. Wednesday told her to bring the same again for everyone, although this time Shadow's mead was to be on the rocks.

'Anyway,' said Wednesday, 'that's what I need of you.'

'Would you like to know what I want?' asked Shadow.

'Nothing could make me happier.'

The waitress brought the drink. Shadow sipped his mead on the rocks. The ice did not help – if anything it sharpened the sourness, and made the taste linger in the mouth after the mead was swallowed. However, Shadow consoled himself, it did not taste particularly alcoholic. He was not ready to be drunk. Not yet.

He took a deep breath.

'Okay,' said Shadow. 'My life, which for three years has been a long way from being the greatest life there has ever been, just took a distinct and sudden turn for the worse. Now there are a few things I need to do. I want to go to Laura's funeral. I want to say goodbye. I should wind up her stuff. If you still need me, I want to start at five hundred dollars a week.' The figure was a stab in the dark. Wednesday's eyes revealed nothing. 'If we're happy working together, in six months' time you raise it to a thousand a week.'

He paused. It was the longest speech he'd made in years. 'You say you may need people to be hurt. Well, I'll hurt people if they're trying to hurt you. But I don't hurt people for fun or for profit. I won't go back to prison. Once was enough.'

'You won't have to,' said Wednesday.

'No,' said Shadow. 'I won't.' He finished the last of the mead. He wondered, suddenly, somewhere in the back of his head, whether the mead was responsible for loosening his tongue. But the words were coming out of him like the water spraying from a broken fire hydrant in summer, and he could not have stopped them if he had tried. 'I don't like you, Mister Wednesday, or whatever your real name may be. We are not friends. I don't know how you got off that plane without me seeing you, or how you trailed me here. But I'm at a loose end right now. When we're done, I'll be gone. And if you piss me off, I'll be gone too. Until then, I'll work for you.'

'Very good,' said Wednesday. 'Then we have a compact. And we are agreed.'

'What the hell,' said Shadow. Across the room, Mad Sweeney was feeding quarters into the juke box. Wednesday spat in his hand and extended it. Shadow shrugged. He spat in his own palm. They clasped hands. Wednesday began to squeeze. Shadow squeezed back. After a few seconds his hand began to hurt. Wednesday held the grip a little longer, and then he let go.

'Good,' he said. 'Good. Very good. So, one last glass of evil, vile fucking mead to seal our deal, and then we are done.'

'It'll be a Southern Comfort and Coke for me,' said Sweeney, lurching back from the juke box.

The juke box began to play the Velvet Underground's 'Who Loves the Sun?' Shadow thought it a strange song to find on a juke box. It seemed very unlikely. But then, this whole evening had become increasingly unlikely.

Shadow took the quarter he had used for the coin-toss from the table, enjoying the sensation of a freshly milled coin against his fingers, producing it in his right hand between forefinger and thumb. He appeared to take it into his left hand in one smooth movement, while casually finger-palming it. He closed his left hand on the imaginary quarter. Then he took a second quarter in his right hand, between finger and thumb, and, as he pretended to drop that coin into the left hand, he let the palmed quarter fall into his right hand, striking the quarter he held there on the way. The chink confirmed the illusion that both coins were in his left hand, while they were now both held safely in his right.

'Coin tricks is it?' asked Sweeney, his chin raising, his scruffy beard bristling. 'Why, if it's coin tricks we're doing, watch this.'

He took an empty glass from the table. Then he reached out and took a large coin, golden and shining, from the air. He dropped it into the glass. He took another gold coin from the air and tossed it into the glass, where it clinked against the first. He took a coin from the candle flame of a candle on the wall, another from his beard, a third from Shadow's empty left hand, and dropped them, one by one, into the glass. Then he curled his fingers over the glass, and blew hard, and several more golden coins dropped into the glass from his hand. He tipped the glass of sticky coins into his jacket pocket, and then tapped the pocket to show, unmistakably, that it was empty.

'There,' he said. '*That's* a coin trick for you.'

Shadow, who had been watching closely, put his head on one side. 'I need to know how you did it.'

'I did it,' said Sweeney, with the air of one confiding a huge secret, 'with panache and style. That's how I did it.' He laughed, silently, rocking on his heels, his gappy teeth bared.

'Yes,' said Shadow. 'That is how you did it. You've got to teach me. All the ways of doing the Miser's Dream that I've read, you'd be hiding the coins in the hand that holds the glass, and dropping them in while you produce and vanish the coin in your right hand.'

'Sounds like a hell of a lot of work to me,' said Mad Sweeney. 'It's easier just to pick them out of the air.'

Wednesday said, 'Mead for you, Shadow. I'll stick with Mister Jack Daniel's, and for the freeloading Irishman . . . ?'

'A bottled beer, something dark for preference,' said Sweeney. 'Freeloader, is it?' He picked up what was left of his drink, and raised it to Wednesday in a toast. 'May the storm pass over us, and leave us hale and unharmed,' he said, and knocked the drink back.

'A fine toast,' said Wednesday. 'But it won't.'

Another mead was placed in front of Shadow.

'Do I have to drink this?'

'I'm afraid you do. It seals our deal. Third time's the charm, eh?'

'Shit,' said Shadow. He swallowed the mead in two large gulps. The pickled honey taste filled his mouth.

'There,' said Mr Wednesday 'you're my man, now.'

'So,' said Sweeney, 'you want to know the trick of how it's done?'

'Yes,' said Shadow. 'Were you loading them in your sleeve?'

'They were never in my sleeve,' said Sweeney. He chortled to himself, rocking and bouncing as if he were a lanky, bearded volcano preparing to erupt with delight at his own brilliance. 'It's the simplest trick in the world. I'll fight you for it.'

Shadow shook his head. 'I'll pass.'

'Now *there's* a fine thing,' said Sweeney to the room. 'Old Wednesday gets himself a bodyguard, and the feller's too scared too put up his fists, even.'

'I won't fight you,' agreed Shadow.

Sweeney swayed and sweated. He fiddled with the peak of his baseball cap. Then he pulled one of his coins out of the air and placed it on the table. 'Real gold, if you were wondering,' said Sweeney. 'Win or lose – and you'll lose – it's yours if you fight me. A big fellow like you – who'd'a thought you'd be a fucken coward?'

'He's already said he won't fight you,' said Wednesday. 'Go away, Mad Sweeney. Take your beer and leave us in peace.'

Sweeney took a step closer to Wednesday. 'Call me a freeloader, will you, you doomed old creature? You cold-blooded, heartless old tree-hanger.' His face was turning a deep, angry red.

Wednesday put out his hands, palms up, pacific. 'Foolishness, Sweeney. Watch where you put your words.'

Sweeney glared at him. Then he said, with the gravity of the very drunk, 'You've hired a coward. What would he do if I hurt you, do you think?'

Wednesday turned to Shadow. 'I've had enough of this,' he said. 'Deal with it.'

Shadow got to his feet and looked up into Mad Sweeney's face: how tall *was* the man? he wondered. 'You're bothering us,' he said. 'You're drunk. I think you ought to leave now.'

A slow smile spread over Sweeney's face. 'There, now,' he said. He swung a huge fist at Shadow's. Shadow jerked back: Sweeney's hand caught him beneath the right eye. He saw blotches of light, and felt pain.

And with that, the fight began.

Sweeney fought without style, without science, with nothing but enthusiasm for the fight itself: huge, barreling roundhouse blows that missed as often as they connected.

Shadow fought defensively, carefully, blocking Sweeney's blows or avoiding them. He became very aware of the audience around them. Tables were pulled out of the way with protesting groans, making a space for the men to spar. Shadow was aware at all times of Wednesday's eyes upon him, of Wednesday's humorless grin. It was a test, that was obvious, but what kind of a test?

In prison Shadow had learned there were two kinds of fights: *don't fuck with me* fights, where you made it as showy and impressive as you could, and private fights, *real* fights which were fast and hard and nasty, and always over in seconds.

'Hey, Sweeney,' said Shadow, breathless, 'why are we fighting?'

'For the joy of it,' said Sweeney, sober now, or at least, no longer visibly drunk. 'For the sheer unholy fucken delight of it. Can't you feel the joy in your own veins, rising like the sap in the springtime?' His lip was bleeding. So was Shadow's knuckle.

'So how'd you do the coin production?' asked Shadow. He swayed back and twisted, took a blow on his shoulder intended for his face.

'I told you how I did it when first we spoke,' grunted Sweeney. 'But there's none so blind – ow! Good one! – as those who will not listen.'

Shadow jabbed at Sweeney, forcing him back into a table; empty glasses and ashtrays crashed to the floor. Shadow could have finished him off then.

Shadow glanced at Wednesday, who nodded. Shadow looked down at Mad Sweeney. 'Are we done?' he asked. Mad Sweeney hesitated, then nodded. Shadow let go of him, and took several steps backward. Sweeney, panting, pushed himself back up to a standing position.

'Not on yer ass!' he shouted. 'It ain't over till I say it is!' Then he grinned, and threw himself forward, swinging at Shadow. He stepped onto a fallen ice-cube, and his grin turned to open-mouthed dismay as his feet went out from under him, and he fell backward. The back of his head hit the barroom floor with a definite thud.

Shadow put his knee into Mad Sweeney's chest. 'For the second time, are we done fighting?' he asked.

'We may as well be, at that,' said Sweeney, raising his head from the floor, 'for the joy's gone out of me now, like the pee from a small boy in a swimming pool on a hot day.' And he spat the blood from his mouth and closed his eyes and began to snore, in deep and magnificent snores.

Somebody clapped Shadow on the back. Wednesday put a bottle of beer into his hand.

It tasted better than mead.

Shadow woke up stretched out in the back of a sedan car. The morning sun was dazzling, and his head hurt. He sat up awkwardly, rubbing his eyes.

Wednesday was driving. He was humming tunelessly as he drove. He had a paper cup of coffee in the cup holder. They were heading along an interstate highway. The passenger seat was empty.

'How are you feeling, this fine morning?' asked Wednesday, without turning around.

'What happened to my car?' asked Shadow. 'It was a rental.'

'Mad Sweeney took it back for you. It was part of the deal the two of you cut last night. After the fight.'

Conversations from the night before began to jostle uncomfortably in Shadow's head. 'You got any more of that coffee?'

The big man reached beneath the passenger seat and passed back an unopened bottle of water. 'Here. You'll be dehydrated. This will help more than coffee, for the moment. We'll stop at the next gas station and get you some breakfast. You'll need to clean yourself up, too. You look like something the goat dragged in.'

'Cat dragged in,' said Shadow.

'Goat,' said Wednesday. 'Huge rank stinking goat with big teeth.'

Shadow unscrewed the top of the water and drank. Something clinked heavily in his jacket pocket. He put his hand into the pocket and pulled out a coin, the size of a half dollar. It was heavy, and a deep yellow in colour.

In the gas station Shadow bought a Clean-U-Up Kit, which contained a razor, a sachet of shaving cream, a comb and a disposable tooth-brush packed with a tiny tube of toothpaste. Then he walked into the men's restroom and looked at himself in the mirror.

He had a bruise under one eye – when he prodded it, experimentally, with one finger, he found it hurt deeply, – and a swollen lower lip.

Shadow washed his face with the restroom's liquid soap, then he lathered his face and shaved. He cleaned his teeth. He wet his hair and combed it back. He still looked rough.

He wondered what Laura would say when she saw him, and then he remembered that Laura wouldn't say anything ever again and he saw his face, in the mirror, tremble, but only for a moment.

He went out.

'I look like shit,' said Shadow.

'Of course you do,' agreed Wednesday.

Wednesday took an assortment of snack-food up to the cash register, and paid for that and their gas, changing his mind twice about whether he was doing it with plastic or with cash, to the irritation of the gum-chewing young lady behind the till. Shadow watched as Wednesday became increasingly flustered and apologetic. He seemed very old, suddenly. The girl gave him his cash back, and put the purchase on the card, and then gave him the card receipt and took his cash, then returned the cash and took a different card. Wednesday was obviously on the verge of tears, an old man made helpless by the implacable plastic march of the modern world.

They walked out of the warm gas station, and their breath steamed in the air.

On the road once more: browning grass meadows slipped past on each side of them. The trees were leafless and dead. Two black birds stared at them from a telegraph wire.

'Hey, Wednesday.'

'What?'

'The way I saw it in there, you never paid for the gas.'

'Oh?'

'The way I saw it, she wound up paying you for the privilege of having you in her gas station. You think she's figured it out yet?'

'She never will.'

'So what are you? A two-bit con artist?'

Wednesday nodded. 'Yes,' he said. 'I suppose I am. Among other things.'

He swung out into the left lane to pass a truck. The sky was a bleak and uniform grey.

'It's going to snow,' said Shadow.

'Yes.'

'Sweeney. Did he actually show me how he did that trick with the gold coins?'

'Oh yes.'

'I can't remember.'

'It'll come back. It was a long night.'

Several small snowflakes brushed the windshield, melting in seconds.

'Your wife's body is on display at Wendell's Funeral Parlor at present,' said Wednesday. 'Then after lunch they will take her from there to the graveyard for the interment.'

'How do you know?'

'I called ahead while you were in the john. You know where Wendell's Funeral Parlor is?'

Shadow nodded. The snowflakes whirled and dizzied in front of them.

'This is our exit,' said Shadow. The car stole off the interstate, and past the cluster of motels to the north of Eagle Point.

Three years had passed. Yes. There were more stoplights, unfamiliar storefronts. Shadow asked Wednesday to slow as they drove past the Muscle Farm. CLOSED INDEFINITELY, said the hand-lettered sign on the door, DUE TO BEREAVEMENT.

Left on Main Street. Past a new tattoo parlor and the Armed Forces Recruitment Centre, then the Burger King, and, familiar and unchanged, Olsen's Drug Store, finally the yellow-brick facade of Wendell's Funeral Parlor. A neon sign in the front window said 'House of Rest'. Blank tombstones stood unchristened and uncarved in the window beneath the sign.

Wednesday pulled up in the parking lot.

'Do you want me to come in?' he asked.

'Not particularly.'

'Good.' The grin flashed, without humour. 'There's business I can be getting on with while you say your goodbyes. I'll get rooms for us at the Motel America. Meet me there when you're done.'

Shadow got out of the car, and watched it pull away. Then he walked in. The dimly lit corridor smelled of flowers and of furniture polish, with just the slightest tang of formaldehyde. At the far end was the Chapel of Rest.

Shadow realised that he was palming the gold coin, moving it compulsively from a back palm to a front palm to a Downs palm, over and over. The weight was reassuring in his hand.

His wife's name was on a sheet of paper beside the door at the far end of the corridor. He walked into the Chapel of Rest. Shadow knew most of the people in the room: Laura's workmates, several of her friends.

They all recognised him. He could see it in their faces. There were no smiles, though, no hellos.

At the end of the room was a small dais, and, on it, a cream-coloured casket with several displays of flowers arranged about it: scarlets and yellows and whites and deep, bloody purples. He took a step forward. He could see Laura's body from where he was standing. He did not want to walk forward; he did not dare to walk away.

A man in a dark suit – Shadow guessed he worked at the funeral home – said, 'Sir? Would you like to sign the condolence and remembrance book?' and pointed him to a leather-bound book, open on a small lectern.

He wrote SHADOW and the date in his precise handwriting, then, slowly, he wrote (PUPPY) beside it, putting off walking toward the end of the room, where the people were, and the casket, and the thing in the cream casket that was no longer Laura.

A small woman walked in through the door, and hesitated. Her hair was a coppery red, and her clothes were expensive, and very black. *Widow's weeds*, thought Shadow, who knew her well: Audrey Burton, Robbie's wife.

Audrey was holding a sprig of violets, wrapped at the base with silver foil. It was the kind of thing a child would make in June, thought Shadow. But violets were out of season.

She walked across the room, to Laura's casket. Shadow followed her.

Laura lay with her eyes closed, and her arms folded across her chest. She wore a conservative blue suit he did not recognise. Her long brown hair was out of her eyes. It was his Laura and it was not: her repose, he realised, was what was unnatural. Laura was always such a restless sleeper.

Audrey placed her sprig of summer violets on Laura's chest. Then she worked her mouth for a moment and spat, hard, onto Laura's dead face.

The spit caught Laura on the cheek, and began to drip down toward her ear.

Audrey was already walking toward the door. Shadow hurried after her.

'Audrey?' he said.

'Shadow? Did you escape? Or did they let you out?'

He wondered if she were taking tranquilisers. Her voice was distant and detached.

'Let me out yesterday. I'm a free man,' said Shadow. 'What the hell was that all about?'

She stopped in the dark corridor. 'The violets? They were always her favorite flower. When we were girls we used to pick them together.'

'Not the violets.'

'Oh, *that*,' she said. She wiped a speck of something invisible from the corner of her mouth. 'Well, I would have thought that was obvious.'

'Not to me, Audrey.'

'They didn't tell you?' Her voice was calm, emotionless. 'Your wife died with my husband's cock in her mouth, Shadow.'

He went back in to the funeral home. Someone had already wiped away the spit.

After lunch – Shadow ate at the Burger King – was the burial. Laura's cream-coloured coffin was interred in the small non-denominational cemetery on the edge of town: unfenced, a hilly woodland meadow filled with black granite and white marble headstones.

He rode to the cemetery in the Wendells' hearse, with Laura's mother. Mrs McCabe seemed to feel that Laura's death was Shadow's fault. 'If you'd been here,' she said, 'this would never have happened. I don't know why she married you. I told her. Time and again, I told her. But they don't listen to their mothers, do they?' She stopped, looked more closely at Shadow's face. 'Have you been fighting?'

'Yes,' he said.

'Barbarian,' she said, then she set her mouth, raised her head so her chins quivered, and stared straight ahead of her.

To Shadow's surprise Audrey Burton was also at the funeral,

standing toward the back. The short service ended, the casket was lowered into the cold ground. The people went away.

Shadow did not leave. He stood there with his hands in his pockets, shivering, staring at the hole in the ground.

Above him the sky was iron-grey, featureless and flat as a mirror. It continued to snow, erratically, in ghost-like tumbling flakes.

There was something he wanted to say to Laura, and he was prepared to wait until he knew what it was. The world slowly began to lose light and colour. Shadow's feet were going numb, while his hands and face hurt from the cold. He burrowed his hands into his pockets for warmth, and his fingers closed about the gold coin.

He walked over to the grave.

'This is for you,' he said.

Several shovels of earth had been emptied onto the casket, but the hole was far from full. He threw the gold coin into the grave with Laura, then he pushed more earth into the hole, to hide the coin from acquisitive grave-diggers. He brushed the earth from his hands, and said, 'Goodnight Laura.' Then he said 'I'm sorry'. He turned his face toward the lights of the town, and began to walk back into Eagle Point.

His motel was a good two miles away, but after spending three years in prison he was relishing the idea that he could simply walk and walk, forever if need be. He could keep walking north, and wind up in Alaska, or head south, to Mexico and beyond. He could walk to Patagonia, or to Tierra del Fuego.

A car drew up beside him. The window hummed down.

'You want a lift, Shadow?' asked Audrey Burton.

'No,' he said. 'And not from you.'

He continued to walk. Audrey drove beside him at three miles an hour. Snowflakes danced in the beams of her headlights.

'I thought she was my best friend,' said Audrey. 'We'd talk every day. When Robbie and I had a fight, she'd be the first one to know – we'd go down to Chi-Chi's for margaritas and to talk about what scumpots men can be. And all the time she was fucking him behind my back.'

'Please go away, Audrey.'

'I just want you to know I had good reason for what I did.'

He said nothing.

'Hey!' she shouted. 'Hey! I'm talking to you!'

Shadow turned. 'Do you want me to tell you that you were right when you spit in Laura's face? Do you want me to say it didn't hurt? Or that what you told me made me hate her more than I miss her? It's not going to happen, Audrey.'

She drove beside him for another minute, not saying anything. Then she said, 'So, how was prison, Shadow?'

'It was fine,' said Shadow. 'You would have felt right at home.'

She put her foot down on the gas then, making the engine roar, and drove on and away.

With the headlights gone, the world was dark. Twilight faded into night. Shadow kept expecting the act of walking to warm him, to spread warmth through his icy hands and feet. It didn't happen.

Back in prison, Low Key Lyesmith had once referred to the little prison cemetery out behind the infirmary as the Bone Orchard, and the image had taken root in Shadow's mind. That night he had dreamed of an orchard under the moonlight, of skeletal white trees, their branches ending in bony hands, their roots going deep down into the graves. There was fruit that grew upon the trees in the bone orchard, in his dream, and there was something very disturbing about the fruit in the dream, but on waking he could no longer remember what strange fruit grew on the trees, nor why he found it so repellent.

Cars passed him. Shadow wished that there was a sidewalk. He tripped on something that he could not see in the dark and sprawled into the ditch on the side of the road, his right hand sinking into several inches of cold mud. He climbed to his feet and wiped his hands on the leg of his pants. He stood there, awkwardly. He had only enough time to observe that there was someone beside him before something wet was forced over his nose and mouth, and he tasted harsh, chemical fumes.

This time the ditch seemed warm and comforting.

Shadow's temples felt as if they had been re-attached to the rest of his skull with roofing nails. His hands were bound behind his back with what felt like some kind of straps. He was in a car, sitting on leather upholstery. For a moment he wondered if there was something wrong with his depth perception and then he understood that, no, the other seat really *was* that far away.

There were people sitting beside him, but he could not turn to look at them.

The fat young man at the other end of the stretch limo took a can of diet Coke from the cocktail bar and popped it open. He wore a long black coat, made of some silky material, and he appeared barely out of his teens: a spattering of acne glistened on one cheek. He smiled when he saw that Shadow was awake.

'Hello Shadow,' he said. 'Don't fuck with me.'

'Okay,' said Shadow. 'I won't. Can you drop me off at the Motel America, up by the interstate?'

'Hit him,' said the young man to the person on Shadow's left. A punch was delivered to Shadow's solar plexus, knocking the breath from him, doubling him over. He straightened up, slowly.

'I said don't fuck with me. That was fucking with me. Keep your answers short and to the point or I'll fucking kill you. Or maybe I won't kill you. Maybe I'll have the children break every bone in your fucking body. There are two hundred and six of them. So don't fuck with me.'

'Got it,' said Shadow.

The ceiling lights in the limo changed colour from violet to blue then to green and to yellow.

'You're working for Wednesday,' said the young man.

'Yes,' said Shadow.

'What the fuck is he after? I mean, what's he doing here? He must have a plan. What's the game plan?'

'I started working for Mr Wednesday this morning,' said Shadow. 'I'm an errand boy.'

'You're saying you don't know?'

'I'm saying I don't know.'

The boy opened his jacket and took out a silver cigarette case from an inside pocket. He opened it, and offered a cigarette to Shadow. 'Smoke?'

Shadow thought about asking for his hands to be untied, but decided against it. 'No thank you,' he said.

The cigarette appeared to have been hand rolled, and when the boy lit it, with a matt black Zippo lighter, it smelled a little like burning electrical parts.

The boy inhaled deeply, then held his breath. He let the smoke trickle out from his mouth, pulled it back into his nostrils. Shadow suspected that he had practised that in front of a mirror for a while before doing it in public. 'If you've lied to me,' said the boy, as if from a long way away, 'I'll fucking kill you. You know that.'

'So you said.'

The boy took another long drag on his cigarette. 'You say you're staying at the Motel America?' He tapped on the driver's window, behind him. The glass window lowered. 'Hey. Motel America, up by the interstate. We need to drop off our guest.'

The driver nodded, and the glass rose up again.

The glinting fibre-optic lights inside the limo continued to change, cycling through their set of dim colours. It seemed to Shadow that the boy's eyes were glinting too, the green of an antique computer monitor.

'You tell Wednesday this, man. You tell him he's history. He's forgotten. He's old. Tell him that we are the future and we don't give a fuck about him or anyone like him. He has been consigned to the dumpster of history while people like me ride our limos down the superhighway of tomorrow.'

'I'll tell him,' said Shadow. He was beginning to feel lightheaded. He hoped that he was not going to be sick.

'Tell him that we have fucking reprogrammed reality. Tell him that language is a virus and that religion is an operating system and that prayers are just so much fucking spam. Tell him that or I'll fucking kill you,' said the young man mildly, from the smoke.

'Got it,' said Shadow. 'You can let me out here. I can walk the rest of the way.'

The young man nodded. 'Good talking to you,' he said. The smoke had mellowed him. 'You should know that if we do fucking kill you then we'll just delete you. You got that? One click and you're over-written with random ones and zeros. Undelete is not an option.' He tapped on the window behind him. 'He's getting off here,' he said. Then he turned back to Shadow, pointed to his cigarette. 'Synthetic toad-skins,' he said. 'You know they can synthesize bufotenin now?'

The car stopped, and the door was opened. Shadow climbed out awkwardly. His bonds were cut. Shadow turned around. The inside of the car was now one writhing cloud of smoke in which two lights glinted, now copper-coloured, like the beautiful eyes of a toad. 'It's all about the dominant fucking paradigm, Shadow. Nothing else is important. And hey, sorry to hear about your old lady.'

The door closed, and the stretch limo drove off, quietly. Shadow was a couple of hundred yards away from his motel, and he walked there, breathing the cold air, past red and yellow and blue lights advertising every kind of fast food a man could imagine, as long as it was a hamburger; and he reached the Motel America without incident.

3

Every hour wounds. The last one kills.
– Old Saying

There was a thin young woman behind the counter at the Motel America. She told Shadow he had already been checked in by his friend, and gave him his rectangular plastic room key. She had pale blonde hair and a rodent-like quality to her face that was most apparent when she looked suspicious, and eased when she smiled. She refused to tell him Wednesday's room number, and insisted on telephoning Wednesday on the house phone to let him know his guest was here.

Wednesday came out of a room down the hall, and beckoned to Shadow.

'How was the funeral?' he asked.

'It's over,' said Shadow.

'You want to talk about it?'

'No,' said Shadow.

'Good.' Wednesday grinned. 'Too much talking these days. Talk talk talk. This country would get along much better if people learned how to suffer in silence.'

Wednesday led the way back to his room, which was across the hall from Shadow's. There were maps all over the room, unfolded, spread out on the bed, taped to the walls. Wednesday had drawn all over the maps in bright marking pens, fluorescent greens and painful pinks and vivid oranges.

'I got hijacked by a fat kid,' said Shadow. 'He says to tell you that you have been consigned to the dungheap of history while people like him ride in their limos down the superhighways of life. Something like that.'

'Little snot,' said Wednesday.

'You know him?'

Wednesday shrugged. 'I know who he is.' He sat down, heavily, on the room's only chair. 'They don't have a clue,' he said. 'They don't have a fucking clue. How much longer do you need to stay in town?'

'I don't know. Maybe another week. I guess I need to wrap up Laura's affairs. Take care of the apartment, get rid of her clothes, all that. It'll drive her mother nuts, but the woman deserves it.'

Wednesday nodded his huge head. 'Well, the sooner you're done, the sooner we can move out of Eagle Point. Goodnight.'

Shadow walked across the hall. His room was a duplicate of Wednesday's room, down to the print of a bloody sunset on the wall above the bed. He ordered a cheese and meatball pizza, then he ran a bath, pouring all the motel's little plastic bottles of shampoo into the water, making it foam.

He was too big to lie down in the bathtub, but he sat in it and luxuriated as best he could. Shadow had promised himself a bath when he got out of prison, and Shadow kept his promises.

The pizza arrived shortly after he got out of the bath, and Shadow ate it, washing it down with a can of root beer.

Shadow lay in bed, thinking, *This is my first bed as a free man*, and the thought gave him less pleasure than he had imagined that it would. He left the drapes open, watched the lights of the cars and of the fast food joints through the window glass, comforted to know there was another world out there, one he could walk to any time he wanted.

Shadow could have been in his bed at home, he thought, in the apartment that he had shared with Laura – in the bed that he had shared with Laura. But the thought of being there without her, surrounded by her things, her scent, her life, was simply too painful . . .

Don't go there, thought Shadow. He decided to think about something else. He thought about coin tricks. Shadow knew that he did not have the personality to be a magician: he could not weave the stories that were so necessary for belief, nor did he wish to do card tricks, or produce paper flowers. But he just wanted to manipulate coins; he liked the craft of it. He started to list the coin vanishes he had mastered, which reminded him of the coin he had tossed into Laura's grave, and then, in his head, Audrey was telling him that Laura had died with Robbie's cock in her mouth, and once again he felt a small hurt in his heart.

Every hour wounds. The last one kills. Where had he heard that?

He thought of Wednesday's comment and smiled, despite himself: Shadow had heard too many people telling each other not to repress their feelings, to let their emotions out, let the pain go. Shadow thought there was a lot to be said for bottling up emotions. If you did it long enough and deep enough, he suspected, pretty soon you wouldn't feel anything at all.

Sleep took him then, without Shadow noticing.

He was walking . . .

He was walking through a room bigger than a city, and everywhere he looked there were statues and carvings and rough-hewn images. He was standing beside a statue of a woman-like thing: her naked breasts hung, flat and pendulous on her chest, around her waist was a chain of severed hands, both of her own hands held sharp knives, and, instead of a head, rising from her neck there were twin serpents, their bodies arched, facing each other, ready to attack. There was something profoundly disturbing about the statue, a deep and violent wrongness. Shadow backed away from it.

He began to walk through the hall. The carved eyes of those statues that had eyes seemed to follow his every step.

In his dream, he realised that each statue had a name burning on the floor in front of it. The man with the white hair, with a necklace of teeth about his neck, holding a drum, was *Leucotios*; the broad-hipped woman with monsters dropping from the vast gash between her legs was *Hubur*; the ram-headed man holding the golden ball was *Hershef*.

A precise voice, fussy and exact, was speaking to him, in his dream, but he could see no-one.

'These are gods who have been forgotten, and now might as well be dead. They can be found only in dry histories. They are gone, all gone, but their names and their images remain with us.'

Shadow turned a corner, and knew himself to be in another room, even vaster than the first. It went on further than the eye could see. Close to him was the skull of a mammoth, polished and brown, and a hairy ochre cloak, being worn by a small woman with a deformed left hand. Next to that were three women, each carved from the same granite boulder, joined at the waist: their faces had an unfinished, hasty look to them, although their breasts and genitalia had been carved with elaborate care; and there was a flightless bird which Shadow did not recognise, twice his height, with a beak like a vulture's, but with human arms: and on, and on.

The voice spoke once more, as if it were addressing a class, saying, 'These are the gods who have passed out of memory. Even their names are lost. The people who worshipped them are as forgotten as their gods. Their totems are long since broken and cast down. Their last priests died without passing on their secrets.

'Gods die. And when they truly die they are unmourned and unremembered. Ideas are more difficult to kill than people, but they can be killed, in the end.'

There was a whispering noise that began then to run through the hall, a low susurrus that caused Shadow, in his dream, to experience a chilling and inexplicable fear. An all-engulfing panic took him, there in the halls of the gods whose very existence had been forgotten – octopus-faced gods and gods who were only mummified hands or falling rocks or forest fires . . .

Shadow woke with his heart jackhammering in his chest, his forehead clammy, entirely awake. The red numerals on the bedside clock told him the time was 1:03 a.m. The light of the Motel America sign outside shone through his bedroom window. Disoriented, Shadow got up and walked into the tiny motel bathroom. He pissed without turning on the lights, and returned to the bedroom. The dream was still fresh and vivid in his mind's eye, but he could not explain to himself why it had scared him so.

The light that came into the room from outside was not bright, but Shadow's eyes had become used to the dark. There was a woman sitting on the side of his bed.

He knew her. He would have known her in a crowd of a thousand, or of a hundred thousand. She was still wearing the navy-blue suit they had buried her in.

Her voice was a whisper, but a familiar one. 'I guess,' said Laura, 'you're going to ask what I'm doing here.'

Shadow said nothing.

He sat down on the room's only chair, and, finally, asked, 'Babe? Is that you?'

'Yes,' she said. 'I'm cold, puppy.'

'You're dead, babe.'

'Yes,' she said. 'Yes. I am.' She patted the bed next to her. 'Come and sit by me,' she said.

'No,' said Shadow. 'I think I'll stay right here for now. We have some unresolved issues to address.'

'Like me being dead?'

'Possibly, but I was thinking more of how you died. You and Robbie.'

'Oh,' she said. 'That.'

Shadow could smell – or perhaps, he thought, he simply imagined that he smelled – an odour of rot, of flowers and preservatives. His wife – his ex-wife . . . no, he corrected himself, his *late* wife – sat on the bed and stared at him, unblinking.

'Puppy,' she said. 'Could you – do you think you could possibly get me – a cigarette?'

'I thought you gave them up.'

'I did,' she said. 'But I'm no longer concerned about the health risks. And I think it would calm my nerves. There's a machine in the lobby.'

Shadow pulled on his jeans and a tee shirt and went, barefoot, into the lobby. The night clerk was a middle-aged man, reading a book by John Grisham. Shadow bought a pack of Virginia Slims from the machine. He asked the night clerk for a book of matches.

'You're in a non-smoking room,' said the clerk. 'You make sure you open the window, now.' He passed Shadow a book of matches and a plastic ashtray with the Motel America logo on it.

'Got it,' said Shadow.

He went back into his bedroom. She had stretched out now, on top of his rumpled covers. Shadow opened the window and then passed her the cigarettes and the matches. Her fingers were cold. She lit a match and he saw that her nails, usually pristine, were battered and chewed, and there was mud under them.

Laura lit the cigarette, inhaled, blew out the match. She took another puff. 'I can't taste it,' she said. 'I don't think this is doing anything.'

'I'm sorry,' he said.

'Me too,' said Laura.

When she inhaled the cigarette tip glowed, and he was able to see her face.

'So,' she said. 'They let you out.'

'Yes.'

The tip of the cigarette glowed orange. 'I'm still grateful. I should never have got you mixed up in it.'

'Well,' he said, 'I agreed to do it. I could have said no.' He wondered why he wasn't scared of her: why a dream of a museum could leave him terrified, while he seemed to be coping with a walking corpse without fear.

'Yes,' she said. 'You could have. You big galoot.' Smoke wreathed her face. She was very beautiful in the dim light. 'You want to know about me and Robbie?'

'I guess.'

She stubbed out the cigarette in the ashtray. 'You were in prison,' she said. 'And I needed someone to talk to. I needed a shoulder to cry on. You weren't there. I was upset.'

'I'm sorry.' Shadow realised something was different about her voice, and he tried to figure out what it was.

'I know. So we'd meet for coffee. Talk about what we'd do when you got out of prison. How good it would be to see you again. He really liked you, you know. He was looking forward to giving you back your old job.'

'Yes.'

'And then Audrey went to visit her sister for a week. This was, oh, a year, thirteen months after you'd gone away.' Her voice lacked expression; each word was flat and dull, like pebbles dropped, one by one, into a deep well. 'Robbie came over. We got drunk together. We did it on the floor of the bedroom. It was good. It was really good.'

'I didn't need to hear that.'

'No? I'm sorry. It's harder to pick and choose when you're dead. It's like a photograph, you know. It doesn't matter as much.'

'It matters to me.'

Laura lit another cigarette. Her movements were fluid and competent, not stiff. Shadow wondered, for a moment, if she was dead at all. Perhaps this was some kind of elaborate trick. 'Yes,' she said. 'I see that. Well, we carried on our affair – although we didn't call it that, we did not call it anything – for most of the last two years.'

'Were you going to leave me for him?'

'Why would I do that? You're my big bear. You're my puppy. You did what you did for me. I waited three years for you to come back to me. I love you.'

He stopped himself from saying *I love you, too*. He wasn't going to say that. Not any more. 'So what happened the other night?'

'The night I was killed?'

'Yes.'

'Well, Robbie and I went out to talk about your welcome back surprise party. It would have been so good. And I told him that we were done. Finished. That now that you were back that was the way it had to be.'

'Mm. Thank you.'

'You're welcome, darling.' The ghost of a smile crossed her face. 'We got maudlin. It was sweet. We got stupid. I got very drunk. He didn't. He had to drive. We were driving home and I announced that I was going to give him a goodbye blowjob, one last time with feeling, and I unzipped his pants, and I did.'

'Big mistake.'

'Tell me about it. I knocked the gearshift with my shoulder, and then Robbie was trying to push me out of the way to put the car back in gear, and we were swerving, and there was a loud crunch and I remember the world started to roll and to spin, and I thought "I'm going to die." It was very dispassionate. I remember that. I wasn't scared. And then I don't remember anything more.'

There was a smell like burning plastic. It was the cigarette, Shadow realised: it had burned down to the filter. Laura did not seem to have noticed.

'What are you doing here, Laura?'

'Can't a wife come and see her husband?'

'You're dead. I went to your funeral this afternoon.'

'Yes.' She stopped talking, stared into nothing. Shadow stood up and walked over to her. He took the smouldering cigarette butt from her fingers and threw it out of the window.

'Well?'

Her eyes sought his. 'I don't know much more than I did when I was alive. Most of the stuff I know now that I didn't know then I can't put into words.'

'Normally people who die stay in their graves,' said Shadow.

'Do they? Do they really, puppy? I used to think they did too. Now I'm not so sure. Perhaps.' She climbed off the bed and walked over to the window. Her face, in the light of the motel sign, was as beautiful as it had ever been. The face of the woman he had gone to prison for.

His heart hurt in his chest as if someone had taken it in a fist and squeezed. 'Laura . . . ?'

She did not look at him. 'You've gotten yourself mixed up in some bad things, Shadow. You're going to screw it up, if someone isn't there to watch out for you. I'm watching out for you. And thank you for my present.'

'What present?'

She reached into the pocket of her blouse, and pulled out the gold coin he had thrown into the grave earlier that day. There was still black dirt on it. 'I may have it put on a chain. It was very sweet of you.'

'You're welcome.'

She turned then and looked at him with eyes that seemed both to see and not to see him. 'I think there are several aspects of our marriage we're going to have to work on.'

'Babes,' he told her. 'You're dead.'

'That's one of those aspects, obviously.' She paused. 'Okay,' she said. 'I'm going now. It will be better if I go.' And, naturally and easily, she turned and put her hands on Shadow's shoulders, and went up on tiptoes to kiss him goodbye, as she had always kissed him goodbye.

Awkwardly he bent to kiss her on the cheek, but she moved her mouth as he did so and pushed her lips against his. Her breath smelled, faintly, of mothballs.

Laura's tongue flickered into Shadow's mouth. It was cold, and dry, and it tasted of cigarettes and of bile. If Shadow had had any doubts as to whether his wife was dead or not, they ended then.

He pulled back.

'I love you,' she said, simply. 'I'll be looking out for you.' She walked over to the motel room door. There was a strange taste in his mouth. 'Get some sleep, puppy,' she told him. 'And stay out of trouble.'

She opened the door to the hall. The fluorescent light in the hallway was not kind: beneath it, Laura looked dead, but then, it did that to everyone.

'You could have asked me to stay the night,' she said, in her cold-stone voice.

'I don't think I could,' said Shadow.

'You will, hon,' she said. 'Before all this is over. You will.' She turned away from him, and walked down the corridor.

Shadow looked out of the doorway. The nightclerk kept on reading his John Grisham novel, and barely looked up as she walked past him. There was thick graveyard mud clinging to her shoes. And then she was gone.

Shadow breathed out, a slow sigh. His heart was pounding arrhythmically in his chest. He walked across the hall, and knocked on Wednesday's door. As he knocked he got the weirdest notion, that he was being buffeted by black wings, as if an enormous crow was flying through him, out into the hall and the world beyond.

Wednesday opened the door. He had a white motel towel wrapped around his waist, but was otherwise naked. 'What the hell do you want?' he asked.

'Something you should know,' said Shadow. 'Maybe it was a dream – but it wasn't – or maybe I inhaled some of the fat kid's synthetic toadskin smoke, or probably I'm just going mad . . .'

'Yeah, yeah. Spit it out,' said Wednesday. 'I'm kind of in the middle of something here.'

Shadow glanced into the room. He could see that there was someone in the bed, watching him. A sheet pulled up over small breasts. Pale blonde hair, something rattish about the face. He lowered his voice. 'I just saw my wife,' he said. 'She was in my room.'

'A ghost, you mean? You saw a ghost?'

'No. Not a ghost. She was solid. It was her. She's dead all right, but it wasn't any kind of a ghost. I touched her. She kissed me.'

'I see.' Wednesday darted a look at the woman in the bed. 'Be right back, m'dear,' he said.

They crossed the hall to Shadow's room. Wednesday turned on the lamps. He looked at the cigarette butt in the ashtray. He scratched his chest. His nipples were dark, old-man nipples, and his chest hair was grizzled. There was a white scar down one side of his torso. He sniffed the air. Then he shrugged.

'Okay,' he said. 'So your dead wife showed up. You scared?'

'A little.'

'Very wise. The dead always give me the screaming mimis. Anything else?'

'I'm ready to leave Eagle Point. Laura's mother can sort out the apartment, all that. She hates me anyway. I'm ready to go when you are.'

Wednesday smiled. 'Good news, my boy. We'll leave in the morning. Now, you should get some sleep. I have some scotch in my room, if you need help sleeping. Yes?'

'No. I'll be fine.'

'Then do not disturb me further. I have a long night ahead of me.'

'Good night,' said Shadow.

'Exactly,' said Wednesday, and he closed the door as he went out.

Shadow sat down on the bed. The smell of cigarettes and preservatives lingered in the air. He wished that he were mourning Laura: it seemed more appropriate than being troubled by her or, he admitted it to himself now that she had gone, just a little scared by her. It was time to mourn. He turned the lights out, and lay on the bed, and thought of Laura as she was before he went to prison. He remembered their marriage when they were young and happy and stupid and unable to keep their hands off each other.

It had been a very long time since Shadow had cried, so long he thought he had forgotten how. He had not even cried when his mother died.

But he began to cry now, in painful, lurching sobs, and for the first time since he was a small boy, Shadow cried himself to sleep.

COMING TO AMERICA
813 AD

They navigated the green sea by the stars and by the shore, and when the shore was only a memory and the night sky was overcast and dark they navigated by faith, and they called on the all-father to bring them safely to land once more.

A bad journey they had of it, their fingers numb and with a shiver in their bones that not even wine could burn off. They would wake in the morning to see that the hoar-frost had touched their beards, and, until the sun warmed them, they looked like old men, white-bearded before their time.

Teeth were loosening and eyes were deep-sunken in their sockets when they made landfall on the green land to the west. The men said, 'We are far, far from our homes and our hearths, far from the seas we know and the lands we love. Here on the edge of the world we will be forgotten by our gods.'

Their leader clambered to the top of a great rock, and he mocked them for their lack of faith. 'The all-father made the world,' he shouted. 'He built it with his hands from the shattered bones and the flesh of Ymir, his grandfather. He placed Ymir's brains in the sky as clouds, and his salt blood became the seas we crossed. If he made the world, do you not realise that he created this land as well? And if we die here as men, shall we not be received into his hall?'

And the men cheered and laughed. They set to, with a will, to build a hall out of split trees and mud, inside a small stockade of sharpened logs, although as far as they knew they were the only men in the new land.

On the day that the hall was finished there was a storm: the sky at mid-day became as dark as night, and the sky was rent with forks of white flame, and the thunder-crashes were so loud that the men were almost deafened by them, and the ship's cat they had brought with them for good fortune hid beneath their beached longboat. The storm was hard enough and vicious enough that the men laughed and clapped each other on the back, and they said 'The thunderer is here with us, in this distant land,' and they gave thanks, and rejoiced, and they drank until they were reeling.

In the smoky darkness of their hall, that night, the bard sang them the old songs. He sang of Odin, the all-father, who was sacrificed to himself as bravely and as nobly as others were sacrificed to him. He sang of the nine days that the all-father hung from the world-tree, his side pierced and dripping from the spear-point's wound, and he sang them all the things the all-father had learned in his agony: nine names, and nine runes, and twice-nine charms. When he told them of the spear piercing Odin's side, the bard shrieked in pain as the all-father himself had called out in his agony, and all the men shivered, imagining his pain.

They found the scraeling the following day, which was the all-father's own day. He was a small man, his long hair black as a crow's wing, his skin the colour of rich red clay. He spoke in words none of them could understand, not even their bard who had been on a ship that had sailed through the pillars of Hercules, and who could speak the trader's pidgin men spoke all across the Mediterranean. The stranger was dressed in feathers and in furs, and there were small bones braided into his long hair.

They led him into their encampment, and they gave him roasted meat to eat, and strong drink to quench his thirst. They laughed riotously at the man as he stumbled and sang, at the way his head rolled and lolled, and this on less than a drinking-horn of mead. They gave him more drink, and soon enough he lay beneath the table with his head curled under his arm.

Then they picked him up, a man at each shoulder, a man at each leg, carried him at shoulder height, the four men making him an eight-legged horse, and they carried him at the head of a procession to an ash tree on the hill overlooking the bay, where they put a rope around his neck and hung him high in the wind, their tribute to the all-father, the gallows lord. The scraeling's body swung in the wind, his face blackening, his tongue protruding, his eyes popping, his penis hard enough to hang a leather helmet on, while the men cheered and shouted and laughed, proud to be sending their sacrifice to the Heavens.

And, the next day, when two huge ravens landed upon the screaling's corpse, one on each shoulder, and commenced to peck at its cheeks and eyes, the men knew their sacrifice had been accepted.

It was a long winter, and they were hungry, but they were cheered by the thought that, when spring came, they would send the boat back to the northlands, and it would bring settlers, and bring women. As the weather became colder, and the days became shorter, some of the men took to searching for the screaling village, hoping to find food, and women. They found nothing, save for the places where fires had been, where small encampments had been abandoned.

One mid-winter's day, when the sun was as distant and cold as a dull silver coin, they saw that the remains of the screaling's body had been removed from the ash-tree. That afternoon it began to snow, in huge, slow flakes.

The men from the northlands closed the gates of their encampment, retreated behind their wooden wall.

The screaling war party fell upon them that night: five hundred men to thirty. They climbed the wall, and, over the following seven days they killed each of the thirty men, in thirty different ways. And the sailors were forgotten, by history and their people.

The wall they tore down, and the village they burned. The long-boat, upside down and pulled high on the shingle, they also burned, hoping that the pale strangers had but one boat, and that by burning it they were ensuring that no other Northmen would come to their shores.

It was more than a hundred years before Leif the Fortunate, son of Erik the Red, rediscovered that land, which he would call Vineland. His gods were already waiting for him when he arrived: Tyr, one-handed, and grey Odin gallows-god, and Thor of the thunders.

They were there.

They were waiting.

Let the Midnight Special
Shine its light on me
Let the Midnight Special
Shine its ever-lovin' light on me
– traditional, *The Midnight Special*

Shadow and Wednesday ate breakfast at a Country Kitchen across the street from their motel. It was eight in the morning, and the world was misty and chill.

'You still ready to leave Eagle Point?' asked Wednesday. 'I have some calls to make, if you are. Friday today. Friday's a free day. A woman's day. Saturday tomorrow. Much to do on Saturday.'

'I'm ready,' said Shadow. 'Nothing keeping me here.'

Wednesday heaped his plate high with several kinds of breakfast meats. Shadow took some melon, a bagel, and a packet of cream cheese. They went and sat down in a booth.

'That was some dream you had last night,' said Wednesday.

'Yes,' said Shadow. 'It was.' Laura's muddy footprints had been visible on the motel carpet when he got up that morning, leading from his bedroom to the lobby and out the door.

'So,' said Wednesday. 'Why'd they call you Shadow?'

Shadow shrugged. 'It's a name,' he said. Outside the plate glass the world in the mist had become a pencil drawing executed in a dozen different greys with, here and there, a smudge of electric red or pure white. 'How'd you lose your eye?'

Wednesday shoveled half a dozen pieces of bacon into his mouth, chewed, wiped the fat from his lips with the back of his hand. 'Didn't lose it,' he said. 'I still know exactly where it is.'

'So what's the plan?'

Wednesday looked thoughtful. He ate several vivid pink slices of ham, picked a fragment of meat from his beard, dropped it onto his plate. 'Plan is as follows. Tomorrow night we shall be meeting with a number of persons preeminent in their respective fields – do not let their demeanor intimidate you. We shall meet at one of the most important places in the entire country. Afterward we shall wine and dine them. I need to enlist them in my current enterprise.'

'And where is this most important place?'

'You'll see, m' boy. I said one of them. Opinions are justifiably divided. I have sent word to my colleagues. We'll stop off in Chicago on the way, as I need to pick up some money. Entertaining, in the manner we shall need to entertain, will take more ready cash than I currently have available. Then on to Madison.' Wednesday paid and they left, walked back across the road to the motel parking lot. Wednesday tossed Shadow the car keys. He drove down to the freeway and out of town.

'You going to miss it?' asked Wednesday. He was sorting through a folder filled with maps.

'The town? No. I didn't really ever have a life here. I was never in one place too long as a kid, and I didn't get here until I was in my twenties. So this town is Laura's.'

'Let's hope she stays here,' said Wednesday.

'It was a dream,' said Shadow. 'Remember.'

'That's good,' said Wednesday. 'Healthy attitude to have. Did you fuck her last night?'

Shadow took a breath. Then, 'That is none of your damn business. And no.'

'Did you want to?'

Shadow said nothing at all. He drove north, toward Chicago. Wednesday chuckled, and began to pore over his maps, unfolding and refolding them, making occasional notes on a yellow legal pad with a large silver ballpoint pen.

Eventually he was finished. He put his pen away, put the folder on the back seat. 'The best thing about the states we're heading for,' said Wednesday, 'Minnesota, Wisconsin, all around there, is it has the kind of women I liked when I was younger. Pale-skinned and blue-eyed, hair so fair it's almost white, wine-coloured lips, and round, full breasts with the veins running through them like a good cheese.'

'Only when you were younger?' asked Shadow. 'Looked like you were doing pretty good last night.'

'Yes.' Wednesday smiled. 'Would you like to know the secret of my success?'

'You pay them?'

'Nothing so crude. No, the secret is charm. Pure and simple.'

'Charm, huh? Well, like they say, you either got it or you ain't.'

'Charms can be learnt,' said Wednesday.

Shadow tuned the radio to an oldies station, and listened to songs that were current before he was born. Bob Dylan sang about a hard rain that was going to fall, and Shadow wondered if that rain had fallen yet, or if it was something that was still going to happen. The road ahead of them was empty and the ice crystals on the asphalt glittered like diamonds in the morning sun.

Chicago happened slowly, like a migraine. First they were driving through countryside, then, imperceptibly, the occasional town became a low suburban sprawl, and the sprawl became the city.

They parked outside a squat black brownstone. The sidewalk was clear of snow. They walked to the lobby. Wednesday pressed the top button on the gouged metal intercom box. Nothing happened. He pressed it again. Then, experimentally, he began to press the other buttons, for other tenants, with no response.

'It's dead,' said a gaunt old woman, coming down the steps. 'Doesn't work. We call the super, ask him when he going to fix, when he going to mend the heating, he does not care, goes to Arizona for the winter for his chest.' Her accent was thick, Eastern European, Shadow guessed.

Wednesday bowed low. 'Zorya, my dear, may I say how unutterably beautiful you look? A radiant creature. You have not aged.'

The old woman glared at him. 'He don't want to see you. I don't want to see you neither. You bad news.'

'That's because I don't come if it isn't important.'

The woman sniffed. She carried an empty string shopping bag, and wore an old red coat, buttoned up to her chin. She looked at Shadow suspiciously.

'Who is the big man?' she asked Wednesday. 'Another one of your murderers?'

'You do me a deep disservice, good lady. This gentleman is called Shadow. He is working for me, yes, but on your behalf. Shadow, may I introduce you to the lovely Miss Zorya Vechernyaya.'

'Good to meet you,' said Shadow.

Bird-like, the old woman peered up at him. 'Shadow,' she said. 'A good name. When the shadows are long, that is my time. And you are the long shadow.' She looked him up and down, then she smiled. 'You may kiss my hand,' she said, and extended a cold hand to him.

Shadow bent down and kissed her thin hand. She had a large amber ring on her middle finger.

'Good boy,' she said. 'I am going to buy groceries. You see, I am the only one of us who brings in any money. The other two cannot make money fortune-telling. This is because they only tell the truth, and the truth is not what people want to hear. It is a bad thing, and it troubles people, so they do not come back. But I can lie to them, tell them what they want to hear. So I bring home the bread. Do you think you will be here for supper?'

'I would hope so,' said Wednesday.

'Then you had better give me some money to buy more food,' she said. 'I am proud, but I am not stupid. The others are prouder than I am, and *he* is the proudest of all. So give me money and do not tell them that you give me money.'

Wednesday opened his wallet, and reached in. He took out a twenty. Zorya Vechernyaya plucked it from his fingers, and waited. He took out another twenty and gave it to her.

'Is good,' she said. 'We will feed you like princes. Now, go up the stairs to the top. Zorya Utrennyaya is awake, but our other sister is still asleep, so do not be making too much noise.'

Shadow and Wednesday climbed the dark stairs. The landing two storeys up was half filled with black plastic garbage bags and it smelled of rotting vegetables.

'Are they gypsies?' asked Shadow.

'Zorya and her family? Not at all. They're not *Rom*. They're Russian. Slavs, I believe.'

'But she does fortune-telling.'

'Lots of people do fortune-telling. I dabble in it myself.' Wednesday was panting as they went up the final flight of stairs. 'I'm out of shape.'

The landing at the top of the stairs ended in a single door painted red, with a peephole in it.

Wednesday knocked at the door. There was no response. He knocked again, louder this time.

'Okay! Okay! I heard you! I heard you!' The sound of locks being undone, of bolts being pulled, the rattle of a chain. The red door opened a crack.

'Who is it?' A man's voice, old and cigarette-roughened.

'An old friend, Czernobog. With an associate.'

The door opened as far as the security chain would allow. Shadow could see a grey face, in the shadows, peering out at them. 'What do you want, Votan?'

'Initially, simply the pleasure of your company. And I have information to share. What's that phrase . . . oh yes. You may learn something to your advantage.'

The door opened all the way. The man in the dusty bathrobe was short, with iron-grey hair, and craggy features. He wore grey pinstripe pants, shiny from age, and slippers. He held an unfiltered cigarette with square-tipped fingers, sucking the tip while keeping it cupped in his fist – like a convict, thought Shadow, or a soldier. He extended his left hand to Wednesday. 'Welcome then, Votan.'

'They call me Wednesday these days,' he said, shaking the old man's hand.

A narrow smile; a flash of yellow teeth. 'Yes,' he said. 'Very funny. And this is?'

'This is my associate. Shadow, meet Mr Czernobog.'

'Well met,' said Czernobog. He shook Shadow's left hand with his own. His hands were rough and calloused, and the tips of his fingers were as yellow as if they had been dipped in iodine.

'How do you do, Mr Czernobog.'

'I do old. My guts ache, and my back hurts, and I cough my chest apart every morning.'

'Why you are standing at the door?' asked a woman's voice. Shadow looked over Czernobog's shoulder, at the old woman standing behind him. She was smaller and frailer than her sister, but her hair was long and still golden. 'I am Zorya Utrennyaya,' she said. 'You must not stand there in the hall. You must go in, sit down. I will bring you coffee.'

Through the doorway into an apartment that smelled like over-boiled cabbage and cat-box and unfiltered foreign cigarettes, and they were ushered through a tiny hallway past several closed doors to the sitting room at the far end of the corridor, and were seated on a huge old horsehair sofa, disturbing an elderly grey cat in the process, who stretched, stood up, and walked, stiffly, to a distant part of the sofa, where he lay down, warily stared at each of them in turn, then closed one eye and went back to sleep. Czernobog sat in an armchair across from them.

Zorya Utrennyaya found an empty ashtray and placed it beside Czernobog. 'How you want your coffee?' she asked her guests. 'Here we take it black as night, sweet as sin.'

'That'll be fine, ma'am,' said Shadow. He looked out of the window, at the buildings across the street.

Zorya Utrennyaya went out. Czernobog stared at her as she left. 'That's a good woman,' he said. 'Not like her sisters. One of them is a harpy, the other, all she does is sleep.' He put his slippered feet up on a long, low coffee table, a chess board inset in the middle, cigarette burns and mug rings on its surface.

'Is she your wife?' asked Shadow.

'She's nobody's wife.' The old man sat in silence for a moment, looking down at his rough hands. 'No. We are all relatives. We come over here together, long time ago.'

From the pocket of his bathrobe, Czernobog produced a pack of unfiltered cigarettes. Wednesday pulled out a narrow gold lighter, and lit the old man's cigarette. 'First we come to New York,' said Czernobog. 'All our countrymen go to New York. Then, we come out here, to Chicago. Everything got very bad. Even in the old country, they had nearly forgotten me. Here, I am just a bad memory. You know what I did when I got to Chicago?'

'No,' said Shadow.

'I get a job in the meat business. On the kill floor. When the steer comes up the ramp, I was a knocker. You know why we are called knockers? Is because we take the sledgehammer and we *knock* the cow down with it. *Bam!* It takes strength in the arms. Yes? Then the shackler chains the beef up, hauls it up, then they cut the throat. They drain the blood first before they cut the head off. We were the strongest, the knockers.' He pushed up the sleeve of his bathrobe, flexed his upper arm to display the muscles still visible under the old skin. 'Is not just strong though. There was an art to it. To the blow. Otherwise the cow is just stunned, or angry. Then, in the fifties, they give us the bolt gun. You put it to the forehead, *bam! bam!* Now you think, anybody can kill. Not so.' He mimed putting a metal bolt through a cow's head. 'It still takes skill.' He smiled at the memory, displaying an iron-coloured tooth.

'Don't tell them cow-killing stories.' Zorya Utrennyaya carried in their coffee on a red wooden tray, in small brightly-enameled cups. She gave them each a cup, then sat beside Czernobog.

'Zorya Vechernyaya is doing shopping,' she said. 'She will be soon back.'

'We met her downstairs,' said Shadow. 'She says she tells fortunes.'

'Yes,' said her sister. 'In the twilight, that is the time for lies. I do not tell good lies, so I am a poor fortune-teller. And our sister, Zorya Polunochnaya, she can tell no lies at all.'

The coffee was even sweeter and stronger than Shadow had expected.

Shadow excused himself to use the bathroom – a closet-like room, hung with several brown-spotted framed photographs of men and women in stiff Victorian poses. It was early afternoon, but already the daylight was beginning to fade. He heard voices raised from down the hall. He washed his hands in icy-cold water with a sickly-smelling sliver of pink soap.

Czernobog was standing in the hall, as Shadow came out.

'You bring trouble!' he was shouting. 'Nothing but trouble! I will not listen! You will get out of my house!'

Wednesday was still sitting on the sofa, sipping his coffee, stroking the grey cat. Zorya Utrennyaya stood on the thin carpet, one hand nervously twining in and out of her long yellow hair.

'Is there a problem?' asked Shadow.

'*He* is the problem!' shouted Czernobog. '*He* is! You tell him that there is nothing will make me help him! I want him to go! I want him out of here! Both of you go!'

'Please,' said Zorya Utrennyaya, 'please be quiet, you wake up Zorya Polunochnaya.'

'You are like him, you want me to join his madness!' shouted Czernobog. He looked as if he was on the verge of tears. A pillar of ash tumbled from his cigarette onto the threadbare hall carpet.

Wednesday stood up, walked over to Czernobog. He rested his hand on Czernobog's shoulder. 'Listen,' he said, peaceably. 'Firstly, it's not madness. It's the only way. Secondly, everyone will be there. You would not want to be left out, would you?'

'You know who I am,' said Czernobog. 'You know what these hands have done. You want my brother, not me. And he's gone.'

A door in the hallway opened, and a sleepy female voice said, 'Is something wrong?'

'Nothing is wrong, my sister,' said Zorya Utrennyaya, 'Go back to sleep.' Then she turned to Czernobog. 'See? See what you do with all your shouting? You go back in there and sit down. Sit!' Czernobog looked as if he were about to protest; and then the fight went out of him. He looked frail, suddenly: frail, and lonely.

The three men went back into the shabby sitting room. There was a brown nicotine ring around that room that ended about a foot from the ceiling, like the tide-line in an old bathtub.

'It doesn't have to be for you,' said Wednesday to Czernobog, unfazed. 'If it is for your brother, it's for you as well. That's one place you dualistic types have it over the rest of us, eh?'

Czernobog said nothing.

'Speaking of Bielebog, have you heard anything from him?'

Czernobog shook his head. He looked up at Shadow. 'Do you have a brother?'

'No,' said Shadow. 'Not that I know of.'

'I have a brother. They say, you put us together, we are like one person, you know? When we are young, his hair, it is very blond, very light, his eyes are blue, and people say, he is the good one. And my hair it is very dark, darker than yours even, and people say I am the rogue, you know? I am the bad one. And now time passes, and my hair is grey. His hair, too, I think, is grey. And you look at us, you would not know who was light, who was dark.'

'Were you close?' asked Shadow.

'Close?' asked Czernobog. 'No. How could we be? We cared about such different things.'

There was a clatter from the end of the hall, and Zorya Vechernyaya came in. 'Supper in one hour,' she said. Then she went out.

Czernobog sighed. 'She thinks she is a good cook,' he said. 'She was brought up, there were servants to cook. Now, there are no servants. There is nothing.'

'Not nothing,' said Wednesday. 'Never nothing.'

'You,' said Czernobog. 'I shall not listen to you.' He turned to Shadow. 'Do you play checkers?' he asked.

'Yes,' said Shadow.

'Good. You shall play checkers with me,' he said, taking a wooden box of pieces from the mantlepiece, and shaking them out onto the table. 'I shall play black.'

Wednesday touched Shadow's arm. 'You don't have to do this, you know,' he said.

'Not a problem. I want to,' said Shadow. Wednesday shrugged, and picked up an old copy of the *Reader's Digest* from a small pile of yellowing magazines on the window-sill.

Czernobog's brown fingers finished arranging the pieces on the squares, and the game began.

In the days that were to come, Shadow often found himself remembering that game. Some nights he dreamed of it. His flat, round pieces were the colour of old, dirty wood, nominally white. Czernobog's were a dull, faded black. Shadow was the first to move. In his dreams, there was no conversation as they played, just the loud click as the pieces were put down, or the hiss of wood against wood as they were slid from square to adjoining square.

For the first half dozen moves each of the men slipped pieces out onto the board, into the centre, leaving the back rows untouched. There were pauses between the moves, long, chess-like pauses, while each man watched, and thought.

Shadow had played checkers in prison: it passed the time. He had played chess, too, but he was not temperamentally suited to planning ahead. He preferred picking the perfect move for the moment. You could win in checkers like that, sometimes.

There was a click, as Czernobog picked up a black piece and

jumped it over one of Shadow's white pieces. The old man picked up Shadow's white piece and put it on the table at the side of the board.

'First blood. You have lost,' said Czernobog. 'The game is done.'

'No,' said Shadow. 'Game's got a long way to go yet.'

'Then would you care for a wager? A little side bet, to make it more interesting?'

'No,' said Wednesday, without looking up from a *Humor In Uniform* column. 'He wouldn't.'

'I am not playing with you, old man. I play with him. So, you want to bet on the game, Mister Shadow?'

'What were you two arguing about, before?' asked Shadow.

Czernobog raised a craggy eyebrow. 'Your master wants me to come with him. To help him with his nonsense. I would rather die.'

'You want to bet? Okay. If I win, you come with us.'

The old man pursed his lips. 'Perhaps,' he said. 'But only if you take my forfeit, when you lose.'

'And that would be?'

There was no change in Czernobog's expression. 'If I win, I get to knock your brains out. With the sledgehammer. First you go down on your knees. Then I hit you a blow with it, so you don't get up again.' Shadow looked at the man's old face, trying to read him. He was not joking, Shadow was certain of that: there was a hunger there for something, for pain, or death or retribution.

Wednesday closed the *Reader's Digest*. 'This is ridiculous,' he said. 'I was wrong to come here. Shadow, we're leaving.' The grey cat, disturbed, got to its feet and stepped onto the table beside the checkers game. It stared at the pieces, then leapt down onto the floor and, tail held high, it stalked from the room.

'No,' said Shadow. He was not scared of dying. After all, it was not as if he had anything to live for. 'It's fine. I accept. If you win the game, you get the chance to knock my brains out with one blow of your sledgehammer,' and he moved his next white piece to the adjoining square on the edge of the board.

Nothing more was said, but Wednesday did not pick up his *Reader's Digest* again. He watched the game with his glass eye and his true eye, with an expression that betrayed nothing.

Czernobog took another of Shadow's pieces. Shadow took two of

Czernobog's. From the corridor came the smell of unfamiliar foods cooking. While not all of the smells were appetizing, Shadow realised suddenly how hungry he was.

The two men moved their pieces, black and white, turn and turn-about. A flurry of pieces taken, a blossoming of two-piece-high kings: no longer forced to move only forward on the board, a sideways slip at a time, the kings could move forward or back, which made them doubly dangerous. They had reached the furthest row, and could go where they wanted. Czernobog had three kings, Shadow had two.

Czernobog moved one of his kings around the board, eliminating Shadow's remaining pieces, while using the other two kings to keep Shadow's pieces pinned down.

And then Czernobog made a fourth king, and returned down the board to Shadow's two kings, and, unsmiling, took them both. And that was that.

'So,' said Czernobog. 'I get to knock out your brains. And you will go on your knees willingly. Is good.' He reached out an old hand, and patted Shadow's arm with it.

'We've still got time before dinner's ready,' said Shadow. 'You want another game? Same terms?'

Czernobog lit another cigarette, from a kitchen box of matches. 'How can it be same terms? You want I should kill you twice?'

'Right now, you have one blow, that's all. You told me yourself that it's not just strength, it's skill too. This way, if you win this game, you get two blows to my head.'

Czernobog glowered. 'One blow, is all it takes, one blow. That is the art.' He patted his upper right arm, where the muscles were, with his left, scattering grey ash from the cigarette in his left hand.

'It's been a long time. If you've lost your skill you might simply bruise me. How long has it been since you swung a killing hammer in the stockyards? Thirty years? Forty?'

Czernobog said nothing. His closed mouth was a grey slash across his face. He tapped his fingers on the wooden table, drumming out a rhythm with them. Then he pushed the twenty-four checkers pieces back to their home squares on the board.

'Play,' he said. 'Again, you are light. I am dark.'

Shadow pushed his first piece out. Czernobog pushed one of his own pieces forward. And it occurred to Shadow that Czernobog was going to try to play the same game again, the one that he had just won, that this would be his limitation.

This time Shadow played recklessly. He snatched tiny opportunities, moved without thinking, without a pause to consider. And this time, as he played, Shadow smiled; and whenever Czernobog moved a piece, Shadow smiled wider.

Soon, Czernobog was slamming his pieces down as he moved them, banging them down on the wooden table so hard that the remaining pieces shivered on their black squares.

'There,' said Czernobog, taking one of Shadow's men with a crash, slamming the black piece down. 'There. What do you say to that?'

Shadow said nothing: he simply smiled, and jumped the piece that Czernobog had put down, and another, and another, and a fourth, clearing the centre of the board of black pieces. He took a white piece from the pile beside the board and kinged his man.

After that, it was just a mopping up exercise: another handful of moves, and the game was done.

Shadow said, 'Best of three?'

Czernobog simply stared at him, his grey eyes like points of steel. And then he laughed, clapped his hands on Shadow's shoulders. 'I like you!' he exclaimed. 'You have balls.'

Then Zorya Utrennyaya put her head around the door to tell them that dinner was ready, and they should clear their game away, and put the tablecloth down on the table.

'We have no dining room,' she said, 'I am sorry. We eat in here.'

Serving dishes were placed on the table. Each of the diners was given a small painted tray on which was some tarnished cutlery, to hold on his or her lap.

Zorya Vechernyaya took five wooden bowls and placed an unpeeled boiled potato in each, then ladled in a healthy serving of a ferociously crimson borscht. She plopped a spoonful of white sour cream in, and handed the bowls to each of them.

'I thought there were six of us,' said Shadow.

'Zorya Polunochnaya is still asleep,' said Zorya Vechernyaya. 'We keep her food in the refrigerator. When she wakes, she will eat.'

The borscht was vinegary, and tasted like pickled beets. The boiled potato was mealy.

The next course was a leathery pot-roast, accompanied by greens of some description – although they had been boiled so long and so thoroughly that they were no longer, by any stretch of the imagination, greens, and were in fact well on their way to becoming browns.

Then there were cabbage leaves stuffed with ground meat and rice, cabbage leaves of such a toughness that they were almost impossible to cut without spattering ground meat and rice all over the carpet. Shadow pushed his around his plate.

'We played checkers,' said Czernobog, hacking himself another lump of pot roast. 'The young man and me. He won a game, I won a game. Because he won a game, I have agreed to go with him and Wednesday, and help them in their madness. And because I won a game, when this is all done, I get to kill the young man, with a blow of a hammer.'

The two Zoryas nodded gravely. 'Such a pity,' Zorya Vechernyaya told Shadow. 'In my fortune for you, I should have said you would have a long life and a happy one, with many children.'

'That is why you are a good fortune teller,' said Zorya Utrennyaya. She looked sleepy, as if it were an effort for her to be up so late. 'You tell the best lies.'

At the end of the meal, Shadow was still hungry. Prison food had been pretty bad, and prison food was better than this.

'Good food,' said Wednesday, who had cleaned his plate with every evidence of enjoyment. 'I thank you ladies. And now, I am afraid that it is incumbent upon us to ask you to recommend to us a fine hotel in the neighborhood.'

Zorya Vechernyaya looked offended at this. 'Why should you go to a hotel?' she said. 'We are not your friends?'

'I couldn't put you to any trouble . . .' said Wednesday.

'Is no trouble,' said Zorya Utrennyaya, one hand playing with her incongruously golden hair, and she yawned.

'*You* can sleep in Bielebog's room,' said Zorya Vechernyaya, pointing to Wednesday. 'Is empty. And for you, young man, I make up a bed on sofa. You will be more comfortable than in feather bed. I swear.'

'That would be really kind of you,' said Wednesday. 'We accept.'

'And you pay me only no more than what you pay for hotel,'

said Zorya Vechernyaya, with a triumphant toss of her head. 'A hundred dollars.'

'Thirty,' said Wednesday.

'Fifty.'

'Thirty-five.'

'Forty-five.'

'Forty.'

'Is good. Forty-five dollar.' Zorya Vechernyaya reached across the table and shook Wednesday's hand. Then she began to clean the pots off the table. Zorya Utrennyaya yawned so hugely Shadow worried that she might dislocate her jaw, and announced that she was going to bed before she fell asleep with her head in the pie, and she said goodnight to them all.

Shadow helped Zorya Vechernyaya to take the plates and dishes into the little kitchen. To his surprise there was an elderly dish-washing machine beneath the sink, and he filled it. Zorya Vechernyaya looked over his shoulder, tutted, and removed the wooden borscht-bowls. 'Those, in the sink,' she told him.

'Sorry.'

'Is not to worry. Now, back in there, we have pie,' she said.

The pie – it was an apple pie – had been bought in a store and oven-warmed, and was very, very good. The four of them ate it with ice-cream, and then Zorya Vechernyaya made everyone go out of the sitting room, and made up a very fine-looking bed on the sofa for Shadow.

Wednesday spoke to Shadow, as they stood in the corridor.

'What you did in there, with the checkers game,' he said.

'Yes?'

'That was good. Very, very stupid of you. But good. Sleep safe.'

Shadow brushed his teeth and washed his face in the cold water of the little bathroom, and then walked back down the hall to the sitting room, turned out the light, and was asleep before his head touched the pillow.

There were explosions in Shadow's dream: he was driving a truck through a mine-field, and bombs were going off on each side of him. The windshield shattered and he felt warm blood running down his face.

Someone was shooting at him.

A bullet punctured his lung, a bullet shattered his spine, another hit his shoulder. He felt each bullet strike. He collapsed across the steering wheel.

The last explosion ended in darkness.

I must be dreaming, thought Shadow, alone in the darkness. *I think I just died.* He remembered hearing and believing, as a child, that if you died in your dreams, you would die in real life. He did not feel dead. He opened his eyes, experimentally.

There was a woman in the little sitting room, standing against the window, with her back to him. His heart missed a half-beat, and he said, 'Laura?'

She turned, framed by the moonlight. 'I'm sorry,' she said. 'I did not mean to wake you.' She had a soft, east-European accent. 'I will go.'

'No, it's okay,' said Shadow. 'You didn't wake me. I had a dream.'

'Yes,' she said. 'You were crying out, and moaning. Part of me wanted to wake you, but I thought, no, I should leave him.'

Her hair was pale and colorless in the moon's thin light. She wore a white cotton nightgown, with a high, lace neck, and a hem that swept the ground. Shadow sat up, entirely awake. 'You are Zorya Polu . . .,' he hesitated. 'The sister who was asleep.'

'I am Zorya Polunochnaya, yes. And you are called Shadow, yes? That was what Zorya Vechernyaya told me, when I woke.'

'Yes. What were you looking at, out there?'

She looked at him, then she beckoned him to join her by the window. She turned her back while he pulled on his jeans. He walked over to her. It seemed a long walk, for such a small room.

He could not tell her age. Her skin was unlined, her eyes were dark, her lashes were long, her hair was to her waist, and white. The moonlight drained colours into ghosts of themselves. She was taller than either of her sisters.

She pointed up into the night sky. 'I was looking at that,' she said, pointing to the Big Dipper. 'See?'

'Ursa Major,' he said. 'The Great Bear.'

'That is one way of looking at it,' she said. 'But it is not the way from where I come from. I am going to sit on the roof. Would you like to come with me?'

She lifted the window and clambered, barefoot, out onto the fire escape. A freezing wind blew through the window. Something was bothering Shadow, but he did not know what it was; he hesitated, then pulled on his sweater, socks and shoes and followed her out onto the rusting fire escape. She was waiting for him. His breath steamed in the chilly air. He watched her bare feet pad up the icy metal steps, and followed her up to the roof.

The wind gusted cold, flattening her nightgown against her body, and Shadow became uncomfortably aware that Zorya Polunochnaya was wearing nothing at all underneath.

'You don't mind the cold?' he said, as they reached the top of the fire escape, and the wind whipped his words away.

'Sorry?'

She bent her face close to his. Her breath was sweet.

'I said, doesn't the cold bother you?'

In reply, she held up a finger: *wait*. She stepped, lightly, over the side of the building and onto the flat roof. Shadow stepped over a little more clumsily, and followed her across the roof, to the shadow of the water-tower. There was a wooden bench waiting for them there, and she sat down on it, and he sat down beside her. The water-tower acted as a windbreak, for which Shadow was grateful.

'No,' she said. 'The cold does not bother me. This time is my time: I could no more feel uncomfortable in the night than a fish could feel uncomfortable in the deep water.'

'You must like the night,' said Shadow, wishing that he had said something wiser, more profound.

'My sisters are of their times. Zorya Utrennyaya is of the dawn. In the old country she would wake to open the gates, and let our father drive his – uhm, I forget the word, like a car but with horses?'

'Chariot?'

'His chariot. Our father would ride it out. And Zorya Vechernyaya, she would open the gates for him at dusk, when he returned to us.'

'And you?'

She paused. Her lips were full, but very pale. 'I never saw our father. I was asleep.'

'Is it a medical condition?'

She did not answer. The shrug, if she shrugged, was imperceptible.

'So. You wanted to know what I was looking at.'

'The Big Dipper.'

She raised an arm to point to it, and the wind flattened her night-gown against her body. Her nipples, every goose-bump on the areolae, were visible momentarily, dark against the white cotton. Shadow shivered.

'Odin's Wain, they call it. And the Great Bear. Where we come from, we believe that is a, a thing, a, not a god, but like a god, a bad thing, chained up in those stars. If it escapes, it will eat the whole of everything. And there are three sisters who must watch the sky, all the day, all the night. If he escapes, the thing in the stars, the world is over. *Pf!*, like that.'

'And people believe that?'

'They did. A long time ago.'

'And you were looking to see if you could see the monster in the stars?'

'Something like that. Yes.'

He smiled. If it were not for the cold, he decided, he would have thought he was dreaming. Everything felt so much like a dream.

'Can I ask how old you are? Your sisters seem so much older.'

She nodded her head. 'I am the youngest. Zorya Utrennyaya was born in the morning, and Zorya Vechernyaya was born in the evening, and I was born at midnight. I am the midnight sister: Zorya Polunochnaya. Are you married?'

'My wife is dead. She died last week in a car accident. It was her funeral yesterday.'

'I'm so sorry.'

'She came to see me last night.' It was not hard to say, in the darkness and the moonlight; it was not as unthinkable as it was by daylight.

'Did you ask her what she wanted?'

'No. Not really.'

'Perhaps you should. It is the wisest thing to ask the dead. Sometimes they will tell you. Zorya Vechernyaya tells me that you played checkers with Czernobog.'

'Yes. He won the right to knock in my skull with a sledge.'

'In the old days, they would take people up to the top of the mountains. To the high places. They would smash the back of their skulls with a rock. For Czernobog.'

Shadow glanced about. No, they were alone on the roof.

Zorya Polunochnaya laughed. 'Silly, he is not here. And you won a game also. He may not strike his blow until this is all over. He said he would not. And you will know. Like the cows he killed. They always know, first. Otherwise, what is the point?'

'I feel,' Shadow told her, 'like I'm in a world with its own sense of logic. Its own rules. Like when you're in a dream, and you know there are rules you mustn't break. Even if you don't know what they mean. I'm just going along with it, you know?'

'I know,' she said. She held his hand, with a hand that was icy cold. 'You were given protection once. You were given the sun itself. But you lost it already. You gave it away. All I can give you is much weaker protection. The daughter, not the father. But all helps. Yes?' Her white hair blew about her face in the chilly wind.

'Do I have to fight you? Or play checkers?' he asked.

'You do not even have to kiss me,' she told him. 'Just take the moon from me.'

'How?'

'Take the moon.'

'I don't understand.'

'Watch,' said Zorya Polunochnaya. She raised her left hand and held it in front of the moon, so that her forefinger and thumb seemed to be grasping it. Then, in one smooth movement, she plucked at it. For a moment, it looked like she had taken the moon from the sky, but then Shadow saw that the moon shone still, and Zorya Polunochnaya opened her hand to display a silver Liberty-head dollar resting between finger and thumb.

'That was beautifully done,' said Shadow. 'I didn't see you palm it. And I don't know how you did that last bit.'

'I did not palm it,' she said. 'I took it. And now I give it you, to keep safe. Here. Don't give this one away.'

She placed it in his right hand and closed his fingers around it. The coin was cold in his hand. Zorya Polunochnaya leaned forward, and closed his eyes with her fingers, and kissed him, lightly, once upon each eyelid.

* * *

Shadow awoke on the sofa, fully dressed. A narrow shaft of sunlight streamed in through the window, making the dust-motes dance.

He got out of bed, and walked over to the window. The room seemed much smaller in the daylight.

The thing that had been troubling him since last night came into focus as he looked out and down and across the street. There was no fire escape outside this window: no balcony, no rusting metal steps.

Still, held tight in the palm of his hand, bright and shiny as the day it had been minted, was a 1922 Liberty-head silver dollar.

'Oh. You're up,' said Wednesday, putting his head around the door. 'That's good. You want coffee? We're going to rob a bank.'

COMING TO AMERICA
1721

The important thing to understand about American history, *wrote Mr Ibis, in his leather-bound journal,* is that it is fictional, a charcoal-sketched simplicity for the children, or the easily bored. For the most part it is uninspected, unimagined, unthought, a representation of the thing, and not the thing itself. It is a fine fiction, *he continued, pausing for a moment to dip his pen in the inkwell, and to collect his thoughts,* that America was founded by pilgrims, seeking the freedom to believe as they wished, that they came to the Americas, spread and bred and filled the empty land.

In truth, the American colonies were as much a dumping ground as an escape, a forgetting place. In the days where you could be hanged in London from Tyburn's triple-crowned tree for the theft of twelve pennies, the Americas became a symbol of clemency, of a second chance. But the conditions of transportation were such that, for some, it was easier to take the leap from the leafless and dance on nothing until the dancing was done. Transportation it was called: for five years, for ten years, for life. That was the sentence.

You were sold to a captain, and would ride in his ship, crowded tight as a slaver's, to the colonies or to the West Indies; off the boat the captain would sell you on as an indentured servant to one who would take the cost of your skin out in your labour until the years of your indenture were done. But at least you were not waiting to hang in an English prison (for in those days prisons were places where you stayed until you were freed, transported or hanged: you were not sentenced there for a term), and you were free to make the best of your new world. You were also free to bribe a sea-captain to return you to England before the terms of your transportation were over and done. People did. And if the authorities caught you returning from transportation – if an old enemy, or an old friend with a score to settle, saw you and peached on you, – then you were hanged without a blink.

I am reminded, *he continued, after a short pause, during which he refilled the inkwell on his desk from the bottle of umber ink from the closet, and dipped his pen once more,* of the life of Essie Tregowan, who came from a chilly little cliff-top village in Cornwall, in the Southwest of England, where her family had lived from time out of mind. Her father was a fisherman, and it was rumoured that he was one of the wreckers – those who would hang their lamps high on the dangerous coast when the storm winds raged, luring ships onto the rocks, for the goods on shipboard. Essie's mother was in service as a cook at the Squire's house, and, at the age of twelve, Essie began to work there, in the scullery. She was a thin little thing, with wide brown eyes and dark brown hair; and she was not a hard worker but was forever slipping off and away to listen to stories and tales, if there was anyone who would tell them: tales of the piskies and the spriggans, of the black dogs of the moors and the seal-women of the Channel. And, though the Squire laughed at such things, the kitchen-folk always put out a china saucer of the creamiest milk at night, put it outside the kitchen door, for the piskies.

Several years passed, and Essie was no longer a thin little thing: now she curved and billowed like the swell of the green sea, and her brown eyes laughed, and her chestnut hair tossed and curled. Essie's eyes lighted on Bartholomew, the Squire's eighteen-year old son, home from Rugby, and she went at night to the standing stone on the edge of the woodland, and she put some bread that Bartholomew had been eating but had left unfinished on the stone, wrapped in a cut strand of her own hair. And on the very next day Bartholomew came and talked to her, and looked on her approvingly with his own eyes, the dangerous blue of a sky when a storm is coming, while she was cleaning out the grate in his bedroom.

He had such dangerous eyes, said Essie Tregowan.

Soon enough Bartholomew went up to Oxford, and, when Essie's condition became apparent, she was dismissed. But the babe was stillborn, and, as a favour to Essie's mother, who was a very fine cook, the Squire's wife prevailed upon her husband to return the former maiden to her former position in the scullery.

But Essie's love for Bartholomew had turned to hatred for his family, and, within the year she took for her new beau a man from a neighboring village, with a bad reputation, who went by the name of Josiah Horner. And one night, when the family slept, Essie arose in the night and unbolted the side door, to let her lover in. He rifled the house while the family slept on.

Suspicion immediately fell upon someone in the house, for it was apparent that someone must have opened the door (which the Squire's wife distinctly remembered having bolted herself) and someone must have known where the squire kept his silver plate, and the drawer in which he kept his coins and his promissory notes. Still, Essie, by resolutely denying everything, was convicted of nothing until Master Josiah Horner was caught, in a chandler's in Exeter, passing one of the Squire's notes. The Squire identified it as his, and Horner and Essie went to trial.

Horner was convicted at the local Assizes, and was, as the slang of the time so cruelly and so casually had it, *turned off*, but the judge took pity on Essie, because of her age or her chestnut hair, and he sentenced her to seven years' transportation. She was to be transported on a ship called the Neptune, under the command of one Captain Clarke. So Essie went to the Carolinas; and on the way she conceived an alliance with the selfsame Captain, and prevailed upon him to return her to England with him, as his wife, and to take her to his mother's house in London, where no man knew her. The journey back, when the human cargo had been exchanged for cotton and tobacco, was a peaceful time, and a happy one, for the Captain and his new bride, who were as two lovebirds or courting butterflies, unable to cease from touching each other or giving each other little gifts and endearments.

When they reached London, Captain Clarke lodged Essie with his mother, who treated her in all ways as her son's new wife. Eight weeks later, the Neptune set sail again, and the pretty young bride with the chestnut hair waved her husband goodbye from dockside. Then she returned to her mother-in-law's house where, the old woman being absent, Essie helped herself to a length of silk, several gold coins, and a silver pot in which the old woman kept her buttons, and pocketing these things Essie vanished into the stews of London.

Over the following two years Essie became an accomplished shoplifter, her wide skirts capable of concealing a multitude of sins, consisting chiefly of stolen bolts of silk and lace, and she lived life to the full. Essie gave thanks for her escapes from her vicissitudes to all the creatures that she had been told of as a child, to the piskies (whose influence, she was certain, extended as far as London), and she would put a wooden bowl of milk on a window-ledge each night, although her friends laughed at her; but she had the last laugh, as her friends got the pox or the clap and Essie remained in the peak of health.

She was a year shy of her twentieth birthday when fate dealt her an ill-blow: she sat in the Crossed Forks Inn off Fleet Street, in Bell Yard, when she saw a young man enter and seat himself near the fire-place, fresh down from the University. 'Oho! A pigeon ripe for the plucking,' thinks Essie to herself, and she sits next to him, and tells him what a fine young man he is, and with one hand she begins to stroke his knee, while her other hand, more carefully, goes in search of his pocket-watch. And then he looked her full in the face, and her heart leapt and sank as eyes the dangerous blue of the summer sky before a storm gazed back into hers, and Master Bartholomew said her name.

She was taken to Newgate and charged with returning from transportation. Found guilty, Essie shocked no-one by pleading her belly, although the town matrons, who assessed such claims (which were usually spurious) were surprised when they were forced to agree that Essie was indeed with child; although who the father was, Essie declined to say.

Her sentence of death was once more commuted to transportation, this time for life.

She rode out this time on the Sea-Maiden. There were two hundred transportees on that ship, packed into the hold like so many fat hogs on their way to market. Fluxes and fevers ran rampant; there was scarcely room to sit, let alone to lie down; a woman died in childbirth in the back of the hold, and, the people being pushed in too tightly to pass her body forward, she and the infant were forced out of a small porthole in the back, directly into the choppy grey sea. Essie was eight months gone, and it was a wonder she kept the baby, but keep it she did.

In her life ever after she would have nightmares of her time in that hold, and she would wake up screaming with the taste and stench of the place in her throat.

The Sea-Maiden landed at Norfolk in Virginia, and Essie's indenture was bought by a 'small planter', a tobacco farmer named John

Richardson, for his wife had died of the childbirth fever a week after giving birth to his daughter, and he had need of a wet-nurse and a maid of all work upon his smallholding.

So Essie's baby boy, whom she called Anthony, after, she said, her late husband his father (knowing there was none there to contradict her, and perhaps she had known an Anthony once), sucked at Essie's breast alongside of Phyllida Richardson, and her employer's child always got first suck, so she grew into a healthy child, tall and strong, while Essie's son grew weak and rickety on what was left.

And along with the milk, the children as they grew drank Essie's tales: of the knockers and the blue-caps who live down the mines; of the Bucca, the tricksiest spirit of the land, much more dangerous than the red-headed, snub-nosed piskies, for whom the first fish of the catch was always left upon the shingle, and for whom a fresh-baked loaf of bread was left in the field, at reaping time, to ensure a fine harvest; she told them of the apple-tree men – old apple trees who talked when they had a mind, and who needed to be placated with the first cider of the crop, which was poured onto their roots as the year turned, if they were to give you a fine crop for the next year. She told them, in her mellifluous Cornish drawl, which trees they should be wary of, in the old rhyme:

Elm, he do brood
And Oak, he do hate,
But the willow-man goes walking,
If you stays out late.

She told them all these things, and they believed, because she believed.

The farm prospered, and Essie Tregowan placed a china saucer of milk outside the back door, each night, for the piskies. And after eight months John Richardson came a-knocking quietly on Essie's bedroom door, and asked her for favours of the kind a woman shows a man, and Essie told him how shocked and hurt she was, a poor widow-woman, and an indentured servant no better than a slave, to be asked to prostitute herself for a man whom she had had so much respect for – and an indentured servant could not marry, so how he could even think to torment an indentured transportee girl so she could not bring herself to think – and her nut-brown eyes filled with tears, such that Richardson found himself apologising to her, and the upshot of it was that John Richardson wound up, in that corridor, of that hot summer's night, going down on one knee to Essie Tregowan and proposing an end to her indenture and offering his hand in marriage. Now, although she accepted him, she would not sleep a night with him until it was legal, whereupon she moved from the little room in the attic to the master bedroom in the front of the house; and if some of Farmer Richardson's friends and their wives cut him when next they saw him in town, many more of them were of the opinion that the new Mistress Richardson was a damn fine looking woman, and that Johnnie Richardson had done quite well for himself.

Within a year, she was delivered of another child, another boy, but as blond as his father and his half-sister, and they named him John, after his father.

The three children went to the local church to hear the travelling preacher on Sundays, and they went to the little school to learn their letters and their numbers with the children of the other small farmers; while Essie also made sure they knew the mysteries of the piskies, which were the most important mysteries there were: red-headed men, with eyes and clothes as green as a river, and turned-up noses, funny, squinting men who would, if they got a mind to, turn you and twist you and lead you out of your way, unless you had salt in your pocket, or a little bread. When the children went off to school, they each of them carried a little salt in one pocket, a little bread in the other, the old symbols of life and the earth, to make sure they came safely home once more, and they always did.

The children grew in the lush Virginia hills, grew tall and strong (although Anthony, her first son, was always weaker, paler, more prone to disease and bad airs) and the Richardsons were happy; and Essie loved her husband as best she could. They had been married a decade when John Richardson developed a toothache so bad it made him fall from his horse. She took him to the nearest town, where his tooth was pulled; but it was too late, and the blood-poisoning carried him off, black-faced and groaning, and they buried him beneath his favorite willow tree.

The Widow Richardson was left the farm to manage until Richardson's two children were of age: she managed the indentured servants and the slaves, and brought in the tobacco crop, year in, year out; she poured cider on the roots of the apple trees on New Year's Eve, and placed a loaf of new-baked bread in the fields at harvest-time, and she always left a saucer of milk at the back door. The farm flourished, and the Widow Richardson gained a reputation as a hard bargainer, but one whose crop was always good, and who never sold shoddy for better merchandise.

So all went well for another ten years; but after that was a bad year, for Anthony, her son, slew Johnnie, his half-brother, in a furious quarrel over the future of the farm and the disposition of Phyllida's hand; and some said he had not meant to kill his brother, and that it was a foolish blow that struck too deep, and some said otherwise. Anthony fled, leaving Essie to bury her youngest son beside his father. Now, some said Anthony fled to Boston, and some said he went south, to Florida, and his mother was of the opinion that he had taken ship to England, to enlist in George's army and fight the rebel Scots. But with both sons gone the farm was an empty place, and a sad one, and Phyllida pined and plained as if her heart had been broken, while nothing that her stepmother could say or do would put a smile back on her lips again.

But heartbroken or not, they needed a man about the farm, and so Phyllida married Harry Soames, a ship's carpenter by profession, who had tired of the sea and who dreamed of a life on land on a farm like the Lincolnshire farm upon which he had grown up. And although the Richardsons' farm was little enough like that, Harry Soames found correspondences enough to make him happy. Five children were born to Phyllida and Harry, three of whom lived.

The Widow Richardson missed her sons, and she missed her husband, although he was now little more than a memory of a fair man who treated her kindly. Phyllida's children would come to Essie for tales, and she would tell them of the Black Dog of the Moors, and of Raw-Head and Bloody-Bones, or the Apple Tree Man, but they were not interested; they only wanted tales of Jack – Jack up the Beanstalk, or Jack Giant-killer, or Jack and his Cat and the King. She loved those children as if they were her own flesh and blood, although sometimes she would call them by the names of those long dead.

It was May, and she took her chair out into the kitchen garden, to pick peas and to shuck them in the sunlight, for even in the lush heat of Virginia the cold had entered her bones as the frost had entered her hair, and a little warmth was a fine thing.

As the Widow Richardson shucked the peas with her old hands, she got to thinking about how fine it would be to walk once more on the moors and the salty cliffs of her native Cornwall, and she thought of sitting on the shingle as a little girl, waiting for her father's ship to return from the grey seas. Her hands, blue-knuckled and clumsy, opened the pea-pods, forced the full peas into an earthenware bowl, while she dropped the empty pea-pods onto her aproned lap. And then she found herself remembering, as she had not remembered for a long time, a life well lost: how she had twitched purses and filched silks with her clever fingers; and now she remembers the warden of Newgate telling her that it will be a good twelve weeks before her case would be heard, and that she could escape the gallows if she could plead her belly, and what a pretty thing she was – and how she had turned to the wall and bravely lifted her skirts, hating herself and hating him, but knowing he was right; and the feel of the life, quickening inside her that meant that she could cheat death for a little longer . . .

'Essie Tregowan?' said the stranger.

The Widow Richardson looked up, shading her eyes in the May sunshine. 'Do I know you?' she asked. She had not heard him approach.

The man was dressed all in green: dusty green trews, green jacket and a dark green coat. His hair was a carroty red, and he grinned at her all lopsided. There was something about the man that made her happy to look at him, and something else that whispered of danger. 'You might say that you know me,' he said.

He squinted down at her, and she squinted right back up at him, searching his moon-face for a clue to his identity. He looked as young as one of her own grandchildren, yet he had called her by her old name, and there was a burr in his voice she knew from her childhood, from the rocks and the moors of her home.

'You're a Cornishman?' she asked.

'That I am, a Cousin Jack,' said the red-haired man, 'or rather, that I was, but now I'm here in this new world, where nobody puts out ale or milk for an honest fellow, or a loaf of bread come harvest time.'

The old woman steadied the bowl of peas upon her lap. 'If you're who I think you are,' she said, 'then I've no quarrel with you.' In the house, she could hear Phyllida grumbling to the housekeeper.

'Nor I with you,' said the red-haired fellow, a little sadly, 'although it was you that brought me here, you and a few like you, into this land with no time for magic and no place for piskies and such folk.'

'You've done me many a good turn,' she said.

'Good and ill,' said the squinting stranger. 'We're like the wind. We blows both ways.'

Essie nodded.

'Will you take my hand, Essie Tregowan?' And he reached out a hand to her. Freckled it was, and although Essie's eyesight was going she could see each orange hair on the back of his hand, glowing golden in the afternoon sunlight. She bit her lip. Then, hesitantly, she placed her blue-knotted hand in his.

She was still warm when they found her, although the life had fled her body and only half the peas were shelled.

5

Madam Life's a piece in bloom
Death goes dogging everywhere:
She's the tenant of the room,
He's the ruffian on the stair.
– W.E. Henley, *Madam Life's a Piece in Bloom*

Only Zorya Utrennyaya was awake to say goodbye to them, that Saturday morning. She took Wednesday's forty-five dollars, and insisted on writing him out a receipt for it in wide, looping hand-writing, on the back of an expired soft-drink coupon. She looked quite doll-like in the morning light, with her old face carefully made-up, and her golden hair piled high upon her head.

Wednesday kissed her hand. 'Thank you for your hospitality, dear lady,' he said. 'You and your lovely sisters remain as radiant as the sky itself.'

'You are a bad old man,' she told him, and shook a finger at him. Then she hugged him. 'Keep safe,' she told him. 'I would not like to hear that you were gone for good.'

'It would distress me equally, my dear.'

She shook hands with Shadow. 'Zorya Polunochnaya thinks very highly of you,' she said. 'I also.'

'Thank you,' said Shadow. 'Thanks for the dinner.'

She raised an eyebrow at him. 'You liked? You must come again.'

Wednesday and Shadow walked down the stairs. Shadow put his hands in his jacket pocket. The silver dollar was cold in his hand. It was bigger and heavier than any coins he'd used so far. He classic-palmed it, let his hand hang by his side naturally then straightened his hand as the coin slipped down to a front-palm position. It felt natural there, held between his forefinger and his little finger by the slightest of pressure.

'Smoothly done,' said Wednesday.

'I'm just learning,' said Shadow. 'I can do a lot of the technical stuff. The hardest part is making people look at the wrong hand.'

'Is that so?'

'Yes,' said Shadow. 'It's called misdirection.' He slipped his middle fingers under the coin, pushing it into a back palm, and fumbled his grip on it, ever-so-slightly. The coin dropped from his hand to the stairwell with a clatter and bounced down half a flight of stairs. Wednesday reached down and picked it up.

'You cannot afford to be careless with people's gifts,' said Wednesday. 'Something like this, you need to hang onto it. Don't go throwing it about.' He examined the coin, looking first at the eagle side, then at the face of Liberty on the obverse. 'Ah, Lady Liberty. Beautiful, is she not?' He tossed the coin to Shadow, who picked it from the air, did a slide vanish – seeming to drop it into his left hand while actually keeping it in his right, – and then appeared to pocket it with his left hand. The coin sat in the palm of his right hand, in plain view. It felt comforting there.

'Lady Liberty,' said Wednesday. 'Like so many of the gods that Americans hold dear, a foreigner. In this case, a Frenchwoman, although, in deference to American sensibilities, the French covered up her magnificent bosom on that statue they presented to New York. Liberty,' he continued, wrinkling his nose at the used condom that lay on the bottom flight of steps, toeing it to the side of the stairs with distaste – 'Someone could slip on that. Break their necks,' he muttered, interrupting himself. 'Like a banana peel, only with bad taste and irony thrown in.' He pushed open the door, and the sunlight hit them. 'Liberty,' boomed Wednesday, as they walked to the car, 'is a bitch who must be bedded on a mattress of corpses.'

'Yeah?' said Shadow.

'Quoting,' said Wednesday. 'Quoting someone French. That's who they have a statue to, in their New York harbor: a bitch, who liked to be fucked on the refuse from the tumbril. Hold your torch as high as you want to, m'dear, there's still rats in your dress and cold jism dripping down your leg.' He unlocked the car, and pointed Shadow to the passenger seat.

'I think she's beautiful,' said Shadow, holding the coin up close. Liberty's silver face reminded him a little of Zorya Polunochnaya.

'That,' said Wednesday, driving off, 'is the eternal folly of man. To be chasing after the sweet flesh, without realising that it is simply a pretty cover for the bones. Worm food. At night, you're rubbing yourself against worm food. No offense meant.'

Shadow had never seen Wednesday quite so expansive. His new boss, he decided, went through phases of extroversion followed by periods of intense quiet. 'So you aren't American?' asked Shadow.

'Nobody's American,' said Wednesday. 'Not originally. That's my point.' He checked his watch. 'We still have several hours to kill before the banks close. Good job last night with Czernobog, by the way. I would have closed him on coming eventually, but you enlisted him more wholeheartedly than I could ever have.'

'Only because he gets to kill me afterward.'

'Not necessarily. As you yourself so wisely pointed out, he's old, and the killing stroke might merely leave you, well, paralyzed for life, say. A hopeless invalid. So you have much to look forward to, should Mister Czernobog survive the coming difficulties.'

'And there is some question about this?' said Shadow, echoing Wednesday's manner, then hating himself for it.

'Fuck yes,' said Wednesday. He pulled up in the parking lot of a bank. 'This,' he said, 'is the bank I shall be robbing. They don't close for another few hours. Let's go in and say hello.'

He gestured to Shadow. Reluctantly, Shadow got out of the car. If the old man was going to do something stupid, Shadow could see no reason why his face should be on the camera. But curiosity pulled him in, and he walked into the bank. He looked down at the floor, rubbed his nose with his hand, doing his best to keep his face hidden.

'Deposit forms, Ma'am?' said Wednesday to the lone teller.

'Over there.'

'Very good. And if I were to need to make a night deposit . . . ?'

'Same forms.' She smiled at him. 'You know where the night deposit slot is, hon? Left out the main door, it's on the wall.'

'My thanks.'

Wednesday picked up several deposit forms. He grinned a goodbye at the teller, and he and Shadow walked out.

Wednesday stood there on the sidewalk for a moment, scratching his beard meditatively. Then he walked over to the ATM machine and to the night safe, set in the side of the wall, and inspected them. He led Shadow across the road to the supermarket, where he bought a chocolate fudge popsicle for himself and a cup of hot chocolate for Shadow. There was a payphone set in the wall of the entry way, below a notice board with rooms to rent, and puppies and kittens in need of good homes. Wednesday wrote down the telephone number of the payphone. They crossed the road once more. 'What we need,' said Wednesday, suddenly, 'is snow. A good, driving, irritating snow. Think "snow" for me, will you?'

'Huh?'

'Concentrate on making those clouds – the ones over there, in the west, – making them bigger and darker. Think grey skies and driving winds coming down from the arctic. Think snow.'

'I don't think it will do any good.'

'Nonsense. If nothing else, it will keep your mind occupied,' said Wednesday, unlocking the car. 'Kinko's next. Hurry up.'

Snow, thought Shadow, in the passenger seat, sipping his hot chocolate. *Huge, dizzying, clumps and clusters of snow falling through the air, patches of white against an iron-grey sky, snow that touches your tongue with cold and winter, that kisses your face with its hesitant touch before freezing you to death. Twelve cotton-candy inches of snow, creating a fairy-tale world, making everything unrecognizably beautiful . . .*

Wednesday was talking to him.

'I'm sorry?' said Shadow.

'I said we're here,' said Wednesday. 'You were somewhere else.'

'I was thinking about snow,' said Shadow.

In Kinko's, Wednesday set about photocopying the deposit slips from the bank. He had the clerk instant print him two sets of ten business cards. Shadow's head had begun to ache, and there was an uncomfortable feeling between his shoulder blades; he wondered if he had slept wrong, if the headache was an awkward legacy of the night before's sofa.

Wednesday sat at the computer terminal, composing a letter, and, with the clerk's help, making several large-sized signs.

Snow, thought Shadow. *High in the atmosphere, perfect, tiny crystals that form about a minute piece of dust, each a lace-like work of fractal art.*

And the snow crystals clump together into flakes as they fall, covering Chicago in their white plenty, inch upon inch . . .

'Here,' said Wednesday. He handed Shadow a cup of Kinko's coffee, a half-dissolved lump of non-dairy creamer powder floating on the top. 'I think that's enough, don't you?'

'Enough what?'

'Enough snow. Don't want to immobilize the city, do we?'

The sky was a uniform battleship grey. Snow was coming. Yes.

'I didn't really do that?' said Shadow. 'I mean, I didn't. Did I?'

'Drink the coffee,' said Wednesday. 'It's foul stuff, but it will ease the headache.' Then he said, 'Good work.'

Wednesday paid the Kinko's clerk, and he carried his signs and letters and cards outside to the car. He opened the trunk of his car, put the papers in a large black metal case of the kind carried by payroll guards, and closed the trunk. He passed Shadow a business card.

'Who,' said Shadow, 'is A. Haddock, Director of Security, A1 Security Services?'

'You are.'

'A. Haddock?'

'Yes.'

'What does the A. stand for?'

'Alfredo? Alphonse? Augustine? Ambrose? Your call entirely.'

'Oh. I see.'

'I'm James O'Gorman,' said Wednesday. 'Jimmy to my friends. See? I've got a card too.'

They got back in the car. Wednesday said, 'If you can think "A. Haddock", as well as you thought "snow", we should have plenty of lovely money with which to wine and dine my friends of tonight.'

'I'm not going back to prison.'

'You won't be.'

'I thought we had agreed that I wouldn't be doing anything illegal.'

'You aren't. Possibly aiding and abetting, a little conspiracy to commit, followed of course by receiving stolen money, but trust me, you'll come out of this smelling like a rose.'

'Is that before or after your elderly Slavic Charles Atlas crushes my skull with one blow?'

'His eyesight's going,' said Wednesday. 'He'll probably miss you entirely. Now, we still have a little time to kill – the bank closes at midday on Saturdays, after all. Would you like lunch?'

'Yes,' said Shadow. 'I'm starving.'

'I know just the place,' said Wednesday. He hummed as he drove, some cheerful song that Shadow could not identify. Snowflakes began to fall, just as Shadow had imagined them, and he felt strangely proud. He knew, rationally, that he had nothing to do with the snow, just as he knew the silver dollar he carried in his pocket was not, and never had been the moon. But still . . .

They stopped outside a large shed-like building. A sign said that the all-U-can-eat lunch buffet was $4.99. 'I love this place,' said Wednesday.

'Good food?' asked Shadow.

'Not particularly,' said Wednesday. 'But the ambience is unmiss-able.'

The ambience that Wednesday loved, it turned out, once lunch had been eaten – Shadow had the fried chicken, and enjoyed it – was the business that took up the rear of the shed: it was, the hanging flag across the centre of the room announced, a Bankrupt and Liquidated Stock Clearance Depot.

Wednesday went out to the car, and reappeared with a small suit-case, which he took into the men's room. Shadow figured he'd learn soon enough what Wednesday was up to, whether he wanted to or not, and so he prowled the liquidation aisles, staring at the things for sale: Boxes of coffee 'for use in airline filters only', Teenage Mutant Ninja Turtle toys and Xena: Warrior Princess Harem dolls, teddy bears that played patriotic tunes on the xylophone when plugged in, cans of processed meat, galoshes and sundry overshoes, marshmallows, Bill Clinton presidential wristwatches, artificial miniature Christmas trees, salt and pepper shakers in the shapes of animals, body parts, fruit and nuns, and, Shadow's favorite, a 'just add real carrot' snowman kit, with plastic coal eyes, a corncob pipe, and a plastic hat.

Shadow thought about how you made the moon seem to come out of the sky and become a silver dollar, and what made a woman get out of her grave and walk across town to talk to you.

'Isn't it a wonderful place?' asked Wednesday, when he came out of the men's room. His hands were still wet, and he was drying them off on a handkerchief. 'They're out of paper towels in there,' he said. He had changed his clothes. He was now wearing a dark blue jacket, with matching trousers, a blue knit tie, a thick blue sweater, a white shirt, and black shoes. He looked like a security guard, and Shadow said so.

'What can I possibly say to that, young man,' said Wednesday, picking up a box of floating plastic aquarium fish (*'they'll never fade – and you'll never have to feed them!!'*), 'other than to congratulate you on your perspicacity. How about Arthur Haddock? Arthur's a good name.'

'Too mundane.'

'Well, you'll think of something. There. Let us return to town. We should be in perfect time for our bank robbery, and then I shall have a little spending money.'

'Most people,' said Shadow, 'would simply take it from the ATM.'

'Which is, oddly enough, more or less exactly what I was planning to do.'

Wednesday parked the car in the supermarket lot across the street from the bank. From the trunk of the car Wednesday brought out the metal case and a clipboard, and a pair of handcuffs. He handcuffed the case to his left wrist. The snow continued to fall. Then he put a peaked blue cap on, and velcroed a patch to the breast pocket of his jacket. 'A1 Security' was written on the cap and the patch. He put the deposit slips on his clipboard. Then he slouched. He looked like a retired beat cop, and appeared somehow to have gained himself a paunch.

'Now,' he said, 'You do a little shopping in the food store, then hang out by the phone. If anyone asks, you're waiting for a call from your girlfriend, whose car has broken down.'

'So why's she calling me there?'

'How the hell should you know?'

Wednesday put on a pair of faded pink ear-muffs. He closed the trunk. Snowflakes settled on his dark blue cap, and on his ear-muffs.

'How do I look?' he asked.

'Ludicrous,' said Shadow.

'Ludicrous?'

'Or goofy, maybe,' said Shadow.

'Mm. Goofy and ludicrous. That's good.' Wednesday smiled. The ear-muffs made him appear, at the same time, reassuring, amusing, and, ultimately, loveable. He strode across the street and walked along the block to the bank building, while Shadow walked into the supermarket hall and watched.

Wednesday taped a large red Out of Order notice to the ATM. He put a red ribbon across the night deposit slot, and he taped a photocopied sign up above it. Shadow read it with amusement.

FOR YOUR CONVENIENCE it said WE ARE WORKING TO MAKE ONGOING IMPROVEMENTS. WE APOLOGIZE FOR THE TEMPORARY INCONVENIENCE.

Then Wednesday turned around and faced the street. He looked cold and put-upon.

A young woman came over to use the ATM. Wednesday shook his head, explained that it was out of order. She cursed, apologised for cursing, and ran off.

A car drew up, and a man got out holding a small grey sack, and a key. Shadow watched as Wednesday apologised to the man, then made him sign the clipboard, checked his deposit slip, painstakingly wrote him out a receipt and puzzled over which copy to keep, and, finally, opened his big black metal case and put the man's sack inside.

The man shivered in the snow, stamping his feet, waiting for the old security guard to be done with this administrative nonsense, so he could leave his takings and get out of the cold and be on his way, then he took his receipt and got back into his warm car and drove off.

Wednesday walked across the street carrying the metal case, and bought himself a coffee at the supermarket.

'Afternoon, young man,' he said, with an avuncular chuckle, as he passed Shadow. 'Cold enough for you?'

He walked back across the street, and took grey sacks and envelopes from people coming to deposit their earnings or their takings on this Saturday afternoon, a fine old security man in his funny pink ear-muffs.

Shadow bought some things to read – *Turkey Hunting, People,* and because the cover picture of Bigfoot was so endearing, the *Weekly World News* – and stared out of the window.

'Anything I can do to help?' asked a middle aged black man with a white moustache. He seemed to be the manager.

'Thanks, man, but no. I'm waiting for a phone call. My girlfriend's car broke down.'

'Probably the battery,' said the man. 'People forget those things only last three, maybe four years. It's not like they cost a fortune.'

'Tell me about it,' said Shadow.

'Hang in there, big guy,' said the manager, and he went back into the supermarket.

The snow had turned the street scene into the interior of a snow-globe, perfect in all its details.

Shadow watched, impressed. Unable to hear the conversations across the street, he felt it was like watching a fine silent movie performance, all pantomime and expression: the old security guard was gruff, earnest – a little bumbling perhaps, but enormously well-meaning. Everyone who gave him their money walked away a little happier from having met him.

And then the cops drew up outside the bank, and Shadow's heart sank. Wednesday tipped his cap to them, and ambled over to the police car. He said his Hellos and shook hands through the open window, and nodded, then hunted through his pockets until he found a business card and a letter, and passed them through the window of the car. Then he sipped his coffee.

The telephone rang. Shadow picked up the handpiece and did his best to sound bored. 'A1 Security Services,' he said.

'Can I speak to A. Haddock?' asked the cop across the street.

'This is Andy Haddock speaking,' said Shadow.

'Yeah, Mr Haddock, this is the police,' said the cop in the car across the street. 'You've got a man at the First Illinois Bank on the corner of Market and Second.'

'Uh, yeah. That's right. Jimmy O'Gorman. And what seems to be the problem, officer? Jim behaving himself? He's not been drinking?'

'No problem, sir. Your man is just fine, sir. Just wanted to make certain everything was in order.'

'You tell Jim that if he's caught drinking again, officer, he's fired. You got that? Out of a job. Out on his ass. We have zero tolerance at A1 Security.'

'I really don't think it's really my place to tell him that, sir. He's doing a fine job. We're just concerned because something like this really ought to be done by two personnel. It's risky, having one unarmed guard dealing with such large amounts of money.'

'Tell me about it. Or more to the point, you tell those cheapskates down at the First Illinois about it. These are my men I'm putting on the line, officer. Good men. Men like you.' Shadow found himself warming to this identity. He could feel himself becoming Andy Haddock, chewed cheap cigar in his ashtray, a stack of paperwork to get to this Saturday afternoon, a home in Schaumburg and a mistress in a little apartment on Lake Shore Drive. 'Y'know, you sound like a bright young man, officer, uh . . .'

'Myerson.'

'Officer Myerson. You need a little weekend work, or you wind up leaving the force, any reason, you give us a call. We always need good men. You got my card?'

'Yes sir.'

'You hang onto it,' said Andy Haddock. 'You call me.'

The police car drove off, and Wednesday shuffled back through the snow to deal with the small line of people who were waiting to give him their money.

'She okay?' asked the manager, putting his head around the door. 'Your girlfriend?'

'It was the battery,' said Shadow. 'Now I just got to wait.'

'Women,' said the manager. 'I hope yours is worth waiting for.'

Winter darkness descended, the afternoon slowly greying into night. Lights went on. More people gave Wednesday their money. Suddenly, as if at some signal Shadow could not see, Wednesday walked over to the wall, removed the Out of Order signs, and trudged across the slushy road, heading for the car park. Shadow waited a minute, then followed him.

Wednesday was sitting in the back of the car. He had opened the metal case, and was methodically laying everything he had been given out on the back seat in neat piles.

'Drive,' he said. 'We're heading for the First Illinois Bank over on State Street.'

'Repeat performance?' asked Shadow. 'Isn't that kind of pushing your luck?'

'Not at all,' said Wednesday. 'We're going to do a little banking.'

While Shadow drove, Wednesday sat in the back seat and removed the bills from the deposit bags in handfuls, leaving the checks and the credit card slips, and taking the cash from some, although not all, of the envelopes. He dropped the cash back into the metal case. Shadow pulled up outside the bank, stopping the car about fifty yards down the road, well out of camera range. Wednesday got out of the car, and pushed the envelopes through the night deposit slot. Then he opened the night safe, and dropped in the grey bags. He closed it again.

He climbed into the passenger seat. 'You're heading for I-90,' said Wednesday. 'Follow the signs west for Madison.'

Shadow began to drive.

Wednesday looked back at the bank they were leaving. 'There, my boy,' he said, cheerfully, 'that will confuse everything. Now, to get the really big money, you need to do that at about four thirty on a Sunday morning, when the clubs and the bars drop off their Saturday night's takings. Hit the right bank, the right guy making the drop off – they tend to pick them big and honest, and sometimes have a couple of bouncers accompany them, but they aren't necessarily smart – and you can walk away with a quarter of a million dollars for an evening's work.'

'If it's that easy,' said Shadow, 'how come everybody doesn't do it?'

'It's not an entirely risk-free occupation,' said Wednesday, 'especially not at four thirty in the morning.'

'You mean the cops are more suspicious at four thirty in the morning?'

'Not at all. But the bouncers are. And things can get awkward.'

He flicked through a sheaf of fifties, added a smaller stack of twenties, weighed them in his hand, then passed them over to Shadow. 'Here,' he said. 'Your first week's wages.'

Shadow pocketed the money without counting it. 'So, that's what you do?' he asked. 'To make money?'

'Rarely. Only when a great deal of cash is needed fast. On the whole, I make my money from people who never know they've been taken, and who never complain, and who will frequently line up to be taken when I come back that way again.'

'That Sweeney guy said you were a hustler.'

'He was right. But that is the least of what I am. And the least of what I need you for, Shadow.'

* * *

Snow spun through their headlights and into the windshield as they drove through the darkness. The effect was almost hypnotic.

'This is the only country in the world,' said Wednesday, into the stillness, 'that worries about what it is.'

'What?'

'The rest of them know what they are. No-one ever needs to go searching for the heart of Norway. Or looks for the soul of Mozambique. They know what they are.'

'And . . . ?'

'Just thinking out loud.'

'So you've been to lots of other countries, then?'

Wednesday said nothing. Shadow glanced at him. 'No,' said Wednesday, with a sigh. 'No. I never have.'

They stopped for gas, and Wednesday went into the restroom in his security guard jacket and his suitcase, and came out in a crisp, pale suit, brown shoes, and a knee-length brown coat that looked like it might be Italian.

'So when we get to Madison, what then?'

'Take Highway 14 west to Spring Green. We'll be meeting everyone at a place called the House on the Rock. You been there?'

'No,' said Shadow. 'But I've seen the signs.'

The signs for the House on the Rock were all around that part of the world: oblique, ambiguous signs all across Illinois and Minnesota and Wisconsin, probably as far away as Iowa, Shadow suspected, signs alerting you to the existence of the House on the Rock. Shadow had seen the signs, and wondered about them. Did the House balance perilously upon the Rock? What was so interesting about the Rock? About the House? He had given it a passing thought, but then forgotten it. Shadow was not in the habit of visiting roadside attractions.

They left the interstate at Madison, and drove past the dome of the capitol building, another perfect snow-globe scene in the falling snow, and then they were off the interstate, and driving down country roads. After almost an hour, of driving through towns with names like Black Earth, they turned down a narrow driveway, past several enormous, snow-dusted flower pots entwined with lizard-like dragons. The tree-lined parking lot was almost empty.

'They'll be closing soon,' said Wednesday.

'So what is this place?' asked Shadow, as they walked through the parking lot toward a low, unimpressive wooden building.

'This is a roadside attraction,' said Wednesday. 'One of the finest. Which means it is a place of power.'

'Come again?'

'It's perfectly simple,' said Wednesday. 'In other countries, over the years, people recognised the places of power. Sometimes it would be a natural formation, sometimes it would just be a place that was, somehow, special. They knew that something important was happening there, that there was some focusing point, some channel, some window to the Immanent. And so they would build temples, or cathedrals, or erect stone circles, or . . . well, you get the idea.'

'There are churches all across the States, though,' said Shadow.

'In every town. Sometimes on every block. And about as significant, in this context, as dentists' offices. No, in the USA, people still get the call, or some of them, and they feel themselves being called to from the transcendent void, and they respond to it by building a model out of beerbottles of somewhere they've never visited, or by erecting a gigantic bat-house in some part of the country that bats have traditionally declined to visit. Roadside attractions: people feel themselves being pulled to places where, in other parts of the world, they would recognise that part of themselves that is truly transcendent, and buy a hot dog and walk around, feeling satisfied on a level they cannot truly describe, and profoundly dissatisfied on a level beneath that.'

'You have some pretty whacked out theories,' said Shadow.

'Nothing theoretical about it, young man,' said Wednesday. 'You should have figured that out by now.'

There was only one ticket window open. 'We stop selling tickets in half an hour,' said the girl. 'It takes at least two hours to walk around, you see.'

Wednesday paid for their tickets in cash.

'Where's the rock?' asked Shadow.

'Under the house,' said Wednesday.

'Where's the house?'

Wednesday put his finger to his lips, and they walked forward. Further in, a player piano was playing something that was intended to have been Ravel's *Bolero*. The place seemed to be a geometrically reconfigured 1960s bachelor pad, with open stone work, pile carpeting, and magnificently ugly mushroom-shaped stained glass lampshades. Up a winding staircase was another room, filled with knick-knacks.

'They say this was built by Frank Lloyd Wright's evil twin,' said Wednesday. 'Frank Lloyd Wrong.' He chuckled at his joke.

'I saw that on a tee shirt,' said Shadow.

Up and down more stairs, and now they were in a long, long room, made of glass, that protruded, needle-like, out over the leafless black-and-white countryside hundreds of feet below them. Shadow stood and watched the snow tumble and spin.

'This is the House on the Rock?' he asked, puzzled.

'More or less. This is the Infinity Room, part of the actual house, although a late addition. But no, my young friend, we have not scratched the tiniest surface of what the house has to offer.'

'So according to your theory,' said Shadow, 'Walt Disney World would be the holiest place in America.'

Wednesday frowned, and stroked his beard. 'Walt Disney bought some orange groves in the middle of Florida and built a tourist town on them. No magic there of any kind. I think there might be something real in the original Disneyland. There may be some power there, although twisted, and hard to access. But some parts of Florida are filled with real magic. You just have to keep your eyes open. Ah, for the mermaids of Weeki Wachee . . . Follow me, this way.'

Everywhere was the sound of music: jangling, awkward, music, ever-so slightly off the beat and out of time. Wednesday took a five dollar bill and put it into a change machine, receiving a handful of brass-coloured metal coins in return. He tossed one to Shadow, who caught it, and, realising that a small boy was watching him, held it up between forefinger and thumb and vanished it. The small boy ran over to his mother, who was inspecting one of the ubiquitous Santa Clauses – over 6000 on display! the signs said – and he tugged, urgently at the hem of her coat.

Shadow followed Wednesday outside briefly, and then followed the signs to the Streets of Yesterday.

'Forty years ago Alex Jordan – his face is on the token you have palmed in your right hand, Shadow, – began to build a house on a high jut of rock in a field he did not own, and even he could not have told you why. And people came to see him build it – the curious, and the puzzled, and those who were neither and who could not honestly have told you why they came. So he did what any sensible American male of his generation would do: he began to charge them money – nothing much. A nickel each, perhaps. Or a quarter. And he continued building, and the people kept coming.

'So he took those quarters and nickels and made something even bigger and stranger. He built these warehouses on the ground beneath the house, and filled them with things for people to see, and then the people came to see them. Millions of people come here every year.'

'Why?'

But Wednesday simply smiled, and they walked into the dimly lit, treelined Streets of Yesterday. Prim-lipped Victorian china dolls stared in profusion through dusty store windows, like so-many props from respectable horror films. Cobblestones under their feet, the darkness of a roof above their heads, jangling mechanical music in the background. They passed a glass box of broken puppets, and an overgrown golden music box in a glass case. They passed the dentist's and the drugstore ('Restore potency! Use O'Leary's Magnetical belt!').

At the end of the street was a large glass box with a female mannequin inside it, dressed as a gypsy fortune teller.

'Now,' boomed Wednesday, over the mechanical music, 'at the start of any quest or enterprise it behooves us to consult the Norns. So let us designate this Sybil our *Urd*, eh?' He dropped a brass-coloured House on the Rock coin into the slot. With jagged, mechanical motions, the gypsy lifted her arm and lowered it once more. A slip of paper chunked out of the slot.

Wednesday took it, read it, grunted, folded it up and put it in his pocket.

'Aren't you going to show it to me? I'll show you mine,' said Shadow.

'A man's fortune is his own affair,' said Wednesday, stiffly. 'I would not ask to see yours.'

Shadow put his own coin in the slot. He took his slip of paper. He read it.

EVERY ENDING IS A NEW BEGINNING.
YOUR LUCKY NUMBER IS NONE.
YOUR LUCKY COLOUR IS DEAD.
    Motto:
LIKE FATHER, LIKE SON.

Shadow made a face. He folded the fortune up and put it in his inside pocket.

They went farther in, down a red corridor, past rooms filled with empty chairs upon which rested violins and violas and cellos which played themselves, or seemed to, when fed a coin. Keys depressed, cymbals crashed, pipes blew compressed air into clarinets and oboes. Shadow observed, with a wry amusement, that the bows of the stringed instruments, played by mechanical arms, never actually touched the strings, which were often loose or missing. He wondered whether all the sounds he heard were made by wind and percussion, or whether there were tapes as well.

They had walked for what felt like several miles when they came to a room called the Mikado, one wall of which was a nineteenth century pseudo-Oriental nightmare, in which beetle-browed mechanical drummers banged cymbals and drums while staring out from their dragon-encrusted lair. Currently, they were majestically torturing Saint-Saëns's *Danse Macabre*.

Czernobog sat on a bench in the wall facing the Mikado machine, tapping out the time with his fingers. Pipes fluted, bells jangled.

Wednesday sat next to him. Shadow decided to remain standing. Czernobog extended his left hand, shook Wednesday's, shook Shadow's. 'Well met,' he said. Then he sat back, apparently enjoying the music.

The *Danse Macabre* came to a tempestuous and discordant end. That all the artificial instruments were ever-so-slightly out of tune added to the otherworldliness of the place. A new piece began.

'How was your bank robbery?' asked Czernobog. 'It went well?' He stood, reluctant to leave the Mikado and its thundering, jangling music.

'Slick as a snake in a barrel of butter,' said Wednesday.

'I get a pension from the slaughterhouse,' said Czernobog. 'I do not ask for more.'

'It won't last forever,' said Wednesday. 'Nothing does.'

More corridors, more musical machines. Shadow became aware that they were not following the path through the rooms intended for tourists, but seemed to be following a different route of Wednesday's own devising. They were going down a slope, and Shadow, confused, wondered if they had already been that way.

Czernobog grasped Shadow's arm. 'Quickly, come here,' he said, pulling him over to a large glass box by a wall. It contained a diorama of a tramp asleep in a churchyard in front of a church door. THE DRUNKARD'S DREAM, said the label, explaining that it was a nineteenth century penny-in-the-slot machine, originally from an English railway station. The coin slot had been modified to take the brass House on the Rock coins.

'Put in the money,' said Czernobog.

'Why?' asked Shadow.

'You must see. I show you.'

Shadow inserted his coin. The drunk in the graveyard raised his bottle to his lips. One of the gravestones flipped over, revealing a grasping corpse; a headstone turned around, flowers replaced by a grinning skull. A wraith appeared on the right of the church, while on the left of the church *something* with a half-glimpsed, pointed, unsettlingly bird-like face, a pale, Boschian nightmare, glided smoothly from a headstone into the shadows and was gone. Then the church door opened, a priest came out, and the ghosts, haunts and corpses vanished, and only the priest and the drunk were left alone in the graveyard. The priest looked down at the drunk disdainfully, and backed through the open door, which closed behind him, leaving the drunk on his own.

The clockwork story was deeply unsettling. Much more unsettling, thought Shadow, than clockwork has any right to be.

'You know why I show that to you?' asked Czernobog.

'No.'

'That is the world as it is. That is the real world. It is there, in that box.'

They wandered through a blood-coloured room filled with old theatrical organs, huge organ pipes, and what appeared to be enormous copper brewing vats, liberated from a brewery.

'Where are we going?' asked Shadow.

'The carousel,' said Czernobog.

'But we've passed signs to the carousel a dozen times already.'

'He goes his way. We travel a spiral. The quickest way is some-times the longest.'

Shadow's feet were beginning to hurt, and he found this senti-ment to be extremely unlikely.

A mechanical machine played *Octopus's Garden* in a room that went up for many storeys, the centre of which was filled entirely with a replica of a great black whale-like beast, with a life-sized replica of a boat in its vast fibre-glass mouth. They passed on from there to a Travel Hall, where they saw the car covered with tiles and the functioning Rube Goldberg chicken device and the rusting Burma Shave ads on the wall.

Life is Hard
It's Toil and Trouble
Keep your Jawline
Free from Stubble
Burma Shave

read one, and

He undertook to overtake
The road was on a bend
From now on the Undertaker
Is his only friend
Burma Shave

and they were at the bottom of a ramp now, with an ice-cream shop in front of them. It was nominally open, but the girl washing down the surfaces had a closed look on her face, so they walked past it into the pizzeria-cafeteria, empty but for an elderly black man, wearing a bright check suit and canary-yellow gloves. He was a small man, the kind of little old man who looked as if the passing of the years had shrunk him, eating an enormous, many-scooped ice-cream sundae, drinking a supersized mug of coffee. A black ciga-rillo was burning in the ashtray in front of him.

'Three coffees,' said Wednesday to Shadow. He went to the rest room.

Shadow bought the coffees, and took them over to Czernobog, who was sitting with the old black man, and was smoking a cigarette surreptitiously, as if he were scared of being caught. The other man, happily toying with his sundae, mostly ignored his cigarillo, but as Shadow approached he picked it up, inhaled deeply, and blew two smoke rings – first one large one, then another, smaller one, which passed neatly through the first – and he grinned, as if he were astonishingly pleased with himself.

'Shadow, this is Mister Nancy,' said Czernobog.

The old man got to his feet, and thrust out his yellow-gloved right hand. 'Good to meet you,' he said with a dazzling smile. 'I know who you must be. You're workin' for the old one-eye bastard, aren't you?' There was a faint twang in his voice, a hint of a patois that might have been West Indian.

'I work for Mister Wednesday,' said Shadow. 'Yes. Please, sit down.'

Czernobog inhaled on his cigarette.

'I think,' he pronounced, gloomily, 'that our kind, we like the cigarettes so much because they remind us of the offerings that once they burned for us, the smoke rising up as they sought our approval or our favour.'

'They never gave me nothin' like that,' said Nancy. 'Best I could hope for was a pile of fruit to eat, maybe curried goat, something slow and cold and tall to drink, and a big old high-titty woman to keep me company.' He grinned white teeth, and winked at Shadow.

'These days,' said Czernobog, his expression unchanged, 'we have nothing.'

'Well, I don't get anywhere near as much fruit as I used to,' said Mr Nancy, his eyes shining. 'But there still ain't nothin' out there in the world for my money that can beat a big old high-titty woman. Some folk you talk to, they say it's the booty you got to inspect at first, but I'm here to tell you that it's the titties that still crank my engine on a cold morning.' Nancy began to laugh, a wheezing, rattling, good-natured laugh, and Shadow found himself liking the old man despite himself.

Wednesday returned from the rest room, and shook hands with

Nancy. 'Shadow, you want something to eat? A slice of pizza? Or a sandwich?'

'I'm not hungry,' said Shadow.

'Let me tell you somethin',' said Mr Nancy. 'It can be a long time between meals. Someone offers you food, you say yes. I'm no longer young as I was, but I can tell you this, you never say no to the opportunity to piss, to eat, or to get half an hour's shut-eye. You follow me?'

'Yes. But I'm really not hungry.'

'You're a big one,' said Nancy, staring into Shadow's light-grey eyes with old eyes the colour of mahogany, 'a tall drink of water, but I got to tell you, you don't look too bright. I got a son, stupid as a man who bought his stupid at a two-for-one sale, and you remind me of him.'

'If you don't mind, I'll take that as a compliment,' said Shadow.

'Being called dumb as a man who slept late the mornin' they handed out brains?'

'Being compared to a member of your family.'

Mr Nancy stubbed out his cigarillo, then he flicked an imaginary speck of ash off his yellow gloves. 'You may not be the worst choice old one-eye could have made, come to that.' He looked up at Wednesday. 'You got any idea how many of us there's goin' to be here tonight?'

'I sent the message out to everyone I could find,' said Wednesday. 'Obviously not everyone is going to be able to come. And some of them,' with a pointed look at Czernobog, 'might not want to. But I think we can confidently expect several dozen of us. And the word will travel.'

They made their way past a display of suits of armour ('Victorian fake,' pronounced Wednesday as they passed the glassed-in display, 'modern fake, twelfth century helm on a seventeenth-century repro-duction, fifteenth century left gauntlet . . .') and then Wednesday pushed through an exit door, circled them around the outside of the building ('I can't be doin' with all these ins and outs,' said Nancy, 'I'm not as young as I used to be, and I come from warmer climes,') along a covered walkway, in through another exit door, and they were in the Carousel room.

Calliope music played: a Strauss waltz, stirring and occasionally discordant. The wall as they entered was hung with antique carousel horses, hundreds of them, some in need of a lick of paint, others in need of a good dusting; above them hung dozens of winged angels constructed rather obviously from female store-window mannequins; some of them bared their sexless breasts; some had lost their wigs and stared baldly and blindly down from the darkness.

And then there was the carousel.

A sign proclaimed it was the largest in the world, said how much it weighed, how many thousand lightbulbs were to be found in the chandeliers that hung from it in gothic profusion, and forbade anyone from climbing on it or from riding on the animals.

And such animals! Shadow stared, impressed in spite of himself, at the hundreds of full-sized creatures who circled on the platform of the carousel. Real creatures, imaginary creatures, and transformations of the two: each creature was different – he saw mermaid and merman, centaur and unicorn, elephants (one huge, one tiny), bulldog, frog and phoenix, zebra, tiger, manticore and basilisk, swans pulling a carriage, a white ox, a fox, twin walruses, even a sea serpent, all of them brightly coloured and more than real: each rode the platform as the waltz came to an end and a new waltz began. The carousel did not even slow down.

'What's it for?' asked Shadow. 'I mean, okay, world's biggest, hundreds of animals, thousands of lightbulbs, and it goes around all the time, and no-one ever rides it.'

'It's not there to be ridden, not by people,' said Wednesday. 'It's there to be admired. It's there to *be*.'

'Like a prayer wheel goin' round and round,' said Mr Nancy. 'Accumulating power.'

'So where are we meeting everyone?' asked Shadow. 'I thought you said that we were meeting them here. But the place is empty.'

Wednesday grinned his scary grin. 'Shadow,' he said. 'You're asking too many questions. You are not paid to ask questions.'

'Sorry.'

'Now, stand over here and help us up,' said Wednesday, and he walked over to the platform on one side, with a description of the carousel on it, and a warning that the carousel was not to be ridden.

Shadow thought of saying something, but instead he helped them, one by one, up onto the ledge. Wednesday seemed profoundly heavy,

Czernobog climbed up himself, only using Shadow's shoulder to steady himself, Nancy seemed to weigh nothing at all. Each of the old men climbed out onto the ledge, and then, with a step and a hop, they walked out onto the circling carousel platform.

'Well?' barked Wednesday. 'Aren't you coming?'

Shadow, not without a certain amount of hesitation, and a hasty look around for any House on the Rock personnel who might be watching, swung himself up onto the ledge beside the World's Largest Carousel. Shadow was amused, and a little puzzled, to realise that he was far more concerned about breaking the rules by climbing onto the carousel than he had been aiding and abetting this afternoon's bank robbery.

Each of the old men selected a mount. Wednesday climbed onto a golden wolf. Czernobog climbed onto an armored centaur, its face hidden by a metal helmet. Nancy, chuckling, slithered up onto the back of an enormous, leaping lion, captured by the sculptor mid-roar. He patted the side of the lion. The Strauss waltz carried them around, majestically.

Wednesday was smiling, and Nancy was laughing delightedly, an old man's cackle, and even the dour Czernobog seemed to be enjoying himself. Shadow felt as if a weight were suddenly lifted from his back: three old men were enjoying themselves, riding the world's biggest carousel. So what if they did all get thrown out of the place? Wasn't it worth it, worth anything, to say that you had ridden on the World's Largest Carousel? Wasn't it worth it to have travelled on one of those glorious monsters?

Shadow inspected a bulldog, and a mer-creature, and an elephant with a golden howdah, and then he climbed on the back of a creature with an eagle's head and the body of a tiger, and held on tight.

The rhythm of the Blue Danube waltz rippled and rang and sang in his head, the lights of a thousand chandeliers glinted and prismed, and for a heartbeat Shadow was a child again, and all it took to make him happy was to ride the carousel: he stayed perfectly still, riding his eagle-tiger at the centre of everything, and the world revolved around him.

Shadow heard himself laugh, over the sound of the music. He was happy. It was as if the last thirty six hours had never happened, as if the last three years had not happened, as if his life had evaporated into the daydream of a small child, riding the carousel in Golden Gate Park in San Francisco, on his first trip back to the States, a marathon journey by ship and by car, his mother standing there, watching him proudly, and himself sucking his melting popsicle, holding on tightly, hoping that the music would never stop, the carousel would never slow, the ride would never end. He was going around and around and around again . . .

Then the lights went out, and Shadow saw the gods.

Wide open and unguarded stand our gates,
And through them passes a wild motley throng.
Men from Volga and Tartar steppes.
Featureless figures from the Hoang-ho,
Malayan, Scythian, Teuton, Kelt and Slav,
Flying the Old World's poverty and scorn;
These bringing with them unknown gods and rites,
Those tiger passions here to stretch their claws,
In street and alley what strange tongues are these,
Accents of menace in our ear,
Voices that once the Tower of Babel knew.
– Thomas Bailey Aldrich, *The Unguarded Gates* 1882

One moment Shadow was riding the World's Largest Carousel, holding onto his eagle-headed tiger, and then the red and white lights of the carousel stretched and shivered and went out, and he was falling through an ocean of stars, while the mechanical waltz was replaced by a pounding rhythmic roll and crash, as of cymbals or the breakers on the shores of a far ocean.

The only light was starlight, but it illuminated everything with a cold clarity. Beneath him his mount stretched, and padded, its warm fur under his left hand, its feathers beneath his right.

'It's a good ride, isn't it?' The voice came from behind him, in his ears and in his mind.

Shadow turned, slowly, streaming images of himself as he moved, frozen moments, each him captured in a fraction of a second, every tiny movement lasting for an infinite period. The images that reached his mind made no sense: it was like seeing the world through the multifaceted jeweled eyes of a dragonfly, but each facet saw something completely different, and he was unable to combine the things he was seeing, or thought he was seeing, into a whole that made any sense.

He was looking at Mr Nancy, an old black man with a pencil moustache, in his check sports jacket and his lemon-yellow gloves, riding a carousel lion as it rose and lowered, high in the air; and, at the same time, in the same place, he saw a jeweled spider as high as a horse, its eyes an emerald nebula, strutting, staring down at him; and simultaneously he was looking at an extraordinarily tall man with teak-coloured skin and three sets of arms, wearing a flowing ostrich-feather headdress, his face painted with red stripes, riding an irritated golden lion, two of his six hands holding on tightly to the beast's mane; and he was also seeing a young black boy, dressed in rags, his left foot all swollen and crawling with blackflies; and last of all, and behind all these things, Shadow was looking at a tiny brown spider, hiding under a withered ochre leaf.

Shadow saw all these things, and he knew they were the same thing.

'If you don't close your mouth,' said the many things that were Mr Nancy, 'somethin's goin' to fly in there.'

Shadow closed his mouth and swallowed, hard.

There was a wooden hall on a hill, a mile or so from them. They were trotting toward the hall, their mounts' hooves and feet padding noiselessly on the dry sand at the sea's edge.

Czernobog trotted up on his centaur. He tapped the human arm of his mount. 'None of this is truly happening,' he said to Shadow. He sounded miserable. 'Is all in your head. Best not to think of it.'

Shadow saw a grey-haired old East-European immigrant, with a shabby raincoat and one iron-coloured tooth, true. But he also saw a squat black thing, darker than the darkness that surrounded them, its eyes two burning coals; and he saw a prince, with long flowing black hair, and long black moustaches, blood on his hands and his face, riding, naked but for a bear-skin over his shoulder, on a creature half-man, half-beast, his face and torso blue-tattooed with swirls and spirals.

'Who are you?' asked Shadow. 'What are you?'

Their mounts padded along the shore. Waves broke and crashed implacably on the night beach.

Wednesday guided his wolf – now a huge and charcoal-grey beast with green eyes – over to Shadow. Shadow's mount caracoled away from it, and Shadow stroked its neck and told it not to be afraid. Its tiger tail swished, aggressively. It occurred to Shadow that there was another wolf, a twin to the one that Wednesday was riding, keeping pace with them in the sand dunes, just a moment out of sight.

'Do you know me, Shadow?' said Wednesday. He rode his wolf with his head high. His right eye glittered and flashed, his left eye was dull. He wore a cloak, with a deep, monk-like cowl, and his face stared out from the shadows. 'I told you I would tell you my names. This is what they call me. I am called Glad-of-War, Grim, Raider, and Third. I am One-eyed. I am called Highest, and True-Guesser. I am Grimnir, and I am the Hooded One. I am All-Father, and I am Gondlir Wand-bearer. I have as many names as there are winds, as many titles as there are ways to die. My ravens are Huginn and Muninn: Thought and Memory; my wolves are Freki and Geri; my horse is the gallows.' Two ghostly grey ravens, like transparent skins of birds, landed on Wednesday's shoulders, pushed their beaks *into* the side of Wednesday's head as if tasting his mind, and flapped out into the world once more.

What should I believe? thought Shadow, and the voice came back to him from somewhere deep beneath the world, in a bass rumble: *Believe everything.*

'Odin?' said Shadow, and the wind whipped the word from his lips.

'Odin,' whispered Wednesday, and the crash of the breakers on the beach of skulls was not loud enough to drown that whisper. 'Odin,' said Wednesday, tasting the sound of the words in his mouth. 'Odin,' said Wednesday, his voice a triumphant shout which echoed from horizon to horizon. His name swelled and grew and filled the world like the pounding of blood in Shadow's ears.

And then, as in a dream, they were no longer riding toward a distant hall. They were already there, and their mounts were tied in the shelter beside the building.

The hall was huge but primitive. The roof was thatched, the walls were wooden. There was a fire burning in the centre of the hall, and the smoke stung Shadow's eyes.

'We should have done this in my mind, not in his,' muttered Mr Nancy to Shadow. 'It would have been warmer there.'

'We're in his mind?'

'More or less. This is Valaskjalf. It's his old hall.'

Shadow was relieved to see that Nancy was now once more an old man wearing yellow gloves, although his shadow shook and shivered and changed in the flames of the fire, and what it changed into was not always entirely human.

There were wooden benches against the walls, and, sitting on them or standing beside them, perhaps ten people. They kept their distance from each other: a mixed lot, who included a dark-skinned, matronly woman in a red sari, several shabby-looking businessmen, and others, too close to the fire for Shadow to be able to make them out.

'Where are they?' whispered Wednesday fiercely, to Nancy. 'Well? Where are they? There should be scores of us here. Dozens!'

'You did all the invitin',' said Nancy. 'I think it's a wonder you got as many here as you did. You think I should tell a story, to start things off?'

Wednesday shook his head. 'Out of the question.'

'They don't look very friendly,' said Nancy. 'A story's a good way of gettin' someone on your side. And you don't have a bard to sing to them.'

'No stories,' said Wednesday. 'Not now. Later, there will be time for stories. Not now.'

'No stories. Right. I'll just be the warm-up man.' And Mr Nancy strode out into the firelight with an easy smile.

'I know what you are all thinking,' he said. 'You are thinking, What is Compé Anansi doing, coming out to talk to you all, when the All-Father called you all here, just like he called me here? Well, you know, sometimes people need reminding of things. I look around when I come in, and I thought, where's the rest of us? But then I thought, just because we are few and they are many, we are weak, and they are powerful, it does not mean that we are lost.

'You know, one time I saw Tiger down at the water-hole: he had the biggest testicles of any animal, and the sharpest claws, and two front teeth as long as knives and as sharp as blades. And I said to him, Brother Tiger, you go for a swim, I'll look after your balls for you. He was so proud of his balls. So he got into the water-hole for a swim, and I put his balls on, and left him my own little spider-balls. And then, you know what I did? I ran away, fast as my legs would take me.

'I didn't stop till I got to the next town. And I saw Old Monkey there. You lookin' mighty fine, Anansi, said Old Monkey. I said to him, you know what they all singin' in the town over there? What are they singin'? he asks me. They singin' the funniest song, I told him. Then I did a dance, and I sings,

Tiger's balls, yeah,
I ate Tiger's balls
Now ain't nobody gonna stop me ever at all
Nobody put me up against the big black wall
'Cos I ate that Tiger's testimonials
I ate Tiger's balls.

'Old Monkey he laughs fit to bust, holding his side and shakin', and stampin', then he starts singin' *Tiger's balls, I ate tiger's balls,* snappin' his fingers, spinnin' around on his two feet. That's a fine song, he says, I'm going to sing it to all my friends. You do that, I tell him, and I head back to the water-hole.

'There's Tiger, down by the water-hole, walking up and down, with his tail switchin' and swishin' and his ears and the fur on his neck up as far as they can go, and he's snappin' at every insect comes by with his huge old saber-teeth, and his eyes flashin' orange fire. He looks mean and scary and big, but danglin' between his legs, there's the littlest balls in the littlest blackest most wrinkledy ball-sack you ever did see.

'Hey, Anansi, he says, when he sees me. You were supposed to be guarding my balls while I went swimming. But when I got out of the swimming hole, there was nothing on the side of the bank but these little black shrivelled-up good-for-nothing spider balls I'm wearing.

'I done my best, I tells him, but it was those monkeys, they come by and eat your balls all up, and when I tell them off, then they pulled off my own little balls. And I was so ashamed I ran away.

'You a liar, Anansi, says Tiger. I'm going to eat your liver. But then he hears the monkeys coming from their town to the water-hole. A dozen happy monkeys, boppin' down the path, clickin' their fingers and singin' as loud as they could sing,

Tiger's balls, yeah,
I ate Tiger's balls
Now ain't nobody gonna stop me ever at all
Nobody put me up against the big black wall
'Cos I ate that Tiger's testimonials
I ate Tiger's balls.

'And Tiger, he growls, and he roars and he's off into the forest after them, and the monkeys screech and head for the highest trees. And I scratch my nice new big balls, and damn they felt good hangin' between my skinny legs, and I walk on home. And even today, Tiger keeps chasin' monkeys. So you all remember: just because you're small, doesn't mean you got no power.'

Mr Nancy smiled, and bowed his head, and spread his hands, accepting the applause and laughter like a pro, and then he turned and walked back to where Shadow and Czernobog were standing.

'I thought I said no stories,' said Wednesday.

'You call that a story?' said Nancy. 'I barely cleared my throat. Just warmed them up for you. Go knock them dead.'

Wednesday walked out into the firelight, a big old man with a glass eye in a brown suit and an old Armani coat. He stood there, looking at the people on the wooden benches, saying nothing for longer than Shadow could believe someone could comfortably say nothing. And, finally, he spoke.

'You know me,' he said. 'You all know me. Some of you have no cause to love me, but love me or not, you know me.'

There was a rustling, a stir among the people on the benches.

'I've been here longer than most of you. Like the rest of you, I figured we could get by on what we got. Not enough to make us happy, but enough to keep going.

'That may not be the case any more. There's a storm coming, and it's not a storm of our making.'

He paused. Now he stepped forward, and folded his arms across his chest.

'When the people came to America they brought us with them. They brought me, and Loki and Thor, Anansi and the Lion-God, Leprechauns and Kobolds and Banshees, Kubera and Frau Holle and Ashtaroth, and they brought you. We rode here in their minds, and we took root. We travelled with the settlers to the new lands across the ocean.

'The land is vast. Soon enough, our people abandoned us, remembered us only as creatures of the old land, as things that had not come with them to the new. Our true believers passed on, or stopped believing, and we were left, lost and scared and dispossessed, only what little smidgens of worship or belief we could find. And to get by as best we could.

'So that's what we've done, gotten by, out on the edges of things, where no-one was watching us too closely.

'We have, let us face it and admit it, little influence. We prey on them, and we take from them, and we get by; we strip and we whore and we drink too much; we pump gas and we steal and we cheat and we exist in the cracks at the edges of society. Old gods, here in this new land without gods.'

Wednesday paused. He looked from one to another of his listeners, grave and statesmanlike. They stared back at him impassively, their faces mask-like and unreadable. Wednesday cleared his throat, and he spat, hard into the fire. It flared and flamed, illuminating the inside of the hall.

'Now, as all of you will have had reason aplenty to discover for yourselves, there are new gods growing in America, clinging to growing knots of belief: gods of credit-card and freeway, of internet and telephone, of radio and hospital and television, gods of plastic and of beeper and of neon. Proud gods, fat and foolish creatures, puffed up with their own newness and importance.

'They are aware of us, and they fear us, and they hate us,' said Odin. 'You are fooling yourselves if you believe otherwise. They will destroy us, if they can. It is time for us to band together. It is time for us to act.'

The old woman in the red sari stepped into the firelight. On her forehead was a small dark blue jewel. She said, 'You called us here for this nonsense?' And then she snorted, a snort of mingled amusement and irritation.

Wednesday's brows lowered. 'I called you here, yes. But this is sense, Mama-ji, not nonsense. Even a child could see that.'

'So I am a child, am I?' She wagged a finger at him. 'I was old in Kalighat before you were dreamed of, you foolish man. I am a child?

Then I *am* a child, for there is nothing in your foolish talk to see.'

Again, a moment of double-vision: Shadow saw the old woman her dark face pinched with age and disapproval, but behind her he saw something huge, a naked woman with skin as black as a new leather jacket, and lips and tongue the bright red of arterial blood. Around her neck were skulls, and her many hands held knives, and swords, and severed heads.

'I did not call you a child, Mama-ji,' said Wednesday, peaceably. 'But it seems self-evident—'

'The only thing that seems self-evident,' said the old woman, pointing (as behind her, through her, above her, a black finger, sharp-taloned, pointed in echo), 'is your own desire for glory. We've lived in peace in this country for a long time. Some of us do better than others, I agree. I do well. Back in India, there is an incarnation of me who does much better, but so be it. I am not envious. I've watched the new ones rise, and I've watched them fall again.' Her hand fell to her side. Shadow saw that the others were looking at her: a mixture of expressions – respect, amusement, embarrassment – in their eyes. 'They worshipped the railroads here, only a blink of an eye ago. And now the iron gods are as forgotten as the emerald hunters . . .'

'Make your point, Mama-ji,' said Wednesday.

'My point?' Her nostrils flared. The corners of her mouth turned down. 'I – and I am *obviously* only a child – say that we wait. We do nothing. We don't know that they mean us harm.'

'And will you still counsel waiting when they come in the night and they kill you, or they take you away?'

Her expression was disdainful and amused: it was all in the lips and the eyebrows and the set of the nose. 'If they try such a thing,' she said, 'they will find me hard to catch, and harder still to kill.'

A squat young man sitting on the bench behind her hrrumphed for attention, then said, with a booming voice, 'All-Father, my people are comfortable. We make the best of what we have. If this war of yours goes against us, we could lose everything.'

Wednesday said, 'You have already lost everything. I am offering you the chance to take something back.'

The fire blazed high as he spoke, illuminating the faces of the audience.

I don't really believe, Shadow thought. *I don't believe any of this. Maybe I'm still fifteen. Mom's still alive and I haven't even met Laura yet. Everything that's happened so far has been some kind of especially vivid dream.* And yet he could not believe that either. All we have to believe with is our senses: the tools we use to perceive the world, our sight, our touch, our memory. If they lie to us, then nothing can be trusted. And even if we do not believe, then still we cannot travel in any other way than the road our senses show us; and we must walk that road to the end.

Then the fire burned out, and there was darkness in Valaskjalf, Odin's Hall.

'Now what?' whispered Shadow.

'Now we go back to the carousel room,' muttered Mr Nancy, 'And old One-Eye buys us all dinner, greases some palms, kisses some babies, and no-one says the Gee-word any more.'

'Gee-word?'

'*Gods*. What *were* you doin' the day they handed out brains, boy, anyway?'

'Someone was telling a story about stealing a tiger's balls, and I had to stop and find out how it ended.'

Mr Nancy chuckled.

'But nothing was resolved. Nobody agreed to anything.'

'He's working them slowly. He'll land 'em one at a time. You'll see. They'll come around in the end.'

Shadow could feel that a wind was coming up from somewhere, stirring his hair, touching his face, pulling at him.

They were standing in the room of the biggest carousel in the world, listening to the Emperor Waltz.

There was a group of people, tourists by the look of them, talking with Wednesday over at the other side of the room, as many people as there had been shadowy figures in Wednesday's hall. 'Through here,' boomed Wednesday, and he led them through the only exit, formed to look like the gaping mouth of a huge monster, its sharp teeth ready to rend them all to slivers. He moved among them like a politician, cajoling, encouraging, smiling, gently disagreeing, pacifying.

'Did that happen?' asked Shadow.

'Did what happen, shit-for-brains?' asked Mr Nancy.

'The hall. The fire. Tiger balls. Riding the carousel.'

'Heck, nobody's allowed to ride the carousel. Didn't you see the signs? Now hush.'

The monster's mouth led to the Organ Room, which puzzled Shadow – hadn't they already come through that way? It was no less strange the second time. Wednesday led them all up some stairs, past life-sized models of the four horsemen of the apocalypse hanging from the ceiling, and they followed the signs to an early exit.

Shadow and Nancy brought up the rear. And then they were out of the House on the Rock, walking past the gift store and heading back into the parking lot.

'Pity we had to leave before the end,' said Mr Nancy. 'I was kind of hoping to see the biggest artificial orchestra in the whole world.'

'I've seen it,' said Czernobog. 'It's not so much.'

The restaurant was ten minutes up the road. Wednesday had told each of his guests that tonight's dinner was on him, and had organised rides to the restaurant for any of them that didn't have their own transportation.

Shadow wondered how they had gotten to the House on the Rock in the first place, without their own transportation, and how they were going to get away again, but he said nothing. It seemed the smartest thing to say.

Shadow had a carful of Wednesday's guests to ferry to the restaurant: the woman in the red sari sat in the front seat beside him. There were two men in the back seat: the squat, peculiar-looking young man whose name Shadow had not properly caught, but which sounded like Elvis, and another man, in a dark suit, who Shadow could not remember.

He had stood beside the man as he got into the car, had opened and closed the door for him, and was unable to remember anything about him. He turned around in the driver's seat and looked at him, carefully noting his face, his hair, his clothes, making certain he would know him if he met him again, and turned back to start the car, to find that the man had slipped from his mind. An impression of wealth was left behind, but nothing more.

I'm tired, thought Shadow. He glanced to his right and snuck a glance at the Indian woman. He noted the tiny silver necklace of skulls that circled her neck; her charm bracelet of heads and hands that jangled, like tiny bells, when she moved; the dark blue jewel on her forehead. She smelled of spices, of cardamom and nutmeg and flowers. Her hair was pepper-and-salt, and she smiled when she saw him look at her.

'You call me Mama-ji,' she said.

'I am Shadow, Mama-ji,' said Shadow.

'And what do you think of your employer's plans, Mister Shadow?'

He slowed, as a large black truck sped past, overtaking them with a spray of slush. 'I don't ask, he don't tell,' he said.

'If you ask me, he wants a last stand. He wants us to go out in a blaze of glory. That's what he wants. And we are old enough, or stupid enough, that maybe some of us will say yes.'

'It's not my job to ask questions, Mama-ji,' said Shadow. The inside of the car filled with her tinkling laughter.

The man in the back seat – not the peculiar young man, the other one, – said something, and Shadow replied to him, but a moment later he was damned if he could remember what had been said.

The peculiar-looking young man had said nothing, but now he started to hum to himself, a deep, melodic, bass humming that made the interior of the car vibrate and rattle and buzz.

The peculiar-looking man was of average height, but of an odd shape: Shadow had heard of men who were barrel-chested before, but had no image to accompany the metaphor. This man was barrel chested, and he had legs like, yes, like tree-trunks, and hands like, exactly, ham-hocks. He wore a black parka, with a hood, several sweaters, thick dungarees, and, incongruously, in the winter and with those clothes, a pair of white tennis-shoes, which were the same size and shape as shoe-boxes. His fingers resembled sausages, with flat, squared-off fingertips.

'That's some hum you got,' said Shadow from the driver's seat.

'Sorry,' said the peculiar young man, in a deep, deep voice, embarrassed. He stopped humming.

'No, I enjoyed it,' said Shadow. 'Don't stop.'

The peculiar young man hesitated, then commenced to hum once more, his voice as deep and reverberant as before. This time there were words interspersed in the humming. 'Down down down,' he sang, so deeply that the windows rattled. 'Down down down, down down, down down.'

Christmas lights were draped across the eaves of every house and building that they drove past. They ranged from discrete golden lights that dripped twinkles to giant displays of snowmen and teddy bears and multicolored stars.

Shadow pulled up at the restaurant, a big, barn-like structure, and he let his passengers off by the front door. He drove the car to the back of the parking lot. He wanted to make the short walk back to the restaurant alone, in the cold, to clear his head.

He parked the car beside a black truck. He wondered if it was the same one that had sped past him earlier. He closed the car door, and stood there in the parking lot, his breath steaming.

Inside the restaurant, Shadow could imagine Wednesday already sitting all his guests down around a big table, working the room. Shadow wondered whether he had really had Kali in the front of his car, wondered what he had been driving in the back . . .

'Hey bud, you got a match?' said a voice that was half-familiar, and Shadow turned to apologise and say no, he didn't, but the gun-barrel hit him over the left eye, and he started to fall. He put out an arm to steady himself as he went down. Someone pushed something soft into his mouth, to stop him crying out, and taped it into position: easy, practised moves, like a butcher gutting a chicken.

Shadow tried to shout, to warn Wednesday, to warn them all, but nothing came out of his mouth but a muffled noise.

'The quarry are all inside,' said the half-familiar voice. 'Everyone in position?' A crackle of a voice, half-audible through a radio. 'Let's move in and round them all up.'

'What about the big guy?' said another voice.

'Package him up, take him out,' said the first voice.

They put a bag-like hood over Shadow's head, and bound his wrists and ankles with tape, and put him in the back of a truck, and drove him away.

There were no windows in the tiny room in which they had locked Shadow. There was a plastic chair, a lightweight folding table, and a bucket with a cover on it, which served Shadow as a makeshift toilet. There was also a six foot-long strip of yellow foam on the floor, and a thin blanket, with a long-since crusted brown stain in the centre: blood or shit or food, Shadow didn't know, and didn't care to investigate. There was a naked bulb behind a metal grille high in the room, but no light switch that Shadow had been able to find. The light was always on. There was no door handle on his side of the door.

He was hungry.

The first thing he had done, when the spooks had pushed him into the room, after they'd ripped off the tape from his ankles and wrists and mouth and left him alone, was to walk around the room and inspect it, carefully. He tapped the walls. They sounded dully metallic. There was a small ventilation grid at the top of the room. The door was soundly locked.

He was bleeding above the left eyebrow in a slow ooze. His head ached.

The floor was uncarpeted. He tapped it. It was made of the same metal as the walls.

He took the top off the bucket, pissed in it, and covered it once more. According to his watch only four hours had passed since the raid on the restaurant.

His wallet was gone, but they had left him his coins.

He sat on the chair, at the card-table. The table was covered with a cigarette-burned green baize. Shadow practiced appearing to push coins through the table. Then he took two quarters and made up a Pointless Coin Trick.

He concealed a quarter in his right palm, and openly displayed the other quarter in his left hand, between finger and thumb. Then he appeared to take the quarter from his left hand, while actually letting it drop back into his left hand. He opened his right hand to display the quarter that had been there all along.

The thing about coin manipulation was that it took all Shadow's head to do it; or rather, he could not do it if he was angry or upset, so the action of practising an illusion, even one with, by itself, no possible use – for, he had expended an enormous amount of effort and skill to make it appear that he had moved a quarter from one hand to the other, something that it takes no skill whatever to do for real – calmed him, cleared his mind of turmoil and fear.

He began a trick even more pointless: a one-handed half-dollar to penny transformation, but with his two quarters. Each of the coins was alternately concealed and revealed as the trick progressed: he began with one quarter visible, the other hidden. He raised his hand to his mouth and blew on the visible coin, while slipping it into a classic palm, as the first two fingers took the hidden quarter out and presented it. The effect was that he displayed a quarter in his hand, raised it to his mouth, blew on it, and lowered it again, displaying the same quarter all the while.

He did it over and over and over again.

He wondered if they were going to kill him, and his hand trembled, just a little, and one of the quarters dropped from his fingertip onto the stained green baize of the card-table.

And then, because he just couldn't do it any more, he put the coins away, and took out the Liberty head dollar that Zorya Polunochnaya had given him, and held onto it tightly, and waited.

At three in the morning, by his watch, the spooks returned to interrogate him. Two men in dark suits, with dark hair and shiny black shoes. Spooks. One was square-jawed, wide-shouldered, had great hair, looked like he had played football in high school, badly bitten finger-nails, the other had a receding hairline, silver-rimmed round glasses, manicured nails. While they looked nothing alike, Shadow found himself suspecting that, on some level, possibly cellular, the two men were identical. They stood on each side of the card-table, looking down at him.

'How long have you been working for Cargo, sir?' asked one.

'I don't know what that is,' said Shadow.

'He calls himself Wednesday. Grimm. Olfather. Old guy. You've been seen with him, sir.'

'I've been working for him for a couple of days.'

'Don't lie to us, sir,' said the spook with the glasses.

'Okay,' said Shadow. 'I won't. But it's still a couple of days.'

The clean-jawed spook reached down and twisted Shadow's ear between finger and thumb. He squeezed as he twisted. The pain was intense. 'We told you not to lie to us, sir,' he said, mildly. Then he let go.

Each of the spooks had a gun-bulge under his jacket. Shadow did not try to retaliate. He pretended he was back in prison. *Do your own time*, thought Shadow. *Don't tell them anything they don't know already. Don't ask questions.*

'These are dangerous people you're palling around with, sir,' said the spook with glasses. 'You will be doing your country a service by turning state's evidence.' He smiled, sympathetically: *I'm the good cop*, said the smile.

'I see,' said Shadow.

'And if you don't want to help us, sir,' said the clean-jawed spook, 'you can see what we're like when we're not happy.' He hit Shadow an open handed blow across the stomach, knocking the breath from him. It wasn't torture, Shadow thought, just punctuation: *I'm the bad cop.* He retched.

'I would like to make you happy,' said Shadow, as soon as he could speak.

'All we ask is your cooperation, sir.'

'Can I ask . . .' gasped Shadow (*don't ask questions*, he thought, but it was too late, the words were already spoken), 'can I ask who I'll be cooperating with?'

'You want us to tell you our names?' asked the clean-jawed spook. 'You have to be out of your mind.'

'No, he's got a point,' said the spook with glasses. 'It may make it easier for him to relate to us.' He looked at Shadow and smiled like a man advertising toothpaste. 'Hi. I'm Mister Stone, sir. My colleague is Mister Wood.'

'Actually,' said Shadow, 'I meant, what agency are you with? CIA? FBI?'

Stone shook his head. 'Gee. It's not as easy as that, any more, sir. Things just aren't that simple.'

'The private sector,' said Wood, 'the public sector. You know. There's a lot of interplay these days.'

'But I can assure you,' said Stone, with another smiley smile, 'we *are* the good guys. Are you hungry, sir?' He reached into a pocket of his jacket, pulled out a Snickers bar. 'Here. A gift.'

'Thanks,' said Shadow. He unwrapped the Snickers bar and ate it.

'I guess you'd like something to drink with that. Coffee? Beer?'

'Water, please,' said Shadow.

Stone walked to the door, knocked on it. He said something to the guard on the other side of the door, who nodded and returned a minute later with a polystyrene cup filled with cold water.

'CIA,' said Wood. He shook his head, ruefully. 'Those bozos. Hey, Stone. I heard a new CIA joke. Okay: how can we be sure the CIA weren't involved in the Kennedy assassination?'

'I don't know,' said Stone. 'How *can* we be sure?'

'He's dead, isn't he?' said Wood.

They both laughed.

'Feeling better now, sir?' asked Stone.

'I guess.'

'So why don't you tell us what happened this evening, sir?'

'We did some tourist stuff. Went to the House on the Rock. Went out for some food. You know the rest.'

Stone sighed, heavily. Wood shook his head, as if disappointed, and kicked Shadow in the kneecap. The pain was excruciating. Then Wood pushed a fist slowly into Shadow's back, just above the right kidney, and knuckled it, hard, and the pain was worse than the pain in Shadow's knee.

I'm bigger than either of them, he thought. *I can take them*. But they were armed; and even if he – somehow – killed or subdued them both, he'd still be locked in the cell with them. (But he'd have a gun. He'd have two guns.) (*No.*)

Wood was keeping his hands away from Shadow's face. No marks. Nothing permanent: just fists and feet on his torso and knees. It hurt, and Shadow clutched the Liberty dollar tight in the palm of his hand, and waited for it to be over.

And after far too long a time the beating ended.

'We'll see you in a couple of hours, sir,' said Stone. 'You know, Woody really hated to have to do that. We're reasonable men. Like I said, we are the good guys. You're on the wrong side. Meantime, why don't you try to get a little sleep?'

'You better start taking us seriously,' said Wood.

'Woody's got a point there, sir,' said Stone. 'Think about it.'

The door slammed closed behind them. Shadow wondered if they would turn out the light, but they didn't, and it blazed into the room like a cold eye. Shadow crawled across the floor to the yellow foam-rubber pad, and climbed onto it, pulling the thin blanket over himself, and he closed his eyes, and he held onto nothing, and he held onto dreams.

Time passed.

He was fifteen again, and his mother was dying, and she was trying to tell him something very important, and he couldn't understand her. He moved in his sleep and a shaft of pain moved him from half-sleep to half-waking, and he winced.

Shadow shivered under the thin blanket. His right arm covered his eyes, blocking out the light of the bulb. He wondered whether Wednesday and the others were still at liberty, if they were even still alive. He hoped that they were.

The silver dollar remained cold in his left hand. He could feel it there, as it had been during the beating. He wondered idly why it did not warm to his body temperature. Half-asleep, now, and half-delirious, the coin, and the idea of liberty, and the moon, and Zorya Polunochnaya somehow became intertwined in one woven beam of silver light that shone from the depths to the heavens, and he rode the silver beam up and away from the pain and the heartache and the fear, away from the pain and, blessedly, back into dreams . . .

From far away he could hear some kind of noise, but it was too late to think about it: he belonged to sleep now.

A half-thought: he hoped it was not people coming to wake him up, to hit him or to shout at him. And then, he noticed with pleasure, he was really asleep, and no longer cold.

Somebody somewhere was calling for help, loudly, in his dream or out of it.

Shadow rolled over on the foam rubber, in his sleep, finding new places that hurt as he rolled.

Someone was shaking his shoulder.

He wanted to ask them not to wake him, to let him sleep and leave him be, but it came out as a grunt.

'Puppy?' said Laura. 'You have to wake up. Please wake up, hon.'

And there was a moment's gentle relief. He had had such a strange dream, of prisons and con-men and down-at-heel gods, and now Laura was waking him to tell him it was time for work, and perhaps there would be time enough before work to steal some coffee and a kiss, or more than a kiss; and he put out his hand to touch her.

Her flesh was cold as ice, and sticky.

Shadow opened his eyes.

'Where did all the blood come from?' he asked.

'Other people,' she said. 'It's not mine. I'm filled with formalde-hyde, mixed with glycerin and lanolin.'

'Which other people?' he asked.

'The guards,' she said. 'It's okay. I killed them. You better move. I don't think I gave anyone a chance to raise the alarm. Take a coat from out there, or you'll freeze your butt off.'

'You killed them?'

She shrugged, and half-smiled, awkwardly. Her hands looked as if she had been finger-painting, composing a picture that had been executed solely in crimsons, and there were splashes and spatters on her face and clothes (the same blue suit in which she had been buried) that made Shadow think of Jackson Pollock, because it was less prob-lematic to think of Jackson Pollock than to accept the alternative.

'It's easier to kill people, when you're dead yourself,' she told him. 'I mean, it's not such a big deal. You're not so prejudiced any more.'

'It's still a big deal to me,' said Shadow.

'You want to stay here until the morning crew come?' she said. 'You can if you like. I thought you'd like to get out of here.'

'They'll think I did it,' he said, stupidly.

'Maybe,' she said. 'Put on a coat, hon. You'll freeze.'

He walked out into the corridor. At the end of the corridor was a guardroom. In the guardroom were four dead men: three guards, and the man who had called himself Stone. His friend was nowhere to be seen. From the blood-coloured skid-marks on the floor, two of them had been dragged into the guardroom, and dropped onto the floor.

His own coat was hanging from the coat rack. His wallet was still in the inside pocket, apparently untouched. Laura pulled open a couple of cardboard boxes, filled with candy bars.

The guards, now he could see them properly, were wearing dark camouflage uniforms, but there were no official tags on them, nothing to say for whom they were working. They might have been weekend duck-hunters, dressed for the shoot.

Laura reached out her cold hand, and squeezed Shadow's hand in hers. She had the gold coin he had given her around her neck, on a golden chain.

'That looks nice,' he said.

'Thanks.' She smiled, prettily.

'What about the others,' he asked. 'Wednesday, and the rest of them? Where are they?' Laura passed him a handful of candy bars, and he filled his pockets with them.

'There wasn't anybody else here. A lot of empty cells, and one with you in it. Oh, and one of the men had gone into the cell down there to jack off with a magazine. He got such a shock.'

'You killed him while he was jerking himself off?'

She shrugged. 'I guess,' she said, uncomfortably. 'I was worried they were hurting you. Someone has to watch out for you, and I told you I would, didn't I? Here, take these.' They were chemical hand- and foot-warmers: thin pads – you broke the seal and they heated up and stayed that way for hours. Shadow pocketed them.

'Look out for me. Yes,' he said, 'you did.'

She reached out a finger, stroked him above his left eyebrow. 'You're hurt,' she said.

'I'm okay,' he said.

He opened a metal door in the wall. It swung open slowly. There was a four foot drop to the ground, and he swung himself down to what felt like gravel. He picked up Laura by the waist, swung her down, as he used to swing her, easily, without a second thought. . . .

The moon came out from behind a thick cloud. It was low on the horizon, ready to set, but the light it cast onto the snow was enough to see by.

They had emerged from what turned out to be the black-painted metal car of a long freight train, parked or abandoned in a wood-land siding. The series of wagon-cars went on as far as he could see, into the trees and away. He had been on a train. He should have known.

'How the hell did you find me here?' he asked his dead wife.

She shook her head slowly, amused. 'You shine like a beacon in a dark world,' she told him. 'It wasn't that hard. Now, just go. Go as far and as fast as you can. Don't use your credit cards and you should be fine.'

'Where should I go?'

She pushed a hand through her matted hair, flicking it back out of her eyes. 'The road's that way,' she told him. 'Do whatever you can. Steal a car if you have to. Go south.'

'Laura,' he said, and hesitated. 'Do you know what's going on? Do you know who these people are? Who did you kill?'

'Yeah,' she said. 'I think I do know.'

'I owe you,' said Shadow. 'I'd still be in there if it wasn't for you. I don't think they had anything good planned for me.'

'No,' she said. 'I don't think they did.'

They walked away from the empty train cars. Shadow wondered about the other trains he'd seen, blank windowless metal cars which went on for mile after mile hooting their lonely way through the night. His fingers closed around the Liberty dollar in his pocket, and he remembered Zorya Polunochnaya, and the way she had looked at him in the moonlight. *Did you ask her what she wanted? It is the wisest thing to ask the dead. Sometimes they will tell you.*

'Laura . . . What do you want?' he asked.

'You really want to know?'

'Yes. Please.'

Laura looked up at him with dead blue eyes. 'I want to be alive again,' she said. 'Not in this half-life. I want to be *really* alive. I want to feel my heart pumping in my chest again. I want to feel blood moving through me – hot, and salty, and real. It's weird, you don't think you can feel it, the blood, but believe me, when it stops flowing, you'll know.' She rubbed her eyes, smudging her face with red from the mess on her hands. 'Look, it's hard. You know why dead people only go out at night, puppy? Because it's easier to pass for real, in the dark. And I don't want to have to pass. I want to be alive.'

'I don't understand what you want me to do.'

'Make it happen, hon. You'll figure it out. I know you will.'

'Okay,' he said. 'I'll try. And if I do figure it out, how do I find you?'

But she was gone, and there was nothing left in the woodland but a gentle grey in the sky to show him where east was, and on the bitter December wind a lonely wail that might have been the cry of the last nightbird or the call of the first bird of dawn.

Shadow set his face to the south, and he began to walk.

7

*As the Hindu gods are 'immortal' only in a very particular sense –
for they are born and they die – they experience most of the great
human dilemmas and often seem to differ from mortals in a few
trivial details . . . and from demons even less. Yet they are regarded
by the Hindus as a class of beings by definition totally different
from any other; they are symbols in a way that no human being,
however 'archetypal' his life story, can ever be. They are actors
playing parts that are real only for us; they are the masks behind
which we see our own faces.*
– Wendy Doniger O'Flaherty, *Introduction, HINDU MYTHS*
(Penguin Books 1975)

Shadow had been walking south, or what he hoped was more or
less south, for several hours, heading along a narrow and unmarked
road through the woods somewhere in, he imagined, southern
Wisconsin. Several jeeps came down the road toward him at one
point, headlights blazing, and he ducked into the trees until they
had passed. The early morning mist hung at waist level. The cars
were black.

When, thirty minutes later, he heard the noise of distant helicopters coming from the west, he struck out away from the timber
trail and into the woods. There were two helicopters, and he lay,
crouched in a hollow beneath a fallen tree, and listened to them pass
over. As they moved away, he looked out and looked up, for one
hasty glance at the grey winter sky. He was satisfied to observe that
the helicopters were painted a matt black. He waited beneath the
tree until the noise of the helicopters was completely gone.

Under the trees the snow was little more than a dusting, which crunched underfoot. He was deeply grateful for the chemical hand- and feet-warmers, which kept his extremities from freezing. Beyond that, he was numb: heart-numb, mind-numb, soul-numb. And the numbness, he realised, went a long way down, and a long way back.

So what do I want? he asked himself. He couldn't answer, so he just kept on walking, a step at a time, on and on through the woods. Trees looked familiar, moments of landscape were perfectly deja-vued. Could he be walking in circles? Maybe he would just walk and walk and walk until the warmers and the candy bars ran out and then sit down and never get up again.

He reached a large stream, of the kind the locals called a creek and pronounced *a crick*, and decided to follow it. Streams led to rivers, rivers all led to the Mississippi, and if he kept walking, or stole a boat or built a raft, eventually he'd get to New Orleans, where it was warm, an idea which seemed both comforting and unlikely.

There were no more helicopters. He had the feeling that the ones that had passed overhead had been cleaning up the mess at the freight train siding, not hunting for him, otherwise they would have returned; there would have been tracker dogs and sirens and the whole paraphernalia of pursuit. Instead, there was nothing.

What did *he* want? Not to get caught. Not to get blamed for the deaths of the men on the train. 'It wasn't me,' he heard himself saying, 'it was my dead wife.' He could imagine the expressions on the faces of the law officers. Then people could argue about whether he was crazy or not while he went to the chair . . . He wondered whether Wisconsin had the death penalty. He wondered whether that would matter. He wanted to understand what was going on – and to find out how it was all going to end. And finally, producing a half-rueful grin, he realised that most of all he wanted everything to be normal. He wanted never to have gone to prison, for Laura to still be alive, for none of this ever to have happened.

'I'm afraid that's not exactly an option, m'boy,' he thought to himself, in Wednesday's gruff voice, and he nodded agreement. *Not an option. You burned your bridges. So keep walking. Do your own time . . .*

A distant woodpecker drummed against a rotten tree.

Shadow became aware of eyes on him: a handful of red cardinals stared at him from a skeletal elder bush, then returned to pecking at the clusters of black elderberries. They looked like the illustrations in the Songbirds of North America calendar. He heard the birds' video-arcade trills and zaps and whoops follow him along the side of the creek. Eventually, they faded away.

The dead fawn lay in a glade in the shadow of a hill, and a black bird the size of a small dog was picking at its side with a large, wicked, beak, rending and tearing gobbets of red meat from the corpse. Its eyes were gone, but its head was untouched, and white fawn-spots were visible on its rump. Shadow wondered how it had died.

The black bird cocked its head onto one side, and then said, in a voice like stones being struck, 'You shadow man.'

'I'm Shadow,' said Shadow. The bird hopped up onto the fawn's rump, raised its head, ruffled its crown and neck feathers. It was enormous and its eyes were black beads. There was something intimidating about a bird that size, this close.

'Says he will see you in Kay-ro,' tokked the raven. Shadow wondered which of Odin's ravens this was: Huginn or Muninn – Memory or Thought.

'Kay-ro?' he asked.

'In Egypt.'

'How am I going to go to Egypt?'

'Follow Mississippi. Go south. Find Jackal.'

'Look,' said Shadow, 'I don't want to seem like I'm – Jesus, look . . .' he paused. Regrouped. He was cold, standing in a wood, talking to a big black bird who was currently brunching on Bambi. 'Okay. What I'm trying to say is I don't want mysteries.'

'Mysteries,' agreed the bird, helpfully.

'What I want is explanations. Jackal in Kay-ro. This does not help me. It's a line from a bad spy thriller.'

'Jackal. Friend. *Tok*. Kay-ro.'

'So you said. I'd like a little more information than that.'

The bird half-turned, and pulled another strip of raw venison from the fawn's ribs. Then it flew off into the trees, the red strip dangling from its beak like a long, bloody worm.

'Hey! Can you at least get me back to a real road?' called Shadow.

The raven flew up and away. Shadow looked at the corpse of the baby deer. He decided that if he were a real woodsman, he would slice off a steak and grill it over a wood-fire. Instead, he sat on a fallen tree and ate a Snickers bar and knew that he really wasn't a real woodsman.

The raven cawed from the edge of the clearing.

'You want me to follow you?' asked Shadow. 'Or has Timmy fallen down another well?' The bird cawed again, impatiently. Shadow started walking towards it. It waited until he was close then flapped heavily into another tree, heading somewhat to the left of the way Shadow had originally been going.

'Hey,' said Shadow. 'Huginn or Muninn, or whoever you are.'

The bird turned, head tipped, suspiciously, on one side, and it stared at him with bright eyes.

'Say "Nevermore",' said Shadow.

'Fuck you,' said the raven. It said nothing else as they went through the woodland together.

In half an hour they reached a blacktop road on the edge of a town, and the raven flew back into the wood. Shadow observed a Culvers Frozen Custard Butterburgers sign, and, next to it, a gas station. He went into the Culvers, which was empty of customers. There was a keen young man with shaven head behind the cash register. Shadow ordered two butterburgers and french fries. Then he went into the rest room to clean up. He looked a real mess. He did an inventory of the contents of his pockets: he had a few coins, including the silver Liberty dollar, a disposable toothbrush and toothpaste, three Snickers bars, five chemical heater pads, a wallet (with nothing more in it than his driver's license and a credit card – he wondered how much longer the credit card had to live?), and in the coat's inside pocket, a thousand dollars in fifties and twenties, his take from yesterday's bank job. He washed his face and hands in hot water, slicked down his dark hair, then went back into the restaurant and ate his burgers and fries, and drank his coffee.

He went back to the counter. 'You want frozen custard?' asked the keen young man.

'No. No thanks. Is there anywhere around here I could rent a car? My car died, back down the road a way.'

The young man scratched his head-stubble. 'Not around here, Mister. If your car died you could call triple-A. Or talk to the gas station next door about a tow.'

'A fine idea,' said Shadow. 'Thanks.'

He walked across the melting snow, from the Culvers parking lot to the gas station. He bought candy bars and beef jerky sticks and more chemical hand- and feet-warmers.

'Anywhere hereabouts I could rent a car?' he asked the woman behind the cash register. She was immensely plump, and bespectacled, and was delighted to have someone to talk to.

'Let me think,' she said. 'We're kind of out of the way here. They do that kind of thing over in Madison. Where you going?'

'Kay-ro,' he said. 'Wherever that is.'

'I know where that is,' she said. 'Hand me an Illinois map from that rack over there.' Shadow passed her a plastic-coated map. She unfolded it, then pointed in triumph to the bottom-most corner of the state. 'There it is.'

'Cairo?'

'That's how they pronounce the one in Egypt. But the one in Little Egypt, they call that one Kayro. They got a Thebes down there, all sorts. My sister-in-law comes from Thebes. I asked her about the one in Egypt, she looked at me as if I had a screw loose.' The woman chuckled like a drain.

'Any pyramids?' The city was five hundred miles away, almost directly south.

'Not that they ever told me. They call it Little Egypt because back, oh, mebbe a hundred, hundred and fifty years back, there was a famine all over. Crops failed. But they didn't fail down there. So everyone went there to buy food. Like in the Bible. Joseph and the Technicolor Dreamcoat. Off we go to Egypt, bad-a-boom.'

'So if you were me, and you needed to get there, how would you go?' asked Shadow.

'Drive.'

'Car died a few miles down the road. It was a pieceashit if you'll pardon my language,' said Shadow.

'Pee-Oh-Esses,' she said. 'Yup. That's what my brother-in-law calls 'em. He buys and sells cars in a small way. He'll call me up, say Mattie, I just sold another Pee-Oh-Ess. Say, maybe he'd be interested in your old car. For scrap or something.'

'It belongs to my boss,' said Shadow, surprising himself with the fluency and ease of his lies. 'I need to call him, so he can come pick it up.' A thought struck him. 'Your brother-in-law, is he around here?'

'He's in Muscoda. Ten minutes south of here. Just over the river. Why?'

'Well, does he have a Pee-Oh-Ess he'd like to sell me for, mm, five, six hundred bucks?'

She smiled sweetly. 'Mister, he doesn't have a car on that back lot you couldn't buy with a full tank of gas for five hundred dollars. But don't you tell him I said so.'

'Would you call him?' asked Shadow.

'I'm way ahead of you,' she told him, and she picked up the phone. 'Hon? It's Mattie. You get over here this minute. I got a man here wants to buy a car.'

The piece of shit he chose was a 1983 Chevy Nova, which he bought, with a full tank of gas, for four hundred and fifty dollars. It had almost a quarter of a million miles on the clock, and smelled faintly of bourbon, tobacco, and more strongly of something that might well have been bananas. He couldn't tell what color it was, under the dirt and the snow. Still, of all the vehicles in Mattie's brother-in-law's back lot, it was the only one that looked like it might take him five hundred miles.

The deal was done in cash, and Mattie's brother-in-law never asked for Shadow's name or social security number or for anything except the money.

Shadow drove west, then south, with five hundred and fifty dollars in his pocket, keeping off the interstate. The piece of shit had a radio, but nothing happened when he turned it on. A sign said he'd left Wisconsin and was now in Illinois. He passed a strip-mining works, huge blue arc lights burning in the dim midwinter daylight.

He stopped and ate at a place called Mom's, catching them just before they closed for the afternoon.

Each town he passed through had an extra sign up beside the sign telling him that he was now entering Our Town (pop.720). The extra sign announced that the town's Under-14s team was the third runner-up in the interstate basketball team, or that the town was the home of the Illinois Girl's Under 16s Wrestling semifinalist.

He drove on, head nodding, feeling more drained with every minute that passed. He ran a stop-light, and was nearly side-swiped by a woman in a Dodge. As soon as he got out into open country he pulled off onto an empty tractor path on the side of the road, and he parked by a snow-spotted stubbly field in which a slow procession of fat black wild turkeys walked like a line of mourners; he turned off the engine, stretched out in the back seat, and fell asleep.

Darkness; a sensation of falling – as if he were tumbling down a great hole, like Alice. He fell for a hundred years into darkness. Faces passed him, swimming out of the black, then each face was ripped up and away before he could touch it . . .

Abruptly, and without transition, he was not falling. Now he was in a cave, and he was no longer alone. Shadow stared into familiar eyes: huge, liquid black eyes. They blinked.

Under the earth: yes. He remembered this place. The stink of wet cow. Firelight flickered on the wet cave walls, illuminating the buffalo head, the man's body, skin the colour of brick clay.

'Can't you people leave me be?' asked Shadow. 'I just want to sleep.'

The buffalo man nodded, slowly. His lips did not move, but a voice in Shadow's head said, 'Where are you going, Shadow?'

'Cairo.'

'Why?'

'Where else have I got to go? It's where Wednesday wants me to go. I drank his mead.' In Shadow's dream, with the power of dream-logic behind it, the obligation seemed unarguable: he drank Wednesday's mead three times, and sealed the pact – what other choice of action did he have?

The buffalo-headed man reached a hand into the fire, stirring the embers and the broken branches into a blaze. 'The storm is coming,' he said. Now there was ash on his hands, and he wiped it onto his hairless chest, leaving soot-black streaks.

'So you people keep telling me. Can I ask you a question?'

There was a pause. A fly settled on the furry forehead. The buffalo man flicked it away. 'Ask.'

'Is this true? Are these people really gods? It's all so,' he paused. Then he said, 'impossible,' which was not exactly the word he had been going for but seemed to be the best he could do.

'What are gods?' asked the buffalo man.

'I don't know,' said Shadow.

There was a tapping, relentless and dull. Shadow waited for the buffalo man to say something more, to explain what gods were, to explain the whole tangled nightmare that his life seemed to have become. He was cold.

Tap. Tap. Tap.

Shadow opened his eyes, and, groggily, sat up. He was freezing, and the sky outside the car was the deep luminescent purple that divides the dusk from the night.

Tap. Tap. Someone said 'Hey, Mister,' and Shadow turned his head. The someone was standing beside the car, no more than a darker shape against the darkling sky. Shadow reached out a hand and cranked down the window a few inches. He made some waking-up noises, and then he said 'Hi.'

'You all right? You sick? You been drinking?' The voice was high – a woman's or a boy's.

'I'm fine,' said Shadow. 'Hold on.' He opened the door, and got out, stretching his aching limbs and neck as he did so. Then he rubbed his hands together, to get the blood circulating and to warm them up.

'Whoa. You're pretty big.'

'That's what they tell me,' said Shadow. 'Who are you?'

'I'm Sam,' said the voice.

'Boy Sam or girl Sam?'

'Girl Sam. I used to be Sammi with an i, and I'd do a smiley face over the i, but then I got completely sick of it because like absolutely everybody was doing it, so I stopped.'

'Okay, girl Sam. You go over there, and look out at the road.'

'Why? Are you a crazed killer or something?'

'No,' said Shadow, 'I need to take a leak and I'd like just the smallest amount of privacy.'

'Oh. Right. Okay. Got it. No problem. I am so with you. I can't even pee if there's someone in the next stall. Major shy bladder syndrome.'

'Now, please.'

She walked to the far side of the car, and Shadow took a few steps closer to the field, unzipped his jeans and pissed against a fencepost for a very long time. He walked back to the car. The last of the gloaming had become night.

'You still there?' he asked.

'Yes,' she said. 'You must have a bladder like Lake Erie. I think empires rose and fell in the time it took you to pee. I could hear it the whole time.'

'Thank you. Do you want something?'

'Well, I wanted to see if you were okay. I mean, if you were dead or something I would have called the cops. But the windows were kind of fogged up so I thought, well, he's probably still alive.'

'You live around here?'

'Nope. Hitchhiking down from Madison.'

'That's not safe.'

'I've done it five times a year for three years now. I'm still alive. Where are you headed?'

'I'm going as far as Cairo.'

'Thank you,' she said. 'I'm going to El Paso. Staying with my Aunt for the holidays.'

'I can't take you all the way,' said Shadow.

'Not El Paso, Texas. The other one, in Illinois. It's a few hours south. You know where you are now?'

'No,' said Shadow. 'I have no idea. Somewhere on Highway 52?'

'The next town's Peru,' said Sam. 'Not the one in Peru. The one in Illinois. Let me smell you. Bend down.' Shadow bent down, and the girl sniffed his face. 'Okay. I don't smell booze. You can drive. Let's go.'

'What makes you think I'm giving you a ride?'

'Because I'm a damsel in distress,' she said, 'And you are a knight in whatever. A really dirty car. You know someone wrote *Wash Me!* on your rear window?' Shadow got into the car and opened the passenger door. The light that goes on in cars when the front door is opened did not go on in this car.

'No,' he said, 'I didn't.'

She climbed in. 'It was me,' she said. 'I wrote it. While there was still enough light to see.'

Shadow started the car, turned on the headlights, and headed back onto the road. 'Left,' said Sam helpfully. Shadow turned left, and he drove. After several minutes the heater started to work, and blessed warmth filled the car.

'You haven't said anything yet,' said Sam. 'Say something.'

'Are you human?' asked Shadow. 'An honest to goodness, born of man and woman, living breathing human being?'

'Sure,' she said.

'Okay. Just checking. So what would you like me to say?'

'Something to reassure me, at this point. I suddenly have that *oh shit I'm in the wrong car with a crazy man* feeling.'

'Yeah,' he said. 'I've had that one. What would you find reassuring?'

'Just tell me you're not an escaped convict or a mass murderer or something.'

He thought for a moment. 'You know, I'm really not.'

'You had to think about it though, didn't you?'

'Done my time. Never killed anybody.'

'Oh.'

They entered a small town, lit up by streetlights and blinking Christmas decorations, and Shadow glanced to his right. The girl had a tangle of short dark hair and a face that was both attractive and, he decided, faintly mannish: her features might have been chiseled out of rock. She was looking at him.

'What were you in prison for?'

'I hurt a couple of people real bad. I got angry.'

'Did they deserve it?'

Shadow thought for a moment. 'I thought so at the time.'

'Would you do it again?'

'Hell, no. I lost three years of my life in there.'

'Mm. You got Indian blood in you?'

'Not that I know of.'

'You looked like it, was all.'

'Sorry to disappoint you.'

'S'okay. You hungry?'

Shadow nodded. 'I could eat,' he said.

'There's a good place just past the next set of lights. Good food. Cheap, too.'

Shadow pulled up in the parking lot. They got out of the car. He didn't bother to lock it, although he pocketed the keys. He pulled out some coins to buy a newspaper. 'Can you afford to eat here?' he asked.

'Yeah,' she said, raising her chin. 'I can pay for myself.'

Shadow nodded. 'Tell you what. I'll toss you for it,' he said. 'Heads you pay for my dinner, tails, I pay for yours.'

'Let me see the coin first,' she said, suspiciously. 'I had an uncle had a double-headed quarter.'

She inspected it, satisfied herself there was nothing strange about the quarter. Shadow placed the coin head up on his thumb and cheated the toss, so it wobbled and looked like it was spinning, then he caught it and flipped it over onto the back of his left hand, and uncovered it with his right, in front of her.

'Tails,' she said, happily. 'Dinner's on you.'

'Yup,' he said. 'You can't win them all.'

Shadow ordered the meatloaf, Sam ordered lasagna. Shadow flipped through the newspaper, to see if there was anything in it about dead men in a freight train. There wasn't. The only story of interest was on the cover: crows in record numbers were infesting the town. Local farmers wanted to hang dead crows around the town on public buildings to frighten the others away; ornithologists said that it wouldn't work, that the living crows would simply eat the dead ones. The locals were implacable. 'When they see the corpses of their friends,' said a spokesman, 'they'll know that we don't want them here.'

The food came mounded high on plates and steaming, more than any one person could eat.

'So what's in Cairo?' asked Sam, with her mouth full.

'No idea. I got a message from my boss saying he needs me down there.'

'What do you do?'

'I'm an errand boy.'

She smiled. 'Well,' she said, 'you aren't mafia, not looking like that and driving that piece of shit. Why does your car smell like bananas, anyway?'

He shrugged, carried on eating.

Sam narrowed her eyes. 'Maybe you're a banana smuggler,' she said. 'You haven't asked me what I do yet.'

'I figure you're at school.'

'UW Madison.'

'Where you are undoubtedly studying art history, women's studies, and probably casting your own bronzes. And you probably work in a coffee house to help cover the rent.'

She put down her fork, nostrils flaring, eyes wide. 'How the fuck did you do that?'

'What? Now you say, no, actually I'm studying Romance Languages and ornithology.'

'So you're saying that was a lucky guess or something?'

'What was?'

She stared at him with dark eyes. 'You are one peculiar guy, Mister . . . . I don't know your name.'

'They call me Shadow,' he said.

She twisted her mouth wryly, as if she were tasting something she disliked. She stopped talking, put her head down, finished her lasagna.

'Do you know why it's called Egypt?' asked Shadow, when Sam finished eating.

'Down Cairo way? Yeah. It's in the delta of the Ohio and the Mississippi. Like Cairo in Egypt, in the Nile delta.'

'That makes sense.'

She sat back in her chair, ordered coffee and chocolate cream pie, ran a hand through her black hair. 'You married, Mr Shadow?' And then, as he hesitated, 'Gee. I just asked another tricky question, didn't I?'

'They buried her on Thursday,' he said, picking his words with care. 'She was killed in a car crash.'

'Oh. God. Jesus. I'm sorry.'

'Me too.'

An awkward pause. 'My half-sister lost her kid, my nephew, end of last year. It's rough.'

'Yeah. It is. What did he die of?'

She sipped her coffee. 'We don't know. We don't even really know that he's dead. He just vanished. But he was only thirteen. It was the middle of last winter. My sister was pretty broken up about it.'

'Were there any, any clues?' He sounded like a TV cop. He tried again. 'Did they suspect foul play?' That sounded worse.

'They suspected my non-custodial asshole brother-in-law, his father. Who was asshole enough to have stolen him away. Probably did. But this is in a little town in the North Woods. Lovely, sweet, pretty little town where no-one ever locks their doors.' She sighed, shook her head. She held her coffee cup in both hands.

'Are you sure you aren't part Indian?'

'Not that I know. It's possible. I don't know much about my father. I guess my Ma would have told me if he was Native American, though. Maybe.'

Again the mouth-twist. Sam gave up half-way through her chocolate cream pie: the slice was half the size of her head. She pushed the plate across the table to Shadow. 'You want?' He smiled, said 'Sure,' and finished it off.

The waitress handed them the check, and Shadow paid.

'Thanks,' said Sam.

It was getting colder now. The car coughed a couple of times before it started. Shadow drove back onto the road, and kept going south. 'You ever read a guy named Herodotus?' he asked.

'Jesus. What?'

'Herodotus. You ever read his *Histories*?'

'You know,' she said, dreamily, 'I don't get it. I don't get how you talk, or the words you use or anything. One moment you're a big dumb guy, the next you're reading my friggin' mind, and the next we're talking about Herodotus. So no. I have not read Herodotus. I've heard about him. Maybe on NPR. Isn't he the one they call the father of lies?'

'I thought that was the devil.'

'Yeah, him too. But they were talking about Herodotus saying there were giant ants and gryphons guarding gold mines, and how he made this stuff up.'

'I don't think so. He wrote what he'd been told. It's like, he's writing these histories. And they're mostly pretty good histories. Loads of weird little details – like, did you know, in Egypt, if a particularly beautiful girl, or the wife of a lord or whatever died, they wouldn't send her to the embalmer for three days? They'd let her body spoil in the heat first.'

'Why? Oh, hold on. Okay, I think I know why. Oh, that's disgusting.'

'And there're battles in there, all sorts of normal things. And then there are the gods. Some guy is running back to report on the outcome of a battle and he's running and running, and he sees Pan in a glade. And Pan says "Tell them to build me a temple here". So he says okay, and runs the rest of the way back. And he reports the battle news, and then says, "Oh, and by the way, Pan wants you to build him a temple." It's really matter-of-fact, you know?'

'So there are stories with gods in. What are you trying to say? That these guys had hallucinations?'

'No,' said Shadow. 'That's not it.'

She chewed a hangnail. 'I read some book about brains,' she said. 'My room-mate had it and she kept waving it around. It was like, how five thousand years ago the lobes of the brain fused and before that people thought when the right lobe of the brain said anything it was the voice of some god telling them what to do. It's just brains.'

'I like my theory better,' said Shadow.

'What's your theory?'

'That back then people used to run into the gods from time to time.'

'Oh.' Silence: only the rattling of the car, the roar of the engine, the growling of the muffler – which did not sound healthy. Then, 'Do you think they're still there?'

'Where?'

'Greece. Egypt. The islands. Those places. Do you think if you walked where those people walked you'd see the gods?'

'Maybe. But I don't think people'd know that was what they'd seen.'

'I bet it's like space aliens,' she said. 'These days, people see space aliens. Back then they saw gods. Maybe the space aliens come from the right side of the brain.'

'I don't think the gods ever gave rectal probes,' said Shadow. 'And they didn't mutilate cattle themselves. They got people to do it for them.'

She chuckled. They drove in silence for a few minutes, and then she said, 'Hey, that reminds me of my favorite god story, from Comparative Religion 101. You want to hear it?'

'Sure,' said Shadow.

'Okay. This is one about Odin. The Norse god. You know? There was some Viking King on a Viking ship – this was back in the Viking times, obviously – and they were becalmed, so he says he'll sacrifice one of his men to Odin if Odin will send them a wind, and get them to land. Okay. The wind comes up, and they get to land. So, on land, they draw lots to figure out who gets sacrificed – and it's the king himself. Well, he's not happy about this, but they figure out that they can hang him in effigy and not hurt him. They take a calf's intestines and loop them loosely around the guy's neck, and they tie the other end to a thin branch, and they take a reed instead of a spear and poke him with it and go "Okay, you've been hung" – hanged? – whatever – "you've been sacrificed to Odin."'

The road curved: Another Town, pop. 300, home of the runner-up to the state under 12s speed-skating championship, two huge giant-economy sized funeral parlors on each side of the road, and how many funeral parlors do you need, Shadow wondered, when you only have 300 people . . . ?

'Okay. As soon as they say Odin's name, the reed transforms into a spear and stabs the guy in the side, the calf intestines become a thick rope, the branch becomes the bough of a tree, and the tree pulls up, and the ground drops away, and the king is left hanging there to die with a wound in his side and his face going black. End of story. White people have some fucked-up gods, Mister Shadow.'

'Yes,' said Shadow. 'You're not white?'

'I'm Cherokee,' she said.

'Full-blooded?'

'Nope. Only four pints. My mom was white. My dad was a real reservation Indian. He came out this way, eventually married my mom, had me, then when they split he went back to Oklahoma.'

'He went back to the reservation?'

'No. He borrowed money and opened a Taco Bell knock-off called Taco Bill's. He does okay. He doesn't like me. Says I'm half-breed.'

'I'm sorry.'

'He's a jerk. I'm proud of my Indian blood. It helps pay my college tuition. Hell, one day it'll probably help get me a job, if I can't sell my bronzes.'

'There's always that,' said Shadow.

He stopped in El Paso, IL (Pop. 2500) to let Sam out, in a down-at-heel house on the edge of the town. A large wire-framed model of a reindeer covered in twinkling lights stood in the front yard. 'You want to come in?' she asked. 'My aunt would give you a coffee.'

'No,' he said. 'I've got to keep moving.'

She smiled at him, looking suddenly, and for the first time, vulnerable. She patted him on the arm. 'You're fucked up, mister. But you're cool.'

'I believe that's what they call the human condition,' said Shadow. 'Thanks for the company.'

'No problem,' she said. 'If you see any gods on the road to Cairo, you make sure and say hi to them from me.' She got out of the car, and went to the door of the house. She pressed a doorbell and stood there at the door, without looking back. Shadow waited until the door was opened and she was safely inside before he put his foot down and headed back for the highway. He passed through Normal, and Bloomington, and Lawndale.

At eleven that night Shadow started shaking. He was just entering Middletown. He decided he needed sleep, or just not to drive any longer, and he pulled up in front of a Night's Inn, paid thirty five dollars, cash in advance, for his ground floor room, and went into the bathroom. A sad cockroach lay on its back in the middle of the tiled floor. Shadow took a towel and cleaned off the inside of the tub, then ran the water. In the main room he took off his clothes and put them on the bed. The bruises on his torso were dark and vivid. He sat in the tub, watching the colour of the bathwater change. Then, naked, he washed his socks and briefs and tee shirt in the basin, wrung them out and hung them on the clothes line that pulled out from the wall above the bathtub. He left the cockroach where it was, out of respect for the dead.

Shadow climbed into the bed. He wondered about watching an adult movie, but the pay-per-view device by the phone needed a credit card, and it was too risky. Then again, he was not convinced that it would make him feel any better to watch other people have sex that he wasn't having. He turned on the TV for company, pressed the *Sleep* button on the remote three times, which would make the TV set turn itself off automatically in 45 minutes. It was a quarter to midnight.

The picture was motel-fuzzy, and the colours swam across the screen. He flipped from late show to late show in the televisual wasteland, unable to focus. Someone was demonstrating something that did something in the kitchen, and replaced a dozen other kitchen utensils, none of which Shadow possessed. *Flip*. A man in a suit explained that these were the end times and that Jesus – a four or five syllable word the way the man pronounced it – would make Shadow's business prosper and thrive if Shadow sent him money. *Flip*: an episode of *M*A*S*H* ended and a *Dick Van Dyke Show* began.

Shadow hadn't seen an episode of *The Dick Van Dyke Show* for years, but there was something comforting about the 1965 black and white world it painted, and he put the channel changer down beside the bed, and turned off the bedside light. He watched the show, eyes slowly closing, aware that something was odd. He had not seen many episodes of *The Dick Van Dyke Show*, so he was not surprised that it was an episode he could not remember seeing before. What he found strange was the tone.

All the regulars were concerned about Rob's drinking: he was missing days at work. They went to his home: he had locked himself in the bedroom, and had to be persuaded to come out: he was staggering drunk, but still pretty funny. His friends, played by Maury Amsterdam and Rose Marie left, after getting some good gags in. Then, when Rob's wife went to remonstrate with him, he hit her, hard, in the face. She sat down on the floor and began to cry, not in that famous Mary Tyler Moore wail, but in small, helpless sobs, hugging herself and whispering, 'Don't hit me, please, I'll do anything, just don't hit me any more.'

'What the fuck is this?' said Shadow, aloud.

The picture dissolved into phosphor dot fuzz. When it came back *The Dick Van Dyke Show* had, inexplicably, become *I Love Lucy*. Lucy was trying to persuade Ricky to let her replace their old icebox with a new refrigerator. When he left, however, she walked over to the couch and sat down, crossing her ankles, resting her hands in her lap, and staring out patiently in black and white across the years.

'Shadow?' she said. 'We need to talk.'

Shadow said nothing. She opened her purse and took out a cigarette, lit it with an expensive silver lighter, put the lighter away. 'I'm talking to you,' she said. 'Well?'

'This is crazy,' said Shadow.

'Like the rest of your life is sane? Give me a fucking break.'

'Whatever. Lucille Ball talking to me from the TV is weirder by several orders of magnitude than anything that's happened to me so far,' said Shadow.

'It's not Lucille Ball. It's Lucy Ricardo. And you know something – I'm not even her. It's just an easy way to look, given the context. That's all.' She shifted uncomfortably on the sofa.

'Who are you?' asked Shadow.

'Okay,' she said. 'Good question. I'm the idiot box. I'm the TV. I'm the all-seeing eye and the world of the cathode ray. I'm the boob tube. I'm the little shrine the family gathers to adore.'

'You're the television? Or someone in the television?'

'The TV's the altar. I'm what people are sacrificing to.'

'What do they sacrifice?' asked Shadow.

'Their time, mostly,' said Lucy. 'Sometimes each other.' She raised two fingers, blew imaginary gunsmoke from the tips. Then she winked, a big old *I Love Lucy* wink.

'You're a god?' said Shadow.

Lucy smirked, and took a lady-like puff of her cigarette. 'You could say that,' she said.

'Sam says hi,' said Shadow.

'What? Who's Sam? What are you talking about?'

Shadow looked at his watch. It was twenty-five past twelve. 'Doesn't matter,' he said. 'So, Lucy-on-the-TV. What do we need to talk about? Too many people have needed to talk recently. Normally it ends with someone hitting me.'

The camera moved in for a close-up: Lucy looked concerned; her lips pursed. 'I hate that. I hate that people were hurting you, Shadow. I'd never do that, honey. No, I want to offer you a job.'

'Doing what?

'Working for me. I heard about the trouble you had with the Spookshow, and I was impressed with how you dealt with it. Efficient, no-nonsense, effective. Who'd've thought you had it in you? They are really pissed.'

'Really?'

'They underestimated you, sweetheart. Not a mistake I'm going to make. I want you in my camp.' She stood up, walked toward the camera. 'Look at it like this, Shadow: we are the coming thing. We're shopping malls – your friends are crappy roadside attractions. Hell, we're online malls, while your friends are sitting by the side of the highway selling homegrown produce from a cart. No – they aren't even fruit sellers. Buggy whip vendors. Whalebone corset repairers.

We are now and tomorrow. Your friends aren't even yesterday any more.'

It was a strangely familiar speech. Shadow asked, 'Did you ever meet a fat kid in a limo?'

She spread her hands and rolled her eyes comically, funny Lucy Ricardo washing her hands of a disaster. 'The technical boy? You met the technical boy? Look, he's a good kid. He's one of us. He's just not good with people he doesn't know. When you're working for us, you'll see how amazing he is.'

'And if I don't want to work for you, I-Love-Lucy?'

There was a knock on the door of Lucy's apartment, and Ricky's voice could be heard off-stage, asking Loo-cy what was *keep*in' her so long, they was due down at the club in the next scene; a flash of irritation touched Lucy's cartoonish face. 'Hell,' she said. 'Look, whatever the old guys are paying you, I can pay you double. Treble. A hundred times. Whatever they're giving you, I can give you so much more.' She smiled, a perfect, roguish, Lucy Ricardo smile. 'You name it, honey. What do you need?' She began to undo the buttons of her blouse. 'Hey,' she said. 'You ever wanted to see Lucy's tits?'

The screen went black. The sleep function had kicked in and the set turned itself off. Shadow looked at his watch: it was half past midnight. 'Not really,' said Shadow.

He rolled over in bed, and closed his eyes. It occurred to him that the reason he liked Wednesday and Mr Nancy and the rest of them better than their opposition was pretty straightforward: they might be dirty, and cheap, and their food might taste like shit, but at least they didn't speak in cliches.

And he guessed he would take a roadside attraction, no matter how cheap, how crooked or how sad, over a shopping mall, any day.

Morning found Shadow back on the road, driving through a gently undulating brown landscape of winter grass and leafless trees. The last of the snow had vanished. He filled up the tank of the piece of shit in a town which was home to the runner-up of the State Women's Under Sixteens 300 meter dash, and, hoping that the dirt wasn't all that was holding it together, he ran the car through the gas station car wash. He was surprised to discover that the car was, when clean – against all reason – white, and pretty much free of rust. He drove on.

The sky was impossibly blue, and white industrial smoke rising from factory chimneys was frozen in the sky, like a photograph. A hawk launched itself from a dead tree and flew toward him, wings strobing in the sunlight like a series of stop-motion photographs.

At some point he found himself heading into East St. Louis. He attempted to avoid it and instead found himself driving through what appeared to be a red light district in an industrial park. Eighteen wheelers and huge rigs were parked outside buildings that looked like temporary warehouses, that claimed to be 24 Hour Nite Clubs and, in one case, The Best Peap Show in Town. Shadow shook his head, and drove on. Laura had loved to dance, clothed or naked (and, on several memorable evenings, moving from one state to the other), and he had loved to watch her.

Lunch was a sandwich and a can of Coke in a town called Red Bud.

He passed a valley filled with the wreckage of thousands of yellow bulldozers, tractors and Caterpillars. He wondered if this was the bulldozers' graveyard, where the bulldozers went to die.

He drove past the Pop-a-Top Lounge. He drove through Chester ('Home of Popeye'). He noticed that the houses had started to gain pillars out front, that even the shabbiest, thinnest house now had its white pillars, proclaiming it, in someone's eyes, a mansion. He drove over a big, muddy river, and laughed out loud when he saw that the name of it, according to the sign, was the Big Muddy River. He saw a covering of brown kudzu over three winter-dead trees, twisting them into strange, almost human shapes: they could have been witches, three bent old crones ready to reveal his fortune.

He drove alongside the Mississippi. Shadow had never seen the Nile, but there was a blinding afternoon sun burning on the wide brown river which made him think of the muddy expanse of the Nile: not the Nile as it is now, but as it was long ago, flowing like an artery through the papyrus marshes, home to cobra and jackal and wild cow . . .

A road sign pointed to Thebes.

The road was built up about twelve feet, so he was driving above the marshes. Clumps and clusters of birds in flight were questing back and forth, black dots against the blue sky, moving in some desperate Brownian motion.

In the late afternoon the sun began to lower, gilding the world in elf-light, a thick warm custardy light that made the world feel unearthly and more than real, and it was in this light that Shadow passed the sign telling him he was Now Entering Historical Cairo. He drove under a bridge and found himself in a small port town. The imposing structure of the Cairo court house and the even more imposing customs house looked like enormous freshly-baked cookies in the syrupy gold of the light at the end of the day.

He parked his car in a side street and walked to the embankment at the edge of a river, unsure whether he was gazing at the Ohio or the Mississippi. A small brown cat nosed and sprang among the trash cans at the back of a building, and the light made even the garbage magical.

A lone seagull was gliding along the river's edge, flipping a wing to correct itself as it went.

Shadow realised that he was not alone. A small girl, wearing old tennis shoes on her feet and a man's grey woollen sweater as a dress, was standing on the sidewalk, ten feet away from him, staring at him with the somber gravity of a six year old. Her hair was black, and straight, and long; her skin was as brown as the river.

He grinned at her. She stared back at him, defiantly.

There was a squeal and a yowl from the waterfront, and the little brown cat shot away from a spilled garbage can, pursued by a long-muzzled black dog. The cat scurried under a car.

'Hey,' said Shadow to the girl. 'You ever seen invisible powder before?'

She hesitated. Then she shook her head.

'Okay,' said Shadow. 'Well, watch this.' Shadow pulled out a quarter with his left hand, held it up, tilting it from one side to another, then appeared to toss it into his right hand, closing his hand hard on nothing, and putting the hand forward. 'Now,' he said, 'I just take some invisible powder from my pocket . . .' and he reached his left hand into his breast pocket, dropping the quarter into the pocket as he did so, ' . . . and I sprinkle it on the hand with the coin . . .' and he mimed sprinkling, '. . . and look – now the quarter's invisible too.' He opened his empty right hand, and, in astonishment, his empty left hand as well.

The little girl just stared.

Shadow shrugged, and put his hands back in his pockets, loading a quarter in one hand, a folded up five dollar bill in the other. He was going to produce them from the air, and then give the girl the five bucks: she looked like she needed it. 'Hey,' he said, 'We've got an audience.'

The black dog and the little brown cat were watching him as well, flanking the girl, looking up at him intently. The dog's huge ears were pricked up, giving it a comically alert expression. A crane-like man with gold-rimmed spectacles was coming up the sidewalk toward them, peering from side to side as if he were looking for something. Shadow wondered if he was the dog's owner.

'What did you think?' Shadow asked the dog, trying to put the little girl at her ease. 'Was that cool?'

The black dog licked its long snout. Then it said, in a deep, dry voice, 'I saw Harry Houdini once, and believe me, man, you are no Harry Houdini.'

The little girl looked at the animals, she looked up at Shadow, and then she ran off, her feet pounding the sidewalk as if all the powers of hell were after her. The two animals watched her go. The crane-like man had reached the dog. He reached down and scratched its high, pointed ears.

'Come on,' said the man in the gold-rimmed spectacles to the dog, 'It was only a coin trick. It's not like he was doing an underwater escape.'

'Not yet,' said the dog. 'But he will.' The golden light was done, and the grey of twilight had begun.

Shadow dropped the coin and the folded bill back into his pocket. 'Okay,' he said. 'Which one of you is Jackal?'

'Use your eyes,' said the black dog with the long snout. It began to amble along the sidewalk beside the man in the gold glasses, and, after a moment's hesitation, Shadow followed them. The cat was nowhere to be seen. They reached a large old building on a row of boarded up houses. The sign beside the door said *Ibis and Jacquel. A family firm. Funeral Parlor. Since 1863.*

'I'm Mr Ibis,' said the man in the gold-rimmed glasses. 'I think I should buy you a spot of supper. I'm afraid my friend here has some work that needs doing.'

Somewhere in America

New York scares Salim, and so he clutches his sample case protectively with both hands, holding it to his chest. He is scared of black people, the way they stare at him, and he is scared of the Jews, the ones dressed all in black with hats and beards and side curls he can identify and how many others that he cannot?; he is scared of the sheer quantity of the people, all shapes and sizes of people, as they spill from their high, high, filthy buildings, onto the sidewalks; he is scared of the honking hullabaloo of the traffic, and he is even scared of the air, which smells both dirty and sweet, and nothing at all like the air of Oman.

Salim has been in New York, in America, for a week. Each day he visits two, perhaps three different offices, opens his sample case, shows them the copper trinkets, the rings and bottles and tiny flashlights, the models of the Empire State Building, the Statue of Liberty, the Eiffel Tower, gleaming in copper inside; each night he writes a fax to his brother-in-law, Fuad, at home in Muscat, telling him that he has taken no orders, or, on one happy day, that he had taken several orders (but, as Salim is painfully aware, not yet enough even to cover his airfare and hotel bill).

For reasons Salim does not understand, his brother-in-law's business partners have booked him into the Paramount Hotel on 46th Street. He finds it confusing, claustrophobic, expensive, alien.

Fuad is Salim's sister's husband. He is not a rich man, but he is the co-owner of a small trinket factory. Everything is made for export, to other Arab countries, to Europe, to America. Salim has been working for Fuad for six months. Fuad scares him a little. The tone of Fuad's faxes is becoming harsher. In the evening, Salim sits in his hotel room, reading his Qur'an, telling himself that this will pass, that his stay in this strange world is limited and finite.

His brother-in-law gave him a thousand dollars for miscellaneous traveling expenses and the money, which seemed so huge a sum when first he saw it, is evaporating faster than Salim can believe. When he first arrived, scared of being seen as a cheap Arab, he tipped promiscuously, handing extra dollar bills to everyone he encountered; and then he decided that he was being taken advantage of, that perhaps they were even laughing at him, and he stopped tipping entirely.

On his first and only journey by subway he got lost and confused, and missed his appointment; now he takes taxis only when he has to, and the rest of the time he walks. He stumbles into overheated offices, his cheeks numb from the cold outside, sweating beneath his coat, shoes soaked by slush; and when the winds blow down the avenues (which run from north to south, as the streets run west to east, all so simple, and Salim always knows where to face Mecca) he feels a cold on his exposed skin that is so intense it is like being struck.

He never eats at the hotel (for while the hotel bill is being covered by Fuad's business partners, he must pay for his own food); instead he buys food at falafel houses and at little food stores, smuggles it up to the hotel beneath his coat for days before he realizes that no-one cares. And even then he feels strange about carrying the bags of food into the dimly-lit elevators (Salim always has to bend and squint to find the button to press to take him to his floor) and up to the tiny white room in which he stays.

Salim is upset. The fax that was waiting for him when he woke this morning was curt, and alternately chiding, stern and disappointed: Salim was letting them down – his sister, Fuad, Fuad's business partners, the Sultanate of Oman, the whole Arab world. Unless he was able to get the orders, Fuad would no longer consider it his obligation to employ Salim. They depended upon him. His hotel was too expensive. What was Salim doing with their money, living like a sultan in America? Salim read the fax in his room (which has always been too hot and stifling, so last night he opened a window, and was now too cold) and sat there for a time, his face frozen into an expression of complete misery.

Then Salim walks downtown, holding his sample case as if it contained diamonds and rubies, trudging through the cold for block after block until, on Broadway and 19th street, he finds a squat building over a deli. He walks up the stairs to the fourth floor, to the office of Panglobal Imports.

The office is dingy, but he knows that Panglobal handles almost half of the ornamental souvenirs that enter the US from the Far East. A real order, a significant order from Panglobal could redeem Salim's journey, could make the difference between failure and success, so Salim sits on an uncomfortable wooden chair in an outer office, his sample case balanced on his lap, staring at the middle-aged woman with her hair dyed too bright a red who sits behind the desk, blowing her nose on Kleenex after Kleenex. After she blows her nose she wipes it, and drops the Kleenex into the trash.

Salim got there at 10:30 a.m., half an hour before his appointment. Now he sits there, flushed and shivering, wondering if he is running a fever. The time ticks by so slowly.

Salim looks at his watch. Then he clears his throat.

The woman behind the desk glares at him. 'Yes?' she says. It sounds like *Yed*.

'It is eleven thirty-five,' says Salim.

The woman glances at the clock on the wall, and says 'Yed,' again. 'Id id.'

'My appointment was for eleven,' says Salim with a placating smile.

'Mister Blanding knows you're here,' she tells him, reprovingly. ('Bidter Bladdig dode you're here.')

Salim picks up an old copy of the *New York Post* from the table. He speaks English better than he reads it, and he puzzles his way through the stories like a man doing a crossword puzzle. He waits, a plump young man with the eyes of a hurt puppy, glancing from his watch to his newspaper to the clock on the wall.

At 12:30 several men come out from the inner office. They talk loudly, jabbering away to each other in American. One of them, a big, paunchy man, has a cigar, unlit, in his mouth. He glances at Salim as he comes out. He tells the woman behind the desk to try the juice of a lemon, and zinc, as his sister swears by zinc, and vitamin C. She promises him that she will, and gives him several envelopes. He pockets them and then he, and the other men, go out into the hall. The sound of their laughter disappears down the stairwell.

It is one o'clock. The woman behind the desk opens a drawer and takes out a brown paper bag, from which she removes several sandwiches, an apple, and a Milky Way. She also takes out a small plastic bottle of freshly-squeezed orange juice.

'Excuse me,' says Salim, 'But can you perhaps call Mister Blanding and tell him that I am still waiting?'

She looks up at him as if surprised to see that he is still there, as if they have not been sitting five feet apart for two and a half hours. 'He's at lunch,' she says. *He'd ad dudge.*

Salim knows, knows deep down in his gut, that Blanding was the man with the unlit cigar. 'When will he be back?'

She shrugs, takes a bite of her sandwich. 'He's busy with appointments for the rest of the day,' she says. *He'd biddy wid abboidmeds for the red ob the day.*

'Will he see me, then, when he comes back?' asks Salim.

She shrugs, and blows her nose.

Salim is hungry, increasingly so, and frustrated, and powerless.

At three o'clock the woman looks at him and says 'He wode be gubbig bag.'

'Excuse?'

'Bidder Bladdig. He wode be gubbig bag today.'

'Can I make an appointment for tomorrow?'

She wipes her nose. 'You hab to teddephode. Appoidbeds odly by teddephode.'

'I see,' says Salim. And then he smiles: a salesman, Fuad had told him many times before he left Muscat, is naked in America without his smile. 'Tomorrow I will telephone,' he says. He takes his sample case, and he walks down the many stairs to the street, where the freezing rain is turning to sleet. Salim contemplates the long, cold walk back to the 46th Street hotel, and the weight of the sample case, then he steps to the edge of the sidewalk and waves at every yellow cab that approaches, whether the light on top is on or off, and every cab drives past him.

One of them accelerates as it passes; a wheel dives into a water-filled pot-hole, spraying freezing muddy water over Salim's pants and coat. For a moment, he contemplates throwing himself in front of one of the lumbering cars, and then he realizes that his brother-in-law would be more concerned with the fate of the sample case than of Salim himself, and that he would bring grief to no-one but his beloved sister, Fuad's wife (for he had always been a slight embarrassment to his father and mother, and his romantic encounters had always, of necessity, been both brief and relatively anonymous): also, he doubts that any of the cars is going fast enough actually to end his life.

A battered yellow taxi draws up beside him and, grateful to be able to abandon his train of thought, Salim gets in.

The back-seat is patched with grey duct tape; the half-open Plexiglass barrier is covered with notices warning him not to smoke, telling him how much to pay to get to the various airports. The recorded voice of somebody famous he has never heard of tells him to remember to wear his seatbelt.

'The Paramount Hotel, please,' says Salim.

The cab driver grunts, and pulls away from the kerb, into the traffic. He is unshaven, and he wears a thick, dust-colored sweater, and black plastic sunglasses. The weather is grey, and night is falling: Salim wonders if the man has a problem with his eyes. The wipers smear the street scene into greys and smudged lights.

From nowhere, a truck pulls out in front of them, and the cab driver swears, by the beard of the prophet.

Salim stares at the name on the dashboard, but he cannot make it out from here. 'How long have you been driving a cab, my friend?' he asks the man, in his own language.

'Ten years,' says the driver, in the same tongue. 'Where are you from?'

'Muscat,' says Salim. 'In Oman.'

'From Oman. I have been in Oman. It was a long time ago. Have you heard of the city of Ubar?' asks the taxi driver.

'Indeed I have,' says Salim. 'The Lost City of Towers. They found it in the desert five, ten years ago, I do not remember exactly. Were you with the expedition that excavated it?'

'Something like that. It was a good city,' says the taxi driver. 'On most nights there would be three, maybe four thousand people camped there: every traveler would rest at Ubar, and the music would play, and the wine would flow like water and the water would flow as well, which was why the city existed.'

'That is what I have heard,' says Salim. 'And it perished, what, a thousand years ago? Two thousand?'

The taxi driver says nothing. They are stopped at a red traffic light. The light turns green, but the driver does not move, despite the immediate discordant blare of horns behind them. Hesitantly, Salim reaches through the hole in the Plexiglas and he touches the driver on the shoulder. The man's head jerks up, with a start, and he puts his foot down on the gas, lurching them across the intersection.

'Fuckshitfuckfuck,' he says, in English.

'You must be very tired, my friend,' says Salim.

'I have been driving this Allah-forgotten taxi for thirty hours,' says the driver. 'It is too much. Before that, I sleep for five hours, and I drove fourteen hours before that. We are shorthanded, before Christmas.'

'I hope you have made a lot of money,' says Salim.

The driver sighs. 'Not much. This morning I drove a man from Fifty-first street to Newark Airport. When we got there, he ran off into the airport, and I could not find him again. A fifty dollar fare gone, and I had to pay the tolls on the way back myself.'

Salim nods. 'I had to spend today waiting to see a man who will not see me. My brother-in-law hates me. I have been in America for a week, and it has done nothing but eat my money. I sell nothing.'

'What do you sell?'

'Shit,' says Salim. 'Worthless gewgaws and baubles and tourist trinkets. Horrible, cheap, foolish, ugly shit.'

The taxi driver wrenches the wheel to the right, swings around something, drives on. Salim wonders how he can see to drive, between the rain, the night, and the thick sunglasses.

'You try to sell shit?'

'Yes,' says Salim, thrilled and horrified that he has spoken the truth about his brother-in-law's samples.

'And they will not buy it?'

'No.'

'Strange. You look at the stores here, that is all they sell.'

Salim smiles nervously.

A truck is blocking the street in front of them: a red-faced cop standing in front of it waves and shouts and points them down the nearest street.

'We will go over to Eighth Avenue, come uptown that way,' says the taxi driver. They turn onto the street, where the traffic has stopped completely. There is a cacophony of horns, but the cars do not move.

The driver sways in his seat. His chin begins to descend to his chest, one, two, three times. Then he begins, gently, to snore. Salim reaches out to wake the man, hoping that he is doing the right thing. As he shakes his shoulder, the driver moves, and Salim's hand brushes the man's face, knocking the sunglasses from his face into his lap.

The taxi driver opens his eyes, reaches for, and replaces the black plastic sunglasses, but it is too late. Salim has seen his eyes.

The car crawls forward in the rain. The numbers on the meter increase.

'Are you going to kill me?' asks Salim.

The taxi driver's lips are pressed together. Salim watches his face in the driver's mirror.

'No,' says the driver, very quietly.

The car stops again. The rain patters on the roof.

Salim begins to speak. 'My grandmother swore that she had seen an ifrit, or perhaps a marid, late one evening, on the edge of the desert. We told her that it was just a sandstorm, a little wind, but she said no, she saw its face, and its eyes, like yours, were burning flames.'

The driver smiles, but his eyes are hidden behind the black plastic glasses, and Salim cannot tell whether there is any humor in that smile or not. 'The grandmothers came here too,' he says.

'Are there many jinn in New York?' asks Salim.

'No. Not many of us.'

'There are the angels, and there are men, who Allah made from mud, and then there are the people of the fire, the jinn,' says Salim.

'People know nothing about my people here,' says the driver. 'They think we grant wishes. If I could grant wishes do you think I would be driving a cab?'

'I do not understand.'

The taxi driver seems gloomy. Salim stares at his face in the mirror as he speaks, watching the ifrit's dark lips.

'They believe that we grant wishes. Why do they believe that? I sleep in one stinking room in Brooklyn. I drive this taxi for any stinking freak who has the money to ride in it, and for some who don't. I drive them where they need to go, and sometimes they tip me. Sometimes they pay me.' His lower lip began to tremble. The ifrit seemed on edge. 'One of them shat on the back seat once. I had to clean it before I could take the cab back. How could he do that? I had to clean the wet shit from the seat. Is that right?'

Salim puts out a hand, pats the ifrit's shoulder. He can feel solid flesh through the wool of the sweater. The ifrit raises his hand from the wheel, rests it on Salim's hand for a moment.

Salim thinks of the desert then: red sands blow a dust-storm through his thoughts, and the scarlet silks of the tents that surrounded the lost city of Ubar flap and billow through his mind.

They drive up Eighth Avenue.

'The old believe. They do not piss into holes, because the Prophet told them that jinn live in holes. They know that the angels throw flaming stars at us when we try to listen to their conversations. But even for the old, when they come to this country we are very, very far away. Back there, I did not have to drive a cab.'

'I am sorry,' says Salim.

'It is a bad time,' says the driver. 'A storm is coming. It scares me. I would do anything to get away.'

The two of them say nothing more on their way back to the hotel.

When Salim gets out of the cab he gives the ifrit a twenty dollar bill, tells him to keep the change. Then, with a sudden burst of courage, he tells him his room number. The taxi driver says nothing in reply. A young woman clambers into the back of the cab, and it pulls out into the cold and the rain.

Six o'clock in the evening. Salim has not yet written the fax to his brother-in-law. He goes out into the rain, buys himself this night's kebab and french fries. It has only been a week, but he feels that he is becoming heavier, rounder, softening in this country of New York.

When he comes back to the hotel he is surprised to see the taxi driver standing in the lobby, hands deep into his pockets. He is staring at a display of black and white postcards. When he sees Salim he smiles, self-consciously. 'I called your room,' he says, 'but there was no answer. So I thought I would wait.'

Salim smiles also, and touches the man's arm. 'I am here,' he says.

Together they enter the dim, green-lit elevator, ascend to the fifth floor holding hands. The ifrit asks if he may use Salim's bathroom.

'I feel very dirty,' he says. Salim nods. He sits on the bed, which fills most of the small white room and listens to the sound of the shower running. Salim takes off his shoes, his socks, and then the rest of his clothes.

The taxi driver comes out of the shower, wet, with a towel wrapped about his mid-section. He is not wearing his sunglasses, and in the dim room his eyes burn with scarlet flames.

Salim blinks back tears. 'I wish you could see what I see,' he says.

'I do not grant wishes,' whispers the ifrit, dropping his towel and pushing Salim gently, but irresistibly, down onto the bed.

It is an hour or more before the ifrit comes, thrusting and grinding into Salim's mouth. Salim has already come twice in this time. The jinn's semen tastes strange, fiery, and it burns Salim's throat.

Salim goes to the bathroom, washes out his mouth. When he returns to the bedroom the taxi driver is already asleep in the white bed, snoring peacefully. Salim climbs into the bed beside him, cuddles close to the ifrit, imagining the desert on his skin.

As he starts to fall asleep he realizes that he still has not written his fax to Fuad, and he feels guilty. Deep inside he feels empty and alone: he reaches out, rests his hand on the ifrit's tumescent cock and, comforted, he sleeps.

They wake in the small hours, moving against each other, and they make love again. At one point Salim realizes that he is crying, and the ifrit is kissing away his tears with burning lips. 'What is your name?' Salim asks the taxi driver.

'There is a name on my driving permit, but it is not mine,' the ifrit says.

Afterward, Salim could not remember where the sex had stopped and the dreams began.

When Salim wakes, the cold sun creeping into the white room, he is alone.

Also, he discovers, his sample case is gone, all the bottles and rings and souvenir copper flashlights, all gone, along with his suitcase, his wallet, his passport, and his air tickets back to Oman.

He finds a pair of jeans, the tee shirt, and the dust-colored woollen sweater discarded on the floor. Beneath them he finds a driver's license in the name of Ibrahim bin Irem, a taxi permit in the same name, and a ring of keys with an address written on a piece of paper attached to them in English. The photographs on the license and the permit do not look much like Salim, but then, they did not look much like the ifrit.

The telephone rings: it is the front desk calling to point out that Salim has already checked out, and his guest needs to leave soon so that they can service the room, to get it ready for another occupant.

'I do not grant wishes,' says Salim, tasting the way the words shape themselves in his mouth.

He feels strangely light-headed as he dresses.

New York is very simple: the avenues run north to south, the streets run west to east. *How hard can it be?* he asks himself.

He tosses the car keys into the air and catches them. Then he puts on the black plastic sunglasses he found in the pockets, and leaves the hotel room to go and look for his cab.

He said the dead had souls, but when I asked him
How that could be – I thought the dead were souls,
He broke my trance. Don't that make you suspicious
That there's something the dead are keeping back?
Yes, there's something the dead are keeping back.
– Robert Frost, *Two Witches*

The week before Christmas is often a quiet one in a funeral parlour, Shadow learned, over supper. They were sitting in a small restaurant, two blocks from Ibis and Jacquel's Funeral Home. Shadow's meal consisted of an all-day full breakfast – it came with hushpuppies – while Mr Ibis picked and pecked at a slice of coffee cake. Mr Ibis explained it to him. 'The lingering ones are holding on for one final Christmas,' said Mr Ibis, 'or even for New Year's, while the others, the ones for whom other people's jollity and celebration will prove too painful, have not yet been tipped over the edge by that last showing of *It's a Wonderful Life*, have not quite encountered the final straw, or should I say, the final *sprig of holly* that breaks not the camel's but the *reindeer's* back.' And he made a little noise as he said it, half smirk, half snort, which suggested that he had just uttered a well-honed phrase of which he was particularly fond.

Ibis and Jacquel was a small, family-owned funeral home: one of the last truly independent funeral homes in the area, or so Mr Ibis maintained. 'Most fields of human merchandising value nationwide brand identities,' he said. Mr Ibis spoke in explanations: a gentle, earnest lecturing that put Shadow in mind of a college professor who used to work out at the Muscle Farm and who could not talk, could only discourse, expound, explain. Shadow had figured out within the first few minutes of meeting Mr Ibis that his expected part in any conversation with the funeral director was to say as little as possible. 'This, I believe, is because people like to know what they are getting ahead of time. Thus McDonald's, Wal-Mart, F.W. Woolworth (of blessed memory): store-brands maintained and visible across the entire country. Wherever you go, you will get something that is, with small regional variations, the same.

'In the field of funeral homes, however, things are, perforce, different. You need to feel that you are getting small-town personal service from someone who has a calling to the profession. You want personal attention to you and your loved one in a time of great loss. You wish to know that your grief is happening on a local level, not on a national one. But in all branches of industry – and death is an industry, my young friend, make no mistake about that, – one makes one's money from operating in bulk, from buying in quantity, from centralising one's operations. It's not pretty, but it's true. Trouble is, no-one wants to know that their loved ones are travelling in a cooler-van to some big old converted warehouse where they may have twenty, fifty, a hundred cadavers on the go. No sir. Folks want to think they're going to a family concern, somewhere they'll be treated with respect by someone who'll tip his hat to them if he sees them in the street.'

Mr Ibis wore a hat. It was a sober brown hat that matched his sober brown blazer and his sober brown face. Small gold-rimmed glasses perched on his nose. In Shadow's memory Mr Ibis was a short man; whenever he would stand beside him, Shadow would rediscover that Mr Ibis was well over six feet in height, with a crane-like stoop. Sitting opposite him now, across the shiny red table, Shadow found himself staring into the man's face.

'So when the big companies come in they buy the name of the company, they pay the funeral directors to stay on, they create the apparency of diversity. But that is merely the tip of the gravestone. In reality, they are as local as Burger King. Now, for our own reasons, we *are* truly an independent. We do all our own embalming, and it's the finest embalming in the country, although nobody knows it but us. We don't do cremations, though. We could make more money if we had our own crematorium, but it goes against what we're good at. What my business partner says is, if the Lord gives you a talent or a skill, you have an obligation to use it as best you can. Don't you agree?'

'Sounds good to me,' said Shadow.

'The Lord gave my business partner dominion over the dead, just as he gave me skill with words. Fine things, words. I write books of tales, you know. Nothing literary. Just for my own amusement. Accounts of lives.' He paused. By the time Shadow realised that he should have asked if he might be allowed to read one, the moment had passed. 'Anyway, what we give them here is continuity: there's been an Ibis and Jacquel in business here for almost two hundred years. We weren't always funeral directors, though. We used to be morticians, and before that, undertakers.'

'And before that?'

'Well,' said Mr Ibis, smiling just a little smugly, 'we go back a very long way. Of course, it wasn't until after the War Between the States that we found our niche here. That was when we became the funeral parlour for the coloured folks hereabouts. Before that no-one thought of us as coloured – foreign maybe, exotic and dark, but not coloured. Once the war was done, pretty soon, no-one could remember a time when we weren't perceived as black. My business partner, he's always had darker skin than mine. It was an easy transition. Mostly you are what they think you are. It's just strange when they talk about African-Americans. Makes me think of the people from Punt, Ophir, Nubia. We never thought of ourselves as Africans – we were the people of the Nile.'

'So you were Egyptians,' said Shadow.

Mr Ibis pushed his lower lip upward, then let his head bob from side to side, as if it were on a spring, weighing the pluses and minuses, seeing things from both points of view. 'Well, yes and no. "Egyptians" makes me think of the folk who live there now. The ones who built their cities over our graveyards and palaces. Do they look like me?'

Shadow shrugged. He'd seen black guys who looked like Mr Ibis. He'd seen white guys with tans who looked like Mr Ibis.

'How's your coffee-cake?' asked the waitress, refilling their coffees.

'Best I ever had,' said Mr Ibis. 'You give my best to your ma.'

'I'll do that,' she said, and bustled away.

'You don't want to ask after the health of anyone, if you're a funeral director. They think maybe you're scouting for business,' said Mr Ibis, in an undertone. 'Shall we see if your room is ready?'

Their breath steamed in the night air. Christmas lights twinkled in the windows of the stores they passed. 'It's good of you, putting me up,' said Shadow. 'I appreciate it.'

'We owe your employer a number of favours. And Lord knows, we have the room. It's a big old house. There used to be more of us, you know. Now it's just the three of us. You won't be in the way.'

'Any idea how long I'm meant to stay with you?'

Mr Ibis shook his head. 'He didn't say. But we are happy to have you here, and we can find you work. If you are not squeamish. If you treat the dead with respect.'

'So,' asked Shadow, 'what are you people doing here in Cairo? Was it just the name or something?'

'No. Not at all. Actually this region takes its names from us, although people barely know it. It was a trading post back in the old days.'

'Frontier times?'

'You might call it that,' said Mr Ibis. '*Evening Mizz Simmons! And a Merry Christmas to you too!* The folk who brought me here came up the Mississippi a long time back.'

Shadow stopped in the street, and stared. 'Are you trying to tell me that ancient Egyptians came here to trade five thousand years ago?'

Mr Ibis said nothing, but he smirked loudly. Then he said, 'Three thousand five hundred and thirty years ago. Give or take.'

'Okay,' said Shadow. 'I'll buy it, I guess. What were they trading?'

'Not much,' said Mr Ibis. 'Animal skins. Some food. Copper from the mines in what would now be Michigan's upper peninsula. The whole thing was rather a disappointment. Not worth the effort. They stayed here long enough to believe in us, to sacrifice to us, and for a handful of the traders to die of fever and be buried here, leaving us behind them.' He stopped dead in the middle of the sidewalk, turned around slowly, arms extended. 'This country has been Grand Central for ten thousand years or more. You say to me, what about Columbus?'

'Sure,' said Shadow, obligingly. 'What about him?'

'Columbus did what people had been doing for thousands of years. There's nothing special about coming to America. I've been writing stories about it, from time to time.' They began to walk again.

'True stories?'

'Up to a point, yes. I'll let you read one or two, if you like. It's all there for anyone who has eyes to see it. Personally – and this is speaking as a subscriber to *Scientific American*, here – I feel very sorry for the professionals whenever they find another confusing skull, something that belonged to the wrong sort of people, or whenever they find statues or artifacts that confuse them – for they'll talk about the odd, but they won't talk about the impossible, which is where I feel sorry for them, for as soon as something becomes impossible it slipslides out of belief entirely, whether it's true or not. I mean, here's a skull that shows the Ainu, the Japanese aboriginal race, were in America nine thousand years ago. Here's another that shows there were Polynesians in California nearly two thousand years later. And all the scientists mutter and puzzle over who's descended from whom, missing the point entirely. Heaven knows what'll happen if they ever actually find the Hopi emergence tunnels. That'll shake a few things up, you just wait.

'Did the Irish come to America in the dark ages, you ask me? Of course they did, and the Welsh, and the Vikings, while the Africans from the West Coast, – what in later days they called the slave coast or the ivory coast – they were trading with South America, and the Chinese visited Oregon a couple of times – they called it Fu Sang. The Basque established their secret sacred fishing grounds off the coast of Newfoundland twelve hundred years back. Now, I suppose you're going to say, but Mister Ibis, these people were primitives, they didn't have radio controls and vitamin pills and jet airplanes.'

Shadow hadn't said anything, and hadn't planned to say anything, but he felt it was required of him, so he said, 'Well, weren't they?' The last dead leaves of the autumn crackled underfoot, winter-crisp.

'The misconception is that men didn't travel long distances in boats before the days of Columbus. Yet New Zealand and Tahiti and count-less Pacific Islands were settled by people in boats whose navigation skills would have put Columbus to shame; and the wealth of Africa was from trading, although that was mostly to the east, to India and China. My people, the Nile folk, we discovered early on that a reed boat will take you around the world, if you have the patience and enough jars of sweet water. You see the biggest problem with coming to America in the old days was that there wasn't a lot here that anyone wanted to trade, and it was much too far away.'

They had reached a large house, built in the style people called Queen Anne. Shadow wondered who Queen Anne was, and why she had been so fond of Addams-Family-style houses. It was the only building on the block that wasn't locked up with boarded-over windows. They went through the gate and walked around the back of the building.

Through large double doors, which Mr Ibis unlocked with a key from his key-chain, and they were in a large, unheated room, occupied by two people. They were a very tall, dark-skinned man, holding a large metal scalpel, and a dead girl in her late teens, lying on a long, porcelain table that resembled both a slab and a sink.

There were several photographs of the dead girl pinned up on a corkboard on the wall above the body. She was smiling in one, a high school head shot. In another she was standing in a line with three other girls; they were wearing what might have been prom dresses, and her black hair was tied above her head in an intricate knotwork.

Cold on the porcelain, her hair was down, loose around her shoulders, and matted with dried blood.

'This is my partner, Mr Jacquel,' said Ibis.

'We met already,' said Jacquel. 'Forgive me if I don't shake hands.'

Shadow looked down at the girl on the table. 'What happened to her?' he asked.

'Poor taste in boyfriends,' said Jacquel.

'It's not always fatal,' said Mr Ibis, with a sigh. 'This time it was. He was drunk, and he had a knife, and she told him that she thought she was pregnant. He didn't believe it was his.'

'She was stabbed . . .' said Mr Jacquel, and he counted. There was a click as he stepped on a foot-switch, turning on a small Dictaphone on a nearby table, 'five times. There are three knife wounds in the left anterior chest wall. The first is between the fourth and fifth intercostal spaces at the medial border of the left breast, two point two centimeters in length; the second and third are through the inferior portion of the left mid-breast penetrating at the sixth interspace, overlapping, and measuring three centimeters. There is one wound two centimeters long in the upper anterior left chest in the second interspace, and one wound five centimeters long and a maximum of one point six centimeters deep in the anteromedial left deltoid, a slashing injury. All the chest wounds are deep penetrating injuries. There are no other visible wounds externally.' He released pressure from the foot-switch. Shadow noticed a small microphone dangling above the embalming table by its cord.

'So you're the coroner as well?' asked Shadow.

'Coroner's a political appointment around here,' said Ibis. 'His job is to kick the corpse. If it doesn't kick him back, he signs the death certificate. Jacquel's what they call a prosector. He works for the county medical examiner. He does autopsies, and saves tissue samples for analysis. He's already photographed her wounds.'

Jacquel ignored them. He took a big scalpel and made a deep incision in a large V which began at both collarbones and met at the bottom of her breastbone, and then he turned the V into a Y, another deep incision that continued from her breastbone to her pubis. He picked up what looked like a small, heavy chrome drill with a medallion-sized round saw blade at the business end. He turned it on, and cut through the ribs at both sides of her breastbone.

The girl opened like a purse.

Shadow suddenly was aware of a mild but unpleasantly penetrating, pungent, meaty smell.

'I thought it would smell worse,' said Shadow.

'She's pretty fresh,' said Jacquel. 'And the intestines weren't pierced, so it doesn't smell of shit.'

Shadow found himself looking away, not from revulsion, as he would have expected, but from a strange desire to give the girl some privacy. It would be hard to be nakeder than this open thing.

Jacquel tied off the intestines, glistening and snakelike in her belly, above the stomach and deep in the pelvis. He ran them through his fingers, foot after foot of them, described them as 'normal' to the microphone, put them in a bucket on the floor. He sucked all the blood out of her chest with a vacuum pump, and measured the volume. Then he inspected the inside of her chest. He said to the microphone, 'There are three lacerations in the pericardium, which is filled with clotted and liquefying blood.'

Jacquel grasped her heart, cut it at its top, turned it about in his hand, examining it. He stepped on his switch and said, 'There are two lacerations of the myocardium; a one point five centimeter laceration in the right ventricle and a one point eight centimeter laceration penetrating the left ventricle.'

Jacquel removed each lung. The left lung had been stabbed and was half collapsed. He weighed them, and the heart, and he photographed the wounds. From each lung he sliced a small piece of tissue, which he placed into a jar.

'Formaldehyde,' whispered Mr Ibis, helpfully.

Jacquel continued to talk to the microphone, describing what he was doing, what he saw, as he removed the girl's liver, the stomach, spleen, pancreas, both kidneys, the uterus and the ovaries.

He weighed each organ, reported them as normal and uninjured. From each organ he took a small slice and put it into a jar of formaldehyde.

From the heart, the liver, and from one of the kidneys, he cut an additional slice. These pieces he chewed, slowly, making them last, while he worked.

Somehow it seemed to Shadow a good thing for him to do: respectful, not obscene.

'So you want to stay here with us for a spell?' said Jacquel, masticating the slice of the girl's heart.

'If you'll have me,' said Shadow.

'Certainly we'll have you,' said Mr Ibis. 'No reasons why not and plenty of reasons why. You'll be under our protection as long as you're here.'

'I hope you don't mind sleeping under the same roof as the dead,' said Jacquel.

Shadow thought of the touch of Laura's lips, bitter and cold. 'No,' he said. 'Not as long as they stay dead, anyhow.'

Jacquel turned and looked at him with dark brown eyes as quizzical and cold as a desert dog's. 'They stay dead here,' was all he said.

'Seems to me,' said Shadow. 'Seems to me that the dead come back pretty easy.'

'Not at all,' said Ibis. 'Even zombies, they make them out of the living, you know. A little powder, a little chanting, a little push, and you have a zombie. They live, but they believe they are dead. But to truly bring the dead back to life, in their bodies. That takes power.' He hesitates, then, 'In the old land, in the old days, it was easier then.'

'You could bind the *ka* of a man to his body for five thousand years,' said Jacquel. 'Binding or loosing. But that was a long time ago.' He took all the organs that he had removed and replaced them, respectfully, in the body cavity. He replaced the intestines and the breastbone and pulled the skin edges near each other. Then he took a thick needle and thread and, with deft, quick strokes, he sewed it up, like a man stitching a baseball: the cadaver transformed from meat into girl once again.

'I need a beer,' said Jacquel. He pulled off his rubber gloves and dropped them into the bin. He dropped his dark brown overalls into a hamper. Then he took the cardboard tray of jars filled with little red and brown and purple slices of the organs. 'Coming?'

They walked up the back stairs to the kitchen. It was brown and white, a sober and respectable room that looked to Shadow as if it had last been decorated in 1920. There was a huge Kelvinator rattling to itself by one wall. Jacquel opened the Kelvinator door, put the plastic jars with their slivers of spleen, of kidney, of liver, of heart, inside. He took out three brown bottles. Ibis opened a glass-fronted cupboard, removed three tall glasses. Then he gestured for Shadow to sit down at the kitchen table.

Ibis poured the beer and passed a glass to Shadow, a glass to Jacquel. It was a fine beer, bitter and dark.

'Good beer,' said Shadow.

'We brew it ourselves,' said Ibis. 'In the old days the women did the brewing. They were better brewers than we are. But now it is only the three of us here. Me, him and her.' He gestured toward the small brown cat, fast asleep in a cat-basket in the corner of the room. 'There were more of us, in the beginning. But Set left us to explore, what, two hundred years ago? Must be, by now. We got a postcard from him from San Francisco in 1905, 1906. Then nothing. While poor Horus. . . .' he trailed off, in a sigh, and shook his head.

'I still see him, on occasion,' said Jacquel. 'On my way to a pick up.' He sipped his beer.

'I'll work for my keep,' said Shadow. 'While I'm here. You tell me what you need doing, and I'll do it.'

'We'll find work for you,' agreed Jacquel.

The small brown cat opened her eyes and stretched to her feet. She padded across the kitchen floor and pushed at Shadow's boot with her head. He put down his left hand and scratched her forehead and the back of her ears and the scruff of her neck. She arched, ecstatically, then sprang into his lap, pushed herself up against his chest and touched her cold nose to his. Then she curled up in his lap and went back to sleep. He put his hand down to stroke her: her fur was soft, and she was warm and pleasant in his lap: she acted like she was in the safest place in the world, and Shadow felt comforted.

The beer left a pleasant buzz in Shadow's head.

'Your room is at the top of the stairs, by the bathroom,' said Jacquel. 'Your work clothes will be hanging in the closet – you'll see. You'll want to wash up and shave first, I guess.'

Shadow did. He showered standing in the cast iron tub and he shaved, very nervously, with a straight razor that Jacquel loaned him. It was obscenely sharp, and had a mother-of-pearl handle, and Shadow suspected it was usually used to give dead men their final shave. He had never used a straight razor before, but he did not cut himself. He washed off the shaving cream, looked at himself naked in the fly-specked bathroom mirror. He was bruised: fresh bruises on his chest and arms overlaying the fading bruises that Mad Sweeney had left him. His eyes looked back mistrustfully from the mirror at him.

And then, as if someone else were holding his hand, he raised the straight razor, placed it, blade open, against his throat.

It would be a way out, he thought. An easy way out. And if there's anyone who'd simply take it in their stride, who'd just clean up the mess and get on with things, it's the two guys sitting downstairs at the kitchen table drinking their beer. No more worries. No more Laura. No more mysteries and conspiracies. No more bad dreams. Just peace and quiet and rest forever. One clean slash, ear to ear. That's all it'll take.

He stood there with the razor against his throat. A tiny smudge of blood came from the place where the blade touched the skin. He had not even noticed a cut. See, he told himself, and he could almost hear the words being whispered in his ear. It's painless. Too sharp to hurt. I'll be gone before I know it.

Then the door to the bathroom swung open, just a few inches, enough for the little brown cat to put her head around the door-frame and 'Mrr?' up at him, curiously.

'Hey,' he said to the cat. 'I thought I locked that door.'

He closed the cut-throat razor, put it down on the side of the sink, dabbed at his tiny cut with a toilet paper swab. Then he wrapped a towel around his waist and went into the bedroom next door.

His bedroom, like the kitchen, seemed to have been decorated some time in the 1920s: there was a washstand and a pitcher beside the chest of drawers and mirror. Someone had already laid out clothes for him on the bed: a black suit, white shirt, black tie, white undershirt and underpants, black socks. Black shoes sat on the worn Persian carpet beside the bed.

He dressed himself. The clothes were of good quality, although none of them were new. He wondered who they had belonged to. Was he wearing a dead man's socks? Would he be stepping into a dead man's shoes? He adjusted the tie in the mirror and now it seemed to him that his reflection was smiling at him, sardonically.

Now it seemed inconceivable to him that he had ever thought of cutting his throat. His reflection continued to smile as he adjusted his tie.

'Hey,' he said to it. 'You know something that I don't?' and immediately felt foolish.

The door creaked open and the cat slipped between the doorpost and the door and padded across the room, then up on the windowsill. 'Hey,' he said to the cat. 'I did shut that door. I know I shut that door.' She looked at him, interested. Her eyes were dark yellow, the colour of amber. Then she jumped down from the sill, onto the bed, where she wrapped herself into a curl of fur and went back to sleep, a circle of cat upon the old counterpane.

Shadow left the bedroom door open, so the cat could leave and the room air a little, and he walked downstairs. The stairs creaked and grumbled as he walked down them, protesting his weight, as if they just wanted to be left in peace.

'*Damn* you look good,' said Jacquel. He was waiting at the bottom of the stairs, and was now himself dressed in a black suit, similar to Shadow's. 'You ever driven a hearse?'

'No.'

'First time for everything, then,' said Jacquel. 'It's parked out front.'

An old woman had died. Her name had been Lila Goodchild. At Mr Jacquel's direction, Shadow carried the folded aluminum gurney up the narrow stairs to her bedroom and unfolded it next to her bed. He took out a translucent blue plastic body bag, laid it next to the dead woman on the bed, and unzipped it open. She wore a pink nightgown and a quilted robe. Shadow lifted her and wrapped her, fragile and almost weightless, in a blanket, and placed it onto the bag. He zipped the bag shut and put it on the gurney. While Shadow did this, Jacquel talked to a very old man who had, when she was alive, been married to Lila Goodchild. Or rather, Jacquel listened while the old man talked. As Shadow had zipped Mrs Goodchild away the old man had been explaining how ungrateful his children had been, and grandchildren too, though that wasn't their fault, that was their parents', the apple didn't fall far from the tree, and he thought he'd raised them better than that.

Shadow and Jacquel wheeled the loaded gurney to the narrow flight of stairs. The old man followed them, still talking, mostly about money, and greed, and ingratitude. He wore bedroom slippers. Shadow carried the heavier bottom end of the gurney down the stairs and out onto the street, then he wheeled it along the icy sidewalk to the hearse. Jacquel opened the hearse's rear door. Shadow hesitated, and Jacquel said 'Just push it on in there. The supports'll fold up out of the way.' Shadow pushed the gurney, and the supports snapped up, the wheels rotated, and the gurney rolled right on to the floor of the hearse. Jacquel showed him how to strap it in securely, and Shadow closed up the hearse while Jacquel listened to the old man who had been married to Lila Goodchild, unmindful of the cold, an old man in his slippers and his bathrobe out on the wintery sidewalk telling Jacquel how his children were vultures, no better than hovering vultures, waiting to take what little he and Lila had scraped together, and how the two of them had fled to St. Louis, to Memphis, to Miami, and how they wound up in Cairo, and how relieved he was that Lila had not died in a nursing home, how scared he was that he would.

They walked the old man back into the house, up the stairs to his room. A small TV set droned from one corner of the couple's bedroom. As Shadow passed it he noticed that the newsreader was grinning and winking at him. When he was sure that no-one was looking in his direction he gave the set the finger.

'They've got no money,' said Jacquel when they were back in the hearse. 'He'll come in to see Ibis tomorrow. He'll choose the cheapest funeral. Her friends will persuade him to do her right, give her a proper send-off in the front room, I expect. But he'll grumble. Got no money. Nobody around here's got money these days. Anyway, he'll be dead in six months. A year at the outside.'

Snowflakes tumbled and drifted in front of the headlights. The snow was coming south. Shadow said, 'Is he sick?'

'It ain't that. Women survive their men. Men – men like him – don't live long when their women are gone. You'll see – he'll just start wandering, all the familiar things are going to be gone with her. He gets tired and he fades and then he gives up and then he's gone. Maybe pneumonia will take him or maybe it'll be cancer, or maybe his heart will stop. Old age, and all the fight gone out of you. Then you die.'

Shadow thought. 'Hey, Jacquel?'

'Yeah.'

'Do you believe in the soul?' It wasn't quite the question he had been going to ask, and it took him by surprise to hear it coming from his mouth. He had intended to say something less direct, but there was nothing less direct that he could say.

'Depends. Back in my day, we had it all set up. You lined up when you died, and you answered for your evil deeds and for your good deeds, and if your evil deeds outweighed a feather, we'd feed your soul and your heart to Ammet, the Eater of Souls.'

'He must have eaten a lot of people.'

'Not as many as you'd think. It was a really heavy feather. We had it made special. You had to be pretty damn evil to tip the scales on that baby. Stop here, that gas station. We'll put in a few gallons.'

The streets were quiet, in the way that streets only are when the first snow falls. 'It's going to be a white Christmas,' said Shadow as he pumped the gas.

'Yup. Shit. That boy was one lucky son of a virgin.'

'Jesus?'

'Lucky, lucky guy. He could fall in a cesspit and come up smelling like roses. Hell, it's not even his birthday, you know that? He took it from Mithras. You run into Mithras yet? Red cap. Nice kid.'

'No, I don't think so.'

'Well . . . I've never seen Mithras around here. He was an army brat. Maybe he's back in the Middle East, taking it easy, but I expect he's probably gone by now. It happens. One day every soldier in the empire has to shower in the blood of your sacrificial bull. The next they don't even remember your birthday.'

Swish went the windshield wipers, pushing the snow to the side, bunching the flakes up into knots and swirls of clear ice.

A traffic light turned momentarily yellow and then red, and Shadow put his foot on the brake. The hearse fishtailed and swung around on the empty road before it stopped. 'Hey pilgrim,' said Jacquel, doing John Wayne. 'Mebbe you should lighten up on the pedal. This ol' heap's the only one we got.'

The light turned green. Shadow took the hearse up to ten miles per hour, which seemed enough on the slippery roads. It was perfectly happy cruising in second gear: he guessed it must have spent a lot of its time at that speed, holding up traffic.

'That's good,' said Jacquel. 'So, yeah, Jesus does pretty good over here. But I met a guy who said he saw him hitchhiking by the side of the road in Afghanistan and nobody was stopping to give him a ride. You know? It all depends on where you are.'

'I think a real storm's coming,' said Shadow. He was talking about the weather.

Jacquel, when, eventually, he began to answer, wasn't talking about the weather at all. 'You look at me and Ibis,' he said. 'We'll be out of business in a few years. We got savings put aside for the lean years, but the lean years have been here for a long while, and every year they just get leaner. Horus is crazy, really bugfuck crazy, spends all his time as a hawk, eats road kill, what kind of a life is that? You've seen Bast. And *we're* in better shape than most of them. At least we've got a little belief to be going along with. Most of the suckers out there have barely got that. It's like the funeral business – the big guys are going to buy you up one day, like it or not, because they're bigger and more efficient and because they *work*. Fighting's not going to change a damned thing, because we lost this particular battle when we came to this green land a hundred years ago or a thousand or ten thousand. We arrived and America just didn't care that we'd arrived. So we get bought out, or we press on, or we hit the road. So, yes. You're right. The storm's coming.'

Shadow turned onto the street where the houses were, all but one of them dead, their windows blind and boarded. 'Take the back alley,' said Jacquel.

He backed the hearse up until it was almost touching the double doors at the rear of the house. Ibis opened the hearse, and the mortuary doors, and Shadow unbuckled the gurney and pulled it out. The wheeled supports rotated and dropped as they cleared the bumper. He wheeled the gurney to the embalming table. He picked up Lila Goodchild, cradling her in her opaque bag like a sleeping child, and placed her carefully on the table in the chilly mortuary, as if he were afraid to wake her.

'You know, I have a transfer board,' said Jacquel. 'You don't have to carry her.'

'Ain't nothing,' said Shadow. He was starting to sound more like Jacquel. 'I'm a big guy. It doesn't bother me.'

As a kid Shadow had been small for his age, all elbows and knees. The only photograph of Shadow as a kid that Laura had liked enough to frame showed a solemn child with unruly hair and dark eyes standing beside a table laden high with cakes and cookies. Shadow thought the picture might have been taken at an embassy Christmas party, as he had been dressed in a bowtie and his best clothes.

They had moved too much, his mother and Shadow, first around Europe, from embassy to embassy, where his mother had worked as a communicator in the Foreign Service, transcribing and sending classified telegrams across the world, and then, when he was eight years old, back to the U.S., where his mother, now too sporadically sick to hold down a steady job, had moved from city to city restlessly spending a year here or a year there, temping when she was well enough. They never spent long enough in any place for Shadow to make friends, to feel at home, to relax. And Shadow had been a small child. . . .

He had grown so fast. In the spring of his thirteenth year the local kids had been picking on him, goading him into fights they knew they could not fail to win and after which Shadow would run, angry and often weeping, to the boys' room to wash the mud or the blood from his face before anyone could see it. Then came summer, a long magical, thirteenth summer, which he spent keeping out of the way of the bigger kids, swimming in the local pool, reading library books at poolside. At the start of the summer he could barely swim. By the end of August he was swimming length after length in an easy crawl, diving from the high board, ripening to a deep brown from the sun and the water. In September, he had returned to school to discover that the boys who had made him miserable were small, soft things no longer capable of upsetting him. The two who tried it were taught better manners, hard and fast and painfully, and Shadow found that he had redefined himself: he could no longer be a quiet kid, doing his best to remain unobtrusively at the back of things. He was too big for that, too obvious. By the end of the year he was on the swimming team and the weight-lifting team, and the coach was courting him for the triathlon team. He liked being big and strong. It gave him an identity. He'd been a shy, quiet, bookish kid, and that had been painful; now he was a big dumb guy, and nobody expected him to be able to do anything more than move a sofa into the next room on his own.

Nobody until Laura, anyway.

Mr Ibis had prepared dinner: rice and boiled greens for himself and Mr Jacquel. 'I am not a meat eater,' he explained, 'While Jacquel gets all the meat he needs in the course of his work.' Beside Shadow's place was a carton of chicken pieces from KFC, and a bottle of beer.

There was more chicken than Shadow could eat, and he shared the leftovers with the cat, removing the skin and crusty coating then shredding the meat for her with his fingers.

'There was a guy in prison named Jackson,' said Shadow, as he ate, 'worked in the prison library. He told me that they changed the name from Kentucky Fried Chicken to KFC because they don't serve real chicken any more. It's become this genetically modified mutant thing, like a giant centipede with no head, just segment after segment of legs and breasts and wings. It's fed through nutrient tubes. This guy said the government wouldn't let them use the word *chicken*.'

Mr Ibis raised his eyebrows. 'You think that's true?'

'Nope. Now, my old cellmate, Low Key, he said they changed the name because the word *fried* had become a bad word. Maybe they wanted people to think that the chicken cooked itself.'

After dinner Jacquel excused himself and went down to the mortuary. Ibis went to his study to write. Shadow sat in the kitchen for a little longer, feeding fragments of chicken breast to the little brown cat, sipping his beer. When the beer and the chicken were gone, he washed up the plates and cutlery, put them on the rack to dry, and went upstairs.

By the time he reached the bedroom the little brown cat was once more asleep at the bottom of the bed, curled into a fur crescent. In the middle drawer of the vanity he found several pairs of striped cotton pyjamas. They looked seventy years old, but smelled fresh, and he pulled on a pair which, like the black suit, fitted him as if they had been tailored for him.

There was a small stack of Reader's Digests on the little table beside the bed, none of them dated later than March 1960. Jackson, the library guy – the same one who had sworn to the truth of the Kentucky Fried Mutant Chicken Creature story, who had told him the story of the black freight trains that the government uses to haul political prisoners off to Secret Northern Californian Concentration Camps, moving across the country in the dead of the night, – Jackson had also told him that the CIA used the Reader's Digest as a front for their branch offices around the world. He said that every Reader's Digest office in every country was really CIA.

'A joke,' said the late Mr Wood, in Shadow's memory. 'How can we be certain the CIA weren't involved in the Kennedy assassination?'

Shadow cracked the window open a few inches – enough for fresh air to get in, enough for the cat to be able to get out onto the balcony outside.

He turned on the bedside lamp, climbed into bed and read for a little, trying to turn off his mind, to get the last few days out of his head, picking the dullest-looking articles in the dullest-looking Digests. He noticed he was falling asleep half way through *I Am John's Pancreas*. He barely had time enough to turn out the bedside light and put his head down on the pillow before his eyes closed for the night.

Later he was never able to recollect the sequences and details of that dream: attempts to remember it produced nothing more than a tangle of dark images. There was a girl. He had met her somewhere, and now they were walking across a bridge. It spanned a small lake, in the middle of a town. The wind was ruffling the surface of the lake, making waves tipped with white-caps, which seemed to Shadow to be tiny hands, reaching for him.

– *Down there*, said the woman. She was wearing a leopard-print skirt which flapped and tossed in the wind, and the flesh between the top of her stockings and her skirt was creamy and soft and in his dream, on the bridge, before God and the world, Shadow went down to his knees in front of her, burying his head in her crotch, drinking in the intoxicating jungle female scent of her. He became aware, in his dream, of his erection in real life, a rigid, pounding, monstrous thing as painful in its hardness as the erections he'd had as a boy, when he was crashing into puberty.

He pulled away and looked upward, and still he could not see her face. But his mouth was seeking hers and her lips were soft against his, and his hands were cupping her breasts, and then they were running across the satin smoothness of her skin, pushing into and parting the furs that hid her waist, sliding into the wonderful cleft of her which warmed and wetted and parted for him, opening to his hand like a flower.

The woman purred against him ecstatically, her hand moving down to the hardness of him and squeezing it. He pushed the bed sheets away and rolled on top of her, his hand parting her thighs, her hand guiding him between her legs, where one thrust, one magical push . . .

Now he was back in his old prison cell with her, and he was kissing her deeply. She wrapped her arms tightly around him, clamped her legs about his legs to hold him tight, so he could not pull out, not even if he wanted to.

Never had he kissed lips so soft. He had not known that there were lips so soft in the whole world. Her tongue, though, was sand-paper-rough as it slipped against his.

– *Who are you?* he asked.

She made no answer, just pushed him onto his back and, in one lithe movement, straddled him and began to ride him. No, not to ride him: to insinuate herself against him in series of silken-smooth waves, each more powerful than the one before, strokes and beats and rhythms which crashed against his mind and his body just as the wind-waves on the lake splashed against the shore. Her nails were needle-sharp and they pierced his sides, raking them, but he felt no pain, only pleasure, everything was transmuted by some alchemy into moments of utter pleasure.

He struggled to find himself, struggled to talk, his head now filled with sand dunes and desert winds.

– *Who are you?* he asked again, gasping for the words.

She stared at him with eyes the colour of dark amber, then lowered her mouth to his and kissed him with a passion, kissed him so completely and so deeply that there, on the bridge over the lake, in his prison cell, in the bed in the Cairo funeral home, he almost came. He rode the sensation like a kite riding a hurricane, willing it not to crest, not to explode, wanting it never to end. He pulled it under control. He had to warn her.

– *My wife, Laura. She will kill you.*

– *Not me*, she said.

A fragment of nonsense bubbled up from somewhere in his mind: in medieval days it was said that a woman on top during coitus would conceive a bishop. That was what they called it: trying for a bishop . . .

He wanted to know her name, but he dared not ask her a third time, and she pushed her chest against his, and he could feel the hard nubs of her nipples against his chest, and she was squeezing him, somehow squeezing him *down there* deep inside her and this time he could not ride it or surf it, this time it picked him up and spun and tumbled him away, and he was arching up, pushing into her as deeply as he could imagine, as if they were, in some way, part of the same creature, tasting, drinking, holding, *wanting* . . .

– *Let it happen,* she said, her voice a throaty feline growl. *Give it to me. Let it happen.*

And he came, spasming and dissolving, the back of his mind itself liquefying then sublimating slowly from one state to the next.

Somewhere in there, at the end of it, he took a breath, a clear draught of air he felt all the way down to the depths of his lungs, and he knew that he had been holding his breath for a long time now. Three years, at least. Perhaps even longer.

– *Now rest,* she said, and she kissed his eyelids with her soft lips. *Let it go. Let it all go.*

The sleep he slept after that was deep and dreamless and comforting, and Shadow dived deep and embraced it.

The light was strange. It was, he checked his watch, 6:45 a.m., and still dark outside, but the room was filled with a pale blue dimness. He climbed out of bed. He was certain that he had been wearing pyjamas when he went to bed, but now he was naked, and the air was cold on his skin. He walked to the window and closed it.

There had been a snowstorm in the night: six inches had fallen, perhaps more. The corner of the town that Shadow could see from his window, dirty and rundown, had been transformed into somewhere clean and different: these houses were not abandoned and forgotten, they were frosted into elegance. The streets had vanished completely, lost beneath a white field of snow.

There was an idea that hovered at the edge of his perception. Something about *transience.* It flickered and was gone.

He could see as well as if it were full daylight.

In the mirror, Shadow noticed something strange. He stepped closer, and stared, puzzled. All his bruises had vanished. He touched his side, pressing firmly with his fingertips, feeling for one of the deep pains that told him he had encountered Mr Stone and Mr Wood, hunting for the greening blossoms of bruise that Mad Sweeney had gifted him with, and finding nothing. His face was clear and unmarked. His sides, however, and his back (he twisted to examine it) were scratched with what looked like claw marks.

He hadn't dreamed it, then. Not entirely.

Shadow opened the drawers, and put on what he found: an

ancient pair of blue-denim Levis, a shirt, a thick blue sweater and a black undertaker's coat he found hanging in the wardrobe at the back of the room.

He wore his own old shoes.

The house was still asleep. He crept through it, willing the floorboards not to creak, and then he was outside, and he walked through the snow, his feet leaving deep prints on the sidewalk. It was lighter out than it had seemed from inside the house, and the snow reflected the light from the sky.

After fifteen minutes of walking Shadow came to a bridge, with a big sign on the side of it warning him he was now leaving historical Cairo. A man stood under the bridge, tall and gangling, sucking on a cigarette and shivering continually. Shadow thought he recognised the man.

And then, under the bridge in the winter darkness he was close enough to see the purple smudge of bruise around the man's eye, and he said, 'Good morning, Mad Sweeney.'

The world was so quiet. Not even cars disturbed the snowbound silence.

'Hey man,' said Mad Sweeney. He did not look up. The cigarette had been rolled by hand.

'You keep hanging out under bridges, Mad Sweeney,' said Shadow, 'people gonna think you're a troll.'

This time Mad Sweeney looked up. Shadow could see the whites of his eyes all around his irises. The man looked scared. 'I was lookin' for you,' he said. 'You gotta help me, man. I fucked up bigtime.' He sucked on his hand-rolled cigarette, pulled it away from his mouth. The cigarette paper stuck to his lower lip, and the cigarette fell apart, spilling its contents onto his ginger beard and down the front of his filthy tee shirt. Mad Sweeney brushed it off, convulsively, with blackened hands, as if it were a dangerous insect.

'My resources are pretty much tapped out, Mad Sweeney,' said Shadow. 'But why don't you tell me what it is you need. You want me to get you a coffee?'

Mad Sweeney shook his head. He took out a tobacco pouch and papers from the pocket of his denim jacket and began to roll himself another cigarette. His beard bristled and his mouth moved as he did this, although no words were said aloud. He licked the adhesive side of the cigarette paper and rolled it between his fingers. The result looked only distantly like a cigarette. Then he said, ''M not a troll. Shit. Those bastards're fucken *mean*.'

'I know you're not a troll, Sweeney,' said Shadow, gently. 'How can I help you?'

Mad Sweeney flicked his zippo, and the first inch of his cigarette flamed and then subsided to ash. 'You remember I showed you how to get a coin? You remember?'

'Yes,' said Shadow. He saw the gold coin in his mind's eye, watched it tumble into Laura's casket, saw it glitter around her neck. 'I remember.'

'You took the wrong coin, man.'

A car approached the gloom under the bridge, blinding them with its lights. It slowed as it passed them, then stopped, and a window slid down. 'Everything okay here, gentlemen?'

'Everything's just peachy, thank you, officer,' said Shadow. 'We're just out for a morning walk.'

'Okay now,' said the cop. He did not look as if he believed that everything was okay. He waited. Shadow put a hand on Mad Sweeney's shoulder, and walked him forward, out of town, away from the police car. He heard the window hum closed, but the car remained where it was.

Shadow walked. Mad Sweeney walked, and sometimes he staggered.

The police car cruised past them slowly, then turned, and went back into the city, accelerating down the snowy road.

'Now, why don't you tell me what's troubling you,' said Shadow.

'I did it like he said. I did it all like he said, but I gave you the wrong coin. It wasn't meant to be that coin. That's for royalty. You see? I shouldn't even have been able to take it. That's the coin you'd give to the King of America himself. Not some pissant bastard like you or me. And now I'm in big trouble. Just give me the coin back, man. You'll never see me again, if you do, I sweartofuckenBran, okay? I swear by the years I spent in the fucken trees.'

'You did it like who said, Sweeney?'

'Grimnir. The dude you call Wednesday. You know who he is? Who he really is?'

'Yeah. I guess.'

There was a panicked look in the Irishman's crazy blue eyes. 'It was nothing bad. Nothing you can – nothing bad. He just told me to be there at that bar and to pick a fight with you. He said he wanted to see what you were made of.'

'He tell you do anything else?'

Sweeney shivered and twitched; Shadow thought it was the cold for a moment, then knew where he'd seen that shuddering shiver before. In prison: it was a junkie shiver. Sweeney was in withdrawal from something, and Shadow would have been willing to bet it was heroin. A junkie leprechaun? Mad Sweeney pinched off the burning head of his cigarette, dropped it on the ground, put the unfinished yellowing rest of it into his pocket. He rubbed his dirt-black fingers together, breathed on them to try and rub warmth into them. His voice was a whine now, 'Listen, just give me the fucken coin, man. I'll give you another, just as good. Hell, I'll give you a shitload of the fuckers.'

He took off his greasy baseball cap – then, with his right hand, he stroked the air, producing a large golden coin. He dropped it into his cap. And then he took another from a wisp of breath steam, and another, catching and grabbing them from the still morning air until the baseball cap was brimming with them and Sweeney was forced to hold it with both hands.

He extended the baseball cap filled with gold to Shadow. 'Here,' he said. 'Take them man. Just give me back the coin I gave to you.' Shadow looked down at the cap, wondered how much its contents would be worth.

'Where am I going to spend those coins, Mad Sweeney?' Shadow asked. 'Are there a lot of places you can turn your gold into cash?'

He thought the Irishman was going to hit him for a moment, but the moment passed and Mad Sweeney just stood there, holding out his gold-filled cap with both hands like Oliver Twist. And then tears swelled in his blue eyes and began to spill down his cheeks. He took the cap and put it – now empty of everything except a greasy sweatband – back over his thinning scalp. 'You gotta man,' he was saying. 'Didn't I show you how to do it? I showed you how to take coins from the hoard. I showed you where the hoard was. Just give me that first coin back. It didn't belong to me.'

'I don't have it any more.'

Mad Sweeney's tears stopped, and spots of colour appeared in his cheeks. 'You, you fucken—' he said, and then the words failed him and his mouth opened and closed, wordlessly.

'I'm telling you the truth,' said Shadow. 'I'm sorry. If I had it I'd give it back to you. But I gave it away.'

Sweeney's grimy hands clamped on Shadow's shoulders, and the pale blue eyes stared into his. The tears had made streaks in the dirt on Mad Sweeney's face. 'Shit,' he said. Shadow could smell tobacco and stale beer and whiskey-sweat. 'You're telling the truth, you fucker. Gave it away and freely and of your own will. Damn your dark eyes, you gave it a-fucken-way.'

'I'm sorry.' Shadow remembered the whispering thump the coin had made as it landed in Laura's casket.

'Sorry or not, I'm damned and I'm doomed.' He wiped his nose and his eyes on his sleeves, muddying his face into strange patterns.

Shadow squeezed Mad Sweeney's upper arm in an awkward male gesture.

''Twere better I had never been conceived,' said Mad Sweeney, at length. Then he looked up. 'The fellow you gave it to. Would he give it back?'

'It's a woman. And I don't know where she is. But no, I don't believe she would.'

Sweeney sighed, mournfully. 'When I was but a young pup,' he said, 'there was a woman I met, under the stars, who let me play with her bubbies, and she told me my fortune. She told me that I would be undone and abandoned west of the sunrise, and that a dead woman's bauble would seal my fate. And I laughed and poured more barley wine and played with her bubbies some more, and I kissed her full on her pretty lips. Those were the good days – the first of the grey monks had not yet come to our land, nor had they ridden the green sea to westward. And now.' He stopped, mid-sentence. His head turned and he focused on Shadow. 'You shouldn't trust him,' he said, reproachfully.

'Who?'

'Wednesday. You mustn't trust him.'

'I don't have to trust him. I work for him.'

'Do you remember how to do it?'

'What?' Shadow felt he was having a conversation with half a dozen different people. The self-styled leprechaun sputtered and jumped from persona to persona, from theme to theme, as if the remaining clusters of brain-cells were igniting, flaming, and then going out for good.

'The coins, man. The coins. I showed you, remember?' He raised two fingers to his face, stared at them, then pulled a gold coin from his mouth. He tossed the coin to Shadow, who stretched out a hand to catch it, but no coin reached him.

'I was drunk,' said Shadow. 'I don't remember.'

Sweeney stumbled across the road. It was light now and the world was white and grey. Shadow followed him. Sweeney walked in a long, loping stride, as if he were always falling, but his legs were there to stop him, to propel him into another stumble. When they reached the bridge, he held onto the bricks with one hand, and turned and said, 'You got a few bucks? I don't need much. Just enough for a ticket out of this place. Twenty bucks will do me fine. Just a lousy twenty?'

'Where can you go on a twenty dollar bus-ticket?' asked Shadow.

'I can get out of here,' said Sweeney. 'I can get away before the storm hits. Away from a world in which opiates have become the religion of the masses. Away from.' He stopped, wiped his nose on the side of his hand, then wiped his hand on his sleeve.

Shadow reached into his jeans, pulled out a twenty and passed it to Sweeney. 'Here.'

Sweeney crumpled it up and pushed it deep into the breast pocket of his oil-stained denim jacket, under the sew-on patch showing two vultures on a dead branch and, beneath them, the words *Patience my ass! I'm going to kill something!* He nodded. 'That'll get me where I need to go,' he said.

He leaned against the brick, fumbled in his pockets until he found the unfinished stub of cigarette he had abandoned earlier. He lit it carefully, trying not to burn his fingers or his beard. 'I'll tell you something,' he said, as if he had said nothing that day. 'You're walking on gallows ground, and there's a rope around your neck and a raven-bird on each shoulder, waiting for your eyes, and the gallows tree has deep roots, for it stretches from heaven to hell, and our world is only the branch from which the rope is swinging.' He stopped. 'I'll rest here a spell,' he said, crouching down, his back resting against the black brickwork.

'Good luck,' said Shadow.

'Hell, I'm fucked,' said Mad Sweeney. 'Whatever. Thanks.'

Shadow walked back toward the town. It was 8:00 a.m. and Cairo was waking. He glanced back to the bridge, and saw Sweeney's pale face, striped with tears and dirt, watching him go.

It was the last time Shadow saw Mad Sweeney alive.

The brief winter days leading up to Christmas were like moments of light between the winter darknesses, and they fled fast in the house of the dead.

It was the twenty-third of December, and Jacquel and Ibis's played host to a wake for Lila Goodchild. Bustling women filled the kitchen with tubs and with saucepans and with skillets and with tupperware, and the deceased was laid out in her casket in the funeral home's front room with hothouse flowers around her. There was a table on the other side of the room laden high with coleslaw and beans and cornmeal hush puppies and chicken and ribs and black-eyed peas, and by mid-afternoon the house was filled with people weeping and laughing and shaking hands with the minister, everything being quietly organised and overseen by the sober-suited Messrs Jacquel and Ibis. The burial would be on the following morning.

When the telephone in the hall rang (it was Bakelite and black and had an honest-to-goodness rotary dial on the front) Mr Ibis answered. Then he took Shadow aside. 'That was the police,' he said. 'Can you make a pickup?'

'Sure.'

'Be discreet. Here.' He wrote down an address on a slip of paper, then passed it to Shadow, who read the address, written in perfect copperplate handwriting, and then folded it up and put it in his pocket. 'There'll be a police car,' Ibis added.

Shadow went out back and got the hearse. Both Mr Jacquel and Mr Ibis had made a point, individually, of explaining that, really, the hearse should only be used for funerals, and they had a van that they used to collect bodies, but the van was being repaired, had been for three weeks now, and could he be very careful with the hearse? Shadow drove carefully down the street. The snowploughs had cleaned the roads by now, but he was comfortable driving slowly. It seemed right to go slow in a hearse, although he could barely remember the last time he had seen a hearse on the streets. Death had vanished from the streets of America, thought Shadow; now it happened in hospital rooms and in ambulances. We must not startle the living, thought Shadow. Mr Ibis had told him that they move the dead about in some hospitals on the lower level of apparently empty covered gurneys, the deceased traveling their own paths in their own covered ways.

A dark blue police cruiser was parked on a sidestreet, and Shadow pulled up the hearse behind it. There were two cops inside the cruiser, drinking their coffee from thermos tops. They had the engine running to keep warm. Shadow tapped on the side window.

'Yeah?'

'I'm from the funeral home,' said Shadow.

'We're waiting for the medical examiner,' said the cop. Shadow wondered if it was the same man who had spoken to him under the bridge. The cop, who was black, got out of the car, leaving his colleague in the driver's seat, and walked Shadow back to a dumpster. Mad Sweeney was sitting in the snow beside the dumpster. There was an empty green bottle in his lap, a dusting of snow and ice on his face and baseball cap and shoulders. He didn't blink.

'Dead wino,' said the cop.

'Looks like it,' said Shadow.

'Don't touch anything yet,' said the cop. 'Medical examiner should be here any time now. You ask me, the guy drank himself into a stupor and froze his ass.'

'Yes,' agreed Shadow. 'That's certainly what it looks like.'

He squatted down and looked at the bottle in Mad Sweeney's lap. Jameson Irish whiskey: a twenty dollar ticket out of this place. A small green Nissan pulled up, and a harassed middle-aged man with sandy hair and a sandy moustache got out, walked over. He touched the corpse's neck. *He kicks the corpse*, thought Shadow, *and if it doesn't kick him back . . .*

'He's dead,' said the medical examiner. 'Any ID?'

'He's a John Doe,' said the cop.

The medical examiner looked at Shadow. 'You working for Jacquel and Ibis?' he asked.

'Yes,' said Shadow.

'Tell Jacquel to get dentals and prints for ID and identity photos. We don't need a post. He should just draw blood for toxicology. Got that? Do you want me to write it down for you?'

'No,' said Shadow. 'It's fine. I can remember.'

The man scowled fleetingly, then pulled a business card from his wallet, scribbled on it, and gave it to Shadow, saying, 'Give this to Jacquel.' Then the medical examiner said 'Merry Christmas' to everyone, and was on his way. The cops kept the empty bottle.

Shadow signed for the John Doe and put it on the gurney. The body was pretty stiff, and Shadow couldn't get it out of a sitting position. He fiddled with the gurney, and found out that he could prop up one end. He strapped John Doe, sitting, to the gurney and put him in the back of the hearse, facing forward. Might as well give him a good ride. He closed the rear curtains. Then he drove back to the funeral home.

The hearse was stopped at a traffic light when Shadow heard a voice croak, 'And it's a fine wake I'll be wanting, with the best of everything, and beautiful women shedding tears and their clothes in their distress, and brave men lamenting and telling fine tales of me in my great days.'

'You're dead, Mad Sweeney,' said Shadow. 'You take what you're given when you're dead.'

'Aye, that I shall,' sighed the dead man sitting in the back of the hearse. The junkie whine had vanished from his voice now, replaced with a resigned flatness, as if the words were being broadcast from a long, long way away, dead words being sent out on a dead frequency.

The light turned green and Shadow put his foot gently down on the gas. 'But give me a wake tonight, nonetheless,' said Mad Sweeney. 'Set me a place at table, and give me a stinking drunk wake tonight. You killed me, Shadow, you owe me that much.'

'I never killed you, Mad Sweeney,' said Shadow. *It's twenty dollars,* he thought, *for a ticket out of here.* 'It was the drink and the cold killed you, not me.'

There was no reply, and there was silence in the car for the rest of the journey. After he parked at the back, Shadow wheeled the gurney out of the hearse and into the mortuary. He manhandled

Mad Sweeney onto the embalming table as if he were hauling a side of beef.

He covered the John Doe with a sheet and left him there, with the paperwork beside him. As he went up the back stairs he thought he heard a voice, quiet and muted, like a radio playing in a distant room, which said, 'And what would drink or cold be doing killing me, a leprechaun of the blood? No, it was you losing the little golden sun killed me, Shadow, killed me dead as sure as water's wet and days are long and a friend will always disappoint you in the end.'

Shadow wanted to point out to Mad Sweeney that that was a kind of bitter philosophy, but he suspected it was the being dead that made you bitter.

He went upstairs to the main house, where a number of middle-aged women were putting saranwrap on casserole dishes, popping the tupperware tops onto plastic pots of cooling fried potatoes and macaroni and cheese.

Mr Goodchild, the husband of the deceased, had Mr Ibis against a wall, and was telling him how he knew none of his children would come out to pay their respects to their mother. The apple don't fall far from the tree, he told anyone who would listen to him. The apple don't fall far from the tree.

That evening Shadow laid an extra place at the table. He put a glass at each place, and a bottle of Jameson Gold in the middle of the table. It was the most expensive Irish whiskey they sold at the liquor store. After they ate (a large platter of leftovers left for them by the women) Shadow poured a generous tot into each glass – his, Ibis's, Jacquel's and Mad Sweeney's.

'So what if he's sitting on a gurney in the cellar,' said Shadow, as he poured, 'on his way to a pauper's grave. Tonight we'll toast him, and give him the wake he wanted.'

Shadow raised his glass to the empty place at the table. 'I only met Mad Sweeney twice, alive,' he said. 'The first time I thought he was a world class jerk with the devil in him. The second time I thought he was a major fuckup and I gave him the money to kill himself. He showed me a coin trick I don't remember how to do, gave me some bruises, and claimed he was a leprechaun. Rest in peace, Mad Sweeney.' He sipped the whiskey, letting the smoky taste evaporate in his mouth. The other two drank, toasting the empty chair along with him.

Mr Ibis reached into an inside pocket and pulled out a notebook, which he flipped through until he found the appropriate page, and he read out a summarized version of Mad Sweeney's life.

According to Mr Ibis, Mad Sweeney had started his life as the guardian of a sacred rock in a small Irish glade, over three thousand years ago. Mr Ibis told them of Mad Sweeney's love affairs, his enmities, the madness that gave him his power ('a later version of the tale is still told, although the sacred nature, and the antiquity, of much of the verse has long been forgotten'), the worship and adoration in his own land that slowly transmuted into a guarded respect and then, finally into amusement; he told them the story of the girl from Bantry who came to the New World, and who brought her belief in Mad Sweeney the leprechaun with her, for hadn't she seen him of a night, down by the pool, and hadn't he smiled at her and called her by her own true name? She had become a refugee, in the hold of a ship of people who had watched their potatoes turn to black sludge in the ground, who had watched friends and lovers die of hunger, who dreamed of a land of full stomachs. The girl from Bantry Bay dreamed, specifically, of a city where a girl would be able to earn enough to bring her family over to the New World. Many of the Irish coming in to America thought of themselves as Catholics, even if they knew nothing of the catechism, even if all they knew of religion was the Bean Sidhe, the banshee, who came to wail at the walls of a house where death soon would be, and Saint Bride, who was once Bridget of the two sisters (each of the three was a Brigid, each was the same woman), and tales of Finn, of Oísin, of Conan the Bald – even of the leprechauns, the little people (and was that not the biggest joke of the Irish, for the leprechauns in their day were the tallest of the mound folk) . . .

All this and more Mr Ibis told them in the kitchen that night. His shadow on the wall was stretched and bird-like, and as the whiskey flowed Shadow imagined it the head of a huge water-fowl, beak long and curved, and it was somewhere in the middle of the second glass that Mad Sweeney himself began to throw both details and irrelevancies into Ibis's narrative ('. . . such a girl she was, with breasts cream-coloured and speckled with freckles, with the tips of them the rich reddish pink of the sunrise on a day when it'll be bucketing down before noon but glorious again by supper . . .') and then Sweeney was trying, with both hands, to explain the history of the gods in Ireland, wave after wave of them as they came in from Gaul and from Spain and from every damn place, each wave of them transforming the last gods into trolls and fairies and every damn creature until Holy Mother Church herself arrived and every god in Ireland was transformed into a fairy or a saint or a dead King without so much as a by-your-leave . . .

Mr Ibis polished his gold-rimmed spectacles and explained – enunciating even more clearly and precisely than usual, so Shadow knew he was drunk (his words, and the sweat that beaded on his forehead in that chilly house were the only indications of this) – with forefinger wagging, that he was an artist and that his tales should not be seen as literal constructs but as imaginative recreations, truer than the truth, and Mad Sweeney said 'I'll show you an imaginative recreation, my fist imaginatively recreating your fucken face for starters,' and Mr Jacquel bared his teeth and growled at Sweeney, the growl of a huge dog who's not looking for a fight but can always finish one by ripping out your throat, and Sweeney took the message and sat down and poured himself another glass of whiskey.

'Have you remembered how I do my little coin-trick?' he asked Shadow with a grin.

'I have not.'

'If you can guess how I did it,' said Mad Sweeney, his lips purple, his blue eyes beclouded, 'I'll tell you if you get warm.'

'It's not a palm is it?' asked Shadow.

'It is not.'

'Is it a gadget of some kind? Something up your sleeve or elsewhere that shoots the coins up for you to catch?'

'It is not that neither. More whiskey, anybody?'

'I read in a book about a way of doing the miser's dream with latex covering the palm of your hand, making a skin-coloured pouch for the coins to hide behind.'

'This is a sad wake for Great Sweeney who flew like a bird across all of Ireland and ate watercress in his madness: to be dead and unmourned save for a bird, a dog, and an idiot. No, it is not a pouch.'

'Well, that's pretty much it for ideas,' said Shadow. 'I expect you just take them out of nowhere.' It was meant to be sarcasm, but then he saw the expression on Sweeney's face. 'You *do*,' he said. 'You do take them from nowhere.'

'Well, not exactly nowhere,' said Mad Sweeney. 'But now you're getting the idea. You take them from the hoard.'

'The hoard,' said Shadow, starting to remember. 'Yes.'

'You just have to hold it in your mind, and it's yours to take from. The sun's treasure. It's there in those moments when the world makes a rainbow. It's there in the moment of eclipse and the moment of the storm.'

And he showed Shadow how to do the thing.

This time Shadow got it.

Shadow's head ached and pounded, and his tongue tasted and felt like flypaper. He squinted at the glare of the daylight. He had fallen asleep with his head on the kitchen table. He was fully dressed, although he had at some point taken off his black tie.

He walked downstairs, to the mortuary, and was relieved but unsurprised to see that John Doe was still on the embalming table. Shadow pried the empty bottle of Jameson Gold from the corpse's rigor-mortised fingers, and threw it away. He could hear someone moving about in the house above.

Mr Wednesday was sitting at the kitchen table when Shadow went upstairs. He was eating leftover potato salad from a tupperware container with a plastic spoon. He wore a dark grey suit, a white shirt and a deep grey tie: the morning sun glittered on the silver tie-pin in the shape of a tree. He smiled at Shadow when he saw him.

'Ah, Shadow m'boy, good to see you're up. I thought you were going to sleep forever.'

'Mad Sweeney's dead,' said Shadow.

'So I heard,' said Wednesday. 'A great pity. Of course it will come to all of us, in the end.' He tugged on an imaginary rope, somewhere on the level of his ear, and then jerked his neck to one side, tongue protruding, eyes bulging. As quick pantomimes went, it was disturbing. And then he let go of the rope and smiled his familiar grin. 'Would you like some potato salad?'

'I would not.' Shadow darted a look around the kitchen and out into the hall. 'Do you know where Ibis and Jacquel are?'

'Indeed I do. They are burying Mrs Lila Goodchild – something that they would probably have liked your help in doing, but I asked them not to wake you. You have a long drive ahead of you.'

'We're leaving?'

'Within the hour.'

'I should say goodbye.'

'Goodbyes are overrated. You'll see them again, I have no doubt, before this affair is done with.'

For the first time since that first night, Shadow observed, the small brown cat was curled up in her basket. She opened her incurious amber eyes and watched him go.

So Shadow left the house of the dead. Ice sheathed the winter-black bushes and trees as if they'd been insulated, made into dreams. The path was slippery.

Wednesday led the way to Shadow's white Chevy Nova, parked out on the road. It had been recently cleaned, and the Wisconsin plates had been removed, replaced with Minnesota plates. Wednesday's luggage was already stacked in the back seat. Wednesday unlocked the car with keys that were duplicates of the ones Shadow had in his own pocket.

'I'll drive,' said Wednesday. 'It'll be at least an hour before you're good for anything.'

They drove north, the Mississippi on their left, a wide silver stream beneath a grey sky. Shadow saw, perched on a leafless grey tree beside the road, a huge brown and white hawk, which stared down at them with mad eyes as they drove toward it, then took to the wing and rose in slow and powerful circles.

Shadow realised it had only been a temporary reprieve, his time in the house of the dead; and already it was beginning to feel like something that happened to somebody else, a long time ago.

Part 2

My Ainsel

Not to mention mythic creatures in the rubble . . .
– Wendy Cope, *A Policeman's Lot*

As they drove out of Illinois late that evening, Shadow asked Wednesday his first question. He saw the *Welcome to Wisconsin* sign, and said, 'So who were the guys that grabbed me in the parking lot? Mister Wood and Mister Stone? Who were they?'

The lights of the car illuminated the winter landscape. Wednesday had announced that they were not to take freeways because he didn't know whose side the freeways were on, so Shadow was sticking to back roads. He didn't mind. He wasn't even sure that Wednesday was crazy.

Wednesday grunted. 'Just spooks. Members of the opposition. Black hats.'

'I think,' said Shadow, 'that they think they're the white hats.'

'Of course they do. There's never been a true war that wasn't fought between two sets of people who were certain they were in the right. The really dangerous people believe that they are doing whatever they are doing solely and only because it is without question the right thing to do. And that is what makes them dangerous.'

'And *you*?' asked Shadow. 'Why are *you* doing what you're doing?'

'Because I want to,' said Wednesday. And then he grinned. 'So *that's* all right.'

Shadow said, 'How did you all get away? Or did you all get away?'

'We did,' said Wednesday. 'Although it was a close thing. If they'd not stopped to grab you, they might have taken the lot of us. It convinced several of the people who had been sitting on the fence that I might not be completely crazy.'

'So how did you get out?'

Wednesday shook his head. 'I don't pay you to ask questions,' he said. 'I've told you before.'

Shadow shrugged.

They spent the night in a Super 8 motel, south of La Crosse.

Christmas day was spent on the road, driving north and east. The farmland became pine forest. The towns seemed to come farther and farther apart.

They ate their Christmas lunch late in the afternoon in a hall-like family restaurant in Northern Central Wisconsin. Shadow picked cheerlessly at the dry turkey, jam-sweet red lumps of cranberry sauce, tough-as-wood roasted potatoes and the violently green canned peas. From the way he attacked it, and the way he smacked his lips, Wednesday seemed to be enjoying the food. As the meal progressed he became positively expansive – talking, joking, and, whenever she came close enough, flirting with the waitress, a thin blonde girl who looked scarcely old enough to have dropped out of high school.

'Excuse me, m'dear, but might I trouble you for another cup of your delightful hot chocolate? And I trust you won't think me too forward if I say what a mightily fetching and becoming dress that is. Festive, yet classy.'

The waitress, who wore a bright red and green skirt edged with glittering silver tinsel, giggled and coloured and smiled happily, and went off to get Wednesday another mug of hot chocolate.

'Fetching,' said Wednesday, thoughtfully, watching her go. 'Becoming,' he said. Shadow did not think he was talking about the dress. Wednesday shoveled the final slice of turkey into his mouth, flicked at his beard with his napkin, and pushed his plate forward. 'Aaah. Good.' He looked around him, at the family restaurant. In the background a tape of Christmas songs was playing: the little drummer boy had no gifts to bring, *parupapom-pom, rapappom pom, rapappom pom.*

'Some things may change,' said Wednesday, abruptly. 'People, however . . . people stay the same. Some grifts last forever, others are swallowed soon enough by time and by the world. My favourite grift of all is no longer practical. Still, a surprising number of grifts are timeless – the Spanish Prisoner, the Pigeon Drop, the Fawney Rig (that's the Pigeon Drop but with a gold ring instead of a wallet), the Fiddle Game . . .'

'I've never heard of the Fiddle Game,' said Shadow. 'I think I've heard of the others. My old cellmate said he'd actually done the Spanish Prisoner. He was a grifter.'

'Ah,' said Wednesday, and his left eye sparkled. 'The Fiddle Game was a fine and wonderful con. In its purest form it is a two man grift. It trades on cupidity and greed, as all great grifts do. You *can* always cheat an honest man, but it takes more work. So. We are in a hotel, or an Inn, or a fine restaurant, and, dining there, we find a man – shabby, but shabby genteel, not down-at-heel but certainly down on his luck. We shall call him Abraham. And when the time comes to settle his bill – not a huge bill, you understand, fifty, seventy-five dollars – an embarrassment! Where is his wallet? Good Lord he must have left it at a friend's, not far away. He shall go and obtain his wallet forthwith! But here, mine host, says Abraham, take this old fiddle of mine for security. It's old, as you can see, but it's how I make my living.'

Wednesday's smile when he saw the waitress approaching was huge and predatory. 'Ah, the hot chocolate! Brought to me by my Christmas Angel! Tell me my dear, could I have some more of your delicious bread when you get a moment?'

The waitress – what was she, Shadow wondered: sixteen, seventeen? – looked at the floor and her cheeks flushed crimson. She put down the chocolate with shaking hands and retreated to the edge of the room, by the slowly rotating display of pies, where she stopped and stared at Wednesday. Then she slipped into the kitchen, to fetch Wednesday his bread.

'So. The violin – old, unquestionably, perhaps even a little battered – is placed away in its case, and our temporarily impecunious Abraham sets off in search of his wallet. But a well-dressed gentleman, only just done with his own dinner, has been observing this exchange, and now he approaches our host: could he, perchance, inspect the violin that honest Abraham left behind?

'Certainly he can. Our host hands it over, and the well-dressed man – let us call him Barrington – opens his mouth wide, then remembers himself and closes it, examines the violin reverentially, like a man who has been permitted into a holy sanctum to examine the bones of a prophet. "Why!" he says, "this is – it *must* be – no, it *cannot* be – but *yes*, there it is – my *lord*! But this is *unbelievable*!" and he points to the maker's mark, on a strip of browning paper inside the violin – but still, he says, even without it he would have known it by the colour of the varnish, by the scroll, by the shape.

'Now Barrington reaches inside his pocket and produces an engraved business card, proclaiming him to be a preeminent dealer in rare and antique musical instruments. "So this violin is rare?" asks mine host. "Indeed it is," says Barrington, still admiring it with awe, "and worth in excess of a hundred thousand dollars, unless I miss my guess. Even as a dealer in such things I would pay fifty – no, seventy-five thousand dollars, good cash money for such an exquisite piece. I have a man on the West Coast who would buy it tomorrow, sight unseen, with one telegram, and pay whatever I asked for it." And then he consults his watch, and his face falls. "My train—" he says. "I have scarcely enough time to catch my train! Good sir, when the owner of this inestimable instrument should return, please give him my card, for, alas, I must be away." And with that, Barrington leaves, a man who knows that time and the train wait for no man.

'Mine host examines the violin, curiosity mingling with cupidity in his veins, and a plan begins to bubble up through his mind. But the minutes go by, and Abraham does not return. And now it is late, and through the door, shabby but proud, comes our Abraham, our fiddle-player, and he holds in his hands a wallet, a wallet that has seen better days, a wallet that has never contained more than a hundred dollars on its best day, and from it he takes the money to pay for his meal or his stay, and he asks for the return of his violin.

'Mine host puts the fiddle in its case on the counter, and Abraham takes it like a mother cradling her child. "Tell me," says the host (with the engraved card of a man who'll pay fifty thousand dollars, good cash money, burning in his inside breast pocket) "how much is a violin like this worth? For my niece has a yearning on her to play the fiddle, and it's her birthday coming up in a week or so."

'"Sell this fiddle?" says Abraham. "I could never sell her. I've had her for twenty years I have, fiddled in every state of the union with her. And to tell the truth, she cost me all of five hundred dollars back when I bought her."

'Mine host keeps the smile from his face. "Five hundred dollars? What if I were to offer you a thousand dollars for it, here and now?"

'The fiddle player looks delighted, then crestfallen, and he says "But lordy, I'm a fiddle player sir, it's all I know how to do. This fiddle knows me and she loves me, and my fingers know her so well I could play an air upon her in the dark. Where will I find another that sounds so fine? A thousand dollars is good money, but this is my livelihood. Not a thousand dollars, not for five thousand."

'Mine host sees his profits shrinking, but this is business, and you must spend money to make money. "Eight thousand dollars," he says. "It's not worth that, but I've taken a fancy to it, and I do love and indulge my niece."

'Abraham is almost in tears at the thought of losing his beloved fiddle, but how can he say no to eight thousand dollars? – especially when mine host goes to the wall-safe, and removes, not eight but *nine* thousand dollars, all neatly banded and ready to be slipped into the fiddle player's threadbare pocket. "You're a good man," he tells his host. "You're a saint! But you must swear to take care of my girl!" and, reluctantly, he hands over his violin.'

'But what if mine host simply hands over Barrington's card and tells Abraham that he's come into some good fortune?' asked Shadow.

'Then we're out the cost of two dinners,' said Wednesday. He wiped the remaining gravy and leftovers from his plate with a slice of bread, which he ate with lip-smacking relish.

'Let me see if I've got it straight,' said Shadow. 'So Abraham leaves, nine thousand dollars the richer, and in the parking lot by the train station he and Barrington meet up. They split the money, get into Barrington's Model-A Ford and head for the next town. I guess in the trunk of that car they must have a box filled with hundred-dollar violins.'

'I personally made it a point of honor never to pay more than five dollars for any of them,' said Wednesday. Then he turned to the hovering waitress. 'Now, my dear, regale us with your description of the sumptuous desserts available to us on this, our Lord's natal day.' He stared at her – it was almost a leer – as if nothing that she could offer him would be as toothsome a morsel as herself. Shadow felt deeply uncomfortable: it was like watching an old wolf stalking a fawn too young to know that if it did not run, and run now, it would wind up in a distant glade with its bones picked clean by the ravens.

The girl blushed once more and told them that dessert was apple pie à la mode – 'That's with a scoop of vanilla ice cream' – Christmas Cake à la mode, or a red and green whipped pudding. Wednesday stared into her eyes and told her that he would try the Christmas Cake à la mode. Shadow passed.

'Now, as grifts go,' said Wednesday, 'the fiddle game goes back three hundred years or more. And if you pick your chicken correctly you could still play it anywhere in America tomorrow.'

'I thought you said that your favorite grift was no longer practical,' said Shadow.

'I did indeed. However, that is not my favorite. No, my favorite was one they called The Bishop Game. It had everything: excitement, subterfuge, portability, surprise. Perhaps, I think from time to time, perhaps with a little modification, it might . . .' he thought for a moment, then shook his head. 'No. Its time has passed. It is, let us say, 1920, in a city of medium to large size – Chicago, perhaps, or New York, or Philadelphia. We are in a jeweler's emporium. A man dressed as a clergyman – and not just any clergyman, but a Bishop, in his purple, – enters and picks out a necklace – a gorgeous and glorious confection of diamonds and pearls, and pays for it with a dozen of the crispest hundred dollar bills.

'There's a smudge of green ink on the topmost bill and the store owner, apologetically but firmly, sends the stack of bills to the bank on the corner to be checked. Soon enough, the store clerk returns with the bills. The bank says they are none of them counterfeit. The owner apologises again, and the Bishop is most gracious, he well understands the problem, there are such lawless and ungodly types in the world today, such immorality and lewdness abroad in the world – and shameless women, and now that the underworld has crawled out of the gutter and come to live on the screens of the picture palaces what more could anyone expect? And the necklace is placed in its case, and the store owner does his best not to ponder why a bishop of the church would be purchasing a twelve-hundred dollar diamond necklace, nor why he would be paying good cash money for it.

'The Bishop bids him a hearty farewell, and walks out on the street, only for a heavy hand to descend on his shoulder. "Why Soapy, yez spalpeen, up to your old tricks are you?" and a broad beat cop with an honest Irish face walks the bishop back into the jewelery store.

"Beggin' your pardon, but has this man just bought anything from you?" asks the cop. "Certainly not," says the Bishop. "Tell him I have not." "Indeed he has," says the jeweler. "He bought a pearl and diamond necklace from me – paid for it in cash as well." "Would you have the bills available, sir?" asks the cop.

'So the jeweler takes the twelve hundred dollar bills from the cash register and hands them to the cop, who holds them up to the light and shakes his head in wonder. "Oh Soapy, Soapy," he says, "these are the finest that you've made yet! You're a craftsman, that you are!"

'A self-satisfied smile spreads across the Bishop's face. "You can't prove nothing," says the Bishop. "And the bank said that they were on the level. It's the real green stuff." "I'm sure they did," agrees the cop on the beat, "but I doubt that the bank had been warned that Soapy Sylvester was in town, nor of the quality of the hundred dollar bills he'd been passing in Denver and in St. Louis." And with that he reaches into the Bishop's pocket and pulls out the necklace. "Twelve hundred dollars worth of diamonds and pearls in exchange for fifty cents worth of paper and ink," says the policeman, who is obviously a philosopher at heart. "And passing yourself off as a man of the church. You should be ashamed," he says, as he claps the handcuffs on the Bishop, who is obviously no bishop, and he marches him away, but not before he gives the jeweler a receipt for both the necklace and the twelve hundred counterfeit dollars. It's evidence, after all.'

'Was it really counterfeit?' asked Shadow.

'Of course not! Fresh banknotes, straight from the bank, only with a thumbprint and a smudge of green ink on a couple of them to make them a little more interesting.'

Shadow sipped his coffee. It was worse than prison coffee. 'So the cop was obviously no cop. And the necklace?'

'Evidence,' said Wednesday. He unscrewed the top from the salt-shaker, poured a little heap of salt on the table. 'But the jeweler gets a receipt, and assurance that he'll get the necklace straight back as soon as Soapy comes to trial. He is congratulated on being a good citizen, and he watches, proudly, already thinking of the tale he'll have to tell at the next meeting of the Oddfellows tomorrow night, as the policeman marches the man pretending to be a bishop out of the store, twelve hundred dollars in one pocket, a twelve hundred dollar diamond necklace in the other, on their way to a police station that'll never see hide nor hair of either of them.'

The waitress had returned to clear the table. 'Tell me my dear,' said Wednesday. 'Are you married?'

She shook her head.

'Astonishing that a young lady of such loveliness has not yet been snapped up.' He was doodling with his fingernail in the spilled salt, making squat, blocky rune-like shapes. The waitress stood passively beside him, reminding Shadow less of a fawn and more of a young rabbit caught in a eighteen-wheeler's headlights, frozen in fear and indecision.

Wednesday lowered his voice, so much so that Shadow, only across the table, could barely hear him. 'What time do you get off work?'

'Nine,' she said, and swallowed. 'Nine thirty latest.'

'And what is the finest motel in this area?'

'There's a Motel 6,' she said. 'It's not much.'

Wednesday touched the back of her hand, fleetingly, with the tips of his fingers, leaving crumbs of salt on her skin. She made no attempt to wipe them off. 'To us,' he said, his voice an almost inaudible rumble, 'it shall be a pleasure-palace.'

The waitress looked at him. She bit her thin lips, hesitated, then nodded and fled for the kitchen.

'C'mon,' said Shadow. 'She looks barely legal.'

'I've never been overly concerned about legality,' Wednesday told him. 'And I need her, not as an end in herself, but to wake me up a little. Even King David knew that there is one easy prescription to get warm blood flowing through an old frame: take one virgin, call me in the morning.'

Shadow caught himself wondering if the girl on night duty in the hotel back in Eagle Point had been a virgin. 'Don't you ever worry about disease?' he asked. 'What if you knock her up? What if she's got a brother?'

'No,' said Wednesday. 'I don't worry about diseases. I don't catch them. Unfortunately – for the most part – people like me fire blanks, so there's not a great deal of interbreeding. It used to happen in the old days. Nowadays, it's possible, but so unlikely as to be almost unimaginable. So no worries there. And many girls have brothers, and fathers. It's not my problem. Ninety-nine times out of a hundred, I've left town already.'

'So we're staying here for the night?'

Wednesday rubbed his chin. 'I shall stay in the Motel 6,' he said. Then he put his hand into his coat pocket. He pulled out a front door key, bronze-coloured, with a card tag attached on which was typed an address: *502 Northridge Rd, Apt #3*. 'You, on the other hand, have an apartment waiting for you, in a city far from here.' Wednesday closed his eyes for a moment. Then he opened them, grey and gleaming and fractionally mismatched, and he said 'The Greyhound bus will be coming through town in twenty minutes. It stops at the gas station. Here's your ticket.' He pulled out a folded bus ticket, passed it across the table. Shadow picked it up and looked at it.

'Who's Mike Ainsel?' he asked. That was the name on the ticket.

'You are. Happy Christmas.'

'And where's Lakeside?'

'Your happy home in the months to come. And now, because good things come in threes . . .' He took a small, gift-wrapped package from his pocket, pushed it across the table. It sat beside the ketchup bottle with the black smears of dried ketchup on the top. Shadow made no move to take it.

'Well?'

Reluctantly, Shadow tore open the red wrapping paper, to reveal a fawn-coloured calf-skin wallet, shiny from use. It was obviously somebody's wallet. Inside the wallet was a driver's license with Shadow's photograph on it, in the name of Michael Ainsel, with a Milwaukee address, a MasterCard for M. Ainsel, and twenty crisp fifty dollar bills. Shadow closed the wallet, put it into an inside pocket.

'Thanks,' he said.

'Think of it as a Christmas Bonus. Now, let me walk you down to the Greyhound. I shall wave to you as you ride the grey dog north.'

They walked outside the restaurant. Shadow found it hard to believe how much colder it had gotten in the last few hours. It felt too cold to snow, now. Aggressively cold. This was a bad winter.

'Hey. Wednesday. Both of the scams you were telling me about – the violin scam and the bishop one, the bishop and the cop—' he hesitated, trying to form his thought, to bring it into focus.

'What of them?'

Then he had it. 'They're both two-man scams. One guy on each side. Did you used to have a partner?' Shadow's breath came in clouds. He promised himself that when he got to Lakeside he would spend some of his Christmas bonus on the warmest, thickest winter coat that money could buy.

'Yes,' said Wednesday. 'Yes. I had a partner. A junior partner. But, alas, those days are gone. *There's* the gas station, and *there*, unless my eye deceives me, is the bus.' It was already signaling its turn into the parking lot. 'Your address is on the key,' said Wednesday. 'If anyone asks, I am your Uncle, and I shall be rejoicing in the unlikely name of Emerson Borson. Settle in, in Lakeside, nephew Ainsel. I'll come for you within the week. We shall be travelling together. Visiting the people I have to visit. In the meantime, keep your head down and stay out of trouble.'

'My car—?' said Shadow.

'I'll take good care of it. Have a good time in Lakeside,' said Wednesday. He thrust out his hand, and Shadow shook it. Wednesday's hand was colder than a corpse's.

'Jesus,' said Shadow. 'You're cold.'

'Then the sooner I am making the two-backed beast with the little hotsy-totsy lass from the restaurant in a back room of the Motel 6, the better.' And he reached out his other hand and squeezed Shadow's shoulder.

Shadow experienced a dizzying moment of double vision: he saw the grizzled man facing him, squeezing his shoulder, but he saw something else: so many winters, hundreds and hundreds of winters, and a grey man in a broad-brimmed hat walking from settlement to settlement, leaning on his staff, staring in through windows at the firelight at a joy and a burning life he would never be able to touch, never even be able to feel. . . .

'Go,' said Wednesday, his voice a reassuring growl. 'All is well, and all is well, and all shall be well.'

Shadow showed his ticket to the driver. 'Hell of a day to be travelling,' she said. And then she added, with a certain grim satisfaction, 'Merry Christmas.'

The bus was almost empty. 'When will we get in to Lakeside?' asked Shadow.

'Two hours. Maybe a bit more,' said the driver. 'They say there's a cold snap coming.' She thumbed a switch and the doors closed with a hiss and a thump.

Shadow walked half-way down the bus, put the seat back as far as it would go, and he started to think. The motion of the bus and the warmth combined to lull him, and before he was aware that he was becoming sleepy, he was asleep.

In the earth, and under the earth. The marks on the wall were the red of wet clay: hand prints, finger-marks and, here and there, crude representations of animals and people and birds.

The fire still burned and the buffalo man still sat on the other side of the fire, staring at Shadow with huge eyes, eyes like pools of dark mud. The buffalo lips, fringed with matted brown hair, did not move as the buffalo voice said, 'Well, Shadow? Do you believe yet?'

'I don't know,' said Shadow. His mouth had not moved either, he observed. Whatever words were passing between the two of them were not being spoken, not in any way that Shadow understood speech. 'Are you real?'

'Believe,' said the buffalo man.

'Are you . . .' Shadow hesitated, and then he asked, 'Are you a god too?'

The buffalo man reached one hand into the flames of the fire and he pulled out a burning brand. He held the brand in the middle. Blue and yellow flames licked his red hand, but they did not burn.

'This is not a land for gods,' said the buffalo man. But it was not the buffalo man talking any more, Shadow knew, in his dream: it was the fire speaking, the crackling and the burning of the flame itself that spoke to Shadow in the dark place under the earth.

'This land was brought up from the depths of the ocean by a diver,' said the fire. 'It was spun from its own substance by a spider. It was shat by a raven. It is the body of a fallen father, whose bones are mountains, whose eyes are lakes.

'This is a land of dreams and fire,' said the flame.

The buffalo man put the brand back on the fire.

'Why are you telling me this stuff?' said Shadow. 'I'm not important. I'm not anything. I was an okay physical trainer, a really lousy small-time crook and maybe not so good a husband as I thought I was . . .' He trailed off.

'How do I help Laura?' Shadow asked the buffalo man. 'She wants to be alive again. I said I'd help her. I owe her that.'

The buffalo man said nothing. He pointed up toward the roof of the cave. Shadow's eyes followed. There was a thin, wintery light coming from a tiny opening far above.

'Up there?' asked Shadow, wishing that one of his questions would be answered. 'I'm supposed to go up there?'

The dream took him then, the idea becoming the thing itself, and Shadow was crushed into the rock and earth. He was like a mole, trying to push through the earth, like a badger, climbing through the earth, like a groundhog, pushing the earth out of his way, like a bear, but the earth was too hard, too dense, and his breath was coming in gasps, and soon he could go no further, dig and climb no more, and he knew then that he would die, somewhere in the deep place beneath the world.

His own strength was not enough. His efforts became weaker. He knew that though his body was riding in a hot bus through cold woods if he stopped breathing here, beneath the world, he would stop breathing there as well, that even now his breath was coming in shallow panting gasps.

He struggled and he pushed, ever more weakly, each movement using precious air. He was trapped: could go no further, and could not return the way that he had come.

'Now bargain,' said a voice in his mind.

'What do I have to bargain with?' Shadow asked. 'I have nothing.' He could taste the clay now, thick and mud-gritty in his mouth.

And then Shadow said, 'Except myself. I have myself, don't I?'

It seemed as if everything was holding its breath.

'I offer myself,' he said.

The response was immediate. The rocks and the earth that had surrounded him began to push down on Shadow, squeezed him so hard that the last ounce of air in his lungs was crushed out of him. The pressure became pain, pushing him on every side. He reached the zenith of pain and hung there, cresting, knowing that he could take no more, at that moment the spasm eased and Shadow could breathe again. The light above him had grown larger.

He was being pushed toward the surface.

As the next earth-spasm hit, Shadow tried to ride with it. This time he felt himself being pushed upward.

The pain, on that last awful contraction, was impossible to believe, as he felt himself being squeezed, crushed and pushed through an unyielding rock gap, his bones shattering, his flesh becoming something shapeless. As his mouth and ruined head cleared the hole he began to scream, in fear and pain.

He wondered, as he screamed, whether, back in the waking world, he was also screaming – if he were screaming in his sleep back on the darkened bus.

And as that final spasm ended Shadow was on the ground, his fingers clutching the red earth.

He pulled himself into a sitting position, wiped the earth from his face with his hand and looked up at the sky. It was twilight, a long, purple twilight, and the stars were coming out, one by one, stars so much brighter and more vivid than any stars he had ever seen or imagined.

'Soon,' said the crackling voice of the flame, coming from behind him, 'they will fall. Soon they will fall and the star people will meet the earth people. There will be heroes among them, and men who will slay monsters and bring knowledge, but none of them will be gods. This is a poor place for gods.'

A blast of air, shocking in its coldness, touched his face. It was like being doused in ice water. He could hear the driver's voice saying that they were in Pinewood, anyone who needed a cigarette or wanted to stretch their legs, we'll be stopping here for ten minutes then we'll be back on the road.

Shadow stumbled off the bus. They were parked outside another rural gas station, almost identical to the one they had left. The driver was helping a couple of teenage girls onto the bus, putting their suitcases away in the luggage compartment.

'Hey,' the driver said, when she saw Shadow. 'You're getting off at Lakeside, right?'

Shadow agreed, sleepily, that he was.

'Heck, that's a *good* town,' said the bus-driver. 'I think sometimes that if I were just going to pack it all in, I'd move to Lakeside. Prettiest town I've ever seen. You've lived there long?'

'My first visit.'

'You have a pasty at Mabel's for me, you hear?'

Shadow decided not to ask for clarification. 'Tell me,' said Shadow, 'was I talking in my sleep?'

'If you were, I didn't hear you.' She looked at her watch. 'Back on the bus. I'll call you when we get to Lakeside.'

The two girls – he doubted that either of them was much more than fourteen years old – who had got on in Pinewood were now in the seat in front of him. They were friends, Shadow decided, eaves-dropping without meaning to, not sisters. One of them knew almost nothing about sex, but knew a lot about animals, helped out or spent a lot of time at some kind of animal shelter, while the other was not interested in animals, but, armed with a hundred tidbits gleaned from the internet and from daytime television, thought she knew a great deal about human sexuality. Shadow listened with a horrified and amused fascination to the one who thought she was wise in the ways of the world detail the precise mechanics of using Alka-Seltzer tablets to enhance oral sex.

Shadow started to tune them out, blanked everything except the noise of the road, and now only fragments of conversation would come back every now and again.

Goldie is, like, such a good dog, and he was a purebred retriever, if only my dad would say okay, he wags his tail whenever he sees me.

It's Christmas, he has to let me use the snowmobile.

You can write your name with your tongue on the side of his thing.

I miss Sandy.

Yeah, I miss Sandy too.

Six inches tonight they said, but they just make it up, they make up the weather and nobody ever calls them on it . . .

And then the brakes of the bus were hissing and the driver was shouting 'Lakeside!' and the doors clunked open. Shadow followed the girls out into the floodlit parking lot of a video store and tanning salon that functioned, Shadow guessed, as Lakeside's Greyhound station. The air was dreadfully cold, but it was a fresh cold. It woke him up. He stared at the lights of the town to the south and the west, and pale expanse of a frozen lake to the east.

The girls were standing in the lot, stamping and blowing on their hands dramatically. One of them, the younger one, snuck a look at Shadow, smiled awkwardly when she realised that he had seen her do so.

'Merry Christmas,' said Shadow.

'Yeah,' said the other girl, perhaps a year or so older than the first, 'Merry Christmas to you too.' She had carroty red hair and a snub nose covered with a hundred thousand freckles.

'Nice town you got here,' said Shadow.

'We like it,' said the younger one. She was the one who liked animals. She gave Shadow a shy grin, revealing blue rubber band braces stretching across her front teeth. 'You look like somebody,' she told him, gravely. 'Are you somebody's brother or somebody's son or something?'

'You are such a spaz Alison,' said her friend. 'Everybody's some-body's son or brother or *something*.'

'That wasn't what I meant,' said Alison. Headlights framed them all for one brilliant white moment. Behind the headlights was a station wagon with a mother in it, and in moments it took the girls and their bags away, leaving Shadow standing alone in the parking lot.

'Young man? Anything I can do for you?' The old man was locking up the video store. He pocketed his keys. 'Store ain't open Christmas,' he told Shadow cheerfully. 'But I come down to meet the bus. Make sure everything was okay. Couldn't live with myself if some poor soul'd found 'emselves stranded on Christmas Day.' He was close enough that Shadow could see his face: old but contented, the face of a man who had sipped life's vinegar and found it, by and large, to be mostly whiskey, and good whiskey at that.

'Well, you could give me the number of the local taxi company,' said Shadow.

'I *could*,' said the old man, doubtfully, 'but Tom'll be in his bed this time of night, and even if you could rouse him you'll get no satisfaction – I saw him down at the Buck Stops Here earlier this evening, and he was very merry. Very merry indeed. Where is it you're aiming to go?'

Shadow showed him the address tag on the door key.

'Well,' he said, 'that's a ten, mebbe a twenty minute walk over the bridge and around. But it's no fun when it's this cold, and when you don't know where you're going it always seems longer – you ever notice that? First time takes forever, and then ever after it's over in a flash?'

'Yes,' said Shadow. 'I've never thought of it like that. But I guess it's true.'

The old man nodded. His face cracked into a grin. 'What the heck, it's Christmas. I'll run you over there in Tessie.'

Shadow followed the old man to the road, where a huge old roadster was parked. It looked like something that gangsters might have been proud to drive in the Roaring Twenties, running boards and all. It was a deep dark colour under the sodium lights that might have been red and might have been green. 'This is Tessie,' the old man said. 'Ain't she a beaut?' He patted her proprietorially, where the hood curved up and arched over the front nearside wheel.

'What make is she?' asked Shadow.

'She's a Wendt Phoenix. Wendt went under in 'thirty one, name was bought by Chrysler, but they never made any more Wendts. Harvey Wendt, who founded the company, was a local boy. Went out to California, killed himself in, oh, Nineteen Forty One, Forty Two. Great tragedy.'

The car smelled of leather and old cigarette smoke – not a fresh smell, but as if enough people had smoked enough cigarettes and cigars in the car over the years that the smell of burning tobacco had become part of the fabric of the car. The old man turned the key in the ignition and Tessie started first time.

'Tomorrow,' he told Shadow, 'she goes into the garage. I'll cover her with a dust sheet, and that's where she'll stay until spring. Truth of the matter is I shouldn't be driving her right now, with the snow on the ground.'

'Doesn't she ride well in snow?'

'Rides just fine. It's the salt they put on the roads. Rusts these old beauties faster than you could believe. You want to go door to door, or would you like the moonlight grand tour of the town?'

'I don't want to trouble you—'

'It's no trouble. You get to be my age, you're grateful for the least wink of sleep. I'm lucky if I get five hours a night nowadays – wake up and my mind is just turning and turning. Where are my manners? My name's Hinzelmann. I'd say, call me Richie, but round here folks who know me just call me plain Hinzelmann. I'd shake your hand, but I need two hands to drive Tessie. She knows when I'm not paying attention.'

'Mike Ainsel,' said Shadow. 'Pleased to meet you, Hinzelmann.'

'So we'll go round the lake. Grand tour,' said Hinzelmann.

Main Street, which they were on, was a pretty street, even at night, and it looked old-fashioned in the best sense of the word – as if, for a hundred years, people had been caring for that street and they had not been in a hurry to lose anything they liked.

Hinzelmann pointed out the town's two restaurants as they passed them (a German restaurant and what he described as 'part Greek, part Norwegian, and a popover at every plate'); he pointed out the bakery and the bookstore ('What I say is, a town isn't a town without a bookstore. It may call itself a town, but unless it's got a bookstore, it knows it's not fooling a soul.') He slowed Tessie as they passed the library so Shadow could get a good look at it. Antique gas lights flickered over the doorway – Hinzelmann proudly called Shadow's attention to them. 'Built in the 1870s by John Henning, local lumber baron. He wanted it called the Henning Memorial Library, but when he died they started calling it the Lakeside Library, and I guess it'll be the Lakeside Library now until the end of time. Isn't it a dream?' He couldn't have been prouder of it if he had built it himself. The building reminded Shadow of a castle, and he said so. 'That's right,' agreed Hinzelmann. 'Turrets and all. Henning wanted it to look like that on the outside. Inside they still have all the original pine shelving. Miriam Shultz wants to tear the insides out and modernize, but it's on some register of historic places, and there's not a damn thing she can do.'

They drove around the south side of the lake. The town circled the lake, which was a thirty foot drop below the level of the road. Shadow could see the patches of white ice dulling the surface of the lake with, here and there, a shiny patch of water reflecting the lights of the town.

'Looks like it's freezing over,' he said.

'It's been frozen over for a month now,' said Hinzelmann. 'The dull spots are snowdrifts and the shiny spots are ice. It froze just after Thanksgiving in one cold night, froze smooth as glass. You do much ice-fishing Mr Ainsel?'

'Never.'

'Best thing a man can do. It's not the fish you catch, it's the peace of mind that you take home at the end of the day.'

'I'll remember that.' Shadow peered down at the lake through Tessie's window. 'Can you actually walk on it already?'

'You can walk on it. Drive on it too, but I wouldn't want to risk it yet. It's been cold up here for six weeks,' said Hinzelmann. 'But you also got to allow that things freeze harder and faster up here in Northern Wisconsin than they do most anyplace else there is. I was out hunting once – hunting for deer, and this was oh, thirty, forty years back, and I shot at a buck, missed him and sent him running off through the woods – this was over across the north end of the lake, up near where you'll be living, Mike. Now he was the finest buck I ever did see, twenty point, big as a small horse, no lie. Now, I'm younger and feistier back then than I am now, and though it had started snowing before Hallowe'en that year, now it was Thanksgiving and there was clean snow on the ground, fresh as anything, and I could see the buck's footprints. It looked to me like the big fellow was heading for the lake in a panic.

'Well, only a damn fool tries to run down a buck, but there am I, a damn fool, running after him, and there he is, standing in the lake, in oh, eight, nine inches of water, and he's just looking at me. That very moment, the sun goes behind a cloud, and the freeze comes – temperature must have fallen thirty degrees in ten minutes, not a word of a lie. And that old stag, he gets ready to run, and he can't move. He's frozen into the ice.

'Me, I just walk over to him slowly. You can see he wants to run, but he's iced in and it just isn't going to happen. But there's no way I can bring myself to shoot a defenseless critter when he can't get away – what kind of man would I be if I done that, heh? So I takes my shotgun and I fires off one shell, straight up into the air.

'Well the noise and the shock is enough to make that buck just about jump out of his skin, and seein' that his legs are iced in, that's just what he proceeds to do. He leaves his hide and his antlers stuck to the ice, while he charges back into the woods, pink as a newborn mouse and shivering fit to bust.

'I felt bad enough for that old buck that I talked the Lakeside Ladies Knitting Circle into making him something warm to wear all the winter, and they knitted him an all-over one piece woollen suit, so he wouldn't freeze to death. Course the joke was on us, because they knitted him a suit of bright orange wool so no hunter ever shot at it. Hunters in these parts wear orange at hunting season,' he added, helpfully. 'And if you think there's a word of a lie in that, I can prove it to you. I've got the antlers up on my rec room wall to this day.'

Shadow laughed, and the old man smiled the satisfied smile of a master craftsman. They pulled up outside a brick building with a large wooden deck, from which golden holiday lights hung and twinkled invitingly.

'That's Five-Oh-Two,' said Hinzelmann. 'Apartment three would be on the top floor, round the other side, overlooking the lake. There you go, Mike.'

'Thank you, Mr Hinzelmann. Can I give you anything toward gas?'

'Just Hinzelmann. And you don't owe me a penny. Merry Christmas from me and from Tessie.'

'Are you sure you won't accept anything?'

The old man scratched his chin. 'Tell you what,' he said. 'Sometime in the next week or so I'll come by and sell you some tickets. For our raffle. Charity. For now, young man, you can be getting on to bed.'

Shadow smiled. 'Merry Christmas, Hinzelmann,' he said.

The old man shook Shadow's hand with one red-knuckled hand. It felt as hard and as calloused as an oak-branch. 'Now, you watch the path as you go up there, it's going to be slippery. I can see your door from here, at the side there, see it? I'll just wait in the car down here until you're safely inside. You just give me the thumbs up when you're in okay, and I'll drive off.'

He kept the Wendt idling, until Shadow was safely up the wooden steps on the side of the house, and had opened the apartment door with his key. The door to the apartment swung open. Shadow made a thumbs up sign and the old man in the Wendt – Tessie, thought Shadow, and the thought of a car with a name made him smile one more time – Hinzelmann and Tessie swung around and made their way back across the bridge.

Shadow shut the front door. The room was freezing. It smelled of people who had gone away to live other lives, and of all they had eaten and dreamed. He found the thermostat and cranked it up to 70 degrees. He went into the tiny kitchen, checked the drawers, opened the avocado-coloured refrigerator, but it was empty. No surprise there. At least the fridge smelled clean inside, not musty.

There was a small bedroom with a bare mattress in it, beside the kitchen, next to an even tinier bathroom that was mostly shower stall. An aged cigarette butt sat in the toilet bowl, staining the water brown. Shadow flushed it away.

He found sheets and blankets in a closet, and made the bed. Then he took off his shoes, his jacket and his watch, and he climbed into the bed fully dressed, wondering how long it would take him to get warm.

The lights were off, and there was silence, mostly, nothing but the hum of the refrigerator, and somewhere in the building, a radio playing. He lay there in the darkness, wondering if he had slept himself out on the Greyhound, if the hunger and the cold and the new bed and the craziness of the last few weeks would combine to keep him awake that night.

In the stillness he heard something snap like a shot. A branch, he thought, or the ice. It was freezing out there.

He wondered how long he would have to wait until Wednesday came for him. A day? A week? However long he had, he knew he had to focus on something in the meantime. He would start to work out again, he decided, and practice his coin sleights and palms until he was smooth as anything (*practice all your tricks*, somebody whispered inside his head, in a voice that was not his own, *all of them but one, not the trick that poor dead Mad Sweeney showed you, dead of exposure and the cold and of being forgotten and surplus to requirements, not that trick. Oh not that one*).

But this *was* a good town. He could feel it.

He thought of his dream, if it had been a dream, that first night in Cairo. He thought of Zorya . . . what the hell was her name? The midnight sister.

And then he thought of Laura . . .

It was as if thinking of her opened a window in his mind. He could see her. He could, somehow, see her.

She was in Eagle Point, in the back yard outside her mother's big house.

She stood in the cold, which she did not feel any more, or which she felt all the time, she stood outside the house that her mother had bought in 1989 with the insurance money after Laura's father, Harvey McCabe, had passed on, a heart attack while straining on the can, and she was staring in, her cold hands pressed against the glass, her breath not fogging it, not at all, watching her mother, and her sister and her sister's children and husband in from Texas, home for Christmas. Out in the darkness, that was where Laura was, unable not to look.

Tears prickled in Shadow's eyes, and he rolled over in his bed.

He felt like a Peeping Tom, turned his thoughts away, willed them to come back to him: he could see the lake spread out below him as the wind blew down from the arctic, prying jack-frost fingers a hundred times colder than the fingers of any corpse.

Shadow's breath came shallowly now. He could hear a wind rising, a bitter screaming around the house, and for a moment he thought he could hear words on the wind.

If he was going to be anywhere, he might as well be here, he thought, and then he slept.

Meanwhile. A Conversation.

Dingdong.

'Mizz Crow?'

'Yes.'

'Mizz Samantha Black Crow?'

'Yes.'

'Do you mind if we ask you a few questions, Ma'am.'

'Are you cops? What are you?'

'My name is Town. My colleague here is Mister Road. We're investigating the disappearance of two of our associates.'

'What were their names?'

'I'm sorry.'

'Tell me their names. I want to know what they were called. Your associates. Tell me their names and maybe I'll help you.'

' . . . okay. Their names were Mister Stone, and Mister Wood. Now, can we ask you some questions?'

'Do you guys just see things and pick names? "Oh, you be Mister Sidewalk, he's Mister Carpet, say hello to Mister Airplane"?'

'Very funny, young lady. First question: we need to know if you've seen this man. Here. You can hold the photograph.'

'Whoah. Straight on and profile, with numbers on the bottom . . . And big. He's cute, though. What did he do?'

'He was mixed up in a small town bank robbery, as a driver, some years ago. His two colleagues decided to keep all the loot for themselves and ran out on him. He got angry. Found them. Came close to killing them with his hands. The state cut a deal with the men he hurt: they testified against him. Shadow here got six years. He served three. You ask me, guys like that, they should just lock them up and throw away the key.'

'I've never heard anyone say that in real life, you know. Not out loud.'

'Say what, Mizz Crow?'

'*Loot*. It's not a word you ever hear people say. Maybe in movies people say it. Not for real.'

'This isn't a movie, Mizz Crow.'

'Black Crow. It's Mizz Black Crow. My friends call me Sam.'

'Got it, Sam. Now about this man—'

'But you aren't my friends. You can call me Mizz Black Crow.'

'Listen, you snotnosed little—'

'It's okay, Mister Road. Sam here – pardon, Ma'am, – I mean, Mizz Black Crow wants to help us. She's a law abiding citizen.'

'Ma'am, we know you helped Shadow. You were seen with him, in a white Chevy Nova. He gave you a ride. He bought you dinner. Did he say anything that could help us in our investigation? Two of our best men have vanished.'

'I never met him.'

'You met him. Please don't make the mistake of thinking we're stupid. We aren't stupid.'

'Mm. I meet a lot of people. Maybe I met him and forgot already.'

'Ma'am, it really is to your advantage to cooperate with us.'

'Otherwise, you'll have to introduce me to your friends Mister Thumbscrews and Mister Pentothal?'

'Ma'am, you aren't making this any easier on yourself.'

'Gee. I'm sorry. Now, is there anything else? 'Cos I'm going to say "buh-bye now" and close the door and I figure you two are going to go and get into Mister Car and drive away.'

'Your lack of cooperation has been noted, ma'am.'

'Buh-bye now.'

Click.

10

I'll tell you all my secrets
But I lie about my past
So send me off to bed forever more
— Tom Waits, *Tango Till They're Sore*

A whole life in darkness, surrounded by filth, that was what Shadow dreamed, his first night in Lakeside. A child's life, long ago and far away, in a land across the ocean, in the lands where the sun rose. But this life contained no sunrises, only dimness by day and blindness by night.

Nobody spoke to him. He heard human voices, from outside, but could understand human speech no better than he understood the howling of the owls or the yelps of dogs.

He remembered, or thought he remembered, one night, half a lifetime ago, when one of the big people had entered, quietly, and had not cuffed him or fed him, but had picked him up to her breast and embraced him. She smelled good. Hot drops of water had fallen from her face to his. He had been scared, and had wailed loudly in his fear.

She put him down on the straw, hurriedly, and left the hut, fastening the door behind her.

He remembered that moment, and he treasured it, just as he remembered the sweetness of a cabbage-heart, the tart taste of plums, the crunch of apples, the greasy delight of roasted fish.

And now he saw the faces in the firelight, all of them looking at him as he was led out from the hut for the first time, which was the only time. So that was what people looked like. Raised in darkness, he had never seen faces. Everything was so new. So strange. The bonfire light hurt his eyes. They pulled on the rope around his neck, to lead him to the place where the man waited for him.

And when the first blade was raised in the firelight, what a cheer went up from the crowd. The child from the darkness began to laugh with them, in delight and in freedom.

And then the blade came down.

Shadow opened his eyes and realised that he was hungry and cold, in an apartment with a layer of ice clouding the inside of the window glass. His frozen breath, he thought. He got out of bed, pleased he did not have to get dressed. He scraped at a window with a finger-nail as he passed, felt the ice collect under the nail, then melt to water.

He tried to remember his dream, but remembered nothing but misery and darkness.

He put on his shoes. He figured he would walk into the town centre, walk across the bridge across the northern end of the lake, if he had the geography of the town right. He put on his thin jacket, remembering his promise to himself that he would buy himself a warm winter coat, opened the apartment door and stepped out onto the wooden deck. The cold took his breath away: he breathed in, and felt every hair in his nostrils freeze into rigidity. The deck gave him a fine view of the lake, irregular patches of grey surrounded by an expanse of white.

The cold snap had come, that was for sure. It could not be much above zero, and it would not be a pleasant walk, but he was certain he could make it into town without too much trouble. What did Hinzelmann say last night – a ten minute walk? And Shadow was a big man. He would walk briskly and keep himself warm.

He set off south, heading for the bridge.

Soon he began to cough, a dry, thin cough, as the bitterly cold air touched his lungs. Soon his ears and face and lips hurt, and then his feet hurt. He thrust his ungloved hands deep into his coat pockets, clenched his fingers together trying to find some warmth. He found himself remembering Low Key Lyesmith's tall tales of the Minnesota winters – particularly the one about a hunter treed by a bear during a hard freeze who took out his dick and pissed an arching yellow stream of steaming urine that was already frozen hard before it hit the ground, then slid down the rock-hard frozen-piss-pole to freedom. A wry smile at the memory and another dry, painful cough.

Step after step after step. He glanced back. The apartment building was not as far away as he had expected.

This walk, he decided, was a mistake. But he was already three or four minutes from the apartment, and the bridge over the lake was in sight. It made as much sense to press on as to go home (and then what? Call a taxi on the dead phone? Wait for spring? He had no food in the apartment, he reminded himself).

He kept walking, revising his estimates of the temperature downward as he walked. Minus Ten? Minus Twenty? Minus Forty, maybe, that strange point on the thermometer when Celsius and Fahrenheit say the same thing. Probably not that cold. But then there was wind chill, and the wind was now hard and steady and continuous, blowing over the lake, coming down from the Arctic across Canada.

He remembered, enviously, the chemical hand- and foot-warmers. He wished he had them now.

Ten more minutes of walking, he guessed, and the bridge seemed to be no nearer. He was too cold to shiver. His eyes hurt. This was not simply cold: this was science fiction. This was a story set on the dark side of Mercury, back when they thought Mercury had a dark side. This was somewhere out on rocky Pluto, where the sun is just another star, shining only a little more brightly in the darkness. This, thought Shadow, is just a hair away from the places where air comes in buckets and pours just like beer.

The occasional cars that roared past him seemed unreal: space ships, little freeze-dried packages of metal and glass, inhabited by people dressed more warmly than he was. An old song his mother had loved, *Walking in a Winter Wonderland,* began to run through his head, and he hummed it through closed lips, kept pace to it as he walked.

He had lost all sensation in his feet. He looked down at his black leather shoes, at the thin cotton socks, and began, seriously, to worry about frostbite.

This was beyond a joke. This had moved beyond foolishness, slipped over the line into genuine 24 karat Jesus-Christ-I-screwed-up-bigtime territory. His clothes might as well have been netting or lace: the wind blew through him, froze his bones and the marrow in his bones, froze the lashes of his eyes, froze the warm place under his balls, which were retreating into his pelvic cavity.

Keep walking, he told himself. *Keep walking. I can stop and drink a pail of air when I get home.* A Beatles song started in his head, and he adjusted his pace to match it. It was only when he got to the chorus that he realised that he was humming *Help*.

He was almost at the bridge now. Then he had to walk across it, and he would still be another ten minutes from the stores on the west of the lake – maybe a little more . . .

A dark car passed him, stopped, then reversed in a foggy cloud of exhaust smoke and came to a halt beside him. A window slid down, and the haze and steam from the window mixed with the exhaust to form a dragon's breath that surrounded the car. 'Everything okay here?' said a cop inside.

Shadow's first, automatic instinct was to say *Yup, everything's just fine and jimdandy thank you officer*. But it was too late for that, and he started to say, 'I think I'm freezing. I was walking into Lakeside to buy food and clothes, but I underestimated the length of the walk,' – he was that far through the sentence in his head, when he realised that all that had come out was 'F-f-freezing,' and a chattering noise, and he said, 'So s-sorry. Cold. Sorry.'

The cop pulled open the back door of the car, and said, 'You get in there this moment and warm yourself up, okay?' Shadow climbed in gratefully, and he sat in the back and rubbed his hands together, trying not to worry about frostbitten toes. The cop got back in the driver's seat. Shadow stared at him through the metal grille. Shadow tried not to think about the last time he'd been in the back of a police car, or to notice that there were no door handles in the back, and to concentrate instead on rubbing life back into his hands. His face hurt and his red fingers hurt, and now, in the warmth, his toes were starting to hurt once more. That was, Shadow figured, a good sign.

The cop put the car in drive and moved off. 'You know, that was,' he said, not turning to look at Shadow, just talking a little louder, 'if you'll pardon me saying so, a real stupid thing to do. You didn't hear any of the weather advisories? It's minus thirty out there. God alone knows what the windchill is, minus sixty, minus seventy, although I figure when you're down at minus thirty, windchill's the least of your worries.'

'Thanks,' said Shadow. 'Thanks for stopping. Very, very grateful.'

'Woman in Rhinelander went out this morning to fill her bird-feeder in her robe and carpet slippers and she froze, literally froze, to the sidewalk. She's in intensive care now. It was on the TV this morning. You're new in town.' It was almost a question, but the man knew the answer already.

'I came in on the Greyhound last night. Figured today I'd buy myself some warm clothes, food and a car. Wasn't expecting this cold.'

'Yeah,' said the cop. 'It took me by surprise as well. I was too busy worrying about global warming. I'm Chad Mulligan. I'm the chief of police here in Lakeside.'

'Mike Ainsel.'

'Hi Mike. Feeling any better?'

'A little, yes.'

'So where would you like me to take you first?'

Shadow put his hands down to the hot air stream, painful on his fingers, then he pulled them away. Let it happen in its own time. 'Can you just drop me off in the town centre?'

'Wouldn't hear of it. Long as you don't need me to drive a getaway car for your bank robbery I'll happily take you wherever you need to go. Think of it as the town welcome wagon.'

'Where would you suggest we start?'

'You only moved in last night.'

'That's right.'

'You eaten breakfast yet?'

'Not yet.'

'Well, that seems like a heck of a good starting place to me,' said Mulligan.

They were over the bridge now, and entering the north west side of the town. 'This is Main Street,' said Mulligan, 'and this,' he said, crossing Main Street and turning right, 'is the town square.'

Even in the winter the town square was impressive, but Shadow knew that this place was meant to be seen in summer: it would be a riot of colour, of poppies and irises and flowers of every kind, and the clump of birch trees in one corner would be a green and silver bower. Now it was colourless, beautiful in a skeletal way, the band-shell empty, the fountain turned off for the winter, the brownstone city hall capped by white snow.

' . . . and this,' concluded Chad Mulligan, bringing the car to a stop outside a high glass-fronted old building on the west of the square, 'is Mabel's.'

He got out of the car, opened the passenger door for Shadow. The two men put their heads down against the cold and the wind, and hurried across the sidewalk and into a warm room, fragrant with the smells of new-baked bread, of pastry and soup and bacon.

The place was almost empty. Mulligan sat down at a table and Shadow sat opposite him. He suspected that Mulligan was doing this to get a feel for the stranger in town. Then again, the police chief might simply be what he appeared: friendly, helpful, good.

A woman bustled over to their table, not fat but *big*, a big woman in her sixties, her hair bottle-bronze.

'Hello Chad,' she said. 'You'll want a hot chocolate while you're thinking.' She handed them two laminated menus.

'No cream on the top, though,' he agreed. 'Mabel knows me too well,' he said to Shadow. 'What'll it be, pal?'

'Hot chocolate sounds great,' said Shadow. 'And I'm happy to have the whipped cream on the top.'

'That's good,' said Mabel. 'Live dangerously, hon. Are you going to introduce me, Chad? Is this young man a new officer?'

'Not yet,' said Chad Mulligan, with a flash of white teeth. 'This is Mike Ainsel. He moved to Lakeside last night. Now, if you'll excuse me.' He got up, walked to the back of the room, through the door marked POINTERS. It was next to a door marked SETTERS.

'You're the new man in the apartment up on Northridge Road. The old Pilsen place. Oh yes,' she said, happily, 'I know *just* who you are. Hinzelmann was by this morning for his morning pasty, he told me all about you. You boys only having hot chocolate or you want to look at the breakfast menu?'

'Breakfast for me,' said Shadow. 'What's good?'

'Everything's good,' said Mabel. 'I make it. But this is the furthest south and east of the yoopie you can get pasties, and they are particularly good. Warming and filling too. My speciality.'

Shadow had no idea what a pasty was, but he said that would be fine, and in a few moments Mabel returned with a plate with what looked like a folded-over pie on it. The lower half was wrapped in a paper napkin. Shadow picked it up with the napkin and bit into it: it was warm and filled with meat, potatoes, carrots, onions. 'First pasty I've ever had,' he said. 'It's real good.'

'They're a yoopie thing,' she told him. 'Mostly you need to be at least up Ironwood way to get one. The Cornishmen who came over to work the iron mines brought them over.'

'Yoopie?'

'Upper Peninsula. U.P. Yoopie. It's the little chunk of Michigan to the northeast.'

The chief of police came back. He picked up the hot chocolate and slurped it. 'Mabel,' he said, 'are you forcing this nice young man to eat one of your pasties?'

'It's good,' said Shadow. It was too, a savory delight wrapped in hot pastry.

'They go straight to the belly,' said Chad Mulligan, patting his own stomach. 'I warn you. Okay. So, you need a car?' With his parka off, he was revealed as a lanky man with a round, apple-belly gut on him. He looked harassed and competent, more like an engineer than a cop.

Shadow nodded, mouth full.

'Right. I made some calls. Justin Liebowitz's selling his jeep, wants four thousand dollars for it, will settle for three. The Gunthers have had their Toyota 4-Runner for sale for eight months, ugly sonofabitch, but at this point they'd probably pay you to take it out of their driveway. And if you don't care about ugly, it's got to be a great deal. I used the phone in the men's room, left a message for Missy Gunther down at Lakeside Realty, but she wasn't in yet, probably getting her hair done down at Sheila's.'

The pasty remained good as Shadow chewed his way through it. It was astonishingly filling. 'Stick-to-your-ribs food,' as his mother would have said. 'Sticks to your sides.'

'So,' said Chief of Police Chad Mulligan, wiping the hot chocolate foam from around his lips. 'I figure we stop off next at Hennings Farm and Home Supplies, get you a real winter wardrobe, swing by Dave's Finest Food, so you can fill your larder, then I'll drop you up by Lakeside Realty. If you can put down a thousand up front for the car they'll be happy, otherwise five hundred a month for four months should see them okay. It's an ugly car, like I said, but if the kid hadn't painted it purple it'd be a ten thousand dollar car, and reliable, and you'll need something like that to get around this winter, you ask me.'

'This is very good of you,' said Shadow. 'But shouldn't you be out catching criminals, not helping newcomers? Not that I'm complaining, you understand.'

Mabel chuckled. 'We all tell him that,' she said.

Mulligan shrugged. 'It's a good town,' he said, simply. 'Not much trouble. You'll always get someone speeding within city limits – which is a good thing, as traffic tickets pay my wages. Friday, Saturday nights you get some jerk who gets drunk and beats on a spouse – and that one can go both ways, believe me. Men and women. But out here things are quiet. They call me out when someone's locked their keys in their vehicle. Barking dogs. Every year there's a couple of High School kids caught with weed behind the bleachers. Biggest police case we've had here in five years was when Dan Schwartz got drunk and shot up his own trailer, then he went on the run, down Main Street, in his wheelchair, waving this darn shotgun, shouting that he would shoot anyone who got in his way, that no-one would stop him from getting to the inter-state. I think he was on his way to Washington to shoot the president. I still laugh whenever I think of Dan heading down the interstate in that wheelchair of his with the bumper sticker on the back. "My Juvenile Delinquent is Screwing Your Honor Student". You remember, Mabel?'

She nodded, lips pursed. She did not seem to find it as funny as Mulligan did.

'What did you do?' asked Shadow.

'I talked to him. He gave me the shotgun. Slept it off down at the jail. Dan's not a bad guy, he was just drunk and upset.'

Shadow paid for his own breakfast and, over Chad Mulligan's half-hearted protests, both hot chocolates.

Hennings Farm and Home was a warehouse-sized building on the south of the town that sold everything from tractors to toys (the toys, along with the Christmas Ornaments, were already on sale). The store was bustling with post-Christmas shoppers. Shadow recognised the younger of the girls who had sat in front of him on the bus. She was trailing after her parents. He waved at her and she gave him a hesitant, blue-rubber-banded smile. Shadow wondered idly what she'd look like in ten years' time.

Probably as beautiful as the girl on the Hennings Farm and Home checkout counter, who scanned in his purchases with a chattering hand-held gun, capable, Shadow had no doubt, of ringing up a tractor if someone drove it through.

'Ten pairs of long underwear?' said the girl. 'Stocking up, huh?' She looked like a movie starlet.

Shadow felt fourteen again, and tongue-tied and foolish. He said nothing while she rang up the thermal boots, the gloves, the sweaters and the goose-down-filled coat.

He had no wish to put the credit card that Wednesday had given him to the test, not with Chief of Police Mulligan standing helpfully beside him, so he paid for everything in cash. Then he took his bags into the men's restroom, came out wearing many of his purchases.

'Looking good, big fella,' said Mulligan.

'At least I'm warm,' said Shadow, and outside, in the parking lot, although the wind burned cold on the skin of his face, the rest of him was warm enough. At Mulligan's invitation, he put his shopping bags in the back of the police car, and rode in the passenger seat, in the front.

'So, what do you do, Mr Ainsel?' asked the Chief of Police. 'Big guy like you. What's your profession, and will you be practising it in Lakeside?'

Shadow's heart began to pound, but his voice was steady. 'I work for my uncle. He buys and sells stuff all over the country. I just do the heavy lifting.'

'Does he pay well?'

'I'm family. He knows I'm not going to rip him off, and I'm learning a little about the trade on the way. Until I figure out what it is I really want to do.' It was coming out of him with conviction, smooth as a snake. He knew everything about big Mike Ainsel in that moment, and he liked Mike Ainsel. Mike Ainsel had none of the problems that Shadow had. Ainsel had never been married. Mike Ainsel had never been interrogated on a freight train by Mr Wood and Mr Stone. Televisions did not speak to Mike Ainsel ('You want to see Lucy's tits?' asked a voice in his head.) Mike Ainsel didn't have bad dreams, or believe that there was a storm coming.

He filled his shopping basket at Dave's Finest Foods, doing what he thought of as a gas-station stop – milk, eggs, bread, apples, cheese, cookies. Just some food. He'd do a real one later. As Shadow moved around, Chad Mulligan said hello to people and introduced Shadow to them. 'This is Mike Ainsel, he's taken the empty apartment at the old Pilsen place. Up around the back,' he'd say. Shadow gave up trying to remember names. He just shook hands with people and smiled, sweating a little, uncomfortable in his insulated layers in the hot store.

Chad Mulligan drove Shadow across the street to Lakeside Realty. Missy Gunther, her hair freshly set and lacquered, did not need an introduction – she knew exactly who Mike Ainsel was. Why that nice Mr Borson, his Uncle Emerson, such a nice man, he'd been by, what, about six, eight weeks ago now, and rented the apartment up at the old Pilsen Place, and wasn't the view just to die for up there? Well, honey, just wait until the spring, and we're so lucky, so many of the lakes in this part of the world go bright green from the algae in the summer, it would turn your stomach, but our lake, well, come fourth of July you could still practically *drink* it, and Mr Borson had paid for a whole year's lease in advance, and as for the Toyota 4-Runner, she couldn't believe that Chad Mulligan still remembered it, and yes, she'd be delighted to get rid of it. Tell the truth, she'd pretty much resigned herself to giving it to Hinzelmann as this year's klunker and just taking the tax write-off, not that the car was a *klunker*, far from it, no it was her son's car before he went to school in Green Bay, and, well, he'd painted it purple one day and, ha-ha, she certainly hoped that Mike Ainsel liked purple, that was all she had to say, and if he didn't she wouldn't blame him . . .

Chief of Police Mulligan excused himself near the middle of this litany. 'Looks like they need me back at the office, good meeting you Mike,' he said, and he moved Shadow's shopping bags into the back of Missy Gunther's station wagon.

Missy drove Shadow back to her place, where, in the drive, he saw an elderly SUV. The blown snow had bleached half of it to a blinding white, while the rest of it was painted the kind of drippy purple that someone would need to be very stoned, very often, to even begin to be able to find attractive.

Still, the car started up on the first try, and the heater worked, although it took almost ten minutes of running the engine with the heater on full before the interior of the car changed from unbearably cold to merely chilly. While this was happening, Missy Gunther took Shadow into her kitchen – excuse the mess, but the little ones just leave their toys all over after Christmas and she just didn't have the heart, would he care for some leftover turkey dinner? Well, coffee then, won't take a moment to brew a fresh pot – and Shadow took a large red toy car off a window seat and sat down, while Missy Gunther asked if he had met his neighbours yet, and Shadow confessed that he hadn't.

There were, he was informed, while the coffee dripped, four other inhabitants of his apartment building – back when it was the Pilsen place the Pilsens lived in the downstairs flat and rented out the upper two flats, now their apartment was taken by a couple of young men, Mr Holz and Mr Neiman, they actually are a couple and when she said *couple* Mr Ainsel, Heavens, we have all kinds here, more than one kind of tree in the forest, although mostly those kind of people wind up in Madison or the Twin Cities, but truth to tell, nobody here gives it a second thought. They're in Key West for the winter, they'll be back in April, he'll meet them then. The thing about Lakeside is that it's a good town. Now next door to Mr Ainsel, that's Marguerite Olsen and her little boy, a sweet lady, sweet, sweet lady, but she's had a hard life, still sweet as pie, and she works for the *Lakeside News*. Not the most exciting newspaper in the world, but truth to tell Missy Gunther thought that was probably the way most folk around here liked it.

Oh, she said, and poured him coffee, she just wished that Mr Ainsel could see the town in the summer or late in the spring, when the lilacs and the apple and the cherry blossoms were out, she thought there was nothing like it for beauty, nothing like it anywhere in the world.

Shadow gave her a five hundred dollar deposit, and he climbed up into the car and started to back it up, out of her front yard and onto the driveway proper. Missy Gunther tapped on his front window. 'This is for you,' she said. 'I nearly forgot.' She handed him a buff envelope. 'It's kind of a gag. We had them printed up a few years back. You don't have to look at it now.'

He thanked her, and drove, cautiously, back into the town. He took the road that ran around the lake. He wished he could see it in the spring, or the summer, or the fall: it would be very beautiful, he had no doubt of that.

In ten minutes he was home.

He parked the car out on the street and walked up the outside steps to his cold apartment. He unpacked his shopping, put the food into the cupboards and the fridge, and then he opened the envelope Missy Gunther had given him.

It contained a passport. Blue, plasticated cover and, inside, a proclamation that *Michael Ainsel* (his name handwritten in Missy Gunther's precise handwriting) was a citizen of Lakeside. There was a map of the town on the next page. The rest of it was filled with discount coupons for various local stores.

'I think I may like it here,' said Shadow, aloud. He looked out of the icy window at the frozen lake. 'If it ever warms up.'

There was a bang at the front door at around 2:00p.m. Shadow had been practising the Sucker Vanish with a quarter, tossing it from one hand to the other undetectably. His hands were cold enough and clumsy enough that he kept dropping the coin onto the table-top, and the knock at the door made him drop it again.

He went to the door, and opened it.

A moment of pure fear: the man at the door wore a black mask which covered the lower half of his face. It was the kind of mask that a bank robber might wear on TV, or a serial killer from a cheap movie might wear to scare his victims. The top of the man's head was covered by a black knit cap.

Still, the man was smaller and slighter than Shadow, and he did not appear to be armed. And he wore a bright plaid coat, of the kind that serial killers normally avoid.

'Ih hihelhan,' said the visitor.

'Huh?'

The man pulled the mask downward, to reveal Hinzelmann's cheerful face. 'I said *It's Hinzelmann*. You know, I don't know what we did before they came up with these masks. Well, I do remember what we did. Thick knitted caps that went all around your face, and scarves and you don't want to know what else. I think it's a miracle what they come up with these days. I may be an old man, but I'm not going to grumble about progress, not me.'

He finished this speech by thrusting a basket at Shadow, filled high with local cheeses, bottles, jars, and several small salamis that proclaimed themselves to be venison summer sausage, and by coming inside. 'Merry day after Christmas,' he said. His nose and ears and cheeks were red as raspberries, mask or no mask. 'I hear you already ate a whole one of Mabel's pasties. Brought you a few things.'

'That's very kind of you,' said Shadow.

'Kind, nothing. I'm going to stick it to you next week for the raffle. The Chamber of Commerce runs it, and I run the Chamber of Commerce. Last year we raised almost seventeen thousand dollars for the children's ward of Lakeside Hospital.'

'Well, why don't you put me down for a ticket now?'

'It don't start until the day the klunker hits the ice,' said Hinzelmann. He looked out of Shadow's window toward the lake. 'Cold out there. Must have dropped fifty degrees last night.'

'It happened really fast,' agreed Shadow.

'We used to pray for freezes like this back in the old days,' said Hinzelmann. 'My daddy told me.'

'You'd pray for days like this?'

'Well, yah, it was the only way the settlers survived back then. Weren't enough food for everyone, and you couldn't just go down to Dave's and fill up your shopping trolley in the old days, no sir. So my grampaw, he got to figgerin', and when a really cold day like this come along he'd take my grammaw, and the kids, my uncle and my aunt and my daddy – he was the youngest – and the serving girl and the hired man, and he'd go down with them to the creek, give 'em a little drink of rum and herbs, it was a recipe he'd got from the old country, then he'd pour creek water over them. Course they'd freeze in seconds, stiff and blue as so many popsicles. He'd haul them to a trench they'd already dug and filled with straw, and he'd stack 'em down there, one by one, like so much cordwood in the trench, and he'd pack straw around them, then he'd cover the top of the trench with two-b'-fours to keep the critters out – in those days there were wolves and bears and all sorts you never see any more around here, no hodags though, that's just a story about the hodags and I wouldn't ever stretch your credulity by telling you no stories, no sir, – he'd cover the trench with two-b'-fours and the next snowfall would cover it up completely, save for the flag he'd planted to show him where the trench was.

'Then my grampaw would ride through the winter in comfort and never have to worry about running out of food or out of fuel. And when he saw that the true spring was coming he'd go to the flag, and he'd dig his way down through the snow, and he'd move the two-b'-fours, and he'd carry them in one by one and set the family in front of the fire to thaw. Nobody ever minded except one of the hired men who lost half an ear to a family of mice who nibbled it off one time my grampaw didn't push those two-b'-fours all the way closed. Of course, in those days we had *real* winters. You could do that back then. These pussy winters we get nowadays it don't hardly get cold enough.'

'No?' asked Shadow. He was playing straight-man, and enjoying it enormously.

'Not since the winter of '49 and you'd be too young to remember that one. *That* was a winter. I see you bought yourself a ve-hicle.'

'Yup. What do you think?'

'Truth to tell, I never liked that Gunther boy. I had a trout stream down in the woods a way, on back of my property, way back, well it's town land but I'd put down stones in the river, made little pools and places where the trout liked to live. Caught me some beauties too – one fellow must have been a six, seven pound brook trout, and that little Gunther so-and-so he kicked down each of the pools and threatened to report me to the DNR. Now he's in Green Bay, and soon enough he'll be back here. If there were any justice in the world he'd've gone off into the world as a winter runaway, but nope, sticks like a cockleburr to a woollen vest.' He began to arrange the contents of Shadow's welcome basket on the counter. 'This is Katherine Powdermaker's crabapple jelly. She's been giving me a pot for Christmas for longer than you've been alive, and the sad truth is I've never opened a one. They're down in my basement, forty, fifty pots. Maybe I'll open one and discover that I like the stuff. Meantime, here's a pot for you. Maybe you'll like it.'

'What's a winter runaway?'

'Mm.' The old man pushed his woollen cap above his ears, rubbed his temple with a pink forefinger. 'Well, it ain't unique to Lakeside – we're a good town, better than most, but we're not perfect. Some winters, well, maybe a kid gets a bit stir-crazy, when it gets so cold that you can't go out, and the snow's so dry that you can't make so much as a snowball without it crumbling away . . .'

'They run off?'

The old man nodded, gravely. 'I blame the television, showing all the kids things they'll never have – *Dallas* and *Dynasty*, all of that nonsense. I've not had a television since the fall of '83, except for a black and white set I keep in a closet for if folk come in from out of town and there's a big game on.'

'Can I get you anything, Hinzelmann?'

'Not coffee. Gives me heartburn. Just water.' Hinzelmann shook his head. 'Biggest problem in this part of the world is poverty. Not the poverty we had in the Depression but something more in . . . what's the word, means it creeps in at the edges, like cock-a-roaches?'

'*Insidious?*'

'Yeah. Insidious. Logging's dead. Mining's dead. Tourists don't drive further north than the Dells, 'cept for a handful of hunters and some kids going to camp on the lakes – and they aren't spending their money in the towns.'

'Lakeside seems kind of prosperous, though.'

The old man's blue eyes blinked. 'And believe me, it takes a lot of work,' he said. 'Hard work. But this is a good town, and all the work all the people here put into it is worthwhile. Not that my family weren't poor as kids. Ask me how poor we was as kids.'

Shadow put on his straight-man face and said, 'How poor were you as kids, Mister Hinzelmann?'

'Just Hinzelmann, Mike. We were so poor that we couldn't afford a fire. Come New Year's Eve my father would suck on a peppermint, and us kids, we'd stand around with our hands outstretched, basking in the glow.'

Shadow made a rimshot noise. Hinzelmann put on his ski-mask and did up his huge plaid coat, pulled out his car keys from his pocket and then, last of all, pulled on his great gloves. 'You get too bored up here, you just come down to the store and ask for me. I'll show you my collection of hand-tied fishing flies. Bore you so much that getting back here will be a relief.' His voice was muffled, but audible.

'I'll do that,' said Shadow with a smile. 'How's Tessie?'

'Hibernating. She'll be out in the spring. You take care now, Mr Ainsel.' And he closed the door behind him as he left.

The apartment grew ever colder.

Shadow put on his coat and his gloves. Then he put on his boots. He could hardly see through the windows now for the ice on the inside of the panes which turned the view of the lake into an abstract image.

His breath was clouding in the air.

He went out of his apartment onto the wooden deck and knocked on the door next door. He heard a woman's voice shouting at someone to for heaven's sake shut up and turn that television down – a kid he thought, adults don't shout like that at other adults. The door opened and a tired woman with very long, very black hair was staring at him warily.

'Yes?'

'How do you do, Ma'am. I'm Mike Ainsel. I'm your next door neighbour.'

Her expression did not change, not by a hair. 'Yes?'

'Ma'am. It's freezing in my apartment. There's a little heat coming out of the grate, but it's not warming the place up, not at all.'

She looked him up and down, then a ghost of a smile touched the edges of her lips and she said, 'Come in, then. If you don't there'll be no heat in here, either.'

He stepped inside her apartment. Plastic, multicoloured toys were strewn all over the floor. There were small heaps of torn Christmas wrapping paper by the wall. A small boy sat inches away from the television set, a video of the Disney *Hercules* playing, an animated satyr stomping and shouting his way across the screen. Shadow kept his back to the TV set.

'Okay,' she said. 'This is what you do. First you seal the windows, you can buy the stuff down at Hennings, it's just like Saran Wrap but for windows. Tape it to windows, then if you want to get fancy you run a blow-drier on it, it stays there the whole winter. That stops the heat leaving through the windows. Then you buy a space heater or two. The building's furnace is old, and it can't cope with the real cold. We've had some easy winters recently, I suppose we should be grateful.' Then she put out her hand. 'Marguerite Olsen.'

'Good to meet you,' said Shadow. He pulled off a glove and they shook hands. 'You know ma'am, I'd always thought of Olsens as being blonder than you.'

'My ex-husband was as blond as they came. Pink and blond. Couldn't tan at gunpoint.'

'Missy Gunther told me you write for the local paper.'

'Missy Gunther tells everybody everything. I don't see why we need a local paper with Missy Gunther around.' She nodded.

'Yes. Some news reporting here and there, but my editor writes most of the news. I write the nature column, the gardening column, an opinion column every Sunday and the News From the Community column which tells, in mind-numbing detail, who went to dinner with who for fifteen miles around. Or is that whom?'

'*Whom*,' said Shadow, before he could stop himself. 'It's the objective case.'

She looked at him with her black eyes, and Shadow experienced a moment of pure *déjà vu*. I've been here before he thought.

No, she reminds me of someone.

'Anyway, that's how you heat up your apartment,' she said.

'Thank you,' said Shadow. 'When it's warm you and your little one must come over.'

'His name's Leon,' she said. 'Good meeting you Mister . . . I'm sorry . . .'

'Ainsel,' said Shadow. 'Mike Ainsel.'

'And what sort of a name is Ainsel?' she asked.

Shadow had no idea. 'My name,' he said. 'I'm afraid I was never very interested in family history.'

'Norwegian, maybe?' she said.

'We were never close,' he said. Then he remembered Uncle Emerson Borson, and added, 'on that side, anyway.'

By the time that Mr Wednesday arrived, Shadow had put clear plastic sheeting across all the windows, and had one space heater running in the main room and one in the bedroom at the back. It was practically cosy.

'What the hell is that purple piece of shit you're driving?' asked Wednesday, by way of greeting.

'Well,' said Shadow, 'you drove off with my white piece of shit. Where is it by the way?'

'I traded it in in Duluth,' said Wednesday. 'You can't be too careful. Don't worry – you'll get your share when all this is done.'

'What am I doing here?' asked Shadow. 'In Lakeside, I mean. Not in the world.'

Wednesday smiled his smile, the one that made Shadow want to hit him. 'You're living here because it's the last place they'll look for you. I can keep you out of sight here.'

'By *they* you mean the black hats?'

'Exactly. I'm afraid the House on the Rock is now out of bounds. It's a little difficult, but we'll cope. Now it's just stamping our feet and flag-waving, caracole and saunter until the action starts – a little later than any of us expected. I think they'll hold off until Spring. Nothing big can happen until then.'

'How come?'

'Because they may babble on about micro-milliseconds and virtual worlds and paradigm shifts and what-have-you, but they still inhabit this planet and are still bound by the cycle of the year. These are the dead months. A victory in these months is a dead victory.'

'I have no idea what you're talking about,' said Shadow. That was not entirely true. He had a vague idea, and he hoped it was wrong.

'It's going to be a bad winter, and you and I are going to use our time as wisely as we can. We shall rally our troops and pick our battleground.'

'Okay,' said Shadow. He knew that Wednesday was telling him the truth, or a part of a truth. War was coming. No, that was not it: the war had already begun. The battle was coming. 'Mad Sweeney said that he was working for you when we met him that first night. He said that before he died.'

'And would I have wanted to employ someone who could not even best a sad case like that in a bar fight? But never fear, you've repaid my faith in you a dozen times over. Have you ever been to Las Vegas?'

'Las Vegas, Nevada?'

'That's the one.'

'No.'

'We're flying in there from Madison later tonight, on a gentleman's red-eye, a charter plane for High Rollers. I've convinced them that we should be on it.'

'Don't you ever get tired of lying?' asked Shadow. He said it gently, curiously.

'Not in the slightest. Anyway, it's true. We are playing for the highest stakes of all. It shouldn't take us more than a couple of hours to get to Madison, the roads are clear. So lock your door and turn off the heaters. It would be a terrible thing if you burned down the house in your absence.'

'Who are we going to see in Las Vegas?'

Wednesday told him.

Shadow turned off the heaters, packed some clothes into an overnight bag, then turned back to Wednesday and said, 'Look, I feel kind of stupid. I know you just told me who we're going to see, but I dunno. I just had a brain-fart or something. It's gone. Who is it again?'

Wednesday told him once more.

This time Shadow almost had it. The name was there on the tip of his mind. He wished he'd been paying closer attention when Wednesday told him. He let it go.

'Who's driving?' he asked Wednesday.

'You are,' said Wednesday. They walked out of the house, down the wooden stairs and the icy path to where a black Lincoln town car was parked.

Shadow drove.

Entering the Casino one is beset at every side by invitation – invitations such that it would take a man of stone, heartless, mindless and curiously devoid of avarice, to decline them. Listen: a machine gun rattle of silver coins as they tumble and spurt down into a slot machine tray and over-flow onto monogrammed carpets is replaced by the siren clangor of the slots, the jangling, blippeting chorus swallowed by the huge room, muted to a comforting background chatter by the time one reaches the card tables, the distant sounds only loud enough to keep the adrenalin flowing through the gamblers' veins.

There is a secret that the casinos possess, a secret they hold and guard and prize, the holiest of their mysteries. For most people do not gamble to win money, after all, although that is what is advertised, sold, claimed and dreamed. But that is merely the easy lie that gets them through the enor-mous, ever-open, welcoming doors.

The secret is this: people gamble to lose *money. They come to the casinos for the moment in which they feel alive, to ride the spinning wheel and turn with the cards and lose themselves, with the coins, in the slots. They may brag about the nights they won, the money they took from the casino, but they treasure, secretly treasure, the times they lost. It's a sacrifice, of sorts.*

The money flows through the casino in an uninterrupted stream of green and silver, streaming from hand to hand, from gambler to croupier to cashier to the management to security, finally ending up in the Holy of Holies, the innermost sanctum, the Counting Room. And it is here, in the counting room of this casino, that you come to rest, here, where the greenbacks are sorted, stacked, indexed, here in a space that is slowly becoming redundant as more and more of the money that flows through the casino is imaginary: an electrical sequence of ons and offs, sequences that flow down telephone lines.

In the counting room you see three men, counting money under the glassy stare of the cameras they can see, the insectile gazes of the tiny cameras they cannot see. During the course of one shift each of the men counts more money than he will see in all the pay packets of his life. Each man, when he sleeps, dreams of counting money, of stacks and paper bands and numbers which climb inevitably, which are sorted and lost. Each of the three men has idly wondered, not less than once a week, how to evade the casino's security systems and run off with as much money as he could haul; and, reluctantly, each man has inspected the dream and found it impractical, has settled for a steady paycheck, avoided the twin spectres of prison and an unmarked grave.

And here, in the sanctum sanctorum, there are the three men who count the money, and there are the guards who watch and who bring money and take it away; and then there is another person. His charcoal-grey suit is immaculate, his hair is dark, he is clean-shaven, and his face, and his demeanor, are, in every sense, forgettable. None of the other men has even observed that he is there, or if they have noticed him, they have forgotten him on the instant.

As the shift ends the doors are opened, and the man in the charcoal suit leaves the room and walks, with the guards, through the corridors, their feet shushing along the monogrammed carpets. The money, in strong boxes, is wheeled to an interior loading bay, where it is loaded into armoured cars. As the ramp door swings open, to allow the armored car out onto the early streets of Las Vegas, the man in the charcoal suit walks, unnoticed, through the doorway, and saunters up the ramp, out onto the sidewalk. He does not even glance up to see the imitation of New York on his left.

Las Vegas has become a child's picture book dream of a city – here a story-book castle, there a sphinx-flanked black pyramid beaming white light into the darkness as a landing beam for UFOs, and everywhere neon oracles and twisting screens predicting happiness and good fortune, announcing singers and comedians and magicians in residence or on their way, and the lights always flash and beckon and call. Once every hour a volcano erupts in light and flame. Once every hour a pirate ship sinks a man o' war.

The man in the charcoal suit ambles comfortably along the sidewalk, feeling the flow of the money through the town. In the summer the streets are baking, and each store doorway he passes breathes wintry A/C out into the sweaty warmth and chills the sweat on his face. Now, in the desert winter, there's a dry cold, which he appreciates. In his mind the movement of money forms a fine lattice-work, a three dimensional cat's-cradle of light and motion. What he finds attractive about this desert city is the speed of movement, the way the money moves from place to place and hand to hand: it's a rush for him, a high, and it pulls him like an addict to the street.

A taxi follows him slowly down the street, keeping its distance. He does not notice it; it does not occur to him to notice it: he is so rarely noticed himself that he finds the concept that he could be being followed almost inconceivable.

It's four in the morning, and he finds himself drawn to a hotel and casino that has been out of style for thirty years, still running until tomorrow or six months from now when they'll implode it and knock it down and build a pleasure palace where it was, and forget it forever. Nobody knows him, nobody remembers him, but the lobby bar is tacky and quiet, and the air is blue with old cigarette smoke and someone's about to drop several million dollars on a poker game in a private room upstairs. The man in the charcoal suit settles himself in the bar several floors below the game, and is ignored by a waitress. A Muzak version of Why Can't He Be You? is playing, almost subliminally. Five Elvis Presley impersonators, each man wearing a different coloured jumpsuit, watch a late night rerun of a football game on the bar TV.

A big man in a light grey suit sits at the man in the charcoal suit's table, and, noticing him even if she does not notice the man in the charcoal suit, the waitress, who is too thin to be pretty, too obviously anorectic to work at Luxor or the Tropicana, and who is counting the minutes until she gets off work, comes straight over and smiles. He grins widely at her. 'You're looking a treat tonight, m'dear, a fine sight for these poor old eyes,' he says, and, scenting a large tip, she smiles broadly at him. The man in the light grey suit orders a Jack Daniel's for himself and a Laphroaig and water for the man in the charcoal suit sitting beside him.

'You know,' says the man in the light grey suit, when his drink arrives, 'the finest line of poetry ever uttered in the history of this whole damn country was said by Canada Bill Jones in 1853, in Baton Rouge, while he was being robbed blind in a crooked game of Faro. George Devol, who was, like Canada Bill, not a man who was averse to fleecing the odd sucker, drew Bill aside and asked him if he couldn't see that the game was crooked. And Canada Bill sighed, and shrugged his shoulders, and said "I know. But it's the only game in town." And he went back to the game.'

Dark eyes stare at the man in the light grey suit mistrustfully. The man in the charcoal suit says something in reply. The man in the light suit, who has a greying reddish beard, shakes his head.

'Look,' he says, 'I'm sorry about what went down in Wisconsin. But I got you all out safely, didn't I? No-one was hurt.'

The man in the dark suit sips his Laphroaig and water, savoring the marshy taste, the body-in-the-bog quality of the whisky. He asks a question.

'I don't know. Everything's moving faster than I expected. Everyone's got a hard-on for the kid I hired to run errands – I've got him outside, waiting in the taxi. Are you still in?'

The man in the dark suit replies.

The bearded man shakes his head. 'She's not been seen for two hundred years. If she isn't dead she's taken herself out of the picture.'

Something else is said.

'Look,' says the bearded man, knocking back his Jack Daniel's. 'You come in, be there when we need you, and I'll take care of you. Whaddayou want? Soma? I can get you a bottle of Soma. The real stuff.'

The man in the dark suit stares. Then he nods his head, reluctantly, and makes a comment.

'Of course I am,' says the bearded man, smiling like a knife. 'What do you expect? But look at it this way: it's the only game in town.' He reaches out a paw-like hand and shakes the other man's well-manicured hand. Then he walks away.

The thin waitress comes over, puzzled: there's now only one man at the corner table, a sharply dressed man with dark hair in a charcoal-grey suit. 'You doing okay?' she asks. 'Is your friend coming back?'

The man with the dark hair sighs, and explains that his friend won't be coming back, and thus she won't be paid for her time, or for her trouble. And then, seeing the hurt in her eyes, and taking pity on her, he examines the golden threads in his mind, watches the matrix, follows the money

until he spots a node, and tells her that if she's outside Treasure Island at
six a.m., thirty minutes after she gets off work, she'll meet an oncologist
from Denver who will just have won $40,000 at a craps table, and will
need a mentor, a partner, someone to help him dispose of it all in the 48
hours before he gets on the plane home.

The words evaporate in the waitress's mind, but they leave her happy.
She sighs and notes that the guys in the corner have done a runner, and
have not even tipped her; and it occurs to her that, instead of driving
straight home when she gets off shift, she's going to drive over to Treasure
Island; but she would never, if you asked her, be able to tell you why.

'So who was that guy you were seeing?' asked Shadow as they
walked back down the Las Vegas concourse. There were slot
machines in the airport. Even at this time of the morning people
stood in front of them, feeding them coins. Shadow wondered
if there were those who never left the airport, who got off their
planes, walked along the jetway into the airport building and
stopped there, trapped by the spinning images and the flashing
lights until they had fed their last quarter to the machines, and
then , with nothing left, just turned around and got onto the plane
back home.

And then he realised that he had zoned out just as Wednesday
had been telling him who the man in the dark suit they had followed
in the taxi had been, and he had missed it.

'So he's in,' said Wednesday. 'It'll cost me a bottle of Soma,
though.'

'What's Soma?'

'It's a drink.' They walked onto the charter plane, empty but for
them and a trio of corporate big spenders who needed to be back
in Chicago by the start of the next business day.

Wednesday got comfortable, ordered himself a Jack Daniel's. 'My
kind of people see your kind of people . . .' he hesitated. 'It's like
bees and honey. Each bee makes only a tiny, tiny drop of honey. It
takes thousands of them, millions perhaps, all working together to
make the pot of honey you have on your breakfast table. Now
imagine that you could eat nothing but honey. That's what it's like
for my kind of people . . . we feed on belief, on prayers, on love.'

'And Soma is . . .'

'To take the analogy further, it's a honey wine. Like mead.' He chuckled. 'It's a drink. Concentrated prayer and belief, distilled into a potent liqueur.'

They were somewhere over Nebraska eating an unimpressive in-flight breakfast when Shadow said, 'My wife.'

'The dead one.'

'Laura. She doesn't want to be dead. She told me. After she got me away from the guys on the train.'

'The action of a fine wife. Freeing you from durance vile and murdering those who would have harmed you. You should treasure her, Nephew Ainsel.'

'She wants to be really alive. Can we do that? Is that possible?'

Wednesday said nothing for long enough that Shadow started to wonder if he had heard the question, or if he had, possibly, fallen asleep with his eyes open. Then he said, staring ahead of him as he talked, 'I know a charm that can cure pain and sickness, and lift the grief from the heart of the grieving.

'I know a charm that will heal with a touch.

'I know a charm that will turn aside the weapons of an enemy.

'I know another charm to free myself from all bonds and locks.

'A fifth charm: I can catch an arrow in flight and take no harm from it.'

His words were quiet, urgent. Gone was the hectoring tone, gone was the grin. Wednesday spoke as if he were reciting the words of a religious ritual, or remembering something dark and painful.

'A sixth: spells sent to hurt me will hurt only the sender.

'A seventh charm I know: I can quench a fire simply by looking at it.

'An eighth: if any man hates me, I can win his friendship.

'A ninth: I can sing the wind to sleep and calm a storm for long enough to bring a ship to shore.

'Those were the first nine charms I learned. Nine nights I hung on the bare tree, my side pierced with a spear's point. I swayed and blew in the cold winds and the hot winds, without food, without water, a sacrifice of myself to myself, and the worlds opened to me.

'For a tenth charm, I learned to dispel witches, to spin them around in the skies so that they will never find their way back to their own doors again.

'An eleventh: if I sing it when a battle rages it can take warriors through the tumult unscathed and unhurt, and bring them safely back to their hearth and their home.

'A twelfth charm I know: if I see a hanged man I can bring him down from the gallows to whisper to us all he remembers.

'A thirteenth: if I sprinkle water on a child's head, that child will not fall in battle.

'A fourteenth: I know the names of all the gods. Every damned one of them.

'A fifteenth: I have a dream of power, of glory and of wisdom, and I can make people believe my dreams.'

His voice was so low now that Shadow had to strain to hear it over the plane's engine noise.

'A sixteenth charm I know: if I need love I can turn the mind and heart of any woman.

'A seventeenth, that no woman I want will ever want another.

'And I know an eighteenth charm, and that charm is the greatest of all, and that charm I can tell to no man, for a secret that no-one knows but you is the most powerful secret there can ever be.'

He sighed, and then stopped talking.

Shadow could feel his skin crawl. It was as if he had just seen a door open to another place, somewhere worlds away where hanged men blew in the wind at every crossroads, where witches shrieked overhead in the night.

'Laura,' was all he said.

Wednesday turned his head, stared into Shadow's pale grey eyes with his own. 'I can't make her live again,' he said. 'I don't even know why she isn't as dead as she ought to be.'

'I think I did it,' said Shadow. 'It was my fault.'

Wednesday raised an eyebrow.

'Mad Sweeney gave me a golden coin, back when he showed me how to do that trick. From what he said, he gave me the wrong coin. What he gave me was something more powerful than what he thought he was giving me. I passed it on to Laura.'

Wednesday grunted, lowered his chin to his chest, frowned. Then he sat back. 'That could do it,' he said. 'And no, I can't help you. What you do in your own time is your own affair, of course.'

'What,' asked Shadow, 'is that supposed to mean?'

'It means that I can't stop you from hunting eagle stones and thunderbirds. But I would infinitely prefer that you spend your days quietly sequestered in Lakeside, out of sight, and, I hope, out of mind. When things get hairy we'll need all hands to the wheel.'

He looked very old as he said this, and fragile, and his skin seemed almost transparent, and the flesh beneath was grey.

Shadow wanted, wanted very much, to reach out and put his hand over Wednesday's grey hand. He wanted to tell him that everything would be okay – something that Shadow did not feel, but that he knew had to be said. There were men in black trains out there. There was a fat kid in a stretch limo and there were people in the television who did not mean them well.

He did not touch Wednesday. He did not say anything.

Later, he wondered if he could have changed things, if that gesture would have done any good, if it could have averted any of the harm that was to come. He told himself it wouldn't. He knew it wouldn't. But still, afterward, he wished that, just for a moment on that slow flight home, he had touched Wednesday's hand.

The brief winter daylight was already fading when Wednesday dropped Shadow outside his apartment. The freezing temperature when Shadow opened the car door felt even more science fictional when compared to Las Vegas.

'Don't get into any trouble,' said Wednesday. 'Keep your head below the parapet. Make no waves.'

'All at the same time?'

'Don't get smart with me, m'boy. You can keep out of sight in Lakeside. I pulled in a big favour to keep you here, safe and sound. If you were in a city they'd get your scent in minutes.'

'I'll stay put and keep out of trouble.' Shadow meant it as he said it. He'd had a lifetime of trouble and he was ready to let it go forever.

'When are you coming back?' he asked.

'Soon,' said Wednesday, and he gunned the Lincoln's engine, slid up the window and drove off into the frigid night.

11

Three may keep a secret, if two of them are dead.
– Ben Franklin. *Poor Richard's Almanack*

Three cold days passed. The thermometer never made it up to the zero mark, not even at midday. Shadow wondered how people had survived this weather in the days before electricity, before thermal face masks and lightweight thermal underwear, before easy travel.

He was down at the Video, Tanning, Bait and Tackle store, being shown Hinzelmann's hand-tied trout flies. They were more interesting than he had expected: colourful fakes of life, made of feather and thread, each with a hook hidden inside it.

He asked Hinzelmann.

'For real?' asked Hinzelmann.

'For real,' said Shadow.

'Well,' said the older man. 'Sometimes they didn't survive it, and they died. Leaky chimneys and badly ventilated stoves and ranges killed as many people as the cold. But those days were hard – they'd spend the summer and the fall laying up the food and the firewood for the winter. The worst thing of all was the madness. I heard on the radio, they were saying how it was to do with the sunlight, how there isn't enough of it in the winter. My daddy, he said folk just went stir crazy – winter madness they called it. Lakeside always had it easy, but some of the other towns around here, they had it hard. There was a saying still had currency when I was a kid, that if the serving girl hadn't tried to kill you by February she hadn't any backbone.

'Storybooks were like gold-dust – anything you could read was treasured, back before the town had a lending library. When my grampaw got sent a storybook from his brother in Bavaria, all the Germans in town met up in the town hall to hear him read it, and the Finns and the Irish and the rest of them, they'd make the Germans tell them the stories.

'Twenty miles south of here, in Jibway, they found a woman walking mother-naked in the winter with a dead babe at her breast, and she'd not suffer them to take it from her.' He shook his head meditatively, closed the fly cabinet with a click. 'Bad business. You want a video rental card? Eventually they'll open a Blockbusters here, and then we'll soon be out of business. But for now we got a pretty fair selection.'

Shadow reminded Hinzelmann that he had no television, and no VCR. He enjoyed Hinzelmann's company – the reminiscences, the tall tales, the goblin grin of the old man. It could make things awkward between them were Shadow to admit that television had made him uncomfortable ever since it had started to talk to him.

Hinzelmann fished in a drawer, and took out a tin box – by the look of it, it had once been a Christmas box, of the kind that contained chocolates or cookies: a mottled Santa Claus, holding a tray of Coca-Cola bottles, beamed up from its lid. Hinzelmann eased off the metal top of the box, revealing a notebook and books of blank tickets, and said, 'How many you want me to put you down for?'

'How many of what?'

'Klunker tickets. She'll go out onto the ice today, so we've started selling tickets. Each ticket is five dollars, ten for forty, twenty for seventy five. One ticket buys you five minutes. Of course we can't promise it'll go down in your five minutes, but the person who's closest stands to win five hundred bucks, and if it goes down in your five minutes, you win a thousand dollars. The earlier you buy your tickets, the more times aren't spoken for. You want to see the info sheet?'

'Sure.'

Hinzelmann handed Shadow a photocopied sheet. The klunker was an old car with its engine and fuel tank removed, which would be parked out on the ice for the winter. Sometime in the spring the lake ice would melt, and when it was too thin to bear the car's weight the car would fall into the lake. The earliest the klunker had ever tumbled into the lake was February the twenty-seventh ('That was the winter of 1998. I don't think you could rightly call that a winter at all,') the latest was May the First ('That was 1950. Seemed that year that the only way that winter would end was if somebody hammered a stake through its heart'). The beginning of April appeared to be the most common time for the car to sink – normally in mid-afternoon.

All of the mid-afternoons in April had already gone, marked off in Hinzelmann's lined notebook. Shadow bought a thirty minute period on the morning of March the 23rd, from 9:00 a.m. to 9:30 a.m. He handed Hinzelmann thirty dollars.

'I just wish everybody in town was as easy a sell as you are,' said Hinzelmann.

'It's a thank-you for that ride you gave me that first night I was in town.'

'No, Mike,' said Hinzelmann. 'It's for the children.' For a moment he looked serious, with no trace of impishness on his creased old face. 'Come down this afternoon, you can lend a hand pushing the klunker out onto the lake.'

He passed Shadow six blue cards, each with a date and time written on it in Hinzelmann's old-fashioned handwriting, then entered the details of each in his notebook.

'Hinzelmann,' asked Shadow. 'Have you ever heard of eagle stones?'

'Up north of Rhinelander? Nope, that's Eagle River. Can't say I have.'

'How about thunderbirds?'

'Well, there was the Thunderbird Framing Gallery up on Fifth Street, but that closed down. I'm not helping, am I?'

'Nope.'

'Tell you what, why don't you go look at the library. Good people, although they may be kind of distracted by the library sale on this week. I showed you where the library was, didn't I?'

Shadow nodded, and said so long. He wished he'd thought of the library himself. He got into the purple 4-Runner and drove south on Main Street, following the lake around to the southernmost point, until he reached the castle-like building which housed the city library. He walked inside. A sign pointed to the basement: LIBRARY

SALE, it said. The library proper was on the ground floor, and he stamped the snow off his boots and went in.

A forbidding woman with pursed, crimson-coloured lips asked him pointedly if she could help him.

'I suppose I need a library card,' he said. 'And I want to know all about thunderbirds.'

Native American Beliefs and Traditions were on a single shelf in one castle-like turret. Shadow pulled down some books and sat in the window seat. In several minutes he had learned that thunderbirds were mythical gigantic birds who lived on mountaintops, who brought the lightning and who flapped their wings to make the thunder. There were some tribes, he read, who believed that the thunderbirds had made the world. Another half hour's reading did not turn up anything more, and he could find no mention of eagle stones anywhere in the books' indexes.

Shadow was putting the last of the books back on the shelf when he became aware of someone staring at him. Somebody small and grave was peeking at him from around the heavy shelves. As he turned to look, the face vanished. He turned his back on the boy, then glanced around to see that he was being watched once more.

In his pocket was the Liberty dollar. He took it out of his pocket, held it up in his right hand, making sure the boy could see it. He finger-palmed it into his left hand, displayed both hands empty, raised his left hand to his mouth and coughed once, letting the coin tumble from his left hand into his right.

The boy looked at him wide-eyed and scampered away, returning a few moments later, dragging an unsmiling Marguerite Olsen, who looked at Shadow suspiciously and said, 'Hello Mister Ainsel. Leon says you were doing magic for him.'

'Just a little prestidigitation, Ma'am. Say, I never did say thank you for your advice about heating the apartment. It's warm as toast in there right now.'

'That's good.' Her icy expression had not begun to thaw.

'It's a lovely library,' said Shadow.

'It's a beautiful building. But the city needs something more efficient and less beautiful. You going to the library sale downstairs?'

'I wasn't planning on it.'

'Well, you should. It's for a good cause.'

'I'll make a point of getting down there.'

'Head out into the hall and then go downstairs. Good seeing you, Mister Ainsel.'

'Call me Mike,' he said.

She said nothing, just took Leon's hand and walked the boy over to the children's section.

'But mom,' Shadow heard Leon say, 'It wasn't pressed igitation. It *wasn't*. I *saw* it vanish and then it fell out of his *nose*. I *saw* it.'

An oil portrait of Abraham Lincoln gazed down from the wall at him. Shadow walked down the marble and oak steps to the library basement, through a door into a large room filled with tables, each table covered with books of all kinds, indiscriminately assorted and promiscuously arranged: paperbacks and hardcovers, fiction and non-fiction, periodicals and encyclopedias all side by side upon the tables, spines up or spines out.

Shadow wandered to the back of the room where there was a table covered with old-looking leather-bound books, each with a catalogue number painted in white on the spine. 'You're the first person over in that corner all day,' said the man sitting by the stack of empty boxes and bags and the small, open, metal cashbox. 'Mostly folk just take the thrillers and the children's books and the Harlequin Romances. Jenny Kerton, Danielle Steel, all that.' The man was reading Agatha Christie's *The Murder of Roger Ackroyd*. 'Everything on the tables is fifty cents a book, or you can take three for a dollar.'

Shadow thanked him and continued to browse. He found a copy of Herodotus's *Histories* bound in peeling brown leather. It made him think of the paperback copy he had left behind in prison. There was a book called *Perplexing Parlour Illusions*, which looked like it might have some coin effects. He carried both the books over to the man with the cashbox.

'Buy one more, it's still a dollar,' said the man. 'And if you take another book away, you'll be doing us a favour. We need the shelf-space.'

Shadow walked back to the old leather-bound books. He decided to liberate the book that was least likely to be bought by anyone else, and found himself unable to decide between *Common Diseases of the Urinary Tract with Illustrations by a Medical Doctor* and *Minutes of the Lakeside City Council 1872-1884*. He looked at the illustrations in the medical book and decided that somewhere in the town there was a teenage boy who could use the book to gross out his friends. He took the *Minutes* to the man on the door who took his dollar and put all the books into a Dave's Finest Food brown paper sack.

Shadow left the library. He had a clear view of the lake, all the way back. He could even see his apartment building, like a doll's house, up past the bridge. And there were men on the ice near the bridge, four or five of them, pushing a dark green car into the centre of the white lake.

'March the 23rd,' Shadow said to the lake, under his breath. '9:00 a.m. to 9:30 a.m.' He wondered if the lake or the klunker could hear him – and if they would pay any attention to him, even if they could. He doubted it.

The wind blew bitter against his face.

Officer Chad Mulligan was waiting outside Shadow's apartment when he got back. Shadow's heart began to pound when he saw the police-car, to relax a little when he observed that the policeman was doing paperwork in the front seat.

He walked over to the car, carrying his paper sack of books.

Mulligan lowered his window. 'Library sale?' he said.

'Yes.'

'I bought a box of Robert Ludlum books there two, three years back. Keep meaning to read them. My cousin swears by the guy. These days I figure if I ever get marooned on a desert island and I got my box of Robert Ludlum books with me, I can catch up on my reading.'

'Something particular I can do for you, Chief?'

'Not a damn thing, pal. Thought I'd stop by and see how you were settling in. You remember that Chinese saying, you save a man's life, you're responsible for him. Well, I'm not saying I saved your life last week. But I still thought I should check in. How's the Purple Gunther-mobile doing?'

'Good,' said Shadow. 'It's good. Running fine.'

'Pleased to hear it.'

'I saw my next-door neighbour in the library,' said Shadow. 'Miz Olsen. I was wondering . . .'

'What crawled up her butt and died?'

'If you want to put it like that.'

'Long story. You want to ride along for a spell, and I'll tell you all about it.'

Shadow thought about it for a moment. 'Okay,' he said. He got into the car, sat in the front passenger seat. Mulligan drove north of town. Then he turned off his lights and parked beside the road.

'Darren Olsen met Marge at U.W. Stevens Point and he brought her back north to Lakeside. She was a journalism major. He was studying, shit, hotel management, something like that. When they got here, jaws dropped. This was, what, thirteen, fourteen years ago. She was so beautiful. . . . that black hair . . .' he paused. 'Darren managed the Motel America over in Camden, twenty miles west of here. Except nobody ever seemed to want to stop in Camden and eventually the motel closed. They had two boys. At that time Sandy was eleven. The little one – Leon is it? – was just a babe in arms.

'Darren Olsen wasn't a brave man. He'd been a good high school football player, but that was the last time he was flying high. Whatever. He couldn't find the courage to tell Margie that he'd lost his job. So for a month, maybe for two months, he'd drive off early in the morning, come home late in the evening complaining about the hard day he'd had at the motel.'

'What was he doing?' asked Shadow.

'Mm. Couldn't say for certain. I reckon he was driving up to Ironwood, maybe down to Green Bay. Guess he started out as a job hunter. Pretty soon he was drinking the time away, getting stoned, more than probably meeting the occasional working girl for a little instant gratification. He could have been gambling. What I do know for certain is that he emptied out their joint account in about ten weeks. It was only a matter of time before Margie figured out – there we go!'

He swung the car out, flicked on the siren and the lights, and scared the daylights out of a small man with Iowa plates who had just come down the hill at seventy.

The rogue Iowan ticketed, Mulligan returned to his story.

'Where was I? Okay. So Margie kicks him out, sues for divorce. It turned into a vicious custody battle. That's what they call 'em when they get into *People* magazine. Vicious Custody Battle. She got the kids. Darren got visitation rights and precious little else. Now, back then Leon was pretty small. Sandy was older, a good kid, the kind of boy who worships his daddy. Wouldn't let Margie say nothing bad about him. They lost the house – had a nice place down on Daniels Road. She moved into the apartments. He left town. Came back every few months to make everybody miserable.

'This went on for a few years. He'd come back, spend money on the kids, leave Margie in tears. Most of us just started wishing he'd never come back at all. His mom and pop had moved to Florida when they retired, said they couldn't take another Wisconsin winter. So last year he came out, said he wanted to take the boys to Florida for Christmas. Margie said not a hope, told him to get lost. It got pretty unpleasant – at one point I had to go over there. Domestic dispute. By the time I got there Darren was standing in the front yard shouting stuff, the boys were barely holding it together, Margie was crying.

'I told Darren he was shaping up for a night in the cells. I thought for a moment he was going to hit me, but he was sober enough not to do that. I gave him a ride down to the trailer park south of town, told him to shape up. That he'd hurt her enough . . . Next day he left town.'

'Two weeks later, Sandy vanished. Didn't get onto the school bus. Told his best friend that he'd be seeing his dad soon, that Darren was bringing him a specially cool present to make up for having missed Christmas in Florida. Nobody's seen him since. Non-custodial kidnappings are the hardest. It's tough to find a kid who doesn't want to be found, y'see?'

Shadow said that he did. He saw something else as well. Chad Mulligan was in love with Marguerite Olsen himself. He wondered if the man knew how obvious it was.

Mulligan pulled out once more, lights flashing, and pulled over some teenagers doing sixty. He didn't ticket them, 'just put the fear of God in them'.

That evening Shadow sat at the kitchen table trying to figure out how to transform a silver dollar into a penny. It was a trick he had found in *Perplexing Parlour Illusions* but the instructions were infuriating, unhelpful and vague. Phrases like 'then vanish the penny in the usual way,' occurred every sentence or so. In this context, Shadow wondered, what was 'the usual way?' A French drop? Sleeving it?

Shouting 'Oh my god, look out! – a mountain lion!' and dropping the coin into his side pocket while the audience's attention was diverted?

He tossed his silver dollar into the air, caught it, remembering the moon and the woman who gave it to him, then he attempted the illusion. It didn't seem to work. He walked into the bathroom and tried it in front of the mirror, and confirmed that he was right. The trick as written simply didn't work. He sighed, dropped the coins in his pocket and sat down on the couch. He spread the cheap throw-rug over his legs and flipped open the *Minutes of the Lakeside Council 1872-1884*. The type, in two columns, was so small as to be almost unreadable. He flipped through the book, looking at the reproductions of the photographs of the period, at the several incarnations of the Lakeside City Council therein: long side-whiskers and clay pipes and battered hats and shiny hats, worn with faces which were, many of them, peculiarly familiar. He was unsurprised to see that the portly secretary of the 1882 city council was a Patrick Mulligan: shave him, make him lose twenty pounds and he'd be a dead ringer for Chad Mulligan, his – what, great-great-grandson? He wondered if Hinzelmann's pioneer grandfather was in the photographs, but it did not appear that he had been city council material. Shadow thought he had seen a reference to a Hinzelmann in the text, while flipping from photograph to photograph, but it eluded him when he leafed back for it, and the tiny type made Shadow's eyes ache.

He put the book down on his chest and realised his head was nodding. It would be foolish to fall asleep on the couch he decided, soberly. The bedroom was only a few feet away. On the other hand, the bedroom and the bed would still be there in five minutes, and anyway, he was not going to go to sleep, only to close his eyes for a moment . . .

Darkness roared.

He stood on an open plain. Beside him was the place from which he had once emerged, from which the earth had squeezed him. Stars were still falling from the sky and each star that touched the red earth became a man or a woman. The men had long black hair and high cheekbones. The women all looked like Marguerite Olsen. These were the star people.

They looked at him with dark, proud eyes.

'Tell me about the thunderbirds,' said Shadow. 'Please. It's not for me. It's for my wife.'

One by one they turned their backs on him, and as he lost their faces they were gone, one with the landscape. But the last of them, her hair streaked white on dark grey, pointed before she turned away, pointed into the wine-coloured sky.

'Ask them yourself,' she said. Summer lightning flickered, momentarily illuminating the world from horizon to horizon.

There were high rocks near him, peaks and spires of sandstone, and Shadow began to climb the nearest. The spire was the colour of old ivory. He grabbed at a handhold, and felt it slice into his hand. It's bone, *thought* Shadow. Not stone. It's old dry bone.

It was a dream, and in dreams you have no choices: either there are no decisions to be made, or they were made for you long before ever the dream began. Shadow continued to climb. His hands hurt. Bone popped and crushed and fragmented under his bare feet. The wind tugged at him, and he pressed himself to the spire, and he continued to climb the tower.

It was made of only one kind of bone, he realised, repeated over and over. Each of the bones was dry and ball-like. He thought that they were eggs of some huge bird. But another flare of lightning told him differently: they had holes for eyes, and they had teeth, which grinned without humour.

Somewhere birds were calling. Rain spattered his face.

He was hundreds of feet above the ground, clinging to the side of the tower of skulls, while flashes of lightning burned in the wings of the shadowy birds who circled the spire – enormous black, condor-like birds, each with a ruff of white at its neck. They were huge, graceful, awful birds, and the beats of their wings crashed like thunder on the night air.

They were circling the spire.

They must be fifteen, twenty feet from wingtip to wingtip, *thought* Shadow.

Then the first bird swung out of its glide toward him, blue lightning crackling in its wings. He pushed himself into a crevice of skulls, hollow eye-holes stared at him, a clutter of ivory teeth smiled at him, but he kept climbing, pulling himself up the mountain of skulls, every sharp edge cutting into his skin, feeling revulsion and terror and awe.

Another bird came at him, and one hand-sized talon sank into his arm.

He reached out and tried to grasp a feather from its wing – for if he returned to his tribe without a thunderbird's feather he would be disgraced, he would never be a man – but the bird pulled up, so that he could not grasp a feather. The thunderbird loosened its grip and swung back onto the wind. Shadow continued to climb.

There must be a thousand skulls, *thought Shadow.* A thousand thousand. And not all of them are human. *He stood at last on the top of the spire, the great birds, the thunderbirds, circling him slowly, navigating the gusts of the storm with tiny flicks of their wings.*

He heard a voice, the voice of the buffalo man, calling to him on the wind, telling him who the skulls belonged to . . .

The tower began to tumble, and the biggest bird, its eyes the blinding blue-white of forked lightning, plummeted down toward him in a rush of thunder, and Shadow was falling, tumbling down the tower of skulls . . .

The telephone shrilled. Shadow had not even known that it was connected. Groggy, shaken, he picked it up.

'What the fuck,' shouted Wednesday, angrier than Shadow had ever heard him, 'what the almighty flying fuck do you think you are playing at?'

'I was asleep,' said Shadow into the receiver, stupidly.

'What do you think is the fucking point of stashing you in a hiding place like Lakeside, if you're going to raise such a ruckus that not even a dead man could miss it?'

'I dreamed of thunderbirds . . .' said Shadow. 'And a tower. Skulls . . .' It seemed to him very important to recount his dream.

'I know what you were dreaming. Everybody damn well knows what you were dreaming. Christ Almighty. What's the point in hiding you, if you're going to start to fucking advertise?'

Shadow said nothing.

There was a pause at the other end of the telephone. 'I'll be there in the morning,' said Wednesday. It sounded like the anger had died down. 'We're going to San Francisco. The flowers in your hair are optional.' And the line went dead.

Shadow put the telephone down on the carpet, and sat up, stiffly. It was six a.m. and still night-dark outside. He got up from the sofa, shivering. He could hear the wind as it screamed across the frozen lake. And he could hear somebody nearby, crying, only the thickness of a wall away. He was certain it was Marguerite Olsen, and her sobbing was insistent and low and heart-breaking.

Shadow walked into the bathroom and pissed, then went into his bedroom and closed the door, blocking off the sound of the crying woman. Outside the wind howled and wailed as if it, too, was seeking a lost child.

San Francisco in January was unseasonably warm, warm enough that the sweat prickled on the back of Shadow's neck. Wednesday was wearing a deep blue suit, and a pair of gold-rimmed spectacles that made him look like an entertainment lawyer.

They were walking along Haight Street. The street people and the hustlers and the moochers watched them go by, and no-one shook a paper cup of change at them, no-one asked them for anything at all.

Wednesday's jaw was set. Shadow had seen immediately that the man was still angry, and had asked no questions when the black Lincoln town car had pulled up outside the apartment that morning. They had not talked on the way to the airport. He had been relieved that Wednesday was in first class and he was back in coach.

Now it was late in the afternoon. Shadow, who had not been in San Francisco since he was a boy, who had only seen it since then as a background to movies, was astonished at how familiar it was, how colourful and unique the wooden houses, how steep the hills, how very much it didn't feel like anywhere else.

'It's almost hard to believe that this is in the same country as Lakeside,' he said.

Wednesday glared at him. Then he said, 'It's not. San Francisco isn't in the same country as Lakeside any more than New Orleans is in the same country as New York or Miami is in the same country as Minneapolis.'

'Is that so?' said Shadow, mildly.

'Indeed it is. They may share certain cultural signifiers – money, a federal government, entertainment – it's the same *land*, obviously – but the only things that give it the illusion of being one country are the greenback, *The Tonight Show* and McDonald's.' They were approaching a park at the end of the road. 'Be nice to the lady we are visiting. But not too nice.'

'I'll be cool,' said Shadow.

They stepped onto the grass.

A young girl, no older than fourteen, her hair dyed green and orange and pink, stared at them as they went by. She sat beside a dog, a mongrel, with a piece of string for a collar and a leash. She looked hungrier than the dog did. The dog yapped at them, then wagged its tail.

Shadow gave the girl a dollar bill. She stared at it as if she was not sure what it was. 'Buy dog food with it,' Shadow suggested. She nodded, and smiled.

'Let me put it bluntly,' said Wednesday. 'You must be very cautious around the lady we are visiting. She might take a fancy to you, and that would be bad.'

'Is she your girlfriend or something?'

'Not for all the little plastic toys in China,' said Wednesday, agreeably. His anger seemed to have dissipated, or perhaps to have been invested for the future. Shadow suspected that anger was the engine that made Wednesday run.

There was a woman sitting on the grass, under a tree, with a paper tablecloth spread in front of her, and a variety of Tupperware dishes on the cloth.

She was – not fat, no, far from fat: what she was, a word that Shadow had never had cause to use until now, was *curvaceous*. Her hair was so fair that it was white, the kind of platinum blonde tresses that should have belonged to a long-dead movie starlet, her lips were painted crimson, and she looked to be somewhere between twenty-five and fifty.

As they reached her she was selecting from a plate of devilled eggs. She looked up as Wednesday approached her, and put down the egg she had chosen, and wiped her hand. 'Hello, you old fraud,' she said, but she smiled as she said it, and Wednesday bowed low, took her hand and raised it to his lips.

He said, 'You look divine.'

'How the hell else should I look?' she demanded, sweetly. 'Anyway, you're a liar. New Orleans was *such* a mistake – I put on, what, thirty pounds there? I swear. I knew I had to leave when I started to waddle. The tops of my thighs rub together when I walk now, can you believe that?' This last was addressed to Shadow. He had no idea what to say in reply, and felt a hot flush suffuse his face. The woman laughed delightedly. 'He's *blushing*! Wednesday my sweet, you brought me a *blusher*. How perfectly wonderful of you. What's he called?'

'This is Shadow,' said Wednesday. He seemed to be enjoying Shadow's discomfort. 'Shadow, say hello to Easter.'

Shadow said something that might have been Hello, and the woman smiled at him again. He felt like he was caught in headlights – the blinding kind that poachers use to freeze deer before they shoot them. He could smell her perfume from where he was standing, an intoxicating mixture of jasmine and honeysuckle, of sweet milk and female skin.

'So, how's tricks?' asked Wednesday.

The woman – Easter – laughed a deep and throaty laugh, full-bodied and joyous. How could you not like someone who laughed like that? 'Everything's fine,' she said. 'How about you, you old wolf?'

'I was hoping to enlist your assistance.'

'Wasting your time.'

'At least hear me out before dismissing me.'

'No point. Don't even bother.'

She looked at Shadow. 'Please, sit down here and help yourself to some of this food. Here, take a plate and pile it high. It's all good. Eggs, roast chicken, chicken curry, chicken salad, and over here is lapin – rabbit, actually, but cold rabbit is a delight, and in that bowl over there is the jugged hare, well, why don't I just fill a plate for you?' And she did, taking a plastic plate, piling it high with food and passing it to him. Then she looked at Wednesday. 'Are you eating?' she asked.

'I am at your disposal, my dear,' said Wednesday.

'You,' she told him, 'are so full of shit it's a wonder your eyes don't turn brown.' She passed him an empty plate. 'Help yourself,' she said.

The afternoon sun at her back burned her hair into a platinum aura. 'Shadow,' she said, chewing a chicken leg with gusto. 'That's a sweet name. Why do they call you Shadow?'

Shadow licked his lips to moisten them. 'When I was a kid,' he said. 'We lived, my mother and I, we were, I mean, she was, well, like a secretary, at a bunch of US Embassies, we went from city to city all over Northern Europe. Then she got sick and had to take early retirement and we came back to the states. I never knew what to say to the other kids, so I'd just find adults and follow them around, not saying anything. I just needed the company, I guess. I don't know. I was a small kid.'

'You grew,' she said.

'Yes,' said Shadow. 'I grew.'

She turned back to Wednesday, who was spooning down a bowl of what looked like cold gumbo. 'Is this the boy who's got everybody so upset?'

'You heard?'

'I keep my ears pricked up,' she said. Then to Shadow, 'You keep out of their way. There are too many secret societies out there, and they have no loyalties and no love. Commercial, independent, government, they're all in the same boat. They range from the barely competent to the deeply dangerous. Hey, old wolf, I heard a joke you'd like the other day. How do you know the CIA wasn't involved in the Kennedy Assassination?'

'I've heard it,' said Wednesday.

'Pity.' She turned her attention back to Shadow. 'But the Spookshow, the ones you met, they're something else. They exist because everyone knows they must exist.' She drained a paper cup of something that looked like white wine, and then she got to her feet. 'Shadow's a good name,' she said. 'I want a Mochaccino. Come on.'

She began to walk away. 'What about the food?' asked Wednesday. 'You can't just leave it here.'

She smiled at him, and pointed to the girl sitting by the dog, and then extended her arms to take in the Haight and the world. 'Let it feed them,' she said, and she walked, with Wednesday and Shadow trailing behind her.

'Remember,' she said to Wednesday, as they walked, '*I'm* rich. I'm doing just peachy. Why should I help you?'

'You're one of us,' he said. 'You're as forgotten and as unloved and unremembered as any of us. It's pretty clear whose side you should be on.'

They reached a sidewalk coffee house, went inside, sat down. There was only one waitress, who wore her eyebrow ring as a mark of caste, and a woman making coffee behind the counter. The waitress advanced upon them, smiling automatically, sat them down, took their orders.

Easter put her slim hand on the back of Wednesday's square grey hand. 'I'm telling you,' she said, 'I'm doing *fine*. On my festival days they still feast on eggs and rabbits, on candy and on flesh, to represent rebirth and copulation. They wear flowers in their bonnets and they give each other flowers. They do it in my name. More and more of them every year. In *my* name, old wolf.'

'And you wax fat and affluent on their worship and their love?' he said, drily.

'Don't be an asshole.' Suddenly she sounded very tired. She sipped her Mochaccino.

'Serious question, m'dear. Certainly I would agree that millions upon millions of them give each other tokens in your name, and that they still practice all the rites of your festival, even down to hunting for hidden eggs. But how many of them know who you are? Eh? Excuse me miss?' This to their waitress.

She said, 'You need another espresso?'

'No, my dear. I was just wondering if you could solve a little argument we were having over here. My friend and I were disagreeing over what the word "Easter" means. Would you happen to know?'

The girl stared at him as if green toads had begun to push their way between his lips. Then she said, 'I don't know about any of that Christian stuff. I'm a pagan.'

The woman behind the counter said, 'I think it's like Latin or something for "Christ Has Risen" maybe.'

'Really?' said Wednesday.

'Yeah, sure,' said the woman. 'Easter. Just like the sun rises in the East, you know.'

'The risen son. Of course – a most logical supposition.' The woman smiled and returned to her coffee grinder. Wednesday looked up at their waitress. 'I think I *shall* have another espresso, if you do not mind. And tell me, as a pagan, who do *you* worship?'

'Worship?'

'That's right. I imagine you must have a pretty wide-open field. So to whom do you set up your household altar? To whom do you bow down? To whom do you pray at dawn and at dusk?'

Her lips described several shapes without saying anything before she said, 'The female principle. It's an empowerment thing. You know.'

'Indeed. And this female principle of yours. Does she have a name?'

'She's the goddess within us all,' said the girl with the eyebrow ring, colour rising to her cheek. 'She doesn't need a name.'

'Ah,' said Wednesday, with a wide monkey grin, 'so do you have mighty bacchanals in her honour? Do you drink blood wine under the full moon, while scarlet candles burn in silver candle holders? Do you step naked into the sea-foam, chanting ecstatically to your nameless goddess while the waves lick at your legs, lapping your thighs like the tongues of a thousand leopards?'

'You're making fun of me,' she said. 'We don't do any of that stuff you were saying.' She took a deep breath. Shadow suspected she was counting to ten. 'Any more coffees here? Another Mochaccino for you ma'am?' Her smile was a lot like the one she had greeted them with when they had entered.

They shook their heads, and the waitress turned to greet another customer.

'There,' said Wednesday, 'is one who "*does not have the faith and will not have the fun*". Chesterton. Pagan indeed. So. Shall we go out onto the street, Easter my dear, and repeat the exercise? Find out how many passers-by know that their Easter festival takes its name from Eostre of the Dawn? Let's see – I have it. We shall ask a hundred people. For every one that knows the truth, you may cut off one of my fingers, and when I run out of them, toes; for every twenty who don't know you spend a night making love to me. And the odds are certainly in your favour here – this is San Francisco, after all. There are heathens and pagans and Wiccans aplenty on these precipitous streets.'

Her green eyes looked at Wednesday. They were, Shadow decided, the exact same colour as a leaf in spring with the sun shining through it. She said nothing.

'We *could* try it,' continued Wednesday. 'But I would end up with ten fingers, ten toes, and five nights in your bed. So don't tell me they worship you and keep your festival day. They mouth your name, but it has no meaning to them. Nothing at all.'

Tears stood out in her eyes. 'I know that,' she said, quietly. 'I'm not a fool.'

'No,' said Wednesday. 'You're not.'

He's pushed her too far, thought Shadow.

Wednesday looked down, ashamed. 'I'm sorry,' he said. Shadow could hear the real sincerity in his voice. 'We *need* you. We need your energy. We need your power. Will you fight beside us when the storm comes?'

She hesitated. She had a chain of blue forget-me-nots tattooed around her left wrist.

'Yes,' she said, after a while. 'I guess I will.'

I guess it's true what they say, thought Shadow. *If you can fake sincerity, you've got it made.* Then he felt guilty for thinking it.

Wednesday kissed his finger, touched it to Easter's cheek. He called their waitress over and paid for their coffees, counting out the money carefully, folding it over with the check and presenting it to her.

As she walked away, Shadow said, 'Ma'am? Excuse me? I think you dropped this.' He picked up a ten dollar bill from the floor.

'No,' she said, looking at the wrapped bills in her hand.

'I saw it fall, ma'am,' said Shadow, politely. 'You should count them.'

She counted the money in her hand, looked puzzled and said, 'Jesus. You're right. I'm sorry.' She took the ten dollar bill from Shadow, and walked away.

Easter walked out onto the sidewalk with them. The light was just starting to fade. She nodded to Wednesday, then she touched Shadow's hand and said, 'What did you dream about, last night?'

'Thunderbirds,' he said. 'A mountain of skulls.'

She nodded. 'And do you know whose skulls they were?'

'There was a voice,' he said. 'In my dream. It told me.'

She nodded and waited.

He said, 'It said they were mine. Old skulls of mine. Thousands and thousands of them.'

She looked at Wednesday, and said, 'I think this one's a keeper.' She smiled her bright smile. Then she patted Shadow's arm and walked away down the sidewalk. He watched her go, trying – and failing – not to think of her thighs rubbing together as she walked.

In the taxi on the way to the airport, Wednesday turned to Shadow. 'What the hell was that business with the ten dollars about?'

'You shortchanged her. It comes out of her wages if she's short.'

'What the hell do you care?' Wednesday seemed genuinely irate.

Shadow thought for a moment. Then he said, 'Well, I wouldn't want anyone to do it to me. She hadn't done anything wrong.'

'No?' Wednesday stared off into the middle-distance, and said, 'When she was seven years old she shut a kitten in a closet. She listened to it mew for several days. When it ceased to mew, she took it out of the closet, put it into a shoebox, and buried it in the back yard. She wanted to bury something. She consistently steals from everywhere she works. Small amounts, usually. Last year she visited her grandmother in the nursing home to which the old woman is confined. She took an antique gold watch from her grandmother's bedside table, and then went prowling through several of the other rooms, stealing small quantities of money and personal effects from the twilight folk in their golden years. When she got home she did not know what to do with her spoils, scared someone would come after her, so she threw everything away except the cash.'

'I get the idea,' said Shadow.

'She also has asymptomatic gonorrhea,' said Wednesday. 'She suspects she might be infected but does nothing about it. When her last boyfriend accused her of having given him a disease she was hurt, offended, and refused to see him again.'

'This isn't necessary,' said Shadow. 'I said I get the idea. You could do this to anyone, couldn't you? Tell me bad things about them.'

'Of course,' agreed Wednesday. 'They all do the same things. They may think their sins are original, but for the most part they are petty and repetitive.'

'And that makes it okay for you to steal ten bucks from her?'

Wednesday paid the taxi and the two men walked into the airport, wandered up to their gate. Boarding had not yet begun. Wednesday said, 'What the hell *else* can I do? They don't sacrifice rams or bulls to me. They don't send me the souls of killers and slaves, gallows-hung and raven-picked. *They* made me. *They* forgot me. Now I take a little back from them. Isn't that fair?'

'My mom used to say, *Life isn't fair*,' said Shadow.

'Of course she did,' said Wednesday. 'It's one of those things that moms say, right up there with *if all your friends jumped off a cliff would you do it too?*'

'You stiffed that girl for ten bucks, I slipped her ten bucks,' said Shadow, doggedly. 'It was the right thing to do.'

Someone announced that their plane was boarding. Wednesday stood up. 'May your choices always be so clear,' he said.

The cold snap was easing when Wednesday dropped Shadow off, in the small hours of the morning. It was still obscenely cold in Lakeside, but it was no longer impossibly cold. The lighted sign on the side of the M&I Bank flashed alternately 3:30 a.m. and -5° F as they drove through the town.

It was 9:30 a.m. when Chief of Police Chad Mulligan knocked on the apartment door and asked Shadow if he knew a girl named Alison McGovern.

'I don't think so,' said Shadow, sleepily.

'This is her picture,' said Mulligan. It was a high school photograph. Shadow recognised the person in the picture immediately: the girl with the blue rubber band braces on her teeth, the one who had been learning all about the oral uses of Alka-Seltzer from her friend.

'Oh yeah. Okay. She was on the bus when I came into town.'

'Where were you yesterday, Mister Ainsel?'

Shadow felt his world begin to spin away from him. He knew he had nothing to feel guilty about (*you're a parole-violating felon living under an assumed name*, whispered a calm voice in his mind. *Isn't that enough?*).

'San Francisco,' he said. 'California. Helping my uncle transport a four poster bed.'

'You got any ticket stubs? Anything like that?'

'Sure.' He had both his boarding pass stubs in his back pocket, pulled them out. 'What's going on?'

Chad Mulligan examined the boarding passes. 'Alison McGovern's vanished. She helped out up at the Lakeside Humane Society. Feed animals, walk dogs. She'd come out for a few hours after school. So. Dolly Knopf, who runs the Humane Society, she'd always run her home when they closed up for the night. Yesterday Alison never got there.'

'She's vanished.'

'Yup. Her parents called us last night. Silly kid used to hitchhike up to the Humane Society. It's out on County W, pretty isolated. Her parents told her not to, but this isn't the kind of place where things happen . . . people here don't lock their doors, you know? And you can't tell kids. So, look at the photo again.'

Alison McGovern was smiling. The rubber bands on her teeth in the photograph were red, not blue.

'You can honestly say you didn't kidnap her, rape her, murder her, anything like that?'

'I was in San Francisco. And I wouldn't do that shit.'

'That was what I figured, pal. So you want to come help us look for her?'

'Me?'

'You. We've had the K-9 guys out this morning – nothing so far.' He sighed. 'Heck, Mike. I just hope she turns up in the Twin Cities with some dopy boyfriend.'

'You think it's likely?'

'I think it's possible. You want to join the hunting party?'

Shadow remembered seeing the girl in Hennings Farm and Home Supplies, the flash of a shy blue-braced smile, how beautiful he had known she was going to be, one day. 'I'll come,' he said.

There were two dozen men and women waiting in the lobby of the fire station. Shadow recognised Hinzelmann, and several other faces looked familiar. There were police officers, and some men and women in the brown uniforms of the Lumber County Sheriff's department.

Chad Mulligan told them what Alison was wearing when she vanished (a scarlet snowsuit, green gloves, blue woollen hat under the hood of her snowsuit) and divided the volunteers into groups of three. Shadow, Hinzelmann and a man named Brogan comprised one of the groups. They were reminded how short the daylight period was, told that if, god forbid, they found Alison's body they were not repeat not to disturb anything, just to radio back for help, but that if she was alive they were to keep her warm until help came.

They were dropped off out on County W.

Hinzelmann, Brogan and Shadow walked along the edge of a frozen creek. Each group of three had been issued a small hand-held walkie-talkie before they left.

The cloud cover was low, and the world was grey. No snow had fallen in the last 36 hours. Footprints stood out in the glittering crust of the crisp snow.

Brogan looked like a retired army colonel, with his slim moustache and white temples. He told Shadow he was a retired High School Principal. 'I wasn't getting any younger. These days I still teach a little, do the school play – that was always the high point of the year anyhow – and now I hunt a little and have a cabin down on Pike Lake, spend too much time there.' As they set out Brogan said, 'On the one hand, I hope we find her. On the other, if she's going to be found, I'd be very grateful if it was someone else who got to find her, and not us. You know what I mean?'

Shadow knew exactly what he meant.

The three men did not talk much. They walked, looking for a red snowsuit, or green gloves, or a blue hat, or a white body. Now and again Brogan, who had the walkie-talkie, would check in with Chad Mulligan.

At lunchtime they sat with the rest of the search party on a commandeered school bus and ate hot dogs and drank hot soup. Someone pointed out a red-tailed hawk in a bare tree, and someone else said that it looked more like a falcon, but it flew away and the argument was abandoned.

Hinzelmann told them a story about his grandfather's trumpet, and how he tried playing it during a cold snap, and the weather was so cold outside by the barn, where his grandfather had gone to practice, that no music came out.

'Then after he came inside he put the trumpet down by the wood-stove to thaw. Well, the family're all in bed that night and suddenly the unfrozen tunes start coming out of that trumpet. Scared my grandmother so much she nearly had kittens.'

The afternoon was endless, unfruitful and depressing. The daylight faded slowly: distances collapsed and the world turned indigo and the wind blew cold enough to burn the skin on your face. When it was too dark to continue, Mulligan radioed to them to call it off for the evening, and they were picked up and driven back to the fire station.

In the block next to the fire station was the Buck Stops Here Tavern, and that was where most of the searchers wound up. They were exhausted and dispirited, talking to each other of how cold it had become, how more than likely Alison would show up in a day or so, no idea of how much trouble she'd caused everyone.

'You shouldn't think badly of the town because of this,' said Brogan. 'It *is* a good town.'

'Lakeside,' said a trim woman whose name Shadow had forgotten, if ever they'd been introduced, 'is the best town in the North Woods. You know how many people are unemployed in Lakeside?'

'No,' said Shadow.

'Less than twenty,' she said. 'There's over five thousand people live in and around this town. We may not be rich, but everyone's working. It's not like the mining towns up in the northeast – most of them are ghost towns now. There were farming towns that were killed by the falling cost of milk, or the low price of hogs. You know what the biggest cause of unnatural death is among farmers in the midwest?'

'Suicide?' Shadow hazarded.

She looked almost disappointed. 'Yeah. That's it. They kill themselves.' She shook her head. Then she continued, 'There are too many towns hereabouts that only exist for the hunters and the vacationers, towns that just take their money and send them home with their trophies and their bug bites. Then there are the company towns, where everything's just hunky-dory until Wal-Mart relocates their distribution centre or 3M stops manufacturing CD cases there or whatever and suddenly there's a boatload of folks who can't pay their mortgages. I'm sorry, I didn't catch your name.'

'Ainsel,' said Shadow. 'Mike Ainsel.' The beer he was drinking was a local brew, made with spring water. It was good.

'I'm Callie Knopf,' she said. 'Dolly's sister.' Her face was still ruddy from the cold. 'So what I'm saying is that Lakeside's lucky. We've got a little of everything here – farm, light industry, tourism, crafts. Good schools.'

Shadow looked at her in puzzlement. There was something empty at the bottom of all her words. It was as if he were listening to a salesman, a good salesman, who believed in his product, but still wanted to make sure you went home with all the brushes or the full set of encyclopedias. Perhaps she could see it in his face. She said, 'I'm sorry. When you love something you just don't want to stop talking about it. What do you do Mr Ainsel?'

'My uncle buys and sells antiques all over the country. He uses me to move big, heavy things. It's a good job, but not steady work.' A black cat, the bar mascot, wound between Shadow's legs, rubbing its forehead on his boot. It leapt up beside him onto the bench and went to sleep.

'At least you get to travel,' said Brogan. 'You do anything else?'

'You got eight quarters on you?' asked Shadow. Brogan fumbled for his change. He found five quarters, pushed them across the table to Shadow. Callie Knopf produced another three quarters.

He laid out the coins, four in each row. Then, with scarcely a fumble, he did the Coins Through the Table, appearing to drop half the coins through the wood of the table, from his left hand into his right.

After that, he divided the quarters into two piles of four. He took all eight coins in his right hand, an empty water glass in his left, covered the glass with a napkin and appeared to make the coins vanish, one by one, from his right hand and land in the glass beneath the napkin with an audible clink. Finally he opened his right hand to show it was empty, then swept the napkin away to show the coins in the glass.

He returned their coins – three to Callie, five to Brogan – then took a quarter back from Brogan's hand, leaving four coins. He blew on it, and it was a penny, which he gave to Brogan, who counted his quarters and was dumbfounded to find that he still had all five in his hand.

'You're a Houdini,' cackled Hinzelmann in delight. 'That's what you are!'

'Just an amateur,' said Shadow. 'I've got a long way to go.' Still, he felt a whisper of pride. They had been his first adult audience.

He stopped at the food store on the way home to buy a carton of milk. The ginger-haired girl on the checkout counter looked familiar, and her eyes were red-rimmed from crying. Her face was one big freckle.

'I know you,' said Shadow. 'You're—' and he was about to say the Alka-Seltzer girl, but bit it back and finished, 'You're Alison's friend. From the bus. I hope she's going to be okay.'

She sniffed and nodded. 'Me too.' She blew her nose on a tissue, hard, and pushed it back into her sleeve.

Her badge said '*Hi! I'm* **SOPHIE!** *Ask ME how YOU can lose 20lbs in 30 days!*'

'I spent today looking for her. No luck yet.'

Sophie nodded, blinked back tears. She waved the milk carton in front of a scanner and it chirped its price at them. Shadow passed her two dollars.

'I'm leaving this fucking town,' said the girl in a sudden, choked voice. 'I'm going to live with my mom in Ashland. Alison's gone. Sandy Olsen went last year. Jo Ming the year before that. What if it's me next year?'

'I thought Sandy Olsen was taken by his father.'

'Yes,' said the girl, bitterly. 'I'm sure he was. And Jo Ming went out to California, and Sarah Lindquist got lost on a trail hike and they never found her. Whatever. I want to go to Ashland.'

She took a deep breath and held it for a moment. Then, unexpectedly, she smiled at him. There was nothing insincere about that smile. It was just, he guessed, that she had been told to smile when she gave somebody change. She told him to have a nice day. Then she turned to the woman with the full shopping cart behind him and began to unload-and-scan.

Shadow took his milk and drove away, past the gas station and the klunker on the ice, and over the bridge and home.

COMING TO AMERICA
1778

There was a girl, and her uncle sold her, *wrote Mr Ibis in his perfect copper-plate handwriting.*

That is the tale; the rest is detail.

There are accounts which, if we open our hearts to them, will cut us too deeply. Look – here is a good man, good by his own lights and the lights of his friends: he is faithful and true to his wife, he adores and lavishes attention on his little children, he cares about his country, he does his job punctiliously, as best he can. So, efficiently and good-naturedly, he exterminates Jews: he appreciates the music that plays in the background to pacify them; he advises the Jews not to forget their identification numbers as they go into the showers – many people, he tells them, forget their numbers, and take the wrong clothes when they come out of the showers. This calms the Jews. There will be life, they assure themselves, after the showers. Our man supervises the detail taking the bodies to the ovens; and if there is anything he feels bad about, it is that he still allows the gassing of vermin to affect him. Were he a truly good man, he knows, he would feel nothing but joy as the earth is cleansed of its pests.

There was a girl, and her uncle sold her. Put like that it seems so simple.

No man, proclaimed Donne, *is an Island,* and he was wrong. If we were not islands, we would be lost, drowned in each other's tragedies. We are insulated (a word that means, literally, remember, *made into an island*) from the tragedy of others, by our island nature, and by the repetitive shape and form of the stories. The shape does not change: there was a human being who was born, lived, and then, by some means or another, died. There. You may fill in the details from your own experience. As unoriginal as any other tale, as unique as any other life. Lives are snowflakes: forming patterns we have seen before, as like one another as peas in a pod (and have you ever looked at peas in a pod? I mean, really *looked* at them? There's not a chance you'd mistake one for another, after a minute's close inspection) but still unique.

Without individuals we see only numbers: a thousand dead, a hundred thousand dead, 'casualties may rise to a million'. With individual stories, the statistics become people – but even that is a lie, for the people continue to suffer in numbers that themselves are numbing and meaningless. *Look*, see the child's swollen, swollen belly, the flies that crawl at the corners of his eyes, his skeletal limbs: will it make it easier for you to know his name, his age, his dreams, his fears? To see him from the inside? And if it does, are we not doing a disservice to his sister, who lies in the searing dust beside him, a distorted, distended caricature of a human child? And there, if we feel for them, are they now more important to us than a thousand other children touched by the same famine, a thousand other young lives who will soon be food for the flies' own myriad squirming children?

We draw our lines around these moments of pain, and remain upon our islands, and they cannot hurt us. They are covered with a smooth, safe, nacreous layer to let them slip, pearl-like, from our souls without real pain.

Fiction allows us to slide into these other heads, these other places, and look out through other eyes. And then in the tale we stop before we die, or we die vicariously and unharmed, and in the world beyond the tale we turn the page or close the book, and we resume our lives.

A life, which is, like any other, unlike any other.

And the simple truth is this: *there was a girl and her uncle sold her.*

This is what they used to say, where the girl came from: no man may be certain who fathered a child, but the mother, ah, that you could be certain of. Lineage and property was something that moved in the matrilineal line, but power remained in the hands of the men: a man had complete ownership of his sister's children.

There was a war in that place, and it was a small war, no more than a skirmish between the men of two rival villages. It was almost an argument. One village won the argument, one village lost it.

Life as a commodity, people as possessions. Enslavement had been part of the culture of those parts for thousands of years. The Arab slavers had destroyed the last of the great kingdoms of East Africa, while the West African nations had destroyed each other.

There was nothing untoward or unusual about their uncle selling the twins, although twins were considered magical beings, and their uncle was scared of them, scared enough that he did not tell them that they were to be sold in case they harmed his shadow and killed him. They were twelve years old. She was called Wututu, the messenger bird, he was called Agasu, the name of a dead king. They were healthy children, and, because they were twins, male and female, they were told many things about the gods, and because they were twins they listened to the things that they were told, and they remembered.

Their uncle was a fat and lazy man. If he had owned more cattle, perhaps he would have given up one of his cattle instead of the children, but he did not. He sold the twins. Enough of him: he shall not enter further into this narrative. We follow the twins.

They were marched, with several other slaves taken or sold in the war, for a dozen miles, to a small outpost. Here they were traded, and the twins, along with thirteen others, were bought by six men with spears and knives who marched them to the west, toward the sea, and then for many miles along the coast. There were fifteen slaves now altogether, their hands loosely bound, tied neck to neck.

Wututu asked her brother Agasu what would happen to them.

'I do not know,' he said. Agasu was a boy who smiled often: his teeth were white and perfect, and he showed them as he grinned, his happy smiles making Wututu happy in her turn. He was not smiling now. Instead he tried to show bravery for his sister, his head back and shoulders spread, as proud, as menacing, as comical as a puppy with its hackles raised.

The man in the line behind Wututu, his cheeks scarred, said, 'They will sell us to the white devils, who will take us to their home across the water.'

'And what will they do to us there?' demanded Wututu.

The man said nothing.

'Well?' asked Wututu. Agasu tried to dart a glance over his shoulder. They were not allowed to talk or sing as they walked.

'It is possible they will eat us,' said the man. 'That is what I have been told. That is why they need so many slaves. It is because they are always hungry.'

Wututu began to cry as she walked. Agasu said, 'Do not cry, my sister. They will not eat you. I shall protect you. Our gods will protect you.'

But Wututu continued to cry, walking with a heavy heart, feeling pain and anger and fear as only a child can feel them: raw and overwhelming. She was unable to tell Agasu that she was not worried about the white devils eating her. She would survive, she was certain of it. She cried because she was scared that they would eat her brother, and she was not certain that she could protect him.

They reached a trading post, and they were kept there for ten days. On the morning of the tenth day they were taken from the hut in which they had been imprisoned (it had become very crowded in the final days, as men arrived from far away bringing their own strings and skeins of slaves). They were marched to the harbor, and Wututu saw the ship that was to take them away.

Her first thought was how big a ship it was, her second that it was too small for all of them to fit inside. It sat lightly on the water. The ship's boat came back and forth, ferrying the captives to the ship where they were manacled and arranged in low decks by sailors, some of whom were brick-red or tan skinned, with strange pointy noses and beards that made them look like beasts. Several of the sailors looked like her own people, like the men who had marched her to the coast. The men and the women and the children were separated, forced into different areas on the slave deck. There were too many slaves for the ship to hold easily, so another dozen men were chained up on the deck in the open, beneath the places where the crew would sling their hammocks.

Wututu was put in with the children, not with the women; and she was not chained, merely locked in. Agasu, her brother, was forced in with the men, in chains, packed like herrings. It stank under that deck, although the crew had scrubbed it down since their last cargo. It was a stink that had entered the wood: the smell of fear and bile and diarrhoea and death, of fever and madness and hate. Wututu sat in the hot hold with the other children. She could feel the children on each side of her sweating. A wave tumbled a small boy into her, hard, and he apologised in a tongue that Wututu did not recognise. She tried to smile at him in the semi-darkness.

The ship set sail. Now it rode heavy in the water.

Wututu wondered about the place the white men came from (although none of them were truly white: sea-burned and sunburned they were, and their skins were dark). Were they so short of food that they had to send all the way to her land for people to eat? Or was it that she was to be a delicacy, a rare treat for a people who had eaten so many things that only black-skinned flesh in their cookpots made their mouths water?

On the second day out of port the ship hit a squall, not a bad one, but the ship's decks lurched and tumbled, and the smell of vomit joined the mixed smells of urine and liquid faeces and fear-sweat. Rain poured down on them in bucketloads from the air gratings set in the ceiling of the slave deck.

A week into the voyage, and well out of sight of land, the slaves were allowed out of irons. They were warned that any disobedience, any trouble, and they would be punished more than they had ever imagined.

In the morning the captives were fed beans and ship's biscuits, and a mouthful each of vinegared lime juice, harsh enough that their faces would twist, and they would cough and splutter, and some of them would moan and wail as the lime juice was spooned out. They could not spit it out, though: if they were caught spitting or dribbling it out they were lashed or beaten.

The night brought them salted beef. It tasted unpleasant, and there was a rainbow sheen to the grey surface of the meat. That was at the start of the voyage. As the voyage continued, the meat grew worse.

When they could, Wututu and Agasu would huddle together, talking of their mother and their home and their playfellows. Sometimes Wututu would tell Agasu the stories their mother had told them, like those of Elegba, the trickiest of the gods, who was Great Mawu's eyes and ears in the world, who took messages to Mawu and brought back Mawu's replies.

In the evenings, to while away the monotony of the voyage, the sailors would make the slaves sing for them and dance the dances of their native lands.

Wututu was lucky that she had been put in with the children.

The children were packed in tightly and ignored; the women were not always so fortunate. On some slave ships the female slaves were raped repeatedly by the crew, simply as an unspoken perquisite of the voyage. This was not one of those ships, which is not to say that there were no rapes.

A hundred men, women and children died on that voyage and were dropped over the side; and some of the captives who were dropped over the side had not yet died, but the green chill of the ocean cooled their final fever and they went down flailing, choking, lost.

Wututu and Agasu were travelling on a Dutch ship, but they did not know this, and it might as easily have been British, or Portuguese, or Spanish, or French.

The black crewmen on the ship, their skins even darker than Wututu's told the captives where to go, what to do, when to dance. One morning Wututu caught one of the black guards watching her. When she was eating, the man came over to her and stared down at her, without saying anything.

'Why do you do this?' she asked the man. 'Why do you serve the white devils?'

He grinned at her as if her question was the funniest thing he ever had heard. Then he leaned over, so his lips were almost brushing her ears, so his hot breath on her ear made her suddenly feel sick. 'If you were older,' he told her, 'I would make you scream with happiness from my penis. Perhaps I will do it tonight. I have seen how well you dance.'

She looked at him with her nut-brown eyes and she said, unflinching, smiling even, 'If you put it in me down there I will bite it off with my teeth down there. I am a witch girl, and I have very sharp teeth down there.' She took pleasure in watching his expression change. He said nothing and walked away.

The words had come out of her mouth, but they had not been her words: she had not thought them or made them. No, she realised, those were the words of Elegba the trickster. Mawu had made the world and then, thanks to Elegba's trickery, had lost interest in it. It was Elegba of the clever ways and the iron-hard erection who had spoken through her, who had ridden her for a moment, and that night before she slept she gave thanks to Elegba.

Several of the captives refused to eat. They were whipped until they put food into their mouths and swallowed, although the whipping was severe enough that two men died of it. Still, no-one else on the ship tried to starve themselves to freedom. A man and a woman tried to kill themselves by leaping over the side. The woman succeeded. The man was rescued and he was tied to the mast and lashed for the better part of a day, until his back ran with blood, and he was left there as the day became night. He was given no food to eat, and nothing to drink but his own piss. By the third day he was raving, and his head had swollen and grown soft, like an old melon. When he stopped raving they threw him over the side. Also, for five days following the escape attempt the captives were returned to their manacles and chains.

It was a long journey and a bad one for the captives, and it was not pleasant for the crew, although they had learned to harden their hearts to the business, and pretended to themselves that they were no more than farmers, taking their livestock to the market.

They made harbour on a pleasant, balmy day in Bridgeport, Barbados, and the captives were carried from the ship to the shore in low boats sent out from the dock, and taken to the market square where they were, by dint of a certain amount of shouting and blows from cudgels, arranged into lines. A whistle blew, and the market square filled with men, poking, prodding red-faced men shouting, inspecting, calling, appraising, grumbling.

Wututu and Agasu were separated then. It happened so fast – a big man forced open Agasu's mouth, looked at his teeth, felt his arm muscles, nodded, and two other men hauled Agasu away. He did not fight them. He looked at Wututu and called, 'Be brave,' to her. She nodded, and then her vision smeared and blurred with tears, and she wailed. Together they were twins, magical, powerful. Apart they were two children in pain.

She never saw him again but once, and never in life.

This is what happened to Agasu. First they took him to a seasoning farm, where they whipped him daily for the things he did and didn't do, they taught him a smattering of English and they gave him the name of Inky Jack, for the darkness of his skin. When he ran away they hunted him down with dogs and brought him back, and cut off a toe with a chisel, to teach him a lesson he would not forget.

He would have starved himself to death, but when he refused to eat his front teeth were broken and thin gruel was forced into his mouth, until he had no choice but to swallow or to choke.

Even in those times they preferred slaves born into captivity to those brought over from Africa. The free-born slaves tried to run, or they tried to die, and either way, there went the profits.

When Inky Jack was sixteen he was sold, with several other slaves, to a sugar plantation on the island of St. Domingue. They called him Hyacinth, the big, broken-toothed slave. He met an old woman from his own village on that plantation – she had been a house slave before her fingers became too gnarled and arthritic – who told him that the whites intentionally split up captives from the same towns and villages and regions, to avoid insurrection and revolts. They did not like it when slaves spoke to each other in their own languages.

Hyacinth learned some French, and was taught a few of the teachings of the Catholic Church. Each day he cut sugar-cane from well before the sun rose until after the sun had set.

He fathered several children. He went with the other slaves, in the small hours of the night, to the woods, although it was forbidden, to dance the Calinda, to sing to Damballa-Wedo, the serpent god, in the form of a black snake. He sang to Elegba, to Ogu, Shango, Zaka, and to many others, all the gods the captives had brought with them to the island, brought in their minds and their secret hearts.

The slaves on the sugar plantations of St. Domingue rarely lived more than a decade. The free time they were given – two hours in the heat of noon, and five hours in the dark of the night (from eleven until four) – was also the only time they had to grow and tend the food they would eat (for they were not fed by their masters, merely given small plots of land to cultivate, with which to feed themselves), and it was also the time they had to sleep and to dream. Even so, they would take that time and they would gather and dance, and sing and worship. The soil of St. Domingue was a fertile soil and the gods of Dahomey and the Congo and the Niger put down thick roots there and grew lush and huge and deep, and they promised freedom to those who worshipped them at night in the groves.

Hyacinth was twenty-five years of age when a spider bit the back of his right hand. The bite became infected and the flesh on the back of his hand was necrotic: soon enough his whole arm was swollen and purple, and the hand stank. It throbbed and it burned.

They gave him crude rum to drink, and they heated the blade of a machete in the fire until it glowed red and white. They cut his arm off at the shoulder with a saw, and they cauterized it with the burning blade. He lay in a fever for a week. Then he returned to work.

The one-armed slave called Hyacinth took part in the slave revolt of 1791.

Elegba himself took possession of Hyacinth in the grove, riding him as a white man rode a horse, and spoke through him. He remembered little of what was said, but the others who were with him told him that he had promised them freedom from their captivity. He remembered only his erection, rod-like and painful; and raising both hands – the one he had, and the one he no longer possessed – to the moon.

A pig was killed, and the men and the women of that plantation drank the hot blood of the pig, pledging themselves and binding themselves into a brotherhood. They swore that they were an army of freedom, pledged themselves once more to the gods of all the lands from which they had been dragged as plunder.

'If we die in battle with the whites,' they told each other, 'we will be reborn in Africa, in our homes, in our own tribes.'

There was another Hyacinth in the uprising, so they now called Agasu by the name of Big One-Arm. He fought, he worshipped, he sacrificed, he planned. He saw his friends and his lovers killed, and he kept fighting.

They fought for twelve years, a maddening, bloody struggle with the plantation owners, with the troops brought over from France. They fought, and they kept fighting, and, impossibly, they won.

On January the First, 1804, the independence of St. Domingue, soon to be known to the world as the Republic of Haiti, was declared. Big One-Arm did not live to see it. He had died in August 1802, bayoneted by a French Soldier.

At the precise moment of the death of Big One-Arm (who had once been called Hyacinth, and before that, Inky Jack, and who was forever in his heart Agasu,) his sister, whom he had known as

Wututu, who had been called Mary on her first plantation in the Carolinas, and Daisy when she had become a house slave, and Sukey when she was sold to the Lavere family down the river to New Orleans, felt the cold bayonet slide between her ribs and started to scream and weep uncontrollably. Her twin daughters woke and began to howl. They were cream-and-coffee colored, her new babies, not like the black children she had borne when she was on the plantation and little more than a girl herself – children she had not seen since they were fifteen and ten years old. The middle girl had been dead for a year, when she was sold away from them.

Sukey had been whipped many times since she had come ashore – once, salt had been rubbed into the wounds, on another occasion she had been whipped so hard and for so long that she could not sit, or allow anything to touch her back, for some days. She had been raped several times when younger: by black men who had been ordered to share her wooden palette, and by white men. She had been chained. She had not wept then, though. Since her brother had been taken from her she had only wept once. It was in North Carolina, when she had seen the food for the slave children and the dogs poured into the same trough, and she had seen her little children scrabbling with the dogs for the scraps. She saw that happen one day – and she had seen it before, every day on that plantation, and she would see it again many times before she left – she saw it that one day and it broke her heart.

She had been beautiful for a while. Then the years of pain had taken their toll, and she was no longer beautiful. Her face was lined, and there was too much pain in those brown eyes.

Eleven years earlier, when she was twenty-five, her right arm had withered. None of the white folk had known what to make of it. The flesh seemed to melt from the bones, and now her right arm hung by her side, little more than a skeletal arm covered in skin, and almost immobile. After this she had become a house-slave.

The Casterton family, who had owned the plantation were impressed by her cooking and house skills, but Mrs Casterton found the withered arm unsettling, and so she was sold to the Lavere family who were out for a year from Louisiana: M. Lavere was a fat, cheerful man, who was in need of a cook and a maid of all work, and who was not in the slightest repulsed by the slave Daisy's withered arm. When, a year later, they returned to Louisiana, slave Sukey went with them.

In New Orleans the women came to her, and the men also, to buy cures and love charms and little fetishes, black folks, yes, of course, but white folks too. The Lavere family turned a blind eye to it. Perhaps they enjoyed the prestige of having a slave who was feared and respected. They would not, however, sell her her freedom.

Sukey went into the Bayou late at night, and she danced the Calinda and the Bamboula. Like the dancers of St. Domingue and the dancers of her native land, the dancers in the bayou had a black snake as their *voudon*; even so, the gods of her homeland and of the other African nations did not possess her people as they had possessed her brother and the folk of St. Domingue. She would still invoke them and call their names, to beg them for favours.

She listened when the white folk spoke of the revolt in St. Domingo (as they called it), and how it was doomed to fail – 'think of it! A cannibal land!' – and then she observed that they no longer spoke of it.

Soon, it seemed to her that they pretended that there never had been a place called St. Domingo, and as for Haiti, the word was never mentioned. It was as if the whole American nation had decided that they could, by an effort of belief, command a good-sized Caribbean island to no longer exist merely by willing it so.

A generation of Lavere children grew up under Sukey's watchful eye. The youngest, unable to say 'Sukey' as a child, had called her Mama Zouzou, and the name had stuck. Now the year was 1821, and Sukey was in her mid-fifties. She looked much older.

She knew more of the secrets than old Sanité Dédé, who sold candies in front of the Cabildo, more than Marie Saloppé, who called herself the voodoo queen: both were free women of colour, while Mama Zouzou was a slave, and would die a slave, or so her master had said.

The young woman who came to her to find what had happened to her husband styled herself the Widow Paris. She was high-breasted and young and proud. She had African blood in her, and European blood, and Indian blood. Her skin was reddish, her hair was a gleaming black. Her eyes were black and haughty. Her husband, Jacques Paris, was, perhaps, dead. He was three-quarters white as these things were calculated, and the bastard of a once-proud family, one of the many immigrants who had fled from St Domingo, and as freeborn as his striking young wife.

'My Jacques. Is he dead?' asked the Widow Paris. She was a hairdresser who went from home to home, arranging the coiffures of the elegant ladies of New Orleans before their demanding social engagements.

Mama Zouzou consulted the bones, then shook her head. 'He is with a white woman, somewhere north of here,' she said. 'A white woman with golden hair. He is alive.'

This was not magic. It was common knowledge in New Orleans just with whom Jacques Paris had run off, and the colour of her hair.

Mama Zouzou was surprised to realise that the Widow Paris did not already know that her Jacques was sticking his quadroon little *pipi* into a pink-skinned girl up in Colfax every night. Well, on the nights that he was not so drunk that he could use it for nothing better than pissing.

Perhaps she knew. Perhaps she had another reason for coming.

The Widow Paris came to see the old slave woman one or two times a week. After a month she brought gifts for the old woman: hair ribbons, and a seed-cake, and a black rooster.

'Mama Zouzou,' said the girl, 'It is time for you to teach me what you know.'

'Yes,' said Mama Zouzou, who knew which way the wind blew. And besides, the Widow Paris had confessed that she had been born with webbed toes, which meant that she was a twin and she had killed her twin in the womb. What choice did Mama Zouzou have?

She taught the girl that two nutmegs hung upon a string around the neck until the string breaks will cure heart murmurs, while a pigeon that has never flown, cut open and laid on the patient's head, will draw a fever. She showed her how to make a wishing bag, a small leather bag containing thirteen pennies, nine cotton seeds and the bristles of a black hog, and how to rub the bag to make wishes come true.

The Widow Paris learned everything that Mama Zouzou told her. She had no real interest in the gods, though. Not really. Her interests were in the practicalities. She was delighted to learn that if you dip a live frog in honey and place it in an ants nest, then, when the bones are cleaned and white, a close examination will reveal a flat, heart-shaped bone, and another with a hook on it: the bone with the hook on it must be hooked onto the garment of the one you wish to love you, while the heart-shaped bone must be kept safely (for if it is lost, your loved one will turn on you like an angry dog). Infallibly, if you do this, the one you love will be yours.

She learned that dried snake powder placed in the face powder of an enemy will produce blindness, and that an enemy can be made to drown herself by taking a piece of her underwear, turning it inside out, and burying it at midnight under a brick.

Mama Zouzou showed the Widow Paris the World Wonder Root, the great and the little roots of John the Conqueror, she showed her Dragon's Blood, and valerian and Five-Finger Grass. She showed her how to brew waste-away tea, and follow-me-water and faire-Shingo water.

All these things and more Mama Zouzou showed the Widow Paris. Still, it was disappointing for the old woman. She did her best to teach her the hidden truths, the deep knowledge, to tell her of Papa 'Legba, of Mawu, of Aido-Hwedo the voudon serpent, and the rest, but the Widow Paris (I shall now tell you the name she was born with, and the name she later made famous: it was Marie Laveau. But this was not the great Marie Laveau, the one you have heard of, this was her mother, who eventually became the Widow Glapion) she had no interest in the gods of the distant land. If St Domingo had been a lush black earth for the African gods to grow in, this land, with its corn and its melons, its crawfish and its cotton, was barren and infertile.

'She does not want to know,' complains Mama Zouzou to Clémentine, her confidant, who took in the washing for many of the houses in that district, washing their curtains and coverlets. Clémentine had a blossom of burns on her cheek, and one of her children had been scalded to death when a copper overturned.

'Then do not teach her,' says Clémentine.

'I teach her, but she does not see what is valuable – all she sees is what she can do with it. I give her diamonds, but she cares only for pretty glass. I give her a demi-bouteille of the best claret and she drinks river-water. I give her quail and she wishes to eat only rat.'

'Then why do you persist?' asks Clémentine.

Mama Zouzou shrugs her thin shoulders, causing her withered arm to shake.

She cannot answer. She could say that she teaches because she is grateful to be alive, and she is: she has seen too many die. She could say that she dreams that one day the slaves will rise, as they rose (and were defeated) in LaPlace, but that she knows in her heart that without the gods of Africa, without the favour of 'Legba and Mawu, they will never overcome their white captors, will never return to their homelands.

When she woke, on that terrible night almost twenty years earlier, and felt the cold steel between her ribs, that was when Mama Zouzou's life had ended. Now she was someone who did not live, who simply hated. If you asked her about the hate she would have been unable to tell you about a twelve year old girl on a stinking ship: that had scabbed over in her mind – there had been too many whippings and beatings, too many nights in manacles, too many partings, too much pain. She could have told you about her son, though, and how his thumb had been cut off when their master discovered the boy was able to read and to write. She could have told you of her daughter, twelve years old and already eight months pregnant by an overseer, and how they dug a hole in the red earth to take her daughter's pregnant belly, and then they whipped her until her back had bled. Despite the carefully dug hole, her daughter had lost her baby and her life on a Sunday morning, when all the white folks were in church . . .

Too much pain.

'Worship them,' Mama Zouzou told the young Widow Paris in the Bayou, one hour after midnight. They were both naked to the waist, sweating in the humid night, their skins given accents by the white moonlight.

The Widow Paris's husband Jacques (whose own death, three years later, would have several remarkable features) had told Marie a little about the gods of St Domingo, but she did not care. Power came from the rituals, not from the gods.

Together Mama Zouzou and the Widow Paris crooned and stamped and keened in the swamp. They were singing in the black-snakes, the free woman of colour and the slave woman with the withered arm.

'There is more to it than just, you prosper, your enemies fail,' said Mama Zouzou.

Many of the words of the ceremonies, words she knew once, words her brother had also known, these words had fled from her memory. She told pretty Marie Laveau that the words did not matter, only the tunes and the beats, and there, singing and tapping in the blacksnakes, in the swamp, she has an odd vision. She sees the beats of the songs, the Calinda beat, the Bamboula beat, all the rhythms of equatorial Africa spreading slowly across this midnight land until the whole country shivers and swings to the beats of the old gods whose realms she had left. And even that, she understands somehow, in the swamp, even that will not be enough.

She turns to pretty Marie and sees herself through Marie's eyes, a black-skinned old woman, her face lined, her bony arm hanging stiffly by her side, her eyes the eyes of one who has seen her children fight in the trough for food from the dogs. She saw herself, and she knew then for the first time the revulsion and the fear the younger woman had for her.

Then she laughed, and crouched, and picked up in her good hand a blacksnake as tall as a sapling and as thick as a ship's rope.

'Here,' she said, 'Here will be our *voudon*.'

She dropped the unresisting snake into a basket that yellow Marie was carrying.

And then, in the moonlight, the second sight possessed her for a final time, and she saw her brother Agasu. He was not the twelve-year old boy she had last seen in the Bridgeport market, but a huge man, bald and grinning with broken teeth, his back lined with deep scars. In one hand he held a machete-knife. His right arm was barely a stump.

She reached out her own good left hand.

'Stay, stay a while,' she whispered. 'I will be there. I will be with you soon.'

And Marie Paris thought the old woman was speaking to her.

12

America has invested her religion as well as her morality in sound income-paying securities. She has adopted the unassailable position of a nation blessed because it deserves to be blessed; and her sons, whatever other theologies they may affect or disregard, subscribe unreservedly to this national creed.
– Agnes Repplier, *Times and Tendencies*

Shadow drove west, across Wisconsin and Minnesota and into North Dakota, where the snow-covered hills looked like huge sleeping buffalo, and he and Wednesday saw nothing but nothing and plenty of it for mile after mile. They went south, then, into South Dakota, heading for reservation country.

Wednesday had traded the Lincoln Town Car, which Shadow had liked to drive, for a lumbering and ancient Winnebago, which smelled pervasively and unmistakably of male cat, which he didn't enjoy driving at all.

As they passed their first signpost for Mount Rushmore, still several hundred miles away, Wednesday grunted. 'Now that,' he said, 'is a holy place.'

Shadow had thought Wednesday was asleep. He said, 'I know it used to be sacred to the Indians.'

'It's a holy place,' said Wednesday. 'That's the American Way – they need to give people an excuse to come and worship. These days, people can't just go and see a mountain. Thus, Mister Gutzon Borglum's tremendous presidential faces. Once they were carved, permission was granted, and now the people drive out in their multitudes to see something in the flesh that they've already seen on a thousand postcards.'

'I knew a guy once. He did weight training at the Muscle Farm, years back. He said that the Dakota Indians, the young men climb up the mountain, then form death-defying human chains off the heads, just so that the guy at the end of the chain can piss on the president's nose.'

Wednesday guffawed. 'Oh, fine! Very fine! Is any specific president the particular butt of their ire?'

Shadow shrugged. 'He never said.'

Miles vanished beneath the wheels of the Winnebago. Shadow began to imagine that he was staying still while the American landscape moved past them at a steady sixty-seven miles per hour. A wintery mist fogged the edges of things.

It was midday on the second day of the drive, and they were almost there. Shadow, who had been thinking, said, 'A girl vanished from Lakeside last week. When we were in San Francisco.'

'Mm?' Wednesday sounded barely interested.

'Kid named Alison McGovern. She's not the first kid to vanish there. There have been others. They go in the wintertime.'

Wednesday furrowed his brow. 'It is a tragedy, is it not? The little faces on the milk-cartons – although I can't remember the last time I saw a kid on a milk-carton – and on the walls of freeway rest areas. *Have you seen me?* they ask. A deeply existential question at the best of times. *Have you seen me?* Pull off at the next exit.'

Shadow thought he heard a helicopter pass overhead, but the clouds were too low to see anything.

'Why did you pick Lakeside?' asked Shadow.

'I told you. It's a nice quiet place to hide you away. You're off the board there, under the radar.'

'*Why?*'

'Because that's the way it is. Now hang a left,' said Wednesday.

Shadow turned left.

'There's something wrong,' said Wednesday. 'Fuck. Jesus fucking Christ on a bicycle. Slow down, but don't stop.'

'Care to elaborate?'

'Trouble. Do you know any alternative routes?'

'Not really. This is my first time in South Dakota,' said Shadow. 'And I don't know where we're going.'

On the other side of the hill something flashed redly, smudged by the mist.

'Roadblock,' said Wednesday. He pushed his hand deeply into first one pocket of his suit then another, searching for something.

'I can stop and turn around.'

'We can't turn. They're behind us as well,' said Wednesday. 'Take your speed down to ten, fifteen miles per hour.'

Shadow glanced into the mirror. There were headlights behind them, under a mile back. 'Are you sure about this?' he asked.

Wednesday snorted. 'Sure as eggs is eggs,' he said. 'As the turkey-farmer said when he hatched his first turtle. Ah, success!' and from the bottom of a pocket he produced a small piece of white chalk.

He started to scratch with the chalk on the dashboard of the camper, making marks as if he were solving an algebraic puzzle – or perhaps, Shadow thought, as if he were a hobo, scratching long messages to the other hobos in hobo code – *bad dog here, dangerous town, nice woman, soft jail in which to overnight* . . .

'Okay,' said Wednesday. 'Now increase your speed to thirty. And don't slow down from that.'

One of the cars behind them turned on its lights and siren and accelerated toward them. 'Do not slow down,' repeated Wednesday. 'They just want us to slow before we get to the roadblock.' *Scratch. Scratch. Scratch.*

They crested the hill. The roadblock was less than a quarter of a mile away. Twelve cars arranged across the road, and on the side of the road, police cars, and several big black SUVs.

'There,' said Wednesday, and he put his chalk away. The dash-board of the Winnebago was now covered with rune-like scratch-ings.

The car with the siren was just behind them. It had slowed to their speed, and a amplified voice was shouting, 'Pull over!' Shadow looked at Wednesday.

'Turn right,' said Wednesday. 'Just pull off the road.'

'I can't take this thing off-road. We'll tip.'

'It'll be fine. Take a right. Now!'

Shadow pulled the wheel down with his right hand, and the Winnebago lurched and jolted. For a moment he thought he had been correct, that the camper was going to tip, and then the world through the windshield dissolved and shimmered, like the reflec-tion in a clear pool when the wind brushes the surface.

The clouds and the mist and the snow and the day were gone.

Now there were stars overhead, hanging like frozen spears of light, stabbing the night sky.

'Park here,' said Wednesday. 'We can walk the rest of the way.'

Shadow turned off the engine. He went into the back of the Winnebago, pulled on his coat, his boots and gloves. Then he climbed out of the vehicle and said 'Okay. Let's go.'

Wednesday looked at him with amusement and something else – irritation perhaps. Or pride. 'Why don't you argue?' asked Wednesday. 'Why don't you exclaim that it's all impossible? Why the hell do you just do what I say and take it all so fucking calmly?'

'Because you're not paying me to ask questions,' said Shadow. And then he said, realising the truth as the words came out of his mouth, 'Anyway, nothing's really surprised me since Laura.'

'Since she came back from the dead?'

'Since I learned she was screwing Robbie. That one hurt. Everything else just sits on the surface. Where are we going now?'

Wednesday pointed, and they began to walk. The ground beneath their feet was rock of some kind, slick and volcanic, occasionally glassy. The air was chilly, but not winter-cold. They sidestepped their way awkwardly down a hill. There was a rough path, and they followed it. Shadow looked down to the bottom of the hill.

'What the hell is that?' asked Shadow, but Wednesday touched his finger to his lips, shook his head sharply. Silence.

It looked like a mechanical spider, blue metal, glittering LED lights, and it was the size of a tractor. It squatted at the bottom of the hill. Beyond it were an assortment of bones, each with a flame beside it little bigger than a candle-flame, flickering.

Wednesday gestured for Shadow to keep his distance from these objects. Shadow took an extra step to the side, which was a mistake on that glassy path, as his ankle twisted and he tumbled down the slope, rolling and slipping and bouncing. He grabbed at a rock as he went past, and the obsidian snag ripped his leather glove as if it were paper.

He came to rest at the bottom of the hill, between the mechanical spider and the bones.

He put a hand down to push himself to his feet, and found himself touching what appeared to be a thighbone with the palm of his hand, and he was . . .

. . . standing in the daylight, smoking a cigarette, and looking at his watch. There were cars all around him, some empty, some not. He was wishing he had not had that last cup of coffee, for he dearly needed a piss, and it was starting to become uncomfortable.

One of the local law enforcement people came over to him, a big man with frost in his walrus moustache. He had already forgotten the man's name.

'I don't know how we could have lost them,' says Local Law Enforcement, apologetic and puzzled.

'It was an optical illusion,' he replies. 'You get them in freak weather conditions. The mist. It was a mirage. They were driving down some other road. We thought they were on this one.'

Local Law Enforcement looks disappointed. 'Oh. I thought it was maybe like an X-Files kinda thing,' he says.

'Nothing so exciting, I'm afraid.' He suffers from occasional hemorrhoids and his ass has just started itching in the way that signals that a flare-up is coming. He wants to be back inside the Beltway. He wishes there was a tree to go and stand behind: the urge to piss is getting worse. He drops the cigarette and steps on it.

Local Law Enforcement walks over to one of the police cars and says something to the driver. They both shake their heads.

He pulls out his telephone, touches the menu, pages down and finds the address entry marked 'Laundry' which had amused him so much when he typed it in – a reference to *The Man from U.N.C.L.E*, and as he looks at it he realises that it's not from that at all, that· was a *tailor's*, he's thinking of *Get Smart*, and he still feels weird and slightly embarrassed after all these years about not realising it was a comedy when he was a kid, and just wanting a shoephone . . .

A woman's voice on the phone. 'Yes?'

'This is Mister Town, for Mister World.'

'Hold please. I'll see if he's available.'

There is silence. Town crosses his legs, tugs his belt higher on his belly – *got* to lose these last ten pounds – and away from his bladder. Then an urbane voice says, 'Hello Mister Town.'

'We lost them,' says Town. He feels a knot of frustration in his gut: these were the bastards, the lousy dirty sons of bitches who killed Woody and Stone, for Chrissakes. Good men. Good men. He badly wants to fuck Mrs Wood, but knows it's still too soon after Woody's death to make a move. So he is taking her out for dinner every couple of weeks, an investment in the future, she's just grateful for the attention . . .

'How?'

'I don't know. We set up a roadblock, there was nowhere they could have gone and they went there anyway.'

'Just another one of life's little mysteries. Don't worry. Have you calmed the locals?'

'Told 'em it was an optical illusion.'

'They buy it?'

'Probably.'

There was something very familiar about Mr World's voice – which was a strange thing to think, he'd been working for him directly for two years now, spoken to him every day, of *course* there was something familiar about his voice.

'They'll be far away by now.'

'Should we send people down to the rez to intercept them?'

'Not worth the aggravation. Too many jurisdictional issues, and there are only so many strings I can pull in a morning. We have plenty of time. Just get back here. I've got my hands full at this end trying to organize the policy meeting.'

'Trouble?'

'It's a pissing contest. I've proposed that we have it out here. The techies want it in Austin, or maybe San Jose, the players want it in Hollywood, the intangibles want it on Wall Street. Everybody wants it in their own back yard. Nobody's going to give.'

'You need me to do anything?'

'Not yet. I'll growl at some of them, stroke others. You know the routine.'

'Yes, sir.'

'Carry on, Town.'

The connection is broken.

Town thinks he should have had a S.W.A.T. team to pick off that fucking Winnebago, or land-mines on the road, or a tactical friggin' nukuler device, that would have showed those bastards they meant business. It was like Mr World had once said to him, *We are writing the future in Letters of Fire* and Mr Town thinks that Jesus Christ if he doesn't piss now he'll lose a kidney, it'll just burst, and it was like his Pop had said when they were on long journeys, when Town was a kid, out on the interstate, his Pop would always say 'My back teeth are afloat,' and Mr Town could hear that voice even now, that sharp Yankee accent saying 'I got to take a leak soon. My back teeth are afloat' . . .

. . . and it was then that Shadow felt a hand opening his own hand, prising it open one finger at a time off the thighbone it was clutching. He no longer needed to urinate; that was someone else. He was standing under the stars on a glassy rock plain.

Wednesday made the signal for silence again. Then he began to walk, and Shadow followed.

There was a creak from the mechanical spider, and Wednesday froze. Shadow stopped and waited with him. Green lights flickered and ran up and along its side in clusters. Shadow tried not to breathe too loudly.

He thought about what had just happened. It had been like looking through a window into someone else's mind. And then he thought, *Mr World. It was me who thought his voice sounded familiar. That was my thought, not Town's. That was why that seemed so strange.* He tried to identify the voice in his mind, to put it into the category in which it belonged, but it eluded him.

It'll come to me, thought Shadow. *Sooner or later, it'll come to me.*

The green lights went blue, then red, then faded to a dull red, and the spider settled down on its metallic haunches. Wednesday began to walk forward, a lonely figure beneath the stars, in a broad-brimmed hat, his frayed dark cloak gusting randomly in the nowhere wind, his staff tapping on the glassy rock floor.

When the metallic spider was only a distant glint in the starlight, far back on the plain, Wednesday said, 'It should be safe to speak, now.'

'Where are we?'

'Behind the scenes,' said Wednesday.

'Sorry?'

'Think of it as being behind the scenes. Like in a theatre or something. I just pulled us out of the audience and now we're walking about backstage. It's a shortcut.'

'When I touched that bone I was in the mind of a guy named Town. He's with that spookshow. He hates us.'

'Yes.'

'He's got a boss named Mister World. He reminds me of someone, but I don't know who. I was looking into Town's head – or maybe I was in his head. I'm not certain.'

'Do they know where we're headed?'

'I think they're calling off the hunt right now. They didn't want to follow us to the reservation. Are we going to a reservation?'

'Maybe.' Wednesday leaned on his staff for a moment, then continued to walk.

'What was that spider thing?'

'A pattern manifestation. A search engine.'

'Are they dangerous?'

'You only get to be my age by assuming the worst.'

Shadow smiled. 'And how old would that be?'

'Old as my tongue,' said Wednesday. 'And a few months older than my teeth.'

'You play your cards so close to your chest,' said Shadow, 'That I'm not even sure that they're really cards at all.'

Wednesday only grunted.

Each hill they came to was harder to climb.

Shadow began to feel headachey. There was a pounding quality to the starlight, something that resonated with the pulse in his temples and his chest. At the bottom of the next hill he stumbled, opened his mouth to say something and, without warning, he vomited.

Wednesday reached into an inside pocket, and produced a small hipflask. 'Take a sip of this,' he said. 'Only a sip.'

The liquid was pungent, and it evaporated in his mouth like a good brandy, although it did not taste like alcohol. Wednesday took the flask away, and pocketed it. 'It's not good for the audience to find themselves walking about backstage. That's why you're feeling sick. We need to hurry to get you out of here.'

They walked faster, Wednesday at a solid trudge, Shadow stumbling from time to time, but feeling better for the drink, which had left his mouth tasting of orange peel, of rosemary oil and peppermint and cloves.

Wednesday took his arm. 'There,' he said, pointing to two identical hillocks of frozen rock-glass to their left. 'Walk between those two mounds. Walk beside me.'

They walked, and the cold air and bright daylight smashed into Shadow's face at the same time.

They were standing half-way up a gentle hill. The mist had gone, and the day was sunny and chill, the sky was a perfect blue. At the bottom of the hill was a gravel road, and a red station wagon bounced along it like a child's toy car. A gust of woodsmoke came from a building nearby. It looked as if someone had picked up a mobile home and dropped it on the side of the hill thirty years ago. The home was much repaired, patched, and, in places, added onto.

As they reached the door it opened, and a middle-aged man with sharp eyes and a mouth like a knife-slash looked down at them and said, 'Eyah, I heard that there were two white men on their way to see me. Two whites in a Winnebago. And I heard that they got lost, like white men always get lost if they don't put up their signs everywhere. And now look at these two sorry beasts at the door. You know you're on Lakota land?' His hair was grey, and long.

'Since when were you Lakota, you old fraud?' said Wednesday. He was wearing a coat and a flap-eared cap, and already it seemed to Shadow unlikely that only a few moments ago under the stars he had been wearing a broad-brimmed hat and a tattered cloak. 'So, Whiskey Jack. I'm starving, and my friend here just threw up his breakfast. Are you going to invite us in?'

Whiskey Jack scratched an armpit. He was wearing blue jeans and an undershirt the grey of his hair. He wore moccasins, and he seemed not to notice the cold. Then he said, 'I like it here. Come in, white men who lost their Winnebago.'

There was more woodsmoke in the air inside the trailer, and there was another man in there, sitting at a table. The man wore stained buckskins, and was barefoot. His skin was the colour of bark.

Wednesday seemed delighted. 'Well,' he said, 'It seems our delay was fortuitous. Whiskey Jack and Apple Johnny. Two birds with one stone.'

The man at the table, Apple Johnny, stared at Wednesday, then he reached down a hand to his crotch, cupped it and said, 'Wrong again. I jes' checked and I got both of my stones, jes' where they oughtta be.' He looked up at Shadow, raised his hand, palm out. 'I'm John Chapman. You don't mind anything your boss says about me. He's an asshole. Always was an asshole. Always goin' to be an asshole. Some people is jes' assholes, and that's an end of it.'

'Mike Ainsel,' said Shadow.

Chapman rubbed his stubbly chin. 'Ainsel,' he said. 'That's not a name. But it'll do at a pinch. What do they call you?'

'Shadow.'

'I'll call you Shadow, then. Hey, Whiskey Jack,' – but it wasn't really *Whiskey Jack* he was saying, Shadow realised. Too many syllables. 'How's the food looking?'

Whiskey Jack took a wooden spoon and lifted the lid off a black iron pot, bubbling away on the range of the woodburning stove. 'It's ready for eating,' he said.

He took four plastic bowls and spooned the contents of the pot into the bowls, put them down on the table. Then he opened the door, stepped out into the snow, and pulled a plastic gallon jug from the snowbank. He brought it inside, and poured four large glasses of a cloudy yellow-brown liquid, which he put beside each bowl. Last of all, he found four spoons. He sat down at the table with the other men.

Wednesday raised his glass suspiciously. 'Looks like piss,' he said.

'You still drinking that stuff?' asked Whiskey Jack. 'You white men are crazy. This is better.' Then, to Shadow, 'The stew is mostly wild turkey. John here brought the applejack.'

'It's a soft apple cider,' said John Chapman. 'I never believed in hard liquor. Makes men mad.'

The stew was delicious, and it was very good apple cider. Shadow forced himself to slow down, to chew his food, not to gulp it, but he was more hungry than he would have believed. He helped himself to a second bowl of the stew and a second glass of the cider.

'Dame Rumour says that you've been out talking to all manner of folk, offering them all manner of things. Says you're takin' the old folks on the war path,' said John Chapman. Shadow and Whiskey Jack were washing up, putting the leftover stew into tupperware bowls. Whiskey Jack put the bowls into the snowdrifts outside his front door, and put a milk crate on top of the place he'd pushed them, so he could find them again.

'I think that's a fair and judicious summary of events,' said Wednesday.

'They'll win,' said Whiskey Jack flatly. 'They won already. You lost already. Like the white man and my people. Mostly they won. And when they lost, they made treaties. Then they broke the treaties. So they won again. I'm not fighting for another lost cause.'

'And it's no use you lookin' at me,' said John Chapman, 'for even if I fought for you – which'n I won't – I'm no use to you. Mangy rat-tailed bastards jes' picked me off and clean forgot me.' He stopped. Then he said, 'Paul Bunyan.' He shook his head slowly and he said it again. *'Paul Bunyan.'* Shadow had never heard two such innocuous words made to sound so damning.

'Paul Bunyan?' Shadow said. 'What did he ever do?'

'He took up head space,' said Whiskey Jack. He bummed a cigarette from Wednesday and the two men sat and smoked.

'It's like the idiots who figure that hummingbirds worry about their weight or tooth decay or some such nonsense, maybe they just want to spare hummingbirds the evils of sugar,' explained Wednesday. 'So they fill the hummingbird feeders with fucking NutraSweet. The birds come to the feeders and they drink it. Then they die, because their food contains no calories even though their little tummies are full. That's Paul Bunyan for you. Nobody ever told Paul Bunyan stories. Nobody ever believed in Paul Bunyan. He came staggering out of a New York ad agency in 1910 and filled the nation's myth stomach with empty calories.'

'I like Paul Bunyan,' said Whiskey Jack. 'I went on his ride at the Mall of America, few years back. You see big old Paul Bunyan at the top then you come crashing down. Splash. He's okay by me. I don't mind that he never existed, means he never cut down any trees. Not as good as planting trees though. That's better.'

'You said a mouthful,' said Johnny Chapman.

Wednesday blew a smoke ring. It hung in the air, dissipating slowly in wisps and curls. 'Damn it, Whiskey Jack, that's not the point and you know it.'

'I'm not going to help you,' said Whiskey Jack. 'When you get your ass kicked, you can come back here and if I'm still here I'll feed you again. You get the best food in the fall.'

Wednesday said, 'All the alternatives are worse.'

'You have no idea what the alternatives are,' said Whiskey Jack. Then he looked at Shadow. 'You are hunting,' he said. His voice was roughened by woodsmoke and cigarettes.

'I'm working,' said Shadow.

Whiskey Jack shook his head. 'You are also hunting something,' he said. 'There is a debt that you wish to pay.'

Shadow thought of Laura's blue lips and the blood on her hands, and he nodded.

'Listen. Fox was here first, and his brother was the wolf. Fox said, people will live for ever. If they die they will not die for long. Wolf said, no, people will die, people must die, all things that live must die, or they will spread and cover the world, and eat all the salmon and the caribou and the buffalo, eat all the squash and all the corn. Now one day Wolf died, and he said to the fox, quick, bring me back to life. And Fox said, No, the dead must stay dead. You convinced me. And he wept as he said this. But he said it, and it was final. Now Wolf rules the world of the dead and Fox lives always under the sun and the moon, and he still mourns his brother.'

Wednesday said, 'If you won't play, you won't play. We'll be moving on.'

Whiskey Jack's face was impassive. 'I'm talking to this young man,' he said. 'You are beyond help. He is not.' He turned back to Shadow. 'Tell me your dream,' said Whiskey Jack.

Shadow said, 'I was climbing a tower of skulls. There were huge birds flying around it. They had lightning in their wings. They were attacking me. The tower fell.'

'Everybody dreams,' said Wednesday. 'Can we hit the road?'

'Not everybody dreams of the *Wakinyau*, the thunderbird,' said Whiskey Jack. 'We felt the echoes of it here.'

'I *told* you,' said Wednesday. 'Jesus.'

'There's a clutch of thunderbirds in West Virginia,' said Chapman, idly. 'A couple of hens and an old cock-bird at least. There's also a breeding pair in the land, they used to call it the State of Franklin, but old Ben never got his state, up between Kentucky and Tennessee. 'Course, there was never a great number of them, even at the best of times.'

Whiskey Jack reached out a hand the colour of the red clay, and touched Shadow's face, gently. 'Eyah,' he said. 'It's true. If you hunt the thunderbird you could bring your woman back. But she belongs to the wolf, in the dead places, not walking the land.'

'How do you *know*?' asked Shadow.

Whiskey Jack's lips did not move. 'What did the Buffalo tell you?'

'To believe.'

'Good advice. Are you going to follow it?'

'Kind of. I guess.' They were talking without words, without mouths, without sound. Shadow wondered if, for the other two men in the room, they were standing, unmoving, for a heartbeat or for a fraction of a heartbeat.

'When you find your tribe, come back and see me,' said Whiskey Jack. 'I can help.'

'I shall.'

Whiskey Jack lowered his hand. Then he turned to Wednesday. 'Are you going to fetch your Ho Chunk?'

'My what?'

'*Ho Chunk*. It's what the Winnebago call themselves.'

Wednesday shook his head. 'It's too risky. Retrieving it could be problematic. They'll be looking for it.'

'Is it stolen?'

Wednesday looked affronted. 'Not a bit of it. The papers are in the glove compartment.'

'And the keys?'

'I've got them,' said Shadow.

'My nephew, Harry Bluejay, has an '81 Buick. Why don't you give me the keys to your camper? You can take his car.'

Wednesday bristled. 'What kind of trade is that?'

Whiskey Jack shrugged. 'You know how hard it will be to bring back your camper from where you abandoned it? I'm doing you a favour. Take it or leave it. I don't care.' He closed his knife-wound mouth.

Wednesday looked angry, and then the anger became rue, and he said, 'Shadow, give the man the keys to the Winnebago.' Shadow passed the car keys to Whiskey Jack.

'Johnny,' said Whiskey Jack, 'will you take these men down to find Harry Bluejay? Tell him I said for him to give them his car.'

'Be my pleasure,' said John Chapman.

He got up and walked to the door, picked up a small hessian sack sitting next to it, opened the door and walked outside. Shadow and Wednesday followed him. Whiskey Jack waited in the doorway. 'Hey,' he said to Wednesday. 'Don't come back here, you. You are not welcome.'

Wednesday extended his finger heavenward. 'Rotate on this,' he said affably.

They walked downhill through the snow, pushing their way through the drifts. Chapman walked in front, his bare feet red against the crust-topped snow. 'Aren't you cold?' asked Shadow.

'My wife was Choctaw,' said Chapman.

'And she taught you mystical ways to keep out the cold?'

'Nope. She thought I was crazy,' said Chapman. 'She used t'say, "Johnny, why don't you jes' put on boots?"' The slope of the hill became steeper, and they were forced to stop talking. The three men stumbled and slipped on the snow, using the trunks of birch trees on the hillside to steady themselves, and to stop themselves from falling. When the ground became slightly more level, Chapman said, 'She's dead now, a'course. When she died I guess maybe I went a mite crazy. It could happen to anyone. It could happen to you.' He clapped Shadow on the arm. 'By Jesus and Jehosophat, you're a big man.'

'So they tell me,' said Shadow.

They trudged down that hill for another half an hour, until they reached the gravel road that wound around the base of it, and the three men began to walk along it, toward the cluster of buildings they had seen from high on the hill.

A car slowed and stopped. The woman driving it reached over, wound down the passenger window and said, 'You bozos need a ride?'

'You are very gracious, madam,' said Wednesday. 'We're looking for a Mister Harry Bluejay.'

'He'll be down at the rec hall,' said the woman. She was in her forties, Shadow guessed. 'Get in.'

They got in. Wednesday took the passenger seat, John Chapman and Shadow climbed into the back. Shadow's legs were too long to sit in the back comfortably, but he did the best he could. The car jolted forward, down the gravel road.

'So where did you three come from?' asked the driver.

'Just visiting with a friend,' said Wednesday.

'Lives on the hill back there,' said Shadow.

'What hill?' she asked.

Shadow looked back through the dusty rear window, looking back at the hill. But there was no high hill back there; nothing but clouds on the plains.

'Whiskey Jack,' he said.

'Ah,' she said. 'We call him Inktomi here. I think it's the same guy. My grandfather used to tell some pretty good stories about him. Of course, all the best of them were kind of dirty.' They hit a bump in the road, and the woman swore. 'You okay back there?'

'Yes ma'am,' said Johnny Chapman. He was holding on to the back seat with both hands.

'Rez roads,' she said. 'You get used to them.'

'Are they all like this?' asked Shadow.

'Pretty much,' said the woman. 'All the ones round here. And don't you go asking about all the money from casinos, because who in their right mind wants to come all the way out here to go to a casino? We don't see none of that money out here.'

'I'm sorry.'

'Don't be.' She changed gear with a crash and a groan. 'You know the white population all round here is falling? You go out there, you find ghost towns. How you going to keep them down on the farm, after they seen the world on their television screens? And it's not worth anyone's while to farm the Bad Lands anyhow. They took our lands, they settled here, now they're leaving. They go south. They go west. Maybe if we wait for enough of them to move to New York and Miami and L.A. we can take the whole of the middle back without a fight.'

'Good luck,' said Shadow.

They found Harry Bluejay in the rec hall, at the pool table, doing trick shots to impress a group of several girls. He had a blue jay tattooed on the back of his right hand, and multiple piercings in his right ear.

'Ho hoka, Harry Bluejay,' said John Chapman.

'Fuck off you crazy barefoot white ghost,' said Harry Bluejay, conversationally. 'You give me the creeps.'

There were older men at the far end of the room, some of them playing cards, some of them talking. There were other men, younger men of about Harry Bluejay's age, waiting for their turn at the pool table. It was a full-sized pool table, and a rip in the green baize on one side had been repaired with silver-grey duct tape.

'I got a message from your uncle,' said Chapman, unfazed. 'He says you're to give these two your car.'

There must have been thirty, maybe even forty people in that hall, and now they were every one of them looking intently at their playing cards, or their feet, or their fingernails, and pretending as hard as they could not to be listening.

'He's not my uncle.'

A cigarette-smoke fug hung over the hall. Chapman smiled widely, displaying the worst set of teeth that Shadow had seen in a human mouth. 'You want to tell your uncle that? He says you're the only reason he stays among the Lakota.'

'Whiskey Jack says a lot of things,' said Harry Bluejay, petulantly. But he did not say Whiskey Jack either. It sounded almost the same, to Shadow's ear, but not quite: *Wisakedjak*, he thought. That's what they're saying. Not Whiskey Jack at all.

Shadow said, 'Yeah. And one of the things he said was that we're trading our Winnebago for your Buick.'

'I don't see a Winnebago.'

'He'll bring you the Winnebago,' said John Chapman. 'You know he will.'

Harry Bluejay attempted a trick shot and missed. His hand was not steady enough. 'I'm not the old fox's nephew,' said Harry Bluejay. 'I wish he wouldn't say that to people.'

'Better a live fox than a dead wolf,' said Wednesday, in a voice so deep it was almost a growl. 'Now, will you sell us your car?'

Harry Bluejay shivered, visibly and violently. 'Sure,' he said. 'Sure. I was only kidding. I kid a lot, me.' He put down the pool cue on the pool table, and took a thick jacket, pulling it out from a cluster of similar jackets hanging from pegs by the door. 'Let me get my shit out of the car first,' he said.

He kept darting glances at Wednesday, as if he were concerned that the older man were about to explode.

Harry Bluejay's car was parked a hundred yards away. As they walked toward it, they passed a small whitewashed Catholic church, and a man in a priest's collar who stared at them from the doorway as they went past. He was sucking on a cigarette as if he did not enjoy smoking it.

'Good day to you, father!' called Johnny Chapman, but the man in the dog-collar made no reply; he crushed his cigarette under his heel, picked up the butt and dropped it into the bin beside the door, and went inside.

Harry Bluejay's car was missing its wing mirrors, and its tires were the baldest Shadow had ever seen: perfectly smooth black rubber. Harry Bluejay told them the car drank oil, but as long as you kept pouring oil in, it would just keep running forever, unless it stopped.

Harry Bluejay filled a black garbage bag with shit from the car (said shit including several screw-top bottles of cheap beer, unfinished, a small packet of cannabis resin wrapped in silver foil and badly hidden in the car's ashtray, a skunk-tail, two dozen country and western cassettes and a battered, yellowing copy of *Stranger in a Strange Land*). 'Sorry I was jerking your chain before,' said Harry Bluejay to Wednesday, passing him the car keys. 'You know when I'll get the Winnebago?'

'Ask your uncle. He's the fucking used car dealer,' growled Wednesday.

'Wisakedjak is *not* my uncle,' said Harry Bluejay. He took his black garbage bag and went into the nearest house, and closed the door behind him.

They dropped Johnny Chapman in Sioux Falls, outside a whole-food store.

Wednesday said nothing on the drive. He was in a black sulk, as he had been since they left Whiskey Jack's place.

In a family restaurant just outside St. Paul Shadow picked up a newspaper someone else had put down. He looked at it once, then again, then he showed it to Wednesday.

'Look at that,' said Shadow.

Wednesday sighed, and looked down at the paper. 'I am,' he said, 'delighted that the air-traffic controllers' dispute has been resolved without recourse to industrial action.'

'Not that,' said Shadow. 'Look. It says it's the fourteenth of February.'

'Happy Valentine's Day.'

'So we set out January the what, twentieth, twenty-first. I wasn't keeping track of the dates, but it was the third week of January. We were three days on the road, all told. So how is it the fourteenth of February?'

'Because we walked for almost a month,' said Wednesday. 'In the Badlands. Backstage.'

'Hell of a shortcut,' said Shadow.

Wednesday pushed the paper away. 'Fucking Johnny Appleseed, always going on about Paul Bunyan. In real life Chapman owned fourteen apple orchards. He farmed thousands of acres. Yes, he kept pace with the western frontier, but there's not a story out there about him with a word of truth in it, save that he went a little crazy once. But it doesn't matter. Like the newspapers used to say, if the truth isn't big enough, you print the legend. This country needs its legends. And even the legends don't believe it any more.'

'But you see it.'

'I'm a has-been. Who the fuck cares about me?'

Shadow said softly, 'You're a god.'

Wednesday looked at him sharply. He seemed to be about to say something, and then he slumped back in his seat, and looked down at the menu and said, 'So?'

'It's a good thing to be a god,' said Shadow.

'Is it?' asked Wednesday, and this time it was Shadow who looked away.

In a gas station twenty-five miles outside Lakeside, on the wall by the rest rooms, Shadow saw a home-made photocopied notice: a black and white photo of Alison McGovern and the handwritten question *Have You Seen Me?* above it. Same yearbook photograph: smiling confidently, a girl with rubber band braces on her top teeth who wants to work with animals when she grows up.

Have you seen me?

Shadow bought a Snickers bar, a bottle of water, and a copy of the *Lakeside News*. The above-the-fold story, written by Marguerite Olsen, our Lakeside Reporter, showed a photograph of a boy and an older man, out on the frozen lake, standing by an outhouse-like ice-fishing shack, and between them they were holding a big fish. They were smiling. *Father and Son Catch Local Record Northern Pike. Full story inside.*

Wednesday was driving. He said, 'Read me anything interesting you find in the paper.'

Shadow looked carefully, and he turned the pages slowly, but he couldn't find anything.

Wednesday dropped him off in the driveway outside his apartment. A smoke-coloured cat stared at him from the driveway, then fled when he bent to stroke it.

Shadow stopped on the wooden deck outside his apartment and looked out at the lake, dotted here and there with green and brown ice-fishing huts. Many of them had cars parked beside them. On the ice nearer the bridge sat the old green klunker, just as it had sat in the newspaper. 'March the twenty-third,' said Shadow, encouragingly. 'Round nine fifteen in the morning. You can do it.'

'Not a chance,' said a woman's voice. 'April third. Six p.m. That way the day warms up the ice.' Shadow smiled. Marguerite Olsen was wearing a ski suit. She was at the far end of the deck, refilling the bird feeder.

'I read your article in the *Lakeside News* on the Town Record Northern Pike.'

'Exciting, huh?'

'Well, educational, maybe.'

'I thought you weren't coming back to us,' she said. 'You were gone for a while, huh?'

'My uncle needed me,' said Shadow. 'The time kind of got away from us.'

She placed the last suet brick in its cage, and began to fill a net sock with thistle-seeds from a plastic milk-jug. Several goldfinches, olive in their winter coats, twitted impatiently from a nearby fir-tree.

'I didn't see anything in the paper about Alison McGovern.'

'There wasn't anything to report. She's still missing. There was a rumour that someone had seen her in Detroit, but it turned out to be a false alarm.'

'Poor kid.'

Marguerite Olsen screwed the top back onto the gallon jug. 'I hope she's dead,' she said, matter-of-factly.

Shadow was shocked. 'Why?'

'Because the alternatives are worse.'

The goldfinches hopped frantically from branch to branch of the fir-tree, impatient for the people to be gone.

You aren't thinking about Alison, thought Shadow. *You're thinking of your son. You're thinking of Sandy.*

He remembered someone saying *I miss Sandy.* Who was that?

'Good talking to you,' he said.

'Yeah,' she said. 'You too.'

February passed in a succession of short, grey days. Some days the snow fell, most days it didn't. The weather warmed up, and on the good days it got above freezing. Shadow stayed in his apartment until it began to feel like a prison cell, and then, on the days that Wednesday did not need him to travel, he began to walk.

He would walk for much of the day, long trudges out of the town. He walked, alone, until he reached the national forest to the north and the west, or the corn fields and cow pastures to the south. He walked the Lumber County Wilderness Trail, and he walked along the old railroad tracks, and he walked the backroads. A couple of times he even walked along the frozen lake, from north to south. Sometimes he'd see locals or winter tourists or joggers, and he'd wave and say hi. Mostly he saw nobody at all, just crows and finches and, a few times, he spotted a hawk feasting on a roadkill possum or raccoon. On one memorable occasion he watched an eagle snatch a silver fish from the middle of the White Pine River, the water frozen at the edges, but still rushing and flowing at the center. The fish wriggled and jerked in the eagle's talons, glittering in the midday sun; Shadow imagined the fish freeing itself and swimming off across the sky, and he smiled, grimly.

If he walked, he discovered, he did not have to think, and that was just the way he liked it; when he thought, his mind went to places he could not control, places that made him feel uncomfortable. Exhaustion was the best thing. When he was exhausted, his thoughts did not wander to Laura, or to the strange dreams, or to things that were not and could not be. He would return home from walking, and sleep without difficulty and without dreaming.

He ran into Police Chief Chad Mulligan in George's Barber Shop in the town square. Shadow always had high hopes for haircuts, but they never lived up to his expectations. After every haircut he looked more or less the same, only with shorter hair. Chad, seated in the barber's chair beside Shadow's, seemed surprisingly concerned about his own appearance. When his haircut was finished he gazed grimly at his reflection, as if he were preparing to give it a speeding ticket.

'It looks good,' Shadow told him.

'Would it look good to you if you were a woman?'

'I guess.'

They went across the square to Mabel's together, ordered mugs of hot chocolate. Chad said, 'Hey. Mike. Have you ever thought about a career in law enforcement?'

Shadow shrugged. 'I can't say I have,' he said. 'Seems like there's a whole lot of things you got to know.'

Chad shook his head. 'You know the main part of police work, somewhere like this? It's just keeping your head. Something happens, somebody's screaming at you, screaming blue murder, you simply have to be able to say that you're sure that it's all a mistake, and you'll just sort it all out if they just step outside quietly. And you have to be able to mean it.'

'And then you sort it out?'

'Mostly, that's when you put handcuffs on them. But yeah, you do what you can to sort it out. Let me know if you want a job. We're hiring. And you're the kind of guy we want.'

'I'll keep that in mind, if the thing with my uncle falls through.'

They sipped their hot chocolate. Mulligan said, 'Say, Mike, what would you do if you had a cousin. Like a widow. And she started calling you?'

'Calling you how?'

'On the phone. Long distance. She lives out of state.' His cheeks crimsoned. 'I saw her last year at a family wedding. She was married, back then, though, I mean, her husband was still alive, and she's family. Not a first cousin. Pretty distant.'

'You got a thing for her?'

Blush. 'I don't know about that.'

'Well then, put it another way. Does she have a thing for you?'

'Well, she's said a few things, on the phone. She's a very fine looking woman.'

'So . . . what are you going to do about it?'

'I could ask her out here. I could do that, couldn't I? She's kind of said she'd like to come up here.'

'You're both adults. I'd say go for it.'

Chad nodded, and blushed, and nodded again.

The telephone in Shadow's apartment was still silent and dead. He thought about getting it connected, but could think of no-one he wanted to call. Late one night he picked it up and listened, and was convinced that he could hear a wind blowing and a distant conversation between a group of people talking in voices too low to properly make out. He said, 'Hello?' and 'Who's there?' but there was no reply, only a sudden silence and then the faraway sound of laughter, so faint he was not certain he was not imagining it.

Shadow made more journeys with Wednesday in the weeks that followed.

He waited in the kitchen of a Rhode Island cottage, and listened while Wednesday sat in a darkened bedroom and argued with a woman who would not get out of bed, nor would she let Wednesday or Shadow look at her face. In the refrigerator was a plastic bag filled with crickets, and another filled with the corpses of baby mice.

In a rock club in Seattle, Shadow watched Wednesday shout his greeting, over the noise of the band, to a young woman with short red hair and blue-spiral tattoos. That talk must have gone well, for Wednesday came away from it grinning delightedly.

Five days later Shadow was waiting in the rental when Wednesday walked, scowling, from the lobby of an office building in Dallas. Wednesday slammed the car door when he got in, and sat there in silence, his face red with rage. He said, 'Drive.' Then he said, 'Fucking Albanians. Like anybody cares.'

Three days after that they flew to Boulder, where they had a pleasant lunch with five young Japanese women. It was a meal of pleasantries and politeness, and Shadow walked away from it unsure of whether anything had been agreed to or decided. Wednesday, though, seemed happy enough.

Shadow had begun to look forward to returning to Lakeside. There was a peace there, and a welcome, that he appreciated.

Each morning when he was not travelling he would drive across the bridge to the town square. He would buy two pasties at Mabel's;

he would eat one pasty then and there, and drink a coffee. If someone had left a newspaper out he would read it, although he was never interested enough in the news to purchase a newspaper himself.

He would pocket the second pasty, wrapped in its paper bag, and eat it for his lunch.

He was reading *USA Today* one morning when Mabel said, 'Hey, Mike. Where you going today?'

The sky was pale blue. The morning mist had left the trees covered with hoarfrost. 'I don't know,' said Shadow. 'Maybe I'll walk the wilderness trail again.'

She refilled his coffee. 'You ever gone east on County Q? It's kind of pretty out thataway. That's the little road that starts across from the carpet store on Twentieth Avenue.'

'No. Never have.'

'Well,' she said, 'it's kind of pretty.'

It was extremely pretty. Shadow parked his car at the edge of town, and walked along the side of the road, a winding, country road that curled around the hills to the east of the town. Each of the hills was covered with leafless maple trees, bone-white birches, dark firs and pines.

At one point a small dark cat kept pace with him beside the road. It was the colour of dirt, with white forepaws. He walked over to it. It did not run away.

'Hey cat,' said Shadow, unselfconsciously.

The cat put its head on one side, looked up at him with emerald eyes. Then it hissed – not at him, but at something over on the side of the road, something he could not see.

'Easy,' said Shadow. The cat stalked away across the road, and vanished into a field of old unharvested corn.

Around the next bend in the road Shadow came upon a tiny graveyard. The headstones were weathered, although several of them had sprays of fresh flowers resting against them. There was no wall about the graveyard, and no fence, only low mulberry trees, planted at the margins, bent over with ice and age. Shadow stepped over the piled-up ice and slush at the side of the road. There were two stone gateposts marking the entry to the graveyard, although there was no gate between them. He walked into the graveyard between the two posts.

He wandered around the graveyard, looking at the headstones. There were no inscriptions later than 1969. He brushed the snow from a solid-looking granite angel, and he leaned against it.

He took the paper bag from his pocket, and removed the pasty from it. He broke off the top: it breathed a faint wisp of steam into the wintery air. It smelled really good, too. He bit into it.

Something rustled behind him. He thought for a moment it was the cat, but then he smelled perfume, and under the perfume, the scent of something rotten.

'Please don't look at me,' she said, from behind him.

'Hello, Laura,' said Shadow.

Her voice was hesitant, perhaps, he thought, even a little scared. She said, 'Hello, puppy.'

He broke off some pasty. 'Would you like some?' he asked.

She was standing immediately behind him, now. 'No,' she said. 'You eat it. I don't eat food any more.'

He ate his pasty. It was good. 'I want to look at you,' he said.

'You won't like it,' she told him.

'Please?'

She stepped around the stone angel. Shadow looked at her, in the daylight. Some things were different and some things were the same. Her eyes had not changed, nor had the crooked hopefulness of her smile. And she was, very obviously, very dead. Shadow finished his pasty. He stood up and tipped the crumbs out of the paper bag, then folded it up and put it back into his pocket.

The time he had spent in the funeral home in Cairo made it easier somehow for him to be in her presence. He did not know what to say to her.

Her cold hand sought his, and he squeezed it gently. He could feel his heart beating in his chest. He was scared, and what scared him was the normality of the moment. He felt so comfortable with her at his side that he would have been willing to stand there for ever.

'I miss you,' he admitted.

'I'm here,' she said.

'That's when I miss you most. When you're here. When you aren't here, when you're just a ghost from the past or a dream from another life, it's easier then.'

She squeezed his fingers.

'So,' he asked. 'How's death?'

'Hard,' she said. 'It just keeps going.'

She rested her head on his shoulder, and it almost undid him. He said, 'You want to walk for a bit?'

'Sure.' She smiled up at him, a nervous, crooked smile in a dead face.

They walked out of the little graveyard, and made their way back down the road, toward the town, hand in hand. 'Where have you been?' she asked.

'Here,' he said. 'Mostly.'

'Since Christmas,' she said, 'I kind of lost you. Sometimes I would know where you were, for a few hours, for a few days. You'd be all over. Then you'd fade away again.'

'I was in this town,' he said. 'Lakeside. It's a good little town.'

'Oh,' she said.

She no longer wore the blue suit in which she had been buried. Now she wore several sweaters, a long, dark, skirt, and high, burgundy boots. Shadow commented on them.

Laura ducked her head. She smiled. 'Aren't they great boots? I found them in this great shoe store in Chicago.'

'So what made you decide to come up from Chicago?'

'Oh, I've not been in Chicago for a while, puppy. I was heading south. The cold was bothering me. You'd think I'd welcome it. But it's something to do with being dead, I guess. You don't feel it as cold. You feel it as a sort of *nothing*, and when you're dead I guess the only thing that you're scared of is nothing. I was going to go to Texas. I planned to spend the winter in Galveston. I think I used to winter in Galveston, when I was a kid.'

'I don't think you did,' said Shadow. 'You've never mentioned it before.'

'No? Maybe it was someone else, then. I don't know. I remember seagulls – throwing bread in the air for seagulls, hundreds of them, the whole sky becoming nothing but seagulls as they flapped their wings and snatched the bread from the air.' She paused. 'If I didn't see it, I guess someone else did.'

A car came around the corner. The driver waved them hello. Shadow waved back. It felt wonderfully normal to walk with his wife.

'This feels good,' said Laura, as if she was reading his mind.

'Yes,' said Shadow.

'When the call came I had to hurry back. I was barely into Texas.'

'Call?'

She looked up at him. Around her neck the gold coin glinted. 'It felt like a call,' she said. 'I started to think about you. About how much I needed to see you. It was like a hunger.'

'You knew I was *here*, then?'

'Yes.' She stopped. She frowned, and her upper teeth pressed into her blue lower lip, biting it gently. She put her head on one side and said, 'I did. Suddenly, I did. I thought you were calling me, but it wasn't you, was it?'

'No.'

'You didn't want to see me.'

'It wasn't that.' He hesitated. 'No. I didn't want to see you. It hurts too much.'

The snow crunched beneath their feet and it glittered diamonds as the sunlight caught it.

'It must be hard,' said Laura, 'not being alive.'

'You mean it's hard for you to be dead? Look, I'm still going to figure out how to bring you back, properly. I think I'm on the right track—'

'No,' she said. 'I mean, I'm grateful. And I hope you really can do it. I did a lot of bad stuff . . .' She shook her head. 'But I was talking about you.'

'I'm alive,' said Shadow. 'I'm not dead. Remember?'

'You're not dead,' she said. 'But I'm not sure that you're alive, either. Not really.'

This isn't the way this conversation goes, thought Shadow. *This isn't the way anything goes.*

'I love you,' she said, dispassionately. 'You're my puppy. But when you're really dead you get to see things clearer. It's like there isn't anyone there. You know? You're like this big, solid, man-shaped hole in the world.' She frowned. 'Even when we were together. I loved being with you. You adored me, and you would do anything for me. But sometimes I'd go into a room and I wouldn't think there was anybody in there. And I'd turn the light on, or I'd turn the light off, and I'd realise that you were in there, sitting on your own, not reading, not watching TV, not doing anything.'

She hugged him then, as if to take the sting from her words, and she said, 'The best thing about Robbie was that he was *somebody*. He was a jerk sometimes, and he could be a joke, and he loved to have mirrors around when we made love so he could watch himself fucking me, but he was *alive*, puppy. He *wanted* things. He filled the space.' She stopped, looked up at him, tipped her head a little to one side. 'I'm sorry. Did I hurt your feelings?'

He did not trust his voice not to betray him, so he simply shook his head.

'Good,' she said. 'That's good.'

They were approaching the rest area where he had parked his car. Shadow felt that he needed to say something: *I love you*, or *please don't go*, or *I'm sorry*. The kind of words you use to patch a conversation that had lurched, without warning, into the dark places. Instead he said, 'I'm not dead.'

'Maybe not,' she said. 'But are you sure you're alive?'

'Look at me,' he said.

'That's not an answer,' said his dead wife. 'You'll know it, when you are.'

'What now?' he said.

'Well,' she said, 'I've seen you now. I'm going south again.'

'Back to Texas?'

'Somewhere warm. I don't care.'

'I have to wait here,' said Shadow. 'Until my boss needs me.'

'That's not living,' said Laura. She sighed; and then she smiled, the same smile that had always been able to tug at his heart no matter how many times he saw it. Every time she smiled at him had been the first time all over again.

He went to put his arm around her, but she shook her head and pulled out of his reach. She sat down on the edge of a snow-covered picnic table, and she watched him drive away.

INTERLUDE

The war had begun and nobody saw it. The storm was lowering and nobody knew it.

A falling girder in Manhattan closed a street for two days. It killed two pedestrians, an Arab taxi-driver and the taxi-driver's passenger.

A trucker in Denver was found dead in his home. The murder instrument, a rubber-gripped claw-headed hammer, had been left on the floor beside his corpse. His face was untouched, but the back of his head was completely destroyed, and several words in a foreign alphabet were written on the bathroom mirror in brown lipstick.

In a postal sorting station in Phoenix, Arizona, a man went crazy, *went postal* as they said on the evening news, and shot Terry 'The Troll' Evensen, a morbidly obese, awkward man who lived alone in a trailer. Several other people in the sorting station were fired on, but only Evensen was killed. The man who fired the shots – first thought to be a disgruntled postal worker – was not caught, and was never identified.

'Frankly,' said Terry 'The Troll' Evensen's supervisor, on the *News at Five*, 'if anyone around here was gonna go postal, we would have figured it was gonna be the Troll. Okay worker, but a weird guy. I mean, you never can tell, huh?'

That interview was cut when the segment was repeated, later that evening.

A community of nine anchorites in Montana were found dead. Reporters speculated that it was a mass suicide, but soon the cause of death was reported as carbon monoxide poisoning from an elderly furnace.

A crypt was defiled in the Key West graveyard.

An Amtrak passenger train hit a UPS truck in Idaho, killing the driver of the truck. None of the passengers were seriously injured.

It was still a cold war at this stage, a phony war, nothing that could be truly won or lost.

The wind stirred the branches of the tree. Sparks flew from the fire. The storm was coming.

The Queen of Sheba, half-demon, they said, on her father's side, witch-woman, wise-woman and queen, who ruled Sheba when Sheba was the richest land there ever was, when its spices and its gems and scented woods were taken by boat and camel-back to the corners of the earth, who was worshipped even when she was alive, worshipped as a living goddess by the wisest of kings, stands on the sidewalk of Sunset Boulevard at 2:00 a.m. staring blankly out at the traffic like a slutty plastic bride on a black and neon wedding cake. She stands as if she owns the sidewalk and the night that surrounds her.

When someone looks straight at her, her lips move, as if she is talking to herself. When men in cars drive past her she makes eye-contact and she smiles.

It's been a long night.

It's been a long week, and a long four thousand years.

She is proud that she owes nothing to anyone. The other girls on the street, they have pimps, they have habits, they have children, they have people who take what they make. Not her.

There is nothing holy left in her profession. Not any more.

A week ago the rains began in Los Angeles, slicking the streets into road accidents, crumbling the mud from the hillsides and toppling houses into canyons, washing the world into the gutters and stormdrains, drowning the bums and the homeless camped down in the concrete channel of the river. When the rains come in Los Angeles they always take people by surprise.

Bilquis has spent the last week inside. Unable to stand on the sidewalk, she has curled up in her bed in the room the colour of raw liver, listening to the rain pattering on the metal box of the window air-conditioner and placing personals on the Internet. She has left her invitations on adultfriendfinder.com, LA-escorts.com, Classyhollywoodbabes.com, has given herself an anonymous e-mail address. She was proud of herself for negotiating the new territories, but remains nervous – she has spent a long time avoiding anything that might resemble a paper trail. She has never even taken a small ad in the back pages of the *LA Weekly*, preferring to pick out her own customers, to find by eye and smell and touch the ones who will worship her as she needs to be worshipped, the ones who will let her take them all the way . . .

And it occurs to her now, standing and shivering on the street corner (for the late February rains have left off, but the chill they brought with them remains) that she has a habit as bad as that of the smack whores and the crack whores, and this distresses her, and her lips begin to move again. If you were close enough to her rubyred lips you would hear her say,

'I will rise now and go about the city in the streets, and in the broad ways I will seek the one I love.' She is whispering that, and she whispers, *'By night on my bed I sought him whom my soul loveth. Let him kiss me with the kisses of his mouth. My beloved is mine and I am his.'*

Bilquis hopes that the break in the rains will bring the johns back. Most of the year she walks the two or three blocks on Sunset, enjoying the cool L.A. nights. Once a month she pays off an officer in the LAPD, who replaced the last guy she used to pay off, who had vanished. His name had been Jerry LeBec, and his disappearance had been a mystery to the LAPD. He had become obsessed with Bilquis, had taken to following her on foot. One afternoon she woke, startled by a noise, and opened the door to her apartment, and found Jerry LeBec in civilian clothes kneeling and swaying on the worn carpet, his head bowed, waiting for her to come out. The noise she had heard was the noise of his head, thumping against her door as he rocked back and forth on his knees.

She stroked his hair and told him to come inside, and later she put his clothes into a black plastic garbage bag and tossed them into a dumpster behind a hotel several blocks away. His gun and his wallet she put into a grocery store bag. She poured used coffee grounds and food waste on top of them, folded the top of the bag and dropped it into a trash can at a bus-stop.

She kept no souvenirs.

The orange night-sky glimmers to the west with distant lightning, somewhere out to sea, and Bilquis knows that the rain will be starting soon. She sighs. She does not want to be caught in the rain. She will return to her apartment, she decides, and take a bath, and shave her legs, it seems to her she is always shaving her legs, and sleep.

She begins to walk up a side-street, walking up the hillside to where her car is parked.

Headlights come up behind her, slowing as they approach her, and she turns her face to the street and smiles. The smile freezes when she sees the car is a white stretch limo. Men in stretch limos want to fuck in stretch limos, not in the privacy of Bilquis's shrine. Still, it might be an investment. Something for the future.

A tinted window hums down and Bilquis walks over to the limo, smiling. 'Hey, honey,' she says. 'You looking for something?'

'Sweet loving,' says a voice from the back of the stretch. She peers inside, as much as she can through the open window: she knows a girl who got into a stretch with five drunk football players and got hurt real bad, but there's only one john in there that she can see, and he looks kind of on the young side. He doesn't feel like a worshipper, but money, good money that's passed from his hand to hers, that's an energy in its own right – *baraka* they called it, once on a time, – which she can use and frankly these days, every little helps.

'How much?' he asks.

'Depends on what you want and how long you want it for,' she says. 'And whether you can afford it.' She can smell something smoky drifting out of the limo window. It smells like burning wires and overheating circuit boards. The door is pushed open from inside.

'I can pay for anything I want,' says the john. She leans into the car and looks around. There's nobody else in there, just the john, a puffy-faced kid who doesn't even look old enough to drink. Nobody else, so she gets in.

'Rich kid, huh?' she says.

'Richer than rich,' he tells her, edging along the leather seat towards her. He moves awkwardly. She smiles at him.

'Mm. Makes me hot, honey,' she tells him. 'You must be one of them dot coms I read about?'

He preens then, puffs like a bullfrog. 'Yeah. Among other things. I'm a technical boy.' The car moves off.

'So,' he says. 'Tell me Bilquis, how much just to suck my cock?'

'What you call me?'

'Bilquis,' he says, again. And then he sings, in a voice not made for singing, '*You are an immaterial girl living in a material world.*' There is something rehearsed about his words, as if he's practiced this exchange in front of a mirror.

She stops smiling, and her face changes, becomes wiser, sharper, harder. 'What do you want?'

'I told you. Sweet loving.'

'I'll give you whatever you want,' she says. She needs to get out of the limo. It's moving too fast for her to throw herself from the car, she figures, but she'll do it if she can't talk her way out of this. Whatever's happening here, she doesn't like it.

'What I want. Yes.' He pauses. His tongue runs over his lips. 'I want a clean world. I want to own tomorrow. I want evolution, devolution and revolution. I want to move our kind from the fringes of the slipstream to the higher ground of the mainstream. You people are underground. That's wrong. We need to take the spotlight and shine. Front and centre. You people have been so far underground for so long you've lost the use of your eyes.'

'My name's Ayesha,' she says. 'I don't know what you're talking about. There's another girl on that corner, her name's Bilquis. We could go back to Sunset, you could have both of us . . .'

'Oh, Bilquis,' he says, and he sighs, theatrically. 'There's only so much belief to go around. They're reaching the end of what they can give us. The credibility gap.' And then he sings, once again, in his tuneless nasal voice, '*You are an analog girl, living in a digital world.*' The limo takes a corner too fast, and he tumbles across the seat into her. The driver of the car is hidden behind tinted glass. An irrational conviction strikes her, that nobody is driving the car, that the white limo is driving through Beverly Hills like Herbie the Love Bug, under its own power.

Then the john reaches out his hand and taps on the tinted glass.

The car slows, and before it has stopped moving Bilquis has pushed open the door and she half-jumps, half-falls out onto the blacktop. She's on a hillside road. To the left of her is a steep hill, to the right is a sheer drop. She starts to run down the road.

The limo sits there, unmoving. It starts to rain, and her high heels slip and twist beneath her. She kicks them off, and runs, soaked to the skin, looking for somewhere she can get off the road. She's scared. She has power, true, but it's hunger-magic, cunt-magic. It has kept her alive in this land for so long, but for everything else she uses her sharp eyes and her mind, her height and her presence.

There's a metal guard-rail at knee-height on her right, to stop cars from tumbling over the side of the hill, and now the rain is running down the hill-road turning it into a river, and the soles of her feet have started to bleed.

The lights of L.A. are spread out in front of her, a twinkling electrical map of an imaginary kingdom, the heavens laid out right here on earth, and she knows that all she needs to be safe is to get off the road.

I am black but comely, she mouths to the night and the rain. *I am the rose of Sharon, and the lily of the valleys. Stay me with flagons, comfort me with apples: for I am sick of love.*

A fork of lightning burns greenly across the night sky. She loses her footing, slides several feet, skinning her leg and elbow, and she is getting to her feet when she sees the lights of the car descending the hill toward her. It's coming down too fast for safety and she wonders whether to throw herself to the right, where it could crush her against the hillside, or the left, where she might tumble down the gully. She runs across the road, intending to push herself up the wet earth, to climb, when the white stretch limo comes fishtailing down the slick hillside road, hell it must be doing eighty, maybe even aquaplaning on the surface of the road, and she's pushing her hands into a handful of weeds and earth, and she's going to get up and away, she knows, when the wet earth crumbles and she tumbles back down onto the road.

The car hits her with an impact that crumples the grille and tosses her into the air like a glove puppet. She lands on the road behind the limo, and the impact shatters her pelvis, fractures her skull. Cold rainwater runs over her face.

She begins to curse her killer: curse him silently, as she cannot move her lips. She curses him in waking and in sleeping, in living and in death. She curses him as only someone who is half-demon on her father's side can curse.

A car door slams. Someone approaches her. *'You were an analog girl,'* he sings again, tunelessly, *'living in a digital world.'* And then he says, 'You fucking madonnas. All you fucking madonnas.' He walks away.

The car door slams.

The limo reverses, and runs back over her, slowly, for the first time. Her bones crunch beneath the wheels. Then the limo comes back down the hill toward her.

When, finally, it drives away, down the hill, all it leaves behind on the road is the smeared red meat of roadkill, barely recognisable as human, and soon even that will be washed away by the rain.

Interlude 2

'Hi Samantha.'

'Mags? Is that you?'

'Who else? Leon said that Auntie Sammy called when I was in the shower.'

'We had a good talk. He's such a sweet kid.'

'Yeah. I think I'll keep him.'

A moment of discomfort for both of them, barely a crackle of a whisper over the telephone lines. Then, 'Sammy, how's school?'

'They're giving us a week off. Problem with the furnaces. How are things in your neck of the North Woods?'

'Well, I've got a new next-door neighbour. He does coin tricks. The *Lakeside News* letter column currently features a blistering debate on the potential rezoning of the town land down by the old cemetery on the southeast shore of the lake and yours truly has to write a strident editorial summarising the paper's position on this without offending anybody or in fact giving anyone any idea what our position is.'

'Sounds like fun.'

'It's not. Alison McGovern vanished last week – Jilly and Stan McGovern's oldest. Nice kid. She babysat for Leon a few times.'

A mouth opens to say something, and it closes again, leaving whatever it was to say unsaid, and instead it says, 'That's awful.'

'Yes.'

'So . . .' and there's nothing to follow that with that isn't going to hurt, so she says, 'Is he cute?'

'Who?'

'The neighbour.'

'His name's Ainsel. Mike Ainsel. He's okay. Too young for me. Big guy, looks . . . what's the word. Begins with an M.'

'Mean? Moody? Magnificent? Married?'

A short laugh, then 'Yes, I guess he does look married. I mean, if there's a look that married men have, he kind of has it. But the word I was thinking of was Melancholy. He looks Melancholy.'

'And Mysterious?'

'Not particularly. When he moved in he seemed kinda helpless – he didn't even know to heat-seal the windows. These days he still looks like he doesn't know what he's doing here. When he's here – he's here, then he's gone again. I've seen him out walking from time to time.'

'Maybe he's a bank robber.'

'Uh-huh. Just what I was thinking.'

'You were not. That was my idea. Listen, Mags, how are *you*? Are *you* okay?'

'Yeah.'

'Really?'

'No.'

A long pause then. 'I'm coming up to see you.'

'Sammy, no.'

'It'll be after the weekend before the furnaces are working and school starts again. It'll be fun. You can make up a bed on the couch for me. And invite the mysterious neighbour over for dinner one night.'

'Sam, you're matchmaking.'

'Who's matchmaking? After Claudine-the-bitch-from-hell, maybe I'm ready to go back to boys for a while. I met a nice strange boy when I hitchhiked down to El Paso for Christmas.'

'Oh. Look, Sam, you've got to stop hitchhiking.'

'How do you think I'm going to get to Lakeside?'

'Alison McGovern was hitchhiking. Even in a town like this, it's not safe. I'll wire you the money. You can take the bus.'

'I'll be fine.'

'*Sammy.*'

'Okay Mags. Wire me the money if it'll let you sleep easier.'

'You know it will.'

'Okay, bossy big sister. Give Leon a hug and tell him Auntie Sammy's coming up and he's not to hide his toys in her bed this time.'

'I'll tell him. I don't promise it'll do any good. So when should I expect you?'

'Tomorrow night. You don't have to meet me at the bus station – I'll ask Hinzelmann to run me over in Tessie.'

'Too late. Tessie's in mothballs for the winter. But Hinzelmann will give you a ride anyway. He likes you. You listen to his stories.'

'Maybe you should get Hinzelmann to write your editorial for you. Let's see. *On the Rezoning of the Land by the Old Cemetery, it so happens that in the winter of nought three my grampaw shot a stag down by the old cemetery by the lake. He was out of bullets, so he used a cherry-stone from the lunch my grandmama had packed for him. Creased the skull of the stag and it shot off like a bat out of heck. Two years later he was down that way and he sees this mighty buck with a spreading cherry tree growing between its antlers. Well, he shot it, and grandmama made cherry pies enough that they were still eating them come the next fourth of July . . .*'

And they both laughed, then.

Interlude 3

Jacksonville, Florida. 2:00 a.m.

'The sign says help wanted.'

'We're always hiring.'

'I can only work the night shift. Is that going to be a problem?'

'Shouldn't be. I can get you an application to fill out. You ever worked in a gas station before?'

'No. I figure, how hard can it be?'

'Well, it ain't rocket science, that's for sure. You know, ma'am, you don't mind my saying this, but you do not look well.'

'I know. It's a medical condition. Looks worse than it is. Nothing life-threatening.'

'Okay. You leave that application with me. We are really short handed on the late shift right now. Round here we call it the zombie shift. You do it too long, that's how you feel. Well now . . . is that *Larna*?'

'Laura.'

'Laura. Okay. Well, I hope you don't mind dealing with weirdos. Because they come out at night.'

'I'm sure they do. I can cope.'

13

Hey, old friend.
What do you say, old friend?
Make it okay, old friend,
Give an old friendship a break.
Why so grim?
We're going on forever.
You, me, him,
Too many lives are at stake . . .
– Stephen Sondheim, *Old Friends*

It was Saturday morning. Shadow answered the door.

Marguerite Olsen was there. She did not come in, just stood in the sunlight, looking serious. 'Mr Ainsel . . . ?'

'Mike, please,' said Shadow.

'Mike, yes. Would you like to come over for dinner tonight? About six-ish? It won't be anything exciting, just spaghetti and meatballs.'

'I like spaghetti and meatballs.'

'Obviously, if you have any other plans . . .'

'I have no other plans.'

'Six o'clock.'

'Should I bring flowers?'

'If you must. But this is a social gesture. Not a romantic one.'

He showered. He went for a short walk, down to the bridge and back. The sun was up, a tarnished quarter in the sky, and he was sweating in his coat by the time he got home. He drove the 4-Runner down to Dave's and bought a bottle of wine. It was a twenty dollar bottle, which seemed to Shadow like some kind of guarantee of quality. He didn't know wines, so he bought a Californian cabernet, because Shadow had once seen a bumper sticker, back when he was younger and people still had bumper stickers on their cars, which said 'Life is a Cabernet' and it had made him laugh.

He bought a plant in a pot as a gift. Green leaves, no flowers. Nothing remotely romantic about that.

He bought a carton of milk, which he would never drink, and a selection of fruit, which he would never eat.

Then he drove over to Mabel's and bought a single lunchtime pasty. Mabel's face lit up when she saw him. 'Did Hinzelmann catch up with you?'

'I didn't know he was looking for me.'

'Yup. Wants to take you ice fishing. And Chad Mulligan wanted to know if I'd seen you around. His cousin's here from out of state. His second cousin, what we used to call kissing cousins. Such a sweetheart. You'll love her,' and she dropped the pasty into a brown paper bag, twisted the top over to keep the pasty warm.

Shadow drove the long way home, eating one-handed, the pastry-crumbs tumbling onto his jeans and onto the floor of the 4-Runner. He passed the library on the south shore of the lake. It was a black and white town in the ice and the snow. Spring seemed unimaginably far away: the klunker would always sit on the ice, with the ice-fishing shelters and the pick-up trucks and the snowmobile tracks.

He reached his apartment, parked, walked up the drive, up the wooden steps to his apartment. The goldfinches and nuthatches on the birdfeeder hardly gave him a glance. He went inside. He watered the plant, wondered whether or not to put the wine into the refrigerator.

There was a lot of time to kill until six.

Shadow wished he could comfortably watch television once more. He wanted to be entertained, not to have to think, just to sit and let the sounds and the light wash over him. *Do you want to see Lucy's tits?* something with a Lucy voice whispered in his memory, and he shook his head, although there was no-one there to see him.

He was nervous, he realised. This would be his first real social interaction with other people – normal people, not people in jail, not gods or culture heroes or dreams – since he was first arrested, over three years ago. He would have to make conversation, as Mike Ainsel.

He checked his watch. It was two thirty. Marguerite Olsen had told him to be there at six. Did she mean six *exactly*? Should he be there a little early? A little late? He decided, eventually, to walk next door at five past six.

Shadow's telephone rang.

'Yeah?' he said.

'That's no way to answer the phone,' growled Wednesday.

'When I get my telephone connected I'll answer it politely,' said Shadow. 'Can I help you?'

'I don't know,' said Wednesday. There was a pause. Then he said, 'Organising gods is like herding cats into straight lines. They don't take naturally to it.' There was a deadness, and an exhaustion, in Wednesday's voice that Shadow had never heard before.

'What's wrong?'

'It's hard. It's too fucking hard. I don't know if this is going to work. We might as well cut our throats. Just cut our own throats.'

'You mustn't talk like that.'

'Yeah. Right.'

'Well, if you do cut your throat,' said Shadow, trying to jolly Wednesday out of his darkness, 'maybe it wouldn't even hurt.'

'It would hurt. Even for my kind, pain still hurts. If you move and act in the material world, then the material world acts on you. Pain hurts, just as greed intoxicates and lust burns. We may not die easy and we sure as hell don't die well, but we can die. If we're still loved and remembered, something else a whole lot like us comes along and takes our place and the whole damn thing starts all over again. And if we're forgotten, we're done.'

Shadow did not know what to say. He said, 'So where are you calling from?'

'None of your goddamn business.'

'Are you drunk?'

'Not yet. I just keep thinking about Thor. You never knew him. Big guy, like you. Good hearted. Not bright, but he'd give you the goddamned shirt off his back if you asked him. And he killed himself. He put a gun in his mouth and blew his head off in Philadelphia in 1932. What kind of a way is that for a god to die?'

'I'm sorry.'

'You don't give two fucking cents, son. He was a whole lot like you. Big and dumb.' Wednesday stopped talking. He coughed.

'What's wrong?' said Shadow, for the second time.

'They got in touch.'

'Who did?'

'The opposition.'

'And?'

'They want to discuss a truce. Peace talks. Live and let fucking live.'

'So what happens now?'

'Now I go and drink bad coffee with the modern assholes in a Kansas City Masonic Hall.'

'Okay. You going to pick me up, or shall I meet you somewhere?'

'You stay there and you keep your head down. Don't get into any trouble. You hear me?'

'But—'

There was a click, and the line went dead and stayed dead. There was no dial tone, but then, there never was.

Nothing but time to kill. The conversation with Wednesday had left Shadow with a sense of disquiet. He got up, intending to go for a walk, but already the light was fading, and he sat back down again.

Shadow picked up the *Minutes of the Lakeside City Council 1872-1884* and turned the pages, his eyes scanning the tiny print, not actually reading it, occasionally stopping to scan something that caught his eye.

In July 1874, Shadow learned, the City Council was concerned about the number of itinerant foreign loggers arriving in the town. An opera house was to be built on the corner of Third Street and Broadway. It was to be expected that the nuisances attendant to the damming of the Mill-Creek would abate once the mill-pond had become a lake. The council authorised the payment of seventy dollars to Mr Samuel Samuels, and of eighty-five dollars to Mr Heikki Salminen, in compensation for their land and for the expenses incurred in moving their domiciles out of the area to be flooded.

It had never occurred to Shadow before that the lake was man-made. Why call a town Lakeside, when the lake had begun as a dammed mill-pond? He read on, to discover that a Mr Hinzelmann, originally of Hüdemuhlen in Bavaria, was in charge of the lake-building project, and that the city council had granted him the sum of $370 toward the project, any shortfall to be made up by public subscription. Shadow tore off a strip of paper towel and placed it into the book as a bookmark. He could imagine Hinzelmann's pleasure in seeing the reference to his grandfather. He wondered if the old man knew that his family had been instrumental in building the lake. Shadow flipped forward through the book, scanning for more references to the lake-building project.

They had dedicated the lake in a ceremony in the spring of 1876, as a precursor to the town's centennial celebrations. A vote of thanks to Mr Hinzelmann was taken by the council.

Shadow checked his watch. It was five thirty. He went into the bathroom, shaved, combed his hair. He changed his clothes. Somehow the final fifteen minutes passed. He got the wine and the plant, and he walked next door.

The door opened as he knocked. Marguerite Olsen looked almost as nervous as he felt. She took the wine bottle and the potted plant, and said thank you. The television was on, *The Wizard of Oz* on video. It was still in sepia, and Dorothy was still in Kansas, sitting with her eyes closed in Professor Marvel's wagon as the old fraud pretended to read her mind, and the twister-wind that would tear her away from her life was approaching. Leon sat in front of the screen, playing with a toy fire truck. When he saw Shadow an expression of delight touched his face; he stood up and ran, tripping over his feet in his excitement, into a back bedroom, from which he emerged a moment later, triumphantly waving a quarter.

'Watch Mike Ainsel!' he shouted. Then closed both his hands and he pretended to take the coin into his right hand, which he opened wide. 'I made it disappear Mike Ainsel!'

'You did,' agreed Shadow. 'After we've eaten, if it's okay with your mom, I'll show you how to do it even smoother than that.'

'Do it now if you want,' said Marguerite. 'We're still waiting for Samantha. I sent her out for sour cream. I don't know what's taking her so long.'

And, as if that was her cue, footsteps sounded on the wooden deck, and somebody shouldered open the front door. Shadow did not recognise her at first, then she said, 'I didn't know if you wanted the kind with calories or the kind that tastes like wallpaper paste so I went for the kind with calories,' and he knew her then: the girl from the road to Cairo.

'That's fine,' said Marguerite. 'Sam, this is my neighbour, Mike Ainsel. Mike, this is Samantha Black Crow, my sister.'

I don't know you, thought Shadow desperately. *You've never met me before. We're total strangers.* He tried to remember how he had thought *snow*, how easy and light that had been: this was desperate. He put out his hand and said, 'Pleased to meetcha.'

She blinked, looked up at his face. A moment of puzzlement, then recognition entered her eyes and curved the corners of her mouth into a grin. 'Hello,' she said.

'I'll see how the food is doing,' said Marguerite, in the taut voice of someone who burns things in kitchens if they leave them alone and unwatched even for a moment.

Sam took off her puffy coat and her hat. 'So you're the melancholy but mysterious neighbour,' she said. 'Who'da thunk it?' She kept her voice down.

'And you,' he said, 'Are girl Sam. Can we talk about this later?'

'If you promise to tell me what's going on.'

'Deal.'

Leon tugged at the leg of Shadow's pants. 'Will you show me now?' he asked, and held out his quarter.

'Okay,' said Shadow. 'But if I show you, you have to remember that a master magician never tells anyone how it's done.'

'I promise,' said Leon, gravely.

Shadow took the coin in his left hand, then moved Leon's right hand, showing him how to appear to take the coin in his right hand while actually leaving it in Shadow's left hand. Then he made Leon repeat the movements on his own.

After several attempts the boy mastered the move. 'Now you know half of it,' said Shadow. 'The other half is this: put your attention on the place where the coin *ought* to be. Look at the place it's meant to be. If you act like it's in your right hand, no one will even look at your left hand, no matter how clumsy you are.'

Sam watched all this with her head tipped slightly on one side, saying nothing.

'Dinner!' called Marguerite, pushing her way in from the kitchen with a steaming bowl of spaghetti in her hands. 'Leon, go wash your hands.'

There was crusty garlic bread, thick red sauce, good spicy meatballs. Shadow complimented Marguerite on it.

'Old family recipe,' she told him, 'from the Corsican side of the family.'

'I thought you were Native American.'

'Dad's Cherokee,' said Sam. 'Mag's mom's father came from Corsica.' Sam was the only person in the room who was actually drinking the Cabernet. 'Dad left her when Mags was ten and he moved across town. Six months after that, I was born. Mom and Dad got married when the divorce came through. When I was ten he went away. I think he has a ten-year attention span.'

'Well, he's been out in Oklahoma for ten years,' said Marguerite.

'Now, *my* mom's family were European Jewish,' continued Sam, 'from one of those places that used to be communist and now are just chaos. I think she liked the idea of being married to a Cherokee. Fried bread and chopped liver.' She took another sip of the red wine.

'Sam's mom's a wild woman,' said Marguerite, semi-approvingly.

'You know where she is now?' asked Sam. Shadow shook his head. 'She's in Australia. She met a guy on the Internet, who lived in Hobart. When they met in the flesh she decided he was actually kind of icky. But she really liked Tasmania. So she's living down there, with a woman's group, teaching them to batik cloth and things like that. Isn't that cool? At her age?'

Shadow agreed that it was, and helped himself to more meatballs. Sam told them how all the aboriginal natives of Tasmania had been wiped out by the British, and about the human chain they made across the island to catch them which trapped only an old man and a sick boy. She told him how the thylacines – the Tasmanian tigers – had been killed by farmers, scared for their sheep, how the politicians in the 1930s noticed that the thylacines should be protected only after the last of them was dead. She finished her second glass of wine, poured her third.

'So, Mike,' said Sam, suddenly, her cheeks reddening, 'Tell us about your family. What are the Ainsels like?' She was smiling, and there was mischief in that smile.

'We're real dull,' said Shadow. 'None of us ever got as far as Tasmania. So you're at school in Madison. What's that like?'

'*You* know,' she said. 'I'm studying art history, women's studies, and casting my own bronzes.'

'When I grow up,' said Leon, 'I'm going to do magic. Poof. Will you teach me Mike Ainsel?'

'Sure,' said Shadow. 'If your mom doesn't mind.'

Sam said, 'After we've eaten, while you're putting Leon to bed, Mags, I think I'm going to get Mike to take me to the Buck Stops Here for an hour or so.'

Marguerite did not shrug. Her head moved, an eyebrow raised slightly.

'I think he's interesting,' said Sam. 'And we have lots to talk about.'

Marguerite looked at Shadow, who busied himself in dabbing an imaginary blob of red sauce from his chin with a paper napkin. 'Well, you're grown-ups,' she said, in a tone of voice that implied that they weren't, and that even if they were they shouldn't be.

After dinner Shadow helped Sam with the washing up – he dried – and then he did a trick for Leon, counting pennies into Leon's palm: each time Leon opened his hand and counted them there was one less coin than he had counted in. And as for the final penny – 'Are you squeezing it? Tightly?' – when Leon opened his hand he found it had transformed into a dime. Leon's plaintive cries of 'How'd you *do* that? Momma, how'd he *do* that?' followed him out into the hall.

Sam handed him his coat. 'Come on,' she said. Her cheeks were flushed from the wine.

Outside it was cold.

Shadow stopped in his apartment, tossed the *Minutes of the Lakeside City Council* into a plastic grocery bag and brought it along. Hinzelmann might be down at the Buck, and he wanted to show him the mention of his grandfather.

They walked down the drive side by side.

He opened the garage door, and she started to laugh. 'Omigod,' she said, when she saw the 4-Runner. 'Paul Gunther's car. You bought Paul Gunther's car. Omigod.'

Shadow opened the door for her. Then he went around and got in. 'You know the car?'

'When I came up here two or three years ago to stay with Mags. It was me that persuaded him to paint it purple.'

'Oh,' said Shadow. 'It's good to have someone to blame.'

He drove the car out onto the street. Got out and closed the garage door. Got back into the car. Sam was looking at him oddly as he got in, as if the confidence had begun to leak out of her. He put on his seatbelt, and she said, 'Okay. This is a stupid thing to do, isn't it? Getting into a car with a psycho-killer.'

'I got you safe home last time,' said Shadow.

'You killed two men,' she said. 'You're wanted by the Feds. And now I find out you're living under an assumed name next door to my sister. Unless Mike Ainsel is your real name?'

'No,' said Shadow, and he sighed. 'It's not.' He hated saying it. It was if he was letting go of something important, abandoning Mike Ainsel by denying him; as if he were taking his leave of a friend.

'Did you kill those men?'

'No.'

'They came to my house, and said we'd been seen together. And this guy showed me photographs of you. What was his name – Mister Hat? No. Mister Town. It was like *The Fugitive*. But I said I hadn't seen you.'

'Thank you.'

'So,' she said. 'Tell me what's going on. I'll keep your secrets if you keep mine.'

'I don't know any of yours,' said Shadow.

'Well, you know that it was my idea to paint this thing purple, thus forcing Paul Gunther to become such an object of scorn and derision for several counties around that he was forced to leave town entirely. We were kind of stoned,' she admitted.

'I doubt that bit of it's much of a secret,' said Shadow. 'Everyone in Lakeside must have known. It's a stoner sort of purple.'

And then she said, very quiet, very fast, 'If you're going to kill me please don't hurt me. I shouldn't have come here with you. I am so fucking fucking dumb. I can identify you. Jesus.'

Shadow sighed. 'I've never killed anybody. Really. Now I'm going to take you to the Buck,' he said. 'We'll have a drink. Or if you give the word, I'll turn this car around and take you home. Either way, I'll just have to hope you aren't going to call the cops.'

There was silence as they crossed the bridge.

'Who did kill those men?' she asked.

'You wouldn't believe me if I told you.'

'I *would*.' She sounded angry now. He wondered if bringing the wine to the dinner had been a wise idea. Life was certainly not a cabernet right now.

'It's not easy to believe.'

'I,' she told him, 'can believe anything. You have no *idea* what I can believe.'

'Really?'

'I can believe things that are true and I can believe things that aren't true and I can believe things where nobody knows if they're true or not. I can believe in Santa Claus and the Easter Bunny and Marilyn Monroe and the Beatles and Elvis and Mister Ed. Listen – I believe that people are perfectible, that knowledge is infinite, that the world is run by secret banking cartels and is visited by aliens on a regular basis, nice ones that look like wrinkledy lemurs and bad ones who mutilate cattle and want our water and our women. I believe that the future sucks and I believe that the future rocks and I believe that one day White Buffalo woman is going to come back and kick everyone's ass. I believe that all men are just over-grown boys with deep problems communicating and that the decline in good sex in America is coincident with the decline in Drive-In Movie theatres from state to state. I believe that all politicians are unprincipled crooks and I still believe that they are better than the alternative. I believe that California is going to sink into the sea when the big one comes, while Florida is going to dissolve into madness and alligators and toxic waste. I believe that anti-bacterial soap is destroying our resistance to dirt and disease so that one day we'll all be wiped out by the common cold like the Martians in *War of the Worlds*. I believe that the greatest poets of the last century were Edith Sitwell and Don Marquis, that jade is dried dragon sperm, and that thousands of years ago in a former life I was a one-armed Siberian Shaman. I believe that Mankind's destiny lies in the stars. I believe that candy really did taste better when I was a kid, that it's aerodynamically impossible for a bumble-bee to fly, that light is a wave and a particle, that there's a cat in a box somewhere who's alive and dead at the same time (although if they don't ever open the box to feed it it'll eventually just be two different kinds of dead), and that there are stars in the universe billions of years older than the universe itself. I believe in a personal god who cares about me and worries and oversees everything I do. I believe in an impersonal god who set the universe in motion and went off to hang with her girlfriends and doesn't even know that I'm alive. I believe in an empty and godless universe of causal chaos, background noise and sheer blind luck. I believe that anyone who says that sex is overrated just hasn't done it properly. I believe that anyone who claims to know what's going on will lie about the little things too. I believe in absolute honesty and sensible social lies. I believe in a woman's right to choose, a baby's right to live, that while all human life is sacred there's nothing wrong with the death penalty if you can trust the legal system implicitly, and that no-one but a moron would ever trust the legal system. I believe that life is a game, life is a cruel joke and that life is what happens when you're alive and that you might as well lie back and enjoy it.' She stopped, out of breath.

Shadow almost took his hands off the wheel to applaud. Instead he said, 'Okay. So if I tell you what I've learned you won't think that I'm a nut.'

'Maybe,' she said. 'Try me.'

'Would you believe that all the gods that people have ever imagined are still with us today?'

'. . . maybe.'

'And that there are new gods out there, gods of computers and telephones and whatever, and that they all seem to think there isn't room for them both in the world. And that some kind of war is kind of likely.'

'And these gods killed those two men?'

'No, my wife killed those two men.'

'I thought you said your wife was dead.'

'She is.'

'She killed them before she died, then?'

'After. Don't ask.'

She reached up a hand and flicked her hair from her forehead.

They pulled up on Main Street, outside the Buck Stops Here. The sign over the window showed a surprised looking stag standing on its hind legs holding a glass of beer. Shadow grabbed the bag with the book in it, and got out.

'Why would they have a war?' asked Sam. 'It seems kind of redundant. What is there to win?'

'I don't know,' admitted Shadow.

'It's easier to believe in aliens than in gods,' said Sam. 'Maybe Mister Town and Mister Whatever were Men in Black, only the alien kind.'

They were standing on the sidewalk outside the Buck Stops Here and Sam stopped. She looked up at Shadow, and her breath hung on the night air like a faint cloud. She said, 'Just tell me you're one of the good guys.'

'I can't,' said Shadow. 'I wish I could. But I'm doing my best.'

She looked up at him, and bit her lower lip. Then she nodded. 'Good enough,' she said. 'I won't turn you in. You can buy me a beer.'

Shadow pushed the door open for her, and they were hit by a blast of heat and music. They went inside.

Sam waved at some friends. Shadow nodded to a handful of people whose faces – although not their names – he remembered from the day he had spent searching for Alison McGovern, or who he had met in Mabel's in the morning. Chad Mulligan was standing at the bar, with his arm around the shoulders of a small red-haired woman – the kissing cousin, Shadow figured. He wondered what she looked like, but she had her back to him. Chad's hand raised in a mock salute when he saw Shadow. Shadow grinned, and waved back at him. Shadow looked around for Hinzelmann, but the old man did not seem to be there this evening. He spied a free table at the back and started walking toward it.

Then somebody began to scream.

It was a bad scream, a full-throated, seen-a-ghost hysterical scream, which silenced all conversation. Shadow looked around, certain somebody was being murdered, and then he realised that all the faces in the bar were turning toward him. Even the black cat, who slept in the window during the day, was standing up on top of the juke box with its tail high and its back arched and was staring at Shadow.

Time slowed.

'Get him!' shouted a woman's voice, parked on the verge of

hysteria. 'Oh for god's sake, somebody stop him! Don't let him get away! Please!' It was a voice he knew.

Nobody moved. They stared at Shadow. He stared back at them.

Chad Mulligan stepped forward, walking through the people. The small woman walked behind him warily, her eyes wide, as if she was preparing to start screaming once more. Shadow knew her. Of course he knew her.

Chad was still holding his beer, which he put down on a nearby table. He said, 'Mike.'

Shadow said, 'Chad.'

Audrey Burton took hold of Chad's sleeve. Her face was white, and there were tears in her eyes. 'Shadow,' she said. 'You bastard. You murderous evil bastard.'

'Are you sure that you know this man, hon?' said Chad. He looked uncomfortable.

Audrey Burton looked at him incredulously. 'Are you *crazy*? He worked for Robbie for *years*. His slutty wife was my best *friend*. He's wanted for *murder*. I had to answer *questions*. He's an escaped *convict*.' She was way over the top, her voice trembling with suppressed hysteria, sobbing out her words like a soap actress going for a daytime Emmy. *Kissing cousins*, thought Shadow, unimpressed.

Nobody in the bar said a word. Chad Mulligan looked up at Shadow. 'It's probably a mistake. I'm sure we can sort this all out,' he said, sensibly. Then he said, to the bar, 'It's all fine. Nothing to worry about. We can sort this out. Everything's fine.' Then, to Shadow. 'Let's step outside, Mike.' Quiet competence. Shadow was impressed.

'Sure,' said Shadow.

He felt a hand touch his hand, and he turned to see Sam staring at him. He smiled down at her as reassuringly as he could.

Sam looked at Shadow, then she looked around the bar at the faces staring at them. She said to Audrey Burton, 'I don't know who you are. But. You. Are such. A cunt.' Then she went up on tiptoes and pulled Shadow down to her, and kissed him hard on the lips, pushing her mouth against his for what felt to Shadow like several minutes, and might have been as long as five seconds in real, clock-ticking time.

It was a strange kiss, Shadow thought, as her lips pressed against his: it wasn't intended for him. It was for the other people in the bar, to let them know that she had picked sides. It was a flag-waving kiss. Even as she kissed him, he became certain that she didn't even like him – well, not like that.

Still, there was a tale he had read once, long ago, as a small boy: the story of a traveller who had slipped down a cliff, with man-eating tigers above him and a lethal fall below him, who managed to stop his fall halfway down the side of the cliff, holding on for dear life. There was a clump of strawberries beside him, and certain death above him and below. *What should he do?* went the question.

And the reply was, *Eat the strawberries.*

The story had never made any sense to him as a boy. It did now. So he closed his eyes, threw himself into the kiss and experienced nothing but Sam's lips and the softness of her skin against his, sweet as a wild strawberry.

'C'mon Mike,' said Chad Mulligan, firmly. 'Please. Let's take it outside.'

Sam pulled back. She licked her lips, and smiled, a smile that nearly reached her eyes. 'Not bad,' she said. 'You kiss good for a boy. Okay, go play outside.' Then she turned to Audrey Burton. 'But you,' she said, 'are still a cunt.'

Shadow tossed Sam his car keys. She caught them, one-handed. He walked through the bar, and stepped outside, followed by Chad Mulligan. A gentle snow had begun to fall, the flakes spinning down into the light of the neon bar sign. 'You want to talk about this?' asked Chad.

Audrey had followed them out onto the sidewalk. She looked as if she were ready to start screaming again. She said, 'He killed two men, Chad. The FBI came to my door. He's a psycho. I'll come down to the station with you, if you want.'

'You've caused enough trouble ma'am,' said Shadow. He sounded tired, even to himself. 'Please go away.'

'Chad? Did you hear that? He threatened me!' said Audrey.

'Get back inside, Audrey,' said Chad Mulligan. She looked as if she were about to argue, then she pressed her lips together so hard they went white, and went back into the bar.

'Would you like to comment on anything she said?' asked Chad Mulligan.

'I've never killed anyone,' said Shadow.

Chad nodded. 'I believe you,' he said. 'I'm sure we can deal with these allegations easily enough. You won't give me any trouble, will you Mike?'

'No trouble,' said Shadow. 'This is all a mistake.'

'Exactly,' said Chad. 'So I figure we ought to head down to my office and sort it all out there?'

'Am I under arrest?' asked Shadow.

'Nope,' said Chad. 'Not unless you want to be. I figure, you come with me out of a sense of civic duty, and we'll straighten all this out.'

Chad patted Shadow down, found no weapons. They got into Mulligan's car. Again Shadow sat in the back, looking out through the metal cage. He thought *SOS. Mayday. Help.* He tried to push Mulligan with his mind, as he'd once pushed a cop in Chicago – *this is your old friend Mike Ainsel. You saved his life. Don't you know how silly this is? Why don't you just drop the whole thing?*

'I figure it was good to get you out of there,' said Chad. 'All you needed was some loudmouth deciding that you were Alison McGovern's killer and we'd've had a lynch mob on our hands.'

'Point.'

They were silent for the rest of the drive to the Lakeside police building, which, Chad said as they pulled up outside it, actually belonged to the county sheriff's department. The local police made do with a few rooms in there. Pretty soon the county would build something modern. For now they had to make do with what they had.

They walked inside.

'Should I call a lawyer?' asked Shadow.

'You aren't accused of anything,' said Mulligan. 'Up to you.' They pushed through some swing doors. 'Take a seat over there.'

Shadow took a seat on the wooden chair with cigarette burns on the side. He felt stupid and numb. There was a small poster on the notice board, beside a large NO SMOKING sign: ENDANGERED MISSING it said. The photograph was Alison McGovern's.

There was a wooden table, with old copies of *Sports Illustrated* and *Newsweek* on it. The light was bad. The paint on the wall was yellow, but it might once have been white.

After ten minutes Chad brought him a watery cup of vending

machine hot chocolate. 'What's in the bag?' he asked. And it was only then that Shadow realised he was still holding the plastic bag containing the *Minutes of the Lakeside City Council*.

'Old book,' said Shadow. 'Your grandfather's picture's in here. Or great grandfather maybe.'

'Yeah?'

Shadow flipped through the book until he found the portrait of the town council, and he pointed to the man called Mulligan. Chad chuckled. 'If that don't beat all,' he said.

Minutes passed, and hours, in that room. Shadow read two of the *Sports Illustrateds* and he started in on the *Newsweek*. From time to time Chad would come through, once checking to see if Shadow needed to use the rest-room, once to offer him a ham roll and a small packet of potato chips.

'Thanks,' said Shadow, taking them. 'Am I under arrest yet?'

Chad sucked the air between his teeth. 'Well,' he said, 'Not yet. It doesn't look like you came by the name Mike Ainsel legally. On the other hand, you can call yourself whatever you want in this state, if it's not for fraudulent purposes. You just hang loose.'

'Can I make a phone call?'

'Is it a local call?'

'Long distance.'

'It'll save money if I put it on my calling card, otherwise you'll just be feeding ten bucks worth of quarters into that thing in the hall.'

Sure, thought Shadow. *And this way you'll know the number I dialed, and you'll probably be listening in on an extension.*

'That would be great,' said Shadow. They went into an empty office. The number Shadow gave Chad to dial for him was that of a funeral home in Cairo, Illinois. Chad dialed it, handed Shadow the receiver. 'I'll leave you in here,' he said, and went out.

The telephone rang several times, then it was picked up.

'Jacquel and Ibis? Can I help you?'

'Hi. Mister Ibis, this is Mike Ainsel. I helped out there for a few days over Christmas.'

A moment's hesitation, then, 'Of course. Mike. How *are* you?'

'Not great, Mister Ibis. In a patch of trouble. About to be arrested. Hoping you'd seen my uncle about, or maybe you could get a message to him.'

'I can certainly ask around. Hold on, uh, Mike. There's someone here who wishes a word with you.'

The phone was passed to somebody, and then a smoky female voice said, 'Hi honey. I miss you.'

He was certain he'd never heard that voice before. But he knew her. He was sure that he knew her . . .

Let it go, the smoky voice whispered in his mind, in a dream. *Let it all go.*

'Who's that girl you were kissing, hon? You trying to make me jealous?'

'We're just friends,' said Shadow. 'I think she was trying to prove a point. How did you know she kissed me?'

'I got eyes wherever my folk walk,' she said. 'You take care now, hon. . . .' There was a moment of silence, then Mr Ibis came back on the line and said 'Mike?'

'Yes.'

'There's a problem getting hold of your uncle. He seems to be kind of tied up. But I'll try and get a message to your Aunt Nancy. Best of luck.' The line went dead.

Shadow sat down, expecting Chad to return. He sat in the empty office, wishing he had something to distract him. Reluctantly, he picked up the *Minutes* once more, opened it to somewhere in the middle of the book, and began to read.

An ordinance prohibiting expectoration on sidewalks and on the floors of public buildings, or throwing thereon tobacco in any form was introduced and passed, eight to four, in December of 1876.

Lemmi Hautala was twelve years old and had 'it was feared, wandered away in a fit of delirium' on December the 13th, 1876. 'A search being immediately effected, but impeded by the snows, which are blinding.' The council had voted unanimously to send the Hautala family their condolences.

The fire at Olsen's livery stables the following week was extinguished without any injury or loss of life, human or equine.

Shadow scanned the closely-printed columns. He found no further mention of Lemmi Hautala.

And then, on something slightly more than a whim, Shadow flipped the pages forward to the winter of 1877. He found what he was looking for mentioned as an aside in the January minutes: Jessie Lovat, age not given, 'a Negro child' had vanished on the night of 28th of December. It was believed that she might have been 'abducted by traveling so-called pedlars'. Condolences were not sent to the Lovat family.

Shadow was scanning the minutes of winter 1878 when Chad Mulligan knocked and entered, looking shamefaced, like a child bringing home a bad report card.

'Mister Ainsel,' he said. 'Mike. I'm truly sorry about this. Personally, I like you. But that don't change anything, you know?'

Shadow said he knew.

'I got no choice in the matter,' said Chad, 'but to place you under arrest for violating your parole.' Then Mulligan read Shadow his rights. He filled out some paperwork. He took Shadow's prints. He walked him down the hall to the county jail, on the other side of the building.

There was a long counter and several doorways on one side of the room, two holding cells and a doorway on the other. One of the cells was occupied – a man slept on a cement bed under a thin blanket. The other was empty.

There was a sleepy-looking woman in a brown uniform behind the counter, watching Jay Leno on a small white portable television. She took the papers from Chad, and signed for Shadow. Chad hung around, filled in more papers. The woman came around the counter, patted Shadow down, took all his possessions – wallet, coins, front door key, book, watch – and put them on the counter, then gave him a plastic bag with orange clothes in and told him to go into the open cell and change into them. He could keep his own underwear and socks. He went in and changed into the orange clothes and the shower footwear. It stank evilly in there. The orange top he pulled over his head had LUMBER COUNTY JAIL written on the back, in large black letters.

The metal toilet in the cell had backed up, and was filled to the brim with a brown stew of liquid faeces and sour, beerish urine.

Shadow came back out, gave the woman his clothes, which she put into the plastic bag with the rest of his possessions. He had thumbed through the wallet before he handed it over. 'You take care of this,' he had said to the woman, 'My whole life is in here.' The woman took the wallet from him, and assured him that it would be safe with them. She asked Chad if that wasn't true, and Chad, looking up from the last of his paperwork, said Liz was telling the truth, they'd never lost a prisoner's possessions yet.

Shadow had slipped the four hundred-dollar bills that he had palmed from the wallet into his socks, when he had changed, along with the silver Liberty dollar he had palmed as he had emptied his pockets.

'Say,' Shadow asked, when he came out. 'Would it be okay if I finished reading the book?'

'Sorry, Mike. Rules are rules,' said Chad.

Liz put Shadow's possessions in a bag in the back room. Chad said he'd leave Shadow in Officer Bute's capable hands. Liz looked tired and unimpressed. Chad left. The telephone rang, and Liz – Officer Bute – answered it. 'Okay,' she said. 'Okay. No problem. Okay. No problem. Okay.' She put down the phone and made a face.

'Problem?' asked Shadow.

'Yes. Not really. Kinda. They're sending someone up from Milwaukee to collect you.'

'Why is that a problem?'

'I got to keep you in here with me for three hours,' she said. 'And the cell over there –' she pointed to the cell by the door, with the sleeping man in it, 'that's occupied. He's on suicide watch. I shouldn't put you in with him. But it's not worth the trouble to sign you in to the county and then sign you out again.' She shook her head. 'And you don't want to go in there –' she pointed to the empty cell in which he'd changed his clothes, 'because the can is shot. It stinks in there, doesn't it?'

'Yes. It was gross.'

'It's common humanity, that's what it is. The sooner we get into the new facilities, it can't be too soon for me. One of the women we had in yesterday must've flushed a tampon away. I tell 'em not to. We got bins for that. They clog the pipes. Every damn tampon down that john costs the county a hundred bucks in plumbers' fees. So, I can keep you out here, if I cuff you. Or you can go in the cell.' She looked at him. 'Your call,' she said.

'I'm not crazy about them,' he said. 'But I'll take the cuffs.'

She took a pair from her utility belt, then patted the semiautomatic in its holster, as if to remind him that it was there. 'Hands behind your back,' she said.

The cuffs were a tight fit: he had big wrists. Then she put hobbles on his ankles, and sat him down on a bench on the far side of the counter, against the wall. 'Now,' she said. 'You don't bother me, and I won't bother you.' She tilted the television so that he could see it.

'Thanks,' he said.

'When we get our new offices,' she said, 'there won't be none of this nonsense.'

The Tonight Show finished. An episode of *Cheers* began. Shadow had never watched *Cheers*. He had only ever seen one episode of it – the one where Coach's daughter comes to the bar – although he had seen that several times. Shadow had noticed that you only ever catch one episode of shows you don't watch, over and over, years apart; he thought it must be some kind of cosmic law.

Officer Liz Bute sat back in her chair. She was not obviously dozing, but she was by no means awake, so she did not notice when the gang at Cheers stopped talking and getting off one-liners and just started staring out of the screen at Shadow.

Diane, the blonde barmaid who fancied herself an intellectual, was the first to talk. 'Shadow,' she said. 'We were so *worried* about you. You'd fallen off the world. It's so good to see you again – albeit in bondage and orange *couture*.'

'What I figure, is, the thing to do,' pontificated bar bore Cliff, 'is to escape in hunting season, when everybody's wearing orange anyway.'

Shadow said nothing.

'Ah, cat got your tongue, I see,' said Diane. 'Well, you've led us a merry chase!'

Shadow looked away. Officer Liz had begun, gently, to snore. Carla, the little waitress, snapped, 'Hey, jerk-wad! We interrupt this broadcast to show you something that's going to make you piss in your friggin' pants. You ready?'

The screen flickered and went black. The words 'LIVE FEED' pulsated in white at the bottom left of screen. A subdued female voice said, in voice-over, 'It's certainly not too late to change to the *winning* side. But you know, you *also* have the freedom to stay *just* where you are. That's what it means to *be* an American. *That's* the miracle of America. Freedom to believe means the freedom to believe the wrong thing, after all. Just as freedom of *speech* gives you the right to stay silent.'

The picture now showed a street scene. The camera lurched forward, in the manner of hand-held video cameras in real-life documentaries.

A man with thinning hair, a tan, and a faintly hangdog expression filled the frame. He was standing by a wall sipping a cup of coffee from a plastic cup. He looked into the camera and said 'Terrorists hide behind weasel-words, like *freedom fighter*. You and I know that they are murdering scum, pure and simple. We're risking our lives to make a difference.'

Shadow recognised the voice. He had been inside the man's head once. Mr Town sounded different from inside – his voice was deeper, more resonant – but there was no mistaking it.

The cameras pulled back to show that Mr Town was standing outside a brick building on an American street. Above the door was a set-square and compass framing the letter G.

'In position,' said somebody off-screen.

'*Let's* see if the cameras *inside* the hall are rolling,' said the female voice-over voice.

The words LIVE FEED continued to blink at the bottom left of the screen. Now the picture showed the interior of a small hall: the room was underlit. Two men sat at a table at the far end of the room. One of them had his back to the camera. The camera zoomed in to them awkwardly. For a moment they were out of focus, and then they became sharp once more. The man facing the camera got up and began to pace, like a bear on a chain. It was Wednesday. He looked as if, on some level, he was enjoying this. As they came into focus the sound came on with a pop.

The man with his back to the screen was saying, '– we are offering is the chance to end this, here and now, with no more bloodshed, no more aggression, no more pain, no more loss of life. Isn't that worth giving up a little?'

Wednesday stopped pacing and turned. His nostrils flared. 'First,' he growled, 'you have to understand that you are asking me to speak for all of us. Which is manifestly nonsensical. Secondly, what on earth makes you think that I believe that you people are going to keep your word?'

The man with his back to the camera moved his head. 'You do yourself an injustice,' he said. 'Obviously you people have no leaders. But you're the one they listen to. They pay attention to you. And as for keeping my word, well, these preliminary talks are being filmed and broadcast live,' and he gestured back toward the camera. 'Some of your people are watching as we speak. Others will see videotapes. The camera does not lie.'

'Everybody lies,' said Wednesday.

Shadow recognised the voice of the man with his back to the camera. It was Mr World, the one who had spoken to Town on the cellphone while Shadow was in Town's head.

'You don't believe,' said Mr World, 'that we will keep our word?'

'I think your promises were made to be broken and your oaths to be forsworn. But *I* will keep *my* word.'

'Safe conduct is safe conduct,' said Mr World, 'and a flag of truce is what we agreed. I should tell you, by the way, that your young protégé is once more in our custody.'

Wednesday snorted. 'No,' he said. 'He's not.'

'We were discussing the ways to deal with the coming paradigm shift. We don't *have* to be enemies. Do we?'

Wednesday seemed shaken. He said, 'I will do whatever is in my power . . .'

Shadow noticed something strange about the image of Wednesday on the television screen. A red glint burned on his left eye, the glass one. The dot left a phosphor-dot after-image as he moved. He seemed unaware of it.

'It's a big country,' said Wednesday, marshaling his thoughts. He moved his head and the red laser-pointer dot slipped to his cheek. Then it edged up to his glass eye once more. 'There is room for—'

There was a bang, muted by the television speakers, and the side of Wednesday's head exploded. His body tumbled backward.

Mr World stood up, his back still to the camera, and walked out of shot.

'Let's see that again, in slow motion this time,' said the announcer's voice, reassuringly.

The words LIVE FEED became REPLAY. Slowly now the red laser

pointer traced its bead onto Wednesday's glass eye, and once again the side of his face dissolved into a cloud of blood. Freeze frame.

'Yes, it's still God's Own Country,' said the announcer, a news reporter pronouncing the final tag line. 'The only question is, which gods?'

Another voice – Shadow thought that it was Mr World's, it had that same half-familiar quality – said, 'We now return you to your regularly scheduled programming.'

On *Cheers* Coach assured his daughter that she was truly beautiful, just like her mother.

The telephone rang, and officer Liz sat up with a start. She picked it up. Said 'Okay. Okay. Yes. Okay.' Put the phone down. She got up from behind the counter, and said to Shadow, 'I'm going to have to put you in the cell. Don't use the can. The Lafayette sheriffs' department should be here to collect you soon.'

She removed the cuffs and the hobbles, locked him into the holding cell. The smell was worse, now that the door was closed.

Shadow sat down on the concrete bed, slipped the Liberty dollar from his sock and began moving it from finger to palm, from position to position, from hand to hand, his only aim to keep the coin from being seen by anyone who might look in. He was passing the time. He was numb.

He missed Wednesday, then, sudden and deep. He missed the man's confidence, his attitude. His conviction.

He opened his hand, looked down at Lady Liberty, a silver profile. He closed his fingers over the coin, held it tightly. He wondered if he'd get to be one of those guys who gets life for something they didn't do. If he even made it that far. From what he'd seen of Mr World and Mr Town, they would have little trouble pulling him out of the system. Perhaps he'd suffer an unfortunate accident on the way to the next holding facility. He could be shot while making a break for it. It did not seem at all unlikely.

There was a stir of activity in the room on the other side of the glass. Officer Liz came back in. She pressed a button, a door that Shadow could not see opened, and a black deputy in a brown sheriff's uniform entered and walked briskly over to the desk.

Shadow slipped the dollar coin back into his sock.

The new deputy handed over some papers, Liz scanned them

and signed. Chad Mulligan came in, said a few words to the new man, then he unlocked the cell door and walked inside.

'Okay. Folk are here to pick you up. Seems you're a matter of national security. You know that?'

'It'll make a great front page story for the *Lakeside News*,' said Shadow.

Chad looked at him without expression. 'That a drifter got picked up for parole violations? Not much of a story.'

'So that's the way it is?'

'That's what they tell me,' said Chad Mulligan. Shadow put his hands in front of him this time, and Chad cuffed him. Chad locked on the ankle hobbles, and a rod from the cuffs to the hobbles.

Shadow thought, *they'll take me outside. Maybe I can make a break for it – in hobbles and cuffs and lightweight orange clothes, out into the snow,* and even as he thought it he knew how stupid and hopeless it was.

Chad walked him out into the office. Liz had turned the TV off now. The black deputy looked him over. 'He's a big guy,' he said to Chad. Liz passed the new deputy the paper bag with Shadow's possessions in it, and he signed for it.

Chad looked at Shadow, then at the deputy. He said to the deputy, quietly, but loudly enough for Shadow to hear, 'Look. I just want to say, I'm not comfortable with the way this is happening.'

The deputy nodded. 'You'll have to take it up with the appropriate authorities, sir. Our job is simply to bring him in.'

Chad made a sour face. He turned to Shadow. 'Okay,' said Chad. 'Through that door and into the sally port.'

'What?'

'Out there. Where the car is.'

Liz unlocked the doors. 'You make sure that orange uniform comes right back here,' she said to the deputy. 'The last felon we sent down to Lafayette, we never saw the uniform again. They cost the county money.' They walked Shadow out to the sally port, where a car sat idling. It wasn't a sheriff's department car. It was a black town car. Another deputy, a grizzled white guy with a moustache, stood by the car, smoking a cigarette. He crushed it out underfoot as they came close, and opened the back door for Shadow.

Shadow sat down, awkwardly, his movements hampered by the

cuffs and the hobbles. There was no grille between the back and the front of the car.

The two deputies climbed into the front of the car. The black deputy started the motor. They waited for the sally port door to open.

'Come on, come on,' said the black deputy, his fingers drumming against the steering wheel.

Chad Mulligan tapped on the side window. The white deputy glanced at the driver, then he lowered the window. 'This is wrong,' said Chad. 'I just wanted to say that.'

'Your comments have been noted, and will be conveyed to the appropriate authorities,' said the driver.

The doors to the outside world opened. The snow was still falling, dizzying into the car's headlights. The driver put his foot on the gas, and they were heading back down the street and onto Main Street.

'You heard about Wednesday?' said the driver. His voice sounded different, now, older, and familiar. 'He's dead.'

'Yeah. I know,' said Shadow. 'I saw it on TV.'

'Those fuckers,' said the white officer. It was the first thing he had said, and his voice was rough and accented and, like the driver's, it was a voice that Shadow knew. 'I tell you, they are fuckers, those fuckers.'

'Thanks for coming to get me,' said Shadow.

'Don't mention it,' said the driver. In the light of an oncoming car his face already seemed to look older. He looked smaller, too. The last time Shadow had seen him he had been wearing lemon-yellow gloves and a check jacket. 'We were in Milwaukee. Had to drive like demons when Ibis called.'

'You think we let them lock you up and send you to the chair, when I'm still waiting to break your head with my hammer?' asked the white deputy gloomily, fumbling in his pocket for a pack of cigarettes. His accent was East European.

'The real shit will hit the fan in an hour or less,' said Mr Nancy, looking more like himself with each moment, 'When they *really* turn up to collect you. We'll pull over before we get to Highway 53 and get you out of those shackles and back into your own clothes.' Czernobog held up a handcuff key and smiled.

'I like the moustache,' said Shadow. 'Suits you.'

Czernobog stroked it with a yellowed finger. 'Thank you.'

'Wednesday,' said Shadow. 'Is he really dead? This isn't some kind of trick is it?'

He realised that he had been holding on to some kind of hope, foolish though it was. But the expression on Nancy's face told him all he needed to know, and the hope was gone.

COMING TO AMERICA
14,000 BC

Cold it was, and dark, when the vision came to her, for in the far
north daylight was a grey dim time in the middle of the day that
came, and went, and came again: an interlude between darknesses.

They were not a large tribe as these things were counted then:
nomads of the Northern Plains. They had a god, who was the skull
of a mammoth, and the hide of a mammoth fashioned into a rough
cloak. *Nunyunnini* they called him. When they were not travelling,
he rested on a wooden frame, at man height.

She was the holy woman of the tribe, the keeper of its secrets,
and her name was Atsula, the fox. Atsula walked before the two
tribesmen who carried their god on long poles, draped with
bearskins, that it should not be seen by profane eyes, nor at times
when it was not holy.

They roamed the tundra, with their tents. The finest of the tents
was made of caribou-hide, and it was the holy tent, and there were
four of them inside it: Atsula, the priestess, Gugwei, the tribal elder,
Yanu, the war leader, and Kalanu, the scout. She called them there,
the day after she had her vision.

Atsula scraped some lichen into the fire, then she threw in dried
leaves with her withered left hand: they smoked, with an eye-
stinging grey smoke, and gave off an odour that was sharp and
strange. Then she took a wooden cup from the wooden platform,
and she passed it to Gugwei. The cup was half-filled with a dark
yellow liquid.

Atsula had found the *pungh* mushrooms – each with seven spots,
only a true holy woman could find a seven-spotted mushroom –
and had picked them at the dark of the moon, and dried them on
a string of deer-cartilage.

Yesterday, before she slept, she had eaten the three dried mushroom caps. Her dreams had been confused and fearful things, of
bright lights moving fast, of rock mountains filled with lights

spearing upward like icicles. In the night she had woken, sweating, and needing to make water. She squatted over the wooden cup and filled it with her urine. Then she placed the cup outside the tent, in the snow, and returned to sleep.

When she woke, she picked the lumps of ice out from the wooden cup, leaving a darker, more concentrated liquid behind.

It was this liquid she passed around, first to Gugwei, then to Yanu and to Kalanu. Each of them took a large gulp of the liquid, then Atsula took the final draught. She swallowed it, and poured what was left on the ground in front of their god, a libation to Nunyunnini.

They sat in the smoky tent, waiting for their god to speak. Outside, in the darkness, the wind wailed and breathed.

Kalanu, the scout, was a woman who dressed and walked as a man: she had even taken Dalani, a fourteen year old maiden, to be her wife. Kalanu blinked her eyes tightly, then she got up and walked over to the mammoth skull. She pulled the mammoth-hide cloak over herself, and stood so her head was inside the mammoth-skull.

'There is evil in the land,' said Nunyunnini in Kalanu's voice. 'Evil, such that if you stay here, in the land of your mothers and your mother's mothers, you shall all perish.'

The three listeners grunted.

'Is it the slavers? Or the great wolves?' asked Gugwei, whose hair was long and white, and whose face was as wrinkled as the grey skin of a thorn tree.

'It is not the slavers,' said Nunyunnini, old stone-hide. 'It is not the great wolves.'

'Is it a famine? Is a famine coming?' asked Gugwei.

Nunyunnini was silent. Kalanu came out of the skull and waited with the rest of them.

Gugwei put on the mammoth-hide cloak and put his head inside the skull.

'It is not a famine as you know it,' said Nunyunnini, through Gugwei's mouth, 'although a famine will follow.'

'Then what is it?' asked Yanu. 'I am not afraid. I will stand against it. We have spears, and we have throwing rocks. Let a hundred mighty warriors come against us, still we shall prevail. We shall lead them into the marshes, and split their skulls with our flints.'

'It is not a man thing,' said Nunyunnini, in Gugwei's old voice. 'It will come from the skies, and none of your spears or your rocks will protect you.'

'How can we protect ourselves?' asked Atsula. 'I have seen flames in the skies. I have heard a noise louder than ten thunderbolts. I have seen forests flattened and rivers boil.'

'Ai . . .' said Nunyunnini, but he said no more. Gugwei came out of the skull, bending stiffly, for he was an old man, and his knuckles were swollen and knotted.

There was silence. Atsula threw more leaves on the fire, and the smoke made their eyes tear.

Then Yanu strode to the mammoth-head, put the cloak about his broad shoulders, put his head inside the skull. His voice boomed. 'You must journey,' said Nunyunnini. 'You must travel to sun-ward. Where the sun rises, there you will find a new land, where you will be safe. It will be a long journey: the moon will swell and empty, die and live, twice, and there will be slavers and beasts, but I shall guide you and keep you safe, if you travel toward the sunrise.'

Atsula spat on the mud of the floor, and said, 'No.' She could feel the god staring at her. 'No,' she said. 'You are a bad god to tell us this. We will die. We will all die, and then who will be left to carry you from high place to high place, to raise your tent, to oil your great tusks with fat?'

The god said nothing. Atsula and Yanu exchanged places. Atsula's face stared out through the yellowed mammoth-bone.

'Atsula has no faith,' said Nunyununni in Atsula's voice. 'Atsula shall die before the rest of you enter the new land, but the rest of you shall live. Trust me: there is a land to the east that is manless. This land shall be your land and the land of your children and your children's children, for seven generations, and seven sevens. But for Atsula's faithlessness, you would have kept it forever. In the morning, pack your tents and your possessions, and walk toward the sunrise.'

And Gugwei and Yanu and Kalanu bowed their heads and exclaimed at the power and wisdom of Nunyunnini.

The moon swelled and waned and swelled and waned once more. The people of the tribe walked east, toward the sunrise, struggling through the icy winds which numbed their exposed skin.

Nunyunnini had promised them truly: they lost no-one from the tribe on the journey, save for a woman in childbirth, and women in childbirth belong to the moon, not to Nunyunnini.

They crossed the land-bridge.

Kalanu had left them at first light to scout the way. Now the sky was dark, and Kalanu had not returned, but the night sky was alive with lights, knotting and flickering and winding, flux and pulse, white and green and violet and red. Atsula and her people had seen the northern lights before, but they were still frightened by them, and this was a display like they had never seen before.

Kalanu returned to them, as the lights in the sky formed and flowed.

'Sometimes,' she said to Atsula, 'I feel that I could simply spread my arms and fall into the sky.'

'That is because you are a scout,' said Atsula, the priestess. 'When you die, you shall fall into the sky and become a star, to guide us as you guide us in life.'

'There are cliffs of ice to the east, high cliffs,' said Kalanu, her raven-black hair worn long, as a man would wear it. 'We can climb them, but it will take many days.'

'You shall lead us safely,' said Atsula. 'I shall die at the foot of the cliff, and that shall be the sacrifice that takes you into the new lands.'

To the west of them, back in the lands from which they had come, where the sun had set hours before, there was a flash of sickly yellow light, brighter than lightning, brighter than daylight. It was a burst of pure brilliance that forced the folk on the land-bridge to cover their eyes and spit and exclaim. Children began to wail.

'That is the doom that Nunyunnini warned us of,' said Gugwei the old. 'Surely he is a wise god and a mighty one.'

'He is the best of all gods,' said Kalanu. 'In our new land we shall raise him up on high, and we shall polish his tusks and skull with fish oil and animal fat, and we shall tell our children, and our children's children and our seventh children's children, that Nunyunnini is the mightiest of all gods, and shall never be forgotten.'

'Gods are great,' said Atsula, slowly, as if she were imparting a great secret. 'But the heart is greater. For it is from our hearts they come, and to our hearts they shall return . . .'

And there is no telling how long she might have continued in this blasphemy, had it not been interrupted in a manner that brooked no argument.

The roar that erupted from the west was so loud that ears bled. They could hear nothing for some time, temporarily blinded and deafened but alive, knowing that they were luckier than the tribes to the west of them.

'It is good,' said Atsula, but she could not hear the words inside her head.

Atsula died at the foot of the cliffs when the Spring sun was at its zenith. She did not live to see the New World, and the tribe walked into those lands with no holy woman.

They scaled the cliffs, and they went south and west, until they found a valley with fresh water, and rivers that teemed with silver fish, and deer that had never seen man before and were so tame it was necessary to spit and to apologise to their spirits before killing them.

Dalani gave birth to three boys, and some said that Kalanu had performed the final magic and could do the man-thing with her bride; while others said that old Gugwei was not too old to keep a young bride company when her husband was away; and certainly once Gugwei died, Dalani had no more children.

And the ice times came and the ice times went, and the people spread out across the land, and formed new tribes and chose new totems: ravens and foxes and ground sloths and great cats and buffalo, each a beast that marked a tribe's identity, each beast a god.

The mammoths of the new lands were bigger, and slower, and more foolish than the mammoth of the Siberian plains, and the *pungh* mushrooms, with their seven spots, were not to be found in the new lands, and Nunyunnini did not speak to the tribe any longer.

And in the days of the grandchildren of Dalani and Kalanu's grandchildren, a band of warriors, members of a big and prosperous tribe, returning from a slaving expedition in the north to their home in the south, found the valley of the First People: they killed most of the men, and they took the women and many of the children captive.

One of the children, hoping for clemency, took them to a cave in the hills, in which they found a mammoth-skull, the tattered remnants of a mammoth-skin cloak, a wooden cup, and the preserved head of Atsula the oracle.

While some of the warriors of the new tribe were for taking the sacred objects away with them, stealing the gods of the First People and owning their power, others counseled against it, saying that they would bring nothing but ill-luck, and the malice of their own god (for these were the people of a raven tribe, and ravens are jealous gods).

So they threw the objects down the side of the hill, into a deep ravine, and took the survivors of the First People with them on their long journey south. And the raven tribes, and the fox tribes, grew more powerful in the land, and soon Nunyunnini was entirely forgot.

Part 3

The Moment of the Storm

14

People are in the dark, they don't know what to do
I had a little lantern, oh but it got blown out too.
I'm reaching out my hand. I hope you are too.
I just want to be in the dark with you.
– Greg Brown, *In the Dark With You*

They changed cars at five in the morning, in Minneapolis, in the airport's long term parking lot. They drove to the top floor, where the parking building was open to the sky.

Shadow took the orange uniform and the handcuffs and leg hobbles, put them in the brown paper bag that had briefly held his possessions, folded the whole thing up and dropped it into a garbage can. They had been waiting for ten minutes when a barrel-chested young man came out of an airport door and walked over to them. He was eating a packet of Burger King french fries. Shadow recognised him immediately: he had sat in the back of the car when they had left the House on the Rock, and hummed so deeply the car had vibrated. He was a barrel-chested young man, who now sported a white-streaked winter beard he had not had before. It made him look older.

The man wiped the grease from his hands onto his jeans, extended one huge hand to Shadow. 'I heard of the all-father's death,' he said. 'They will pay, and they will pay dearly.'

'Wednesday was your father?' asked Shadow.

'He was the all-father,' said the man. His deep voice caught in his throat. 'You tell them, tell them all, that when we are needed, my people will be there.'

Czernobog picked at a flake of tobacco from between his teeth and spat it out onto the frozen slush. 'And how many of you is that? Ten? Twenty?'

The barrel-chested man's beard bristled. 'And aren't ten of us worth a hundred of them? Who would stand against even one of my folk, in a battle? But there are more of us than that, at the edge of the cities. There are a few in the mountains. Some in the Catskills, a few living in the carny towns in Florida. They keep their axes sharp. They will come if I call them.'

'You do that, Elvis,' said Mr Nancy. Shadow thought he said Elvis, anyway. Nancy had exchanged the deputy's uniform for a thick brown cardigan, corduroy trousers and brown loafers. 'You call them. It's what the old bastard would have wanted.'

'They betrayed him. They killed him. I laughed at Wednesday, but I was wrong. None of us are safe any longer,' said the man whose name sounded like Elvis. 'But you can rely on us.' He gently patted Shadow on the back and almost sent him sprawling. It was like being gently patted on the back by a wrecking ball.

Czernobog had been looking around the parking lot. Now he said, 'You will pardon me asking, but our new vehicle is which?'

The barrel-chested man pointed. 'There she is,' he said.

Czernobog snorted. 'That?'

It was a 1970 VW bus. There was a rainbow decal in the rear window.

'It's a fine vehicle. And it's the last thing that they'll be expecting you to be driving.'

Czernobog walked around the vehicle. Then he started to cough, a lung-rumbling, old-man, five-in-the-morning smoker's cough. He hawked, and spat, and put his hand to his chest, massaging away the pain. 'Yes. The last car they will suspect. So what happens when the police pull us over, looking for the hippies, and the dope? Eh? We are not here to ride the magic bus. We are to blend in.'

The bearded man unlocked the door of the bus. 'So they take a look at you, they see you aren't hippies, they wave you goodbye. It's the perfect disguise. And it's all I could find at no notice.'

Czernobog seemed to be ready to argue it further, but Mr Nancy intervened smoothly. 'Elvis, you come through for us. We are very grateful. Now, that car needs to get back to Chicago.'

'We'll leave it in Bloomington,' said the bearded man. 'The wolves will take care of it. Don't give it another thought.' He turned back to Shadow. 'Again, you have my sympathy and I share your pain.

Good luck. And if the vigil falls to you, my admiration, and my sympathy.' He squeezed Shadow's hand with his own catcher's mitt fist. It hurt. 'You tell his corpse when you see it. Tell him that Alviss son of Vindalf will keep the faith.'

The VW bus smelled of patchouli, of old incense and rolling tobacco. There was a faded pink carpet glued to the floor and to the walls.

'Who was that?' asked Shadow, as he drove them down the ramp, grinding the gears.

'Just like he said, Alviss son of Vindalf. He's the king of the dwarfs. The biggest, mightiest, greatest of all the dwarf folk.'

'But he's not a dwarf,' pointed out Shadow. 'He's what, five eight? Five nine?'

'Which makes him a giant among dwarfs,' said Czernobog from behind him. 'Tallest dwarf in America.'

'What was that about the vigil?' asked Shadow.

The two old men said nothing. Shadow glanced at Mr Nancy, who was staring out of the window.

'Well? He was talking about a vigil. You heard him.'

Czernobog spoke up from the back seat. 'You will not have to do it,' he said.

'Do what?'

'The vigil. He talks too much. All the dwarfs talk and talk. Is nothing to think of. Better you put it out of your mind.'

Driving south was like driving forward in time. The snows erased, slowly, and were completely gone by the following morning when the bus reached Kentucky. Winter was already over in Kentucky, and spring was on its way. Shadow began to wonder if there were some kind of equation to explain it – perhaps every fifty miles he drove south he was driving a day into the future.

He would have mentioned his idea, but Mr Nancy was asleep in the passenger seat in the front, while Czernobog snored unceasingly in the back.

Time seemed a flexible construct at that moment, an illusion he was imagining as he drove. He found himself becoming painfully aware of birds and animals: he saw the crows on the side of the road, or in the bus's path, picking at roadkill; flights of birds wheeled across the skies in patterns that almost made sense; cats stared at them from front lawns and fence-posts.

Czernobog snorted and woke, sitting up slowly. 'I dreamed a strange dream,' he said. 'I dreamed that I am truly Bielebog. That forever the world imagines that there are two of us, the light god and the dark, but that now we are both old, I find it was only me all the time, giving them gifts, taking my gifts away.' He broke the filter from a Lucky Strike, put it between his lips, and lit it.

Shadow wound down his window.

'Aren't you worried about lung cancer?' he said.

'I *am* cancer,' said Czernobog. 'I do not frighten myself.'

Nancy spoke. 'Folk like us don't get cancer. We don't get arteriosclerosis or Parkinson's Disease or syphilis. We're kind of hard to kill.'

'They killed Wednesday,' said Shadow.

He pulled over for gas, and then parked next door at a restaurant, for an early breakfast. As they entered the payphone in the entrance began to jangle.

They gave their orders to an elderly woman with a worried smile, who had been sitting reading a paperback copy of *What My Heart Meant* by Jenny Kerton. The woman sighed, then walked back and over to the phone, picked it up, said 'Yes'. Then she looked back at the room, said, 'Yep. Looks like they are. You just hold the line now,' and walked over to Mr Nancy.

'It's for you,' she said.

'Okay,' said Mr Nancy. 'Now ma'am, you make sure my fries are real *crisp* now. Think burnt.' He walked over to the payphone. 'This is he.'

'And what makes you think I'm dumb enough to trust you?' he said.

'I can find it,' he said. 'I know where it is.'

'Yes,' he said. 'Of course we want it. You know we want it. And I know you want to get rid of it. So don't give me any shit.'

He hung up the telephone, came back to the table.

'Who was it?' asked Shadow.

'Didn't say.'

'What did they want?'

'They were offerin' us a truce, while they hand over the body.'

'They lie,' said Czernobog. 'They want to lure us in, and then they will kill us. What they did to Wednesday. Is what I always used to do,' he added, with gloomy pride.

'It's on neutral territory,' said Nancy. 'Truly neutral.'

Czernobog chuckled. It sounded like a metal ball rattling in a dry skull. 'I used to say *that* also. Come to a neutral place, I would say, and then in the night we would rise up and kill them all. Those were the good days.'

Mr Nancy shrugged. He crunched down on his dark brown french fries, grinned his approval. 'Mm-mm. These are fine fries,' he said.

'We can't trust those people,' said Shadow.

'Listen, I'm older than you and I'm smarter than you and I'm better lookin' than you,' said Mr Nancy, thumping the bottom of the ketchup bottle, blobbing ketchup over his burnt fries. 'I can get more pussy in an afternoon than you'll get in a year. I can dance like an angel, fight like a cornered bear, plan better than a fox, sing like a nightingale . . .'

'And your point here is . . . ?'

Nancy's brown eyes gazed into Shadow's. 'And they need to get rid of the body as much as we need to take it.'

Czernobog said, 'There is no such neutral place.'

'There's one,' said Mr Nancy. 'It's the centre.'

Determining the exact centre of anything can be problematic at best. With living things – people, for example, or continents – the problem becomes one of intangibles: What is the centre of a man? What is the centre of a dream? And in the case of the continental United States, should one count Alaska when one attempts to find the centre? Or Hawaii?

In the 1930s they made a huge model of the USA, the lower forty-eight states, out of cardboard, and to find the centre they balanced it on a pin, until they found the single place it balanced.

As near as anyone could figure it out, the exact centre of the continental United States was several miles from Lebanon, Kansas, on Johnny Grib's hog farm. The people of Lebanon were all ready to put a monument up in the middle of the hog farm, but Johnny Grib said that he didn't want millions of tourists coming in and tramping all over and upsetting the hogs, so they put the monument to the geographical centre of the United States two miles north of the town. They built a park, and a stone monument to go in the park, and a brass plaque on the monument. They black-topped the road from the town, and, certain of the influx of tourists waiting to arrive, they even built a motel by the monument. Then they waited.

The tourists did not come. Nobody came.

It's a sad little park, now, with a mobile chapel in it that wouldn't fit a small funeral party, and a motel whose windows look like dead eyes.

'Which is why,' concluded Mr Nancy, as they drove into Humansville, Missouri (Population 1084), 'the exact centre of America is a tiny run-down park, an empty church, a pile of stones, and a derelict motel.'

'Hog farm,' said Czernobog. 'You just said that the real centre of America was a hog farm.'

'This isn't about what is,' said Mr Nancy. 'It's about what people *think* is. It's all imaginary anyway. That's why it's important. People only fight over imaginary things.'

'My kind of people?' asked Shadow. 'Or your kind of people?'

Nancy said nothing. Czernobog made a noise that might have been a chuckle, might have been a snort.

Shadow tried to get comfortable in the back of the bus. He had only slept a little. He had a bad feeling in the pit of his stomach. Worse than the feeling he had had in prison, worse than the feeling he had had back when Laura had come to him and told him about the robbery. This was bad. The back of his neck prickled, he felt sick and, several times, in waves, he felt scared.

Mr Nancy pulled over in Humansville, parked outside a super-market. Mr Nancy went inside, and Shadow followed him in. Czernobog waited in the parking lot, smoking his cigarette.

There was a young fair-haired man, little more than a boy, restocking the breakfast cereal shelves.

'Hey,' said Mr Nancy.

'Hey,' said the young man. 'It's true, isn't it? They killed him?'

'Yes,' said Mr Nancy. 'They killed him.'

The young man banged several boxes of Cap'n Crunch down on the shelf. 'They think they can crush us like cockroaches,' he said.

He had a tarnished silver bracelet circling his wrist. 'We don't crush that easy, do we?'

'No,' said Mr Nancy. 'We don't.'

'I'll be there, sir,' said the young man, his pale blue eyes blazing.

'I know you will, Gwydion,' said Mr Nancy.

Mr Nancy bought several large bottles of RC Cola, a six-pack of toilet paper, a pack of evil-looking black cigarillos, a bunch of bananas and a pack of Doublemint chewing gum. 'He's a good boy. Came over in the seventh century. Welsh.'

The bus meandered first to the west and then to the north. Spring faded back into the dead end of winter. Kansas was the cheerless grey of lonesome clouds, empty windows and lost hearts. Shadow had become adept at hunting for radio stations, negotiating between Mr Nancy, who liked talk radio and dance music, and Czernobog, who favoured classical music, the gloomier the better, leavened with the more extreme evangelical religious stations. For himself, Shadow liked oldies.

Toward the end of the afternoon they stopped, at Czernobog's request, on the outskirts of Cherryvale, Kansas (Pop 2,464). Czernobog led them to a meadow outside the town. There were still traces of snow in the shadows of the trees, and the grass was the colour of dirt.

'Wait here,' said Czernobog.

He walked, alone, to the centre of the meadow. He stood there, in the winds of the end of February, for some time. At first he hung his head, then he began gesticulating.

'He looks like he's talking to someone,' said Shadow.

'Ghosts,' said Mr Nancy. 'They worshipped him here, over a hundred years ago. They made blood-sacrifice to him, libations spilled with the hammer. After a time, the townsfolk figured out why so many of the strangers who passed through the town didn't ever come back. This was where they hid some of the bodies.'

Czernobog came back from the middle of the field. His moustache seemed darker now, and there were streaks of black in his grey hair. He smiled, showing his iron tooth. 'I feel good, now. Ahh. Some things linger, and blood lingers longest.'

They walked back across the meadow to where they had parked the VW bus. Czernobog lit a cigarette, but did not cough. 'They did it with the hammer,' he said. 'Votan, he would talk of the gallows and the spear, but for me, it is one thing . . .' He reached out a nicotine-coloured finger and tapped it, hard, in the centre of Shadow's forehead.

'Please don't do that,' said Shadow, politely.

'*Please don't do that,*' mimicked Czernobog. 'One day I will take my hammer and do much worse than that to you, my friend, remember?'

'Yes,' said Shadow. 'But if you tap my head again, I'll break your hand.'

Czernobog snorted. Then he said, 'They should be grateful, the people here. There was such power raised. Even thirty years after they forced my people into hiding, this land, this very land, gave us the greatest movie star of all time. She was the greatest there ever was.'

'Judy Garland?' asked Shadow.

Czernobog shook his head curtly.

'He's talking about Louise Brooks,' said Mr Nancy.

Shadow decided not to ask who Louise Brooks was. Instead he said, 'So, look, when Wednesday went to talk to them, he did it under a truce.'

'Yes.'

'And now we're going to get Wednesday's body from them, as a truce.'

'Yes.'

'And we know that they want me dead or out of the way.'

'They want all of us dead,' said Nancy.

'So what I don't get is, why do we think they'll play fair this time, when they didn't for Wednesday.'

'That,' said Czernobog, 'is why we are meeting at the centre. Is . . .' he frowned. 'What is the word for it? The opposite of sacred?'

'Profane,' said Shadow, without thinking.

'No,' said Czernobog. 'I mean, when a place is less sacred than any other place. Of negative sacredness. Places where they can build no temples. Places where people will not come, and will leave as soon as they can. Places where gods only walk if they are forced to.'

'I don't know,' said Shadow. 'I don't think there is a word for it.'

'All of America has it, a little,' said Czernobog. 'That is why we are not welcome here. But the centre,' said Czernobog. 'The centre is worst. Is like a mine field. We all tread too carefully there to dare break the truce.'

They had reached the bus. Czernobog patted Shadow's upper arm. 'You don't worry,' he said, with gloomy reassurance. 'Nobody else is going to kill you. Nobody but me.'

Shadow found the centre of America at evening that same day, before it was fully dark. It was on a slight hill to the northwest of Lebanon. He drove around the little hillside park, past the tiny mobile chapel and the stone monument, and when Shadow saw the one storey 1950s motel at the edge of the park his heart sank. There was a black Humvee parked in front of it – it looked like a jeep reflected in a fun-house mirror, as squat and pointless and ugly as an armoured car. There were no lights on inside the building.

They parked beside the motel, and as they did so, a man in a chauffeur's uniform and cap walked out of the motel and was illuminated by the headlights of the bus. He touched his cap to them, politely, got into the Humvee, and drove off.

'Big car, tiny dick,' said Mr Nancy.

'Do you think they'll even have beds here?' asked Shadow. 'It's been days since I slept in a bed. This place looks like it's just waiting to be demolished.'

'It's owned by hunters from Texas,' said Mr Nancy. 'Come up here once a year. Damned if I know what they're huntin'. It stops the place being condemned and destroyed.'

They climbed out of the bus. Waiting for them in front of the motel was a woman Shadow did not recognise. She was perfectly made-up, perfectly coiffed. She reminded him of every newscaster he'd ever seen on morning television sitting in a studio that didn't really resemble a living room.

'Lovely to see you,' she said. 'Now, *you* must be Czernobog. I've heard a lot about you. And *you're* Anansi, always up to mischief, eh? You *jolly* old man. And you, you *must* be Shadow. You've certainly led us a merry chase, haven't you?' A hand took his, pressed it firmly, looked him straight in the eye. 'I'm Media. Good to meet you. I hope we can get this evening's business done as *pleasantly* as possible.'

The main doors opened. 'Somehow, Toto,' said the fat kid Shadow had last seen sitting in a limo, 'I don't believe we're in Kansas any more.'

'We're in Kansas,' said Mr Nancy. 'I think we must have drove through most of it today. Damn but this state is flat.'

'This place has no lights, no power, and no hot water,' said the fat kid. 'And, no offense, you people really need the hot water. You just smell like you've been in that bus for a week.'

'I don't think there's *any* need to go there,' said the woman, smoothly. 'We're all friends here. Come on in. We'll show you to your rooms. *We* took the first four rooms. Your late friend is in the fifth. All the ones beyond room five are empty – you can take your pick. I'm afraid it's *not* the Four Seasons, but then, what *is*?'

She opened the door to the motel lobby for them. It smelled of mildew, of damp and dust and of decay.

There was a man sitting in the lobby, in the near darkness. 'You people hungry?' he asked.

'I can always eat,' said Mr Nancy.

'Driver's gone out for a sack of hamburgers,' said the man. 'He'll be back soon.' He looked up. It was too dark to see faces, but he said, 'Big guy. You're Shadow, huh? The asshole who killed Woody and Stone?'

'No,' said Shadow. 'That was someone else. And I know who you are.' He did. He had been inside the man's head. 'You're Town. Have you slept with Wood's widow yet?'

Mr Town fell off his chair. In a movie, it would have been funny; in real life it was simply clumsy. He stood up quickly, came toward Shadow. Shadow looked down at him, and said, 'Don't start anything you're not prepared to finish.'

Mr Nancy rested his hand on Shadow's upper arm. 'Truce, remember?' he said. 'We're at the centre.'

Mr Town turned away, leaned over to the counter and picked up three keys. 'You're down at the end of the hall,' he said. 'Here.'

He handed the keys to Mr Nancy and walked away, into the shadows of the corridor. They heard a motel room door open, and they heard it slam.

Mr Nancy passed a key to Shadow, another to Czernobog. 'Is there a flashlight on the bus?' asked Shadow.

'No,' said Mr Nancy. 'But it's just dark. You mustn't be afraid of the dark.'

'I'm not,' said Shadow. 'I'm afraid of the people in the dark.'

'Dark is good,' said Czernobog. He seemed to have no difficulty seeing where he was going, leading them down the darkened corridor, putting the keys into the locks without fumbling. 'I will be in room ten,' he told them. And then he said, 'Media. I think I have heard of her. Isn't she the one who killed her children?'

'Different woman,' said Mr Nancy. 'Same deal.'

Mr Nancy was in room eight, and Shadow opposite the two of them, in room nine. The room smelled damp, and dusty, and deserted. There was a bed-frame in there, with a mattress on it, but no sheets. A little light entered the room from the gloaming outside the window. Shadow sat down on the mattress, pulled off his shoes, and stretched out at full length. He had driven too much in the last few days.

Perhaps he slept.

He was walking.

A cold wind tugged at his clothes. The tiny snowflakes were little more than a crystalline dust which gusted and flurried in the wind.

There were trees, bare of leaves in the winter. There were high hills on each side of him. It was late on a winter's afternoon: the sky and the snow had attained the same deep shade of purple. Somewhere ahead of him – in this light, distances were impossible to judge – the flames of a bonfire flickered, yellow and orange.

A grey wolf padded through the snow before him.

Shadow stopped. The wolf stopped also, and turned, and waited. One of its eyes glinted yellowish-green. Shadow shrugged and walked toward the flames and the wolf ambled ahead of him.

The bonfire burned in the middle of a grove of trees. There must have been a hundred trees, planted in two rows. There were shapes hanging from the trees. At the end of the rows was a building that looked a little like an overturned boat. It was carved of wood, and it crawled with wooden creatures and wooden faces – dragons, gryphons, trolls and boars – all of them dancing in the flickering light of the fire.

The bonfire was so high that Shadow could barely approach it. The wolf padded around the crackling fire.

In place of the wolf a man came out on the other side of the fire. He was leaning on a tall stick.

'You are in Uppsala, in Sweden,' said the man, in a familiar, gravelly voice. 'About a thousand years ago.'

'Wednesday?' said Shadow.

The man continued to talk, as if Shadow was not there. 'First every year, then, later, when the rot set in, and they became lax, every nine years, they would sacrifice here. A sacrifice of nines. Each day, for nine days, they would hang nine animals from trees in the grove. One of those animals was always a man.'

He strode away from the firelight, toward the trees, and Shadow followed him. As he approached the trees the shapes that hung from them resolved: legs and eyes and tongues and heads. Shadow shook his head: there was something about seeing a bull hanging by its neck from a tree that was darkly sad, and at the same time surreal enough almost to be funny. Shadow passed a hanging stag, a wolfhound, a brown bear, and a chestnut horse with a white mane, little bigger than a pony. The dog was still alive: every few seconds it would kick spasmodically, and it was making a strained whimpering noise as it dangled from the rope.

The man he was following took his long stick, which Shadow realised now, as it moved, was actually a spear, and he slashed at the dog's stomach with it, in one knife-like cut downward. Steaming entrails tumbled onto the snow. 'I dedicate this death to Odin,' said the man, formally.

'It is only a gesture,' he said, turning back to Shadow. 'But gestures mean everything. The death of one dog symbolises the death of all dogs. Nine men they gave to me, but they stood for all the men, all the blood, all the power. It just wasn't enough. One day, the blood stopped flowing. Belief without blood only takes us so far. The blood must flow.'

'I saw you die,' said Shadow.

'In the god business,' said the figure – and now Shadow was certain it was Wednesday, nobody else had that rasp, that deep cynical joy in words, 'it's not the death that matters. It's the opportunity for resurrection. And when the blood flows . . .' He gestured at the animals, at the people, hanging from the trees.

Shadow could not decide whether the dead humans they walked past were more or less horrifying than the animals: at least the humans had known the fate they were going to. There was a deep, boozy smell about the men that suggested that they had been allowed to anaesthetize themselves on their way to the gallows; while the animals would simply have been lynched, hauled up alive and terrified. The faces of the men looked so young: none of them was older than twenty.

'Who am I?' asked Shadow.

'You?' said the man. 'You were an opportunity. You were part of a grand tradition. Although both of us are committed enough to the affair to die for it. Eh?'

'Who are you?' asked Shadow.

'The hardest part is simply surviving,' said the man. The bonfire – and Shadow realised with a strange horror that it truly was a bone-fire: ribcages and fire-eyed skulls stared and stuck and jutted from the flames, sputtering trace-element colours into the night, greens and yellows and blues – was flaring and crackling and burning hotly. 'Three days on the tree, three days in the underworld, three days to find my way back.'

The flames sputtered and flamed too brightly for Shadow to look at directly. He looked down into the darkness beneath the trees.

A knock on the door – and now there was moonlight coming in the window. Shadow sat up with a start. 'Dinner's served,' said Media's voice.

Shadow put his shoes back on, walked over to the door, went out into the corridor. Someone had found some candles, and a dim yellow light illuminated the reception hall. The driver of the Humvee came in holding a cardboard tray and a paper sack. He wore a long black coat and a peaked chauffeur's cap.

'Sorry about the delay,' he said, hoarsely. 'I got everybody the same: a couple of burgers, large fries, large Coke and apple pie. I'll eat mine out in the car.' He put the food down, then walked back outside. The smell of fast food filled the lobby. Shadow took the paper bag and passed out the food, the napkins, the sachets of ketchup.

They ate in silence while the candles flickered and the burning wax hissed.

Shadow noticed that Town was glaring at him. He turned his chair a little, so his back was to the wall. Media ate her burger with a napkin poised by her lips to remove crumbs.

'Oh. Great. These burgers are nearly cold,' said the fat kid. He was still wearing his shades, which Shadow thought pointless and foolish, given the darkness of the room.

'Sorry about that,' said Town. 'The nearest McDonald's is in Nebraska.'

They finished their lukewarm hamburgers and cold fries. The fat kid bit into his single-person apple pie, and the filling spurted down his chin. Unexpectedly, the filling was still hot. 'Ow,' he said. He wiped at it with his hand, licking his fingers to get them clean. 'That stuff burns!' he said. 'Those pies are a class action suit waiting to fucking happen.'

Shadow wanted to hit the kid. He'd wanted to hit him since the kid had his goons hurt him in the limo, after Laura's funeral. He pushed the thought away. 'Can't we just take Wednesday's body and get out of here?' he asked.

'Midnight,' said Mr Nancy and the fat kid, at the same time.

'These things must be done by the rules,' said Czernobog.

'Yeah,' said Shadow. 'But nobody tells me what they are. You keep talking about the goddamn rules, I don't even know what game you people are playing.'

'It's like breaking the street date,' said Media, brightly. 'You know. When things are allowed to be on sale.'

Town said, 'I think the whole thing's a crock of shit. But if their rules make them happy, then my agency is happy and everybody's happy.' He slurped his Coke. 'Roll on midnight. You take the body, you go away. We're all lovey-fucking-dovey and we wave you goodbye. And then we can get on with hunting you down like the rats you are.'

'Hey,' said the fat kid to Shadow. 'Reminds me. I told you to tell your boss he was history. Did you ever tell him?'

'I told him,' said Shadow. 'And you know what he said to me? He said to tell the little snot, if ever I saw him again, to remember that today's future is tomorrow's yesterday.' Wednesday had never said any such thing. Still, these people seemed to like clichés. The black sunglasses reflected the flickering candle-flames back at him, like eyes.

The fat kid said, 'This place is such a fucking dump. No power. Out of wireless range. I mean, when you got to be wired, you're already back in the stone age.' He sucked the last of his Coke through the straw, dropped the cup on the table and walked away down the corridor.

Shadow reached over and placed the fat kid's garbage back into the paper sack. 'I'm going to see the centre of America,' he announced. He got up, and walked outside, into the night. Mr Nancy followed him. They strolled together, across the little park, saying nothing until they reached the stone monument. The wind gusted at them, fitfully, first from one direction, then from another. 'So,' Shadow said. 'Now what?'

The half-moon hung pale in the dark sky.

'Now,' said Nancy, 'you should go back to your room. Lock the door. You try to get some more sleep. At midnight they give us the body. And then we get the hell out of here. The centre is not a stable place for anybody.'

'If you say so.'

Mr Nancy inhaled on his cigarillo. 'This should never have happened,' he said. 'None of this should have happened. Our kind of people, we are . . .' he waved the cigarillo about, as if using it to hunt for a word, then stabbing forward with it, '. . . *exclusive*. We're not social. Not even me. Not even Bacchus. Not for long. We walk by ourselves or we stay in our own little groups. We do not play well with others. We like to be adored and respected and worshipped – me, I like them to be tellin' tales about me, tales showing my cleverness. It's a fault, I know, but it's the way I am. We like to be big. Now, in these shabby days, we are small. The new gods rise and fall and rise again. But this is not a country that tolerates gods for long. Brahma creates, Vishnu preserves, Shiva destroys, and the ground is clear for Brahma to create once more.'

'So what are you saying?' asked Shadow. 'The fighting's over, now? The battle's done?'

Mr Nancy snorted. 'Are you out of your mind? They killed Wednesday. They killed him and they bragged about it. They spread the word. They've showed it on every channel to those with eyes to see it. No, Shadow. It's only just begun.'

He bent down at the foot of the stone monument, stubbed out his cigarillo on the earth, and left it there, like an offering.

'You used to make jokes,' said Shadow. 'You don't any more.'

'It's hard to find the jokes these days. Wednesday's dead. Are you comin' inside?'

'Soon.'

Nancy walked away, toward the motel. Shadow reached out his hand and touched the monument's stones. He dragged his big fingers across the cold brass plate. Then he turned and walked over to the tiny white chapel, walked through the open doorway into the darkness. He sat down in the nearest pew and closed his eyes and lowered his head, and thought about Laura, and about Wednesday, and about being alive.

There was a click from behind him, and a scuff of shoe against earth. Shadow sat up, and turned. Someone stood just outside the open doorway, a dark shape against the stars. Moonlight glinted from something metal.

'You going to shoot me?' asked Shadow.

'Jesus – I wish,' said Mr Town. 'It's only for self defense. So, you're praying? Have they got you thinking that they're gods? They aren't gods.'

'I wasn't praying,' said Shadow. 'Just thinking.'

'The way I figure it,' said Town, 'they're mutations. Evolutionary experiments. A little hypnotic ability, a little hocus pocus, and they can make people believe anything. Nothing to write home about. That's all. They die like men, after all.'

'They always did,' said Shadow. He got up, and Town took a step back. Shadow walked out of the little chapel, and Mr Town kept his distance. 'Hey,' Shadow said. 'Do you know who Louise Brooks was?'

'Friend of yours?'

'Nope. She was a movie star from south of here.'

Town paused. 'Maybe she changed her name, and became Liz Taylor or Sharon Stone or someone,' he suggested, helpfully.

'Maybe.' Shadow started to walk back to the motel. Town kept pace with him.

'You should be back in prison,' said Mr Town. 'You should be on fucking death row.'

'I didn't kill your associates,' said Shadow. 'But I'll tell you something a guy once told me, back when I was in prison. Something I've never forgotten.'

'And that is?'

'There was only one guy in the whole Bible Jesus ever personally promised a place with him in Paradise. Not Peter, not Paul, not any of those guys. He was a convicted thief, being executed. So don't knock the guys on death row. Maybe they know something you don't.'

The driver stood by the Humvee. 'G'night gentlemen,' he said, as they passed.

'Night,' said Mr Town. And then he said, to Shadow, 'I personally don't give a fuck about any of this. What I do, is what Mister World says. It's easier that way.'

Shadow walked down the corridor to room nine.

He unlocked the door, went inside. He said, 'Sorry. I thought this was my room.'

'It is,' said Media. 'I was waiting for you.' He could see her hair in the moonlight, and her pale face. She was sitting on his bed, primly.

'I'll find another room.'

'I won't be here for long,' she said. 'I just thought it might be an appropriate time to make you an *offer*.'

'Okay. Make the offer.'

'Relax,' she said. There was a smile in her voice. 'You have *such* a stick up your butt. Look, Wednesday's *dead*. You don't owe anyone anything. Throw in with us. Time to Come Over to the Winning Team.'

Shadow said nothing.

'We can make you *famous*, Shadow. We can give you power over what people believe and say and wear and dream. You want to be the next Cary Grant? We can make that *happen*. We can make you the next Beatles.'

'I think I preferred it when you were offering to show me Lucy's tits,' said Shadow. 'If that was you.'

'Ah,' she said.

'I need my room back. Good night.'

'And then of course,' she said, not moving, as if he had not spoken, 'we can turn it all around. We can make it *bad* for you. You could be a bad joke forever, Shadow. Or you could be remembered as a monster. You could be remembered forever, but as a Manson, a Hitler . . . how would you *like* that?'

'I'm sorry, ma'am, but I'm kind of tired,' said Shadow. 'I'd be grateful if you'd leave now.'

'I offered you the world,' she said. 'When you're dying in a gutter, you remember that.'

'I'll make a point of it,' he said.

After she had gone her perfume lingered. He lay on the bare mattress and thought about Laura, but whatever he thought about – Laura playing Frisbee, Laura eating a root-beer float without a spoon, Laura giggling and showing off the exotic underwear she had bought when she attended a travel agents' convention in Anaheim – always morphed, in his mind, into Laura sucking Robbie's cock as a truck slammed them off the road and into oblivion. And then he heard her words, and they hurt every time.

You're not dead, said Laura in her quiet voice, in his head. *But I'm not sure that you're alive, either.*

There was a knock. Shadow got up and opened the door. It was the fat kid. 'Those hamburgers,' he said. 'They were just icky. Can you believe it? Fifty miles from McDonald's. I didn't think there was anywhere in the *world* that was fifty miles from McDonald's.'

'This place is turning into Grand Central Station,' said Shadow. 'Okay, so I guess you're here to offer me the freedom of the internet if I come over to your side of the fence. Right?'

The fat kid was shivering. 'No. You're already dead meat,' he said. 'You-you're a fucking illuminated gothic black letter manuscript. You couldn't be hypertext if you tried. I'm . . . I'm synaptic, while, while you're synoptic . . .' He smelled strange, Shadow realised. There was a guy in the cell across the way, whose name Shadow had never known. He had taken off all his clothes in the middle of the day and told everyone that he had been sent to take them away, the truly good ones, like him, in a silver space ship to a perfect place. That had been the last time Shadow had seen him. The fat kid smelled like that guy.

'Are you here for a reason?'

'Just wanted to talk,' said the fat kid. There was a whine in his voice. 'It's creepy in my room. That's all. It's *creepy* in there. Fifty miles to a McDonald's, can you believe that? Maybe I could stay in here with you.'

'What about your friends from the limo? The ones who hit me? Shouldn't you ask them to stay with you?'

'The children wouldn't operate out here. We're in a dead zone.'

Shadow said, 'It's a while until midnight, and it's longer to dawn. I think maybe you need rest. I know I do.'

The fat kid said nothing for a moment, then he nodded, and walked out of the room.

Shadow closed his door, and locked it with the key. He lay back on the mattress.

After a few moments the noise began. It took him a few moments to figure out what it had to be, then he unlocked his door and walked out into the hallway. It was the fat kid, now back in his own room. It sounded like he was throwing something huge against the walls of the room. From the sounds, Shadow guessed that what he was throwing was himself. 'It's just me!' he was sobbing. Or perhaps, 'It's just meat!' Shadow could not tell.

'Quiet!' came a bellow from Czernobog's room, down the hall.

Shadow walked down to the lobby and out of the motel. He was tired.

The driver still stood beside the Humvee, a dark shape in a peaked cap.

'Couldn't sleep, sir?' he asked.

'No,' said Shadow.

'Cigarette, sir?'

'No, thank you.'

'You don't mind if I do?'

'Go right ahead.'

The driver used a Bic Disposable lighter, and it was in the yellow light of the flame that Shadow saw the man's face, actually saw it for the first time, and recognised him, and began to understand.

Shadow knew that thin face. He knew that there would be close-cropped orange-blond hair beneath the black driver's cap, cut close to the scalp. He knew that when the man's lips smiled they would crease into a network of rough scars.

'You're looking good, big guy,' said the driver.

'Low Key?' Shadow stared at his old cell-mate warily.

Prison friendships are good things: they get you through bad places and through dark times. But a prison friendship ends at the prison gates, and a prison friend who reappears in your life is at best a mixed blessing.

'Jesus. Low Key Lyesmith,' said Shadow, and then he heard what he was saying and he understood. 'Loki,' he said. 'Loki Lie-Smith.'

'You're slow,' said Loki, 'but you get there in the end.' And his lips twisted into a scarred smile and embers danced in the shadows of his eyes.

They sat in Shadow's room in the abandoned motel, sitting on the bed, at opposite ends of the mattress. The sounds from the fat kid's room had pretty much stopped.

'You were lucky we were inside together,' said Loki. 'You would never have survived your first year without me.'

'You couldn't have walked out if you wanted?'

'It's easier just to do the time.' He paused. Then, 'You got to understand the god thing. It's not magic. It's about being you, but the *you* that people believe in. It's about being the concentrated, magnified, essence of you. It's about becoming thunder, or the power of a running horse, or wisdom. You take all the belief and become bigger, cooler, more than human. You crystallise.' He paused. 'And then one day they forget about you, and they don't believe in you, and they don't sacrifice, and they don't care, and the next thing you know you're running a three card monte game on the corner of Broadway and Forty-third.'

'Why were you in my cell?'

'Coincidence. Pure and simple.'

'And now you're driving for the opposition.'

'If you want to call them that. It depends where you're standing. The way I figure it, I'm driving for the winning team.'

'But you and Wednesday, you were from the same, you're both –'

'Norse pantheon. We're both from the Norse pantheon. Is that what you're trying to say?'

'Yeah.'

'So?'

Shadow hesitated. 'You must have been friends. Once.'

'No. We were never friends. I'm not sorry he's dead. He was just holding the rest of us back. With him gone, the rest of them are going to have to face up to the facts: it's change or die, evolve or perish. He's gone. War's over.'

Shadow looked at him, puzzled. 'You aren't that stupid,' he said. 'You were always so sharp. Wednesday's death isn't going to end anything. It's just pushed all of the ones who were on the fence over the edge.'

'Mixing metaphors, Shadow. Bad habit.'

'Whatever,' said Shadow. 'It's still true. Jesus. His death did in an instant what he'd spent the last few months trying to do. It united them. It gave them something to believe in.'

'Perhaps.' Loki shrugged. 'As far as I know, the thinking on this side of the fence was that with the troublemaker out of the way, the trouble would also be gone. It's not any of my business, though. I just drive.'

'So tell me,' said Shadow, 'why does everyone care about me? They act like I'm important. Why does it matter what I do.'

'Damned if I know. You were important to us because you were important to Wednesday. As for the why of it . . . I guess it's just another one of life's little mysteries.'

'I'm tired of mysteries.'

'Yeah? I think they add a kind of zest to the world. Like salt in a stew.'

'So you're their driver. You drive for all of them?'

'Whoever needs me,' said Loki. 'It's a living.'

He raised his wristwatch to his face, pressed a button: the dial glowed a gentle blue, which illuminated his face, giving it a haunting, haunted appearance. 'Five to midnight. Time,' said Loki. 'You coming?'

Shadow took a deep breath. 'I'm coming,' he said.

They walked down the dark motel corridor until they reached Room Five.

Loki took a box of matches from his pocket, and thumbed-nailed a match into flame. The momentary flare hurt Shadow's eyes. A candle-wick flickered and caught. And another. Loki lit a new match, and continued to light the candle-stubs: they were on the window-sills and on the headboard of the bed and on the sink in the corner of the room.

The bed had been hauled from its position against the wall into the middle of the motel room, leaving a few feet of space between the bed and the wall on each side. There were sheets draped over the bed, old motel sheets, moth-holed and stained. On top of the sheets lay Wednesday, perfectly still.

He was dressed in the pale suit he had been wearing when he was shot. The right side of his face was untouched, perfect, unmarred by blood. The left side of his face was a ragged mess, and the left shoulder and front of the suit was spattered with dark spots. His hands were at his side. The expression on that wreck of a face was far from peaceful: it looked hurt – a soul-hurt, a real down-deep hurt, filled with hatred and anger and raw craziness. And, on some level, it looked satisfied.

Shadow imagined Mr Jacquel's practiced hands smoothing that hatred and pain away, rebuilding a face for Wednesday with mortician's wax and make-up, giving him a final peace and dignity that even death had denied him.

Still, the body seemed no smaller in death. And it still smelled faintly of Jack Daniel's.

The wind from the plains was rising: he could hear it howling around the old motel at the imaginary centre of America. The candles on the window-sill guttered and flickered.

He could hear footsteps in the hallway. Someone knocked on a door, called 'Hurry up please, it's time,' and they began to shuffle in, heads lowered.

Town came in first, followed by Media and Mr Nancy and Czernobog. Last of all came the fat kid: he had fresh red bruises on his face, and his lips were moving all the time, as if he were reciting some words to himself, but he was making no sound. Shadow found himself feeling sorry for him.

Informally, without a word being spoken, they ranged themselves about the body, each an arm's length away from the next. The atmosphere in the room was religious – deeply religious, in a way that Shadow had never previously experienced. There was no sound but the howling of the wind and the crackling of the candles.

'We are come together, here in this godless place,' said Loki, 'to pass on the body of this individual to those who will dispose of it properly according to the rites. If anyone would like to say something, say it now.'

'Not me,' said Town. 'I never properly met the guy. And this whole thing makes me feel uncomfortable.'

Czernobog said, 'These actions will have consequences. You know that? This can only be the start of it all.'

The fat kid started to giggle, a high-pitched, girlish noise. He said, 'Okay. Okay I've got it.' And then, all on one note, he recited:

'Turning and turning in the widening gyre
The falcon cannot hear the falconer;
Things fall apart; the centre cannot hold . . .'

and then he broke off, his brow creasing. He said, 'Shit. I used to know the whole thing,' and he rubbed his temples and made a face and was quiet.

And then they were all looking at Shadow. The wind was screaming now. He didn't know what to say. He said, 'This whole thing is pitiful. Half of you killed him or had a hand in his death. Now you're giving us his body. Great. He was an irascible old fuck but I drank his mead and I'm still working for him. That's all.'

Media said, 'In a world where people die every day, I think the *important* thing to remember is that for each moment of sorrow we get when people *leave* this world there's a corresponding moment of *joy* when a new baby comes into this world. That first wail is – well, it's *magic*, isn't it? Perhaps it's a *hard* thing to say, but joy and sorrow are like milk and cookies. *That's* how well they go together. I think we should all take a moment to meditate on that.'

And Mr Nancy cleared his throat and said, 'So. I got to say it, because nobody else here will. We are at the centre of this place: a land that has no time for gods, and here at the centre it has less time for us than anywhere. It is a no-man's land, a place of truce, and we observe our truces, here. We have no choice. So. You give us the body of our friend. We accept it. You will pay for this, murder for murder, blood for blood.'

Town said, 'Whatever. You could save yourselves a lot of time and effort by going home and shooting yourselves in the heads. Cut out the middle man.'

'Fuck you,' said Czernobog. 'Fuck you and fuck your mother and fuck the fucking horse you fucking rode in on. You will not even die in battle. No warrior will taste your blood. No one alive will take your life. You will die a soft, poor death. You will die with a kiss on your lips and a lie in your heart.'

'Leave it, old man,' said Town.

'*The blood-dimmed tide is loose,*' said the fat kid. 'I think that comes next.'

The wind howled.

'Okay,' said Loki. 'He's yours. We're done. Take the old bastard away.'

He made a gesture with his fingers, and Town, Media and the fat kid left the room. He smiled at Shadow. 'Call no man happy, huh, kid?' he said. And then he, too, walked away.

'What happens now?' asked Shadow.

'Now we wrap him up,' said Anansi. 'And we take him away from here.'

They wrapped the body in the motel sheets, wrapped it well in its impromptu shroud, so there was no body to be seen, and they could carry it. The two old men walked to each end of the body, but Shadow said, 'Let me see something,' and he bent his knees and slipped his arms around the white-sheeted figure, pushed him up and over his shoulder. He straightened his knees, until he was standing, more or less easily. 'Okay,' he said. 'I've got him. Let's put him into the back of the car.'

Czernobog looked as if he were about to argue, but he closed his mouth. He spat on his forefinger and thumb and began to snuff the candles between his fingertips. Shadow could hear them fizz as he walked from the darkening room.

Wednesday was heavy, but Shadow could cope, if he walked steadily. He had no choice. Wednesday's words were in his head with every step he took along the corridor, and he could taste the sour-sweetness of mead in the back of his throat. *You protect me. You transport me from place to place. You run errands. In an emergency, but only in an emergency, you hurt people who need to be hurt. In the unlikely event of my death, you will hold my vigil . . .*

Mr Nancy opened the motel lobby door for him, then hurried over and opened the back of the bus. The other four were already standing by their Humvee, watching them as if they could not wait to be off. Loki had put his driver's cap back on. The cold wind tugged at Shadow as he walked, whipped at the sheets.

He placed Wednesday down as gently as he could in the back of the bus.

Someone tapped him on the shoulder. He turned. Town stood there with his hand out. He was holding something.

'Here,' said Mr Town, 'Mister World wanted you to have this.'

It was a glass eye. There was a hairline crack down the middle of it, and a tiny chip gone from the front.

'We found it in the Masonic Hall, when we were cleaning up. Keep it for luck. God knows you'll need it.'

Shadow closed his hand around the eye. He wished he could come back with something smart and sharp, but Town was already back at the Humvee, and climbing up into the car; and Shadow still couldn't think of anything clever to say.

They drove east. Dawn found them in Princeton, Missouri. Shadow had not slept yet.

Nancy said, 'Anywhere you want us to drop you? If I were you, I'd rustle up some ID and head for Canada. Or Mexico.'

'I'm sticking with you guys,' said Shadow. 'It's what Wednesday would have wanted.'

'You aren't working for him any more. He's dead. Once we drop his body off, you are free to go.'

'And do what?'

'Keep out of the way, while the war is on,' said Nancy. He flipped his turn signal, and took a left.

'Hide yourself, for a little time,' said Czernobog. 'Then, when this is over, you will come back to me, and I will finish the whole thing.'

Shadow said, 'Where are we taking the body?'

'Virginia. There's a tree,' said Nancy.

'A world tree,' said Czernobog with gloomy satisfaction. 'We had one in my part of the world. But ours grew under the world, not above it.'

'We put him at the foot of the tree,' said Nancy. 'We leave him there. We let you go. We drive south. There's a battle. Blood is shed. Many die. The world changes, a little.'

'You don't want me at your battle? I'm pretty big. I'm good in a fight.'

Nancy turned his head to Shadow and smiled – the first real smile Shadow had seen on Mr Nancy's face since he had rescued Shadow from the Lumber County Jail. 'Most of this battle will be fought in a place you cannot go, and you cannot touch.'

'In the hearts and the minds of the people,' said Czernobog. 'Like at the big roundabout.'

'Huh?'

'The carousel,' said Mr Nancy.

'Oh,' said Shadow. 'Backstage. I got it. Like the desert with the bones in.'

Mr Nancy raised his head. 'Every time I figure you don't have enough sense to bring guts to a bear, you surprise me. Yeah, that's where the real battle will happen. Everything else will just be flash and thunder.'

'Tell me about the vigil,' said Shadow.

'Someone has to stay with the body. It's a tradition. We'll find somebody.'

'He wanted me to do it.'

'No,' said Czernobog. 'It will kill you. Bad, bad, bad idea.'

'Yeah? It'll kill me? To stay with his body?'

'It's not what I'd want at my funeral,' said Mr Nancy. 'When I die, I just want them to plant me somewhere warm. And then when pretty women walk over my grave I would grab their ankles, like in that movie.'

'I never saw that movie,' said Czernobog.

'Of course you did. It's right at the end. It's the high school movie. All the children going to the prom.'

Czernobog shook his head.

Shadow said, 'The film's called *Carrie*, Mr Czernobog. Okay, one of you tell me about the vigil.'

Nancy said, 'You tell him. I'm drivin'.'

'I never heard of no film called *Carrie*. You tell him.'

Nancy said, 'The person on the vigil – gets tied to the tree. Just like Wednesday was. And then they hang there for nine days and nine nights. No food, no water. All alone. At the end they cut the person down, and if they lived . . . well, it could happen. And Wednesday will have had his vigil.'

Czernobog said, 'Maybe Alviss will send us one of his people. A dwarf could survive it.'

'I'll do it,' said Shadow.

'No,' said Mr Nancy.

'Yes,' said Shadow.

The two old men were silent. Then Nancy said, 'Why?'

'Because it's the kind of thing a living person would do,' said Shadow.

'You are crazy,' said Czernobog.

'Maybe. But I'm going to hold Wednesday's vigil.'

When they stopped for gas Czernobog announced he felt sick, and wanted to ride in the front. Shadow didn't mind moving to the back of the bus. He could stretch out more, and sleep.

They drove on in silence. Shadow felt that he'd made a decision; something big and strange.

'Hey. Czernobog,' said Mr Nancy, after a while. 'You check out the technical boy back at the motel? He was not happy. He's been screwin' with something that screwed him right back. That's the biggest trouble with the new kids – they figure they know everythin', and you can't teach them nothin' but the hard way.'

'Good,' said Czernobog.

Shadow was stretched out full length on the seat in the back. He felt like two people, or more than two. There was part of him that felt gently exhilarated: he had *done* something. He had moved. It wouldn't have mattered, if he hadn't wanted to live, but he did want to live, and that made all the difference. He hoped he would live though this, but he was willing to die, if that was what it took to be alive. And, for a moment he thought that the whole thing was funny, just the funniest thing in the world; and he wondered if Laura would appreciate the joke.

There was another part of him – maybe it was Mike Ainsel, he thought, vanished off into nothing at the press of a button in the Lakeside Police Department – who was still trying to figure it all out, trying to see the big picture.

'Hidden Indians,' he said out loud.

'What?' came Czernobog's irritated croak from the front seat.

'The pictures you'd get to colour in as kids. "Can you see the hidden Indians in this picture? There are ten Indians in this picture, can you find them all?" And at first glance you could only see the waterfall and the rocks and the trees, then you see that if you just tip the picture on its side that shadow is an Indian . . .' He yawned.

'Sleep,' suggested Czernobog.

'But the big picture,' said Shadow. Then he slept, and dreamed of hidden Indians.

The tree was in Virginia. It was a long way away from anywhere, on the back of an old farm. To get to the farm they had had to drive for almost an hour south from Blacksburg, to drive roads with names like Pennywinkle Branch and Rooster Spur. They got turned around twice and Mr Nancy and Czernobog both lost their tempers with Shadow and with each other.

They stopped to get directions at a tiny general store, set at the bottom of the hill in the place where the road forked. An old man came out of the back of the store and stared at them: he wore Oshkosh B'Gosh denim overalls and nothing else, not even shoes. Czernobog selected a pickled hog's foot from a jar on the counter and went outside to eat it on the deck, while the man in the overalls drew Mr Nancy maps on the back of napkins, marking off turnings and local landmarks.

They set off once more, with Mr Nancy driving, and they were there in ten minutes. A sign on the gate said ASH.

Shadow got out of the bus, and opened the gate. The bus drove through, jolting through the meadowland. Shadow closed the gate. He walked a little behind the bus, stretching his legs, jogging when the bus got too far in front of him, enjoying the sensation of moving his body.

He had lost all sense of time on the drive from Kansas. Had they been driving for two days? Three days? He did not know.

The body in the back of the bus did not seem to be rotting. He could smell it – a faint odour of Jack Daniel's, overlaid with something that might have been sour honey. But the smell was not unpleasant. From time to time he would take out the glass eye from his pocket and look at it: it was shattered deep inside, fractured from what he imagined was the impact of a bullet, but apart from a chip to one side of the iris the surface was unmarred. Shadow would run it though his hands, palming it, rolling it, pushing it along with his fingers. It was a ghastly souvenir, but oddly comforting: and he suspected that it would have amused Wednesday to know that his eye had wound up in Shadow's pocket.

The farmhouse was dark and shut up. The meadows were overgrown and seemed abandoned. The farm roof was crumbling at the back; it was covered in black plastic sheeting. They jolted over a ridge and Shadow saw the tree.

It was silver-grey and it was higher than the farmhouse. It was the most beautiful tree Shadow had ever seen: spectral and yet utterly real and almost perfectly symmetrical. It also looked instantly familiar: he wondered if he had dreamed it, then realised that no, he had seen it before, or a representation of it, many times. It was Wednesday's silver tie-pin.

The VW bus jolted and bumped across the meadow, and came to a stop about twenty feet from the trunk of the tree.

There were three women standing by the tree. At first glance Shadow thought that they were the Zorya, but no, they were three women he did not know. They looked tired and bored, as if they had been standing there for a long time. Each of them held a wooden ladder. The biggest also carried a brown sack. They looked like a set of Russian dolls: a tall one – she was Shadow's height, or even taller – a middle-sized one, and a woman so short and hunched that at first glance Shadow wrongly supposed her to be a child. They looked so much alike that Shadow was certain that the women must be sisters.

The smallest of the women dropped to a curtsy when the bus drew up. The other two just stared. They were sharing a cigarette, and they smoked it down to the filter before one of them stubbed it out against a root.

Czernobog opened the back of the bus and the biggest of the women pushed past him, and, easily as if it were a sack of flour, she lifted Wednesday's body out of the back and carried it to the tree. She laid it in front of the tree, about ten feet from the trunk. She and her sisters unwrapped Wednesday's body. He looked worse by daylight than he had by candlelight in the motel room, and after one quick glance Shadow looked away. The women arranged his clothes, tidied his suit, then placed him at the corner of the sheet, and wound it around him once more.

Then the women came over to Shadow.

– *You are the one?* the biggest of them asked.

– *The one who will mourn the all-father?* asked the middle-sized one.

– *You have chosen to take the vigil?* asked the smallest.

Shadow nodded. Afterward, he was unable to remember whether he had actually heard their voices. Perhaps he had simply understood what they had meant from their looks and their eyes.

Mr Nancy, who had gone back to the house to use the bathroom, came walking back to the tree. He was smoking a cigarillo. He looked thoughtful.

'Shadow,' he called. 'You really don't have to do this. We can find somebody more suited.'

'I'm doing it,' said Shadow, simply.

'And if you die?' asked Mr Nancy. 'If it kills you?'

'Then,' said Shadow, 'it kills me.'

Mr Nancy flicked his cigarillo into the meadow, angrily. 'I said you had shit for brains, and you still have shit for brains. Can't see when somebody's tryin' to give you an out?'

'I'm sorry,' said Shadow. He didn't say anything else. Nancy walked back to the bus.

Czernobog walked over to Shadow. He did not look pleased. 'You must come through this alive,' he said. 'Come through this safely for me.' And then he tapped his knuckle gently against Shadow's forehead and said *'Bam!'* He squeezed Shadow's shoulder, patted his arm, and went to join Mr Nancy.

The biggest woman, whose name seemed to be Urtha or Urder – Shadow could not repeat it back to her to her satisfaction – told him, in pantomime, to take off his clothes.

'All of them?'

The big woman shrugged. Shadow stripped to his briefs and tee shirt. The women propped the ladders against the tree. One of the ladders – it was painted by hand, with little flowers and leaves twining up the struts – they pointed out to him.

He climbed the nine steps. Then, at their urging, he stepped onto a low branch.

The middle woman tipped out the contents of the sack onto the meadow-grass. It was filled with a tangle of thin ropes, brown with age and dirt, and the woman began to sort them out into lengths, and to lay them carefully on the ground beside Wednesday's body.

They climbed their own ladders now, and they began to knot the ropes, intricate and elegant knots, and they wrapped the ropes first about the tree, and then about Shadow. Unembarrassed, like midwives or nurses or those who lay out corpses, they removed his tee shirt and briefs, then they bound him, never tightly, but firmly and finally. He was amazed at how comfortably the ropes and the knots bore his weight. The ropes went under his arms, between his legs, around his waist, his ankles, his chest, binding him to the tree.

The final rope was tied, loosely, about his neck. It was, initially, uncomfortable, but his weight was well distributed, and none of the ropes cut his flesh.

His feet were five feet above the ground. The tree was leafless and huge, its branches black against the grey sky: its bark a smooth silvery grey.

They took the ladders away. There was a moment of panic as all his weight was taken by the ropes, and he dropped a few inches. Still, he made no sound.

The women moved Wednesday's body, wrapped in its motel-sheet shroud, to the foot of the tree, and they left him there.

They left him there alone.

15

Hang me, O hang me, and I'll be dead and gone,
Hang me, O hang me, and I'll be dead and gone,
I wouldn't mind the hangin', it's bein' gone so long,
It's lyin' in the grave so long.
– Old Song

The first day that Shadow hung from the tree he experienced only discomfort that edged slowly into pain, and fear and, occasionally, an emotion that was somewhere between boredom and apathy: a grey acceptance, a waiting.

He hung.

The wind was still.

After several hours fleeting bursts of colour started to explode across his vision in blossoms of crimson and gold, throbbing and pulsing with a life of their own.

The pain in his arms and legs became, by degrees, intolerable. If he relaxed them, let his body go slack and dangle, if he flopped forward, then the rope around his neck would take up the slack and the world would shimmer and swim. So he pushed himself back against the trunk of the tree. He could feel his heart labouring in his chest, a pounding arrhythmic tattoo as it pumped the blood through his body . . .

Emeralds and sapphires and rubies crystallised and burst in front of his eyes. His breath came in shallow gulps. The bark of the tree was rough against his back. The chill of the afternoon on his naked skin made him shiver, made his flesh prickle and goose.

It's easy, said someone in the back of his head. *There's a trick to it. Either you do it, or you die.*

He was pleased with the thought, and repeated it over and over in the back of his head, part mantra, part nursery rhyme, rattling along to the drumbeat of his heart.

It's easy, there's a trick to it, you do it or you die.
It's easy, there's a trick to it, you do it or you die.
It's easy, there's a trick to it, you do it or you die.
It's easy, there's a trick to it, you do it or you die.

Time passed. The chanting continued. He could hear it. Someone was repeating the words, only stopping when Shadow's mouth began to dry out, when his tongue turned dry and skin-like in his mouth. He pushed himself up and away from the tree with his feet, trying to support his weight in a way that would still allow him to fill his lungs.

He breathed until he could hold himself up no more, and then he fell back into the bonds, and hung from the tree.

When the chattering started – an angry, laughing chattering noise – he closed his mouth, concerned that it was he himself making it; but the noise continued. *It's the world laughing at me, then,* thought Shadow. His head lolled to one side. Something ran down the tree-trunk beside him, stopping beside his head. It chittered loudly in his ear, one word, which sounded a lot like 'ratatosk'. Shadow tried to repeat it, but his tongue stuck to the roof of his mouth. He turned, slowly, and stared into the grey-brown face and pointed ears of a squirrel.

In close up, he learned, a squirrel looks a lot less cute than it does from a distance. The creature was rat-like and dangerous, not sweet or charming. And its teeth looked sharp. He hoped that it would not perceive him as a threat, or as a food source. He did not think that squirrels were carnivorous . . . but then, so many things he had not thought had turned out to be so . . .

He slept.

The pain woke him several times in the next few hours. It pulled him from a dark dream in which dead children rose and came to him, their eyes peeling swollen pearls, and they reproached him for failing them. A spider edged across his face, and he woke. He shook his head, dislodging or frightening it and returned to his dreams –

and now an elephant-headed man, pot-bellied, one tusk broken, was riding toward him on the back of a huge mouse. The elephant-headed man curled his trunk towards Shadow and said, 'If you had invoked me before you began this journey, perhaps some of your troubles might have been avoided.' Then the elephant took the mouse, which had, by some means that Shadow could not perceive, become tiny while not changing in size at all, and passed it from hand to hand to hand, fingers curling about it as the little creature scampered from palm to palm, and Shadow was not at all surprised when the elephant-headed god finally opened all four of his hands to reveal them perfectly empty. He shrugged arm after arm after arm in a peculiar fluid motion, and looked at Shadow, his face unreadable.

'It's in the trunk,' Shadow told the elephant man, who had been watching as the flickering tail vanished.

The elephant man nodded his huge head, and said, 'Yes. In the trunk. You will forget many things. You will give many things away. You will lose many things. But do not lose this,' and then the rain began, and Shadow was tumbled, shivering and wet, from deep sleep into full wakefulness. The shivering intensified until it scared Shadow: he was shivering more violently than he had ever imagined possible, a series of convulsive shudders which built upon each other. He willed himself to stop, but still he shivered, his teeth banging together, his limbs twitching and jerking beyond his control. There was real pain there, too, a deep, knife-like pain that covered his body with tiny, invisible wounds, intimate and unbearable.

He opened his mouth to catch the rain as it fell, moistening his cracked lips and his dry tongue, wetting the ropes that bound him to the trunk of the tree. There was a flash of lightning so bright it felt like a blow to his eyes, transforming the world into an intense panorama of image and after-image. Then the thunder, a crack and a boom and a rumble, and, as the thunder echoed, the rain redoubled. In the rain and the night the shivering abated; the knife-blades were put away. Shadow no longer felt the cold, or rather, he felt only the cold, but the cold had now become part of himself.

Shadow hung from the tree while the lightning flickered and forked across the sky, and the thunder subsided into an omnipresent rumbling, with occasional bangs and roars like distant bombs exploding in the night. The wind tugged at Shadow, trying to pull him from the tree, flaying him, cutting to the bone; and Shadow knew in his soul that the real storm had truly begun.

A strange joy rose within Shadow then, and he started laughing, as the rain washed his naked skin and the lightning flashed and thunder rumbled so loudly that he could barely hear himself laugh. He exulted.

He was alive. He had never felt like this. Ever.

If he did die, he thought, if he died right now, here on the tree, it would be worth it to have had this one, perfect, mad moment.

'Hey!' he shouted, at the storm. 'Hey! It's me! I'm here!'

He trapped some water between his bare shoulder and the trunk of the tree, and he twisted his head over and drank the trapped rainwater, sucking and slurping at it, and he drank more and he laughed, laughed with joy and delight, not madness, until he could laugh no more, until he hung there too exhausted to move.

At the foot of the tree, on the ground, the rain had made the sheet partly transparent, and had lifted it and pushed it forward so that Shadow could see Wednesday's dead hand, waxy and pale, and the shape of his head, and he thought of the shroud of Turin and he remembered the open girl on Jacquel's table in Cairo, and then, as if to spite the cold, he observed that he was feeling warm and comfortable, and the bark of the tree felt soft, and he slept once more, and if he dreamed any dreams this time he could not remember them.

By the following morning the pain was no longer local, not confined to the places where the ropes cut into his flesh, or where the bark scraped his skin. Now the pain was everywhere.

And he was hungry, with empty pangs down in the pit of him. His head was pounding. Sometimes he imagined that he had stopped breathing, that his heart had ceased to beat. Then he would hold his breath until he could hear his heart pounding an ocean in his ears and he was forced to suck air like a diver surfacing from the depths.

It seemed to him that the tree reached from hell to heaven, and that he had been hanging there forever. A brown hawk circled the tree, landed on a broken branch near to him, and then took to the wing, flying west.

The storm, which had abated at dawn, began to return as the day passed. Grey, roiling clouds stretched from horizon to horizon; a slow drizzle began to fall. The body at the base of the tree seemed to have become less, in its stained motel winding sheet, crumbling into itself like a sugar cake left in the rain.

Sometimes Shadow burned, sometimes he froze.

When the thunder started once more he imagined that he heard drums beating, kettledrums in the thunder and the thump of his heart, inside his head or outside, it did not matter.

He perceived the pain in colours: the red of a neon bar-sign, the green of a traffic light on a wet night, the blue of an empty video screen.

The squirrel dropped from the bark of the trunk onto Shadow's shoulder, sharp claws digging into his skin. 'Ratatosk!' it chattered. The tip of its nose touched his lips. 'Ratatosk.' It sprang back onto the tree.

His skin was on fire with pins and needles, a pricking covering his whole body. The sensation was intolerable.

His life was laid out below him, on the motel sheet shroud: literally laid out, like the items at some Dada picnic, a surrealist tableau: he could see his mother's puzzled stare, the American embassy in Norway, Laura's eyes on their wedding day . . .

He chuckled through dry lips.

'What's so funny, puppy?' asked Laura.

'Our wedding day,' he said. 'You bribed the organist to change from playing the Wedding March to the theme-song from *Scooby-Doo* as you walked toward me down the aisle. Do you remember?'

'Of course I remember, darling. "I would have made it too, if it wasn't for those meddling kids".'

'I loved you so much,' said Shadow.

He could feel her lips on his, and they were warm and wet and living, not cold and dead, so he knew that this was another hallucination. 'You aren't here, are you?' he asked.

'No,' she said. 'But you are calling me, for the last time. And I am coming.'

Breathing was harder now. The ropes cutting his flesh were an abstract concept, like free will or eternity.

'Sleep, puppy,' she said, although he thought it might have been his own voice he heard, and he slept.

The sun was a pewter coin in a leaden sky. Shadow was, he realised slowly, awake, and he was cold. But the part of him that understood that seemed very far away from the rest of him. Somewhere in the distance he was aware that his mouth and throat were burning, painful and cracked. Sometimes, in the daylight, he would see stars fall; other times he saw huge birds, the size of delivery trucks, flying toward him. Nothing reached him; nothing touched him.

'Ratatosk. Ratatosk.' The chattering had become a scolding.

The squirrel landed, heavily, with sharp claws, on his shoulder and stared into his face. He wondered if he were hallucinating: the animal was holding a walnut-shell, like a doll's house cup, in its front paws. The animal pressed the shell to Shadow's lips. Shadow felt the water, and, involuntarily, he sucked it in to his mouth, drinking from the tiny cup. He ran the water around his cracked lips, his dry tongue. He wet his mouth with it, and swallowed what was left, which was not much.

The squirrel leapt back to the tree, and ran down it, towards the roots, and then, in seconds, or minutes, or hours, Shadow could not tell which (all the clocks in his mind were broken, he thought, and their gears and cogs and springs were simply a jumble down there in the writhing grass), the squirrel returned with its walnut-shell cup, climbing carefully, and Shadow drank the water it brought to him.

The muddy-iron taste of the water filled his mouth, cooled his parched throat. It eased his fatigue and his madness.

By the third walnut-shell, he was no longer thirsty.

He began to struggle, then, pulling at the ropes, flailing his body, trying to get down, to get free, to get away. He moaned.

The knots were good. The ropes were strong, and they held, and soon he exhausted himself once more.

In his delirium, Shadow became the tree. Its roots went deep into the loam of the earth, deep down into time, into the hidden springs. He felt the spring of the woman called Urd, which is to say, *Past*. She was huge, a giantess, an underground mountain of a woman, and the waters she guarded were the waters of time. Other roots went to other places. Some of them were secret. Now, when he was thirsty, he pulled water from his roots, pulled them up into the body of his being.

He had a hundred arms which broke into a hundred thousand fingers, and all of his fingers reached up into the sky. The weight of the sky was heavy on his shoulders.

It was not that the discomfort was lessened, but the pain belonged to the figure hanging from the tree, rather than to the tree itself. Shadow in his madness was now so much more than the man on the tree. He was the tree, and he was the wind rattling the bare branches of the world tree; he was the grey sky and the tumbling clouds; he was Ratatosk the squirrel running from the deepest roots to the highest branches; he was the mad-eyed hawk who sat on a broken branch at the top of the tree surveying the world; he was the worm in the heart of the tree.

The stars wheeled, and he passed his hundred hands over the glittering stars, palming them, switching them, vanishing them . . .

A moment of clarity, in the pain and the madness: Shadow felt himself surfacing. He knew it would not be for long. The morning sun was dazzling him. He closed his eyes, wishing he could shade them.

There was not long to go. He knew that, too.

When he opened his eyes, Shadow saw that there was a young man in the tree with him.

His skin was dark brown. His forehead was high and his dark hair was tightly curled. He was sitting on a branch high above Shadow's head. Shadow could see him clearly by craning his head. And the man was mad. Shadow could see that at a glance.

'You're naked,' confided the madman, in a cracked voice. 'I'm naked too.'

'I see that,' croaked Shadow.

The madman looked at him, then he nodded and twisted his head down and around, as if he were trying to remove a crick from his neck. Eventually he said, 'Do you know me?'

'No,' said Shadow.

'I know you. I watched you in Cairo. I watched you after. My sister likes you.'

'You are . . .' the name escaped him. *Eats roadkill*. Yes. 'You are Horus.'

The madman nodded. 'Horus,' he said. 'I am the falcon of the morning, the hawk of the afternoon. I am the sun, as you are. And I know the true name of Ra. My mother told me.'

'That's great,' said Shadow, politely.

The madman stared at the ground below them intently, saying nothing. Then he dropped from the tree.

A hawk fell like a stone to the ground, pulled out of its plummet into a swoop, beat its wings heavily and flew back to the tree, a baby rabbit in its talons. It landed on a branch closer to Shadow.

'Are you hungry?' asked the madman.

'No,' said Shadow. 'I guess I should be, but I'm not.'

'I'm hungry,' said the madman. He ate the rabbit rapidly, pulling it apart, sucking, tearing, rending. As he finished with them, he dropped the gnawed bones and the fur to the ground. He walked further down the branch until he was only an arm's length from Shadow. Then he peered at Shadow unselfconsciously, inspecting him with care and caution, from his feet to his head. There was rabbit-blood on his chin and his chest, and he wiped it off with the back of his hand.

Shadow felt he had to say something. 'Hey,' he said.

'Hey,' said the madman. He stood up on the branch, turned away from Shadow and let a stream of dark urine arc out into the meadow below. It went on for a long time. When he had finished he crouched down again on the branch.

'What do they call you?' asked Horus.

'Shadow,' said Shadow.

The madman nodded. 'You are the shadow. I am the light,' he said. 'Everything that is, casts a shadow.' Then he said, 'They will fight soon. I was watching them as they started to arrive.'

And then the madman said, 'You are dying. Aren't you?'

But Shadow could no longer speak. A hawk took wing, and circled slowly upward, riding the updrafts into the morning.

* * *

Moonlight.

A cough shook Shadow's frame, a racking painful cough that stabbed his chest and his throat. He gagged for breath.

'Hey puppy,' called a voice that he knew.

He looked down.

The moonlight burned whitely through the branches of the tree, bright as day, and there was a woman standing in the moonlight on the ground below him, her face a pale oval. The wind rattled in the branches of the tree.

'Hi, puppy,' she said.

He tried to speak, but he coughed instead, deep in his chest, for a long time.

'You know,' she said, helpfully, 'that doesn't sound good.'

He croaked, 'Hello Laura.'

She looked up at him with dead eyes, and she smiled.

'How did you find me?' he asked.

She was silent, for a while, in the moonlight. Then she said, 'You are the nearest thing I have to life. You are the only thing I have left, the only thing that isn't bleak and flat and grey. I could be blindfolded and dropped into the deepest ocean and I would know where to find you. I could be buried a hundred miles underground and I would know where you are.'

He looked down at the woman in the moonlight, and his eyes stung with tears.

'I'll cut you down,' she said, after a while. 'I spend too much time rescuing you, don't I?'

He coughed again. Then, 'No, leave me. I have to do this.'

She looked up at him, and shook her head. 'You're crazy,' she said. 'You're dying up there. Or you'll be crippled, if you aren't already.'

'Maybe,' he said. 'But I'm alive.'

'Yes,' she said, after a moment. 'I guess you are.'

'You told me,' he said. 'In the graveyard.'

'It seems like such a long time ago, puppy,' she said. Then she said, 'I feel better, here. It doesn't hurt as much. You know what I mean? But I'm so dry.'

The wind let up, and he could smell her now: a stink of rotten meat and sickness and decay, pervasive and unpleasant.

'I lost my job,' she said. 'It was a night job, but they said people had complained. I told them I was sick, and they said they didn't care. I'm so thirsty.'

'The women,' he told her. 'They have water. The house.'

'Puppy . . .' she sounded scared.

'Tell them . . . tell them I said to give you water . . .'

The white face stared up at him. 'I should go,' she told him. Then she hacked, and made a face, and spat a mass of something white onto the grass. It broke up when it hit the ground, and wriggled away.

It was almost impossible to breathe. His chest felt heavy, and his head was swaying.

'Stay,' he said, in a breath that was almost a whisper, unsure whether or not she could hear him. 'Please don't go.' He started to cough. 'Stay the night.'

'I'll stop a while,' she said. And then, like a mother to a child she said, 'Nothing's gonna hurt you when I'm here. You know that?'

Shadow coughed once more. He closed his eyes – only for a moment, he thought, but when he opened them again the moon had set and he was alone.

A crashing and a pounding in his head, beyond the pain of migraine, beyond all pain. Everything dissolved into tiny butterflies which circled him like a multicoloured duststorm and then evaporated into the night.

The white sheet wrapped about the body at the base of the tree flapped noisily in the morning wind.

The pounding eased. Everything slowed. There was nothing left to make him keep breathing. His heart ceased to beat in his chest.

The darkness that he entered this time was deep, and lit by a single star, and it was final.

16

I know it's crooked. But it's the only game in town.
– Canada Bill Jones

The tree was gone, and the world was gone, and the morning-grey sky above him was gone. The sky was now the colour of midnight. There was a single cold star shining high above him, a blazing, twinkling light, and nothing else. He took a single step and almost tripped.

Shadow looked down. There were steps cut into the rock, going down, steps so huge that he could only imagine that giants had cut them and descended them a long time ago.

He clambered downward, half jumping, half vaulting from step to step. His body ached, but it was the ache of lack of use, not the tortured ache of a body that has hung on a tree until it was dead.

He observed, without surprise, that he was now fully dressed, in jeans and a white tee shirt. He was barefoot. He experienced a profound moment of *déjà vu*: this was what he had been wearing when he stood in Czernobog's apartment the night when Zorya Polunochnaya had come to him and told him about the constellation called Odin's Wain. She had taken the moon down from the sky for him.

He knew, suddenly, what would happen next. Zorya Polunochnaya would be there.

She was waiting for him at the bottom of the steps. There was no moon in the sky, but she was bathed in moonlight nonetheless: her white hair was moon-pale, and she wore the same lace-and-linen nightdress she had worn that night in Chicago.

She smiled when she saw him, and looked down, as if momentarily embarrassed. 'Hello,' she said.

'Hi,' said Shadow.

'How are you?'

'I don't know,' he said. 'I think this is maybe another strange dream on the tree. I've been having crazy dreams since I got out of prison.'

Her face was silvered by the moonlight (but no moon hung in that plum-black sky, and now, at the foot of the steps, even the single star was lost to view) and she looked both solemn and vulnerable. She said, 'All your questions can be answered, if that is what you want. But once you learn your answers, you can never unlearn them.'

Beyond her, the path forked. He would have to decide which path to take, he knew that. But there was one thing he had to do first. He reached into the pocket of his jeans and was relieved when he felt the familiar weight of the coin at the bottom of the pocket. He eased it out, held it between finger and thumb: a 1922 Liberty dollar. 'This is yours,' he said.

He remembered then that his clothes were really at the foot of the tree. The women had placed his clothes in the canvas sack from which they had taken the ropes, and tied the end of the sack, and the biggest of the women had placed a heavy rock on it to stop it from blowing away. And so he knew that, in reality, the Liberty dollar was in a pocket in that sack, beneath the rock. But still, it was heavy in his hand, at the entrance to the underworld.

She took it from his palm with her slim fingers.

'Thank you. It bought you your liberty twice,' she said. 'And now it will light your way into dark places.'

She closed her hand around the dollar, then she reached up and placed it in the air, as high as she could reach. Then she let go of it. Instead of falling, the coin floated upward until it was a foot or so above Shadow's head. It was no longer a silver coin, though. Lady Liberty and her crown of spikes were gone. The face he saw on the coin was the indeterminate face of the moon in the summer sky.

Shadow could not decide whether he was looking at a moon the size of a dollar, a foot above his head; or whether he was looking at a moon the size of the Pacific Ocean, many thousands of miles away. Nor whether there was any difference between the two ideas. Perhaps it was all a matter of the way you looked at it.

He looked at the forking path ahead of him.

'Which path should I take?' he asked. 'Which one is safe?'

'Take one, and you cannot take the other,' she said. 'But neither path is safe. Which way would you walk – the way of hard truths or the way of fine lies?'

'Truths,' he said. 'I've come too far for more lies.'

She looked sad. 'There will be a price, then,' she said.

'I'll pay it. What's the price.'

'Your name,' she said. 'Your real name. You will have to give it to me.'

'How?'

'Like this,' she said. She reached a perfect hand toward his head. He felt her fingers brush his skin, then he felt them penetrate his skin, his skull, felt them push deep into his head. Something tickled, in his skull and all down his spine. She pulled her hand out of his head. A flame, like a candle-flame but burning with a clear magnesium-white luminance, was flickering on the tip of her forefinger.

'Is that my name?' he asked.

She closed her hand, and the light was gone. 'It was,' she said. She extended her hand, and pointed to the right-hand path. 'That way,' she said. 'For now.'

Nameless, Shadow walked down the right-hand path in the moonlight. When he turned around to thank her, he saw nothing but darkness. It seemed to him that he was deep under the ground, but when he looked up into the darkness above him he still saw the tiny moon.

He turned a corner.

If this was the afterlife, he thought, it was a lot like the House on the Rock: part diorama, part nightmare.

He was looking at himself in prison blues, in the warden's office, as the warden told him that Laura had died in a car crash. He saw the expression on his own face – he looked like a man who had been abandoned by the world. It hurt him to see it, the nakedness and the fear. He hurried on, pushed through the warden's grey office, and found himself looking at the VCR repair store on the outskirts of Eagle Point. Three years ago. Yes.

Inside the store, he knew, he was beating the living crap out of Larry Powers and B.J. West, bruising his knuckles in the process: pretty soon he would walk out of there, carrying a brown supermarket bag filled with twenty dollar bills. The money they could never prove he had taken: his share of the proceeds, and a little more, for they shouldn't have tried to rip him and Laura off like that. He was only the driver, but he had done his part, done everything that she had asked of him . . .

At the trial, nobody mentioned the bank robbery, although everybody wanted to. They couldn't prove a thing, as long as nobody was talking. And nobody was. The prosecutor was forced instead to stick to the bodily damage that Shadow had inflicted on Powers and West. He showed photographs of the two men on their arrival in the local hospital. Shadow barely defended himself in court; it was easier that way. Neither Powers nor West seemed able to remember what the fight had been about, but they each admitted that Shadow had been their assailant.

Nobody talked about the money.

Nobody even mentioned Laura, and that was all that Shadow had wanted.

Shadow wondered whether the path of comforting lies would have been a better one to walk. He walked away from that place, and followed the rock path down into what looked like a hospital room, a public hospital in Chicago and he felt the bile rise in his throat. He stopped. He did not want to look. He did not want to keep walking.

In the hospital bed his mother was dying again, as she'd died when he was sixteen, and, yes, here he was, a large, clumsy sixteen-year old with acne pocking his cream-and-coffee skin, sitting at her bedside, unable to look at her, reading a thick paperback book. Shadow wondered what the book was, and he walked around the hospital bed to inspect it more closely. He stood between the bed and the chair looking from the one to the other, the big boy hunched into his chair, his nose buried in *Gravity's Rainbow*, trying to escape from his mother's death into London during the blitz, the fictional madness of the book no escape and no excuse.

His mother's eyes were closed in a morphine peace: what she had thought was just another sickle-cell crisis, another bout of pain to be endured, had turned out, they had discovered, too late, to be lymphoma. There was a lemonish-grey tinge to her skin. She was in her early thirties, but she looked much older.

Shadow wanted to shake himself, the awkward boy that he once was, get him to hold her hand, talk to her, do *something* before she slips away, as he knows that she will. But he cannot touch himself, and he continues to read; and so his mother died while he sat in the chair next to her, reading a fat book.

After that he had more or less stopped reading. You could not trust fiction. What good were books, if they couldn't protect you from something like that?

Shadow walked away from the hospital room, down the winding corridor, deep into the bowels of the earth.

He sees his mother first and he cannot believe how young she is, not yet twenty-five he guesses, before her medical discharge. They're in their apartment, another embassy rental somewhere in Northern Europe. He looks around for something to give him a clue, and he sees himself: a shrimp of a kid, big pale-grey eyes, and dark hair. They are arguing. Shadow knows without hearing the words what they're arguing about: it was the only thing they quarreled about, after all.

– *Tell me about my father.*

– *He's dead. Don't ask about him.*

– *But who was he?*

– *Forget him. Dead and gone and you ain't missed nothing.*

– *I want to see a picture of him.*

– *I ain't got a picture*, she'd say and her voice would get quiet and fierce, and he knew that if he kept asking her questions she would shout, or even hit him, and he knew that he would not stop asking questions, so he turned away and walked on down the tunnel.

The path he followed twisted and wound and curled back on itself, and it put him in mind of snake-skins and intestines and of deep, deep tree-roots. There was a pool to his left; he heard the *drip, drip* of water into it somewhere at the back of the tunnel, the falling water barely ruffling the mirrored surface of the pool. He dropped to his knees and drank, using his hand to bring the water to his lips. Then he walked on until he was standing in the floating disco-glitter patterns of a mirror-ball. It was like being in the exact centre of the universe with all the stars and planets circling him, and he could not hear anything, not the music, nor the shouted conversations over the music, and now Shadow was staring at a woman who looked just like his mother never looked in all the years he knew her, she's little more than a child, after all . . .

And she is dancing.

Shadow found that he was completely unsurprised when he recognised the man who dances with her. He had not changed that much in thirty-three years.

She is drunk: Shadow could see that at a glance. She is not very drunk, but she is unused to drink, and in a week or so she will take a ship to Norway. They have been drinking margaritas, and she has salt on her lips and salt clinging to the back of her hand.

Wednesday is not wearing a suit and tie, but the pin in the shape of a silver tree he wears over the pocket of his shirt glitters and glints when the mirror-ball light catches it. They make a fine-looking couple, considering the difference in their ages. There is a lupine grace to Wednesday's movements.

A slow dance. He pulls her close to him, and his paw-like hand curves around the seat of her skirt possessively, moving her closer to him. His other hand takes her chin, pushes it upward into his face, and the two of them kiss, there on the floor, as the glitter-ball lights circle them into the centre of the universe.

Soon after, they leave. She sways against him, and he leads her from the dance hall.

Shadow buries his head in his hands, and does not follow them, unable or unwilling to witness his own conception.

The mirror lights were gone, and now the only illumination came from the tiny moon that burned high above his head.

He walked on. At a bend in the path he stopped for a moment, to catch his breath.

He felt a hand run gently up his back, and gentle fingers ruffle the hair on the back of his head.

'Hello,' whispered a smoky feline voice, over his shoulder.

'Hello,' he said, turning to face her.

She had brown hair and brown skin and her eyes were the deep golden-amber of good honey. Her pupils were vertical slits. 'Do I know you?' he asked, puzzled.

'Intimately,' she said, and she smiled. 'I used to sleep on your bed. And my people have been keeping their eyes on you, for me.'

She turned to the path ahead of him, pointed to the three ways he could go. 'Okay,' she said. 'One way will make you wise. One way will make you whole. And one way will kill you.'

'I'm already dead, I think,' said Shadow. 'I died on the tree.'

She made a moue. 'There's dead,' she said, 'and there's dead, and there's dead. It's a relative thing.' Then she smiled again. 'I could make a joke about that, you know. Something about dead relatives.'

'No,' said Shadow. 'It's okay.'

'So,' she said. 'Which way do you want to go?'

'I don't know,' he admitted.

She tipped her head on one side, a perfectly feline gesture. Suddenly, Shadow remembered the claw marks on his shoulder. He felt himself beginning to blush. 'If you trust me,' said Bast, 'I can choose for you.'

'I trust you,' he said, without hesitation.

'Do you want to know what it's going to cost you?'

'I've already lost my name,' he told her.

'Names come and names go. Was it worth it?'

'Yes. Maybe. It wasn't easy. As revelations go, it was kind of personal.'

'All revelations are personal,' she said. 'That's why all revelations are suspect.'

'I don't understand.'

'No,' she said, 'you don't. I'll take your heart. We'll need it later,' and she reached her hand deep inside his chest, and she pulled it back out with something ruby and pulsing held between her sharp fingernails. It was the colour of pigeon's blood, and it was made of pure light. Rhythmically it expanded and contracted.

She closed her hand, and it was gone.

'Take the middle way,' she said.

Shadow nodded, and walked on.

The path was becoming slippery now. There was ice on the rock. The moon above him glittered through the ice-crystals in the air: there was a ring about the moon, a moonbow, diffusing the light. It was beautiful, but it made walking harder. The path was unreliable.

He reached the place where the path divided.

He looked at the first path with a feeling of recognition. It opened into a vast chamber, or a set of chambers, like a dark museum. He knew it already. He could hear the long echoes of tiny noises. He could hear the noise that the dust makes as it settles.

It was the place that he had dreamed of, that first night that Laura had come to him, in the motel so long ago; the endless memorial hall to the gods that were forgotten, and the ones whose very existence had been lost.

He took a step backward.

He walked to the path on the far side, and looked ahead. There was a Disneyland quality to the corridor: black Plexiglas walls with lights set in them. The coloured lights blinked and flashed in the illusion of order, for no particular reason, like the console lights on a television starship.

He could hear something there as well: a deep vibrating bass drone which Shadow felt in the pit of his stomach.

He stopped and looked around. Neither way seemed right. Not any longer. He was done with paths. The middle way, the way the cat-woman had told him to walk, that was his way. He moved toward it.

The moon above him was beginning to fade: the edge of it was pinking and going into eclipse. The path was framed by a huge doorway.

Shadow walked through the arch, in darkness. The air was warm, and it smelled of wet dust, like a city street after the summer's first rain.

He was not afraid.

Not any more. Fear had died on the tree, as Shadow had died. There was no fear left, no hatred, no pain. Nothing left but essence.

Something big splashed, quietly, in the distance, and the splash echoed into the vastness. He squinted, but could see nothing. It was too dark. And then, from the direction of the splashes, a ghost-light glimmered and the world took form: he was in a cavern, and in front of him, mirror-smooth, was water.

The splashing noises came closer and the light became brighter, and Shadow waited on the shore. Soon enough a low, flat boat came into sight, a flickering white lantern burning at its raised prow, another reflected in the glassy black water several feet below it. The boat was being poled by a tall figure, and the splashing noise Shadow had heard was the sound of the pole being lifted and moved as it pushed the craft across the waters of the underground lake.

'Hello there!' called Shadow. Echoes of his words suddenly surrounded him: he could imagine that a whole chorus of people were welcoming him, and calling to him and each of them had his voice.

The person poling the boat made no reply.

The boat's pilot was tall, and very thin. He – if it was a he – wore an unadorned white robe, and the pale head that topped it was so utterly inhuman that Shadow was certain that it had to be a mask of some sort: it was a bird's head, small on a long neck, its beak long and high. Shadow was certain he had seen it before, this ghostly, bird-like figure. He grasped at the memory and then, disappointed, realised that he was picturing the clockwork penny-in-the-slot machine in the House on the Rock, and the pale, bird-like, half-glimpsed figure that glided out from behind the crypt for the drunkard's soul.

Water dripped and echoed from the pole and the prow, and the ship's wake rippled the glassy waters. The boat was made of reeds, bound and tied.

The boat came close to the shore. The pilot leant on its pole. Its head turned slowly, until it was facing Shadow. 'Hello,' it said, without moving its long beak. The voice was male, and, like everything else in Shadow's afterlife so far, familiar. 'Come on board. You'll get your feet wet, I'm afraid, but there's not a thing can be done about that. These are old boats, and if I come in closer I could rip out the bottom.'

Shadow took off his shoes and stepped out into the water. It came half-way up his calves, and was, after the initial shock of wetness, surprisingly warm. He reached the boat, and the pilot put down a hand, and pulled him aboard. The reed boat rocked a little, and water splashed over the low sides of it, and then it steadied.

The pilot poled off away from the shore. Shadow stood there and watched, his pants-legs dripping.

'I know you,' he said to the creature at the prow.

'You do indeed,' said the boatman. The oil lamp which hung at the front of the boat burned more fitfully, and the smoke from the lamp made Shadow cough. 'You worked for me. I'm afraid we had to inter Lila Goodchild without you.' The voice was fussy and precise.

The smoke stung Shadow's eyes. He wiped the tears away with his hand, and, through the smoke, he thought he saw a tall man, in a suit, with gold-rimmed spectacles. The smoke cleared and the boatman was once more a half-human creature with the head of a river-bird.

'Mister Ibis?'

'Good to see you, Shadow,' said the creature, with Mr Ibis's voice. 'Do you know what a *psychopomp* is?'

Shadow thought he knew the word, but it had been a long time. He shook his head.

'It's a fancy term for an escort,' said Mr Ibis. 'We all have so many functions, so many ways of existing. In my own vision of myself, I am a scholar who lives quietly, and pens his little tales, and dreams about a past that may or may not ever have existed. And that is true, as far as it goes. But I am also, in one of my capacities, like so many of the people you have chosen to associate with, a psychopomp. I escort the living to the world of the dead.'

'I thought this was the world of the dead,' said Shadow.

'No. Not *per se*. It's more of a preliminary.'

The boat slipped and slid across the mirror-surface of the underground pool. And then Mr Ibis said, without moving its beak, 'You people talk about the living and the dead as if they were two mutually exclusive categories. As if you cannot have a river that is also a road, or a song that is also a colour.'

'You can't,' said Shadow. 'Can you?' The echoes whispered his words back at him from across the pool.

'What you have to remember,' said Mr Ibis, testily, 'is that life and death are different sides of the same coin. Like the heads and tails of a quarter.'

'And if I had a double-headed quarter?'

'You don't.'

Shadow had a frisson, then, as they crossed the dark water. He imagined he could see the faces of children staring up at him reproachfully from beneath the water's glassy surface: their faces were waterlogged and softened, their blind eyes clouded. There was no wind in that underground cavern to disturb the black surface of the lake.

'So I'm dead,' said Shadow. He was getting used to the idea. 'Or I'm going to be dead.'

'We are on our way to the Hall of the Dead. I requested that I be the one to come for you.'

'Why?'

'You were a hard worker. Why not?'

'Because . . . .' Shadow marshaled his thoughts. 'Because I never believed in you. Because I don't know much about Egyptian Mythology. Because I didn't expect this. What happened to Saint Peter and the Pearly Gates?'

The long-beaked white head shook from side to side, gravely. 'It doesn't matter that you didn't believe in us,' said Mr Ibis. 'We believed in you.'

The boat touched bottom. Mr Ibis stepped off the side, into the pool, and told Shadow to do the same. Mr Ibis took a line from the prow of the boat, and passed Shadow the lantern to carry. It was in the shape of a crescent moon. They walked ashore, and Mr Ibis tied the boat to a metal ring set in the rock floor. Then he took the lamp from Shadow and walked swiftly forward, holding the lamp high as he walked, throwing vast shadows across the rock floor and the high rock walls.

'Are you scared?' asked Mr Ibis.

'Not really.'

'Well, try to cultivate the emotions of true awe and spiritual terror, as we walk. They are the appropriate feelings for the situation at hand.'

Shadow was not scared. He was interested, and apprehensive, but no more. He was not scared of the shifting darkness, nor of being dead, nor even of the dog-headed creature the size of a grain silo who stared at them as they approached. It growled, deep in its throat, and Shadow felt his neck-hairs prickle.

'Shadow,' it said. 'Now is the time of judgment.'

Shadow looked up at the creature. 'Mr Jacquel?' he said.

The hands of Anubis came down, huge dark hands, and they picked Shadow up and brought him close.

The jackal head examined him with bright and glittering eyes; examined him as dispassionately as Mr Jacquel had examined the dead girl on the slab. Shadow knew that all his faults, all his failings, all his weaknesses were being taken out and weighed and measured; that he was, in some way, being dissected, and sliced, and tasted.

We do not always remember the things that do no credit to us. We justify them, cover them in bright lies or with the thick dust of forgetfulness. All of the things that Shadow had done in his life of which he was not proud, all the things he wished he had done otherwise or left undone, came at him then in a swirling storm of guilt and regret and shame, and he had nowhere to hide from them. He was as naked and as open as a corpse on a table, and dark Anubis the jackal god was his prosector and his prosecutor and his persecutor.

'Please,' said Shadow. 'Please stop.'

But the examination did not stop. Every lie he had ever told, every object he had stolen, every hurt he had inflicted on another person, all the little crimes and the tiny murders that make up the day, each of these things and more were extracted and held up to the light by the jackal-headed judge of the dead.

Shadow began to weep, painfully, in the palm of the dark god's hand. He was a tiny child again, as helpless and as powerless as he had ever been.

And then, without warning, it was over. Shadow panted, and sobbed, and snot streamed from his nose; he still felt helpless, but the hands placed him, carefully, almost tenderly, down on the rock floor.

'Who has his heart?' growled Anubis.

'I do,' purred a woman's voice. Shadow looked up. Bast was standing there beside the thing that was no longer Mr Ibis, and she held Shadow's heart in her right hand. It lit her face with a ruby light.

'Give it to me,' said Thoth, the ibis-headed god, and he took the heart in his hands, which were not human hands, and he glided forward.

Anubis placed a pair of golden scales in front of him.

'So is this where we find out what I get?' whispered Shadow to Bast. 'Heaven? Hell? Purgatory?'

'If the feather balances,' she said, 'you get to choose your own destination.'

'And if not?'

She shrugged, as if the subject made her uncomfortable. Then she said, 'Then we feed your heart and your soul to Ammet, the Eater of Souls . . .'

'Maybe,' he said. 'Maybe I can get some kind of a happy ending.'

'Not only are there no happy endings,' she told him. 'There aren't even any endings.'

On one of the pans of the scales, carefully, reverently, Anubis placed a feather.

Anubis put Shadow's heart on the other pan of the scales. Something *moved* in the shadows under the scale, something it made Shadow uncomfortable to examine too closely.

It was a heavy feather, but Shadow had a heavy heart, and the scales tipped and swung worryingly.

But they balanced, in the end, and the creature in the shadows skulked away, unsatisfied.

'So that's that,' said Bast, wistfully. 'Just another skull for the pile. It's a pity. I had hoped that you would do some good, in the current troubles. It's like watching a slow-motion car-crash and being power-less to prevent it.'

'You won't be there?'

She shook her head. 'I don't like other people picking my battles for me,' she said.

There was silence then, in the vast hall of death, where it echoed of water and the dark.

Shadow said, 'So now I get to choose where I go next?'

'Choose,' said Thoth. 'Or we can choose for you.'

'No,' said Shadow. 'It's okay. It's my choice.'

'Well?' roared Anubis.

'I want to rest now,' said Shadow. 'That's what I want. I want nothing. No heaven, no hell, no anything. Just let it end.'

'You're certain?' asked Thoth.

'Yes,' said Shadow.

Mr Jacquel opened the last door for Shadow, and behind that door there was nothing. Not darkness. Not even oblivion. Only nothing.

Shadow accepted it, completely and without reservation, and he walked through the door into nothing with a strange fierce joy.

17

Everything is upon a great scale upon this continent. The rivers are immense, the climate violent in heat and cold, the prospects magnificent, the thunder and lightning tremendous. The disorders incident to the country make every constitution tremble. Our own blunders here, our misconduct, our losses, our disgraces, our ruin, are on a great scale.
– Lord Carlisle, to George Selwyn, 1778

The most important place in the South-Eastern United States is advertised on hundreds of ageing barn-roofs across Georgia and Tennessee and up into Kentucky. On a winding road through a forest a driver will pass a rotting red barn, and see, painted on its roof,

SEE ROCK CITY
THE EIGHTH WONDER OF THE WORLD

and on the roof of a tumbledown milking shed nearby, painted in white block letters,

SEE SEVEN STATES FROM ROCK CITY
THE WORLD'S WONDER

The driver is led by this to believe that Rock City is surely just around the nearest corner, instead of being a day's drive away, on Lookout Mountain, a hair over the state line, in Georgia, just south-west of Chattanooga, Tennessee.

Lookout Mountain is not much of a mountain. It resembles an impossibly high and commanding hill. The Chickamauga, a branch of the Cherokee, lived there when the white men came; they called the mountain Chattotonoogee, which has been translated as *the mountain that rises to a point.*

In the 1830s Andrew Jackson's Indian Relocation Act exiled them from their land – all the Choctaw and Chickamauga and Cherokee and Chickasaw – and U.S. troops forced every one of them they could catch to walk over a thousand miles to the new Indian Territories in what would one day be Oklahoma, down the trail of tears: an act of casual genocide. Thousands of men, women, and children died on the way. When you've won, you've won, and nobody can argue with that.

For whoever controlled Lookout Mountain controlled the land; that was the legend. It was a sacred site, after all, and it was a high place. In the Civil War, the War Between the States, there was a battle there: the Battle Above the Clouds, that was the first day's fighting, and then the Union forces did the impossible, and, without orders, swept up Missionary Ridge and took it. The North took Lookout Mountain and the North took the war.

There are tunnels and caves, some very old, beneath Lookout Mountain. For the most part they are blocked off now, although a local businessman excavated an underground waterfall, which he called Ruby Falls. It can be reached by elevator. It's a tourist attraction, although the biggest tourist attraction of all is at the top of Lookout Mountain. That is Rock City.

Rock City begins as an ornamental garden on a mountainside: its visitors walk a path that takes them through rocks, over rocks, between rocks. They throw corn into a deer enclosure, cross a hanging bridge and peer out through a quarter-a-throw binoculars at a view that promises them seven states on the rare sunny days when the air is perfectly clear. And from there, like a drop into some strange hell, the path takes the visitors, millions upon millions of them every year, down into caverns, where they stare at back-lit dolls arranged into nursery rhyme and fairy tale dioramas. When they leave, they leave bemused, uncertain of why they came, of what they have seen, of whether they had a good time or not.

They came to Lookout Mountain from all across the United States. They were not tourists. They came by car and they came by plane and by bus and by railroad and on foot. Some of them flew – they flew low, and they flew only in the dark of the night. Several of them travelled their own ways beneath the earth. Many of them hitch-hiked, cadging rides from nervous motorists or from truck drivers. Those who had cars or trucks would see the ones who had not walking beside the roads or at rest stations and in diners on the way, and, recognising them for what they were, would offer them rides.

They arrived dust-stained and weary at the foot of Lookout Mountain. Looking up to the heights of the tree-covered slope they could see, or imagine that they could see, the paths and gardens and waterfall of Rock City.

They started arriving early in the morning. A second wave of them arrived at dusk. And for several days they simply kept coming.

A battered U-haul truck pulled up, disgorging several travel-weary *vila* and *rusalka*, their make-up smudged, runs in their stockings, their expressions heavy-lidded and tired.

In a clump of trees at the bottom of the hill, an elderly *wampyr* offered a Marlboro to a naked ape-like creature covered with a tangle of orange fur. It accepted graciously, and they smoked in silence, side by side.

A Toyota Previa pulled over by the side of the road, and seven Chinese men and women got out of it. They looked, above all, clean, and they wore the kind of dark suits that, in some countries, are worn by minor government officials. One of them carried a clip-board, and he checked the inventory as they unloaded large golf-bags from the back of the car: the bags contained ornate swords with lacquer handles, and carved sticks, and mirrors. The weapons were distributed, checked off, signed for.

A once-famous comedian, believed to have died in the 1920s, climbed out of his rusting car, and proceeded to remove his clothing: his legs were goat-legs, and his tail was short and goatish.

Four Mexicans arrived, all smiles, their hair black and very shiny: they passed among themselves a bottle which they kept out of sight in a brown paper bag, its contents a bitter mixture of powdered chocolate, liquor and blood.

A small, dark-bearded man with a dusty black derby on his head, curling *payess* at his temples and a ragged fringed prayer shawl came to them walking across the fields. He was several feet in front of his companion, who was twice his height and was the blank grey colour of good Polish clay: the word inscribed on his forehead meant *life*.

They kept coming. A cab drew up and several *Rakshasas,* the demons of the Indian subcontinent, climbed out and milled around, staring at the people at the bottom of the hill without speaking, until they found Mama-ji, her eyes closed, her lips moving in prayer. She was the only thing here that was familiar to them, but still, they hesitated to approach her, remembering old battles. Her hands rubbed the necklace of skulls about her neck. Her brown skin became slowly black, the glassy black of jet, of obsidian: her lips curled and her long white teeth were very sharp. She opened all her eyes, and beckoned the Rakshasas to her, and greeted them as she would have greeted her own children.

The storms of the last few days, to the north and the east, had done nothing to ease the feeling of pressure and discomfort in the air. Local weather forecasters had begun to warn of cells that might spawn tornados, of high pressure areas that did not move. It was warm by day there, but the nights were cold.

They clumped together in informal companies, banding together sometimes by nationality, by race, by temperament, even by species. They looked apprehensive. They looked tired.

Some of them were talking. There was laughter, on occasion, but it was muted and sporadic. Six-packs of beer were handed around.

Several local men and women came walking over the meadows, their bodies moving in unfamiliar ways: their voices, when they spoke, were the voices of the *Loa* who rode them: a tall, black man spoke in the voice of Papa Legba who opens the gates; while Baron Samedi, the Voudon lord of death, had taken over the body of a teenage goth girl from Chattanooga, possibly because she possessed her own black silk top hat, which sat on her dark hair at a jaunty angle. She spoke in the Baron's own deep voice, smoked a cigar of enormous size, and commanded three of the *Gédé,* the Loa of the dead. The *Gédé* inhabited the bodies of three middle-aged brothers. They carried shotguns and told jokes of such astounding filthiness that only they were willing to laugh at them, which they did, raucously.

Two ageless Chickamauga women, in oil-stained blue jeans and battered leather jackets, walked around, watching the people and the preparations for battle. Sometimes they pointed and shook their heads. They did not intend to take part in the coming conflict.

The moon swelled and rose in the east, a day away from full. It seemed half as big as the sky, as it rose, a deep reddish-orange, immediately above the hills. As it crossed the sky it seemed to shrink and pale until it hung high in the sky like a lantern.

There were so many of them waiting there, in the moonlight, at the foot of Lookout Mountain.

Laura was thirsty.

Sometimes living people burned steadily in her mind like candles and sometimes they flamed like torches. It made them easy to avoid, and it made them easy, on occasion, to find. Shadow had burned so strangely, with his own light, up on that tree.

She had chided him once, when they had walked and held hands, for not being alive. She had hoped, then, to see a spark of raw emotion. To have seen anything.

She remembered walking beside him, wishing that he could understand what she was trying to say.

But dying on the tree, Shadow had been utterly alive. She had watched him as the life had faded, and he had been focused and real. And he had asked her to stay with him, to stay the whole night. He had forgiven her . . . perhaps he had forgiven her. It did not matter. He had changed; that was all she knew.

Shadow had told her to go to the farmhouse, that they would give her water to drink there. There were no lights burning in the farm building, and she could feel nobody at home. But he had told her that they would care for her. She pushed against the door of the farmhouse and it opened, rusty hinges protesting the whole while.

Something moved in her left lung, something that pushed and squirmed and made her cough.

She found herself in a narrow hallway, her way almost blocked by a tall and dusty piano. The inside of the building smelled of old damp. She squeezed past the piano, pushed open a door and found herself in a dilapidated drawing room, filled with ramshackle furniture. An oil lamp burned on the mantelpiece. There was a coal fire burning in the fireplace beneath it, although she had neither seen nor smelled smoke outside the house. The coal fire did nothing to lift the chill she felt in that room, although, Laura was willing to concede, that might not be the fault of the room.

Death hurt Laura, although the hurt consisted mostly of things that were not there: a parching thirst that drained every cell of her, an absence of heat in her bones that was absolute. Sometimes she would catch herself wondering whether the crisp and crackling flames of a pyre would warm her, or the soft brown blanket of the earth; whether the cold sea would quench her thirst . . .

The room, she realised, was not empty.

Three women sat on an elderly couch, as if they had come as a matched set in some peculiar artistic exhibition. The couch was upholstered in threadbare velvet, a faded brown that might, once, a hundred years ago, have been a bright canary yellow. They followed her with their eyes as she entered the room, and they said nothing.

Laura had not known they would be there.

Something wriggled and fell in her nasal cavity. Laura fumbled in her sleeve for a tissue, and she blew her nose into it. She crumpled the tissue and flung it and its contents onto the coals of the fire, watched it crumple and blacken and become orange lace. She watched the maggots shrivel and brown and burn.

This done, she turned back to the women on the couch. They had not moved since she had entered, not a muscle, not a hair. They stared at her.

'Hello. Is this your farm?' she asked.

The largest of the women nodded. Her hands were very red, and her expression was impassive.

'Shadow – that's the guy hanging on the tree. He's my husband – he said I should tell you that he wants you to give me water.' Something large shifted in her bowels. It squirmed, and then was still.

The smallest woman clambered off the couch. Her feet had not previously reached the floor. She scurried from the room.

Laura could hear doors opening and closing, through the farm-house. Then, from outside, she could hear a series of loud creaks. Each was followed by a splash of water.

Soon enough, the small woman returned. She was carrying a brown earthenware jug of water. She put it down, carefully, on the table, and retreated to the couch. She pulled herself up, with a wriggle and a shiver, and was seated beside her sisters once again.

'Thank you.' Laura walked over to the table, looked around for a cup or a glass, but there was nothing like that to be seen. She picked up the jug. It was heavier than it looked. The water in it was perfectly clear.

She raised the jug to her lips and began to drink.

The water was colder than she had ever imagined liquid water could be. It froze her tongue and her teeth and her gullet. Still, she drank, unable to stop, feeling the water freezing its way into her stomach, her bowels, her heart, her veins.

The water flowed into her. It was like liquid ice.

She realised that the jug was empty and, surprised, she put it down on the table.

The women were observing her, dispassionately. Since her death, Laura had not thought in metaphors: things were, or they were not. But now, as she looked at the women on the sofa, she found herself thinking of juries, of scientists observing a laboratory animal.

She shook, suddenly and convulsively. She reached out a hand to the table to steady herself, but the table was slipping and lurching, and it almost avoided her grasp. As she put her hand on the table she began to vomit. She brought up bile and formalin, centipedes, and maggots. And then she felt herself starting to void, and to piss: stuff was being pushed violently, wetly, from her body. She would have screamed if she could; but then the dusty floorboards came up to meet her so fast and so hard that, had she been breathing, they would have knocked the breath from her body.

Time rushed over her and into her, swirling like a dust-devil. A thousand memories began to play at once: she was lost in a department store the week before Christmas and her father was nowhere to be seen; and now she was sitting in the bar at Chi-Chi's, ordering a strawberry daiquiri and checking out her blind date, the big, grave man-child, and wondering how he kissed; and she was in the car as, sickeningly, it rolled and jolted, and Robbie was screaming at her until the metal post finally stopped the car, but not its contents, from moving . . .

The water of time, which comes from the spring of fate, Urd's Well, is not the water of life. Not quite. It feeds the roots of the world tree, though. And there is no other water like it.

When Laura woke in the empty farmhouse room, she was

shivering, and her breath actually steamed in the morning air. There was a scrape on the back of her hand, and a smear of wetness on the scrape, the vivid red of fresh blood.

And she knew where she had to go. She had drunk from the water of time, which comes from the spring of fate. She could see the mountain in her mind.

She licked the blood from the back of her hand, marveling at the film of saliva, and she began to walk.

It was a wet March day, and it was unseasonably cold, and the storms of the previous few days had lashed their way across the southern states, which meant that there were very few real tourists at Rock City on Lookout Mountain. The Christmas lights had been taken down, the summer visitors were yet to start coming.

Still, there were people there. There was even a tour bus, that drew up that morning releasing a dozen men and women with perfect tans and gleaming, reassuring smiles. They looked like news anchors, and one could almost imagine there was a phosphor-dot quality to them: they seemed to blur gently as they moved. A black Humvee was parked in the front lot of Rock City.

The TV people walked intently though Rock City, stationing themselves near the balancing rock, where they talked to each other in pleasant, reasonable voices.

They were not the only people in this wave of visitors. If you had walked the paths of Rock City that day, you might have noticed people who looked like movie stars, and people who looked like aliens and a number of people who looked most of all like the idea of a person and nothing like the reality. You might have seen them, but most likely you would never have noticed them at all.

They came to Rock City in long limousines and in small sports cars and in oversized SUVs. Many of them wore the sunglasses of those who habitually wear sunglasses indoors and out, and do not willingly or comfortably remove them. There were suntans and suits and shades and smiles and scowls. They came in all sizes and shapes, all ages and styles.

All they had in common was a look, a very specific look. It said, *you know me*; or perhaps, *you ought to know me*. An instant familiarity that was also a distance, a look, or an attitude – the confidence that the world existed for them, and that it welcomed them, and that they were adored.

The fat kid moved among them with the shuffling walk of one who, despite having no social skills, has still become successful beyond his dreams. His black coat flapped in the wind.

Something that stood beside the soft drink stand in Mother Goose Court coughed to attract his attention. It was massive, and scalpel-blades jutted from its face and its fingers. Its face was cancerous. 'It will be a mighty battle,' it told him, in a glutinous voice.

'It's not going to be a battle,' said the fat kid. 'All we're facing here is a fucking paradigm shift. It's a shakedown. Modalities like *battle* are so fucking Lao Tzu.'

The cancerous thing blinked at him. 'Waiting,' is all it said in reply.

'Whatever,' said the fat kid. Then, 'I'm looking for Mr World. You seen him?'

The thing scratched itself with a scalpel-blade, a tumorous lower lip pushed out in concentration. Then it nodded. 'Over there,' it said.

The fat kid walked away, without a thank you, in the direction indicated. The cancerous thing waited, saying nothing, until the kid was out of sight.

'It *will* be a battle,' said the cancerous thing to a woman whose face was smudged with phosphor-dots.

She nodded, and leaned closer to it. 'So how does that make you *feel*?' she asked, in a sympathetic voice.

It blinked, and then it began to tell her.

Town's Ford Explorer had a global positioning system, a little screen that listened to the satellites and showed the car its location, but he still got lost once he got south of Blacksburg and onto the country roads: the roads he drove seemed to bear little relationship to the tangle of lines on the map on the screen. Eventually he stopped the car in a country lane, wound down the window and asked a fat white woman being pulled by a wolfhound on its early morning walk for directions to Ashtree farm.

She nodded, and pointed and said something to him. He could not understand what she had said, but he said thanks a million and wound up the window and drove off in the general direction she had indicated.

He kept going for another forty minutes, down country road after country road, none of them the road he sought. Town began to chew his lower lip.

'I'm too old for this shit,' he said aloud, relishing the movie-star world-weariness of the line.

He was pushing fifty. Most of his working life had been spent in a branch of government which went only by its initials, and whether or not he had left his government job a dozen years ago for employment by the private sector was open to debate: some days he thought one way, some days another. Anyway, it was only the joes on the street that really believed there was a difference.

He was on the verge of giving up on the farm when he drove up a hill and saw the sign, hand painted, on the gate. It said simply, as he had been told it would, ASH. He pulled up the Ford Explorer, climbed out and untwisted the wire that held the gate closed. He got back in the car and drove through.

It was like cooking a frog, he thought. You put the frog in the water, and then you turn on the heat. And by the time the frog notices that there's anything wrong, it's already been cooked. The world in which he worked was all too weird. There was no solid ground beneath his feet; the water in the pot was bubbling fiercely.

When he'd been transferred to the Agency it had all seemed so simple. Now it was all so – not complex, he decided; merely bizarre. He had been sitting in Mr World's office at two that morning, and he had been told what he was to do. 'You got it?' said Mr World, handing him the knife in its dark leather sheath. 'Cut me a stick. It doesn't have to be longer than a couple of feet.'

'Affirmative,' he said. And then he said, 'Why do I have to do this, sir?'

'Because I tell you to,' said Mr World, flatly. 'Find the tree. Do the job. Meet me down in Chattanooga. Don't waste any time.'

'And what about the asshole?'

'Shadow? If you see him, just avoid him. Don't touch him. Don't even mess with him. I don't want you turning him into a martyr. There's no room for martyrs in the current game-plan.' He smiled then, his scarred smile. Mr World was easily amused. Mr Town had noticed this on several occasions. It had amused him to play chauffeur, in Kansas, after all.

'Look—'

'No martyrs, Town.'

And Town had nodded, and taken the knife in its sheath, and pushed the rage that welled up inside him down deep and away.

Mr Town's hatred of Shadow had become a part of him. As he was falling asleep he would see Shadow's solemn face, see that smile that wasn't a smile, the way Shadow had of smiling without smiling that made Town want to sink his fist into the man's gut, and even as he fell asleep he could feel his jaws squeeze together, his temples tense, his gullet burn.

He drove the Ford Explorer across the meadow, past an abandoned farmhouse. He crested a ridge and saw the tree. He parked the car a little way past it, and turned off the engine. The clock on the dashboard said it was 6:38 a.m. He left the keys in the car, and walked toward the tree.

The tree was large; it seemed to exist on its own sense of scale. Town could not have said if it was fifty feet high or two hundred. Its bark was the grey of a fine silk scarf.

There was a naked man tied to the trunk a little way above the ground by a webwork of ropes, and there was something wrapped in a sheet at the foot of the tree. Town realised what it was as he passed it. He pushed at the sheet with his foot. Wednesday's ruined half-a-face stared out at him.

Town reached the tree. He walked a little way around the thick trunk, away from the sightless eyes of the farmhouse, then he unzipped his fly and pissed against the trunk of the tree. He did up his fly. He walked back over to the house, found a wooden extension ladder, carried it back to the tree. He leaned it carefully against the trunk. Then he climbed up it.

Shadow hung, limply, from the ropes that tied him to the tree. Town wondered if the man were still alive: his chest did not rise or fall. Dead or almost dead, it did not matter.

'Hello, asshole,' Town said, aloud. Shadow did not move.

Town reached the top of the ladder, and he pulled out the knife. He found a small branch which seemed to meet Mr World's specifications, and hacked at the base of it with the knife-blade, cutting it half-through, then breaking it off with his hand. It was about thirty inches long.

He put the knife back in its sheath. Then he started to climb back down the ladder. When he was opposite Shadow, he paused. 'God, I hate you,' he said. He wished he could just have taken out a gun and shot him, and he knew that he could not. And then he jabbed the stick in the air toward the hanging man, in a stabbing motion. It was an instinctive gesture, containing all the frustration and rage inside Town. He imagined that he was holding a spear and twisting it into Shadow's guts.

'Come on,' he said, aloud. 'Time to get moving.' Then he thought, *First sign of madness. Talking to yourself.* He climbed down a few more steps, then jumped the rest of the way to the ground. He looked at the stick he was holding, and felt like a small boy, holding his stick as a sword or a spear. *I could have cut a stick from any tree, he thought. It didn't have to be this tree. Who the fuck would have known?*

And he thought, *Mr World would have known.*

He carried the ladder back to the farmhouse. From the corner of his eye he thought he saw something move, and he looked in through the window, into the dark room filled with broken furniture, with the plaster peeling from the walls, and for a moment, in a half-dream, he imagined that he saw three women sitting in the dark parlour.

One of them was knitting. One of them was staring directly at him. One of them appeared to be asleep. The woman who was staring at him began to smile, a huge smile that seemed to split her face lengthwise, a smile that crossed from ear to ear. Then she raised a finger and touched it to her neck, and ran it gently from one side of her neck to the other.

That was what he thought he saw, all in a moment, in that empty room, which contained, he saw at a second glance, nothing more than old rotting furniture and fly-spotted prints and dry rot. There was nobody there at all.

He rubbed his eyes.

Town walked back to the brown Ford Explorer and climbed in. He tossed the stick onto the white leather of the passenger seat. He turned the key in the ignition. The dashboard clock said 06:37 a.m. Town frowned, and checked his wristwatch, which blinked that it was 13:58.

Great, he thought. *I was either up on that tree for eight hours, or for minus a minute.* That was what he thought, but what he believed was that both timepieces had, coincidentally, begun to misbehave.

On the tree, Shadow's body began to bleed. The wound was in his side. The blood that came from it was slow and thick and treacle-black.

Clouds covered the top of Lookout Mountain.

Easter sat some distance away from the crowd at the bottom of the mountain, watching the dawn over the hills to the east. She had a chain of blue forget-me-nots tattooed around her left wrist, and she rubbed them, absently, with her right thumb.

Another night had come and gone, and nothing. The folk were still coming, by ones and twos. The last night had brought several creatures from the southwest, including two small boys each the size of an apple tree, and something which she had only glimpsed, but which had looked like a disembodied head the size of a VW bug. They had disappeared into the trees at the base of the mountain.

Nobody bothered them. Nobody from the outside world even seemed to have noticed they were there: she imagined the tourists at Rock City staring down at them through their insert-a-quarter binoculars, staring straight at a ramshackle encampment of things and people at the foot of the mountain, and seeing nothing but trees and bushes and rocks.

She could smell the smoke from a cooking fire, a smell of frying bacon on the chilly dawn wind. Someone at the far end of the encampment began to play the harmonica, which made her, involuntarily, smile and shiver. She had a paperback book in her backpack, and she waited for the sky to become light enough for her to read.

There were two dots in the sky, immediately below the clouds: a small one and a larger one. A spatter of rain brushed her face in the morning wind.

A barefoot girl came out from the encampment, walking toward her. She stopped beside a tree, hitched up her skirts, and squatted. When she had finished, Easter hailed her. The girl walked over.

'Good morning, lady,' she said. 'The battle will start soon now.' The tip of her pink tongue touched her scarlet lips. She had a black crow's wing tied with leather onto her shoulder, a crow's foot on a chain around her neck. Her arms were blue-tattooed with lines and patterns and intricate knots.

'How do you know?'

The girl grinned. 'I am Macha, of the Morrigan. When war comes, I can smell it in the air. I am a war goddess, and I say, blood shall be spilled this day.'

'Oh,' said Easter. 'Well. There you go.' She was watching the smaller dot in the sky as it tumbled down toward them, dropping like a rock.

'And we shall fight them, and we shall kill them, every one,' said the girl. 'And we shall take their heads as trophies, and the crows shall have their eyes and their corpses.' The dot had become a bird, its wings outstretched, riding the gusty morning winds above them.

Easter cocked her head on one side. 'Is that some hidden war goddess knowledge?' she asked. 'The whole who's going to win thing? Who gets whose head?'

'No,' said the girl. 'I can smell the battle, but that's all. But we'll win. Won't we? We *have* to. I saw what they did to the all-father. It's them or us.'

'Yeah,' said Easter. 'I suppose it is.'

The girl smiled again, in the half-light, and made her way back to the camp. Easter put her hand down and touched a green shoot which stabbed up from the earth like a knife blade. As she touched it it grew, and opened, and twisted, and changed, until she was resting her hand on a green tulip head. When the sun was high the flower would open.

Easter looked up at the hawk. 'Can I help you?' she said.

The hawk circled about fifteen feet above Easter's head, slowly, then it glided down to her, and landed on the ground nearby. It looked up at her with mad eyes.

'Hello cutie,' she said. 'Now, what do you really look like, eh?'

The hawk hopped toward her, uncertainly, and then it was no longer a hawk, but a young man. He looked at her, and then looked down at the grass. 'You?' he said. His glance went everywhere, to the grass, to the sky, to the bushes. Not to her.

'Me,' she said. 'What about me?'

'You.' He stopped. He seemed to be trying to muster his thoughts; strange expressions flitted and swam across his face. *He spent too long a bird*, she thought. *He has forgotten how to be a man.* She waited patiently. Eventually, he said, 'Will you come with me?'

'Maybe. Where do you want me to go?'

'The man on the tree. He needs you. A ghost hurt, in his side. The blood came, then it stopped. I think he is dead.'

'There's a war on. I can't just go running away.'

The naked man said nothing, just moved from one foot to another as if he were uncertain of his weight, as if he were used to resting on the air or on a swaying branch, not on the solid earth. Then he said, 'If he is gone forever, it is all over.'

'But the battle—'

'If he is lost, it will not matter who wins.' He looked like he needed a blanket, and a cup of sweet coffee, and someone to take him somewhere he could just shiver and babble until he got his mind back. He held his arms stiffly against his sides.

'Where is this? Nearby?'

He stared at the tulip plant, and shook his head. 'Way away.'

'Well,' she said, 'I'm needed here. And I can't just leave. How do you expect me to get there? I can't fly, like you, you know.'

'No,' said Horus. 'You can't.' Then he looked up, gravely, and pointed to the other dot that circled them, as it dropped from the darkening clouds, growing in size. '*He* can.'

Another several hours' pointless driving, and by now Town hated the global positioning system almost as much as he hated Shadow. There was no passion in the hate, though. He had thought finding his way to the farm, to the great silver ash tree, had been hard; finding his way *away* from the farm was much harder. It did not seem to matter which road he took, which direction he drove down the narrow country lanes – the twisting Virginia backroads which must have begun, he was sure, as deer trails and cowpaths – eventually he would find himself passing the farm once more, and the hand-painted sign, ASH.

This was crazy, wasn't it? He simply had to retrace his way, take a left turn for every right he had taken on his way here, a right turn for every left.

Only that was what he had done last time, and now here he was, back at the farm once more. There were heavy stormclouds coming in, it was getting dark fast, it felt like night, not morning, and he had a long drive ahead of him: he would never get to Chattanooga before afternoon at this rate.

His cellphone gave him only a *No Service* message. The fold-out map in the car's glove compartment showed the main roads, all the interstates and the real highways, but as far as it was concerned nothing else existed.

Nor was there anyone around that he could ask. The houses were set back from the roads; there were no welcoming lights. Now the fuel gauge was nudging Empty. He heard a rumble of distant thunder, and a single drop of rain splashed heavily onto his windshield.

So when Town saw the woman, walking along the side of the road, he found himself smiling, involuntarily. 'Thank God,' he said, aloud, and he drew up beside her. He thumbed down the window. 'Ma'am? I'm sorry. I'm kind of lost. Can you tell me how to get to Highway 81 from here?'

She looked at him through the open passenger-side window and said, 'You know. I don't think I can explain it. But I can show you, if you like.' She was pale, and her wet hair was long and dark.

'Climb in,' said Town. He didn't even hesitate. 'First thing, we need to buy some gas.'

'Thanks,' she said. 'I needed a ride.' She got in. Her eyes were astonishingly blue. 'There's a stick here, on the seat,' she said, puzzled.

'Just throw it in the back. Where are you heading?' he asked. 'Lady, if you can get me to a gas station, and back to a freeway, I'll take you all the way to your own front door.'

She said, 'Thank you. But I think I'm going further than you are. If you can get me to the freeway, that will be fine. Maybe a trucker will give me a ride.' And she smiled, a crooked, determined smile. It was the smile that did it.

'Ma'am,' he said, 'I can give you a finer ride than any trucker.' He could smell her perfume. It was heady and heavy, a cloying scent, like magnolias or lilacs, but he did not mind.

'I'm going to Georgia,' she said. 'It's a long way.'

'I'm going to Chattanooga. I'll take you as far as I can.'

'Mmm,' she said. 'What's your name?'

'They call me Mack,' said Mr Town. When he was talking to women in bars, he would sometimes follow that up with 'And the ones that know me really well call me Big Mack.' That could wait. With a long drive ahead of them, they would have many hours in each other's company to get to know each other. 'What's yours?'

'Laura,' she told him.

'Well Laura,' he said, 'I'm sure we're going to be great friends.'

The fat kid found Mr World in the Rainbow Room – a walled section of the path, its window glass covered in clear plastic sheets of green and red and yellow film. He was walking impatiently from window to window, staring out, in turn, at a golden world, a red world, a green world. His hair was reddish-orange and close-cropped to his skull. He wore a Burberry raincoat.

The fat kid coughed. Mr World looked up.

'Excuse me? Mister World?'

'Yes? Is everything on schedule?'

The fat kid's mouth was dry. He licked his lips, and said, 'I've set up everything. I don't have confirmation on the choppers.'

'The helicopters will be here when we need them.'

'Good,' said the fat kid. 'Good.' He stood there, not saying anything, not going away. There was a bruise on his forehead.

After a while Mr World said, 'Is there anything else I can do for you?'

A pause. The boy swallowed and nodded. 'Something else,' he said. 'Yes.'

'Would you feel more comfortable discussing it in private?'

The boy nodded again.

Mr World walked with the kid back to his operations centre: a damp cave containing a diorama of drunken pixies making moonshine with a still. A sign outside warned tourists away during renovations. The two men sat down on plastic chairs.

'How can I help you?' asked Mr World.

'Yes. Okay. Right, two things, Okay. One. What are we waiting for? And two. Two is harder. Look. We have the guns. Right. We have the firepower. They have. They have fucking swords and knives and fucking hammers and stone axes. And like, tire irons. We have fucking *smart* bombs.'

'Which we will not be using,' pointed out the other man.

'I know that. You said that already. I know that. And that's doable. But. Look, ever since I did the job on that bitch in LA. I've been . . .' He stopped, made a face, seemed unwilling to go on.

'You've been troubled?'

'Yes. Good word. *Troubled*. Yes. Like a home for troubled teens. Funny. Yes.'

'And what exactly is troubling you?'

'Well, we fight, we win.'

'And that is a source of trouble? I find it a matter of triumph and delight, myself.'

'But. They'll die out anyway. They are passenger pigeons and thylacines. Yes? Who cares? This way, it's going to be a bloodbath.'

'Ah.' Mr World nodded.

He was following. That was good. The fat kid said, 'Look, I'm not the only one who feels this way. I've checked with the crew at Radio Modern, and they're all for settling this peacefully; and the intangibles are pretty much in favour of letting market forces take care of it. I'm being. You know. The voice of reason here.'

'You are indeed. Unfortunately, there is information you do not have.' The smile that followed was twisted and scarred.

The boy blinked. He said, 'Mister World? What happened to your lips?'

World sighed. 'The truth of the matter,' he said, 'Is that somebody once sewed them together. A long time ago.'

'Whoa,' said the fat kid. 'Serious *omertà* shit.'

'Yes. You want to know what we're waiting for? Why we didn't strike last night?'

The fat kid nodded. He was sweating, but it was a cold sweat.

'We didn't strike yet, because I'm waiting for a stick.'

'A stick?'

'That's right. A stick. And do you know what I'm going to do with the stick?'

A head shake. 'Okay. I'll bite. What?'

'I could tell you,' said Mr World, soberly. 'But then I'd have to kill you.' He winked, and the tension in the room evaporated.

The fat kid began to giggle, a low, snuffling laugh in the back of his throat and in his nose. 'Okay,' he said. '*Hee. Hee.* Okay. *Hee.* Got it. Message received on Planet Technical. Loud and clear. Ixnay on the Estionsquay.'

Mr World shook his head. He rested a hand on the fat kid's shoulder. 'Hey,' he said. 'You really want to know?'

'Sure.'

'Well,' said Mr World, 'seeing that we're friends, here's the answer: I'm going to take the stick, and I'm going to throw it over the armies as they come together. As I throw it, it will become a spear. And then, as the spear arcs over the battle, I'm going to shout "I dedicate this battle to Odin".'

'Huh?' said the fat kid. 'Why?'

'Power,' said Mr World. He scratched his chin. 'And food. A combination of the two. You see, the outcome of the battle is unimportant. What matters is the chaos, and the slaughter.'

'I don't get.'

'Let me show you. It'll be just like this,' said Mr World, 'Watch!' He took the wooden-bladed hunter's knife from the pocket of his Burberry and, in one fluid movement, he slipped the blade of it into the soft flesh beneath the fat kid's chin, and pushed hard upward, toward the brain. 'I dedicate this death to Odin,' he said, as the knife sank in.

There was a leakage onto his hand of something that was not actually blood, and a sputtering sparking noise behind the fat kid's eyes. The smell on the air was that of burning insulation wire.

The fat kid's hand twitched spastically, and then he fell. The expression on his face was one of puzzlement, and misery. 'Look at him,' said Mr World, conversationally, to the air. 'He looks as if he just saw a sequence of zeroes and ones turn into a flock of brightly coloured birds and fly away.'

There was no reply from the empty rock corridor.

Mr World shouldered the body as if it weighed very little, and he opened the pixie diorama and dropped the body beside the still, covering it with its long black raincoat. He would dispose of it that evening, he decided, and he grinned his scarred grin: hiding a body on a battlefield would almost be too easy. Nobody would ever notice. Nobody would care.

For a little while there was silence in that place. And then a gruff voice, which was not Mr World's cleared its throat in the shadows, and said, 'Good start.'

18

They tried to stand off the soldiers, but the men fired and killed them both. So the song's wrong about the jail, but that's put in for poetry. You can't allus have things like they are in poetry. Poetry ain't what you'd call truth. There ain't room enough in the verses.
– A singer's commentary on "The Ballad of Sam Bass".
A Treasury of American Folklore

None of this can actually be happening. If it makes you more comfortable, you could simply think of it as metaphor. Religions are, by definition, metaphors, after all: God is a dream, a hope, a woman, an ironist, a father, a city, a house of many rooms, a watchmaker who left his prize chronometer in the desert, someone who loves you – even, perhaps, against all evidence, a celestial being whose only interest is to make sure your football team, army, business, or marriage thrives, prospers and triumphs over all opposition.

Religions are places to stand and look and act, vantage points from which to view the world.

So none of this is happening. Such things could not occur. Never a word of it is literally true. Even so, the next thing that happened, happened like this:

At the foot of Lookout Mountain men and women were gathered around a small bonfire in the rain. They were standing beneath the trees, which provided poor cover, and they were arguing.

The lady Kali, with her ink-black skin and her white, sharp teeth, said, 'It is time.'

Anansi, with lemon-yellow gloves and silvering hair shook his head. 'We can wait,' he said. 'While we *can* wait, we *should* wait.'

There was a murmur of disagreement from the crowd.

'No, listen. He's right,' said an old man with iron-grey hair: Czernobog. He was holding a small sledge-hammer, resting the head of it on his shoulder. 'They have the high ground. The weather is against us. This is madness, to begin this now.'

Something that looked a little like a wolf and a little more like a man, grunted and spat on the forest floor. 'When better to attack them, *dedushka*? Shall we wait until the weather clears, when they expect it? I say we go now. I say we move.'

'There are clouds, between us and them,' pointed out Isten of the Hungarians. He had a fine black moustache, a large, dusty black hat, and the grin of a man who makes his living selling aluminum siding and new roofs and gutters to senior citizens but who always leaves town the day after the checks clear whether the work is done or not.

A man in an elegant charcoal suit, who had until now said nothing, put his hands together, stepped into the firelight, and made his point succinctly and clearly. There were nods and mutters of agreement.

A voice came from one of three warrior-women who comprised the Morrigan, standing so close together in the shadows that they had become an arrangement of blue-tattooed limbs and dangling crow's wings. She said, 'It doesn't matter whether this is a good time or a bad time. This is *the* time. They have been killing us. Better to die together, on the attack, like gods, than to die fleeing and singly, like rats in a cellar.'

Another murmur, this time one of deep agreement. She had said it for all of them. Now was the time.

'The first head is mine,' said a very tall Chinese man, with a rope of tiny skulls around his neck. He began to walk, slowly and intently, up the mountain, shouldering a staff with a curved blade at the end of it, like a silver moon.

Even Nothing cannot last forever.

He might have been there, been Nowhere, for ten minutes or for ten thousand years. It made no difference: time was an idea for which he no longer had any need.

He could no longer remember his real name. He felt empty and cleansed, in that place that was not a place.

He was without form, and void.

He was nothing.

And into that nothing a voice said, 'Ho-hoka, cousin. We got to talk.'

And something that might once have been Shadow said, 'Whiskey Jack?'

'Yeah,' said Whiskey Jack, in the darkness. 'You are a hard man to hunt down, when you're dead. You didn't go to any of the places I figured. I had to look all over before I thought of checking here. Say, you ever find your tribe?'

Shadow remembered the man and the girl in the disco beneath the spinning mirror-ball. 'I guess I found my family. But no, I never found my tribe.'

'Sorry to have to disturb you.'

'Let me be. I got what I wanted. I'm done.'

'They are coming for you,' said Whiskey Jack. 'They are going to revive you.'

'But I'm done,' said Shadow. 'It was all over and done.'

'No such thing,' said Whiskey Jack. 'Never any such thing. We'll go to my place. You want a beer?'

He guessed he *would* like a beer, at that. 'Sure.'

'Get me one too. There's a cooler outside the door,' said Whiskey Jack, and he pointed. They were in his shack.

Shadow opened the door to the shack with hands he had not possessed moments before. There was a plastic cooler filled with chunks of river-ice out there, and, in the ice, a dozen cans of Budweiser. He pulled out a couple of cans of beer and then sat in the doorway and looked out over the valley.

They were at the top of a hill, near a waterfall, swollen with melting snow and run-off. It fell, in stages, maybe seventy feet below them, maybe a hundred. The sun reflected from the ice which sheathed the trees that overhung the waterfall basin.

'Where are we?' asked Shadow.

'Where you were last time,' said Whiskey Jack. 'My place. You planning on holding on to my Bud till it warms up?'

Shadow stood up and passed him the can of beer. 'You didn't have a waterfall outside your place last time I was here,' he said.

Whiskey Jack said nothing. He popped the top of the Bud and

drank half the can in one long slow swallow. Then he said, 'You remember my nephew? Henry Bluejay? The poet? He traded his Buick for your Winnebago. Remember?'

'Sure. I didn't know he was a poet.'

Whiskey Jack raised his chin and looked proud. 'Best damn poet in America,' he said.

He drained the rest of his can of beer, belched, and got another can, while Shadow popped open his own can of beer, and the two men sat outside on a rock, by the pale green ferns, in the morning sun, and they watched the falling water and they drank their beer. There was still snow on the ground, in the places where the shadows never lifted.

The earth was muddy and wet.

'Henry was diabetic,' continued Whiskey Jack. 'It happens. Too much. You people came to America, you take our sugar cane, potatoes and corn, then you sell us potato chips and caramel popcorn, and we're the ones who get sick.' He sipped his beer, reflecting. 'He'd won a couple of prizes for his poetry. There were people in Minnesota who wanted to put his poems into a book. He was driving to Minnesota in a sports car to talk to them. He had traded your 'Bago for a yellow Miata. The doctors said they think he went into a coma while he was driving, went off the road, ran the car into one of your road signs. Too lazy to look at where you are, to read the mountains and the clouds, you people need road signs everywhere. And so Henry Bluejay went away forever, went to live with Brother Wolf. So I said, nothing keeping me there any longer. I came north. Good fishing up here.'

'I'm sorry about your nephew.'

'Me too. So now I'm living here in the north. Long way from white man's diseases. White man's roads. White man's road signs. White man's yellow Miatas. White man's caramel popcorn.'

'White man's beer?'

Whiskey Jack looked at the can. 'When you people finally give up and go home, you can leave us the Budweiser breweries,' he said.

'Where are we?' asked Shadow. 'Am I on the tree? Am I dead? Am I here? I thought everything was finished. What's real?'

'Yes,' said Whiskey Jack.

'Yes? What kind of an answer is *Yes*?'

'It's a good answer. True answer, too.'

Shadow said, 'Are you a god as well?'

Whiskey Jack shook his head. 'I'm a culture hero,' he said. 'We do the same shit gods do, we just screw up more and nobody worships us. They tell stories about us, but they tell the ones which make us look bad along with the ones where we came out fairly okay.'

'I see,' said Shadow. And he did see, more or less.

'Look,' said Whiskey Jack. 'This is not a good country for gods. My people figured that out early on. There are creator spirits who found the earth or made it or shit it out, but you think about it: who's going to worship Coyote? He made love to Porcupine Woman and got his dick shot through with more needles than a pincushion. He'd argue with rocks and the rocks would win.

'So, yeah, my people figured that maybe there's something at the back of it all, a creator, a great spirit, and so we say thank you to it, because it's always good to say thank you. But we never built churches. We didn't need to. The land was the church. The land was the religion. The land was older and wiser than the people who walked on it. It gave us salmon and corn and buffalo and passenger pigeons. It gave us wild rice and walleye. It gave us melon and squash and turkey. And we were the children of the land, just like the porcupine and the skunk and the bluejay.'

He finished his second beer and gestured toward the river at the bottom of the waterfall. 'You follow that river for a way, you'll get to the lakes where the wild rice grows. In wild rice time, you go out in your canoe with a friend, and you knock the wild rice into your canoe, and cook it, and store it, and it will keep you for a long time. Different places grow different foods. Go far enough south there are orange trees, lemon trees, and those squashy green guys, look like pears –'

'Avocados.'

'Avocados,' agreed Whiskey Jack. 'That's them. They don't grow up this way. This is wild rice country. Moose country. What I'm trying to say is that America is like that. It's not good growing country for gods. They don't grow well here. They're like avocados trying to grow in wild rice country.'

'They may not grow well,' said Shadow, remembering, 'but they're going to war.'

That was the only time he ever saw Whiskey Jack laugh. It was almost a bark, and it had little humour in it. 'Hey Shadow,' said Whiskey Jack. 'If all your friends jumped off a cliff, would you jump off too?'

'Maybe.' Shadow felt good. He didn't think it was just the beer. He couldn't remember the last time he had felt so alive, and so together.

'It's not going to be a war.'

'Then what is it?'

Whiskey Jack crushed the beer-can between his hands, pressing it until it was flat. 'Look,' he said, and pointed to the waterfall. The sun was high enough that it caught the waterfall spray: a rainbow nimbus hung in the air. Shadow thought it was the most beautiful thing he had ever seen.

'It's going to be a bloodbath,' said Whiskey Jack, flatly.

Shadow saw it then. He saw it all, stark in its simplicity. He shook his head, then he began to chuckle, and he shook his head some more, and the chuckle became a full-throated laugh.

'You okay?'

'I'm fine,' said Shadow. 'I just saw the hidden Indians. Not all of them. But I saw them anyhow.'

'Probably Ho Chunk, then. Those guys never could hide worth a damn.' He looked up at the sun. 'Time to go back,' he said. He stood up.

'It's a two-man con,' said Shadow. 'It's not a war at all, is it?'

Whiskey Jack patted Shadow's arm. 'You're not so dumb,' he said.

They walked back to Whiskey Jack's shack. He opened the door. Shadow hesitated. 'I wish I could stay here with you,' he said. 'This seems like a good place.'

'There are a lot of good places,' said Whiskey Jack. 'That's kind of the point. Listen, gods die when they are forgotten. People too. But the land's still here. The good places, and the bad. The land isn't going anywhere. And neither am I.'

Shadow closed the door. Something was pulling at him. He was alone in the darkness once more, but the darkness became brighter and brighter until it was burning like the sun.

And then the pain began.

* * *

Easter walked through the meadow, and spring flowers blossomed where she had passed.

She walked by a place where, long ago, a farmhouse had stood. Even today several walls were still standing, jutting out of the weeds and the meadow-grass like rotten teeth. A thin rain was falling. The clouds were dark and low, and it was cold.

A little way beyond the place where the farmhouse had been there was a tree, a huge silver-grey tree, winter-dead to all appearances, and leafless, and in front of the tree, on the grass, were frayed clumps of colourless fabric. The woman stopped at the fabric, and bent down, and picked up something brownish-white: it was a much-gnawed fragment of bone which might, once, have been a part of a human skull. She tossed it back down onto the grass.

Then she looked at the man on the tree and she smiled wryly. 'They just aren't as interesting naked,' she said. 'It's the unwrapping that's half the fun. Like with gifts, and eggs.'

The hawk-headed man who walked beside her looked down at his penis and seemed, for the first time, to become aware of his own nakedness. He said, 'I can look at the sun without even blinking.'

'That's very clever of you,' Easter told him, reassuringly. 'Now, let's get him down from there.'

The wet ropes that held Shadow to the tree had long ago weathered and rotted, and they parted easily as the two people pulled on them. The body on the tree slipped and slid down toward the roots. They caught him as he fell, and they took him up, carrying him easily, although he was a very big man, and they put him down in the grey meadow.

The body on the grass was cold, and it did not breathe. There was a patch of dried black blood on its side, as if it had been stabbed with a spear.

'What now?'

'Now,' she said, 'We warm him. You know what you have to do.'

'I know. I cannot.'

'If you are not willing to help, then you should not have called me here.'

She reached out a white hand to Horus, and she touched his black hair. He blinked at her, intently. Then he shimmered, as if in a heat haze.

The hawk eye that faced her glinted orange, as if a flame had just been kindled inside it; a flame that had been long extinguished.

The hawk took to the air, and it swung upward, circling and ascending in a rising gyre, circling the place in the grey clouds where the sun might conceivably be, and as the hawk rose and it became first a dot and then a speck, and then, to the naked eye, nothing at all, something that could only be imagined. The clouds began to thin and to evaporate, creating a patch of blue sky through which the sun glared. The single bright sunbeam penetrating the clouds and bathing the meadow was beautiful, but the image faded as more clouds vanished. Soon the morning sun was blazing down on that meadow like a summer sun at noon, burning the water vapour from the morning's rain into mists and burning the mist off into nothing at all.

The golden sun bathed the body on the floor of the meadow with its radiance and its heat. Shades of pink and of warm brown, touched the dead thing.

The woman dragged the fingers of her right hand lightly across the body's chest. She imagined she could feel a shiver in his breast – something that was not a heartbeat, but still . . . . She let her hand remain there, on his chest, just above his heart.

She lowered her lips to Shadow's lips, and she breathed into his lungs, a gentle in and out, and then the breath became a kiss. Her kiss was gentle, and it tasted of spring rains and meadow flowers.

The wound in his side began to flow with liquid blood once more – a scarlet blood, which oozed like liquid rubies in the sunlight, and then the bleeding stopped.

She kissed his cheek and his forehead. 'Come on,' she said. 'Time to get up. It's all happening. You don't want to miss it.'

His eyes fluttered, and then they opened, two eyes the grey of evening, and he looked at her.

She smiled, and then she removed her hand from his chest.

He said, 'You called me back.' He said it slowly, as if he had forgotten how to speak English. There was hurt in his voice, and puzzlement.

'Yes.'

'I was done. I was judged. It was over. You called me back. You dared.'

'I'm sorry.'

'Yes.'

He sat up, slowly. He winced, and touched his side. Then he looked puzzled: there was a beading of wet blood there, but there was no wound beneath it.

He reached out a hand, and she put her arm around him and helped him to his feet. He looked across the meadow as if he was trying to remember the names of the things he was looking at: the flowers in the long grass, the ruins of the farmhouse, the haze of green buds that fogged the branches of the huge silver tree.

'Do you remember?' she asked. 'Do you remember what you learned?'

' I lost my name, and I lost my heart. And you brought me back.'

'I'm sorry,' she said. 'They are going to fight, soon. The old gods and the new ones.'

'You want me to fight for you? You wasted your time.'

'I brought you back because that was what I had to do,' she said. 'What you do now is whatever you have to do. Your call. I did my part.'

Suddenly, she became aware of his nakedness, and she blushed a burning scarlet flush, and she looked down and away.

In the rain and the cloud, shadows moved up the side of the mountain, up to the rock pathways.

White foxes padded up the hill in company with red-haired men in green jackets. There was a bull-headed minotaur walking beside an iron-fingered dactyl. A pig, a monkey and a sharp-toothed ghoul clambered up the hillside, in company with a blue-skinned man holding a flaming bow, a bear with flowers twined into its fur, and a man in golden chain-mail holding his sword of eyes.

Beautiful Antinous, who was once the lover of Hadrian, walked up the hillside at the head of a company of leather queens, their arms and chests steroid-sculpted into perfect shapes.

A grey-skinned man, his one cyclopean eye a huge cabochon emerald, walked stiffly up the hill, ahead of several squat and swarthy men, their impassive faces as regular as Aztec carvings: they knew the secrets that the jungles had swallowed.

A sniper at the top of the hill took careful aim at a white fox, and fired. There was an explosion, and a puff of cordite, gunpowder scent on the wet air. The corpse was a young Japanese woman with her stomach blown away, and her face all bloody. Slowly, the corpse began to fade.

The people continued up the hill, on two legs, on four legs, on no legs at all.

The drive through the Tennessee mountain country had been startlingly beautiful whenever the storm had eased, and nerve-wracking whenever the rain had pelted down. Town and Laura had talked and talked and talked the whole way. He was so glad he had met her. It was like meeting an old friend, a really good old friend you'd simply never met before. They talked history and movies and music, and she turned out to be the only person, and I mean the *only* other person he had ever met who had seen a foreign film (Mr Town was sure it was Spanish, while Laura was just as certain it was Polish) from the sixties called *The Manuscript Found in Saragossa*, a film he had been starting to believe he had hallucinated.

When Laura pointed out the first SEE ROCK CITY barn to him he chuckled and admitted that that was where he was headed. She said that was so cool. She always wanted to visit those kinds of places, but she never made the time, and always regretted it later. That was why she was on the road right now. She was having an adventure.

She was a travel agent, she told him. Separated from her husband. She admitted that she didn't think they could ever get back together, and said it was her fault.

'I can't believe that.'

She sighed. 'It's true, Mack. I'm just not the woman he married any more.'

Well, he told her, people change, and before he could think he was telling her everything he *could* tell her about his life, he was even telling her about Woody and Stoner, how the three of them were the three musketeers, and the two of them were killed, you think you'd get hardened to that kind of thing in government work, but you never did.

And she reached out one hand – it was cold enough that he turned up the car's heating – and squeezed his hand tightly in hers.

Lunchtime, they ate bad Japanese food while a thunderstorm lowered on Knoxville, and Town didn't care that the food was late, that the miso soup was cold or that the sushi was warm.

He loved the fact that she was out, with him, having an adventure.

'Well,' confided Laura, 'I hated the idea of getting stale. I was just rotting away where I was. So I set off without my car and without my credit cards. I'm just relying on the kindness of strangers.'

'Aren't you scared?' he asked. 'I mean, you could be stranded, you could be mugged, you could starve.'

She shook her head. Then she said, with a hesitant smile, 'I met you, didn't I?' and he couldn't find anything to say.

When the meal was over they ran through the storm to his car holding Japanese language newspapers to cover their heads, and they laughed as they ran, like schoolchildren in the rain.

'How far can I take you?' he asked, when they made it back into the car.

'I'll go as far as you're going, Mack,' she told him, shyly.

He was glad he hadn't used the Big Mack line. This woman wasn't a bar-room one nighter, Mr Town knew that in his soul. It might have taken him fifty years to find her, but this was finally it, this was the one, this wild, magical woman with the long dark hair.

This was love.

'Look,' he said, as they approached Chattanooga. The wipers slooshed the rain across the windshield, blurring the grey of the city. 'How about I find a motel for you tonight? I'll pay for it. And once I make my delivery, we can. Well, we can take a hot bath together, for a start. Warm you up.'

'That sounds wonderful,' said Laura. 'What are you delivering?'

'That stick,' he told her, and chuckled. 'The one on the back seat.'

'Okay,' she said, humouring him. 'Then don't tell me, Mister Mysterious.'

He told her it would be best if she waited in the car in the Rock City parking lot while he made his delivery. He drove up the side of Lookout Mountain in the driving rain, never breaking thirty miles per hour, with his headlights burning.

They parked at the back of the parking lot. He turned off the engine.

'Hey. Mack. Before you get out of the car, don't I get a hug?' asked Laura with a smile.

'You surely do,' said Mr Town, and he put his arms around her, and she snuggled close to him while the rain pattered a tattoo on the roof of the Ford Explorer. He could smell her hair. There was a faintly unpleasant scent beneath the smell of the perfume. Travel would do it, every time. That bath, he decided, was a real must for both of them. He wondered if there was anyplace in Chattanooga where he could get those lavender bath-bombs his first wife had loved so much. Laura raised her head against his, and her hand stroked the line of his neck, absently.

'Mack . . . I keep thinking. You must really want to know what happened to those friends of yours?' she asked. 'Woody and Stone. Do you?'

'Yeah,' he said, moving his lips down to hers, for their first kiss. 'Sure I do.'

So she showed him.

Shadow walked the meadow, making his own slow circles around the trunk of the tree, gradually widening his circle. Sometimes he would stop and pick something up: a flower, or a leaf, or a pebble, or a twig, or a blade of grass. He would examine it minutely, as if concentrating entirely on the *twigness* of the twig, the *leafness* of the leaf.

Easter found herself reminded of the gaze of a baby, at the point where it learns to focus.

She did not dare to talk to him. At that moment, it would have been sacrilegious. She watched him, exhausted as she was, and she wondered.

About twenty feet out from the base of the tree, half-overgrown with long meadow-grass and dead creepers, he found a canvas bag. Shadow picked it up, untied the knots at the top of the bag, loosened the drawstring.

The clothes he pulled out were his own. They were old, but still serviceable. He turned the shoes over in his hands. He stroked the fabric of the shirt, the wool of the sweater, stared at them as if he were looking at them across a million years.

One by one, he put them on.

He put his hands into his pockets, and looked puzzled as he pulled one hand out, holding up what looked to Easter like a white and grey marble.

He said, 'No coins.' It was the first thing he had said in several hours.

'No coins?' echoed Easter.

He shook his head. 'They gave me something to do with my hands.' He bent down to pull on his shoes.

Once he was dressed, he looked more normal. Grave, though. She wondered how far he had travelled, and what it had cost him to return. He was not the first whose return she had initiated; and she knew that, soon enough, the million-year stare would fade, and the memories and the dreams that he had brought back from the tree would be elided by the world of things you could touch. That was the way it always went.

She led their way to the rear of the meadow. Her mount waited in the trees.

'It can't carry both of us,' she told him. 'I'll make my own way home.'

Shadow nodded. He seemed to be trying to remember something. Then he opened his mouth, and he screeched a cry of welcome and of joy.

The thunderbird opened its cruel beak, and it screeched a welcome back at him.

Superficially, at least, it resembled a condor. Its feathers were black, with a purplish sheen, and its neck was banded with white. Its beak was black and cruel: a raptor's beak, made for tearing. At rest, on the ground, with its wings folded away, it was the size of a black bear, and its head was on a level with Shadow's own.

Horus said, proudly, 'I brought him. They live in the mountains.'

Shadow nodded. 'I had a dream of thunderbirds once,' he said. 'Damnedest dream I ever had.'

The thunderbird opened its beak and made a surprisingly gentle noise, *crawroo?* 'You heard my dream too?' asked Shadow.

He reached out a hand and rubbed it gently against the bird's head. The thunderbird pushed up against him like an affectionate pony. He scratched it from the nape of its neck up to the crown.

Shadow turned to Easter. 'You rode him here?'

'Yes,' she said. 'You can ride him back, if he lets you.'

'How do you ride him?'

'It's easy,' she said. 'If you don't fall. Like riding the lightning.'

'Will I see you back there?'

She shook her head. 'I'm done, honey,' she told him. 'You go do what you need to do. I'm tired. Good luck.'

Shadow nodded. 'Whiskey Jack. I saw him. After I passed on. He came and found me. We drank beer together.'

'Yes,' she said. 'I'm sure you did.'

'Will I ever see you again?' asked Shadow.

She looked at him with eyes the green of ripening corn. She said nothing. Then, abruptly, she shook her head. 'I doubt it,' she said.

Shadow clambered awkwardly onto the thunderbird's back. He felt like a mouse on the back of a hawk. There was an ozone taste in his mouth, metallic and blue. Something crackled. The thunderbird extended its wings, and began to flap them, hard.

As the ground fell away beneath them, Shadow clung on, his heart pounding in his chest like a wild thing.

It was exactly like riding the lightning.

Laura took the stick from the back seat of the car. She left Mr Town in the front seat of the Ford Explorer, and climbed out of the car, and walked through the rain to Rock City. The ticket office was closed. The door to the gift shop was not locked and she walked through it, past the rock candy and the display of SEE ROCK CITY birdhouses, into the Eighth Wonder of the World.

Nobody challenged her, although she passed several men and women on the path, in the rain. Many of them looked faintly artificial; several of them were translucent. She walked across a swinging rope bridge. She passed the white deer gardens, and pushed herself through the Fat Man's Squeeze, where the path ran between two rock walls.

And, in the end, she stepped over a chain, with a sign on it telling her that this part of the attraction was closed, and she went into a cavern, and she saw a man sitting on a plastic chair, in front of a diorama of drunken gnomes. He was reading the *Washington Post* by the light of a small electric lantern. When he saw her he folded the paper and placed it beneath his chair. He stood up, a tall man with close-cropped orange hair in an expensive raincoat, and he gave her a small bow.

'I shall assume that Mister Town is dead,' he said. 'Welcome, spear-carrier.'

'Thank you. I'm sorry about Mack,' she said. 'Were you friends?'

'Not at all. He should have kept himself alive, if he wanted to keep his job. But you brought his stick.' He looked her up and down with eyes that glimmered like the orange embers of a dying fire. 'I am afraid you have the advantage of me. They call me Mister World, here at the top of the hill.'

'I'm Shadow's wife.'

'Of course. The lovely Laura,' he said. 'I should have recognised you. He had several photographs of you up above his bed, in the cell that once we shared. And, if you don't mind my saying so, you are looking lovelier than you have any right to look. Shouldn't you be further along on the whole road to rot and ruin business by now?'

'I was,' she said simply. 'But those women, in the farm, they gave me water from their well.'

An eyebrow raised. 'Urd's Well? Surely not.'

She pointed to herself. Her skin was pale, and her eye-sockets were dark, but she was manifestly whole: if she was indeed a walking corpse, she was freshly dead.

'It won't last,' said Mr World. 'The Norns gave you a little taste of the past. It will dissolve into the present soon enough, and then those pretty blue eyes will roll out of their sockets and ooze down those pretty cheeks, which will, by then, of course, no longer be so pretty. By the way, you have my stick. Can I have it, please?'

He pulled out a pack of Lucky Strikes, took a cigarette, lit it with a disposable black Bic.

She said, 'Can I have one of those?'

'Sure. I'll give you a cigarette if you give me my stick.'

'If you want it, it's worth more than just a cigarette.'

He said nothing.

She said, 'I want answers. I want to know things.'

He lit a cigarette and passed it to her. She took it and inhaled. Then she blinked. 'I can almost taste this one,' she said. 'I think maybe I can.' She smiled. 'Mm. Nicotine.'

'Yes,' he said. 'Why did you go to the women in the farmhouse?'

'Shadow told me to go to them,' she said. 'He said to ask them for water.'

'I wonder if he knew what it would do. Probably not. Still, that's the good thing about having him dead on his tree. I know where he is at all times, now. He's off the board.'

'You set up my husband,' she said. 'You set him up all the way, you people. He has a good heart, you know that?'

'Yes,' said Mr World. 'I know. When this is all done with, I guess I'll sharpen a stick of mistletoe and go down to the ash tree, and ram it through his eye. Now. My stick, please.'

'Why do you want it?'

'It's a souvenir of this whole sorry mess,' said Mr World. 'Don't worry, it's not mistletoe.' He flashed a grin. 'It symbolizes a spear, and in this sorry world, the symbol *is* the thing.'

The noises from outside grew louder.

'Which side are you on?' she asked.

'It's not about sides,' he told her. 'But since you asked, I'm on the winning side. Always.'

She nodded, and she did not let go of the stick.

She turned away from him, and looked out of the cavern door. Far below her, in the rocks, she could see something that glowed and pulsed. It wrapped itself around a thin, mauve-faced bearded man, who was beating at it with a squeegee stick, the kind of squeegee that people like him use to smear across car windshields at traffic lights. There was a scream, and they both disappeared from view.

'Okay. I'll give you the stick,' she said.

Mr World's voice came from behind her. 'Good girl,' he said reassuringly, in a way that struck her as being both patronising and indefinably male. It made her skin crawl.

She waited in the rock doorway until she could hear his breath in her ear. She had to wait until he got close enough. She had that much figured out.

* * *

The ride was more than exhilarating; it was electric.

They swept through the storm like jagged bolts of lightning, flashing from cloud to cloud; they moved like the thunder's roar, like the swell and rip of the hurricane. It was a crackling, impossible journey. There was no fear: only the power of the storm, unstoppable and all-consuming, and the joy of the flight.

Shadow dug his fingers into the thunderbird's feathers, feeling the static prickle on his skin. Blue sparks writhed across his hands like tiny snakes. Rain washed his face.

'This is the best,' he shouted, over the roar of the storm.

As if it understood him, the bird began to rise higher, every wing-beat a clap of thunder, and it swooped and dove and tumbled through the dark clouds.

'In my dream, I was hunting you,' said Shadow, his words ripped away by the wind. 'In my dream. I had to bring back a feather.'

Yes. The word was a static crackle in the radio of his mind. *They came to us for feathers, to prove that they were men; and they came to us to cut the stones from our heads, to gift their dead with our lives.*

An image filled his mind then: of a thunderbird – a female, he assumed, for her plumage was brown, not black – lying freshly-dead on the side of a mountain. Beside it was a woman. She was breaking open its skull with a knob of flint. She picked through the wet shards of bone and the brains until she found a smooth clear stone the tawny colour of garnet, opalescent fires flickering in its depths. *Eagle stones,* thought Shadow. She was going to take it to her infant son, dead these last three nights, and she would lay it on his cold breast. By the next sunrise the boy would be alive and laughing, and the jewel would be grey and clouded and as dead as the bird it had been stolen from.

'I understand,' he said to the bird.

The bird threw back its head and crowed, and its cry was the thunder.

The world beneath them flashed past in one strange dream.

Laura adjusted her grip on the stick, and she waited for the man she knew as Mr World to come to her. She was facing away from him, looking out at the storm, and the dark green hills below.

In this sorry world, she thought, *the symbol is the thing. Yes.*

She felt his hand close softly onto her right shoulder.

Good, she thought. *He does not want to alarm me. He is scared that I will throw his stick out into the storm, that it will tumble down the mountainside, and he will lose it.*

She leaned back, just a little, until she was touching his chest with her back. His left arm curved around her. It was an intimate gesture. His left hand was open in front of her. She closed both of her hands around the top of the stick, exhaled, concentrated.

'Please. My stick,' he said, in her ears.

'Yes,' she said. 'It's yours.' And then, not knowing if it would mean anything, she said, 'I dedicate this death to Shadow,' and she stabbed the stick into her chest, just below the breastbone, felt it writhe and change in her hands as the stick became a spear.

The boundary between sensation and pain had diffused since she had died. She felt the spear head penetrate her chest, felt it push out through her back. A moment's resistance – she pushed harder – and the spear pushed into Mr World. She could feel the warm breath of him on the cool skin of her neck, as he wailed in hurt and surprise, impaled on the spear.

She did not recognise the words he spoke, nor the language he said them in. She pushed the shaft of the spear further in, forcing it through her body, into and through his.

She could feel his hot blood spurting onto her back.

'Bitch,' he said, in English. 'You fucking bitch.' There was a wet gurgling quality to his voice. She guessed that the blade of the spear must have sliced a lung. Mr World was moving now, or trying to move, and every move he made rocked her too: they were joined by the pole, impaled together like two fish on a single spear. He now had a knife in one hand, she saw, and he stabbed her chest and breasts randomly and wildly with the knife, unable to see what he was doing.

She did not care. What are knife-cuts to a corpse?

She brought her fist down, hard, on his waving wrist, and the knife went flying to the floor of the cavern. She kicked it away.

And now he was crying and wailing. She could feel him pushing against her, his hands fumbling at her back, his hot tears on her neck. His blood was soaking her back, spurting down the back of her legs.

'This must look so undignified,' she said, in a dead whisper, not without a certain dark amusement.

She felt Mr World stumble behind her, and she stumbled too, and then she slipped in the blood – all of it his – that was puddling on the floor of the cave, and they both went down.

The thunderbird landed in the Rock City parking lot. Rain was falling in sheets. Shadow could barely see a dozen feet in front of his face. He let go of the thunderbird's feathers and half-slipped, half-tumbled to the wet tarmac.

Lightning flashed, and the bird was gone.

Shadow climbed to his feet.

The parking lot was three-quarters empty. Shadow started toward the entrance. He passed a brown Ford Explorer, parked against a rock wall. There was something deeply familiar about the car, and he glanced up at it curiously, noticing the man inside the car, slumped over the steering wheel as if asleep.

Shadow pulled open the driver's-side door.

He had last seen Mr Town standing outside the motel in the centre of America. The expression on his face now was one of surprise. His neck had been expertly broken. Shadow touched the man's face. Still warm.

Shadow could smell a scent on the air in the car; it was faint, like the perfume of someone who left a room years before, but Shadow would have known it anywhere. He slammed the door of the Explorer and made his way across the parking lot.

As he walked he felt a twinge in his side, a sharp, jabbing pain that lasted for only a second, or less, and then it was gone.

There was nobody selling tickets. He walked through the building and out into the gardens of Rock City.

Thunder rumbled, and it rattled the branches of the trees and shook deep inside the huge rocks, and the rain fell with cold violence. It was late afternoon, but it was dark as night.

A trail of lightning speared across the clouds, and Shadow wondered if that was the thunderbird returning to its high crags, or just an atmospheric discharge, or whether the two ideas were, on some level, the same thing.

And of course they were. That was the point, after all.

Somewhere a man's voice called out. Shadow heard it. The only words he recognised or thought he recognised were ' . . . *to Odin!*'

Shadow hurried across Seven States Flag Court, the flagstones now running fast with rainwater. Once he slipped on the slick stone. There was a thick layer of cloud surrounding the mountain, and in the gloom and the storm beyond the courtyard he could see no states at all.

There was no sound. The place seemed utterly abandoned.

He called out, and imagined he heard something answering. He walked toward the place from which he thought the sound had come.

Nobody. Nothing. Just a chain marking the entrance to a cave as off-limits to guests.

Shadow stepped over the chain.

He looked around, peering into the darkness.

His skin prickled.

A voice from behind him, in the shadows, said, very quietly, 'You have never disappointed me.'

Shadow did not turn. 'That's weird,' he said. 'I disappointed myself all the way. Every time.'

'Not at all,' said the voice. 'You did everything you were intended to do, and more. You took everybody's attention, so they never looked at the hand with the coin in it. It's called misdirection. And there's power in the sacrifice of a son – power enough, and more than enough, to get the whole ball rolling. To tell the truth, I'm proud of you.'

'It was crooked,' said Shadow. 'All of it. None of it was for real. It was just a set-up for a massacre.'

'Exactly,' said Wednesday's voice from the shadows. 'It was crooked. But it was the only game in town.'

'I want Laura,' said Shadow. 'I want Loki. Where are they?'

There was only silence. A spray of rain gusted at him. Thunder rumbled somewhere close at hand.

He walked further in.

Loki Lie-Smith sat on the ground with his back to a metal cage. Inside the cage, drunken pixies tended their still. He was covered with a blanket. Only his face showed, and his hands, white and long, came around the blanket. An electric lantern sat on a chair beside him. The lantern's batteries were close to failing, and the light it cast was faint and yellow.

He looked pale, and he looked rough.

His eyes, though. His eyes were still fiery, and they glared at Shadow as he walked through the cavern.

When Shadow was several paces from Loki, he stopped.

'You are too late,' said Loki. His voice was raspy and wet. 'I have thrown the spear. I have dedicated the battle. It has begun.'

'No shit,' said Shadow.

'No shit,' said Loki. 'So it does not matter what you do any more.'

Shadow stopped and thought. Then he said, 'The spear you had to throw to kick off the battle. Like the whole Uppsala thing. This is the battle you'll be feeding on. Am I right?'

Silence. He could hear Loki breathing, a ghastly rattling inhalation.

'I figured it out,' said Shadow. 'Kind of. I'm not sure when I figured it out. Maybe when I was hanging on the tree. Maybe before. It was from something Wednesday said to me, at Christmas.'

Loki just stared at him from the floor, saying nothing.

'It's just a two-man con,' said Shadow. 'Like the Bishop with the diamond necklace and the cop who arrests him. Like the guy with the fiddle, and the guy who wants to buy the fiddle. Two men, who appear to be on opposite sides, playing the same game.'

Loki whispered, 'You are ridiculous.'

'Why? I liked what you did at the motel. That was smart. You needed to be there, to make sure that everything went according to plan. I saw you. I even realised who you were. And I still never twigged that you were their Mister World.'

Shadow raised his voice. 'You can come out,' he said, to the cavern. 'Wherever you are. Show yourself.'

The wind howled in the opening of the cavern, and it drove a spray of rainwater in toward them. Shadow shivered.

'I'm tired of being played for a sucker,' said Shadow. 'Just show yourself. Let me see you.'

There was a change in the shadows at the back of the cave. Something became more solid; something shifted. 'You know too damned much, m'boy,' said Wednesday's familiar rumble.

'So they didn't kill you.'

'They killed me,' said Wednesday, from the shadows. 'None of this would have worked if they hadn't.' His voice was faint – not actually quiet, but there was a quality to it that made Shadow think of an old radio not quite tuned in to a distant station. 'If I hadn't died for real, we could never have got them here,' said Wednesday. 'Kali and the Morrigan and the fucking Albanians and – well, you've seen them all. It was my death that drew them all together. I was the sacrificial lamb.'

'No,' said Shadow. 'You were the Judas Goat.'

The wraith-shape in the shadows swirled and shifted. 'Not at all. That implies that I was betraying the old gods for the new. Which was not what we were doing.'

'Not at all,' whispered Loki.

'I can see that,' said Shadow. 'You two weren't betraying either side. You were betraying both sides.'

'I guess we were at that,' said Wednesday. He sounded pleased with himself.

'You wanted a massacre. You needed a blood sacrifice. A sacrifice of gods.'

The wind grew stronger; the howl across the cave door became a screech, as if of something immeasurably huge in pain.

'And why the hell not? I've been trapped in this damned land for almost twelve hundred years. My blood is thin. I'm hungry.'

'And you two feed on death,' said Shadow.

He thought he could see Wednesday, now. He was a shape made of darkness, who became more real only when Shadow looked away from him, taking shape in his peripheral vision. 'I feed on death that is dedicated to me,' said Wednesday.

'Like my death on the tree,' said Shadow.

'That,' said Wednesday, 'was special.'

'And do you also feed on death?' asked Shadow, looking at Loki. Loki shook his head, wearily.

'No, of course not,' said Shadow. '*You* feed on chaos.'

Loki smiled at that, a brief pained smile, and orange flames danced in his eyes, and flickered like burning lace beneath his pale skin.

'We couldn't have done it without you,' said Wednesday, from the corner of Shadow's eye. 'I'd been with so many women . . .'

'You needed a son,' said Shadow.

Wednesday's ghost-voice echoed. 'I needed *you*, my boy. Yes. My own boy. I knew that you had been conceived, but your mother left the country. It took us so long to find you. And when we did find you, you were in prison. We needed to find out what made you tick. What buttons we could press to make you move. Who you were.' Loki looked, momentarily, pleased with himself. 'And you had a wife to go back home to. It was unfortunate, but not insurmountable.'

'She was no good for you,' whispered Loki. 'You were better off without her.'

'If it could have been any other way,' said Wednesday, and this time Shadow knew what he meant.

'And if she'd had – the grace – to stay dead,' panted Loki. 'Wood and Stone – were good men. You were going – to be allowed to escape – when the train crossed the Dakotas . . .'

'Where is she?' asked Shadow.

Loki reached a pale arm, and pointed to the back of the cavern.

'She went that-a-way,' he said. Then, without warning, he tipped forward, his body collapsing onto the rock floor.

Shadow saw what the blanket had hidden from him; the pool of blood, the hole through Loki's back, the fawn raincoat soaked black with blood. 'What happened?' he said.

Loki said nothing.

Shadow did not think he would be saying anything any more.

'Your wife happened to him, m'boy,' said Wednesday's distant voice. He had become harder to see, as if he was fading back into the ether. 'But the battle will bring him back. As the battle will bring me back for good. I'm a ghost, and he's a corpse, but we've still won. The game was rigged.'

'Rigged games,' said Shadow, remembering, 'are the easiest to beat.'

There was no answer. Nothing moved in the shadows.

Shadow said, 'Goodbye,' and then he said, 'Father.' But by then there was no trace of anybody else in the cavern. Nobody at all.

Shadow walked back up to the Seven States Flag Court, but saw nobody, and heard nothing but the crack and whip of the flags in the storm-wind. There were no people with swords at the Thousand

Ton Balanced Rock, no defenders of the Swing-a-long bridge. He was alone.

There was nothing to see. The place was deserted. It was an empty battlefield.

No. Not deserted. Not exactly.

This was Rock City. It had been a place of awe and worship for thousands of years; today the millions of tourists who walked through the gardens and swung their way across the Swing-a-long bridge had the same effect as water turning a million prayer wheels. Reality was thin here. And Shadow knew where the battle must be taking place.

With that, he began to walk. He remembered how he had felt on the carousel, tried to feel like that . . .

He remembered turning the Winnebago, shifting it at right angles to *everything*. He tried to capture that sensation –

And then, easily and perfectly, it happened.

It was like pushing through a membrane, like plunging up from deep water into air. With one step he had moved from the tourist path on the mountain to . . .

To somewhere real. He was Backstage.

He was still on the top of a mountain, that much remained the same. But it was so much more than that. This mountaintop was the quintessence of place, the heart of things as they were. Compared to it, the Lookout Mountain he had left was a painting on a backdrop, or a papier-mâché model seen on a TV screen – merely a representation of the thing, not the thing itself.

This was the true place.

The rock walls formed a natural amphitheatre. Paths of stone that wound around and across it, forming twisty natural bridges that Eschered through and across the rock walls.

And the sky . . .

The sky was dark. It was lit, and the world beneath it was illuminated by a burning greenish-white streak, brighter than the sun, which forked crazily across the sky from end to end, like a white rip in the darkened sky.

It was lightning, Shadow realised. Lightning held in one frozen moment that stretched into forever. The light it cast was harsh and unforgiving: it washed out faces, hollowed eyes into dark pits.

This was the moment of the storm.

The paradigms were shifting. He could feel it. The old world, a world of infinite vastness and illimitable resources and future was being confronted by something else – a web of energy, of opinions, of gulfs.

People believe, thought Shadow. It's what people do. They believe. And then they will not take responsibility for their beliefs; they conjure things, and do not trust the conjurations. People populate the darkness; with ghosts, with gods, with electrons, with tales. People imagine, and people believe: and it is that belief, that rock-solid belief, that makes things happen.

The mountaintop was an arena; he saw that immediately. And on each side of the arena he could see them arrayed.

They were too big. Everything was too big in that place.

There were old gods in that place: gods with skins the brown of old mushrooms, the pink of chicken-flesh, the yellow of autumn leaves. Some were crazy and some were sane. Shadow recognised the old gods. He'd met them already, or he'd met others like them. There were ifrits and piskies, giants and dwarfs. He saw the woman he had met in the darkened bedroom in Rhode Island, saw the writhing green snake-coils of her hair. He saw Mama-ji, from the carousel, and there was blood on her hands and a smile on her face. He knew them all.

He recognised the new ones, too.

There was somebody who had to be a railroad baron, in an antique suit, his watch-chain stretched across his vest. He had the air of one who had seen better days. His forehead twitched.

There were the great grey gods of the airplanes, heirs to all the dreams of heavier-than-air travel.

There were car gods there: a powerful, serious-faced contingent, with blood on their black gloves and on their chrome teeth: recipients of human sacrifice on a scale undreamed-of since the Aztecs. Even they looked uncomfortable. Worlds change.

Others had faces of smudged phosphors; they glowed gently, as if they existed in their own light.

Shadow felt sorry for them all.

There was an arrogance to the new ones. Shadow could see that. But there was also a fear.

They were afraid that unless they kept pace with a changing world, unless they remade and redrew and rebuilt the world in their image, their time would already be over.

Each side faced the other with bravery. To each side, the opposition were the demons, the monsters, the damned.

Shadow could see an initial skirmish had taken place. There was already blood on the rocks.

They were readying themselves for the real battle; for the real war. It was now or never, he thought. If he did not move now, it would be too late.

In America everything goes on forever, said a voice in the back of his head. *The 1950s lasted for a thousand years. You have all the time in the world.*

Shadow walked in something that was half a stroll, half controlled stumble, into the centre of the arena.

He could feel eyes on him, eyes and things that were not eyes. He shivered.

The buffalo voice said, *You are doing just fine.*

Shadow thought, *Damn right. I came back from the dead this morning. After that, everything else should be a piece of cake.*

'You know,' said Shadow, to the air, in a conversational voice, 'This is not a war. This was never intended to be a war. And if any of you think this is a war, you are deluding yourselves.' He heard grumbling noises from both sides. He had impressed nobody.

'We are fighting for our survival,' lowed a minotaur from one side of the arena.

'We are fighting for our existence,' shouted a mouth in a pillar of glittering smoke, from the other.

'This is a bad land for gods,' said Shadow. As an opening statement it wasn't *Friends, Romans, Countrymen*, but it would do. 'You've probably all learned that, in your own way. The old gods are ignored. The new gods are as quickly taken up as they are abandoned, cast aside for the next big thing. Either you've been forgotten, or you're scared you're going to be rendered obsolete, or maybe you're just getting tired of existing on the whim of people.'

The grumbles were fewer now. He had said something they agreed with. Now, while they were listening, he had to tell them the story.

'There was a god who came here from a far land, and whose power and influence waned as belief in him faded. He was a god who took his power from sacrifice, and from death, and especially from war. The deaths of those who fell in war were dedicated to him – whole battlefields which had given him in the Old Country power and sustenance.

'Now he was old. He made his living as a grifter, working with another god from his pantheon, a god of chaos and deceit. Together they rooked the gullible. Together they took people for all they'd got.

'Somewhere in there – maybe fifty years ago, maybe a hundred, they put a plan into motion, a plan to create a reserve of power they could both tap into. Something that would make them stronger than they had ever been. After all, what could be more powerful than a battlefield covered with dead gods? The game they played was called "Let's You and Him Fight".

'Do you see?

'The battle you came here for isn't something that any of you can win or lose. The winning and the losing are unimportant to him, to them. What matters is that enough of you die. Each of you that falls in battle gives him power. Every one of you that dies, feeds him. Do you understand?'

The roaring, *whoompf*ing sound of something catching fire echoed across the arena. Shadow looked to the place the noise came from. An enormous man, his skin the deep brown of mahogany, his chest naked, wearing a top hat, cigar sticking rakishly from his mouth, spoke in a voice as deep as the grave. Baron Samedi said, 'Okay. But Odin. He *died*. At the peace talks. Motherfuckers killed him. He died. I *know* death. Nobody going to fool me about death.'

Shadow said, 'Obviously. He had to die for real. He sacrificed his physical body to make this war happen. After the battle he would have been more powerful than he had ever been.'

Somebody called, 'Who are you?'

'I am – I was – I am his son.'

One of the new gods – Shadow suspected it was a drug from the way it smiled and spangled, said, 'But Mister World said . . .'

'There *was* no Mister World. There never was any such person. He was just another one of you bastards trying to feed on the chaos he created.'

They believed him, and he could see the hurt in their eyes.

Shadow shook his head. 'You know,' he said. 'I think I would rather be a man than a god. We don't need anyone to believe in us. We just keep going anyhow. It's what we do.'

There was silence, in the high place.

And then, with a shocking crack, the lightning bolt frozen in the sky crashed to the mountaintop, and the arena went entirely dark.

They glowed, many of those presences, in the darkness.

Shadow wondered if they were going to argue with him, to attack him, to try to kill him. He waited for some kind of response.

And then Shadow realised that the lights were going out. The gods were leaving that place, first in handfuls, and then by scores, and finally in their hundreds.

A spider the size of a rottweiler scuttled heavily toward him, on seven legs; its cluster of eyes glowed faintly.

Shadow held his ground, although he felt slightly sick.

When the spider got close enough, it said, in Mr Nancy's voice. 'That was a good job. Proud of you. You done good, kid.'

'Thank you,' said Shadow.

'We should get you back. Too long in this place is goin' to mess you up.' It rested one brown-haired spider-leg on Shadow's shoulder . . .

. . . and, back on Seven States Flag Court, Mr Nancy coughed. His right hand rested on Shadow's shoulder. The rain had stopped. Mr Nancy held his left hand across his side, as if it hurt. Shadow asked if he was okay.

'I'm tough as old nails,' said Mr Nancy. 'Tougher.' He did not sound happy. He sounded like an old man in pain.

There were dozens of them, standing or sitting on the ground or on the benches. Some of them looked badly injured.

Shadow could hear a rattling noise in the sky, approaching from the south. He looked at Mr Nancy. 'Helicopters?'

Mr Nancy nodded. 'Don't you worry about them. Not any more. They'll just clean up the mess, and leave.'

'Got it.'

Shadow knew that there was one part of the mess he wanted to see for himself, before it was cleaned up. He borrowed a flashlight from a grey-haired man who looked like a retired news anchor and began to hunt.

He found Laura stretched out on the ground in a side-cavern, beside a diorama of mining gnomes straight out of Snow White. The floor beneath her was sticky with blood. She was on her side, where Loki must have dropped her after he had pulled the spear out of them both.

One of Laura's hands clutched her chest. She looked dreadfully vulnerable. She looked dead, but then, Shadow was almost used to that by now.

Shadow squatted beside her, and he touched her cheek with his hand, and he said her name. Her eyes opened, and she lifted her head and turned it until she was looking at him.

'Hello, puppy,' she said. Her voice was thin.

'Hi, Laura. What happened here?'

'Nothing,' she said. 'Just stuff. Did they win?'

'I stopped the battle they were trying to start.'

'My clever puppy,' she said. 'That man, Mister World, he said he was going to put a stick through your eye. I didn't like him at all.'

'He's dead. You killed him, hon.'

She nodded. She said, 'That's good.'

Her eyes closed. Shadow's hand found her cold hand, and he held it in his. In time she opened her eyes again.

'Did you ever figure out how to bring me back from the dead?' she asked.

'I guess,' he said. 'I know one way, anyway.'

'That's good,' she said. She squeezed his hand with her cold hand. And then she said, 'And the opposite? What about that?'

'The opposite?'

'Yes,' she whispered. 'I think I must have earned it.'

'I don't want to do that.'

She said nothing. She simply waited.

Shadow said, 'Okay.' Then he took his hand from hers and put it to her neck.

She said, 'That's my husband.' She said it proudly.

'I love you, babes,' said Shadow.

'Love you, puppy,' she whispered.

He closed his hand around the golden coin that hung around her neck. He tugged, hard, at the chain, which snapped easily. Then he took the gold coin between his finger and thumb, and blew on it, and opened his hand wide.

The coin was gone.

Her eyes were still open, but they did not move.

He bent down then, and kissed her, gently, on her cold cheek, but she did not respond. He did not expect her to. Then he got up and walked out of the cavern, to stare into the night.

The storms had cleared. The air felt fresh and clean and new once more.

Tomorrow, he had no doubt, would be one hell of a beautiful day.

Part 4

Epilogue:

Something that the Dead are Keeping Back

19

One describes a tale best by telling the tale. You see? The way one describes a story, to oneself or to the world, is by telling the story. It is a balancing act and it is a dream. The more accurate the map, the more it resembles the territory. The most accurate map possible would be the territory, and thus would be perfectly accurate and perfectly useless.

The tale is the map which is the territory.

You must remember this.

– From the Notebooks of Mr Ibis

The two of them were in the VW bus, heading down to Florida on I-75. They'd been driving since dawn; or rather, Shadow had driven, and Mr Nancy had sat up front in the passenger seat and, from time to time, and with a pained expression on his face, offered to drive. Shadow always said no.

'Are you happy?' asked Mr Nancy, suddenly. He had been staring at Shadow for several hours. Whenever Shadow glanced over to his right, Mr Nancy was looking at him with his earth-brown eyes.

'Not really,' said Shadow. 'But I'm not dead yet.'

'Huh?'

'*Call no man happy until he is dead.* Herodotus.'

Mr Nancy raised a white eyebrow, and he said, '*I'm* not dead yet, and, mostly *because* I'm not dead yet, I'm happy as a clamboy.'

'The Herodotus thing. It doesn't mean that the dead are happy,' said Shadow. 'It means that you can't judge the shape of someone's life until it's over and done.'

'I don't even judge then,' said Mr Nancy. 'And as for happiness, there's a lot of different kinds of happiness, just as there's a hell of a lot of different kinds of dead. Me, I'll just take what I can get when I can get it.'

Shadow changed the subject. 'Those helicopters,' he said. 'The ones that took away the bodies, and the injured.'

'What about them?'

'Who sent them? Where did they come from?'

'You shouldn't worry yourself about that. They're like valkyries or buzzards. They come because they have to come.'

'If you say so.'

'The dead and the wounded will be taken care of. You ask me, old Jacquel's going to be very busy for the next month or so. Tell me somethin', Shadow-boy.'

'Okay.'

'You learn anythin' from all this?'

Shadow shrugged. 'I don't know. Most of what I learned on the tree I've already forgotten,' he said. 'I think I met some people. But I'm not certain of anything any more. It's like one of those dreams that changes you. You keep some of the dream forever, and you know things down deep inside yourself, because it happened to you, but when you go looking for details they kind of just slip out of your head.'

'Yeah,' said Mr Nancy. And then he said, grudgingly, 'You're not so dumb.'

'Maybe not,' said Shadow. 'But I wish I could have kept more of what passed through my hands, since I got out of prison. I was given so many things, and I lost them again.'

'Maybe,' said Mr Nancy, 'You kept more than you think.'

'No,' said Shadow.

They crossed the border into Florida, and Shadow saw his first palm tree. He wondered if they'd planted it there on purpose, at the border, just so that you knew you were in Florida now.

Mr Nancy began to snore, and Shadow glanced over at him. The old man still looked very grey, and his breath was rasping. Shadow wondered, not for the first time, if he had sustained some kind of chest or lung injury in the fight. Nancy had refused any medical attention.

Florida went on for longer than Shadow had imagined, and it was late by the time he pulled up outside a small, one storey wooden house, its windows tightly shuttered, on the outskirts of Fort Pierce. Nancy, who had directed him through the last five miles, invited him to stay the night.

'I can get a room in a motel,' said Shadow. 'It's not a problem.'

'You *could* do that, and I'd be hurt. Obviously I wouldn't say anythin'. But I'd be real hurt, real bad,' said Mr Nancy. 'So you better stay here, and I'll make you a bed up on the couch.'

Mr Nancy unlocked the hurricane shutters, and pulled open the windows. The house smelled musty and damp, and a little sweet, as if it were haunted by the ghosts of long-dead cookies.

Shadow agreed, reluctantly, to stay the night there, just as he agreed, even more reluctantly, to walk with Mr Nancy to the bar at the end of the road, for just one late night drink while the house aired out.

'Did you see Czernobog?' asked Nancy, as they strolled through the muggy Floridian night. The air was alive with whirring palmetto bugs and the ground crawled with creatures that scuttled and clicked. Mr Nancy lit a cigarillo, and coughed and choked on it. Still, he kept right on smoking.

'He was gone when I came out of the cave.'

'He will have headed home. He'll be waitin' for you there, you know.'

'Yes.'

They walked in silence to the end of the road. It wasn't much of a bar, but it was open.

'I'll buy the first beers,' said Mr Nancy.

'We're only having one beer, remember,' said Shadow.

'What are you,' asked Mr Nancy. 'Some kind of cheapskate?'

Mr Nancy bought them their first beers, and Shadow bought the second round. He stared in horror as Mr Nancy talked the barman into turning on the karaoke machine, and then watched in fascinated embarrassment as the old man belted his way through 'What's New Pussycat?' before crooning out a moving, tuneful version of 'The Way You Look Tonight'. He had a fine voice, and by the end the handful of people still in the bar were cheering and applauding him.

When he came back to Shadow at the bar he was looking brighter. The whites of his eyes were clear, and the grey pallor that had touched his skin was gone. 'Your turn,' he said.

'Absolutely not,' said Shadow.

But Mr Nancy had ordered more beers, and was handing Shadow a stained printout of songs from which to choose. 'Just pick a song you know the words to.'

'This is not funny,' said Shadow. The world was beginning to swim, a little, but he couldn't muster the energy to argue, and then Mr Nancy was putting on the backing tapes to 'Don't Let Me Be Misunderstood', and pushing – literally *pushing* – Shadow up onto the tiny makeshift stage at the end of the bar.

Shadow held the mike as if it was probably live, and then the backing music started and he croaked out the initial '*Baby . . .*' Nobody in the bar threw anything in his direction. And it felt good. '*Can you understand me now?*' His voice was rough but melodic, and rough suited the song just fine. '*Sometimes I feel a little mad. Don't you know that no-one alive can always be an angel . . .*'

And he was still singing it as they walked home through the busy Florida night, the old man and the young, stumbling and happy.

'*I'm just a soul whose intentions are good,*' he sang to the crabs and the spiders and the palmetto beetles and the lizards and the night. '*Oh lord, please don't let me be misunderstood.*'

Mr Nancy showed him to the couch. It was much smaller than Shadow, who decided to sleep on the floor, but by the time he had finished deciding to sleep on the floor he was already fast asleep, half-sitting, half lying, on the tiny sofa.

At first, he did not dream. There was just the comforting darkness. And then he saw a fire burning in the darkness and he walked toward it.

'You did well,' whispered the Buffalo Man without moving his lips.

'I don't know what I did,' said Shadow.

'You made peace,' said the Buffalo Man. 'You took our words and made them your own. They never understood that *they* were here – and the people who worshipped them were here – because it suits us that they are here. But we can change our minds. And perhaps we will.'

'Are you a god?' asked Shadow.

The buffalo-headed man shook his head. Shadow thought, for a moment, that the creature was amused. 'I am the land,' he said.

And if there was more to that dream then Shadow did not remember it.

He heard something sizzling. His head was aching, and there was a pounding behind his eyes.

Mr Nancy was already cooking breakfast: a towering stack of pancakes, sizzling bacon, perfect eggs and coffee. He looked in the peak of health.

'My head hurts,' said Shadow.

'You get a good breakfast inside you, you'll feel like a new man.'

'I'd rather feel like the same man, just with a different head,' said Shadow.

'Eat,' said Mr Nancy.

Shadow ate.

'How do you feel now?'

'Like I've got a headache, only now I've got some food in my stomach and I think I'm going to throw up.'

'Come with me.' Beside the sofa, on which Shadow had spent the night, covered with an African blanket, was a trunk, made of some dark wood, which looked like an undersized pirate chest. Mr Nancy undid the padlock, and opened the lid. Inside the trunk there were a number of boxes. Nancy rummaged among the boxes. 'It's an ancient African herbal remedy,' he said. 'It's made of ground willow bark, things like that.'

'Like aspirin?'

'Yup,' said Mr Nancy. 'Just like that.' From the bottom of the trunk he produced a giant economy-sized bottle of generic aspirin. He unscrewed the top, and shook out a couple of white pills. 'Here.'

'Nice trunk,' said Shadow. He took the bitter pills, swallowed them with a glass of water.

'My son sent it to me,' said Mr Nancy. 'He's a good boy. I don't see him as much as I'd like.'

'I miss Wednesday,' said Shadow. 'Despite everything he did. I keep expecting to see him. But I look up and he's not there.' He kept staring at the pirate trunk, trying to figure out what it reminded him of.

You will lose many things. Do not lose this. Who said that?

'You miss him? After what he put you through? Put us all through?'

'Yes,' said Shadow. 'I guess I do. Do you think he'll be back?'

'I think,' said Mr Nancy, 'that wherever two men are gathered together to sell a third man a twenty dollar violin for ten thousand dollars, he will be there in spirit.'

'Yes, but—'

'We should get back into the kitchen,' said Mr Nancy, his expression becoming stony. 'Those pans won't wash themselves.'

Mr Nancy washed the pans and the dishes. Shadow dried them, and put them away. Somewhere in there the headache began to ease. They went back into the sitting room.

Shadow stared at the old trunk some more, willing himself to remember. 'If I don't go to see Czernobog,' he said, 'What will happen?'

'You'll see him,' said Mr Nancy flatly. 'Maybe he'll find you. Or maybe he'll bring you to him. But one way or another, you'll see him.'

Shadow nodded. Something started to fall into place. A dream, on the tree. 'Hey,' he said. 'Is there a god with an elephant's head?'

'Ganesh? He's a Hindu god. He removes obstacles, and makes journeys easier. Good cook, too.'

Shadow looked up. '. . . *it's in the trunk,*' he said. 'I knew it was important, but I didn't know why. I thought maybe it meant the trunk of the tree. But he wasn't talking about that at all, was he?'

Mr Nancy frowned. 'You lost me.'

'It's in the trunk,' said Shadow. He knew it was true. He did not know why it should be true, not quite. But of that he was completely certain.

He got to his feet. 'I got to go,' he said. 'I'm sorry.'

Mr Nancy raised an eyebrow. 'Why the hurry?'

'Because,' said Shadow, simply, 'the ice is melting.'

20

it's
   spring
   and
      the
        goat-footed
balloonMan whistles
   far
   and
   wee
– e.e.cummings

Shadow drove the rental out of the forest, about 8:30 in the morning. He came down the hill doing under 45mph, and entered the town of Lakeside three weeks after he was certain he had left it for good.

He drove through the city, surprised at how little it had changed in the last few weeks, which were a lifetime, and he parked half-way down the driveway that led to the lake. Then he got out of the car.

There were no more ice-fishing huts on the frozen lake any longer, no SUVs, no men sitting at a fishing hole with a line and a twelve-pack. The lake was dark: no longer covered with a blind white layer of snow, now there were reflective patches of water on the surface of the ice, and the water beneath the ice was black, and the ice itself was clear enough that the darkness beneath showed through. The sky was grey, but the icy lake was bleak and empty.

Almost empty.

There was one car remaining on the ice, parked out on the frozen lake almost beneath the bridge, so that anyone driving through the town, anyone crossing the town, could not help but see it. It was a dirty green in colour; the sort of car that people abandon in parking lots. It had no engine. It was a symbol of a wager, waiting for the ice to become rotten enough, and soft enough, and dangerous enough to allow the lake to take it forever.

There was a chain across the short driveway that led down to the lake, and a warning sign forbidding entrance to people or to vehicles. *Thin ice*, it said. Beneath it was a hand painted sequence of pictograms with lines through them: no cars, no pedestrians, no snowmobiles. *Danger.*

Shadow ignored the warnings and scrambled down the bank. It was slippery – the snow had already melted, turning the earth to mud under his feet, and the brown grass barely offered traction. He skidded and slid down to the lake and walked, carefully, out onto a short wooden jetty, and from there he stepped down onto the ice.

The layer of water on the ice, made up of melted ice and melted snow, was deeper than it had looked from above, and the ice beneath the water was slicker and more slippery than any skating rink, so that Shadow was forced to fight to keep his footing. He splashed though the water, as it covered his boots to the laces and seeped inside. Ice-water. It numbed where it touched. He felt strangely distant as he trudged across the frozen lake, as if he were watching himself on a movie screen – a movie in which he was the hero: a detective, perhaps.

He walked toward the klunker, painfully aware that the ice was too rotten for this, and that the water beneath the ice was as cold as water could be without freezing. He kept walking, and he slipped and slid. Several times he fell.

He passed empty beer bottles and cans left to litter the ice, and he passed round holes cut into the ice, for fishing, holes that had not frozen again, each hole filled with black water.

The klunker seemed further away than it had looked from the road. He heard a loud crack from the south of the lake, like a stick breaking, followed by the sound of something huge thrumming, as if a bass string the size of a lake was vibrating. Massively, the ice creaked and groaned, like an old door protesting being opened. Shadow kept walking, as steadily as he could.

This is suicide, whispered a sane voice in the back of his mind. *Can't you just let it go?*

'No,' he said, aloud. 'I have to *know*.' And he kept right on walking.

He arrived at the klunker, and even before he reached it he knew that he had been right. There was a miasma that hung about the car, something that was at the same time a faint, foul smell and was also a bad taste in the back of his throat. He walked around the car, looking inside. The seats were stained, and ripped. The car was obviously empty. He tried the doors. They were locked. He tried the trunk. Also locked.

He wished that he had brought a crowbar.

He made a fist of his hand, inside his glove. He counted to three, then smashed his hand, hard, against the driver's side window-glass.

His hand hurt, but the side-window was undamaged.

He thought about running at it – he could kick the window in, he was certain, if he didn't skid and fall on the wet ice. But the last thing he wanted to do was to disturb the klunker enough that the ice beneath it would crack.

He looked at the car. Then he reached for the radio antenna – it was the kind which was supposed to go up and down, but which had stuck in the up position a decade ago – and, with a little waggling, he broke it off at the base. He took the thin end of the antenna – it had once had a metal button on the end, but that was lost in time, and, with strong fingers, he bent it back up into a makeshift hook.

Then he rammed the extended metal antenna down between the rubber and the glass of the front window, deep into the mechanism of the door. He fished in the mechanism, twisting, moving, pushing the metal antenna about until it caught: and then he pulled up.

He felt the improvised hook sliding from the lock, uselessly.

He sighed. Fished again, slower, more carefully. He could imagine the ice grumbling beneath his feet as he shifted his weight. And slow . . . and . . .

He *had* it. He pulled up on the antenna and the front door locking mechanism popped up. Shadow reached down one gloved hand and took the door handle, pressed the button and pulled. The door did not open.

It's stuck, he thought, *iced up. That's all.*

He tugged, sliding on the ice, and suddenly the door of the klunker flew open, ice scattering everywhere.

The miasma was worse inside the car, a stench of rot and sickness. Shadow felt ill.

He reached under the dashboard, found the black plastic handle that opened the trunk, and tugged on it, hard.

There was a thunk from behind him as the trunk door released.

Shadow walked out onto the ice, slipped and splashed around the car, holding on to the side of it as he went.

It's in the trunk, he thought.

The trunk was open an inch. He reached down and opened it the rest of the way, pulling it up.

The smell was bad, but it could have been much worse: the bottom of the trunk was filled with an inch or so of half-melted ice. There was a girl in the trunk. She wore a scarlet snowsuit, now stained, and her mousey hair was long and her mouth was closed, so Shadow could not see the blue rubber-band braces, but he knew that they were there. The cold had preserved her, kept her as fresh as if she had been in a freezer.

Her eyes were wide open, and she looked as if she had been crying when she died, and the tears that had frozen on her cheeks had still not melted.

'You were here all the time,' said Shadow to Alison McGovern's corpse. 'Every single person who drove over that bridge saw you. Everyone who drove through the town saw you. The ice fishermen walked past you every day. And nobody knew.'

And then he realised how foolish that was.

Somebody knew. Somebody had put her here.

He reached in to the trunk – to see if he could pull her out. He put his weight on the car, as he leaned in. Maybe that was what did it.

The ice beneath the front wheels went at that moment, perhaps from his movements, perhaps not. The front of the car lurched downward several feet into the dark water of the lake. Water began to pour into the car through the open driver's door. Lake water splashed about Shadow's ankles, although the ice he stood on was still solid. He looked around urgently, wondering how to get away – and then it was too late, and the ice tipped precipitously, throwing him against the car and the dead girl in the trunk; and the back of the car went down, and Shadow went down with it, into the cold waters of the lake. It was ten past nine in the morning, on March the twenty-third.

He took a deep breath before he went under, closing his eyes, but the cold of the lake water hit him like a wall, knocking the breath from his body.

He tumbled downward into the murky ice-water, pulled down by the car.

He was under the lake, down in the darkness and the cold, weighed down by his clothes and his gloves and his boots, trapped and swathed in his coat which seemed to have become heavier and bulkier than he could have imagined.

He was falling, still. He tried to push away from the car, but it was pulling him with it, and then there was a bang which he could hear with his whole body, not his ears, and his left foot was wrenched at the ankle, the foot twisted and trapped beneath the car as it settled on the lake-bottom, and panic took him.

He opened his eyes.

He knew it was dark down there: rationally, he knew it was too dark to see anything, but still, he could see; he could see everything. He could see Alison McGovern's white face staring at him from the open trunk. He could see other cars as well – the klunkers of bygone years, rotten hulk shapes in the darkness, half-buried in the lake mud.

Each one, he knew, without any question, had a dead child in the trunk. There were more than a hundred of them . . . each had sat out on the ice, in front of the eyes of the world, all through the cold winter. Each had tumbled into the cold waters of the lake, when the winter was done.

This was where they rested: Lemmi Hautala and Jessie Lovat and Sandy Olsen and Jo Ming and Sarah Lindquist and all the rest of them. Down where it was silent and cold . . .

He pulled at his foot. It was stuck fast, and the pressure in his lungs was becoming unbearable. There was a sharp, terrible, hurt in his ears. He exhaled slowly, and the air bubbled around his face.

Soon, he thought, *soon I'll have to breathe. Or I'll choke.*

He reached down, put both hands around the bumper of the

klunker, and pushed, with everything he had, leaning into it. Nothing happened.

It's only the shell of a car, he told himself. *They took out the engine. That's the heaviest part of the car. You can do it. Just keep pushing.*

He pushed.

Agonisingly slowly, a fraction of an inch at a time, the car slipped forward in the mud, and Shadow pulled his foot from the mud beneath the car, and kicked, and tried to push himself out into the cold lake water. He didn't move. *The coat*, he told himself. *It's the coat. It's stuck, or caught on something.* He pulled his arms from his coat, fumbled with numb fingers at the frozen zipper. Then he pulled both hands on each side of the zipper, felt the coat give and rend. Hastily, he freed himself from its embrace, and pushed upward, away from the car.

There was a rushing sensation but no sense of up, no sense of down, and he was choking and the pain in his chest and in his head was too much to bear, so that he was certain that he was going to have to inhale, to breathe in the cold water, to die. And then his head hit something solid.

Ice. He was pushing against the ice on the top of the lake. He hammered at it with his fists, but there was no strength left in his arms, nothing to hold onto, nothing to push against. The world had dissolved into the chill blackness beneath the lake. There was nothing left but cold.

This is ridiculous, he thought. And he thought, remembering some old Tony Curtis film he'd seen as a kid, *I should roll onto my back and push the ice upward and press my face to it, and find some air, I could breathe again, there's air there somewhere*, but he was just floating and freezing and he could no longer move a muscle, not if his life depended on it, which it did.

The cold became bearable. Became warm. And he thought, *I'm dying*. There was anger there this time, a deep fury, and he took the pain and the anger and reached with it, flailed, forced muscles to move that were ready never to move again.

He pushed up with his hand, and felt it scrape the edge of the ice and move up into the air. He flailed for a grip, and felt another hand take his own, and pull.

His head banged against the ice, his face scraped the underneath of the ice, and then his head was up in the air, and he could see that he was coming up through a hole in the ice, and for a moment all he could do was breathe, and let the black lake water run from his nose and his mouth, and blink his eyes, which could see nothing more than a blinding daylight and shapes, and someone was pulling him, now, forcing him out of the water, saying something about how he'd freeze to death, so come on, man, *pull*, and Shadow wriggled and shook like a bull seal coming ashore, shaking and coughing and shuddering.

He breathed deep gasps of air, stretched flat out on the creaking ice, and even that would not hold for long, he knew, but it was no good. His thoughts were coming with difficulty, syrupy-slow.

'Just leave me,' he tried to say. 'I'll be fine.' His words were a slur, and everything was drawing to a halt.

He just needed to rest for a moment, that was all, just rest, and then he would get up and move on. Obviously he could not just lie there forever.

There was a jerk; water splashed his face. His head was lifted up. Shadow felt himself being hauled across the ice, sliding on his back across the slick surface, and he wanted to protest, to explain that he just needed a little rest – maybe a little sleep, was that asking for so much? – and he would be just fine. If they just left him alone.

He did not believe that he had fallen asleep, but he was standing on a vast plain, and there was a man there with the head and shoulders of a buffalo, and a woman with the head of an enormous condor, and there was Whiskey Jack standing between them, looking at him sadly, shaking his head.

Whiskey Jack turned and walked slowly away from Shadow. The Buffalo Man walked away beside him. The Thunderbird Woman also walked, and then she ducked and kicked and she was gliding out into the skies.

Shadow felt a sense of loss. He wanted to call to them, to plead with them to come back, not to give up on him, but everything was becoming formless and without shape: they were gone, and the plains were fading, and everything became void.

The pain was intense: it was as if every cell in his body, every nerve, was melting and waking, and advertising its presence by burning him and hurting him.

There was a hand at the back of his head, gripping it by the hair, and another hand beneath his chin. He opened his eyes, expecting to find himself in some kind of hospital.

His feet were bare. He was wearing jeans. He was naked from the waist up. There was steam in the air. He could see a shaving mirror on the wall facing him, and a small basin, and a blue toothbrush in a toothpaste-stained glass.

Information was processed slowly, one datum at a time.

His fingers burned. His toes burned.

He began to whimper from the pain.

'Easy now, Mike. Easy there,' said a voice he knew.

'What?' he said, or tried to say. 'What's happening?' It sounded strained and strange to his ears.

He was in a bathtub. The water was hot. He thought the water was hot, although he could not be certain. The water was up to his neck.

'Dumbest thing you can do with a fellow freezing to death is to put him in front of a fire. The second dumbest thing you can do is to wrap him in blankets – especially if he's in cold wet clothes already. Blankets insulate him – keep the cold in. The third dumbest thing – and this is my private opinion – is to take the fellow's blood out, warm it up and put it back. That's what doctors do these days. Complicated, expensive. Dumb.' The voice was coming from above and behind his head.

'The smartest, quickest thing you can do is what sailors have done to men overboard for hundreds of years. You put the fellow in hot water. Not *too* hot. Just hot. Now, just so you know, you were basically dead, when I found you on the ice back there. How are you feeling now, Houdini?'

'It hurts,' said Shadow. 'Everything hurts. You saved my life.'

'I guess maybe I did, at that. Can you hold your head up on your own now?'

'Maybe.'

'I'm going to let you go. If you start sinking below the water I'll pull you back up again.'

The hands released their grip on his head.

He felt himself sliding forward in the tub. He put out his hands, pressed them against the side of the tub, and leaned back. The bathroom was small. The tub was metal, and the enamel was stained and scratched.

An old man moved into his field of vision. He looked concerned.

'Feeling better?' asked Hinzelmann. 'You just lay back and relax. I've got the den nice and warm. You tell me when you're ready, I got a robe you can wear, and I can throw your jeans into the drier with the rest of your clothes. Sound good, Mike?'

'That's not my name.'

'If you say so.' The old man's goblin face twisted into an expression of discomfort.

Shadow had no real sense of time: he lay in the bathtub until the burning stopped and his toes and fingers flexed without real discomfort. Hinzelmann helped Shadow to his feet and let out the warm water. Shadow sat on the side of the bathtub and together they pulled off his jeans.

He squeezed, without much difficulty, into a terrycloth robe too small for him, and, leaning on the old man, he went into the den, and flopped down on an ancient sofa. He was tired and weak: deeply fatigued, but alive. A log fire burned in the fireplace. A handful of puzzled-looking deer heads peered down dustily from around the walls, where they jostled for space with several large varnished fish.

Hinzelmann went away with Shadow's jeans, and from the room next door Shadow could hear a brief pause in the rattle of a clothes drier, before it resumed. The old man returned with a steaming mug.

'It's coffee,' he said, 'Which is a stimulant. And I splashed a little Schnapps into it. Just a little. That's what we always did in the old days. A doctor wouldn't recommend it.'

Shadow took the coffee with both hands. On the side of the mug was a picture of a mosquito and the message, *Give Blood – Visit Wisconsin!!*

'Thanks,' he said.

'It's what friends are for,' said Hinzelmann. 'One day, you can save my life. For now, forget about it.'

Shadow sipped the coffee. 'I thought I was dead.'

'You were lucky. I was up on the bridge – I'd pretty much figured that today was going to be the big day, you get a feel for it, when you get to my age – so I was up there with my old pocket watch, and I saw you heading out onto the lake. I shouted, but I sure as heck don't think you coulda heard me. I saw the car go down, and I saw you go down with it, and I thought I'd lost you, so I went out onto the ice. Gave me the heeby jeebies. You must have been under the water for the best part of two minutes. Then I saw your hand come up through the place where the car went down – it was like seeing a ghost, seeing you there . . .' He trailed off. 'We were both damn lucky that the ice took our weight as I dragged you back to the shore.'

Shadow nodded.

'You did a good thing,' he told Hinzelmann, and the old man beamed all over his goblin face.

Somewhere in the house, Shadow heard a door close. He sipped at his coffee.

Now that he was able to think clearly, he was starting to ask himself questions.

He wondered how an old man, a man half his height and perhaps a third his weight, had been able to drag him, unconscious, across the ice, or get him up the bank to a car. He wondered how Hinzelmann had gotten Shadow into the house and the bathtub.

Hinzelmann walked over to the fire, picked up the tongs and placed a thin log, carefully, onto the blazing fire.

'Do you want to know what I was doing out on the ice?'

Hinzelmann shrugged. 'None of my business.'

'You know what I don't understand . . .' said Shadow. He hesitated, putting his thoughts in order. 'I don't understand why you saved my life.'

'Well,' said Hinzelmann, 'the way I was brought up, if you see another fellow in trouble—'

'No,' said Shadow. 'That's not what I mean. I mean, you killed all those kids. Every winter. I was the only one to have figured it out. You must have seen me open the trunk. Why didn't you just let me drown?'

Hinzelmann tipped his head on one side. He scratched his nose, thoughtfully, rocked back and forth as if he were thinking. 'Well,' he said. 'That's a good question. I guess it's because I owed a certain party a debt. And I'm good for my debts.'

'Wednesday?'

'That's the fellow.'

'There was a reason he hid me in Lakeside, wasn't there? There was a reason nobody should have been able to find me here.'

Hinzelmann said nothing. He unhooked a heavy black poker from its place on the wall, and he prodded at the fire with it, sending up a cloud of orange sparks and smoke. 'This is my home,' he said, petulantly. 'It's a *good* town.'

Shadow finished his coffee. He put the cup down on the floor. The effort was exhausting. 'How long have you been here?'

'Long enough.'

'And you made the lake?'

Hinzelmann peered at him, surprised. 'Yes,' he said. 'I made the lake. They were calling it a lake when I got here, but it weren't nothing more than a spring and a mill pond and a creek.' He paused. 'I figured, that this country is hell on my kind of folk. It eats us. I didn't want to be eaten. So I made a deal. I gave them a lake, and I gave them prosperity . . .'

'And all it cost them was one child every winter.'

'Good kids,' said Hinzelmann, shaking his old head, slowly. 'They were all good kids. I'd only pick ones I liked. Except for Charlie Nelligan. He was a bad seed, that one. He was, what, 1924? 1925? Yeah. That was the deal.'

'The people of the town,' said Shadow. 'Mabel. Marguerite. Chad Mulligan. Do they *know*?'

Hinzelmann said nothing. He pulled the poker from the fire: the first six inches at the tip glowed a dull orange. Shadow knew that the handle of the poker must be too hot to hold, but it did not seem to bother Hinzelmann, and he prodded the fire again. He put the poker back into the fire, tip first, and left it there. Then he said, 'They know that they live in a good place. While every other town and city in this county, heck, in this part of the state, is crumbling into nothing. They know that.'

'And that's your doing?'

'This town,' said Hinzelmann. 'I care for it. Nothing happens here that I don't want to happen. You understand that? Nobody comes here that I don't want to come here. That was why your father sent you here. He didn't want you out there in the world, attracting attention. That's all.'

'And you betrayed him.'

'I did no such thing. He was a crook. But I always pay my debts.'

'I don't believe you,' said Shadow.

Hinzelmann looked offended. One hand tugged at the clump of white hair at his temple. 'I keep my word.'

'No. You don't. Laura came here. She said something was calling her here. And what about the coincidence that brought Sam Black Crow and Audrey Burton here, on the same night? I don't believe in coincidence any more.

'Sam Black Crow and Audrey Burton. Two people who both knew who I really was, and that there were people out there looking for me. I guess if one of them failed, there was always the other. And if all of them had failed, who else was on their way to Lakeside, Hinzelmann? My old prison warden, up here for a weekend's ice fishing? Laura's mother?' Shadow realised that he was angry. 'You wanted me out of your town. You just didn't want to have to tell Wednesday that was what you were doing.'

In the firelight, Hinzelmann seemed more like a gargoyle than an imp. 'This is a good town,' he said. Without his smile he looked waxen and corpse-like. 'You could have attracted too much attention. Not good for the town.'

'You should have left me back there on the ice,' said Shadow. 'You should have left me in the lake. I opened the trunk of the klunker. Right now Alison is still iced into the trunk. But the ice will melt, and her body'll float out and up to the surface. And then they'll go down and look and see what else they can find down there. Find your whole stash of kids. I guess some of those bodies are pretty well preserved.'

Hinzelmann reached down and picked up the poker. He made no pretense of stirring the fire with it any longer; he held it like a sword, or a baton, the glowing orange-white tip of it waving in the air. It smoked. Shadow was very aware that he was next-to-naked, and he was still tired, and clumsy, and far from able to defend himself.

'You want to kill me?' said Shadow. 'Go ahead. Do it. I'm a dead man anyway. I know you own this town – it's your little world. But if you think no-one's going to come looking for me, you're living in a dream world. It's over, Hinzelmann. One way or another, it's done.'

Hinzelmann pushed himself to his feet, using the poker as a

walking stick. The carpet charred and smoked where he rested the red-hot tip, as he got up. He looked at Shadow and there were tears in his pale blue eyes. 'I love this town,' he said. 'I really like being a cranky old man, and telling my stories and driving Tessie and ice fishing. Remember what I told you, it's not the fish you bring home from a day's fishing. It's the peace of mind.'

He extended the tip of the poker in Shadow's direction: Shadow could feel the heat of it from a foot away.

'I could kill you,' said Hinzelmann, 'I could fix it. I've done it before. You're not the first to figure it out. Chad Mulligan's father, he figured it out. I fixed him, and I can fix you.'

'Maybe,' said Shadow. 'But for how long, Hinzelmann? Another year? Another decade? They have computers now, Hinzelmann. They aren't stupid. They pick up on patterns. Every year a kid's going to vanish. Sooner or later they'll come sniffing about here. Just like they'll come looking for me. Tell me – how old *are* you?' He curled his fingers around a sofa cushion, and prepared to pull it over his head: it would deflect a first blow.

Hinzelmann's face was expressionless. 'They were giving their children to me before the Romans came to the Black Forest,' he said. 'I was a god before ever I was a kobold.'

'Maybe it's time to move on,' said Shadow. He wondered what a kobold was.

Hinzelmann stared at him. Then he took the poker, and pushed the tip of it back into the burning embers. 'It's not that simple. What makes you think I can leave this town, even if I want to, Shadow? I'm part of this town. You going to make me go, Shadow? You ready to kill me? So I can leave?'

Shadow looked down at the floor. There were still glimmers and sparks in the carpet, where the poker-tip had rested. Hinzelmann followed the look with his own, and crushed the embers out with his foot, twisting. In Shadow's mind came, unbidden, children, more than a hundred of them, staring at him with bone-blind eyes, the hair twisting slowly around their faces like fronds of seaweed. They were looking at him reproachfully.

He knew that he was letting them down. He just didn't know what else to do.

Shadow said, 'I can't kill you. You saved my life.'

He shook his head. He felt like crap, in every way he could feel like crap. He didn't feel like a hero or a detective any more – just another fucking sell-out, waving a stern finger at the darkness before turning his back on it.

'You want to know a secret?' asked Hinzelmann.

'Sure,' said Shadow, with a heavy heart. He was ready to be done with secrets.

'Watch this.'

Where Hinzelmann had been standing stood a male child, no more than five years old. His hair was dark brown, and long. He was perfectly naked, save for a worn leather band around his neck. He was pierced with two swords, one of them going through his chest, the other entering at his shoulder, with the point coming out beneath the rib-cage. Blood flowed through the wounds without stopping and ran down the child's body to pool and puddle on the floor. The swords looked unimaginably old.

The little boy stared up at Shadow with eyes that held only pain.

And Shadow thought to himself, *of course*. That's as good a way as any other of making a tribal god. He did not have to be told. He knew.

You take a baby and you bring it up in the darkness, letting it see no-one, touch no-one, and you feed it well as the years pass, feed it better than any of the village's other children, and then, five winters on, when the night is at its longest, you drag the terrified child out of its hut and into the circle of bonfires, and you pierce it with blades of iron and of bronze. Then you smoke the small body over charcoal fires until it is properly dried, and you wrap it in furs and carry it with you from encampment to encampment deep in the Black Forest, sacrificing animals and children to it, making it the luck of the tribe. When, eventually, the thing falls apart from age, you place its fragile bones in a box, and you worship the box; until one day the bones are scattered and forgotten, and the tribes who worshipped the child-god of the box are long gone; and the child-god, the luck of the village, will be barely remembered, save as a ghost or a brownie: a kobold.

Shadow wondered which of the people who had come to northern Wisconsin a hundred and fifty years ago, a woodcutter, perhaps, or a mapmaker, had crossed the Atlantic with Hinzelmann living in his head.

And then the bloody child was gone, and the blood, and there was only an old man with a fluff of white hair and a goblin smile, his sweater-sleeves still soaked from putting Shadow into the bath that had saved his life.

'Hinzelmann?' the voice came from the doorway of the den.

Hinzelmann turned. Shadow turned too.

'I came over to tell you,' said Chad Mulligan, and his voice was strained, 'that the klunker went through the ice. I saw it had gone down when I drove over that way, and thought I'd come over and let you know, in case you'd missed it.'

He was holding his gun. It was pointed at the floor.

'Hey Chad,' said Shadow.

'Hey pal,' said Chad Mulligan. 'They sent me a note said you'd died in custody. Heart attack.'

'How about that?' said Shadow. 'Seems like I'm dying all over the place.'

'He came down here, Chad,' said Hinzelmann. 'He threatened me.'

'No,' said Chad Mulligan. 'He didn't. I've been here for the last ten minutes, Hinzelmann. I heard everything you said. About my old man. About the lake.' He walked further into the den. He did not raise the gun. 'Jesus, Hinzelmann. You can't drive through this town without seeing that goddamned lake. It's at the centre of every-thing. So what the hell am I supposed to do?'

'You got to arrest him. He said he was going to kill me,' said Hinzelmann, a scared old man in a dusty den. 'Chad, I'm pleased you're here.'

'No,' said Chad Mulligan. 'You're not.'

Hinzelmann sighed. He bent down, as if resigned, and he pulled the poker out from the fire. The tip of it was burning bright orange.

'Put that down, Hinzelmann. Just put it down slowly, keep your hands in the air where I can see them, and turn and face the wall.'

There was an expression of pure fear on the old man's face, and Shadow would have felt sorry for him, but he remembered the frozen tears on the cheeks of Alison McGovern. Hinzelmann did not move. He did not put down the poker. He did not turn to the wall. Shadow was about to reach for Hinzelmann, to try to take the poker away from him, when the old man threw the burning poker at Mulligan.

Hinzelmann threw it awkwardly – lobbing it across the room as if for form's sake – and as he threw it he was already hurrying for the door.

The poker glanced off Mulligan's left arm.

The noise of the shot, in the close quarters of the old man's room, was deafening.

One shot to the head, and that was all.

Mulligan said, 'Better get your clothes on.' His voice was dull and dead.

Shadow nodded. He walked to the room next door, opened the door of the clothes drier and pulled out his clothes. The jeans were still damp, but he put them on anyway. By the time he got back to the den, fully dressed – except for his coat, which was somewhere deep in the freezing mud of the lake, and his boots, which he could not find – Mulligan had already hauled several smouldering logs out from the fireplace.

Mulligan said, 'It's a bad day for a cop when he has to commit arson, just to cover up a murder.' Then he looked up at Shadow. 'You need boots,' he said.

'I don't know where he put them,' said Shadow.

'Hell,' said Mulligan. Then he said, 'Sorry about this, Hinzelmann,' and he picked the old man up by the collar and by the belt buckle, and he swung him forward, dropped the body with its head resting in the open fireplace. The white hair crackled and flared, and the room began to fill with the smell of charring flesh.

'It wasn't murder. It was self-defense,' said Shadow.

'I know what it was,' said Mulligan, flatly. He had already turned his attention to the smoking logs he had scattered about the room. He pushed one of them to the edge of the sofa, picked up an old copy of the *Lakeside News* and pulled it into its component pages, which he crumpled up and dropped onto the log. The newspaper pages browned and then burst into flame.

'Get outside,' said Chad Mulligan.

He opened the windows as they walked out of the house, and he sprang the lock on the front door to lock it before he closed it.

Shadow followed him out to the police car in his bare feet. Mulligan opened the front passenger door for him, and Shadow got in and wiped his feet off on the mat. Then he put on his socks, which were pretty much dry by now.

'We can get you some boots at Hennings Farm and Home,' said Chad Mulligan.

'How much did you hear in there?' asked Shadow.

'Enough,' said Mulligan. Then he said, 'Too much.'

They drove to Hennings Farm and Home in silence. When they got there the police chief said, 'What size feet?'

Shadow told him.

Mulligan walked into the store. He returned with a pair of thick woollen socks, and a pair of leather farm-boots. 'All they had left in your size,' he said. 'Unless you wanted gumboots. I figured you didn't.'

Shadow pulled on the socks and the boots. They fitted fine. 'Thanks,' he said.

'You got a car?' asked Mulligan.

'It's parked by the road down to the lake. Near the bridge.'

Mulligan started the car and pulled out of the Hennings parking lot.

'What happened to Audrey?' asked Shadow.

'Day after they took you away, she said she liked me as a friend, but it would never work out between us, us being family and all, and she went back to Eagle Point. Broke my gosh-darn heart.'

'Makes sense,' said Shadow. 'And it wasn't personal. Hinzelmann didn't need her here any more.'

They drove back past Hinzelmann's house. A thick plume of white smoke was coming up from the chimney.

'She only came to town because he wanted her here. She helped him get me out of town. I was bringing attention he didn't need.'

'I thought she liked me.'

They pulled up beside Shadow's rental car. 'What are you going to do now?' asked Shadow.

'I don't know,' said Mulligan, his normally harassed face was starting to look more alive than it had at any point since Hinzelmann's den. It also looked more troubled. 'I figure, I got a couple of choices. Either I'll . . .,' and he made a gun of his first two fingers, and put the fingertips into his open mouth, and removed them, '. . . put a bullet through my brain. Or I'll wait another couple of days until the ice is mostly gone, and tie a concrete block to my leg and jump off the bridge. Or pills. Sheesh. Maybe I should just drive a while, out to one of the forests. Take pills out there. I don't want to make one of my guys have to do the clean up. Leave it for the county, huh?' He sighed, and shook his head.

'You didn't kill Hinzelmann, Chad. He died a long time ago, a long way from here.'

'Thanks for saying that, Mike. But I killed him. I shot a man in cold blood, and I covered it up. And if you asked me why I did it, why I really did it, I'm darned if I could tell you.'

Shadow put out a hand, touched Mulligan on the arm. 'Hinzelmann owned this town,' he said. 'I don't think you had a lot of choice about what happened back there. I think he brought you there. He wanted you to hear what you heard. He set you up. I guess it was the only way he could leave.'

Mulligan's miserable expression did not change. Shadow could see that the police chief had barely heard anything that he had said. He had killed Hinzelmann, and built him a pyre, and now, obeying the last of Hinzelmann's desires, he would commit suicide.

Shadow closed his eyes, remembering the place in his head that he had gone when Wednesday had told him to make snow: that place that pushed, mind to mind, and he smiled a smile he did not feel and he said, 'Chad. Let it go.' There was a cloud in the man's mind, a dark, oppressive cloud, and Shadow could almost see it and, concentrating on it, imagined it fading away like a fog in the morning. 'Chad,' he said, fiercely, trying to penetrate the cloud, 'This town is going to change now. It's not going to be the only good town in a depressed region any more. It's going to be a lot more like the rest of this part of the world. There's going to be a lot more trouble. People out of work. People out of their heads. More people getting hurt. More bad shit going down. They are going to need a police chief with experience. The town needs you.' And then he said, 'Marguerite needs you.'

Something shifted in the stormcloud that filled the man's head. Shadow could feel it change. He *pushed* then, envisioning Marguerite Olsen's practical brown hands and her dark eyes, and her long, long black hair. He pictured the way she tipped her head on one side and half-smiled when she was amused. 'She's waiting for you,' said Shadow, and he knew it was true as he said it.

'Margie?' said Chad Mulligan.

And at that moment, although he could never tell you how he had done it, and he doubted that he could ever do it again, Shadow reached in to Chad Mulligan's mind, easy as anything, and he plucked the events of that afternoon away from it as precisely and dispassionately as a raven picks an eye from roadkill.

The creases in Chad's forehead smoothed, and he blinked, sleepily.

'Go see Margie,' said Shadow. 'It's been good seeing you, Chad. Take care of yourself.'

'Sure,' yawned Chad Mulligan.

A message crackled over the police radio, and Chad reached out for the handset. Shadow got out of the car.

Shadow walked over to his rental car. He could see the grey flatness of the lake at the centre of the town. He thought of the dead children who waited at the bottom of the water.

Soon, Alison would float to the surface . . .

As Shadow drove past Hinzelmann's place he could see the plume of smoke had already turned into a blaze. He could hear a siren wail.

He drove south, heading for Highway 51. He was on his way to keep his final appointment. But before that, he thought, he would stop off in Madison, for one last goodbye.

Best of everything, Samantha Black Crow liked closing up the Coffee House at night. It was a perfectly calming thing to do: it gave her a feeling that she was putting order back into the world. She would put on an Indigo Girls CD, and she would do her final chores of the night at her own pace and in her own way. First, she would clean the espresso machine. Then she would do the final rounds, ensuring that any missed cups or plates were deposited back in the kitchen, and that the newspapers that were always scattered around the Coffee House by the end of each day were collected together and piled neatly by the front door, all ready for recycling.

She loved the Coffee House. It was a long, winding series of rooms filled with armchairs and sofas and low tables, on a street lined with second-hand bookstores.

She covered the leftover slices of cheesecake and put them into the large refrigerator for the night, then she took a cloth and wiped the last of the crumbs away. She enjoyed being alone.

A tapping on the window jerked her attention from her chores back to the real world. Sam went to the door, opened it, to admit a woman of about her own age, with pigtailed magenta hair. Her name was Natalie.

'Hello,' said Natalie. She went up on tiptoes and kissed Sam, depositing the kiss snugly between Sam's cheek and the corner of her mouth. You can say a lot of things with a kiss like that. 'You done?'

'Nearly.'

'You want to see a movie?'

'Sure. Love to. I've got a good five minutes left here, though. Why don't you sit and read the *Onion*?'

'I saw this week's already.' She sat on a chair near the door, ruffled through the pile of newspapers put aside for recycling until she found something, and she read it, while Sam bagged up the last of the money in the till and put it in the safe.

They had been sleeping together for a week now. Sam wondered if this was it, the relationship she'd been waiting for all her life. She told herself that it was just brain chemicals and pheremones that made her happy when she saw Natalie, and perhaps that was what it was; still, all she knew for sure was that she smiled when she saw Natalie, and that when they were together she felt comfortable and comforted.

'This paper,' said Natalie, 'has another one of those articles in it. "Is America Changing?"'

'Well, is it?'

'They don't say. They say that maybe it is, but they don't know how and they don't know why, and maybe it isn't happening at all.'

Sam smiled broadly. 'Well,' she said, 'That covers every option, doesn't it?'

'I guess.' Natalie's brow creased and she went back to her newspaper.

Sam washed the dishcloth and folded it. 'I think it's just that, despite the government and whatever, everything just feels suddenly good right now. Maybe it's just spring coming a little early. It was a long winter, and I'm glad it's over.'

'Me too.' A pause. 'It says in the article that lots of people have been reporting weird dreams. I haven't really had any weird dreams. Nothing weirder than normal.'

Sam looked around to see if there was anything she had missed.

Nope. It was a good job well done. She took off her apron, hung it back in the kitchen. Then she came back and started to turn off the lights. 'I've had some weird dreams recently,' she said. 'They got weird enough that I actually started keeping a dream journal. I write them down when I wake up. But when I read them, they don't mean anything at all.'

She put on her street coat, and her one-size-fits-all woollen gloves.

'I did some dream work,' said Natalie. Natalie had done a little of everything, from arcane self-defense disciplines and sweat lodges to feng shui and jazz dancing. 'Tell me. I'll tell you what they mean.'

'Okay.' Sam unlocked the door and turned the last of the lights off. She let Natalie out, and she walked out onto the street and locked the door to the Coffee House firmly behind her. 'Sometimes I have been dreaming of people who fell from the sky. Sometimes I'm underground, talking to a woman with a buffalo head. And some-times I dream about this guy I kissed in a bar last month.'

Natalie made a noise. 'Something you should have told me about?'

'Maybe. But not like that. It was a Fuck Off Kiss.'

'You were telling him to fuck off?'

'No, I was telling everyone else they could fuck off. You had to be there, I guess.'

Natalie's shoes clicked down the sidewalk. Sam padded on next to her. 'He owns my car,' said Sam.

'That purple thing you got at your sister's?'

'Yup.'

'What happened to him? Why doesn't he want his car?'

'I don't know. Maybe he's in prison. Maybe he's dead.'

'Dead?'

'I guess.' Sam hesitated. 'A few weeks back, I was certain he was dead. ESP. Or whatever. Like, I knew. But then, I started to think maybe he wasn't. I don't know. I guess my ESP isn't that hot.'

'How long are you going to keep his car?'

'Until someone comes for it. I think it's what he would have wanted.'

Natalie looked at Sam, then she looked again. Then she said, 'Where did you get *those* from?'

'What?'

'The flowers. The ones you're *holding*, Sam. Where did they come from? Did you have them when we left the Coffee House? I would have seen them.'

Sam looked down. Then she grinned. 'You are so sweet. I should have said something when you gave them to me, shouldn't I?' she said. 'They are lovely. Thank you so much. But wouldn't red have been more appropriate?'

They were roses, their stems wrapped in paper. Six of them, and white.

'I didn't give them to you,' said Natalie, her lips firming.

And neither of them said another word until they reached the movie theatre.

When she got home that night Sam put the roses in an improvised vase. Later, she cast them in bronze, and she kept to herself the tale of how she got them, although she told Caroline, who came after Natalie, the story of the ghost-roses one night when they were both very drunk, and Caroline agreed with Sam that it was a really, really strange and spooky story, and, deep down, did not actually believe a word of it, so that was all right.

Shadow had parked near a payphone. He called information, and they gave him the number.

No, he was told. She isn't here. She's probably still at the Coffee House.

He stopped on the way to the Coffee House to buy flowers.

He found the Coffee House, then he crossed the road and stood in the doorway of a used bookstore, and waited, and watched.

The place closed at eight, and at ten past eight Shadow saw Sam Black Crow walk out of the Coffee House in the company of a smaller woman whose pigtailed hair was a peculiar shade of red. They were holding hands tightly, as if simply holding hands could keep the world at bay, and they were talking – or rather, Sam was doing most of the talking while her friend listened. Shadow wondered what Sam was saying. She smiled as she talked.

The two women crossed the road, and they walked past the place where Shadow was standing. The pigtailed girl passed within a foot of him; he could have reached out and touched her, and they didn't see him at all.

He watched them walking away from him down the street, and felt a pang, like a minor chord being played inside him.

It had been a good kiss, Shadow reflected, but Sam had never looked at him the way she was looking at the pigtailed girl, and she never would.

'What the hell. We'll always have Peru,' he said, under his breath, as Sam walked away from him. 'And El Paso. We'll always have that.'

Then he ran after her, and put the flowers into Sam's hands. He hurried away, so she could not give them back.

Then he walked up the hill, back to his car, and he followed the signs to Chicago. He drove at or slightly under the speed limit.

It was the last thing he had to do.

He was in no hurry.

Shadow spent the night in a Motel 6. He got up the next morning, and realised his clothes still smelled like the bottom of the lake. He put them on anyway. He figured he wouldn't need them much longer.

Shadow paid his bill. He drove to the brownstone apartment building. He found it without any difficulty. It was smaller than he remembered.

He walked up the stairs steadily, not fast, that would have meant he was eager to go to his death, and not slow, that would have meant he was afraid. Someone had cleaned the stairwell: the black garbage bags had gone. The place smelled of the chlorine-smell of bleach, no longer of rotting vegetables.

The red-painted door at the top of the stairs was wide open: the smell of old meals hung in the air. Shadow hesitated, then he pressed the doorbell.

'I come!' called a woman's voice, and, dwarf-small and dazzlingly blonde, Zorya Utrennyaya came out of the kitchen and bustled towards him, wiping her hands on her apron. She looked different, Shadow realised. She looked happy. Her cheeks were rouged red, and there was a sparkle in her old eyes. When she saw him her mouth became an O and she called out 'Shadow? You came back to us?' and she hurried toward him with her arms outstretched. He bent down and embraced her, and she kissed his cheek. 'So good to see you!' she said. 'Now you must go away.'

Shadow stepped into the apartment. All the doors in the apartment (except, unsurprisingly, Zorya Polunochnaya's) were wide open, and all the windows he could see were open as well. A gentle breeze blew fitfully through the corridor.

'You're spring cleaning,' he said to Zorya Utrennyaya.

'We have a guest coming,' she told him. 'Now, you must go away. First, you want coffee?'

'I came to see Czernobog,' said Shadow. 'It's time.'

Zorya Utrennyaya shook her head violently. 'No, no,' she said. 'You *don't* want to see him. Not a good idea.'

'I know,' said Shadow. 'But you know, the only thing I've really learned about dealing with gods is that if you make a deal, you keep it. They get to break all the rules they want. We don't. Even if I tried to walk out of here, my feet would just bring me back.'

She pushed up her bottom lip, then said, 'Is true. But go today. Come back tomorrow. He will be gone then.'

'Who is it?' called a woman's voice, from further down the corridor. 'Zorya Utrennyaya, to who are you talking? This mattress, I cannot turn on my own, you know.'

Shadow walked down the corridor, and said 'Good morning, Zorya Vechernyaya. Can I help?' which made the woman in the room squeak with surprise and drop her corner of the mattress.

The bedroom was thick with dusk: it covered every surface, the wood and the glass, and motes of it floated and danced through the beams of sunshine coming through the open window, disturbed by occasional breezes and the lazy flapping of the yellowed lace curtains.

He remembered this room. This was the room they had given to Wednesday, that night. Bielebog's room.

Zorya Vechernyaya eyed him uncertainly. 'The mattress,' she said. 'It needs to be turned.'

'Not a problem,' said Shadow. He reached out and took the mattress, lifted it with ease and turned it over. It was an old wooden bed, and the feather mattress weighed almost as much as a man. Dust flew and swirled as the mattress went down.

'Why are you here?' asked Zorya Vechernyaya. It was not a friendly question, the way she asked it.

'I'm here,' said Shadow, 'because back in December a young man played a game of checkers with an old god, and he lost.'

The old woman's grey hair was up on the top of her head in a tight bun. She pursed her lips. 'Come back tomorrow,' said Zorya Vechernyaya.

'I can't,' he said, simply.

'Is your funeral. Now, you go and sit down. Zorya Utrennyaya will bring you coffee. Czernobog will be back soon.'

Shadow walked along the corridor to the sitting room. It was just as he remembered, although now the window was open. The grey cat slept on the arm of the sofa. It opened an eye as Shadow came in and then, unimpressed, it went back to sleep.

This was where he had played checkers with Czernobog; this was where he had wagered his life to get the old man to join them on Wednesday's last doomed grift. The fresh air gusted in through the open window, blowing the stale air away.

Zorya Utrennyaya came in with a red wooden tray. A small enameled cup of steaming black coffee sat on the tray, beside a saucer filled with small chocolate-chip cookies. She put it down on the table in front of him.

'I saw Zorya Polunochnaya again,' he said. 'She came to me under the world, and she gave me the moon to light my way. And she took something from me. But I don't remember what.'

'She likes you,' said Zorya Utrennyaya. 'She dreams so much. And she guards us all. She is so brave.'

'Where's Czernobog?'

'He says the spring-cleaning makes him uncomfortable. He goes out to buy newspaper, sit in the park. Buy cigarettes. Perhaps he will not come back today. You do not have to wait. Why don't you go? Come back tomorrow.'

'I'll wait,' said Shadow. There was no magic forcing him to wait, he knew that. This was *him*. It was one last thing that needed to happen, and if it was *the* last thing that happened, well, he was going there of his own volition. After this there would be no more obligations, no more mysteries, no more ghosts.

He sipped the hot coffee, as black and as sweet as he remembered.

He heard a deep male voice in the corridor, and he sat up straighter. He was pleased to see that his hand was not trembling. The door opened.

'Shadow?'

'Hi,' said Shadow. He stayed sitting down.

Czernobog walked into the room. He was carrying a folded copy of the *Chicago Sun-Times*, which he put down on the coffee table. He stared at Shadow, then he put his hand out, tentatively. The two men shook hands.

'I came,' said Shadow. 'Our deal. You came through with your part of it. This is my part.'

Czernobog nodded. His brow creased. The sunlight glinted on his grey hair and moustache, making them appear almost golden. 'Is . . .' He frowned. 'Is not . . .' He broke off. 'Maybe you should go. Is not a good time.'

'Take as long as you need,' said Shadow. 'I'm ready.'

Czernobog sighed. 'You are a very stupid boy. You know that?'

'I guess.'

'You are a stupid boy. And on the mountaintop, you did a very good thing.'

'I did what I had to do.'

'Perhaps.'

Czernobog walked to the old wooden sideboard, and, bending down, pulled an attache case from underneath it. He flipped the catches on the case. Each one sprang back with a satisfying thump. He opened the case. He took a hammer out, and hefted it, experimentally. The hammer looked like a scaled down sledgehammer; its wooden haft was stained.

Then he stood up. He said, 'I owe you much. More than you know. Because of you, things are changing. This is spring time. The true spring.'

'I know what I did,' said Shadow. 'I didn't have a lot of choice.'

Czernobog nodded. There was a look in his eyes that Shadow did not remember seeing before. 'Did I ever tell you about my brother?'

'Bielebog?' Shadow walked to the centre of the ash-stained carpet. He went down on his knees. 'You said you hadn't seen him in a long time.'

'Yes,' said the old man, raising the hammer. 'It has been a long winter, boy. A very long winter. But the winter is ending, now.' And he shook his head, slowly, as if he were remembering something. And he said, 'Close your eyes.'

Shadow closed his eyes and raised his head, and he waited.

The head of the sledgehammer was cold, icy cold, and it touched his forehead as gently as a kiss.

'*Pock*! There,' said Czernobog. 'Is done.' There was a smile on his face that Shadow had never seen before, an easy, comfortable smile, like sunshine on a summer's day. The old man walked over to the case, and he put the hammer away, and closed the bag, and pushed it back under the sideboard.

'Czernobog?' asked Shadow. Then, '*Are* you Czernobog?'

'Yes. For today,' said the old man. 'By tomorrow, it will all be Bielebog. But today, is still Czernobog.'

'Then why? Why didn't you kill me when you could?'

The old man took out an unfiltered cigarette from a packet in his pocket. He took a large box of matches from the mantelpiece and lit the cigarette with a match. He seemed deep in thought. 'Because,' said the old man, after some time, 'there is blood. But there is also gratitude. And it has been a long, long winter.'

Shadow got to his feet. There were dusty patches on the knees of his jeans, where he had knelt, and he brushed the dust away.

'Thanks,' he said.

'You're welcome,' said the old man. 'Next time you want to play checkers, you know where to find me. *This* time, I play white.'

'Thanks. Maybe I will,' said Shadow. 'But not for a while.' He looked into the old man's twinkling eyes, and he wondered if they had always been that cornflower shade of blue. They shook hands, and neither of them said goodbye.

Shadow kissed Zorya Utrennyaya on the cheek on his way out, and he kissed Zorya Vechernyaya on the back of her hand, and he took the stairs out of that place two at a time.

Postscript

Reykjavik in Iceland is a strange city, even for those who have seen many strange cities. It is a volcanic city – the heat for the city comes from deep underground.

There are tourists, but not as many of them as you might expect, not even in early July. The sun was shining, as it had shone for weeks now: it ceased shining for an hour or two in the small hours of the morning. There would be a dusky dawn of sorts between two and three in the morning, and then the day would begin once more.

The big tourist had walked most of Reykjavik that morning, listening to people talk in a language that had changed little in a thousand years. The natives here could read the ancient sagas as easily as they could read a newspaper. There was a sense of continuity on this island that scared him, and that he found desperately reassuring. He was very tired: the unending daylight had made sleep almost impossible, and he had sat in his hotel room through the whole long nightless night alternately reading a guidebook and *Bleak House*, a novel he had bought in an airport in the last few weeks, but which airport he could no longer remember. Sometimes he had stared out of the window.

Finally the clock as well as the sun proclaimed it morning.

He bought a bar of chocolate at one of the many candy stores, walked the sidewalk, occasionally finding himself reminded of the volcanic nature of Iceland: he would turn a corner and notice, for a moment, a sulphurous quality to the air. It put him in mind not of Hades but of rotten eggs.

Many of the women he passed were very beautiful: slender and pale. The kind of women that Wednesday had liked. Shadow wondered what could have attracted Wednesday to Shadow's mother, who had been beautiful, but had been neither of those things.

Shadow smiled at the pretty women, because they made him feel pleasantly male, and he smiled at the other women too, because he was having a good time.

He was not sure when he became aware that he was being observed. Somewhere on his walk through Reykjavik he became certain that someone was watching him. He would turn, from time to time, trying to get a glimpse of who it was, and he would stare into store windows and out at the reflected street behind him, but he saw no-one out of the ordinary, no-one who seemed to be observing him.

He went into a small restaurant, where he ate smoked puffin and cloudberries and arctic char and boiled potatoes, and he drank Coca-Cola, which tasted sweeter, more sugary than he remembered it tasting back in the States.

When the waiter brought his bill, he said, 'Excuse me. You are American?'

'Yes.'

'Then, happy fourth of July,' said the waiter. He looked pleased with himself.

Shadow had not realised that it was the fourth. Independence Day. Yes. He liked the idea of independence. He left the money and a tip on the table, and walked outside. There was a cool breeze coming in off the Atlantic, and he buttoned up his coat.

He sat down on a grassy bank and looked at the city that surrounded him, and thought, one day he would have to go home. And one day he would have to make a home to go back to. He wondered whether home was a thing that happened to a place after a while; or if it was something that you found in the end, if you simply walked and waited and willed it long enough.

An old man came striding across the hillside toward him: he wore a dark grey cloak, ragged at the bottom, as if he had done a lot of travelling, and he wore a broad-brimmed blue hat, with a seagull feather tucked into the band at a jaunty angle. He looked like an ageing hippie, thought Shadow. Or a long-retired gunfighter. The old man was ridiculously tall.

The man squatted beside Shadow on the hillside. He nodded, curtly, to Shadow. He had a piratical black eyepatch over one eye, and a jutting white chin-beard. Shadow wondered if the man was going to hit him up for a cigarette.

'*Hvernig gengur? Manst þú eftir mér?*' said the old man.

'I'm sorry,' said Shadow. 'I don't speak Icelandic.' Then he said, awkwardly, the phrase he had learned from his phrase book in the daylight of the small hours of that morning: '*Ég tala bara ensku.*' *I speak only English.* And then, 'American.'

The old man nodded slowly. He said, 'My people went from here to America a long time ago. They went there, and then they returned to Iceland. They said it was a good place for men, but a bad place for gods. And without their gods they felt too . . . alone.' His English was fluent, but the pauses and the beats of the sentence were strange. Shadow looked at him: close-up, the man seemed older than Shadow had imagined possible. His skin was lined with tiny wrinkles and cracks, like the cracks in granite.

The old man said, 'I do know you, boy.'

'You do?'

'You and I, we have walked the same path. I also hung on the tree for nine days, a sacrifice of myself to myself. I am the lord of the Aes. I am the god of the gallows.'

'You are Odin,' said Shadow.

The man nodded thoughtfully, as if weighing up the name. 'They call me many things, but, yes, I am Odin, Bor's son', he said.

'I saw you die,' said Shadow. 'I stood vigil for your body. You tried to destroy so much, for power. You would have sacrificed so much for yourself. You did that.'

'I did not do that.'

'Wednesday did. He was you.'

'He was me, yes. But I am not him.'

The man scratched the side of his nose. His gull-feather bobbed. 'Will you go back?' asked the Lord of the Gallows. 'To America?'

'Nothing to go back for,' said Shadow, and as he said it he knew it was a lie.

'Things wait for you there,' said the old man. 'But they will wait until you return.'

A white butterfly flew crookedly past them. Shadow said nothing.

He had had enough of gods and their ways to last him several life-times. He would take the bus to the airport, he decided, and change his ticket. Get a plane to somewhere he had never been. He would keep moving.

'Hey,' said Shadow. 'I have something for you.' His hand dipped into his pocket, and palmed the object he needed. 'Hold your hand out,' he said.

Odin looked at him strangely and seriously. Then he shrugged, and extended his right hand, palm down. Shadow reached over and turned it so the palm was upward.

He opened his own hands, showed them, one after the other, to be completely empty. Then he pushed the glass eye into the leathery palm of the old man's hand and left it there.

'How did you do that?'

'Magic,' said Shadow, without smiling.

The old man grinned and laughed and clapped his hands together. He looked at the eye, holding it between finger and thumb, and nodded, as if he knew exactly what it was, and then he slipped it into a leather bag that hung by his waist. '*Takk kærlega*. I shall take care of this.'

'You're welcome,' said Shadow. He stood up, brushed the grass from his jeans.

'Again,' said the Lord of Asgard, with an imperious motion of his head, his voice deep and commanding. 'More. Do again.'

'You people,' said Shadow. 'You're never satisfied. Okay. This is one I learned from a guy who's dead now.'

He reached into nowhere, and took a gold coin from the air. It was a normal sort of gold coin. It couldn't bring back the dead or heal the sick, but it was a gold coin sure enough.

'And that's all there is,' he said, displaying it between finger and thumb. 'That's all she wrote.'

He tossed the coin into the air with a flick of his thumb.

It spun golden at the top of its arc, in the sunlight, and it glittered and glinted and hung there in the midsummer sky as if it was never going to come down. Maybe it never would. Shadow didn't wait to see. He walked away and he kept on walking.

Acknowledgments:

It's been a long book, and a long journey, and I owe many people a great deal.

Mrs Hawley lent me her Florida house to write in, and all I had to do in return was scare away the vultures. She lent me her Irish house to finish it in, and cautioned me not to scare away the ghosts. My thanks to her and Mr Hawley for all their kindness and generosity. Jonathan and Jane lent me their house and hammock to write in, and all I had to do was fish the occasional peculiar Floridian beastie out of the lizard pool. I'm very grateful to them all.

Dan Johnson, M.D., gave me medical information whenever I needed it, pointed out stray and unintentional anglicisms (everybody else did this as well), answered the oddest questions, and, one July day, even flew me around northern Wisconsin in a tiny plane. In addition to keeping my life going by proxy while I wrote this book, my assistant, the fabulous Lorraine Garland, became very blasé about finding out the population of small American towns for me; I'm still not sure quite how she did it. (She's part of a girl group called the Flash Girls: buy their new record, *Play Each Morning, Wild Queen*, and make her happy.) Terry Pratchett helped unlock a knotty plot point for me on the train to Gothenburg. Eric Edelman answered my diplomatic questions. Anna Sunshine Ison unearthed a bunch of stuff for me on the West Coast Japanese internment camps, which will have to wait for another book to be written, for it never quite fitted into this one. I took the best line of dialogue in the epilogue from Gene Wolfe, to whom, my thanks. Sergeant Kathy Ertz graciously answered even my weirdest police procedural questions and Deputy Sheriff Marshall Multhauf took me on a drive-along. Pete Clark submitted to some ridiculously personal questioning with grace and good humor. Dale Robertson was the book's consulting hydrologist. I appreciated Dr Jim Miller's comments about people, language and fish, as I did the linguistic help of Margret Rodas. Jamy Ian Swiss made sure that the coin magic was magical. Any mistakes in the book are mine, not theirs.

Many good people read the manuscript and offered valuable suggestions, corrections, encouragement, and information. I am especially grateful to Colin Greenland and Susanna Clarke, John Clute, and Samuel R. Delany. I'd also like to thank Owl Goingback (who really does have the world's coolest name), Iselin Røsjø Evensen, Peter Straub, Jonathan Carroll, Kelli Bickman, Dianna Graf, Lenny Henry, Pete Atkins, Amy Horsting, Chris Ewen, Teller, Kelly Link, Barb Gilly, Will Shetterly, Connie Zastoupil, Rantz Hoseley, Diana Schutz, Steve Brust, Kelly Sue DeConnick, Roz Kaveney, Ian McDowell, Karen Berger, Wendy Japhet, Terje Nordberg, Gwenda Bond, Therese Littleton, Lou Aronica, Hy Bender, Mark Askwith, Alan Moore (who graciously lent me *Litvinoff's Book*), and the original Joe Sanders. Thanks also go to Rebecca Wilson, and particular thanks to Stacy Weiss, for her insight. After she read the first draft Diana Wynne Jones warned me what kind of book this was, and the perils I risked writing it, and she's been right on every count so far.

I wish Professor Frank McConnell were still with us. I think he would have enjoyed this one.

Once I'd written the first draft I realized that a number of other people had tackled these themes before ever I got to them: in particular my favourite unfashionable author, James Branch Cabell; the late Roger Zelazny; and, of course, the inimitable Harlan Ellison in his collection *Deathbird Stories*, which burned itself onto the back of my head when I was still of an age where a book could change me forever.

I can never quite see the point of noting down for posterity the music you listened to while writing a book, and there was an awful lot of music listened to while I was writing this. Still, without Greg Brown's *Dream Café* and the Magnetic Fields' *69 Love Songs* it would have been a different book, so thanks to Greg and to Stephin. And

I feel it my duty to tell you that you can experience the music of the House on the Rock on tape or CD, including that of the Mikado machine and of the World's Largest Carousel. It's unlike, although certainly not better than, anything else you've heard. Write to: The House on the Rock, Spring Green, WI 53588 USA, or telephone them in the U.S. on 608-935-3639.

My agents – Merrilee Heifetz at Writers House, Jon Levin and Erin Culley La Chapelle at CAA – were invaluable as sounding boards and pillars of wisdom.

Many people, who were waiting for things I had promised them just as soon as I finished writing this book, were astonishingly patient. I'd like to thank the good folk at Warner Brothers pictures (particularly Kevin McCormick and Lorenzo di Bonaventura), at Village Roadshow, at Sunbow, and at Miramax; and Shelly Bond, who put up with a lot.

The two people without whom: Jennifer Hershey at Harper Collins in the US and Doug Young at Hodder Headline in the UK. I'm lucky to have good editors, and these are two of the best editors I've known. Not to mention two of the most uncomplaining, patient and, as the deadlines whirled past us like dry leaves in a gust of wind, positively stoic.

Bill Massey came in at the end, at Headline, and lent the book his editorial eagle eye. Kelly Notaras helped shepherd it through production with grace and aplomb.

Lastly, I want to thank my family, Mary, Mike, Holly, and Maddy, who were the most patient of all, who loved me, and who, for long periods during the writing of this book, put up with my going away both to write and to find America – which, turned out, when I eventually found it, to have been in America all along.

Neil Gaiman
near Kinsale, County Cork
15 January 2001

Anansi Boys

Dedication

You know how it is. You pick up a book, flip to the dedication, and find that, once again, the author has dedicated a book to someone else and not to you.

Not this time.

Because we haven't yet met/have only a glancing acquaintance/ are just crazy about each other/haven't seen each other in much too long/are in some way related/will never meet, but will, I trust, despite that, always think fondly of each other . . .

This one's for you.

With you know what, and you probably know why.

Note: the author would like to take this opportunity to tip his hat respectfully to the ghosts of Zora Neale Hurston, Thorne Smith, P. G. Wodehouse, and Frederick 'Tex' Avery.

Chapter One

Which Is Mostly about Names and Family Relationships

I t begins, as most things begin, with a song.

In the beginning, after all, were the words, and they came with a tune. That was how the world was made, how the void was divided, how the lands and the stars and the dreams and the little gods and the animals, how all of them came into the world.

They were sung.

The great beasts were sung into existence, after the Singer had done with the planets and the hills and the trees and the oceans and the lesser beasts. The cliffs that bound existence were sung, and the hunting grounds, and the dark.

Songs remain. They last. The right song can turn an emperor into a laughing stock, can bring down dynasties. A song can last long after the events and the people in it are dust and dreams and gone. That's the power of songs.

There are other things you can do with songs. They do not only make worlds or recreate existence. Fat Charlie Nancy's father, for example, was simply using them to have what he hoped and expected would be a marvellous night out.

Before Fat Charlie's father had come into the bar, the barman had been of the opinion that the whole karaoke evening was going to be an utter bust; but then the little old man had sashayed into the room, walked past the table of several blonde women with the fresh sunburns and smiles of tourists who were sitting by the little makeshift stage in the corner. He had tipped his hat to them, for he wore a hat, a spotless green fedora, and lemon-yellow gloves, and then he walked over to their table. They giggled.

'Are you enjoyin' yourselves, ladies?' he asked.

They continued to giggle and told him they were having a good time, thank you, and that they were here on vacation. He said to them, it gets better, just you wait.

He was older than they were, much, much older, but he was charm itself, like something from a bygone age when fine manners and courtly gestures were worth something. The barman relaxed. With someone like this in the bar, it was going to be a good evening.

There was karaoke. There was dancing. The old man got up to sing, on the makeshift stage, not once, that evening, but twice. He had a fine voice, and an excellent smile, and feet that twinkled when he danced. The first time he got up to sing, he sang 'What's New Pussycat?' The second time he got up to sing, he ruined Fat Charlie's life.

* * *

Fat Charlie was only ever fat for a handful of years, from shortly before the age of ten, which was when his mother announced to the world that if there was one thing she was over and done with (and if the gentleman in question had any argument with it he could just stick it you know where) it was her marriage to the elderly goat that she had made the unfortunate mistake of marrying and she would be leaving in the morning for somewhere a long way away and he had better not try to follow, to the age of fourteen, when Fat Charlie grew a bit and exercised a little more. He was not fat. Truth to tell, he was not really even chubby, simply slightly soft-looking around the edges. But the name Fat Charlie clung to him, like chewing gum to the sole of a tennis shoe. He would introduce himself as Charles, or, in his early twenties, Chaz, or, in writing, as C. Nancy, but it was no use: the name would creep in, infiltrating the new part of his life just as cockroaches invade the cracks and the world behind the fridge in a new kitchen, and like it or not – and he didn't – he would be Fat Charlie again.

It was, he knew, irrationally, because his father had given him the nickname, and when his father gave things names, they stuck.

There was a dog who had lived in the house across the way, in the Florida street on which Fat Charlie had grown up. It was a chestnut-coloured boxer, long-legged and pointy-eared, with a face that looked like the beast had, as a puppy, run face-first into a wall. Its head was raised, its tail-nub erect. It was, unmistakably, an aristocrat amongst canines. It had entered dog shows. It had rosettes for Best of Breed, and for Best in Class, and even one rosette marked Best in Show. This dog rejoiced in the name of Campbell's Macinrory Arbuthnot the Seventh, and its owners, when they were feeling familiar, called it Kai. This lasted until the day that Fat Charlie's father, sitting out on their dilapidated porch-swing, sipping his beer, noticed the dog as it ambled back and forth across the neighbour's yard, on a leash that ran from a palm tree to a fence-post.

'Hell of a goofy dog,' said Fat Charlie's father. 'Like that friend of Donald Duck's. Hey, Goofy.'

And what once had been Best in Show suddenly slipped and shifted. For Fat Charlie, it was as if he saw the dog through his father's eyes, and darned if he *wasn't* a pretty goofy dog, all things considered. Almost rubbery.

It didn't take long for the name to spread up and down the street. Campbell's Macinrory Arbuthnot the Seventh's owners struggled with it, but they might as well have stood their ground and argued with a hurricane. Total strangers would pat the once-proud boxer's head, and say, 'Hello, Goofy. How's a boy?' The dog's owners stopped entering him in dog shows soon after that. They didn't have the heart. 'Goofy-looking dog,' said the judges.

Fat Charlie's father's names for things stuck. That was just how it was.

That was far from the worst thing about Fat Charlie's father.

There had been, during the years that Fat Charlie was growing up, a number of candidates for the worst thing about his father: his roving eye and equally as adventurous fingers, at least according to the young ladies of the area, who would complain to Fat Charlie's mother, and then there would be trouble; the little black cigarillos, which he called cheroots, which he smoked, the smell of which clung to everything he touched; his fondness for a peculiar shuffling form of tap-dancing only ever fashionable, Fat Charlie suspected, for half an hour in Harlem in the 1920s; his total and invincible ignorance about current world affairs, combined with his apparent conviction that sitcoms were half-hour-long insights into the lives and struggles of real people. None of these, individually, as far as Fat Charlie was concerned, was the worst thing about Fat Charlie's father, although each of them had contributed to the worst thing.

The worst thing about Fat Charlie's father was simply this: he was embarrassing.

Of course, everyone's parents are embarrassing. It goes with the territory. The nature of parents is to embarrass merely by existing, just as it is the nature of children of a certain age to cringe with embarrassment, shame and mortification should their parents so much as speak to them on the street.

Fat Charlie's father, of course, had elevated this to an art form, and he rejoiced in it, just as he rejoiced in practical jokes, from the simple – Fat Charlie would never forget the first time he had climbed into an apple-pie bed – to the unimaginably complex.

'Like what?' asked Rosie, Fat Charlie's fiancée, one evening, when Fat Charlie, who normally did not talk about his father, had attempted, stumblingly, to explain why he believed that simply inviting his father to their upcoming wedding would be a horrendously bad idea. They were in a small wine bar in South London at the time. Fat Charlie had long been of the opinion that four thousand miles and the Atlantic Ocean were both good things to keep between himself and his father.

'Well . . .' said Fat Charlie, and he remembered a parade of indignities, each one of which made his toes curl involuntarily. He settled upon one of them. 'Well, when I changed schools, when I was a kid, my dad made a point of telling me how much he had always looked forward to Presidents' Day, when he was a boy, because it's the law that on Presidents' Day, the kids who go to school dressed as their favourite presidents get a big bag of candy.'

'Oh. That's a nice law,' said Rosie. 'I wish we had something like that in England.' Rosie had never been out of the UK, if you didn't count a Club 18-30 holiday to an island in, she was fairly certain, the Mediterranean. She had warm brown eyes and a good heart, even if geography was not her strongest suit.

'It's *not* a nice law,' said Fat Charlie. 'It's not a law at all. He made it up. Most states don't even have school on Presidents' Day, and even for the ones that do, there is no tradition of going to school on Presidents' Day dressed as your favourite president. Kids dressed as presidents do not get big bags of candy by an Act of Congress, nor is your popularity in the years ahead, all through middle school and high school, decided entirely by which president you decided to dress as – the average kids dress as the obvious presidents, the Lincolns and Washingtons and Jeffersons, but the ones who would become popular, they dressed as John Quincy Adams or Warren Gamaliel Harding, or someone like that. And it's bad luck to talk about it before the day. Or rather it isn't, but he said it was.'

'Boys *and* girls dress up as presidents?'

'Oh yes. Boys and girls. So I spent the week before Presidents' Day reading everything there was to read about presidents in the *World Book Encyclopedia*, trying to choose the right one.'

'Didn't you ever suspect that he was pulling your leg?'

Fat Charlie shook his head. 'It's not something you think about, when my dad starts to work you over. He's the finest liar you'll ever meet. He's convincing.'

Rosie took a sip of her Chardonnay. 'So which president did you go to school as?'

'Taft. He was the twenty-seventh president. I wore a brown suit my father had found somewhere, with the legs all rolled up and a pillow stuffed down the front. I had a painted-on moustache. My dad took me to school himself that day. I walked in so proudly. The other kids just screamed and pointed, and somewhere in there I locked myself in a cubicle in the boys' room and cried. They wouldn't let me go home to change. I went through the day like that. It was Hell.'

'You should have made something up,' said Rosie. 'You were going to a costume party afterwards or something. Or just told them the truth.'

'Yeah,' said Fat Charlie meaningfully and gloomily, remembering.

'What did your dad say, when you got home?'

'Oh, he hooted with laughter. Chuckled and chortled and, and chittered and all that. Then he told me that maybe they didn't do that Presidents' Day stuff any more. Now, why didn't we go down to the beach together and look for mermaids?'

'Look for . . . mermaids?'

'We'd go down to the beach, and walk along it, and he'd be as embarrassing as any human being on the face of this planet has ever been – he'd start singing, and he'd start doing a shuffling sort of sand-dance on the sand, and he'd just talk to people as he went – people he didn't even know, people he'd never met, and I hated it, except he told me there were mermaids out there in the Atlantic, and if I looked fast enough and sharp enough, I'd see one.

' "There!" he'd say. "Did you see her? She was a big ol' redhead, with a green tail." And I looked, and I looked, but I never did.'

He shook his head. Then he took a handful of mixed nuts from the bowl on the table and began to toss them into his mouth, chomping down on them as if each nut was a twenty-year-old indignity that could never be erased.

'Well,' said Rosie, brightly, 'I think he sounds lovely, a real character! We have to get him to come over for the wedding. He'd be the life and soul of the party.'

Which, Fat Charlie explained, after briefly choking on a Brazil nut, was really the last thing you wanted at your wedding, after all, wasn't it, your father turning up and being the life and soul of the party? He said that his father was, he had no doubt, still the most embarrassing person on God's Green Earth. He added that he was perfectly happy not to have seen the old goat for several years, and that the best thing his mother ever did was to leave his father and come to England to stay with her Aunt Alanna. He buttressed this by stating categorically that he was damned, double damned, and quite possibly even thrice damned if he was going to invite his father. In fact, said Fat Charlie in closing, the best thing about getting married was not having to invite his dad to their wedding.

And then Fat Charlie saw the expression on Rosie's face and the icy glint in her normally friendly eyes, and he corrected himself hurriedly, explaining that he meant the second-best, but it was already much too late.

'You'll just have to get used to the idea,' said Rosie. 'After all, a wedding is a marvellous opportunity for mending fences and building bridges. It's your opportunity to show him that there are no hard feelings.'

'But there *are* hard feelings,' said Fat Charlie. 'Lots.'

'Do you have an address for him?' asked Rosie. 'Or a phone number? You probably ought to phone him. A letter's a bit impersonal when your only son is getting married . . . you are his only son, aren't you? Does he have e-mail?'

'Yes. I'm his only son. I have no idea if he has e-mail or not. Probably not,' said Fat Charlie. Letters were good things, he thought. They could get lost in the post for a start.

'Well, you must have an address or a phone number.'

'I don't,' said Fat Charlie, honestly. Maybe his father had moved away. He could have left Florida and gone somewhere they didn't have telephones. Or addresses.

'Well,' said Rosie, sharply, 'who does?'

'Mrs Higgler,' said Fat Charlie, and all the fight went out of him.

Rosie smiled sweetly. 'And who is Mrs Higgler?' she asked.

'Friend of the family,' said Fat Charlie. 'When I was growing up, she used to live next door.'

He had spoken to Mrs Higgler several years earlier, when his mother was dying. He had, at his mother's request, telephoned Mrs Higgler to pass on the message to Fat Charlie's father, and to tell him to get in touch. And several days later there had been a message on Fat Charlie's answering machine, left while he was at work, in a voice that was unmistakably his father's, even if it did sound rather older, and a little drunk.

His father said that it was not a good time, and that business

affairs would be keeping him in America. And then he added
that, for everything, Fat Charlie's mother was a damn fine woman.
Several days later a vase of assorted flowers had been delivered to
the hospital ward. Fat Charlie's mother had snorted when she
read the card.

'Thinks he can get around me that easily?' she said. 'He's got
another think coming, I can tell you that.' But she had had the
nurse put the flowers in a place of honour by her bed, and,
several times since, had asked Fat Charlie if he had heard
anything about his father coming and visiting her before it was all
over.

Fat Charlie said he hadn't. He grew to hate the question, and his
answer, and the expression on her face when he told her that, no,
his father wasn't coming.

The worst day, in Fat Charlie's opinion, was the day that the
doctor, a gruff little man, had taken Fat Charlie aside and told him
that it would not be long now, that his mother was fading fast,
and it had become a matter of keeping her comfortable until the
end.

Fat Charlie had nodded, and gone in to his mother. She had
held his hand, and was asking him whether or not he had
remembered to pay her gas bill, when the noise began in the
corridor – a clashing, parping, stomping, rattling, brass and bass
and drum sort of noise, of the kind that tends not to be heard in
hospitals, where signs in the stairwells request quiet and the icy
glares of the nursing staff enforce it.

The noise was getting louder.

For one moment Fat Charlie thought it might be terrorists. His
mother, though, smiled weakly at the cacophony. 'Yellow bird,'
she whispered.

'What?' said Fat Charlie, scared that she had stopped making
sense.

' "Yellow Bird",' she said, louder and more firmly. 'It's what
they're playing.'

Fat Charlie went to the door, and looked out.

Coming down the hospital corridor, ignoring the protests of
nurses, the stares of patients in pyjamas and of their families, was
what appeared to be a very small New Orleans jazz band. There

was a saxophone, and a sousaphone and a trumpet. There was an enormous man with what looked like a double bass strung around his neck. There was a man with a bass drum, which he banged. And at the head of the pack, in a smart checked suit, wearing a fedora hat and lemon-yellow gloves, came Fat Charlie's father. He played no instrument, but was doing a soft-shoe shuffle along the polished linoleum of the hospital floor, lifting his hat to each of the medical staff in turn, shaking hands with anyone who got close enough to talk or to attempt to complain.

Fat Charlie bit his lip, and prayed to anyone who might be listening that the Earth would open and swallow him up, or failing that, that he might suffer a brief, merciful and entirely fatal heart attack. No such luck. He remained among the living, the brass band kept coming, his father kept dancing, and shaking hands, and smiling.

If there is any justice in the world, thought Fat Charlie, *my father will keep going down the corridor and he'll go straight past us and into the genito-urinary department*; however, there was no justice, and his father reached the door of the oncology ward and stopped.

'Fat Charlie,' he said, loudly enough that everyone in the ward – on that floor – in the hospital – was able to comprehend that this was someone who knew Fat Charlie. 'Fat Charlie, get out of the way. Your father is here.'

Fat Charlie got out of the way.

The band, led by Fat Charlie's father, snaked their way through the ward to Fat Charlie's mother's bed. She looked up at them as they approached, and she smiled.

' "Yellow Bird",' she said, weakly. 'It's my favourite song.'

'And what kind of man would I be if I forgot that?' asked Fat Charlie's father.

She shook her head slowly, and she reached out her hand and squeezed his hand in its lemon-yellow glove.

'Excuse me,' said a small white woman with a clipboard, 'are these people with you?'

'No,' said Fat Charlie, his cheeks heating up. 'They're not. Not really.'

'But that *is* your mother, isn't it?' said the woman, with a basilisk glance. 'I must ask you to make these people vacate the ward momentarily, and without incurring any further disturbance.'

Fat Charlie muttered.

'What was that?'

'I said, I'm pretty sure I can't make them do anything,' said Fat Charlie. He was consoling himself that things could not possibly get any worse, when his father took a plastic carrier bag from the drummer, and began producing cans of brown ale and handing them out, to his band, to the nursing staff, to the patients. Then he lit a cheroot.

'Excuse me,' said the woman with the clipboard, when she saw the smoke, and she launched herself across the room at Fat Charlie's father like a Scud missile with its watch on upside down.

Fat Charlie took that moment to slip away. It seemed the wisest course of action.

He sat at home that night, waiting for the phone to ring or for a knock on the door in much the same spirit that a man kneeling at the guillotine might wait for the blade to kiss his neck; still, the doorbell did not ring.

He barely slept, and slunk in to the hospital the following afternoon, prepared for the worst.

His mother, in her bed, looked happier and more comfortable than she had looked in months. 'He's gone back,' she told Fat Charlie, when he came in. 'He couldn't stay. I have to say, Charlie, I do wish you hadn't just gone like that. We wound up having a party here. We had a fine old time.'

Fat Charlie could think of nothing worse than having to attend a party in a cancer ward, thrown by his father with a jazz band. He didn't say anything.

'He's not a bad man,' said Fat Charlie's mother, with a twinkle in her eye. Then she frowned. 'Well, that's not exactly true. He's certainly not a good man. But he did me a power of good last night,' and she smiled a real smile and, for just a moment, looked young again.

The woman with the clipboard was standing in the doorway, and she crooked her finger at him. Fat Charlie beetled down the ward towards her, apologising before she was even properly within earshot. Her look, he realised, as he got closer to her, was no longer that of a basilisk with stomach cramps. Now she looked positively kittenish. 'Your father,' she said.

'I'm sorry,' said Fat Charlie. It was what he had always said, growing up, when his father was mentioned.

'No, no, no,' said the former basilisk. 'Nothing to apologise for. I was just wondering. Your father. In case we need to get in touch with him – we don't have a telephone number or an address on file. I should have asked him last night, but it completely got away from me.'

'I don't think he has a phone number,' said Fat Charlie. 'And the best way to find him is to go to Florida, and to drive up Highway A1A – that's the coast road that runs up most of the east of the state. In the afternoon you may find him fishing off a bridge. In the evening he'll be in a bar.'

'Such a charming man,' she said, wistfully. 'What does he do?'

'I told you. He says it's the miracle of the loafs and the fishes.'

She stared at him blankly, and he felt stupid. When his father said it, people would laugh. 'Um. Like in the Bible. The miracle of the loaves and the fishes. Dad used to say that he loafs and fishes, and it's a miracle that he still makes money. It was a sort of joke.'

A misty look. 'Yes. He told the funniest jokes.' She clucked her tongue, and once more was all business. 'Now, I need you back here at five-thirty.'

'Why?'

'To pick up your mother. And her belongings. Didn't Dr Johnson tell you we were discharging her?'

'You're sending her home?'

'Yes, Mr Nancy.'

'What about the, about the cancer?'

'It seems to have been a false alarm.'

Fat Charlie couldn't understand how it could have been a false alarm. Last week they'd been talking about sending his mother to a hospice. The doctor had been using phrases like 'weeks not months' and 'making her as comfortable as possible while we wait for the inevitable'.

Still, Fat Charlie came back at 5.30 and picked up his mother, who seemed quite unsurprised to learn that she was no longer dying. On the way home she told Fat Charlie that she would be using her life's savings to travel around the world.

'The doctors were saying I had three months,' she said. 'And I remember I thought, if I get out of this hospital bed then I'm going to see Paris and Rome and places like that. I'm going back to Barbados, and to Saint Andrews. I may go to Africa. And China. I like Chinese food.'

Fat Charlie wasn't sure what was going on, but whatever it was, he blamed his father. He accompanied his mother and a serious suitcase to Heathrow airport, and waved her goodbye at the International Departures gate. She was smiling hugely as she went through, clutching her passport and tickets, and she looked younger than he remembered her looking in many years.

She sent him postcards from Paris, and from Rome and from Athens, and from Lagos and Cape Town. Her postcard from Nanking told him that she certainly didn't like what passed for Chinese food in China, and that she couldn't wait to come back to London and eat *proper* Chinese food.

She died in her sleep, in a hotel in Williamstown, on the Caribbean island of Saint Andrews.

At the funeral, at a South London crematorium, Fat Charlie kept expecting to see his father: perhaps the old man would make an entrance at the head of a jazz band, or be followed down the aisle by a clown troupe or a half-dozen tricycle-riding cigar-puffing chimpanzees; even during the service Fat Charlie kept glancing back over his shoulder, towards the chapel door. But Fat Charlie's father was not there, only his mother's friends and distant relations, mostly big women in black hats, blowing their noses and dabbing at their eyes and shaking their heads.

It was during the final hymn, after the button had been pressed and Fat Charlie's mother had trundled off down the conveyor belt to her final reward, that Fat Charlie noticed a man of about his own age standing at the back of the chapel. It was not his father, obviously. It was someone he did not know, someone he might not even have noticed, at the back, in the shadows, had he not been looking for his father . . . and then there was the stranger, in an elegant black suit, his eyes lowered, his hands folded.

Fat Charlie let his glance linger a moment too long, and the stranger looked at Fat Charlie and flashed him a joyless smile of the kind that suggested that they were both in this together. It was not the kind of expression you see on the faces of strangers, but still, Fat Charlie could not place the man. He turned his face back to the front of the chapel. They sang 'Swing Low, Sweet Chariot', a song Fat Charlie was pretty sure his mother had always disliked, and the Reverend Wright invited them back to Fat Charlie's Great-Aunt Alanna's for something to eat.

There was nobody at his Great-Aunt Alanna's whom he did not already know. In the years since his mother had died, he had sometimes wondered about that stranger: who he was, why he was there. Sometimes Fat Charlie thought that he had simply imagined him . . .

'So,' said Rosie, draining her Chardonnay, 'you'll call your Mrs Higgler, and give her my mobile number. Tell her about the wedding and the date . . . that's a thought: do you think we should invite her?'

'We can if we like,' said Fat Charlie. 'I don't think she'll come. She's an old family friend. She knew my dad back in the Dark Ages.'

'Well, sound her out. See if we should send her an invitation.'

Rosie was a good person. There was in Rosie a little of the essence of Francis of Assisi, of Robin Hood, of Buddha and of Glinda the Good: the knowledge that she was about to bring together her true love and his estranged father gave her forthcoming wedding an extra dimension, she decided. It was no longer simply a wedding: it was now practically a humanitarian mission, and Fat Charlie had known Rosie long enough to know never to stand between his fiancée and her need to Do Good.

'I'll call Mrs Higgler tomorrow,' he said.

'Tell you what,' said Rosie, with an endearing wrinkle of her nose, 'call her tonight. It's not late in America, after all.'

Fat Charlie nodded. They walked out of the wine bar together, Rosie with a spring in her step, Fat Charlie like a man going to the gallows. He told himself not to be silly. After all, perhaps Mrs

Higgler had moved, or had her phone disconnected. It was possible. Anything was possible.

They went up to Fat Charlie's place, the upstairs half of a smallish house in Maxwell Gardens, just off the Brixton Road.

'What time is it in Florida?' Rosie asked.

'Late afternoon,' said Fat Charlie.

'Well. Go on then.'

'Maybe we should wait a bit. In case she's out.'

'And maybe we should call now, before she has her dinner.'

Fat Charlie found his old paper address book, and under H was a scrap of an envelope, in his mother's handwriting, with a telephone number on it and, beneath that, 'Callyanne Higgler'.

The phone rang and rang.

'She's not there,' he said to Rosie, but at that moment the phone at the other end was answered, and a female voice said 'Yes? Who is this?'

'Um. Is that Mrs Higgler?'

'Who is this?' said Mrs Higgler. 'If you're one of they damn telemarketers, you take me off your list right now or I sue. I know my rights.'

'No. It's me. Charles Nancy. I used to live next door to you.'

'Fat Charlie? If that don't beat all. I been looking for your number all this morning. I turn this place upside down, looking for it, and you think I could find it? What I think happen was I had it written in my old accounts book. Upside down I turn the place. And I say to myself, Callyanne, this is a good time to just pray and hope the Lord hear you and see you right, and I went down on my knees, well, my knees are not so good any more, so I just put my hands together, but anyway, I still don't find your number, but look at how you just phone me up, and that's even better from some points of view, particularly because I ain't made of money and I can't afford to go phoning no foreign countries even for something like this, although I was going to phone you, don't you worry, given the circumstances—'

And she stopped, suddenly, either to take a breath, or to take a sip from the huge mug of too-hot coffee she always carried in her left hand, and during the brief quiet Fat Charlie said, 'I want to ask my dad to come to my wedding. Getting married.' There was silence at the end of the line. 'It's not till the end of the year, though,' he said. Still silence. 'Her name's Rosie,' he added, helpfully. He was starting to wonder if they had been cut off; conversations with Mrs Higgler were normally somewhat one-sided affairs, often with her doing your lines for you, and here she was, letting him say three whole things uninterrupted. He decided to go for a fourth. 'You can come too if you want,' he said.

'Lord, Lord, Lord,' said Mrs Higgler. 'Nobody tell you?'

'Told me what?'

So she told him, at length and in detail, while he stood there and said nothing at all, and when she was done he said, 'Thank you, Mrs Higgler.' He wrote something down on a scrap of paper, then he said, 'Thanks. No, really, thanks,' again, and he put down the phone.

'Well?' asked Rosie. 'Have you got his number?'

Fat Charlie said, 'Dad won't be coming to the wedding.' Then he said, 'I have to go to Florida.' His voice was flat, and without emotion. He might have been saying, 'I have to order a new cheque book.'

'When?'

'Tomorrow.'

'Why?'

'Funeral. My dad's. He's dead.'

'Oh. I'm sorry. I'm so sorry.' She put her arms around him, and held him. He stood in her arms like a shop-window dummy. 'How did it, did he . . . was he ill?'

Fat Charlie shook his head. 'I don't want to talk about it,' he said.

And Rosie squeezed him tightly, and then she nodded, sympathetically, and let him go. She thought he was too over-come with grief to talk about it.

He wasn't. That wasn't it at all. He was too embarrassed.

* * *

There must be a hundred thousand respectable ways to die. Leaping off a bridge into a river to save a small child from drowning, for example, or being mown down in a hail of bullets while single-handedly storming a nest of criminals. Perfectly respectable ways to die.

Truth to tell, there were even some less-than-respectable ways to die that wouldn't have been so bad. Spontaneous human combustion, for example: it's medically dodgy and scientifically unlikely, but even so, people persist in going up in smoke, leaving nothing behind but a charred hand still clutching an unfinished cigarette. Fat Charlie had read about it in a magazine: he wouldn't have minded if his father had gone like that. Or even if he'd had a heart attack running down the street after the men who had stolen his beer money.

This is how Fat Charlie's father died.

He had arrived in the bar early, and had launched the karaoke evening by singing 'What's New Pussycat?', which song he had belted out, according to Mrs Higgler, who had not been there, in a manner that would have caused Tom Jones to be festooned in flung feminine undergarments, and which brought Fat Charlie's father a complimentary beer, courtesy of the several blonde tourists from Michigan who thought he was just about the cutest thing they'd ever seen.

'It was their fault,' said Mrs Higgler, bitterly, over the phone. 'They was en*cour*agin' him!' They were women who had squeezed into tube tops, and they had reddish too-much-sun-too-early tans, and they were all young enough to be his daughters.

So pretty soon he's down at their table, smoking his cheroots and hinting strongly that he was in army intelligence during the war, although he was careful not to say which war, and that he could kill a man in a dozen different ways with his bare hands without breaking a sweat.

Now he takes the bustiest and blondest of the tourists on a quick spin around the dance floor, such as it was, while one of her friends warbled 'Strangers in the Night' from the stage. He appeared to be having a fine time, although the tourist was somewhat taller than he was, and his grin was on a level with her bosom.

And then, the dance done, he announced it was his turn again, and, because if there was one thing you could say about Fat Charlie's father, it was that he was secure in his heterosexuality, he sang 'I Am What I Am' to the room, but particularly to the blondest tourist on the table just below him. He gave it everything he had. He had just got as far as explaining to anyone listening that as far as he was concerned his life would not actually be worth a damn unless he was able to tell everybody that he was what he was, when he made an odd face, pressed one hand to his chest, stretched the other hand out, and toppled, as slowly and as gracefully as a man could topple, off the makeshift stage and on to the blondest holidaymaker, and from her on to the floor.

'It was how he always would have wanted to go,' sighed Mrs Higgler.

And then she told Fat Charlie how his father had, with his final gesture, as he fell, reached out and grasped at something, which turned out to be the blonde tourist's tube top, so that at first some people thought he had made a lust-driven leap from the stage with the sole purpose of exposing the bosom in question, because there she was, screaming, with her breasts staring at the room, while the music for 'I Am What I Am' kept playing, only now without anyone singing.

When the onlookers realised what had actually happened they had two minutes' silence, and Fat Charlie's father was carried out and put into an ambulance while the blonde tourist had hysterics in the ladies' room.

It was the breasts that Fat Charlie couldn't get out of his head. In his mind's eye they followed him accusatively around the room, like the eyes in a painting. He kept wanting to apologise to a roomful of people he had never met. And the knowledge that his father would have found it hugely amusing simply added to Fat Charlie's mortification. It's worse when you're embarrassed about something you were not even there to see: your mind keeps embroidering the events, and going back to it and turning it over and over, and examining it from every side. Well, yours might not, but Fat Charlie's certainly did.

As a rule, Fat Charlie felt embarrassment in his teeth, and in the upper pit of his stomach. If something that even looked like it might be embarrassing was about to happen on his television screen Fat Charlie would leap up and turn it off. If that was not possible, say if other people were present, he would leave the room on some pretext and wait until the moment of embarrassment was sure to be over.

Fat Charlie lived in South London. He had arrived, at the age of ten, with an American accent, which he had been relentlessly teased about, and had worked very hard to lose, slowly extirpating the last of the soft consonants and rich Rs, while learning the correct use and placement of the word 'innit'. He had finally succeeded in losing his American accent for good as he had turned sixteen, just as his schoolfriends discovered that they needed very badly to sound like they came from the 'hood. Soon all of them except Fat Charlie sounded like people who wanted to sound like Fat Charlie had talked when he'd come to England in the first place, except that he could never have used language like that in public without his mum giving him a swift clout round the ear.

It was all in the voice.

Once the embarrassment over his father's method of passing began to fade, Fat Charlie just felt empty.

'I don't have any family,' he said to Rosie, almost petulantly.

'You've got me,' she said. That made Fat Charlie smile. 'And you've got my mum,' she added, which stopped the smile in its tracks. She kissed him on the cheek.

'You could stay over for the night,' he suggested. 'Comfort me, all that.'

'I could,' she agreed, 'but I'm not going to.'

Rosie was not going to sleep with Fat Charlie until they were married. She said it was her decision, and she had made it when she was fifteen; not that she had known Fat Charlie then, but she had decided. So she gave him another hug, a long one. And she said, 'You need to make your peace with your dad, you know.' And then she went home.

He spent a restless night, sleeping sometimes, then waking, and wondering, and falling back asleep again.

He was up at sunrise. When people got in to work he would ring his travel agent and ask about bereavement fares to Florida, and he would phone the Grahame Coats Agency and tell them that, due to a death in the family, he would have to take a few days off and yes, he knew it came out of his sick leave or his holiday time. But for now he was glad that the world was quiet.

He went along the corridor to the tiny spare room at the back of the house, and looked down into the gardens below. The dawn chorus had begun, and he could see blackbirds, and small hedge-hopping sparrows, a single spotted-breasted thrush in the boughs of a nearby tree. Fat Charlie thought that a world in which birds sang in the morning was a normal world, a sensible world, a world he didn't mind being a part of.

Later, when birds were something to be afraid of, Fat Charlie would still remember that morning as something good and something fine, but also as the place where it all started. Before the madness; before the fear.

Chapter Two

Which Goes into Some of the Things that Happen after Funerals

Fat Charlie puffed his way through the Memorial Garden of Rest, squinting at the Florida sunshine. Sweat stains were spreading across his suit, beginning with the armpits and the chest. Sweat began to pour down his face as he ran.

The Memorial Garden of Rest did, in fact, look very much like a garden, but a very odd garden, in which all the flowers were artificial and they grew from metal vases protruding from metal plaques set in the ground. Fat Charlie ran past a sign. 'FREE Burial Space for all Honorably Discharged Veterans!' it said. He ran through Babyland, where multicoloured windmills and sodden blue and pink teddy bears joined the artificial flowers on the Florida turf. A mouldering Winnie-the-Pooh stared up wanly at the blue sky.

Fat Charlie could see the funeral party now, and he changed direction, finding a path that allowed him to run towards it. There were thirty people, perhaps more, standing around the grave. The women wore dark dresses, and big black hats trimmed with black lace, like fabulous flowers. The men wore suits without sweat stains. The children looked solemn. Fat Charlie slowed his pace to a respectful walk, still trying to hurry without moving fast enough for anyone to notice that he was in fact hurrying, and, having reached the group of mourners, he attempted to edge his way to the front ranks without attracting too much attention. Seeing that by now he was panting like a walrus who had just had to tackle a flight of stairs, was dripping with sweat, and trod on several feet as he went by, this attempt proved a failure.

There were glares, which Fat Charlie tried to pretend he did not notice. Everyone was singing a song that Fat Charlie did not know. He moved his head in time with the song and tried to make it look as if he was sort of singing, moving his lips in a way that might have meant that he was actively singing along, *sotto voce*, and he might have been muttering a prayer under his breath, and it might just have been random lip motion. He took the opportunity to look down at the casket. He was pleased to see that it was closed.

The casket was a glorious thing, made of what looked like heavy-duty, reinforced steel, gun-metal grey. In the event of the glorious resurrection, thought Fat Charlie, when Gabriel blows his mighty horn and the dead escape their coffins, his father was going to be stuck in his grave, banging away futilely at the lid, wishing that he had been buried with a crowbar and possibly an oxyacetylene torch.

A final, deeply melodic hallelujah faded away. In the silence that followed, Fat Charlie could hear someone shouting at the other end of the memorial gardens, back near where he had come in.

The preacher said, 'Now, does anyone have anything they want to say in memory of the dear departed?'

By the expressions on the faces of those nearest to the grave, it was obvious that several of them were planning to say things. But Fat Charlie knew it was a now or never moment. *You need to make your peace with your dad, you know*. Right.

He took a deep breath and a step forward, so he was right at the edge of the grave, and he said, 'Um. Excuse me. Right. I think I have something to say.'

The distant shouting was getting louder. Several of the

mourners were casting glances back over their shoulders to see where it was coming from. The rest of them were staring at Fat Charlie.

'I was never what you would call close to my father,' said Fat Charlie. 'I suppose we didn't really know how. I've not been part of his life for twenty years, and he hasn't been part of mine. There's a lot of things it's hard to forgive, but then one day you turn around and you've got no family left.' He wiped a hand across his forehead. 'I don't think I've ever said "I love you, Dad" in my whole life. All of you, you all probably knew him better than I did. Some of you may have loved him. You were part of his life and I wasn't. So I'm not ashamed that any of you should hear me say it. Say it for the first time in at least twenty years.' He looked down at the impregnable metal casket lid. 'I love you,' he said. 'And I'll never forget you.'

The shouting got even louder, and now it was loud enough, and clear enough, in the silence that followed Fat Charlie's statement, for everyone to be able to make out the words being bellowed across the memorial gardens.

'Fat Charlie! You stop botherin' those people and get your ass over here *this* minute!'

Fat Charlie stared at the sea of unfamiliar faces, their expressions a seething stew of shock, puzzlement, anger and horror; ears burning, he realised the truth.

'Er. Sorry. Wrong funeral,' he said.

A small boy with big ears and an enormous smile said, proudly, 'That was my gramma.'

Fat Charlie backed through the small crowd mumbling barely coherent apologies. He wanted the world to end now. He knew it was not his father's fault, but also knew that his father would have found it hilarious.

Standing on the path, her hands on her hips, was a large woman with grey hair and thunder in her face. Fat Charlie walked towards her as he would have walked across a minefield, nine years old again, and in trouble.

'You don't hear me yellin?' she asked. 'You went right on past me. Makin' a embarrassment of yourself!' The way she said 'embarrassment', it began with the letter H. 'Back this way,' she

said. 'You miss the service and everythin'. But there's a shovelful
of dirt waiting for you.'

Mrs Higgler had barely changed in the last two decades: she
was a little fatter, a little greyer. Her lips were pressed tightly
together, and she led the way down one of the memorial garden's
many paths. Fat Charlie suspected that he had not made the best
possible first impression. She led the way and, in disgrace, Fat
Charlie followed.

A lizard zapped up one of the struts of the metal fence at the
edge of the memorial garden, then poised itself at the top of a
spike, tasting the thick Florida air. The sun had gone behind a
cloud, but, if anything, the afternoon was getting hotter. The
lizard puffed its neck out into a bright orange balloon.

Two long-legged cranes he had taken initially for lawn
ornaments looked up at him as he passed. One of them darted its
head down, rose up again with a large frog dangling from its beak.
It began, in a series of gulping movements, to try to swallow the
frog, which kicked and flailed in the air.

'Come on,' said Mrs Higgler. 'Don't dawdle. Bad enough you
missing your own father's funeral.'

Fat Charlie suppressed the urge to say something about having
come four thousand miles already that day, and having rented a
car and driven down from Orlando, and how he had got off at the
wrong exit and whose idea was it anyway to tuck a garden of rest
behind a Wal-Mart on the very edge of town? They kept walking,
past a large concrete building that smelled of formaldehyde,
until they reached an open grave at the very furthest reaches of
the property. There was nothing beyond this but a high fence,
and, beyond that, a wilderness of trees and palms and greenery.
In the grave was a modest wooden coffin. It had several mounds
of dirt on it already. Beside the grave was a pile of mud, and a
shovel.

Mrs Higgler picked up the shovel and handed it to Fat Charlie.

'It was a pretty service,' she said. 'Some of your daddy's old
drinkin' buddies were there, and all the ladies from our street.
Even after he moved down the road we still kept in touch. He
would have liked it. Of course, he would have liked it more if
you'd been there.' She shook her head. 'Now, shovel,' she said.

'And if you got any goodbyes, you can say them while you're shovellin' down the dirt.'

'I thought I was just meant to do one or two spadefuls of dirt,' he said. 'To show willing.'

'I give the man thirty bucks to go away,' said Mrs Higgler. 'I tell him that the departed's son is flying in all the way from Hingland, and that he would want to do right by his father. Do the right thing. Not just "show willing".'

'Right,' said Fat Charlie. 'Absolutely. Got it.' He took off his suit jacket and hung it on the fence. He loosened his tie, pulled it over his head, and put it into the jacket pocket. He shovelled the black dirt into the open grave, in Florida air as thick as soup.

After a while it sort of began to rain, which is to say that it was the kind of rain that never comes to a decision about whether it's actually raining or not. Driving in it, you would never have been certain whether or not to turn on your wipers. Standing in it, shovelling in it, you simply got sweatier, damper, more uncomfortable. Fat Charlie continued to shovel, and Mrs Higgler stood there with her arms folded across her gargantuan bosom, with the almost-rain misting her black dress and her straw hat with one black silk rose on it, watching him, as he filled in the hole.

The earth became mud, and became, if anything, heavier.

After what seemed like a lifetime, and a very uncomfortable one at that, Fat Charlie patted down the final shovelful of dirt.

Mrs Higgler walked over to him. She took his jacket off the fence, and handed it to him.

'You're soaked to the skin, and covered in dirt and sweat, but you grew up. Welcome home, Fat Charlie,' she said, and she smiled and she held him to her vast breast.

'I'm not crying,' said Fat Charlie.

'Hush now,' said Mrs Higgler.

'It's the rain on my face,' said Fat Charlie.

Mrs Higgler didn't say anything. She just held him, and swayed backward and forward, and after a while Fat Charlie said 'It's OK. I'm better now.'

'There's food back at my house,' said Mrs Higgler. 'Let's get you fed.'

He wiped the mud from his shoes in the parking lot, then he got into his grey rental car, and he followed Mrs Higgler in her maroon station wagon down streets that had not existed twenty years earlier. Mrs Higgler drove like a woman who had just discovered an enormous and much-needed mug of coffee and whose primary mission was to drink as much coffee as she was able to while driving as fast as possible, and Fat Charlie drove along behind her, keeping up as best he could, racing from traffic light to traffic light while trying to figure out more or less where they were.

And then they turned down a street, and, with mounting apprehension, he realised he recognised it. This was the street he had lived on as a boy. Even the houses looked more or less the same, although most of them had now grown impressive wire-mesh fences around their front yards.

There were several cars already parked in front of Mrs Higgler's house. He pulled up behind an elderly grey Ford. Mrs Higgler walked up to the front door, opened it with her key.

Fat Charlie looked down at himself, muddy and sweat-soaked. 'I can't go in looking like this,' he said.

'I seen worse,' said Mrs Higgler. Then she sniffed. 'I tell you what, you go in there, go straight into the bathroom, you can wash off your hands and face, clean yourself up, and when you're ready we'll all be in the kitchen.'

He went into the bathroom. Everything smelled like jasmine. He took off his muddy shirt, and washed his face and hands with jasmine-scented soap, in a tiny washbasin. He took a wash-cloth, and wiped down his chest, and scrubbed at the muddiest lumps on his suit trousers. He looked at the shirt, which had been white when he put it on this morning and was now a particularly grubby brown, and decided not to put it back on. He had more shirts in his bag, in the back seat of the rental car. He would slip back out of the house, put on a clean shirt, then face the people in the house.

He unlocked the bathroom door, and opened it.

Four elderly ladies were standing in the corridor, staring at him. He knew them. He knew all of them.

'What you doing now?' asked Mrs Higgler.

'Changing shirt,' said Fat Charlie. 'Shirt in car. Yes. Back soon.'

He raised his chin high, and strode down the corridor and out of the front door.

'What kind of language was that he was talkin?' asked little Mrs Dunwiddy, behind his back, loudly.

'That's not something you see every day,' said Mrs Bustamonte, although, this being Florida's Treasure Coast, if there was something you did see every day, it was topless men, although not usually with muddy suit trousers on.

Fat Charlie changed his shirt by the car, and went back into the house. The four ladies were in the kitchen, industriously packing away into Tupperware containers what looked like it had until recently been a large spread of food.

Mrs Higgler was older than Mrs Bustamonte, and both of them were older than Miss Noles and none of them was older than Mrs Dunwiddy. Mrs Dunwiddy was old, and she looked it. There were geological ages that were probably younger than Mrs Dunwiddy.

As a boy, Fat Charlie had imagined Mrs Dunwiddy in Equatorial Africa, peering disapprovingly though her thick spectacles at the newly erect hominids. 'Keep out of my front yard,' she would tell a recently evolved and rather nervous specimen of *Homo habilis*, 'or I going to belt you around your ear-hole, I can tell you.' Mrs Dunwiddy smelled of violet-water and beneath the violets she smelled of very old woman indeed. She was a tiny old lady who could outglare a thunderstorm, and Fat Charlie, who had, over two decades ago, followed a lost tennis ball into her yard, and then broken one of her lawn ornaments, was still quite terrified of her.

Right now, Mrs Dunwiddy was eating lumps of curry goat with her fingers from a small Tupperware bowl. 'Pity to waste it,' she said, and dropped the bits of goat-bone into a china saucer.

'Time for you to eat, Fat Charlie?' asked Miss Noles.

'I'm fine,' said Fat Charlie. 'Honest.'

Four pairs of eyes stared at him reproachfully through four pairs of spectacles. 'No good starvin' yourself in your grief,' said Mrs Dunwiddy, licking her fingertips, and picking out another brown fatty lump of goat.

'I'm not. I'm just not hungry. That's all.'

'Misery going to shrivel you away to pure skin and bones,' said Miss Noles, with gloomy relish.

'I don't think it will.'

'I putting a plate together for you at the table over there,' said Mrs Higgler. 'You go and sit down now. I don't want to hear another word out of you. There's more of everything, so don't you worry about that.'

Fat Charlie sat down where she pointed, and within seconds there was placed in front of him a plate piled high with stew peas and rice, and sweet potato pudding, jerk pork, curry goat, curry chicken, fried plantains, and a pickled cow foot. Fat Charlie could feel the heartburn beginning, and he had not even put anything in his mouth yet.

'Where's everyone else?' he said.

'Your daddy's drinking buddies, they gone off drinking. They going to have a memorial fishing trip off a bridge, in his memory.' Mrs Higgler poured the remaining coffee out of her bucket-sized travelling mug into the sink, and replaced it with the steaming contents of a freshly brewed jug of coffee.

Mrs Dunwiddy licked her fingers clean with a small purple tongue, and she shuffled over to where Fat Charlie was sitting, his food as yet untouched. When he was a little boy he had truly believed that Mrs Dunwiddy was a witch. Not a nice witch, more the kind kids had to push into ovens to escape from. This was the first time he'd seen her in more than twenty years, and he was still having to quell an inner urge to yelp and hide under the table.

'I seen plenty people die,' said Mrs Dunwiddy. 'In my time. Get old enough, you will see it your own self too. Everybody going to be dead one day, just give them time.' She paused. 'Still. I never thought it would happen to your daddy.' And she shook her head.

'What was he like?' asked Fat Charlie. 'When he was young?'

Mrs Dunwiddy looked at him through her thick, thick spectacles, and her lips pursed, and she shook her head. 'Before my time,' was all she said. 'Eat your cow foot.'

Fat Charlie sighed, and he began to eat.

* * *

It was late afternoon, and they were alone in the house.

'Where you going to sleep tonight?' asked Mrs Higgler.

'I thought I'd get a motel room,' said Fat Charlie.

'When you got a perfectly good bedroom here? And a perfectly good house down the road? You haven't even looked at it yet. You ask me, your father would have wanted you to stay there.'

'I'd rather be on my own. And I don't think I feel right about sleeping at my dad's place.'

'Well, it's not my money I'm throwin' away,' said Mrs Higgler. 'You're goin' to have to decide what you're goin' to do with your father's house anyway. And all his things.'

'I don't care,' said Fat Charlie. 'We could have a garage sale. Put them on eBay. Haul them to the dump.'

'Now, what kind of an attitude is that?' She rummaged in a kitchen drawer, and pulled out a front door key with a large paper label attached to it. 'He give me a spare key when he move,' she said. 'In case he lose his, or lock it inside, or something. He used to say, he could forget his head if it wasn't attached to his neck. When he sell the house next door, he tell me, don't you worry, Callyanne, I won't go far, he'd live in that house as long as I remember, but now he decide it's too big and he need to move house . . .' and still talking she walked him down to the kerb, and drove them down several streets in her maroon station wagon, until they reached a one-storey wooden house.

She unlocked the front door and they went inside.

The smell was familiar: faintly sweet, as if chocolate-chip cookies had been baked there the last time the kitchen was used, but that had been a long time ago. It was too hot in there. Mrs Higgler led them into the little sitting room, and she turned on a window-fitted air-conditioning unit. It rattled and shook, and smelled like a wet sheepdog, and moved the warm air around.

There were stacks of books piled around a decrepit sofa Fat Charlie remembered from his childhood, and there were photographs in frames: one, in black and white, of Fat Charlie's mother when she was young, with her hair up on top of her head all black and shiny, wearing a sparkly dress; beside it, a photo of Fat Charlie himself, aged perhaps five or six years old, standing beside a mirrored door, so it looked at first glance as if two little

Fat Charlies, side by side, were staring seriously out of the photograph at you.

Fat Charlie picked up the top book in the pile. It was a book on Italian architecture.

'Was he interested in architecture?'

'Passionate about it. Yes.'

'I didn't know that.'

Mrs Higgler shrugged and sipped her coffee.

Fat Charlie opened the book, and saw his father's name neatly written on the first page. He closed the book.

'I never knew him,' said Fat Charlie. 'Not really.'

'He was never an easy man to know,' said Mrs Higgler. 'I knew him for what, nearly sixty years? And I didn't know him.'

'You must have known him when he was a boy.'

Mrs Higgler hesitated. She seemed to be remembering. Then she said, very quietly, 'I knew him when I was a girl.'

Fat Charlie felt that he should be changing the subject, so he pointed to the photo of his mother. 'He's got Mum's picture there,' he said.

Mrs Higgler took a slurp of her coffee. 'Them take it on a boat,' she said. 'Back before you was born. One of those boats that you had dinner on, and they would sail out three miles, out of territorial waters, and then there was gamblin'. Then they come back. I don't know if they still run those boats. Your mother say it was the first time she ever eat steak.'

Fat Charlie tried to imagine what his parents had been like before he was born.

'He always was a good-looking man,' mused Mrs Higgler, as if she were reading his mind. 'All the way to the end. He had a smile that could make a girl squeeze her toes. And he was always such a very fine dresser. All the ladies loved him.'

Fat Charlie knew the answer before he asked the question. 'Did you . . . ?'

'What kind of a question is that to be asking a respectable widow-woman?' She sipped her coffee. Fat Charlie waited for the answer. She said, 'I kissed him. Long, long time ago, before he ever met your mother. He was a fine, fine kisser. I hoped that he'd call, take me dancing again, instead he vanish. He was gone for what, a year? Two years? And by the time he come back, I was married to Mr Higgler, and he's bringing back your mother. Is out on the islands he meet her.'

'Were you upset?'

'I was a married woman.' Another sip of coffee. 'And you couldn't hate him. Couldn't even be properly angry with him. And the way he look at her – damn, if he did ever look at me like that I could have died happy. You know, at their wedding, is me was your mother's matron of honour?'

'I didn't know.'

The air-conditioning unit was starting to bellow out cold air. It still smelled like a wet sheepdog.

He asked, 'Do you think they were happy?'

'In the beginning.' She hefted her huge thermal mug, seemed about to take a sip of coffee and then changed her mind. 'In the beginning. But not even she could keep his attention for very long. He had so much to do. He was very busy, your father.'

Fat Charlie tried to work out if Mrs Higgler was joking or not. He couldn't tell. She didn't smile, though.

'So much to do? Like what? Fish off bridges? Play dominoes on the porch? Await the inevitable invention of karaoke? He wasn't busy. I don't think he ever did a day's work in all the time I knew him.'

'You shouldn't say that about your father!'

'Well, it's true. He was crap. A rotten husband and a rotten father.'

'Of course he was!' said Mrs Higgler, fiercely, 'But you can't judge him like you would judge a man. You got to remember, Fat Charlie, that your father was a god.'

'A god among men?'

'No. Just a god.' She said it without any kind of emphasis, as flatly and as normally as she might have said 'he was diabetic' or simply 'he was black'.

Fat Charlie wanted to make a joke of it, but there was that look in Mrs Higgler's eyes, and suddenly he couldn't think of anything funny to say. So he said, softly, 'He wasn't a god. Gods are special. Mythical. They do miracles and things.'

'That's right,' said Mrs Higgler. 'We wouldn't have told you while he was alive, but now he is gone, there can't be any harm in it.'

'He was not a god. He was my dad.'

'You can be both,' she said. 'It happens.'

It was like arguing with a crazy person, thought Fat Charlie. He realised that he should just shut up, but his mouth kept going. Right now his mouth was saying, 'Look. If my dad was a god, he would have had godlike powers.'

'He did. Never did a lot with them, mind you. But he was old. Anyway, how do you think he got away with not working? Whenever he needed money, he'd play the lottery, or go down to Hallendale and bet on the dogs or the horses. Never win enough to attract attention. Just enough to get by.'

Fat Charlie had never won anything in his whole life. Nothing whatsoever. In the various office sweepstakes he had taken part in, he was only able to rely on his horse never making it out of the starting gate, or his team being relegated to some hitherto unheard-of division somewhere in the elephants' graveyard of organised sport. It rankled.

'If my dad was a god – something which I do not for one moment concede in any way, I should add – then why aren't *I* a god too? I mean, you're saying I'm the son of a god, aren't you?'

'Obviously.'

'Well then, why can't I bet on winning horses or do magic or miracles or things?'

She sniffed. 'Your brother got all that god stuff.'

Fat Charlie found that he was smiling. He breathed out. It was a joke after all, then.

'Ah. You know, Mrs Higgler, I don't actually have a brother.'

'Of course you do. That's you and him, in the photograph.'

Although he knew what was in it, Fat Charlie glanced over at the photograph. She was mad all right. Absolutely barking. 'Mrs Higgler,' he said, as gently as possible, 'that's *me*. Just me when I was a kid. It's a mirrored door. I'm standing next to it. It's me, and my reflection.'

'It is you, and it is also your brother.'

'I never had a brother.'

'Sure you did. I don't miss him. You were always the good one, you know. He was a handful when he was here.' And before Fat Charlie could say anything else she added. 'He went away, when you are just a little boy.'

Fat Charlie leaned over. He put his big hand on Mrs Higgler's bony hand, the one that wasn't holding the coffee mug. 'It's not true,' he said.

'Louella Dunwiddy made him go,' she said. 'He was scared of her. But he still came back, from time to time. He could be charming when he wanted to be.' She finished her coffee.

'I always wanted a brother,' said Fat Charlie. 'Somebody to play with.'

Mrs Higgler got up. 'This place isn't going to clean itself up,' she said. 'I've got garbage bags in the car. I figure we'll need a lot of garbage bags.'

'Yes,' said Fat Charlie.

He stayed in a motel that night. In the morning, he and Mrs Higgler met, back at his father's house, and they put garbage into big black garbage bags. They assembled bags of objects to be donated to Goodwill. They also filled a box with things Fat Charlie wanted to hold on to for sentimental reasons, mostly photographs from his childhood and before he was born.

There was an old trunk, like a small pirate's treasure chest, filled with documents and old papers. Fat Charlie sat on the floor going through them. Mrs Higgler came in from the bedroom, with another black garbage bag filled with moth-eaten clothes.

'It's your brother give him that trunk,' said Mrs Higgler, out of the blue. It was the first time she had mentioned any of her fantasies of the previous night.

'I wish I did have a brother,' said Fat Charlie, and he did not realise he had said it aloud until Mrs Higgler said, 'I already told you. You *do* have a brother.'

'So,' he said. 'Where would I find this mythical brother of mine?' Later, he would wonder why he had asked her this. Was he humouring her? Teasing her? Was it just that he had to say something to fill the void? Whatever the reason, he said it. And she was chewing her lower lip, and nodding.

'You got to know. It's your heritage. It's your bloodline.' She walked over to him and crooked her finger. Fat Charlie bent down.

The old woman's lips brushed his ear as she whispered, '. . . need him . . . tell a . . .'

'What?'

'I say,' she said, in her normal voice, 'if you need him, just tell a spider. He'll come running.'

'Tell a spider?'

'That's what I said. You think I just talkin' for my health? Exercisin' my lungs? You never hear of talkin' to the bees? When I was a girl in Saint Andrews, before my folks came here, you would go tell the bees all your good news. Well, this is just like that. Talk to spider. It was how I used to send messages to your father, when he would vanish off.'

' . . . Right.'

'Don't you say "right" like that.'

'Like what?'

'Like I'm a crazy old lady who don't know the price of fish. You think I don't know which way is up?'

'Um. I'm quite sure you do. Honestly.'

Mrs Higgler was not mollified. She was far from gruntled. She picked up her coffee mug from the table, and cradled it, disapprovingly. Fat Charlie had done it now, and Mrs Higgler was determined to make sure that he knew it.

'I don't got to do this, you know,' she said. 'I don't got to help you. I'm only doing it because your father, he was special, and because your mother, she was a fine woman. I'm telling you big things. I'm telling you important things. You should listen to me. You should believe me.'

'I do believe you,' said Fat Charlie, as convincingly as he could.

'Now you're just humouring an old woman.'

'No,' he lied. 'I'm not. Honestly I'm not.' His words rang with honesty, sincerity and truth. He was thousands of miles from home, in his late father's house, with a crazy old woman on the verge of an apoplectic seizure. He would have told her that the moon was just some kind of unusual tropical fruit if it would have calmed her down, and meant it, as best he could.

She sniffed.

'That's the trouble with you young people,' she said. 'You think because you ain't been here long, you know everything. In my life

I already forget more than you ever know. You don't know nothin' about your father, you don't know nothin' about your family. I tell you your father is a god, you don't even ask me what god I talking about.'

Fat Charlie tried to remember the names of some gods. 'Zeus?' he suggested.

Mrs Higgler made a noise like a kettle suppressing the urge to boil. Fat Charlie was fairly sure that Zeus had been the wrong answer. 'Cupid?'

She made another noise, which began as a sputter and ended in a giggle. 'I can just picture your dad wearing nothin' but one of them fluffy diapers, with a big bow and arrow.' She giggled some more. Then she swallowed some coffee.

'Back when he was a god,' she told him. 'Back then, they called him Anansi.'

* * *

Now, probably you know some Anansi stories. Probably there's no one in the whole wide world doesn't know some Anansi stories.

Anansi was a spider, when the world was young, and all the stories were being told for the first time. He used to get himself into trouble, and he used to get himself out of trouble. The story of the tar-baby, the one they tell about Brer Rabbit? That was Anansi's story first. Some people think he was a rabbit. But that's their mistake. He wasn't a rabbit. He was a spider.

Anansi stories go back as long as people been telling each other stories. Back in Africa, where everything began, even before people were painting cave-lions and bears on rock walls, even then they were telling stories, about monkeys and lions and buffalo: big dream stories. People always had those proclivities. That was how they made sense of their worlds. Everything that ran or crawled or swung or snaked got to walk through those stories, and different tribes of people would venerate different creatures.

Lion was the king of beasts, even then, and Gazelle was the fleetest of foot, and Monkey was the most foolish, and Tiger was the most terrible, but it wasn't stories about them people wanted to hear.

Anansi gave his name to stories. Every story is Anansi's. Once, before the stories were Anansi's, they all belonged to Tiger (which is the name the people of the islands call all the big cats), and back then the tales were dark and evil, and filled with pain, and none of them ended happily. But that was a long time ago. These days, the stories are Anansi's.

Seeing we were just at a funeral, let me tell you a story about Anansi, the time his grandmother died. (It's OK: she was a very old woman, and she went in her sleep. It happens.) She died a long way from home, so Anansi, he goes across the island with his handcart, and he gets his grandmother's body, and puts it on the handcart, and he wheels it home. He's going to bury her by the banyan tree out the back of his hut, you see.

Now, he's passing through the town, after pushing his grandmother's corpse in the cart all morning, and he thinks, *I need some whisky.* So he goes into the shop, for there is a shop in that village, a store that sells everything, where the shopkeeper is a very hasty-tempered man. Anansi, he goes in and he drinks some whisky. He drinks a little more whisky, and he thinks, I shall play a trick on this fellow, so he says to the shopkeeper, go take some whisky to my grandmother, sleeping in the cart outside. You may have to wake her, for she's a sound sleeper.

So the shopkeeper, he goes out to the cart with a bottle, and he says to the old lady in the cart, hey, here's your whisky, but the old lady she not say anything. And the shopkeeper, he's just getting angrier and angrier, for he was such a hasty-tempered man, saying get up old woman, get up and drink your whisky, but the old woman she says nothing. Then she does something that the dead sometimes do in the heat of the day: she flatulates loudly. Well, the shopkeeper, he's so angry with this old woman for flatulating at him that he hits her, and then he hits her again, and now he hits her one more time and she tumbles down from the handcart on to the ground.

Anansi, he runs out and he starts a-crying and a-wailing and a-carrying on, and saying my grandmother, she's a dead woman, look what you did! Murderer! Evil-doer! Now the shopkeeper, he says to Anansi, don't you tell anyone I done this, and he gives Anansi five whole bottles of whisky, and a bag of gold, and a sack of plantains and pineapples and mangos, to make him hush his carrying-on, and to go away.

(He thinks he killed Anansi's grandmother, you see.)

So Anansi, he wheels his handcart home, and he buries his grandmother underneath the banyan tree.

Now the next day, Tiger, he's passing by Anansi's house, and he smells cooking smells. So he invites himself over, and there's Anansi having a feast, and Anansi, having no other option, asks Tiger to sit and eat with them.

Tiger says, Brother Anansi, where did you get all that fine food from, and don't you lie to me? And where did you get these bottles of whisky from, and that big bag filled with gold pieces? If you lie to me, I'll tear out your throat.

So Anansi, he says, I cannot lie to you, Brother Tiger. I got them all for I take my dead grandmother to the village on a handcart. And the storekeeper gave me all these good things for bringing him my dead grandmother.

Now, Tiger, he didn't have a living grandmother, but his wife had a mother, so he goes home and he calls his wife's mother out to see him, saying, Grandmother, you come out now, for you and I must have a talk. And she comes out and peers around, and says what is it? Well, Tiger, he kills her, even though his wife loves her, and he places her body on a handcart.

Then he wheels his handcart to the village, with his dead mother-in-law on it. Who want a dead body? he calls. Who want a dead grandmother? But all the people they just jeered at him, and they laughed at him, and they mocked him and when they saw that he was serious and he wasn't going anywhere, they pelted him with rotten fruit until he ran away.

It wasn't the first time Tiger was made a fool of by Anansi, and it wouldn't be the last time. Tiger's wife never let him forget how he killed her mother. Some days it's better for Tiger if he's never been born.

That's an Anansi story.

'Course, all stories are Anansi stories. Even this one.

Olden days, all the animals wanted to have stories named after them, back in the days when the songs that sung the world were still being sung, back when they were still singing the sky and the rainbow and the ocean. It was in those days when animals were people as well as animals that Anansi the spider tricked all of them, especially Tiger, because he wanted all the stories named after him.

Stories are like spiders, with all they long legs, and stories are like spider-webs, which man gets himself all tangled up in but which look so pretty when you see them under a leaf in the morning dew and in the elegant way that they connect to one another, each to each.

What's that? You want to know if Anansi looked like a spider? Sure he did, except when he looked like a man.

No, he never changed his shape. It's just a matter of how you tell the story. That's all.

Chapter Three

In Which There Is a Family Reunion

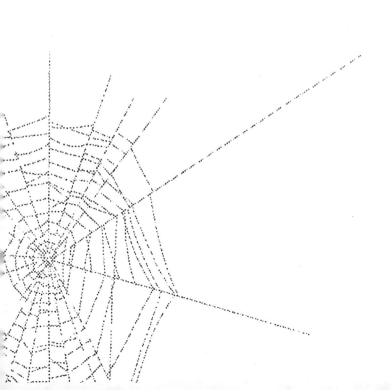

Fat Charlie flew home to England; as home as he was going to get, anyway.

Rosie was waiting for him as he came out of the Customs Hall carrying a small suitcase and a large taped-up cardboard box. She gave him a huge hug. 'How was it?' she asked.

He shrugged. 'Could've been worse.'

'Well,' she said, 'at least you don't have to worry about him coming to the wedding and embarrassing you any more.'

'There is that.'

'My mum says that we ought to put off the wedding for a few months as a mark of respect.'

'Your mum just wants us to put off the wedding, full stop.'

'Nonsense. She thinks you're quite a catch.'

'Your mother wouldn't describe a combination of Brad Pitt, Bill Gates and Prince William as "quite a catch". There is nobody walking the earth good enough to be her son-in-law.'

'She likes you,' said Rosie, dutifully, and without conviction.

Rosie's mother did not like Fat Charlie, and everybody knew it. Rosie's mother was a highly strung bundle of barely thought-through prejudices, worries, and feuds. She lived in a magnificent flat in Wimpole Street with nothing in the enormous fridge but bottles of vitaminised water and rye crackers. Wax fruit sat in the bowls on the antique sideboards, and was dusted twice a week.

Fat Charlie had, on his first visit to Rosie's mother's place, taken a bite from one of the wax apples. He had been extremely nervous, nervous enough that he had picked up an apple – in his defence, an extremely realistic apple – and had bitten into it. Rosie had signed frantically. Fat Charlie spat out the lump of wax into his hand and thought about pretending that he liked wax fruit, or that he'd known all along and had just done it to be funny; however, Rosie's mother had raised an eyebrow, walked over, taken the remains of the apple from him, explained shortly just how much real wax fruit cost these days, if you could find it, and then dropped the apple into the bin. He sat on the sofa for the rest of the afternoon, with his mouth tasting like the inside of a candle, while Rosie's mother stared at him to ensure that he did not try to take another bite out of her precious wax fruit, or attempt to gnaw on the leg of a Chippendale chair.

There were large colour photographs in silver frames on the sideboard of Rosie's mother's flat: photographs of Rosie as a girl, and of Rosie's mother and father, and Fat Charlie had studied them intently, looking for clues to the mystery that was Rosie. Her father, who had died when Rosie was fifteen, had been an enormous man. He had been first a cook, then a chef, then a restaurateur. He was perfectly turned-out in every photograph, as if dressed by a wardrobe department before each shot, rotund and smiling, his arm always crooked for Rosie's mother to hold.

'He was an amazing cook,' Rosie said. In the photographs, Rosie's mother had been curvaceous, and smiling. Now, twelve years on, she resembled a skeletal Eartha Kitt, and Fat Charlie had never seen her smile.

'Does your mum ever cook?' Fat Charlie had asked, after that first time.

'I don't know. I've never seen her cook anything.'

'What does she eat? I mean, she can't live on crackers and water.'

Rosie said, 'I think she sends out for things.'

Fat Charlie thought it highly likely that Rosie's mum went out at night in bat form to suck the blood from sleeping innocents. He had mentioned this theory to Rosie once, but she had failed to see the humour in it.

Rosie's mother had told Rosie that she was certain that Fat Charlie was marrying her for her money.

'What money?' asked Rosie.

Rosie's mother gestured to the apartment, a gesture that took in the wax fruit, the antique furniture, the paintings on the walls, and pursed her lips.

'But this is all yours,' said Rosie, who lived on her wages working for a London charity, and her wages were not large, so to supplement them Rosie had dipped into the money her father had left her in his will. It had paid for a small flat, which Rosie shared with a succession of Australians and New Zealanders, and for a second-hand VW Golf.

'I won't live for ever,' sniffed her mother, in a way that implied that she had every intention of living for ever, getting harder and thinner and more stonelike as she went, and eating less and less, until she would be able to live on nothing more than air and wax fruit and spite.

Rosie, driving Fat Charlie home from Heathrow, decided that the subject should be changed. She said, 'The water's gone off in my flat. It's out in the whole building.'

'Why's that then?'

'Mrs Klinger downstairs. She said something sprung a leak.'

'Probably Mrs Klinger.'

'*Char*lie. So, I was wondering – could I take a bath at your place tonight?'

'Do you need me to sponge you down?'

'*Char*lie.'

'Sure. Not a problem.'

Rosie stared at the back of the car in front of her, then she took her hand off the gear stick, and reached out, and squeezed Fat Charlie's huge hand. 'We'll be married soon enough,' she said.

'I know,' said Fat Charlie.

'Well, I mean,' she said, 'there'll be plenty of time for all that, won't there?'

'Plenty,' said Fat Charlie.

'You know what my mum once said?' said Rosie.

'Er. Was it something about bringing back hanging?'

'It was *not*. She said that if a just-married couple put a coin in a jar every time they make love in their first year, and take a coin out for every time that they make love in the years that follow, the jar will never be emptied.'

'And this means . . . ?'

'Well,' she said. 'It's interesting, isn't it? I'll be over at eight tonight with my rubber duck. How are you for towels?'

'Um . . .'

'I'll bring my own towel.'

Fat Charlie did not believe it would be the end of the world if an occasional coin went into the jar before they tied the knot and sliced the wedding cake, but Rosie had her own opinions on the matter, and there the matter ended. The jar remained perfectly empty.

* * *

The problem, Fat Charlie realised, once he got home, with arriving back in London after a brief trip away, is that if you arrive in the early morning, there is nothing much to do for the rest of the day.

Fat Charlie was a man who preferred to be working. He regarded lying on a sofa watching *Countdown* as a reminder of his interludes as a member of the unemployed. He decided that the sensible thing to do would be to go back to work a day early. In the Aldwych offices of the Grahame Coats Agency, up on the fifth and topmost floor, he would feel part of the swim of things. There would be interesting conversation with his fellow workers in the tea-room. The whole panoply of life would unfold before him, majestic in its tapestry, implacable and relentless in its industry. People would be pleased to see him.

'You're not back until tomorrow,' said Annie the receptionist, when Fat Charlie walked in. 'I told people you wouldn't be back until tomorrow. When they phoned.' She was not amused.

'Couldn't keep away,' said Fat Charlie.

'Obviously not,' she said, with a sniff. 'You should phone Maeve Livingstone back. She's been calling every day.'

'I thought she was one of Grahame Coats's people.'

'Well, he wants you to talk to her. Hang on.' She picked up the phone.

Grahame Coats came with both names. Not Mr Coats. Never just Grahame. It was his agency, and it represented people, and took a percentage of what they earned for the right to have represented them.

Fat Charlie went back to his office, which was a tiny room he shared with a number of filing cabinets. There was a yellow Post-it note stuck to his computer screen with 'See me. GC' on it, so he went down the hall to Grahame Coats's enormous office. The door was closed. He knocked, and then, unsure if he had heard anyone say anything or not, opened the door and put his head inside.

The room was empty. There was nobody there. 'Um, hello?' said Fat Charlie, not very loudly. There was no reply. There was a certain amount of disarrangement in the room, however: the bookcase was sticking out of the wall at a peculiar angle, and from the space behind it he could hear a thumping sound that might have been hammering.

He closed the door as quietly as he could, and went back to his desk.

His telephone rang. He picked it up.

'Grahame Coats here. Come and see me.'

This time Grahame Coats was sitting behind his desk, and the bookcase was flat against the wall. He did not invite Fat Charlie to sit down. He was a middle-aged white man with receding very fair hair. If you happened to see Grahame Coats and immediately found yourself thinking of an albino ferret in an expensive suit, you would not be the first.

'You're back with us, I see,' said Grahame Coats. 'As it were.'

'Yes,' said Fat Charlie. Then, because Grahame Coats did not seem particularly pleased with Fat Charlie's early return, he added, 'Sorry.'

Grahame Coats pinched his lips together, looked down at a

paper on his desk, looked up again. 'I was given to understand that you were not, in fact, returning until tomorrow. Bit early, aren't we?'

'We – I mean, I – got in this morning. From Florida. I thought I'd come in. Lots to do. Show willing. If that's all right.'

'Absatively,' said Grahame Coats. The word – a car crash between *absolutely* and *positively* – always set Fat Charlie's teeth on edge. 'It's your funeral.'

'My father's, actually.'

A ferret-like neck twist. 'You're still using one of your sick days.'

'Right.'

'Maeve Livingstone. Worried widow of Morris. Needs reassurance. Fair words and fine promises. Rome was not built in a day. The actual business of sorting out Morris Livingstone's estate and getting money to her continues unabated. Phones me practically daily for hand-holding. Meanwhilst, I turn the task over to you.'

'Right,' said Fat Charlie. 'So, um. No rest for the wicked.'

'Another day, another dollar,' said Grahame Coats, with a wag of his finger.

'Nose to the grindstone?' suggested Fat Charlie.

'Shoulder to the wheel,' said Grahame Coats. 'Well, delightful chatting with you. But we both have much work to do.'

There was something about being in the vicinity of Grahame Coats that always made Fat Charlie a) speak in clichés and b) begin to daydream about huge black helicopters first opening fire upon, then dropping buckets of flaming napalm on to the offices of the Grahame Coats Agency. Fat Charlie would not be in the office in those daydreams. He would be sitting in a chair outside a little café on the other side of the Aldwych, sipping a frothy coffee and occasionally cheering at an exceptionally well-flung bucket of napalm.

From this you would presume that there is little you need to know about Fat Charlie's employment, save that he was unhappy in it, and, in the main, you would be right. Fat Charlie had a facility for figures which kept him in work, and an awkwardness and a diffidence which kept him from pointing out to people what it was that he actually did, and how much he actually did. All about him, Fat Charlie would see people ascending implacably to their levels of incompetence, while he remained in entry-level positions, performing essential functions until the day he rejoined the ranks of the unemployed and started watching daytime television again. He was never out of a job for long, but it had happened far too often in the last decade for Fat Charlie to feel particularly comfortable in any position. He did not, however, take it personally.

He telephoned Maeve Livingstone, widow of Morris Livingstone, once the most famous short Yorkshire comedian in Britain and a long-time client of the Grahame Coats Agency. 'Hello,' he said. 'This is Charles Nancy, from the accounts department of the Grahame Coats Agency.'

'Oh,' said a woman's voice at the other end of the line. 'I thought Grahame would be phoning me himself.'

'He's a bit tied up. So he's um, delegated it,' said Fat Charlie. 'To me. So. Can I help?'

'I'm not sure. I was rather wondering – well, the bank manager was wondering – when the rest of the money from Morris's estate would be coming through – Grahame Coats explained to me, the last time – well, I think it was the last time – when we spoke – that it was invested – I mean, I understand that these things take time – he said otherwise I could lose a lot of money—'

'Well,' said Fat Charlie, 'I know he's on it. But these things do take time.'

'Yes,' she said. 'I suppose they must do. I called the BBC and they said they'd made several payments since Morris's death. You know, they've released the whole of *Morris Livingstone, I Presume* on DVD now? And they're bringing out both series of *Short Back and Sides* for Christmas.'

'I didn't know,' admitted Fat Charlie. 'But I'm sure Grahame Coats does. He's always on top of that kind of thing.'

'I had to buy my own DVD,' she said, wistfully. 'Still, it brought it all back. The roar of the greasepaint, the smell of the BBC club. Made me miss the spotlight, I can tell you that for nothing. That was how I met Morris, you know. I was a dancer. I had my own career.'

Fat Charlie told her that he'd let Grahame Coats know that her bank manager was a bit concerned, and he put down the phone.

He wondered how anyone could ever miss the spotlight.

In Fat Charlie's worst nightmares, a spotlight shone down upon him from a dark sky, on to a wide stage, and unseen figures would try to force Fat Charlie to stand in the spotlight and sing. And no matter how far or how fast he ran, or how well he hid, they would find him, and drag him back on to the stage, in front of dozens of expectant faces. He would always awake before he actually had to sing, sweating and trembling, his heart beating a cannonade in his chest.

A day's work passed. Fat Charlie had worked there almost two years. He had been there longer than anyone except Grahame Coats himself, for the staff turnover at the Grahame Coats Agency tended to be high. And still, nobody had been pleased to see him.

Fat Charlie would sometimes sit at his desk and stare out of the window, as the loveless grey rain rattled against the glass, and he would imagine himself on a tropical beach somewhere, with the breakers crashing from an impossibly blue sea on to the impossibly yellow sands. Often Fat Charlie would wonder if the people on the beach in his imagination, watching the white fingers of the waves as they wriggled towards the shore, listening to the tropical birds whistling in the palm trees, whether they ever dreamed of being in England, in the rain, in a cupboard-sized room in a fifth-floor office, a safe distance from the dullness of the pure golden sand and the hellish boredom of a day so perfect that not even a creamy drink containing slightly too much rum and a red paper umbrella can do anything to alleviate it. It comforted him.

He stopped at the off-licence on the way home, and bought a bottle of German white wine, and a patchouli-scented candle from the tiny supermarket next door, and picked up a pizza from the Pizza Place nearby.

Rosie phoned from her yoga class at 7.30 p.m. to let him know that she was going to be a little late, then from her car at 8.00 p.m. to let him know she was stuck in traffic, at 9.15 to let him know that she was now just around the corner, by which time Fat Charlie had drunk most of the bottle of white wine on his own, and consumed all but one lonely triangle of pizza.

Later, he wondered if it was the wine that made him say it.

Rosie arrived at 9:20, with towels, and a Tesco bag filled with shampoos, soaps and a large pot of hair mayonnaise. She said no, briskly but cheerfully, to a glass of the white wine and the slice of pizza – she had, she explained, eaten in the traffic jam. She had ordered in. So Fat Charlie sat in the kitchen, and poured himself the final glass of white wine, and picked the cheese and the pepperoni from the top of the cold pizza while Rosie went off to run the bath and then started, suddenly and quite loudly, to scream.

Fat Charlie made it to the bathroom before the first scream had finished dying away, and while Rosie was filling her lungs for the second. He was convinced that he would find her dripping with blood. To his surprise and relief, she was not bleeding. She was wearing a blue bra and panties, and was pointing to the bath, in the centre of which sat a large brown garden spider.

'I'm sorry,' she wailed. 'It took me by surprise.'

'They can do that,' said Fat Charlie. 'I'll just wash it away.'

'Don't you dare,' said Rosie, fiercely. 'It's a living thing. Take it outside.'

'Right,' said Fat Charlie.

'I'll wait in the kitchen,' she said. 'Tell me when it's all over.'

When you have drunk an entire bottle of white wine, coaxing a rather skittish garden spider into a clear plastic tumbler using only an old birthday card becomes more of a challenge to hand-eye coordination than it is at other times; a challenge that is not helped by a partially unclothed fiancée on the edge of hysterics, who, despite her announcement that she would wait in the kitchen, is instead leaning over your shoulder and offering advice.

But soon enough, despite the help, he had the spider inside the tumbler, the mouth of which was firmly covered by a card from an old schoolfriend which told him, 'YOU ARE ONLY AS OLD AS YOU FEEL' (and, on the inside humorously topped this with 'SO STOP FEELING YOURSELF YOU SEX MANIAC – HAPPY BIRTHDAY').

He took the spider downstairs and out of the front door, into the tiny front garden, which consisted of a hedge, for people to throw up in, and several large flagstones with grass growing up between them. He held the tumbler up. In the yellow sodium light, the spider was black. He imagined it was staring at him.

'Sorry about that,' he said to the spider, and, white wine slooshing comfortably around inside him, he said it aloud.

He put the card and the tumbler down on a cracked flagstone, and he lifted the tumbler, and waited for the spider to scuttle away. Instead, it simply sat, unmoving, on the face of the cheerful cartoon teddy bear on the birthday card. The man and the spider regarded each other.

Something that Mrs Higgler said came to him then, and the words were out of his mouth before he could stop them. Perhaps it was the devil in him. Probably it was the alcohol.

'If you see my brother,' said Fat Charlie to the spider, 'tell him he ought to come by and say hello.'

The spider remained where it was, and raised one leg, almost as if it was thinking it over, then it scuttled across the flagstone towards the hedge, and was gone.

* * *

Rosie had her bath, and she gave Fat Charlie a lingering peck on the cheek, and she went home.

Fat Charlie turned on the TV, but he found himself nodding, so he turned it off, and went to bed, where he dreamed a dream of such vividness and peculiarity that it would remain with him for the rest of his life.

One way that you know something is a dream is that you are somewhere you have never been in real life. Fat Charlie had never been to California. He had never been to Beverly Hills. He had seen it enough, though, in movies and on television to feel a comfortable thrill of recognition. A party was going on.

The lights of Los Angeles glimmered and twinkled beneath them.

The people at the party seemed to divide neatly into the ones with the silver plates, covered with perfect canapés, and the ones who picked things off the silver plates, or who declined to. The ones who were being fed moved around the huge house gossiping, smiling, talking, each as certain of his or her relative importance in the world of Hollywood as were the courtiers in the court of ancient Japan – and, just as in the ancient Japanese court, each of them was certain that, just one rung up the ladder, they would be safe. There were actors who wished to be stars, stars who wanted to be independent producers, independent producers who craved the safety of a studio job, directors who wanted to be stars, studio bosses who wanted to be the bosses of other, less precarious studios, studio lawyers who wanted to be liked for themselves, or, failing that, just wanted to be liked.

In Fat Charlie's dream, he could see himself from inside and outside at the same time, and he was not himself. In Fat Charlie's usual dreams he was probably just sitting down for an exam on double-entry book-keeping that he had forgotten to study for in circumstances which made it a certainty that when he finally stood up he would discover that he had somehow neglected to put anything on below the waist when he got dressed that morning. In his dreams, Fat Charlie was himself, only clumsier.

Not in this dream.

In this dream, Fat Charlie was cool, and beyond cool. He was slick, he was fly, he was smart, he was the only person at the party without a silver tray who had not received an invitation. And (this was something that was a source of astonishment to the sleeping Fat Charlie, who could think of nothing more embarrassing than being anywhere without an invitation) he was having a marvellous time.

He told each person who asked him a different story about who he was and why he was there. After half an hour, most of the people at the party were convinced that he was the representative of a foreign investment house, seeking to buy outright one of the studios, and after another half an hour it was common knowledge at the party that he would be putting in a bid for Paramount.

His laugh was raucous and infectious, and he seemed to be having a better time than any of the other people at the party, that was for certain. He instructed the barman in the preparation of a cocktail he called a 'Double Entendre' which, while it seemed to begin with a base of champagne, he explained was actually scientifically non-alcoholic. It contained a splash of this and a splash of that until it went a vivid purple colour, and he handed them out to the partygoers, pressing them upon them with joy and enthusiasm until even the people who had been sipping fizzy water warily, as if it might go off, were knocking back the purple drinks with pleasure.

And then, with the logic of dreams, he was leading them all down to the pool, and was proposing to teach them the trick of Walking on the Water. It was all a matter of confidence, he told them, of attitude, of attack, of knowing how to do it. And it seemed to the people at the party that Walking on the Water would be a very fine trick to master, something they had always known how to do, deep down in their souls, but they had forgotten, and that this man would remind them of the technique of it.

Take off your shoes, he said to them, so they took off their shoes, Sergio Rossis and Christian Louboutins and René Caovillas lined up side by side with Nikes and Doc Martens and anonymous black leather agent-shoes, and he led them, in a sort of a conga line, around the side of the swimming pool and then out on to its surface. The water was cool to the touch, and it quivered, like thick jelly, under their feet; some women, and several men, tittered at this, and a couple of the younger agents began jumping up and down on the surface of the pool, like children at a bouncy castle. Far below them the lights of Los Angeles shone through the smog, like distant galaxies.

Soon every inch of the pool was taken up with partygoers – standing, dancing, shaking or bouncing up and down on the water. The press of the crowd was so strong that the fly guy, the Charlie-in-his-dream, stepped back on to the concrete poolside to take a falafel-sashimi ball from a silver plate.

A spider dropped from a jasmine plant on to the fly guy's shoulder. It scuttled down his arm and on to the palm of his hand, where he greeted it with a delighted *Heyyy*.

There was a silence, as if he was listening to something the spider was saying, something only he could hear, then he said, *Ask, and you shall receive. Ain't that the truth?*

He placed the spider down, carefully, on a jasmine leaf.

And at that selfsame moment, each of the people standing barefoot on the surface of the swimming pool remembered that water was a liquid and not a solid, and that there was a reason why people did not commonly walk, let alone dance or even bounce on water, viz., its impossibility.

They were the movers and the shakers of the dream machine, those people, and suddenly they were flailing, fully dressed, in from four to twelve feet of water, wet and scrabbling and terrified.

Casually, the fly guy walked across the pool, treading on the heads of people, and on the hands of other people, and never once losing his balance. Then, when he reached the far end of the pool, where everything dropped into a steep hill, he took one huge jump and dived into the lights of Los Angeles at night, which shimmered and swallowed him like an ocean.

The people in the pool scrambled out, angry, upset, confused, wet, and in some cases, half drowned . . .

It was early in the morning in South London. The light was blue-grey.

Fat Charlie got out of bed, troubled by his dream, and walked to the window. The curtains were open. He could see the sunrise beginning, a huge blood orange of a morning sun surrounded by grey clouds tinged with scarlet. It was the kind of sky that makes even the most prosaic person discover a deeply buried urge to start painting in oils.

Fat Charlie looked at the sunrise. *Red sky in the morning*, he thought, *sailor's warning*.

His dream had been so strange. *A party in Hollywood. The secret of Walking on the Water. And that man, who was him and was not him* . . .

Fat Charlie realised that he knew the man in his dream, knew him from somewhere, and he also realised that this would irritate him for the rest of the day if he let it, like a snag of dental floss caught between two teeth, or the precise difference between the words 'lubricious' and 'lascivious', it would sit there, and it would irritate him.

He stared out of the window.

It was barely 6.00 in the morning, and the world was quiet. An early dog-walker, at the end of the road, was encouraging a

Pomeranian to defecate. A postman ambled from house to house and back to his red van. And then something moved, on the pavement beneath his house, and Fat Charlie looked down.

A man was standing by the hedge. When he saw that Fat Charlie, in pyjamas, was looking down at him, he grinned, and waved. A moment of recognition that shocked Fat Charlie to the core: he was familiar with both the grin and the wave, although he could not immediately see how. Something of the dream still hung about Fat Charlie's head, making him uncomfortable, making the world seem unreal. He rubbed his eyes, and now the person by the hedge was gone. Fat Charlie hoped that the man had moved on, wandered down the road into the remnants of the hanging morning mist, taking whatever awkwardnesses and irritants and madnesses he had brought away with him.

And then the doorbell rang.

Fat Charlie pulled on his dressing gown, and he went downstairs.

He had never fastened the safety chain before opening a door, never in his life, but before he turned the handle he clicked the head of the chain into place, and he pulled the front door open six inches.

'Morning?' he said, warily.

The smile that came through the crack in the door could have illuminated a small village.

'You called me and I came,' said the stranger. 'Now. You going to open this door for me, Fat Charlie?'

'Who are you?' As he said it, he knew where he had seen the man before: at his mother's funeral service, in the little chapel at the crematorium. That was the last time he had seen that smile. And he knew the answer, knew it even before the man could say the words.

'I'm your brother,' said the man.

Fat Charlie closed the door. He slipped off the safety chain and opened the door all the way. The man was still there.

Fat Charlie was not entirely sure how to greet a potentially imaginary brother he had not previously believed in. So they stood there, one on one side of the door, one on the other, until his brother said, 'You can call me Spider. You going to invite me in?'

'Yes. I am. Of course I am. Please. Come in.'

Fat Charlie led the man upstairs.

Impossible things happen. When they do happen, most people just deal with it. Today, like every day, roughly five thousand people on the face of the planet will experience one-chance-in-a-million things, and not one of them will refuse to believe the evidence of their senses. Most of them will say the equivalent, in their own language, of 'funny old world, isn't it?' and just keep going. So while part of Fat Charlie was trying to come up with logical, sensible, sane explanations for what was going on, most of him was simply getting used to the idea that a brother he hadn't known he had was walking up the staircase behind him.

They got to the kitchen and stood there.

'Would you like a cup of tea?'

'Got any coffee?'

'Only instant, I'm afraid.'

'That's fine.'

Fat Charlie turned on the kettle. 'You come far, then?' he asked.

'Los Angeles.'

'How was the flight?'

The man sat down at the kitchen table. Now he shrugged. It was the kind of shrug that could have meant anything.

'Um. You planning on staying long?'

'I haven't really given it much thought.' The man – Spider – looked around Fat Charlie's kitchen, as if he had never been in a kitchen before.

'How do you take your coffee?'

'Dark as night, sweet as sin.'

Fat Charlie put the mug down in front of him, and passed him a sugarbowl. 'Help yourself.'

While Spider spooned teaspoon after teaspoon of sugar into his coffee, Fat Charlie sat opposite him, and stared.

There was a family resemblance between the two men. That was unarguable, although that alone did not explain the intense feeling of familiarity that Fat Charlie felt on seeing Spider. His brother looked like Fat Charlie wished he looked in his mind, unconstrained by the faintly disappointing fellow that he saw, with monotonous regularity, in the bathroom mirror. Spider was taller, and leaner, and cooler. He was wearing a black and scarlet leather jacket, and black leather leggings, and he looked at home in them. Fat Charlie tried to remember if this was what the fly guy had been wearing in his dream. There was something larger than life about him: simply being on the other side of the table to this man made Fat Charlie feel awkward and badly constructed, and slightly foolish. It wasn't the clothes Spider wore, but the knowledge that if Fat Charlie put them on he would look as if he were wearing some kind of unconvincing drag. It wasn't the way Spider smiled – casually, delightedly – but Fat Charlie's cold, incontrovertible certainty that he himself could practise smiling in front of a mirror from now until the end of time and never manage a single smile one-half so charming, so cocky, or so twinklingly debonair.

'You were at Mum's cremation,' said Fat Charlie.

'I thought about coming over to talk to you after the service,' said Spider. 'I just wasn't certain that it would be a good idea.'

'I wish you had.' Fat Charlie thought of something. He said, 'I would have thought you would have been at Dad's funeral.'

Spider said 'What?'

'His funeral. It was in Florida. Couple of days ago.'

Spider shook his head. 'He's not dead,' he said. 'I'm pretty sure I'd know if he were dead.'

'He's dead. I buried him. Well, I filled the grave. Ask Mrs Higgler.'

Spider said, 'How'd he die?'

'Heart failure.'

'That doesn't mean anything. That just means he died.'

'Well, yes. He did.'

Spider had stopped smiling. Now he was staring down into his coffee as if he suspected he was going to be able to find an answer in there. 'I ought to check this out,' said Spider. 'It's not that I don't believe you. But when it's your old man. Even when your old man is my old man.' And he made a face. Fat Charlie knew what that face meant. He had made it himself, from the inside, enough times, when the subject of his father came up. 'Is she still living in the same place? Next door to where we grew up?'

'Mrs Higgler? Yes. Still there.'

'You don't have anything from there, do you? A picture? Maybe a photograph?'

'I brought home a box of them.' Fat Charlie had not opened the large cardboard box yet. It was still sitting in the hall. He carried the box into the kitchen and put it down on the table. He took a kitchen knife and cut the packing tape that surrounded it, Spider reached into the box with his thin fingers, riffling through the photographs like playing cards, until he pulled out one of their mother and Mrs Higgler, sitting on Mrs Higgler's porch, twenty-five years earlier.

'Is that porch still there?'

Fat Charlie tried to remember. 'I think so,' he said.

Later, he was unable to remember whether the picture grew very big, or Spider grew very small. He could have sworn that neither of those things had actually happened; nevertheless, it was unarguable that Spider had walked into the photograph, and it had shimmered and rippled and swallowed him up.

Fat Charlie rubbed his eyes. He was alone in the kitchen at six in the morning. There was a box filled with photographs and papers on the kitchen table, along with an empty mug, which he placed in the sink. He walked along the hall to his bedroom, lay down on his bed and slept until the alarm went off at 7.15.

Chapter Four

Which Concludes
With an Evening of
Wine, Women and Song

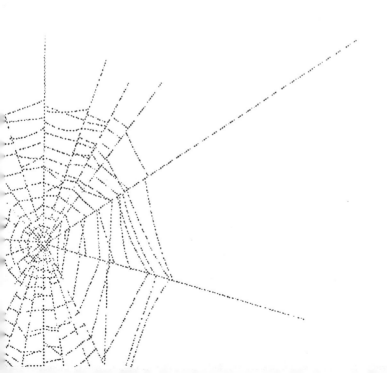

Fat Charlie woke up.

Memories of dreams of a meeting with some film-star brother mingled with a dream in which President Taft had come to stay, bringing with him the entire cast of the cartoon *Tom and Jerry*. He showered, and he took the tube to work.

All through the work day something was nagging at the back of his head, and he didn't know what it was. He misplaced things. He forgot things. At one point, he started singing, at his desk, not because he was happy, but because he forgot not to. He only realised he was doing it when Grahame Coats himself put his head around the door of Fat Charlie's closet to chide him. 'No radios, Walkmans, MP3 players or similar instruments of music at the office,' said Grahame Coats, with a ferrety glare. 'It bespeaks a lackadaisical attitude, of the kind one abhors in the workaday world.'

'It wasn't the radio,' admitted Fat Charlie, his ears burning.

'No? Then what, pray tell, was it?'

'It was me,' said Fat Charlie.

'You?'

'Yes. I was singing. I'm sorry—'

'I could have sworn it was the radio. And yet I was wrong. Good Lord. Well, with such a wealth of talents at your disposal, with such remarkable skills, perhaps you should leave us to tread the boards, entertain the multitudes, possibly do an end-of-the-pier show, rather than cluttering up a desk in an office where other people are trying to work. Eh? A place where people's careers are being managed.'

'No,' said Fat Charlie. 'I don't want to leave. I just wasn't thinking.'

'Then,' said Grahame Coats, 'you must learn to refrain from singing – save in the bath, the shower, or perchance the stands as you support your favourite football team. I myself am a Crystal Palace supporter. Or you will find yourself seeking gainful employment elsewhere.'

Fat Charlie smiled, then realised that smiling wasn't what he wanted to do at all, and looked serious, but by that point Grahame Coats had left the room, so Fat Charlie swore under his breath, folded his arms on the desk and put his head on them.

'Was that you singing?' It was one of the new girls in the Artist Liaison Department. Fat Charlie never managed to learn their names. They were always gone before then.

'I'm afraid so.'

'What were you singing? It was pretty.'

Fat Charlie realised he didn't know. He said, 'I'm not sure. I wasn't listening.'

She laughed at that, although quietly. 'He's right. You should be making records, not wasting your time here.'

Fat Charlie didn't know what to say. Cheeks burning, he started crossing out numbers and making notes and gathering up Post-it notes with messages on them and putting those messages up on the screen, until he was sure that she had gone.

Maeve Livingstone phoned: could Fat Charlie *please* ensure that Grahame Coats phoned her bank manager. He said he'd do his best. She told him pointedly to see that he did.

Rosie called him on his mobile at four in the afternoon, to let him know that the water was now back on again in her flat, and to tell him that, good news, her mother had decided to take an interest in the upcoming wedding, and had asked her to come round that evening and discuss it.

'Well,' said Fat Charlie, 'if she's organising the dinner, we'll save a fortune on food.'

'That's not nice. I'll call you tonight and let you know how it went.'

Fat Charlie told her that he loved her, and he clicked the phone off. Someone was looking at him. He turned round.

Grahame Coats said, 'He who maketh personal phone calls on company time, lo he shall reap the whirlwind. Do you know who said that?'

'You did?'

'Indeed I did,' said Grahame Coats. 'Indeed I did. And never a truer word was spoken. Consider this a formal warning.' And he smiled then, the kind of self-satisfied smile that forced Fat Charlie to ponder the various probable outcomes of sinking his fist into Grahame Coats's comfortably padded mid-section. He decided that it would be a toss-up between being fired and an action for assault. Either way, he thought, it would be a fine thing . . .

Fat Charlie was not by nature a violent man; still, he could dream. His daydreams tended to be small and comfortable things. He would like to have enough money to eat in good restaurants whenever he wished. He wanted a job in which nobody could tell him what to do. He wanted to be able to sing without embarrassment, somewhere there were never any people around to hear him.

This afternoon, however, his daydreams assumed a different shape: he could fly, for a start, and bullets bounced off his mighty chest as he zoomed down from the sky and rescued Rosie from a band of kidnapping scoundrels and dastards. She would hold him tightly as they flew off into the sunset, off to his Fortress of Cool, where she would be so overwhelmed with feelings of gratitude that she would enthusiastically decide not to bother with the whole waiting until they were married bit, and would start to see how high and how fast they could fill their jar . . .

The daydream eased the stress of life in the Grahame Coats Agency, of telling people that their cheques were in the post, of calling in money the agency was owed.

At 6.00 p.m. Fat Charlie turned off his computer, and walked down the five flights of stairs to the street. It had not rained. Overhead, the starlings were wheeling and cheeping: the dusk chorus of a city. Everyone on the pavement was hurrying somewhere. Most of them, like Fat Charlie, were walking up Kingsway to Holborn tube. They had their heads down, and the look about them of people who wanted to get home for the night.

There was one person on the pavement who wasn't going anywhere, though. He stood there, facing Fat Charlie and the remaining commuters, and his leather jacket flapped in the wind. He was not smiling.

Fat Charlie saw him from the end of the street. As he walked towards him everything became unreal. The day melted, and he realised what he had spent the day trying to remember.

'Hello, Spider,' he said, when he got close.

Spider looked like a storm was raging inside him. He might have been about to cry. Fat Charlie didn't know. There was too much emotion on his face, in the way he stood, so the people on the street looked away, ashamed.

'I went out there,' he said. His voice was jagged. 'I saw Mrs Higgler. She took me to the grave. My father died, and I didn't know.'

Fat Charlie said, 'He was my father too, Spider.' He wondered how he could have forgotten Spider, how he could have dismissed him so easily as a dream.

'True.'

The dusk sky was cross-hatched with starlings; they wheeled and crossed from rooftop to rooftop.

Spider jerked, and stood straight. He seemed to have come to a decision. 'You are so right,' he said. 'We got to do this together.'

'Exactly,' said Fat Charlie. Then he said, 'Do what?' but Spider had already hailed a cab.

'We are men with troubles,' said Spider to the world. 'Our father is no more. Our hearts are heavy in our chests. Sorrow settles upon us like pollen in hay fever season. Darkness is our lot, and misfortune our only companion.'

'Right, gentlemen,' said the cabbie, brightly. 'Where am I taking you?'

'To where the three remedies for darkness of the soul may be found,' said Spider.

'Maybe we could get a curry,' suggested Fat Charlie.

'There are three things, and three things only, that can lift the pain of mortality and ease the ravages of life,' said Spider. 'These things are wine, women and song.'

'Curry's nice too,' pointed out Fat Charlie, but nobody was listening to him.

'In any particular order?' asked the cabbie.

'Wine first,' Spider announced. 'Rivers and lakes and vast oceans of wine.'

'Right you are,' said the cabbie, and he pulled out into the traffic.

'I have a particularly bad feeling about all this,' said Fat Charlie, helpfully.

Spider nodded. 'A bad feeling,' he said. 'Yes. We both have a bad feeling. Tonight we shall take our bad feelings and share them, and face them. We shall mourn. We shall drain the bitter dregs of mortality. Pain shared, my brother, is pain not doubled, but halved. No man is an island.'

'Seek not to ask for whom the bell tolls,' intoned the cabbie. 'It tolls for thee.'

'Whoa,' said Spider. 'Now that's a pretty heavy koan you got there.'

'Thank you,' said the cabbie.

'That's how it ends, all right. You are some kind of philosopher. I'm Spider. This is my brother, Fat Charlie.'

'Charles,' said Fat Charlie.

'Steve,' said the cabbie. 'Steve Burridge.'

'Mr Burridge,' said Spider. 'How would you like to be our personal driver, this evening?'

Steve Burridge explained that he was coming up to the end of his shift, and would now be driving his cab home for the night, that dinner with Mrs Burridge and all the little Burridges awaited him.

'You hear that?' said Spider. 'A family man. Now, my brother and I are all the family that we have left. And this is the first time we've met.'

'Sounds like quite a story,' said the cabbie. 'Was there a feud?'

'Not at all. He simply did not know that he had a brother,' said Spider.

'Did *you*?' asked Fat Charlie. 'Know about me?'

'I may have done,' said Spider. 'But things like that can slip a guy's mind so easily.'

The cab pulled over to the kerb. 'Where are we?' asked Fat Charlie. They hadn't gone very far. He thought they were somewhere just off Fleet Street.

'What he asked for,' said the cabbie. 'Wine.'

Spider got out of the cab and stared at the grubby oak and grimy glass exterior of the ancient wine bar. 'Perfect,' he said. 'Pay the man, brother.'

Fat Charlie paid the cabbie. They went inside: down wooden steps to a cellar where rubicund barristers drank side by side with pallid money market fund managers. There was sawdust on the floor, and a wine list chalked illegibly on a blackboard behind the bar.

'What are you drinking?' asked Spider.

'Just a glass of house red, please,' said Fat Charlie.

Spider looked at him gravely. 'We are the final scions of Anansi's line. We do not mourn our father's passing with house red.'

'Er. Right. Well, I'll have what you're having then.'

Spider went up to the bar, easing his way through the crush of people as if it was not there. In several minutes he returned, carrying two wine glasses, a corkscrew and an extremely dusty wine bottle. He opened the bottle with an ease that left Fat Charlie, who always wound up picking fragments of cork from his wine, deeply impressed. Spider poured from the bottle a wine so tawny it was almost black. He filled each glass, then put one in front of Fat Charlie.

'A toast,' he said. 'To our father's memory.'

'To Dad,' said Fat Charlie, and he clinked his glass against Spider's – managing, miraculously, not to spill any as he did so – and he tasted his wine. It was peculiarly bitter, and herby, and salty. 'What is this?'

'Funeral wine, the kind you drink for gods. They haven't made it for a long time. It's seasoned with bitter aloes and rosemary, and with the tears of broken-hearted virgins.'

'And they sell it in a Fleet Street wine bar?' Fat Charlie picked up the bottle, but the label was too faded and dusty to read. 'Never heard of it.'

'These old places have the good stuff, if you ask for it,' said Spider. 'Or maybe I just think they do.'

Fat Charlie took another sip of his wine. It was powerful and pungent.

'It's not a sipping wine,' said Spider. 'It's a mourning wine. You drain it. Like this.' He took a huge swig. Then he made a face. 'It tastes better that way, too.'

Fat Charlie hesitated, then took a large mouthful of the strange wine. He could imagine that he was able to taste the aloes and the rosemary. He wondered if the salt was really tears.

'They put in the rosemary for remembrance,' said Spider, and he began to top up their glasses. Fat Charlie started to try to explain that he wasn't really up for too much wine tonight, and that he had to work tomorrow, but Spider cut him off. 'It's your turn to make a toast,' he said.

'Er. Right,' said Fat Charlie. 'To Mum.'

They drank to their mother. Fat Charlie found that the taste of the bitter wine was beginning to grow on him; he found his eyes prickling, and a sense of loss, profound and painful, ran through him. He missed his mother. He missed his childhood. He even missed his father. Across the table, Spider was shaking his head; a tear ran down Spider's face, and plopped into the wineglass; he reached for the bottle and poured more wine for them both.

Fat Charlie drank.

Grief ran through him as he drank, filling his head and his body with loss and with the pain of absence, swelling through him like waves on the ocean.

His own tears were running down his face, splashing into his drink. He fumbled in his pockets for a tissue. Spider poured out the last of the black wine, for both of them.

'Did they really sell this wine here?'

'They had a bottle they didn't know they had. They just needed to be reminded.'

Fat Charlie blew his nose. 'I never knew I had a brother,' he said.

'I did,' admitted Spider. 'I always meant to look you up, but I got distracted. You know how it is.'

'Not really.'

'Things came up.'

'What kind of things?'

'Things. They came up. That's what things do. They come up. I can't be expected to keep track of them all.'

'Well, give me a f'rinstance.'

Spider drank more wine. 'OK. The last time I decided that you and I should meet, I, well, I spent days planning it. Wanted it to go perfectly. I had to choose my wardrobe. Then I had to decide what I'd say to you when we met. I knew that the meeting of two brothers, well, it's the subject of epics, isn't it? I decided that the only way to treat it with the appropriate gravity would be to do it in verse. But what kind of verse? Am I going to rap it? Declaim it? I mean, I'm not going to greet you with a limerick. So. It had to be something dark, something powerful, rhythmic, epic. And then, I had it. The perfect first line. *Blood calls to blood like sirens in the night*. It says so much. I knew I'd be able to get everything in there – people dying in alleys, sweat and nightmares, the power of free spirits uncrushable. Everything was going to be there. And then I had to come up with a second line, and the whole thing completely fell apart. The best I could come up with was *Tum-tumpty-tumpty-tumpty got a fright*.'

Fat Charlie blinked. 'Who exactly is Tum-tumpty-tumpty-tumpty?'

'It's not anybody. It's just there to show you where the words ought to be. But I never really got any further on it than that, and I couldn't turn up with just a first line, some tumpties and three words of an epic poem, could I? That would have been disrespecting you.'

'Well . . .'

'Exactly. So I went to Hawaii for the week instead. Like I said, something came up.'

Fat Charlie drank more of his wine. He was beginning to like it. Sometimes strong tastes fit strong emotions, and this was one of those times. 'It couldn't *always* have been the second line of a poem, though,' he said.

Spider put his thin hand on top of Fat Charlie's larger hand. 'Enough about me,' he said. 'I want to hear about you.'

'Not much to tell,' said Fat Charlie. He told his brother about his life. About Rosie and Rosie's mother, about Grahame Coats and the Grahame Coats Agency, and his brother nodded his head. It didn't sound like much of a life, now that Fat Charlie was putting it into words.

'Still,' Fat Charlie said, philosophically, 'I figure that there are those people you read about in the gossip pages of newspapers. And they are always saying how dull and empty and pointless their lives are.' He held the wine bottle above his glass, hoping there was just enough of the wine left for another mouthful, but there was barely a drip. The bottle was empty. It had lasted longer than it had any right to have lasted, but now there was nothing left at all.

Spider stood up. 'I've met those people,' he said. 'The ones from the glossy magazines. I've walked among them. I have seen, first-hand, their callow empty lives. I have watched them from the shadows when they thought themselves alone. And I can tell you this: I'm afraid there is not one of them who would swap lives with you at gunpoint, my brother. Come on.'

'Whuh? Where are you going?'

'We are going. We have accomplished the first part of tonight's triune mission. Wine has been drunk. Two parts left to go.'

'Er . . .'

Fat Charlie followed Spider outside, hoping the cool night air would clear his head. It didn't. Fat Charlie's head was feeling like it might float away if it wasn't firmly tied down.

'Women next,' said Spider. 'Then song.'

* * *

It is possibly worth mentioning that in Fat Charlie's world, women did not simply turn up. You needed to be introduced to them; you needed to pluck up the courage to talk to them; you needed to find a subject to talk about when you did, and then, once you had achieved those heights, there were further peaks to scale. You needed to dare to ask them if they were doing anything on Saturday night, and then when you did, mostly they had hair that needed washing that night, or diaries to update, or cockatiels to groom, or they simply needed to wait by the phone for some other man not to call.

But Spider lived in a different world.

They wandered towards the West End, stopping when they reached a crowded pub. The patrons spilled out on to the pavement, and Spider stopped and said hello to what turned out to be a birthday celebration for a young lady named Sybilla, who was only too flattered when Spider insisted on buying a birthday round of drinks for her and for her friends. Then he told jokes ('. . . and the duck says, *Put it on my bill? WhaddayathinkIam? Some kinda perrvert?*') and he laughed at his own jokes, a booming, joyful laugh. He could remember the names of all the people around him. He talked to people, and listened to what they said. When Spider announced it was time to find another pub, the entire birthday group decided, as one woman, that they were coming with him . . .

By the time they reached their third pub, Spider resembled someone from a rock video. He was draped with girls. They snuggled in. Several of them had kissed him, half-joking, half-seriously. Fat Charlie watched in envious horror.

'You his bodyguard?' asked one of the girls.

'What?'

'His bodyguard. *Are* you?'

'No,' said Fat Charlie. 'I'm his brother.'

'Wow,' she said. 'I didn't know he had a brother. I think he's amazing.'

'Me too,' said another, who had spent some time cuddling Spider, until forced away by the press of other bodies with similar ideas. She noticed Fat Charlie for the first time. 'Are you his manager?'

'No. He's the brother,' said the first girl. 'He was just telling me,' she added, pointedly.

The second ignored her. 'Are you from the States as well?' she asked. 'You've sort of got a bit of an accent.'

'When I was younger,' said Fat Charlie, 'we lived in Florida. My dad was American, my mum was from, well, she was originally from Saint Andrews, but she grew up in . . .'

Nobody was listening.

When they moved on from there, the remnants of the birthday celebration accompanied them. The women surrounded Spider, enquiring where they were going next. Restaurants were suggested, as were nightclubs. Spider simply grinned and kept walking.

Fat Charlie trailed along behind them, feeling more left out than ever.

They stumbled through the neon and striplight world. Spider had his arms around several of the women. He would kiss them, as he walked, indiscriminately, like a man taking a bite from first one summer fruit, then another. None of them seemed to mind.

It's not normal, thought Fat Charlie. *That's what it's not.* He was not even trying to keep up, merely attempting not to be left behind.

He could still taste the bitter wine on his tongue.

He became aware that a girl was walking along beside him. She was small, and pretty in a pixyish sort of way. She tugged at his sleeve. 'What are we doing?' she asked. 'Where are we going?'

'We're mourning my father,' he said, 'I think.'

'Is it a reality TV show?'

'I hope not.'

Spider stopped and turned. The gleam in his eyes was disturbing. 'We are here,' he announced. 'We have arrived. It is what he would have wanted.' There was a handwritten message on a sheet of bright orange paper on the door outside the pub. It said on it: 'Tonight. Upstair's. KAROAKE.'

'Song,' said Spider. Then he said, 'It's showtime!'

'No,' said Fat Charlie. He stopped where he was.

'It's what he loved,' said Spider.

'I don't sing. Not in public. And I'm drunk. And, I really don't think this is a really good idea.'

'It's a *great* idea.' Spider had a perfectly convincing smile. Properly deployed, a smile like that could launch a holy war. Fat Charlie, however, was not convinced.

'Look,' he said, trying to keep the panic from his voice. 'There are things that people don't do. Right? Some people don't fly. Some people don't have sex in public. Some people don't turn into smoke and blow away. I don't do any of those things, and I don't sing either.'

'Not even for Dad?'

'Especially not for Dad. He's not going to embarrass me from beyond the grave. Well, not any more than he has already.'

''Scuse me,' said one of the young women. ''Scuse me but are we going in? 'Cause I'm getting cold out here, and Sybilla needs to wee.'

'We're going in,' said Spider, and he smiled at her.

Fat Charlie wanted to protest, to stand his ground, but he found himself swept inside, hating himself.

He caught up with Spider on the stairs. 'I'll go in,' he said. 'But I won't sing.'

'You're already in.'

'I know. But I'm not singing.'

'Not much point in saying you won't go in if you're already in.'

'I can't sing.'

'You telling me I inherited all the musical talent as well?'

'I'm telling you that if I have to open my mouth in order to sing in public, I'll throw up.'

Spider squeezed his arm, reassuringly. 'You watch how I do it,' he said.

The birthday girl and two of her friends stumbled up on to the little dais, and giggled their way through 'Dancing Queen'. Fat Charlie drank a gin and tonic somebody had put into his hand, and he winced at every note they missed, at every key-change that didn't happen. There was a round of applause from the rest of the birthday group.

Another of the women took the stage. It was the pixyish one who had asked Fat Charlie where they were going. The opening chords sounded to 'Stand By Me', and she began, using the phrase in its most approximate and all-encompassing way, to sing along: she missed every note, came in too soon or too late on every line, and misread most of them. Fat Charlie felt for her.

She climbed down from the stage, and came towards the bar.

Fat Charlie was going to say something sympathetic, but she was glowing with joy. 'That was *so* great,' she said. 'I mean, that was just a*maz*ing.' Fat Charlie bought her a drink, a large vodka and orange. 'That was *such* a laugh,' she told him. 'Are you going to do it? Go on. You have to do it. I bet you won't be any crapper than I was.'

Fat Charlie shrugged, in a way that, he hoped, indicated that he contained within him depths of crap as yet unplumbed.

Spider walked over to the little stage as if a spotlight was following him.

'I bet this will be good,' said the vodka and orange. 'Did someone say you were his brother?'

'No,' muttered Fat Charlie, ungraciously. 'I said that *he* was *my* brother.'

Spider began to sing. It was 'Under the Boardwalk'.

It wouldn't have happened if Fat Charlie had not liked the song so much. When Fat Charlie was thirteen he had believed that 'Under the Boardwalk' was the greatest song in the world. (By the time he was a jaded and world-weary fourteen-year-old, it had become Bob Marley's 'No Woman No Cry'.) And now Spider was singing his song, and singing it well. He sang it in tune, he sang it as if he meant it. People stopped drinking, stopped talking, and they looked at him, and they listened.

When Spider finished singing, people cheered. Had they been wearing hats, they might well have flung them into the air.

'I can see why you wouldn't want to follow that,' said the vodka and orange to Fat Charlie. 'I mean, you can't follow that, can you?'

'Well . . .' said Fat Charlie.

'I mean,' she said with a grin, 'you can see who's got all the talent in your family.' She tipped her head, as she said it, and tilted her chin. It was the chin-tilt that did it.

Fat Charlie headed toward the stage, putting one foot in front of the other in an impressive display of physical dexterity. He was sweating.

The next few minutes passed in a blur. He spoke to the DJ, chose his song from the list – 'Unforgettable' – waited for what seemed like a brief eternity, and was handed a microphone.

His mouth was dry. His heart was fluttering in his chest.

On the screen was his first word: *Unforgettable* . . .

Now, Fat Charlie could *really* sing. He had range and power and expression. When he sang his whole body became an instrument.

The music started . . .

In Fat Charlie's head, he was all ready to open his mouth, and to sing. '*Unforgettable*,' he would sing. He would sing it to his dead father and to his brother and the night, telling them all that they were things it was impossible to forget.

Only he couldn't do it. There were people looking up at him. Barely two dozen of them, in the upstairs room of a pub. Many of them were women. In front of an audience, Fat Charlie couldn't even open his mouth.

He could hear the music playing, but he just stood there. He felt very cold. His feet seemed a long way away.

He forced his mouth open.

'I think,' he said, very distinctly, into the microphone, over the music, and heard his words echoing back from every corner of the room. 'I think I'm going to be sick.'

There was no graceful exit from the stage.

After that, everything got a bit wobbly.

* * *

There are myth-places. They exist, each in their own way. Some of them are overlaid on the world; others exist beneath the world as it is, like an underpainting.

There are mountains. They are the rocky places you will reach before you come to the cliffs that border the end of the world, and there are caves in those mountains, deep caves that were inhabited long before the first men walked the earth.

They are inhabited still.

Chapter Five

In Which We Examine the Many Consequences of the Morning After

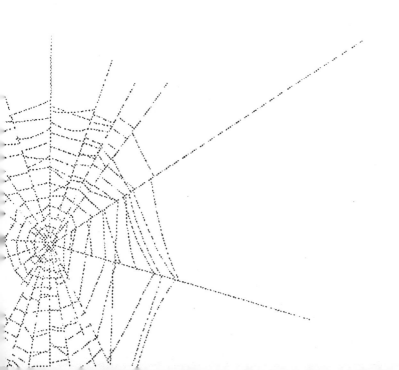

Fat Charlie was thirsty.

Fat Charlie was thirsty and his head hurt.

Fat Charlie was thirsty and his head hurt and his mouth tasted evil and his eyes were too tight in his head and all his teeth twinged and his stomach burned and his back was aching in a way that started around his knees and went up to his forehead and his brains had been removed and replaced with cotton balls and needles and pins which was why it hurt to try and think, and his eyes were not just too tight in his head but they must have rolled out in the night and been reattached with roofing nails; and now he noticed that anything louder than the gentle Brownian motion of air molecules drifting softly past each other was above his pain threshold. Also, he wished he were dead.

Fat Charlie opened his eyes, which was a mistake, in that it let daylight in, which hurt. It also told him where he was (in his own bed, in his bedroom) and because he was staring at the clock on his bedside table, it told him that the time was 11.30.

That, he thought, one word at a time, was about as bad as things could get: he had the kind of hangover that an Old

Testament God might have smitten the Midianites with, and the next time he saw Grahame Coats he would undoubtedly learn that he had been fired.

He wondered if he could sound convincingly sick over the phone, then realised that the challenge would be convincingly sounding anything else.

He could not remember getting home last night.

He would phone the office, the moment he was able to remember the telephone number. He would apologise – crippling twenty-four-hour flu, flat on his back, nothing that could be done . . .

'You know,' said someone in the bed next to him, 'I think there's a bottle of water on your side. Could you pass it over here?'

Fat Charlie wanted to explain that there was no water on his side of the bed, and that there was, in fact, no water closer than the bathroom sink, if he disinfected the toothbrush mug first, but he realised he was staring at one of several bottles of water, sitting on the bedside table. He reached his hand out, and closed fingers that felt like they belonged to someone else around one of them, then, with the sort of effort people usually reserve for hauling themselves up the final few feet of a sheer rock face, he rolled over in bed.

It was the vodka and orange.

Also, she was naked. At least, the bits of her he could see were.

She took the water, and pulled the sheet up to cover her chest. 'Ta. He said to tell you,' she said, 'when you woke, not to worry about calling work and telling them you were ill. He said to tell you he's already taken care of it.'

Fat Charlie's mind was not put at rest. His fears and worries were not allayed. Then again, in the condition he was in, he only had room in his head for a single thing to worry about at once, and right now he was worrying about whether or not he would make it to the bathroom in time.

'You'll need more liquids,' said the girl. 'You'll need to replenish your electrolytes.'

Fat Charlie made it to the bathroom in time. Afterwards, seeing he was there already, he stood under the shower until the room stopped undulating, and then he brushed his teeth without throwing up.

When he returned to the bedroom, the vodka and orange was no longer there, which was a relief to Fat Charlie, who had started to hope that she might have been an alcohol-induced delusion, like pink elephants or the nightmarish idea that he had taken to the stage to sing on the previous evening.

He could not find his dressing gown, so he pulled on a tracksuit, in order to feel dressed enough to visit the kitchen, at the far end of the hall.

His phone chimed, and he rummaged through his jacket, which was on the floor beside the bed, until he found it, and flipped it open. He grunted into it, as anonymously as he could, just in case it was someone from the Grahame Coats Agency trying to discern his whereabouts.

'It's me,' said Spider's voice. 'Everything's OK.'

'You told them I was dead?'

'Better than that. I told them I was you.'

'But.' Fat Charlie tried to think clearly. 'But you're not me.'

'Hey. I know that. I told them I was.'

'You don't even look like me.'

'Brother of mine, you are harshing a potential mellow here. It's all taken care of. Oops. Gotta go. The big boss needs to talk to me.'

'Grahame Coats? Look, Spider—'

But Spider had put down the phone, and the screen blanked.

Fat Charlie's dressing gown came through the door. There was a girl inside it. It looked significantly better on her than it ever had on him. She was carrying a tray, on which was a water-glass with a fizzing Alka-Seltzer in it, along with something in a mug.

'Drink both of these,' she told him. 'The mug first. Just knock it back.'

'What's in the mug?'

'Egg yolk, Worcestershire sauce, Tabasco, salt, dash of vodka, things like that,' she said. 'Kill or cure. Now,' she told him, in tones that brooked no argument. 'Drink.'

Fat Charlie drank.

'Oh my God,' he said.

'Yeah,' she agreed. 'But you're still alive.'

He wasn't sure about that. He drank the Alka-Seltzer anyway. Something occurred to him.

'Um,' said Fat Charlie. 'Um. Look. Last night. Did we. Um.'

She looked blank.

'Did we what?'

'Did we. You know. *Do* it?'

'You mean you don't remember?' Her face fell. 'You said it was the best you'd ever had. That it was as if you'd never made love to a woman before. You were part god, part animal, and part unstoppable sex machine . . .'

Fat Charlie didn't know where to look. She giggled.

'I'm just winding you up,' she said. 'I'd helped your brother get you home, we cleaned you up, and, after that, you know.'

'No,' he said. 'I don't know.'

'Well,' she said, 'you were completely out cold, and it's a big bed. I'm not sure where your brother slept. He must have the constitution of an ox. He was up at the crack of dawn, all bright and smiling.'

'He went into work,' said Fat Charlie. 'He told them he was me.'

'Wouldn't they be able to tell the difference? I mean, you're not exactly twins.'

'Apparently not.' He shook his head. Then he looked at her. She stuck out a small, extremely pink tongue at him.

'What's your name?'

'You mean you've forgotten? I remember your name. You're Fat Charlie.'

'Charles,' he said. 'Just Charles is fine.'

'I'm Daisy,' she said, and stuck out her hand. 'Pleased to meet you.'

They shook hands solemnly.

'I feel a bit better,' said Fat Charlie.

'Like I said,' she said. 'Kill or cure.'

***

Spider was having a great day at the office. He almost never worked in offices. He almost never worked. Everything was new, everything was marvellous and strange, from the tiny lift that

lurched him up to the fifth floor, to the warrenlike offices of the
Grahame Coats Agency. He stared, fascinated, at the glass case in
the lobby filled with dusty awards. He wandered through the
offices, and when anyone asked him who he was, he would say
'I'm Fat Charlie Nancy', and he'd say it in his god-voice, which
would make whatever he said practically true.

He found the tea-room, and made himself several cups of tea.
Then he carried them back to Fat Charlie's desk, and arranged
them around it in an artistic fashion. He started to play with the
computer network. It asked him for a password. 'I'm Fat Charlie
Nancy,' he told the computer, but there were still places it didn't
want him to go, so he said, 'I'm Grahame Coats,' and it opened to
him like a flower.

He looked at things on the computer until he got bored.

He dealt with the contents of Fat Charlie's in-basket. He dealt
with Fat Charlie's pending basket.

It occurred to him that Fat Charlie would be waking up around
now, so he called him at home, in order to reassure him; he just
felt that he was making a little headway when Grahame Coats put
his head round the door, ran his fingers across his stoat-like lips,
and beckoned.

'Gotta go,' Spider said to his brother. 'The big boss needs to talk
to me.' He put down the phone.

'Making private phone calls on company time, Nancy,' stated
Grahame Coats.

'Abso-friggin'-lutely,' agreed Spider.

'And was that myself you were referring to as "the big boss"?'
asked Grahame Coats. They walked to the end of the hallway, and
into his office.

'You're the biggest,' said Spider. 'And the bossest.'

Grahame Coats looked puzzled; he suspected he was being
made fun of, but he was not certain, and this disturbed him.

'Well, sit ye down, sit ye down,' he said.

Spider sat him down.

It was Grahame Coats's custom to keep the turnover of staff at
the Grahame Coats Agency fairly constant. Some people came
and went. Others came, and remained until just before their jobs
would begin to carry some kind of employment protection. Fat

Charlie had been there longer than anyone: one year and eleven months. One month to go before redundancy payments or industrial tribunals could become a part of his life.

There was a speech that Grahame Coats gave, before he fired someone. He was very proud of his speech.

'Into each life,' he began, 'a little rain must fall. There's no cloud without a silver lining.'

'It's an ill wind,' offered Spider, 'that blows no one good.'

'Ah. Yes. Yes indeed. Well. As we pass through this vale of tears, we must pause to reflect that—'

'The first cut,' said Spider, 'is the deepest.'

'What? Oh.' Grahame Coats scrabbled to remember what came next. 'Happiness,' he pronounced, 'is like a butterfly.'

'Or a bluebird,' agreed Spider.

'Quite. If I may finish?'

'Of course. Be my guest,' said Spider, cheerfully.

'And the happiness of every soul at the Grahame Coats Agency is as important to me as my own.'

'I cannot tell you,' said Spider, 'how happy that makes me.'

'Yes,' said Grahame Coats.

'Well, I better get back to work,' said Spider. 'It's been a blast, though. Next time you want to share some more, just call me. You know where I am.'

'Happiness,' said Grahame Coats. His voice was taking on a faintly strangulated quality. 'And what I wonder, Nancy, Charles, is this – are you happy here? And do you not agree that you might be rather happier elsewhere?'

'That's not what I wonder,' said Spider. 'You want to know what I wonder?'

Grahame Coats said nothing. It had never gone like this before. Normally, at this point, their faces fell, and they went into shock. Sometimes they cried. Grahame Coats had never minded when they cried.

'What I wonder,' said Spider, 'is what the accounts in the Cayman Islands are for. You know, because it almost sort of looks like money that should go to our client accounts sometimes just goes into the Cayman Island accounts instead. And it seems a funny sort of way to organise the finances, for the money coming in to rest in those accounts. I've never seen anything like it before. I was hoping you could explain it to me.'

Grahame Coats had gone off-white – one of those colours that turn up in paint catalogues with names like Parchment or Magnolia. He said, 'How did you get access to those accounts?'

'Computers,' said Spider. 'Do they drive you as nuts as they drive me? What can you do?'

Grahame Coats thought for several long moments. He had always liked to imagine that his financial affairs were so deeply tangled that, even if the Fraud Squad were ever able to conclude that financial crimes had been committed, they would find it extremely difficult to explain to a jury exactly what kind of crimes they were.

'There's nothing illegal about having offshore accounts,' he said, as carelessly as possible.

'Illegal?' said Spider. 'I should hope not. I mean, if I saw anything illegal, I should have to report it to the appropriate authorities.'

Grahame Coats picked up a pen from his desk, then he put it down again. 'Ah,' he said. 'Well, delightful though it is to chat, converse, spend time and otherwise hobnob with you, Charles, I suspect that both of us have work we should be getting on with. Time and tide, after all, wait for no man. Procrastination is the thief of time.'

'Life is a rock,' suggested Spider, 'but the radio rolled me.'

'Whatever.'

* * *

Fat Charlie was starting to feel human again. He was no longer in pain; slow, intimate waves of nausea were no longer sweeping over him. While he was not yet convinced that the world was a fine and joyous place, he was no longer in the ninth circle of hangover hell, and this was a good thing.

Daisy had taken over the bathroom. He had listened to the taps running, and then to some contented splashes.

He knocked on the bathroom door.

'I'm in here,' said Daisy. 'I'm in the bath.'

'I know,' said Fat Charlie. 'I mean, I didn't know, but I thought you probably were.'

'Yes?' said Daisy.

'I just wondered,' he said, through the door. 'I wondered why you came back here. Last night.'

'Well,' she said. 'You were a bit the worse for wear. And your brother looked like he needed a hand. I'm not working this morning, so. *Voilà.*'

'*Voilà,*' said Fat Charlie. On the one hand, she felt sorry for him. And on the other, she really liked Spider. Yes. He'd only had a brother for a little over a day, and already he felt there would be no surprises left in this new family relationship. Spider was the cool one; he was the other one.

She said, 'You have a lovely voice.'

'What?'

'You were singing in the taxi, when we were going home. "Unforgettable". It was lovely.'

He had somehow put the karaoke incident out of his mind, placed it in the dark places one disposes of inconvenient things. Now it came back, and he wished it hadn't.

'You were great,' she said. 'Will you sing to me, later?'

Fat Charlie thought desperately, and then was saved from thinking desperately by the doorbell.

'Someone at the door,' he said.

He went downstairs and opened the door and things got worse. Rosie's mother gave him a look that would have curdled milk. She said nothing. She was holding a large white envelope.

'Hello,' said Fat Charlie. 'Mrs Noah. Nice to see you. Um.'

She sniffed and held the envelope in front of her. 'Oh,' she said. 'You're here. So. You going to invite me in?'

That's right, thought Fat Charlie. *Your kind always have to be invited. Just say no, and she'll have to go away.* 'Of course, Mrs Noah. Please, come in.' *So that's how vampires do it.* 'Would you like a cup of tea?'

'Don't think you can get around me like that,' she said. 'Because you can't.'

'Er. Right.'

Up the narrow stairs and into the kitchen. Rosie's mother

looked around and made a face as if to indicate that it did not meet her standards of hygiene, containing, as it did, edible foodstuffs. 'Coffee? Water?' *Don't say wax fruit.* 'Wax fruit?' *Damn.*

'I understand from Rosie that your father recently passed away,' she said.

'Yes. He did.'

'When Rosie's father passed, they did a four-page obituary in *Cooks and Cookery*. They said he was solely responsible for the arrival of Caribbean Fusion Cuisine in this country.'

'Oh,' he said.

'It's not like he left me badly off, neither. He had life insurance, and he owned a share of two successful restaurants. I'm a very well-off woman. When I die, it will all go to Rosie.'

'When we're married,' said Fat Charlie, 'I'll be looking after her. Don't you worry.'

'I'm not saying you're only after Rosie for my money,' said Rosie's mother, in a tone of voice that made it clear that that was exactly what she did believe.

Fat Charlie's headache started coming back. 'Mrs Noah, is there anything I can help you with?'

'I've been talking to Rosie, and we've decided that I should start helping with your wedding plans,' she said, primly. 'I need a list of your relations and friends. The ones you were hoping to invite. Names, addresses, e-mail and phone numbers. I've made a form for you to fill out. I thought I'd save on postage and drop it off myself, since I was going to be passing by Maxwell Gardens anyway. I was not expecting to find you home.' She handed him the large white envelope. 'There will be a total of ninety people at the wedding. You will be permitted a total of eight family members and six personal friends. The personal friends, and four family members will comprise Table H. The rest of your group will be at Table C. Your father would have been seated with us at the head table, but seeing that he has passed over, we have allocated his seat to Rosie's Aunt Winifred. Have you decided on your best man, yet?'

Fat Charlie shook his head.

'Well, when you do, make certain he knows that there won't be any crude stuff in his speech. I don't want to hear nothing from your best man I wouldn't hear in a church. You understand me?'

Fat Charlie wondered what Rosie's mother would usually hear in a church. Probably just cries of 'Back! Foul beast of Hell!' followed by gasps of 'Is it alive?' and a nervous enquiry as to whether anybody had remembered to bring the stakes and hammers.

'I think,' said Fat Charlie, 'I have more than eight relations. I mean, there are cousins, and great-aunts and things.'

'What you obviously fail to grasp,' said Rosie's mother, 'is that weddings cost money. I've allocated £175 a person to tables A to D – Table A is the head table – which takes care of Rosie's closest relations and my women's club, and £125 to tables E to G, which are, you know, more distant acquaintances, the children and so on and so forth.'

'You said my friends would be at Table H,' said Fat Charlie.

'That's the next tier down. They won't be getting the avocado shrimp starters or the sherry trifle.'

'When Rosie and I talked about it last, we thought we'd be going for a sort of a general West Indian theme to the food.'

Rosie's mother sniffed. 'She sometimes doesn't know her own mind, that girl. But she and I are now in full agreement.'

'Look,' said Fat Charlie, 'I think maybe I ought to talk to Rosie about all this, and get back to you.'

'Just fill out the forms,' said Rosie's mother. Then she said, suspiciously, 'Why aren't you at work?'

'I'm. Um. I'm not in. That is to say, I'm off this morning. Not going in today. I'm. Not.'

'I hope you told Rosie that. She was planning to see you for lunch, she told me. That was why she could not have lunch with me.'

Fat Charlie took this information in. 'Right,' he said. 'Well, thanks for popping over, Mrs Noah. I'll talk to Rosie, and—'

Daisy came into the kitchen. She wore a towel wrapped around her head, and Fat Charlie's dressing gown, which clung to her damp body. She said 'There's orange juice, isn't there? I know I saw some, when I was poking around before. How's your head?

Any better?' She opened the fridge door, and poured herself a tall glass of orange juice.

Rosie's mother cleared her throat. It did not sound like a throat being cleared. It sounded like pebbles rattling down a beach.

'Hullo,' said Daisy. 'I'm Daisy.'

The temperature in the kitchen began to drop. 'Indeed?' said Rosie's mother. Icicles hung from the final D.

'I wonder what they would have called oranges,' said Fat Charlie into the silence, 'if they weren't orange. I mean, if they were some previously unknown blue fruit, would they have been called *blues*? Would we be drinking blue juice?'

'What?' asked Rosie's mother.

'Bless. You should hear the things that come out of your mouth,' said Daisy, cheerfully. 'Right. I'm going to see if I can find my clothes. Lovely meeting you.'

She went out. Fat Charlie did not resume breathing.

'Who,' said Rosie's mother, perfectly calmly. 'Was. That.'

'My sis-cousin. My cousin,' said Fat Charlie. 'I just think of her as my sister. We were very close, growing up. She just decided to crash here last night. She's a bit of a wild child. Well. Yes. You'll see her at the wedding.'

'I'll put her down for Table H,' said Rosie's mother. 'She'll be more comfortable there.' She said it in the same way most people would say things like, 'Do you wish to die quickly, or shall I let Mongo have his fun first?'

'Right,' said Fat Charlie. 'Well,' he said. 'Lovely to see you. Well,' he said, 'you must have lots of things to be getting on with. And,' he said, 'I need to be getting to work.'

'I thought you had the day off.'

'Morning. I've got the morning off. And it's nearly over. And I should be getting off to work now so goodbye.'

She clutched her handbag to her, and she stood up. Fat Charlie followed her out into the hall.

'Lovely seeing you,' he said.

She blinked, as a nictitating python might blink before striking. 'Goodbye, Daisy,' she called. 'I'll see you at the wedding.'

Daisy, now wearing panties and a bra, and in the process of

pulling on a T-shirt, leaned out into the hall. 'Take care,' she said, and went back into Fat Charlie's bedroom.

Rosie's mother said nothing else as Fat Charlie led her down the stairs. He opened the door for her, and as she went past him, he saw on her face something terrible, something that made his stomach knot more than it was knotting already: the thing that Rosie's mother was doing with her mouth. It was pulled up at the corners in a ghastly rictus. Like a skull with lips, Rosie's mother was smiling.

He closed the door behind her and he stood and shivered in the downstairs hall. Then, like a man going to the electric chair, he went back up the hall steps.

'Who was that?' asked Daisy, who was now almost dressed.

'My fiancée's mother.'

'She's a real bundle of joy, isn't she?' She was dressed in the same clothes she had worn the previous night.

'You going to work like that?'

'Oh. Bless. No, I'll go home and change. This isn't how I look at work, anyway. Can you ring a taxi?'

'Where are you headed?'

'Hendon.'

He called a local taxi service. Then he sat on the floor in the hallway and contemplated various future scenarios, all of them uncontemplatable.

Someone was standing next to him. 'I've got some B vitamins in my bag,' she said. 'Or you could try sucking on a spoonful of honey. It's never done anything for me, but my flatmate swears by it for hangovers.'

'It's not that,' said Fat Charlie. 'I told her you were my cousin. So she wouldn't think you were my, that we, you know, a strange girl in the apartment, all that.'

'Cousin, is it? Well, not to worry. She'll probably forget all about me, and if she doesn't, tell her I left the country mysteriously. You'll never see me again.'

'Really? Promise?'

'You don't have to sound so pleased about it.'

A car horn sounded in the street outside. 'That'll be my taxi. Stand up and say goodbye.'

He stood up.

'Not to worry,' she said. She hugged him.

'I think my life is over,' he said.

'No. It's not.'

'I'm doomed.'

'Thanks,' she said. She leaned up, and she kissed him on the lips, longer and harder than could possibly fit within the bounds of recent introduction. Then she smiled, and walked jauntily down the stairs and let herself out.

'This,' said Fat Charlie out loud, when the door closed, 'probably isn't really happening.'

He could still taste her on his lips, all orange-juice and raspberries. That was a kiss. That was a serious kiss. There was an oomf behind that kiss that he had never in his whole life had before, not even from—

'Rosie,' he said.

He flipped open his phone, and speed-dialled her.

'This is Rosie's phone,' said Rosie's voice. 'I'm busy or I've lost the phone again. And you're in voicemail. Try me at home or leave me a message.'

Fat Charlie closed the phone. Then he put on his coat over his tracksuit and, wincing just a little at the terrible unblinking daylight, he went out into the street.

***

Rosie Noah was worried, which in itself worried her. It was, as so many things in Rosie's world were, whether she would admit it to herself or not, Rosie's mother's fault.

Rosie had become quite used to a world in which her mother hated the idea of her marrying Fat Charlie Nancy. She took her mother's opposition to the marriage as a sign from the heavens that she was probably doing something right, even when she was not entirely sure in her own mind that this was actually the case.

And she loved him, of course. He was solid, reassuring, sane . . .

Her mother's about-turn on the matter of Fat Charlie had Rosie worried, and her mother's sudden enthusiasm for wedding organisation troubled her deeply.

She had phoned Fat Charlie the previous night to discuss the matter, but he was not answering his phones. Rosie thought perhaps he had had an early night.

It was why she was giving up her lunch time to talk to him.

The Grahame Coats Agency occupied the top floor of a grey Victorian building in the Aldwych, and was at the top of five flights of stairs. There was a lift, though, which had been installed a hundred years before by theatrical agent Rupert 'Binky' Butterworth. It was an extremely small, slow, juddery lift, whose design and function peculiarities only became comprehensible when you discovered that Binky Butterworth had possessed the size, shape and ability to squeeze into small spaces of a portly young hippopotamus, and had designed the lift to fit, at a squeeze, Binky Butterworth and one other, much slimmer, person – a chorus girl, for example, or a chorus boy, Binky was not picky. All it took to make Binky happy was someone seeking theatrical representation squeezed into the lift with him, and a very slow and juddery journey up all six storeys to the top. It was often the case that by the time he reached the top floor, Binky would be so overcome by the pressures of the journey that he would need to go and have a little lie-down, leaving the chorus girl or chorus boy to cool his or her heels in the waiting room, concerned that the red-faced panting and uncontrolled gasping for breath that Binky had been suffering from as they reached the final floors meant that he had been having some kind of early Edwardian embolism.

People would go into the lift with Binky Butterworth once, but after that they used the stairs.

Grahame Coats, who had purchased the remains of the Butterworth Agency from Binky's granddaughter more than twenty years before, maintained the lift was part of history.

Rosie slammed the inner accordion door, closed the outer door, and went into reception, where she told the receptionist she wanted to see Charles Nancy. She sat down, beneath the photographs of Grahame Coats with people he had represented: she recognised Morris Livingstone, the comedian; some once-famous boy bands; and a clutch of sports stars who had, in their later years, become 'personalities' – the kind who got as much fun out of life as they could until a new liver became available.

A man came into reception. He did not look much like Fat Charlie. He was darker, and he was smiling as if he were amused by everything – deeply, dangerously amused.

'I'm Fat Charlie Nancy,' said the man.

Rosie walked over to Fat Charlie and gave him a peck on the cheek. He said, 'Do I know you?' which was an odd thing to say, and then he said, 'Of course I do. You're Rosie. And you get more beautiful every day,' and he kissed her in return, touching his lips to hers. Their lips only brushed, but Rosie's heart began to beat like Binky Butterworth's after a particularly juddery lift-journey pressed up against a chorine.

'Lunch,' squeaked Rosie. 'Passing. Thought maybe we could. Talk.'

'Yeah,' said the man who Rosie now thought of as Fat Charlie. 'Lunch.'

He put a comfortable arm around Rosie. 'Anywhere you want to go for lunch?'

'Oh,' she said. 'Just. Wherever you want.' It was the way he smelled, she thought. Why had she never before noticed how much she liked the way he smelled?

'We'll find somewhere,' he said. 'Shall we take the stairs?'

'If it's all the same to you,' she said, 'I think I'd rather take the lift.'

She banged home the accordion door, and they rode down to street level slowly and shakily, pressed up against each other.

Rosie couldn't remember the last time she had been so happy.

When they got out on to the street Rosie's phone beeped to let her know she had missed a call. She ignored it.

They went into the first restaurant they came to. Until the previous month it had been a high-tech sushi restaurant, with a conveyor belt that ran around the room carrying small raw-fishy nibbles priced according to plate colour. The Japanese restaurant had gone out of business, and had been instantly replaced, in the way of London restaurants, by a Hungarian restaurant, which had kept the conveyor belt as a high-tech addition to the world of Hungarian cuisine, which meant that rapidly cooling bowls of goulash, paprika dumplings, and pots of sour cream made their way in stately fashion around the room.

Rosie didn't think it was going to catch on.

'Where were you last night?' she asked.

'I went out,' he said. 'With my brother.'

'You're an only child,' she said.

'I'm not. It turns out I'm half of a matched set.'

'Really? Is this more of your dad's legacy?'

'Honey,' said the man she thought of as Fat Charlie, 'you don't know the half of it.'

'Well,' she said. 'I hope he'll be coming to the wedding.'

'I don't believe he would miss it for the world.' He closed his hand around hers, and she nearly dropped her goulash spoon. 'What are you doing for the rest of the afternoon?'

'Not much. Things are practically dead back at the office right now. Couple of fund-raising phone calls to make, but they can wait. Is there. Um. Were you. Um. Why?'

'It's such a beautiful day. Do you want to go for a walk?'

'That,' said Rosie, 'would be quite lovely.'

They wandered down to the Embankment, and began to walk along the northern back of the Thames, a slow, hand-in-hand amble, talking about nothing much in particular.

'What about *your* work?' asked Rosie, when they stopped to buy an ice cream.

'Oh,' he said. 'They won't mind. They probably won't even notice that I'm not there.'

* * *

Fat Charlie ran up the stairs to the Grahame Coats Agency. He always took the stairs. It was healthier, for a start, and it meant he would never again have to worry about finding himself wedged into the lift with someone else, too close to pretend they weren't there.

He walked into reception, panting slightly. 'Has Rosie been in, Annie?'

'Did you lose her?' said the receptionist.

He walked back to his office. His desk was peculiarly tidy. The clutter of undealt-with correspondence was gone. There was a yellow Post-it note on his computer screen, with 'See me. GC' on it.

He knocked on Grahame Coats's office door. This time a voice said 'Yes?'

'It's me,' he said.

'Yes,' said Grahame Coats. 'Come ye in, Master Nancy. Pull up a pew. I've been giving our conversation of this morning a great deal of thought. And it seems to me that I have misjudged you. You have been working here, for, how long . . . ?'

'Nearly two years.'

'You have been working long and hard. And now your father's sad passing . . .'

'I didn't really know him.'

'Ah. Brave soul, Nancy. Given that it is currently the fallow season, how would you react to an offer of a couple of weeks off? With, I hardly need to add, full pay?'

'Full pay?' said Fat Charlie.

'Full pay, but, yes, I see your point. Spending money. I'm sure you could do with a little spending money, couldn't you?'

Fat Charlie tried to work out what universe he was in. 'Am I being fired?'

Grahame Coats laughed then, like a weasel with a sharp bone stuck in its throat. 'Absatively not. Quite the reverse. In fact I believe,' he said, 'that we now understand each other perfectly. Your job is safe and sound. Safe as houses. As long as you remain the model of circumspection and discretion you have been so far.'

'How safe are houses?' asked Fat Charlie.

'Extremely safe.'

'It's just that I read somewhere that most accidents occur in the home.'

'Then,' said Grahame Coats, 'I think it vitally important that you are encouraged to return to your own house with all celerity.' He handed Fat Charlie a piece of rectangular paper. 'Here,' he said. 'A small thank you for two years of devoted service to the Grahame Coats Agency.' Then, because it was what he always said when he gave people money, 'Don't spend it all at once.'

Fat Charlie looked at the piece of paper. It was a cheque. 'Two thousand pounds. Gosh. I mean, I won't.'

Grahame Coats smiled at Fat Charlie. If there was triumph in that smile, Fat Charlie was too puzzled, too shaken, too bemused, to see it.

'Go well,' said Grahame Coats.

Fat Charlie went back to his office.

Grahame Coats leaned around the door, casually, like a mongoose leaning idly against a snake-den. 'An idle question. If, while you are off enjoying yourself and relaxing – a course of action I cannot press upon you strongly enough – if, during this time, I should need to access your files, could you let me know your password?'

'I think your password should get you anywhere in the system,' said Fat Charlie.

'Without doubt it will,' agreed Grahame Coats, blithely. 'But just in case. You know computers, after all.'

'It's Mermaid,' said Fat Charlie. 'M-E-R-M-A-I-D.'

'Excellent,' said Grahame Coats. 'Excellent.' He didn't rub his hands together, but he might as well have done.

Fat Charlie walked down the stairs with a cheque for two thousand pounds in his pocket, wondering how he could have so misjudged Grahame Coats for the last two years.

He walked round the corner to his bank, and deposited the cheque into his account.

Then he walked down to the Embankment, to breathe, and to think.

He was two thousand pounds richer. His headache of this morning had completely gone. He was feeling solid and prosperous. He wondered if he could talk Rosie into coming on a short holiday with him. It was short notice, but still . . .

And then he saw Spider and Rosie, walking hand in hand, on the other side of the road. Rosie was finishing an ice cream. Then she stopped, and dropped the remainder of the ice cream into a bin, and pulled Spider towards her and, with an ice-creamy mouth, began to kiss him with enthusiasm and gusto.

Fat Charlie could feel his headache coming back. He felt paralysed.

He watched them kissing. He was of the opinion that sooner or later they would have to come up for air, but they didn't, so he walked in the other direction, feeling miserable, until he reached the tube.

And he went home.

By the time he got home, Fat Charlie felt pretty wretched, so he got on to a bed that still smelled faintly of Daisy, and he closed his eyes.

Time passed, and now Fat Charlie was walking along a sandy beach with his father. They were barefoot. He was a kid again, and his father was ageless.

So, his father was saying, *how are you and Spider getting on?*

This is a dream, pointed out Fat Charlie, *and I don't want to talk about it.*

You boys, said his father, shaking his head. *Listen. I'm going to tell you something important.*

What?

But his father did not answer. Something on the edge of the waves had caught his eye, and he reached down and picked it up. Five pointed legs flexed languidly.

Starfish, said his father, musing. *When you cut one in half, they just grow into two new starfish.*

I thought you said you were going to tell me something important.

His father clutched his chest, and he collapsed on to the sand, and stopped moving. Worms came out of the sand and devoured him in moments, leaving nothing but bones.

Dad?

Fat Charlie woke up in his bedroom, his cheeks wet with tears. Then he stopped crying. He had nothing to be upset about. His father had not died; it had simply been a bad dream.

He decided that he would invite Rosie over tomorrow night. They would have steak. He would cook. All would be well.

He got up and got dressed.

He was in the kitchen, twenty minutes later, spooning down a Pot Noodle, when it occurred to him that, although what had happened on the beach had been a dream, his father was still dead.

* * *

Rosie stopped in at her mother's flat in Wimpole Street, late that afternoon.

'I saw your boyfriend today,' said Mrs Noah. Her given name had been Eutheria, but in the last three decades nobody had used it to her face but her late husband, and following his death it had atrophied, and was unlikely to be used again in her lifetime.

'So did I,' said Rosie. 'My God I love that man.'

'Well, of course. You're marrying him, aren't you?'

'Well, yes. I mean, I always knew I loved him, but today I really saw how much I loved him. Everything about him.'

'Did you find out where he was last night?'

'Yes. He explained it all. He was out with his brother.'

'I didn't know he had a brother.'

'He hadn't mentioned him before. They aren't very close.'

Rosie's mother clicked her tongue. 'Must be quite a family reunion going on. Did he mention his cousin, too?'

'Cousin?'

'Or maybe his sister. He didn't seem entirely sure. Pretty thing, in a trashy sort of way. Looked a bit Chinese. No better than she should be, if you ask me. But that's that whole family for you.'

'Mum. You haven't met his family.'

'I met her. She was in his kitchen this morning, walking about that place damn near naked. Shameless. *If* she was his cousin.'

'Fat Charlie wouldn't lie.'

'He's a man, isn't he?'

'*Mum!*'

'And why wasn't he at work today, anyway?'

'He was. He was at work today. We had lunch together.'

Rosie's mother examined her lipstick in a pocket mirror, then, with her forefinger, rubbed the scarlet smudges off her teeth.

'What else did you say to him?' asked Rosie.

'We just talked about the wedding, how I didn't want his best man making one of them near-the-knuckle speeches. He looked to me like he'd been drinking. You know how I warned you about marrying a drinking man.'

'Well, he looked perfectly fine when I saw him,' said Rosie, primly. Then, 'Oh, Mum, I had the most wonderful day. We walked and we talked and – oh, have I told you how wonderful he *smells*? And he has the softest hands.'

'You ask me,' said her mother, 'he smells fishy. Tell you what, next time you see him, you ask him about this cousin of his. I'm not saying she is his cousin, and I'm not saying she's not. I'm just saying that if she is, then he has hookers and strippers and good-time girls in his family, and is not the kind of person you should be seeing romantically.'

Rosie felt more comfortable, now her mother was once more coming down against Fat Charlie. 'Mum. I won't hear another word.'

'All right. I'll hold my tongue. It's not me that's marrying him, after all. Not me that's throwing my life away. Not me that'll be weeping into my pillow while he's out all night drinking with his fancy women. It's not me that'll be waiting, day after day, night after empty night, for him to get out of prison.'

'Mum!' Rosie tried to be indignant, but the thought of Fat Charlie in prison was too funny, too silly, and she found herself stifling a giggle.

Rosie's phone trilled. She answered it, and said, 'Yes,' and, 'I'd love to. That would be wonderful.' She put her phone away.

'That was him,' she said to her mother. 'I'm going over there tomorrow night. He's cooking for me. How sweet is that?' And then she said, 'Prison indeed.'

'I'm a mother,' said her mother, in her foodless flat where the dust did not dare to settle, 'and I know what I know.'

* * *

Grahame Coats sat in his office, while the day faded into dusk, staring at a computer screen. He brought up document after document, spreadsheet after spreadsheet. Some of them he changed. Most of them he deleted.

He was meant to be travelling to Birmingham that evening, where a former footballer, a client of his, was to open a nightclub. Instead he called and apologised: some things were unavoidable.

Soon the light outside the window was gone entirely. Grahame Coats sat in the cold glow of the computer screen, and he changed, and he overwrote, and he deleted.

* * *

Here's another story they tell about Anansi.

Once, long long ago, Anansi's wife planted a field of peas. They were the finest, the fattest, the greenest peas you ever did see. It would have made your mouth water just to look at them.

From the moment Anansi saw the pea field, he wanted them. And he didn't just want some of them, for Anansi was a man of enormous appetites. He did not want to share them. He wanted them all.

So Anansi lay down on his bed and he sighed, long and loud, and his wife and his sons all came a-running. 'I'm a-dying,' said Anansi, in this little weeny-weedy-weaky voice, 'and my life is all over and done.'

At this his wife and his sons began to cry hot tears.

In his weensy-weak voice, Anansi says, 'On my deathbed, you have to promise me two things.'

'Anything, anything,' says his wife and his sons.

'First, you got to promise me you will bury me down under the big breadfruit tree.'

'The big breadfruit tree down by the pea patch, you mean?' asks his wife.

'Of course that's the one I mean,' says Anansi. Then, in his weensy-weak voice, he says, 'And you got to promise something else. Promise me that, as a memorial to me, you going to make a little fire at the foot of my grave. And, to show you ain't forgotten me, you going to keep the little fire burning, and not ever let it go out.'

'We will! We will!' said Anansi's wife and children, wailing and sobbing.

'And on that fire, as mark of your respect and your love, I want to see a lickle pot, filled with salt water, to remind you all of the hot salt tears you shed over me as I lay dying.'

'We shall! We shall!' they wept, and Anansi, he closed his eyes, and he breathed no more.

Well, they carried Anansi down to the big breadfruit tree that grew beside the pea patch, and they buried him six feet down, and at the foot of the grave they built a little fire, and they put a pot beside it, filled with salt water.

Anansi, he waits down there all the day but when night falls he climbs out of the grave, and he goes into the pea patch, where he picks him the fattest, sweetest, ripest peas. He gathers them up and he boils them up in his pot, and he stuffs himself with them till his tummy swells and tightens like a drum.

Then, before dawn, he goes back under the ground, and he goes back to sleep. He sleeps as his wife and his sons find the peas gone, he sleeps through them seeing the pot empty of water and refilling it, he sleeps through their sorrow.

Each night Anansi comes out of his grave, dancing and delighting at the cleverness of him, and each night he fills the pot with peas, and he fills his tummy with peas, and he eats until he cannot eat another thing.

Days go by, and Anansi's family gets thinner and thinner, for nothing ever ripens that isn't picked in the night by Anansi, and they got nothing to eat.

Anansi's wife, she looks down at the empty plates, and she says to her sons, 'What would your father do?'

Her sons, they think and they think, and they remember every tale that Anansi ever told them. Then they go down to the tar-pits, and they buy them sixpennyworth of tar, enough to fill four big buckets, and they take that tar back to the pea patch. And down in the middle of the pea patch, they make them a man out of tar: tar face, tar eyes, tar arms, tar fingers, and tar chest. It was a fine man, as black and as proud as Anansi himself.

That night, old Anansi, fat as he has ever been in his whole life, he scuttles up out of the ground, and, plump and happy, stomach swollen like a drum, he strolls over to the pea patch.

'Who you?' he says to the tar man.

The tar man, he don't say one word.

'This is my place,' said Anansi to the tar man. 'It's my pea patch. You better get going, if you know what's good for you.'

The tar man, he don't say one word, he don't move a muscle.

'I'm the strongest, mightiest, most powerful fellow there is or was or ever will be,' says Anansi to the tar man. 'I'm fiercer than Lion, faster than Cheetah, stronger than Elephant, more terrible than Tiger.' He swelled up with pride at his power and strength and fierceness, and he forgot he was just a little spider. 'Tremble,' says Anansi. 'Tremble and run.'

The tar man, he didn't tremble and he didn't run. Tell the truth, he just stood there.

So Anansi hits him.

Anansi's fist, it sticks solid.

'Let go of my hand,' he tells the tar man. 'Let go my hand, or I'm going to hit you in the face.'

The tar man, he says not a word, and he doesn't move the tiniest muscle, and Anansi hits him, bash, right in the face.

'OK,' says Anansi, 'a joke's a joke. You can keep hold of my hands if you like, but I got four more hands, and two good legs, and you can't hold them all, so you let me go and I'll take it easy on you.'

The tar man, he doesn't let go of Anansi's hands, and he doesn't say a word, so Anansi hits him with all his hands and then kicks him with his feet, one after another.

'Right,' says Anansi. 'You let me go, or I *bite* you.' The tar fills his mouth, and covers his nose and his face.

So that's how they find Anansi, the next morning, when his wife and his sons come down to the pea patch, by the old breadfruit tree: all stuck to the tar man, and dead as history.

They weren't surprised to see him like that.

Those days, you used to find Anansi like that all the time.

Chapter Six

In Which Fat Charlie
Fails to Get Home,
Even by Taxi

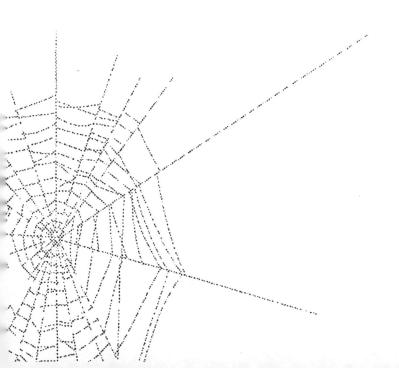

D aisy woke up to the alarm. She stretched in her bed like a
kitten. She could hear the shower, which meant that her
flatmate was already up. She put on a pink fuzzy dressing
gown and went into the hall.

'You want porridge?' she called through the bathroom door.

'Not much. If you're making it, I'll eat it.'

'You certainly know how to make a girl feel wanted,' said Daisy,
and she went into the kitchenette and put the porridge on to cook.

She went back into her bedroom, pulled on her work clothes,
then looked at herself in the mirror. She made a face. She put her
hair up into a tight bun at the back.

Her flatmate, Carol, a thin-faced white woman from Preston,
stuck her head around the bedroom door. She was towelling her
hair vigorously. 'Bathroom's all yours. What's the word on the
porridge?'

'Probably needs a stir.'

'So where were you the other night anyway? You said you were
going off to Sybilla's birthday drinks, and I know you never came
back.'

'None of your beeswax, innit.' Daisy went into the kitchen and stirred the porridge. She added a pinch of salt and stirred it some more. She glopped the porridge into bowls and placed them on the counter.

'Carol? Porridge is getting cold.'

Carol came in, sat down, stared at the porridge. She was only half-dressed. ''S not a proper breakfast, is it? You ask me, a proper breakfast is fried eggs, sausages, black pudden and grilled tomatoes.'

'You cook it,' said Daisy, 'I'll eat it.'

Carol sprinkled a dessertspoonful of sugar on her porridge. She looked at it. Then she sprinkled another one on. 'No, you bloody won't. You say that you will. But you'll start rabbiting on about cholesterol or what fried food is doing to your kidneys.' She tasted the porridge as if it might bite her back. Daisy passed her a cup of tea. 'You and your kidneys. Actually, that might be nice for a change. You ever eaten kidneys, Daisy?'

'Once,' said Daisy. 'If you ask me, you can get the same effect by grilling half a pound of liver, then weeing all over it.'

Carol sniffed. 'That wasn't called for,' she said.

'Eat your porridge.'

They finished their porridge, and their tea. They put the bowls in the dishwasher, and, because it was not yet full, did not turn it on. Then they drove in to work. Carol, who was now in uniform, did the driving.

Daisy went up to her desk, in a room filled with empty desks.

The phone rang as she sat down. 'Daisy? You're late.'

She looked at her watch. 'No,' she said. 'I'm not, sir. Now is there anything else I can do for you this morning?'

'Too right. You can call a man named Coats. He's a friend of the chief super. Fellow Crystal Palace supporter. He's already texted me about it twice this morning. Who taught the chief super to text, that's what I want to know?'

Daisy took down the details, and called the number. She put on her most businesslike and efficient tone of voice, and said, 'Detective Constable Day. How can I help you?'

'Ah,' said a man's voice. 'Well, as I was telling the chief superintendent last night, a lovely man, old friend. Good man. He suggested I talk to someone in your office. I wish to report. Well, I'm not actually certain that a crime has been committed. Probably a perfectly sensible explanation. There have been certain irregularities, and, well, to be perfectly frank with you, I've given my book-keeper a couple of weeks' leave, while I try to come to grips with the possibility that he may have been involved in certain, mm, financial irregularities.'

'Suppose we get the details,' said Daisy. 'What's your full name, sir? And the book-keeper's name?'

'My name is Grahame Coats,' said the man on the other end of the telephone. 'Of the Grahame Coats Agency. My book-keeper is a man named Nancy. Charles Nancy.'

She wrote both names down. They did not ring any bells.

***

Fat Charlie had planned to have an argument with Spider as soon as Spider came home. He had rehearsed the argument in his head, over and over, and had won it, both fairly and decisively, every time.

Spider had not, however, come home last night, and Fat Charlie had eventually fallen asleep in front of the television, half watching a raucous game show for horny insomniacs, which seemed to be called *Show Us Your Bum!*

He woke up on the sofa, when Spider pulled open the curtains. 'Beautiful day,' said Spider.

'You!' said Fat Charlie. 'You were kissing Rosie. Don't try to deny it.'

'I had to,' said Spider.

'What do you mean, you had to? You didn't have to.'

'She thought I was you.'

'Well, you knew you weren't me. You shouldn't have kissed her.'

'But if I had refused to kiss her, she would have thought it was you not kissing her.'

'But it wasn't me.'

'She didn't know that. I was just trying to be helpful.'

'Being helpful,' said Fat Charlie, from the sofa, 'is something you do that, generally speaking, involves *not* kissing my fiancée. You could have said you had a toothache.'

'That,' said Spider, virtuously, 'would have been lying.'

'But you were lying already! You were pretending to be me!'

'Well, it would have been compounding the lie, anyway,' explained Spider. 'Something I only did because you were in no shape to go to work. No,' he said, 'I couldn't have lied further. I would have felt dreadful.'

'Well, I *did* feel dreadful. I had to watch you kissing her.'

'Ah,' said Spider. 'But she *thought* she was kissing *you*.'

'Don't keep saying that!'

'You should feel flattered,' Spider said. 'Do you want lunch?'

'Of course I don't want lunch. What time is it?'

'Lunch time,' said Spider. 'And you're late for work again. It's a good thing I didn't cover for you again, if this is all the thanks I get.'

' 'S OK,' said Fat Charlie. 'I've been given two weeks off. And a bonus.'

Spider raised an eyebrow.

'Look,' said Fat Charlie, feeling like it was time to move to the second round of the argument, 'it's not like I'm trying to get rid of you or anything, but I was wondering when you were thinking of leaving.'

Spider said, 'Well, when I came here, I'd only planned to visit for a day. Maybe two days. Long enough to meet my little brother and then I'd be on my way. I'm a busy man.'

'So you're leaving today.'

'That *was* my plan,' said Spider. 'But then I met you. I cannot believe that we have let almost an entire lifetime go by without each other's company, my brother.'

'I can.'

'The ties of blood,' said Spider, 'are stronger than water.'

'Water's not strong,' objected Fat Charlie.

'Stronger than vodka, then. Or volcanoes. Or, or ammonia. Look, my point is that meeting you – well, it's a privilege. We've never been part of each other's lives, but that was yesterday. Let's start a new tomorrow, today. We'll put yesterday behind us and forge new bonds – the bonds of brotherhood.'

'You're totally after Rosie,' said Fat Charlie.

'Totally,' agreed Spider. 'What do you plan to do about it?'

'Do about it? Well, she's *my* fiancée.'

'Not to worry. She thinks I'm you.'

'Will you stop saying that . . . ?'

Spider spread his hands, in a saintly gesture, then ruined the effect by licking his lips.

'So,' said Fat Charlie, 'what are you planning to do next? Marry her, pretending to be me?'

'Marry?' Spider paused and thought for a moment. 'What. A horrible. Idea.'

'Well, I was quite looking forward to it, actually.'

'Spider does not marry. I'm not the marrying kind.'

'So my Rosie's not good enough for you, is that what you're saying?'

Spider did not answer. He walked out of the room.

Fat Charlie felt like he'd scored, somehow, in the argument. He got up from the sofa, picked up the empty foil cartons that had, the previous evening, held a chicken chow mein and crispy pork balls, and he dropped them into the bin. He went into his bedroom, where he took off the clothes he had slept in in order to put on clean clothes, discovered that, due to not doing the laundry, he had no clean clothes, so brushed yesterday's clothes down vigorously – dislodging several stray strands of chow mein – and put them back on.

He went into the kitchen.

Spider was sitting at the kitchen table, enjoying a steak large enough for two people.

'Where did you get that from?' said Fat Charlie, although he was certain that he already knew.

'I asked you if you wanted lunch,' said Spider, mildly.

'Where did you get the steak?'

'It was in the fridge.'

'That,' declaimed Fat Charlie, wagging his finger like a prosecuting attorney going in for the kill, '*that* was the steak I bought for dinner tonight. For dinner tonight for me and Rosie. The dinner I was going to be cooking for her! And you're just sitting there like a, a person eating a steak, and, and eating it, and—'

'It's not a problem,' said Spider.

'What do you mean, not a problem?'

'Well,' said Spider, 'I called Rosie this morning already, and I'm taking her out to dinner tonight. So you wouldn't have needed the steak anyway.'

Fat Charlie opened his mouth. He closed it again. 'I want you out,' he said.

'It's a good thing for man's desire to out-strip his something or other – grasp or reach or something – or what else is Heaven for?' said Spider, cheerfully, between mouthfuls of Fat Charlie's steak.

'What the hell does that mean?'

'It means I'm not going anywhere. I like it here. ' He hacked off another lump of steak, shovelled it down.

'Out,' said Fat Charlie, and then the hall telephone rang. Fat Charlie sighed, walked into the hall and answered it. '*What?*'

'Ah. Charles. Good to hear your voice. I know you're currently enjoying your well-earned, but do you think it might be within the bounds of possibility for you to swing by for, oh, half an hour or so, tomorrow morning? Say, around ten-ish?'

'Yeah. Course,' said Fat Charlie. 'Not a problem.'

'Delighted to hear it. I'll need your signature on some papers. Well, until then.'

'Who was that?' asked Spider. He had cleaned his plate, and was blotting his mouth with a paper towel.

'Grahame Coats. He wants me to pop in tomorrow.'

Spider said, 'He's a bastard.'

'So? You're a bastard.'

'Different kind of bastard. He's not good news. You should find another job.'

'I love my job!' Fat Charlie meant it when he said it. He had managed entirely to forget how much he disliked his job, and the Grahame Coats Agency, and the ghastly, lurking-behind-every-door presence of Grahame Coats.

Spider stood up. 'Nice piece of steak,' he said. 'I've set my stuff up in your spare room.'

'You've what?'

Fat Charlie hurried down to the end of the hall, where there was a room that technically qualified his residence as a two-bedroom flat. The room contained several boxes of books, a box containing an elderly Scalextric set, a tin box filled with Hot Wheels cars (most of them missing tyres), and various other battered remnants of Fat Charlie's childhood. It might have been a good-sized bedroom for a normal-sized garden gnome or an undersized dwarf, but for anyone else it was a closet with a window.

Or rather, it used to be, but it wasn't. Not any more.

Fat Charlie pulled the door open and stood in the hallway, blinking.

There was a room, yes; that much was still true, but it was an enormous room. A magnificent room. There were windows at the far end, huge picture windows, looking out over what appeared to be a waterfall. Beyond the waterfall, the tropical sun was low on the horizon, and it burnished everything in its golden light. There was a fireplace large enough to roast a pair of oxen, upon which three burning logs crackled and spat. There was a hammock in one corner, along with a perfectly white sofa and a four-poster bed. Near the fireplace was something that Fat Charlie, who had only ever seen them in magazines, suspected was probably some kind of Jacuzzi. There was a zebra-skin rug, and a bear-pelt hanging on one wall, and there was the kind of advanced audio equipment that mostly consists of a black piece of polished plastic that you wave at. On one wall hung a flat television screen that was the width of the room that should have been there. And there was more . . .

'What have you done?' asked Fat Charlie. He did not go in.

'Well,' said Spider from behind him, 'seeing as I'm going to be here for a few days, I thought I'd bring my stuff over.'

'Bring your stuff? "Bringing your stuff" is a couple of carrier bags filled with laundry, some PlayStation games and a spider plant. This is . . . *this* is . . .' He was out of words.

Spider patted Fat Charlie's shoulder as he pushed past. 'If you need me,' he said to his brother, 'I'll be in my room.' And he shut the door behind him.

Fat Charlie shook the doorknob. The door was now locked.

He went into the TV room, got the phone from the hall, and dialled Mrs Higgler's number.

'Who the hell is this at this time of the morning?' she said.

'It's me. Fat Charlie. I'm sorry.'

'Well? What you callin' about?'

'Well, I was calling to ask your advice. You see, my brother came out here.'

'Your brother.'

'Spider. You told me about him. You said to ask a spider if I wanted to see him, and I did and he's here.'

'Well,' she said, noncommittally, 'that's good.'

'It's not.'

'Why not? He's family, isn't he?'

'Look, I can't go into it now. I just want him to go away.'

'Have you tried asking him nicely?'

'We just got through with all that. He says he isn't going. He's set up something that looks like the pleasure dome of Kublai Khan in my boxroom, and I mean, round here you need the council's permission just to put in double glazing. He's got some kind of waterfall in there. Not in there, it's on the other side of the window. And he's after my fiancée.'

'How do you know?'

'He said so.'

Mrs Higgler said, 'I'm not at my best before I have my coffee.'

'I just need to know how to make him go away.'

'I don't know,' said Mrs Higgler. 'I will talk to Mrs Dunwiddy about it.' She hung up.

Fat Charlie went back down to the end of the corridor, and knocked on the door.

'What is it now?'

'I want to talk.'

The door clicked and swung open. Fat Charlie went inside. Spider was reclining, naked, in the hot tub. He was drinking something more or less the colour of electricity from a long, frosted glass. The huge picture windows were now wide open, and the roar of the waterfall contrasted with the low, liquid jazz that emanated from hidden speakers somewhere in the room.

'Look,' said Fat Charlie, 'you have to understand, this is my house.'

Spider blinked. '*This?*' he asked. '*This* is your house?'

'Well, not exactly. But the principle's the same. I mean, we're in my spare room, and you're a guest. Um.'

Spider sipped his drink, and luxuriated deeper in the hot water. 'They say,' he said, 'that house guests are like fish. They both stink after three days.'

'Good point,' said Fat Charlie.

'But it's hard,' said Spider. 'Hard when you've gone a lifetime not seeing your brother. Hard when he didn't even know you existed. Harder still when you finally see him and learn that, as far as he's concerned, you're no better than a dead fish.'

'But,' said Fat Charlie.

Spider stretched in the tub. 'I'll tell you what,' he said. 'I can't stay here for ever. Chill. I'll be gone before you know it. And, for my part, I will never think of you as a dead fish. And I appreciate that we're both under a lot of stress. So let's say no more about it. Why don't you go and get yourself some lunch – leave your front-door key behind – and then go and see a movie?'

Fat Charlie put on his jacket and went outside. He put his door-key down beside the sink. The fresh air was wonderful, although the day was grey and the sky was spitting drizzle. He bought a newspaper to read. He stopped at the chippie and bought a large bag of chips and a battered saveloy for his lunch. The drizzle stopped, so he sat on a bench in a churchyard, and read his newspaper and ate his saveloy and chips.

He very much wanted to see a film.

He wandered into the Odeon, bought a ticket for the first thing showing. It was an action adventure, and it was already on when he went inside. Things blew up. It was great.

Halfway through the film it occurred to Fat Charlie that there was something that he was not remembering. It was in his head somewhere, like an itch an inch behind his eyes, and it kept distracting him.

The film ended.

Fat Charlie realised that, although he had enjoyed it, he had not actually managed to keep much of the film he had just seen in his head. So he bought a large bag of popcorn and sat through it again. It was even better the second time.

And the third.

After that, he thought that perhaps he ought to think about getting home, but there was a late-night double feature of *Eraserhead* and *True Stories*, and he had never actually seen either film, so he watched them both, although he was, by now, really quite hungry, which meant that by the end he was unsure of what *Eraserhead* had actually been about, or what the lady was doing in the radiator and he wondered if they'd let him stay and watch it again, but they explained, very patiently, over and over, that they were going to close for the night, and enquired as to whether he didn't have a home to go to, and wasn't it time for him to be in bed?

And of course, he did, and it was, although the fact of it had slipped his mind for a while. So he walked back to Maxwell Gardens, and was slightly surprised to see that the light was on in his bedroom.

The curtains were drawn as he reached the house. Still, there were silhouettes on the window, moving about. He thought he recognised both of the silhouettes.

They came together; they blended into one shadow.

Fat Charlie uttered one deep and terrible howl.

*   *   *

In Mrs Dunwiddy's house there were many plastic animals. The dust moved slowly through the air in that place, as if it were better used to the sunbeams of a more leisurely age, and could not be bothered with all this fast modern light. There was a transparent plastic cover on the sofa, and chairs that crackled when you sat down on them.

In Mrs Dunwiddy's house there was pine-scented hard toilet paper. Mrs Dunwiddy believed in economy, and pine-scented hard toilet paper was at the bottom of her economy drive. You could still get hard toilet paper, if you looked long enough and were prepared to pay more for it.

Mrs Dunwiddy's house smelled of violet-water. It was an old house. People forget that the first children born to settlers in Florida were already old men and women when the dour Puritans landed at Plymouth Rock. The house didn't go that far back; it had been built in the 1920s, during a Florida land development scheme, to be the show house, to represent the hypothetical houses that all the other buyers would find themselves eventually unable to build on the plots of gatory swamp they were being sold. Mrs Dunwiddy's house had survived hurricanes without losing a roof-tile.

When the doorbell rang, Mrs Dunwiddy was stuffing a small turkey. She tutted, and washed her hands, then walked down the corridor to her front door, peering out at the world through her thick, thick glasses, her left hand trailing on the wallpaper.

She opened the door a crack and peered out.

'Louella? It's me.' It was Callyanne Higgler.

'Come in.' Mrs Higgler followed Mrs Dunwiddy back to the kitchen. Mrs Dunwiddy ran her hands under the tap, then recommenced taking handfuls of soggy corn-bread stuffing and pushing them deep into the turkey.

'You expectin' company?'

Mrs Dunwiddy, made a noncommittal noise. 'It always a good idea to be prepared,' she said. 'Now, suppose you tell me what's going on?'

'Nancy's boy. Fat Charlie.'

'What about him?'

'Well, I tell him about his brother, when he out here last week.'

Mrs Dunwiddy pulled her hand out of the turkey. 'That's not the end of the world,' she said.

'I tell him how he can contact his brother.'

'Ahh,' said Mrs Dunwiddy. She could disapprove with just that one syllable. 'And?'

'He's turned up in Hingland. Boy's at his wits' end.'

Mrs Dunwiddy took a large handful of wet cornbread and rammed it into the turkey with a force that would have made the turkey's eyes water, if it still had any. 'Can't get him to go away?'

'Nope.'

Sharp eyes peered through thick lenses. Then Mrs Dunwiddy said, 'I done it once. Can't do it again. Not that way.'

'I know. But we got to do something.'

Mrs Dunwiddy sighed. 'It's true what they say. Live long enough, you see all your birds come home to roost.'

'Isn't there another way?'

Mrs Dunwiddy finished stuffing the turkey. She picked up a skewer, pinned the flap of skin closed. Then she covered the bird with silver foil.

'I reckon,' she said, 'I put it on to cook late tomorrow morning. It be done in the afternoon, then I put it back into a hot oven early evening, to get it all ready for dinner.'

'Who you got comin' to dinner?' asked Mrs Higgler.

'You,' said Mrs Dunwiddy, 'Zorah Bustamonte, Bella Noles. And Fat Charlie Nancy. By the time that boy gets here, he have a real appetite.'

Mrs Higgler said, 'He's coming here?'

'Aren't you listening, girl?' said Mrs Dunwiddy. Only Mrs Dunwiddy could have called Mrs Higgler 'girl' without sounding foolish. 'Now, help me get this turkey into the fridge.'

* * *

It would be fair to say that Rosie had, that evening, just had the most wonderful night of her life: magical, perfect, utterly fine. She could not have stopped smiling, not even if she had wanted to. The food had been fabulous and, once they had eaten, Fat Charlie had taken her dancing. It was a proper dance hall, with a small orchestra, and people in pastel clothes who glided across the floor. She felt as if they had travelled in time together and were visiting a gentler age. Rosie had enjoyed dancing lessons from the age of five, but had no one to dance with.

'I didn't know you could dance,' she told him.

'There are so many things about me you do not know,' he said.

And that made her happy. Soon enough, she and this man would be married. There were things about him she did not know? Excellent. She would have a lifetime in which to find them out. All sorts of things.

She noticed the way other women, and other men, looked at Fat Charlie as she walked beside him, and she was happy she was the woman on his arm.

They walked through Leicester Square, and Rosie could see the stars shining up above them, the starlight somehow crisply twinkling, despite the glare of the streetlights.

For a brief moment, she found herself wondering why it had never been like this with Fat Charlie before. Sometimes, somewhere deep inside herself, Rosie had suspected that perhaps she had only kept going out with Fat Charlie because her mother disliked him so much; that she had only said 'yes' when he had asked her to marry him because her mother would have wanted her to say 'no' . . .

Fat Charlie had taken her out to the West End, once. They'd gone to the theatre. It was a birthday surprise for her, but there had been a mix-up on the tickets, which, it turned out, had actually been issued for the day before; the management were both understanding and extremely helpful, and they had managed to find Fat Charlie a seat behind a pillar in the stalls, while Rosie took a seat in the upper circle behind a violently giggly hen party from Norwich. It had not been a success, not as these things were counted.

This evening, though, this evening had been magic. Rosie had not had many perfect moments in her life, but whatever the total was, it had just gone up by one.

She loved how she felt, when she was with him.

And once the dancing was done, after they had stumbled out into the night, giddy on movement and champagne, then Fat Charlie – and, she thought, why did she think of him as Fat Charlie anyway? for he wasn't the least bit fat – put his arm around her and said, 'Now, you're coming back to my place,' in a voice so deep and real it made her abdomen vibrate; and she said nothing about working the next day, nothing about there'd be time enough for that kind of thing when they were married, nothing at all, in fact, while all the time she thought about how much she didn't want the evening to end, and how very very much she wished, no, she *needed*, to kiss this man on the lips, and to hold him.

And then, remembering she had to say something, she said 'Yes'.

In the cab back to his flat, her hands held his, and she leaned against him and stared at him as the light from passing cars and streetlamps illuminated his face.

'You have a pierced ear,' she said. 'Why didn't I ever notice before that you have a pierced ear?'

'Hey,' he said with a smile, his voice a deep bass thrum, 'how do you think it makes me feel, when you've never even noticed something like that, even when we've been together for, what is it now?'

'Eighteen months,' said Rosie.

'For eighteen months,' said her fiancé.

She leaned against him, breathed him in. 'I love the way you smell,' she told him. 'Are you wearing some kind of cologne?'

'That's just me,' he told her.

'Well, you should bottle it.'

She paid the taxi, while he opened the front door. They went up the stairs together. When they got to the top of the stairs, he seemed to be heading along the corridor, towards the spare room at the back.

'You know,' she said, 'the bedroom's here, silly. Where are you going?'

'Nowhere. I knew that,' he said. They went into Fat Charlie's bedroom. She closed the curtains. Then she just looked at him, and was happy.

'Well,' she said, after a while, 'aren't you going to try to kiss me?'

'I guess I am,' he said, and he did. Time melted and stretched and curved. She might have kissed him for a moment, or for an hour, or for a lifetime. And then—

'What was that?'

He said, 'I didn't hear anything.'

'It sounded like someone in pain.'

'Cats fighting, maybe?'

'It sounded like a person.'

'Could have been an urban fox. They can sound a lot like people.'

She stood there with her head tipped to one side, listening intently. 'It's stopped now,' she said. 'Hmm. You want to know the strangest thing?'

'Uh-huh,' he said, his lips now nuzzling her neck. 'Sure, tell me the strangest thing. But I've made it go away now. It won't bother you again.'

'The strangest thing,' said Rosie, 'is that it sounded like you.'

* * *

Fat Charlie walked the streets, trying to clear his head. The obvious course of action was to bang on his own front door until Spider came down and let him in, then to give Spider and Rosie a piece of his mind. That was obvious. Perfectly, utterly obvious.

He just needed to go back to his flat and explain the whole thing to Rosie, and shame Spider into leaving him alone. That was all he had to do. How hard could that be?

Harder than it ought to be, that was for certain. He was not quite sure why he had walked away from his flat. He was even less certain how to find his way back. Streets he knew, or thought he knew, seemed to have reconfigured themselves. He found himself walking down dead ends, exploring endless cul-de-sacs, stumbling through the tangle of late-night London residential streets.

Sometimes, he saw the main road. There were traffic lights on it, and the lights of fast-food places. He knew that once he got on to the main road he would be able to find his way back to his house, but whenever he walked to the main road he would wind up somewhere else.

Fat Charlie's feet were starting to hurt. His stomach rumbled, violently. He was angry, and as he walked he became angrier and angrier.

The anger cleared his head. The cobwebs surrounding his thoughts began to evaporate; the web of streets he was walking began to simplify. He turned a corner and found himself on the main road, next to the all-night New Jersey Fried Chicken outlet. He ordered a family pack of chicken, and sat and finished it off without any help from anyone else in his family. When that was done he stood on the pavement until the friendly orange light of a FOR HIRE sign, attached to a large black cab, came into view, and he hailed the cab. It pulled up next to him, and the window rolled down.

'Where to?'

'Maxwell Gardens,' said Fat Charlie.

'You taking the mickey or something?' asked the cab driver. 'That's just round the corner.'

'Will you take me there? I'll give you an extra fiver. Honest.'

The cabbie breathed in loudly through his clenched teeth: it was the noise a car mechanic makes before asking you whether you're particularly attached to that engine for sentimental reasons.

'It's your funeral,' said the cabbie. 'Hop in.'

Fat Charlie hopped. The cabbie pulled out, waited for the lights to change, went around the corner.

'Where did you say you wanted to go?' asked the cabbie.

'Maxwell Gardens,' said Fat Charlie. 'Number thirty-four. It's just past the off-licence.'

He was wearing yesterday's clothes, and he wished he wasn't. His mother had always told him to wear clean underwear, in case he was hit by a car, and to brush his teeth, in case they needed to identify him by his dental records.

'I know where it is,' said the cabbie. 'It's just before you get to Park Crescent.'

'That's right,' said Fat Charlie. He was falling asleep in the back seat.

'I must have taken a wrong turning,' said the cabbie. He sounded irritated. 'I'll turn off the meter, all right? Call it a fiver.'

'Sure,' said Fat Charlie, and he snuggled down on the back seat of the taxi, and he slept. The taxi drove on through the night, trying to get just round the corner.

* * *

Detective Constable Day, currently on a twelve-month secondment to the Fraud Squad, arrived at the offices of the Grahame Coats Agency at 9.30 a.m. Grahame Coats was waiting for her in reception, and he walked her back into his office.

'Would you care for a coffee, tea?'

'No, thank you. I'm fine.' She pulled out a notebook, and sat looking at him expectantly.

'Now, I cannot stress enough that discretion must needs be the essence of your investigations. The Grahame Coats Agency has a reputation for probity and fair dealing. At the Grahame Coats Agency, a client's money is a sacrosanct trust. I must tell you, that when I first began to entertain suspicions about Charles Nancy, I dismissed them as unworthy of a decent man and a hard worker. Had you asked me a week ago what I thought about Charles Nancy, I would have told you that he was the very salt of the earth.'

'I'm sure you would. So when did you become aware that money might have been diverted from clients' accounts?'

'Well, I'm still not certain. I hesitate to cast aspersions. Or first stones, for that matter. Judge not, lest ye be judged.'

On television, thought Daisy, they say 'just give me the facts'. She wished she could say it, but she didn't.

She did not like this man.

'I've printed out all the anomalous transactions here,' he said. 'As you'll see, they were all made from Nancy's computer. I must again stress that discretion is of the essence here: clients of the Grahame Coats Agency include a number of prominent public figures, and, as I said to your superior, I would count it as a personal favour if this matter could be dealt with as quietly as possible. Discretion must be your watchword. If, perchance, we can persuade our Master Nancy simply to return his ill-gotten gains, I would be perfectly satisfied to let the matter rest there. I have no desire to prosecute.'

'I can do my best, but at the end of the day, we gather information and turn it over to the Crown Prosecution Service.' She wondered how much pull he really had with the chief super. 'So what attracted your suspicions?'

'Ah, yes. Frankly and in all honesty, it was certain peculiarities of behaviour. The dog that failed to bark in the night time. The depth the parsley had sunk into the butter. We detectives find significance in the smallest things, do we not, Detective Day?'

'Er. Detective Constable Day, really. So, if you can give me the print-outs,' she said, 'along with any other documentation, bank records all that. We may actually need to pick up his computer, to look at the hard disk.'

'Absatively,' he said. His desk phone rang, and – 'If you'll excuse me?' – he answered it. 'He is? Good Lord. Well, tell him to just wait for me in reception. I'll come out and see him in a moment.'

He put down the phone. 'That,' he said to Daisy, 'is what I believe you would call, in police circles, a right turn-up for the books.'

She raised an eyebrow.

'That is the aforementioned Charles Nancy himself, here to see me. Shall we show him in? If you need to, you may use my offices as an interview room. I'm sure I even have a tape recorder you might borrow.'

Daisy said, 'That won't be necessary. And the first thing I'll need to do is go through all the paperwork.'

'Righto,' he said. 'Silly of me. Um, would you . . . would you like to look at him?'

'I don't see that that would accomplish anything,' said Daisy.

'Oh, I wouldn't tell him you were investigating him,' Grahame Coats assured her. 'Otherwise he'd be off to the Costa Del Crime before we could say "prima-facie evidence". Frankly, I like to think of myself as being extremely sympathetic to the problems of contemporary policing.'

Daisy caught herself thinking that anyone who would steal money from this man could not be all bad, which was, she knew, no way for a police officer to think.

'I'll lead you out,' he said to her.

In the waiting room a man was sitting. He looked as if he had slept in his clothes. He was unshaven, and he looked a little confused. Grahame Coats nudged Daisy, and inclined his head towards the man. Aloud, he said, 'Charles, Good Lord, man, look at the state of you. You look terrible.'

Fat Charlie looked at him blearily. 'Didn't get home last night,' he said. 'Bit of a mix-up with the taxi.'

'Charles,' said Grahame Coats, 'this is Detective Constable Day, of the Metropolitan Police. She is just here on routine business.'

Fat Charlie realised there was someone else there. He focused, saw the sensible clothes that might as well have been a uniform. Then he saw the face. 'Er,' he said.

'Morning,' said Daisy. That was what she said with her mouth. Inside her head she was going *ohbollocks ohbollocks ohbollocks*, over and over.

'Nice to meet you,' said Fat Charlie. Puzzled, he did something he had never done before: he imagined a plain-clothes police officer with no clothes on, and found his imagination was providing him with a fairly accurate representation of the young lady beside whom he had woken up in bed, the morning after his father's wake. The sensible clothes made her look slightly older, more severe, and much scarier, but it was her all right.

Like all sentient beings, Fat Charlie had a weirdness quotient. For some days the needle had been over in the red, occasionally banging jerkily against the pin. Now the meter broke. From this moment on, he suspected, nothing would surprise him. He could no longer be outweirded. He was done.

He was wrong, of course.

Fat Charlie watched Daisy leave, and he followed Grahame Coats back into his office.

Grahame Coats closed the door firmly. Then he perched his bottom against his desk, and smiled like a weasel who has just realised that he's been accidentally locked into the henhouse for the night.

'Let us be blunt,' he said. 'Cards on the table. No beating about the bush. Let us,' he elaborated, 'let us call a spade a spade.'

'All right,' said Fat Charlie, 'let's. You said you had something for me to sign?'

'No longer an operative statement. Dismiss it from your mind. No, let us now discuss something you pointed out to me several days ago. You alerted me to certain unorthodox transactions occurring here.'

'I did?'

'Two, as they say, Charles, two can play at that game. Naturally, my first impulse was to investigate. Thus the visit this morning from Detective Constable Day. And what I found will, I suspect, not come as a shock to you.'

'It won't?'

'No indeed. There are, as you pointed out, definite indicators of financial irregularities, Charles. But alas, there is only one place to which the fickle finger of suspicion unerringly points.'

'There is?'

'There is.'

Fat Charlie felt completely at sea. 'Where?'

Grahame Coats attempted to look concerned, or at least, to look as if he were trying to look concerned, managing an expression which, in babies, always indicates that they are in need of a good burping. 'You, Charles. The police suspect you.'

'Yes,' said Fat Charlie. 'Of course they do. It's been that sort of a day.'

And he went home.

* * *

Spider opened the front door. It had started raining, and Fat Charlie stood there looking rumpled and wet.

'So,' said Fat Charlie. 'I'm allowed home now, am I?'

'I wouldn't do anything to stop you,' said Spider. 'It's your home, after all. Where were you all night?'

'You know perfectly well where I was. I was failing to come home. I don't know what kind of magic 'fluence you were using on me.'

'It wasn't magic,' said Spider, offended. 'It was a miracle.'

Fat Charlie pushed past him and stomped up the stairs. He walked into the bathroom, put in the plug and turned on the taps. He leaned out into the hall. 'I don't care what it's called. You're doing it in my house, and you stopped me coming home last night.'

He took off the day-before-yesterday's clothes. Then he put his head back around the door. 'And the police are investigating me at work. Did you tell Grahame Coats that there were financial irregularities going on?'

'Of course I did,' said Spider.

'Hah! Well, he only suspects me, that's what.'

'Oh, I don't think he does,' said Spider.

'Shows all you know,' said Fat Charlie. 'I talked to him. The police are involved. And then there's Rosie. And you and I are going to have a very long conversation about Rosie, when I get out of the bath. But first of all, I'm going to get into the bath. I spent yesterday night wandering around. I got the only sleep of the night in the back seat of a taxi. By the time I woke up it was five in the morning and my taxi driver was turning into Travis Bickle. He was conducting a monologue. I told him he might as well give up looking for Maxwell Gardens, and that it obviously wasn't a

Maxwell Gardens kind of night, and eventually he agreed so we went and had breakfast in one of those places taxi drivers have breakfast. Eggs and beans and sausages and toast, and tea you could stand a spoon up in. When he told the other taxi drivers he'd been driving all around last night looking for Maxwell Gardens, well, I thought blood was going to be spilled. It wasn't. But it looked a pretty close thing for a minute there.'

Fat Charlie stopped to take a breath. Spider looked guilty.

'*After*,' said Fat Charlie. '*After* my bath.' He shut the bathroom door.

He climbed into the bath.

He made a whimpering noise.

He climbed out of the bath.

He turned off the taps.

He wrapped a towel around his midriff and opened the bathroom door. 'No hot water,' he said, much, much too calmly. 'Do you have any idea why we have no hot water?'

Spider was still standing in the hallway. He hadn't moved. 'My hot tub,' he said. 'Sorry.'

Fat Charlie said, 'Well, at least Rosie doesn't. I mean, she wouldn't have—' And then he caught the expression on Spider's face.

Fat Charlie said, 'I want you out of here. Out of my life. Out of Rosie's life. Gone.'

'I like it here,' said Spider.

'You're ruining my bloody life.'

'Tough.' Spider walked down the hallway and opened the door to Fat Charlie's spare room. Golden tropical sunlight flooded the hallway momentarily, then the door was closed.

Fat Charlie washed his hair in cold water. He brushed his teeth. He rummaged through his laundry hamper until he found a pair of jeans and a T-shirt that were, by virtue of being at the bottom, practically clean once more. He put them on, along with a purple sweater with a teddy bear on it his mother had once given him that he had never worn but had never got around to giving away.

He went down to the end of the corridor.

The *boom-chagga-boom* of a bass and drums penetrated the door.

Fat Charlie rattled the doorhandle. It didn't budge. 'If you don't open this door,' he said, 'I'm going to break it down.'

The door opened, without warning, and Fat Charlie lurched inward, into the empty boxroom at the end of the hall. The view through the window was the back of the house behind, what little you could see of it through the rain that was now lashing the windowpane.

Still, from somewhere only a wall's thinness away, a stereo was playing too loudly: everything in the boxroom vibrated to a distant *boom-chagga-boom*.

'Right,' said Fat Charlie conversationally. 'You realise, of course, that this means war?' It was the traditional war-cry of the rabbit when pushed too far. There are places in which people believe that Anansi was a trickster rabbit. They are wrong, of course; he was a spider. You might think the two creatures would be easy to keep separate, but they still get confused more often than you would expect.

Fat Charlie went into his bedroom. He retrieved his passport from the drawer by his bed. He found his wallet where he had left it, in the bathroom.

He walked down to the main road, in the rain, and hailed a taxi.

'Where to?'

'Heathrow,' said Fat Charlie.

'Right you are,' said the cabbie. 'Which terminal?'

'No idea,' said Fat Charlie, who knew that, really, he ought to know. It had only been a few days, after all. 'Where do they leave for Florida?'

***

Grahame Coats had begun planning his exit from the Grahame Coats Agency back when John Major was Prime Minister. Nothing good lasts for ever, after all. Sooner or later, as Grahame Coats himself would have delighted in assuring you, even if your goose habitually lays golden eggs, it will still be cooked. While his planning had been good – one never knew when one might need to leave at a moment's notice – and he was not unaware that events were massing, like grey clouds on the horizon, he wished to put off the moment of leaving until it could be delayed no longer.

What was important, he had long ago decided, was not leaving, but vanishing, evaporating, disappearing without trace.

In the concealed safe in his office – a walk-in room he was extremely proud of – on a shelf he had put up himself, and had recently needed to put up again when it fell down, was a leather vanity case, containing two passports, one in the name of Basil Finnegan, the other in the name of Roger Bronstein. Each of the men had been born about fifty years ago, just as Grahame Coats had, but had died in their first year of life. Both of the passport photographs in the passports were of Grahame Coats. The case also contained two wallets, each with its own set of credit cards and photographic identification in the name of one of the names of the passport holders. Each name was a signatory to the funnel accounts in the Caymans, which themselves funnelled to other accounts in the British Virgin Islands, Switzerland and Liechtenstein.

Grahame Coats had been planning to leave for good on his fiftieth birthday, a little more than a year from now, and he was brooding on the matter of Fat Charlie.

He did not actually expect Fat Charlie to be arrested or imprisoned, although he would not have greatly objected to either scenario, had it occurred. He wanted him scared, discredited, and gone.

Grahame Coats truly enjoyed milking the clients of the Grahame Coats Agency, and he was good at it. He had been pleasantly surprised to discover that, as long as he picked his clientele with care, the celebrities and performers he represented had very little sense of money, and were relieved to find someone who would represent them and manage their financial affairs and make sure that they didn't have to worry. And if sometimes statements or cheques were late in coming, or if they weren't always what the clients were expecting, or if there were unidentified direct debits from client accounts, well, Grahame Coats had a high staff turnover, particularly in the book-keeping department, and there was nothing that couldn't easily be blamed on the incompetence of a previous employee, or, rarely, made right with a case of champagne and a large and apologetic cheque.

It wasn't that people liked Grahame Coats, or that they trusted him. Even the people he represented thought he was a weasel. But they believed that he was *their* weasel, and in that they were wrong.

Grahame Coats was his own weasel.

The telephone on his desk rang and he picked it up. 'Yes?'

'Mr Coats? It's Maeve Livingstone on the phone. I know you said to put her through to Fat Charlie, but he's off this week, and I wasn't sure what to say. Shall I tell her you're out?'

Grahame Coats pondered. Before a sudden heart attack had carried him off, Morris Livingstone, once the best-loved short Yorkshire comedian in the country, had been the star of such television series as *Short Back and Sides* and his own Saturday night variety-game show, *Morris Livingstone, I Presume*. He had even had a top-ten single back in the eighties, with the novelty song, 'It's Nice Out (But Put It Away)'. Amiable, easy-going, he had not only left all his financial affairs in the control of the Grahame Coats Agency, but he had also appointed, at Grahame Coats's suggestion, Grahame Coats himself as trustee of his estate.

It would have been criminal not to give in to a temptation like that.

And then there was Maeve Livingstone. It would be fair to say that Maeve Livingstone had, without knowing it, featured for many years in starring and co-starring roles in a number of Grahame Coats's most treasured and private fantasies.

Grahame Coats said, 'Please. Put her through,' and then, solicitously, 'Maeve, how lovely to hear from you. How are you?'

'I'm not sure,' she said.

Maeve Livingstone had been a dancer when she met Morris, and had always towered over the little man. They had adored each other.

'Well, why don't you tell me about it?'

'I spoke to Charles a couple of days ago. I was wondering. Well, the bank manager was wondering. The money from Morris's estate. We were told we would be seeing something by now.'

'Maeve,' said Grahame Coats, in what he thought of as his dark velvet voice, the one he believed that women responded to, 'the problem is not that the money is not there – it's merely a matter of liquidity. As I've told you, Morris made a number of unwise investments towards the end of his life, and although, following my advice, he made some sound ones as well, we do need to allow the good ones to mature: we cannot pull out now without losing almost everything. But worry ye not, worry ye not. Anything for a good client. I shall write you a cheque from my own bank account in order to keep you solvent and comfortable. How much does the bank manager require?'

'He says that he's going to have to start bouncing cheques,' she said. 'And the BBC tell me that they've been sending money from the DVD releases of the old shows. *That's* not invested, is it?'

'That's what the BBC said? Actually, *we've* been chasing *them* for money. But I wouldn't want to put all the blame on BBC Worldwide. Our book-keeper's pregnant, and things have been all at sixes and sevens. And Charles Nancy, who you spoke to, has been rather distraught – his father died, and he has been out of the country a great deal—'

'Last time we spoke,' she pointed out, 'you were putting in a new computer system.'

'Indeed we were, and please, do not get me started on the subject of book-keeping programs. What is it they say – to err is human, but to really, er, mess things up, you need a computer. Something like that. I shall investigate this forcefully, by hand if necessary, the old-fashioned way, and your moneys shall be wending their way to you. It's what Morris would have wanted.'

'My bank manager says I need ten thousand pounds in right now, just to stop them bouncing cheques.'

'Ten thousand pounds shall be yours. I am writing a cheque for you even as we speak.' He drew a circle on his note-pad, with a line going off the top of it. It looked a bit like an apple.

'I'm very grateful,' said Maeve, and Grahame Coats preened. 'I hope I'm not becoming a bother.'

'You are never a bother,' said Grahame Coats. 'No sort of bother at all.'

He put down the phone. The funny thing, Grahame Coats

always thought, was that Morris's comedic persona had always been that of a hard-headed Yorkshireman, proud of knowing the location of every penny.

It had been a fine game, thought Grahame Coats, and he added two eyes to the apple, and a couple of ears. It now looked, he decided, more or less like a cat. Soon enough it would be time to exchange a life of milking hard-to-please celebrities for a life of sunshine, swimming pools, fine meals, good wines and, if possible, enormous quantities of oral sex. The best things in life, Grahame Coats was convinced, could all be bought and paid for.

He drew a mouth on the cat, and filled it with sharp teeth, so it looked a little like a mountain lion, and as he drew he began to sing, in a reedy tenor voice,

> 'When I were a young man my father would say
> It's lovely outside, you should go out to play,
> But now that I'm older, the ladies all say,
> It's nice out, but put it away . . .'

Morris Livingstone had bought and paid for Grahame Coats's penthouse flat on the Copacabana, and for the installation of the swimming pool on the island of Saint Andrews, and you must not imagine that Grahame Coats was not grateful.

> 'It's nice out, but put it awaaaay.'

* * *

Spider felt odd.

There was something going on: a strange feeling, spreading like a mist through his life, and it was ruining his day. He could not identify it, and he did not like it.

And if there was one thing that he was definitely *not* feeling, it was guilty. It simply wasn't the kind of thing he ever felt. He felt excellent. Spider felt cool. He did not feel guilty. He would not have felt guilty if he was caught red-handed holding up a bank.

And yet there was, all about him, a faint miasma of discomfort.

Until now Spider had believed that gods were different: they had no consciences, nor did they need them. A god's relationship to the world, even a world in which he was walking, was about as emotionally connected as that of a computer gamer playing with knowledge of the overall shape of the game, and armed with a complete set of cheat codes.

Spider kept himself amused. That was what he did. That was the important bit. He would not have recognised guilt if he had an illustrated guide to it, with all the component parts clearly labelled. It was not that he was feckless – more that he had simply not been around the day they handed out feck. But something had changed – inside him or outside, he was not sure – and it bothered him. He poured himself another drink. He waved a hand and made the music louder. He changed it from Miles Davis to James Brown. It still didn't help.

He lay on the hammock, in the tropical sunshine, listening to the music, basking in how extremely cool it was to be him . . . and for the first time even that, somehow, wasn't enough.

He climbed out of the hammock and wandered over to the door. 'Fat Charlie?'

There was no answer. The flat felt empty. Outside the windows of the flat there was a grey day, and rain. Spider liked the rain. It seemed appropriate.

Shrill and sweet, the telephone rang. Spider picked it up.

Rosie said, 'Is that you?'

'Hullo, Rosie.'

'Last night,' she said. Then she didn't say anything. Then she said, 'Was it as wonderful for you as it was for me?'

'I don't know,' said Spider. 'It was pretty wonderful for me. So, I mean, that's probably a yes.'

'Mmm,' she said.

They didn't say anything.

'Charlie?' said Rosie.

'Uh-huh?'

'I even like not saying anything, just knowing you're on the other end of the phone.'

'Me too,' said Spider.

They enjoyed the sensation of not saying anything for a while longer, savouring it, making it last.

'Do you want to come over to my place tonight?' asked Rosie. 'My flatmates are in the Cairngorms.'

'That,' said Spider, 'may be a candidate for the most beautiful phrase in the English language. *My flatmates are in the Cairngorms*. Perfect poetry.'

She giggled. 'Twit. Um. Bring your toothbrush . . . ?'

'Oh. *Oh*. OK.'

And after several minutes of 'you put down the phone', and 'no *you* put down the phone' that would have done credit to a pair of hormonally intoxicated fifteen-year-olds, the phone was eventually put down.

Spider smiled like a saint. The world, given that it had Rosie in it, was the best world that any world could possibly be. The fog had lifted, the world had ungloomed.

It did not even occur to Spider to wonder where Fat Charlie had gone. Why should he care about such trivia? Rosie's flatmates were in the Cairngorms, and tonight? Why, tonight he would be bringing his toothbrush.

***

Fat Charlie's body was on a plane to Florida; it was crushed in a seat in the middle of a row of five people, and it was fast asleep. This was a good thing: the rear toilets had malfunctioned as soon as the plane was in the air, and although the cabin attendants had hung 'out of order' signs on the doors, this did nothing to alleviate the smell which spread slowly across the back of the plane like a low-level chemical fug. There were babies crying, and adults grumbling and children whining. One faction of the passengers, en route to Walt Disney World, who felt that their holidays began the moment they got on the plane, had got settled into their seats then began a sing-song. They sang 'Bibbidi-Bobbidi-Boo' and 'The Wonderful Thing about Tiggers', and 'Under the Sea' and 'Heigh-Ho, Heigh-Ho, It's Off to Work We Go', and even, under the impression that it was a Disney song as well, 'We're Off to See the Wizard'.

Once the plane was in the air it was discovered that, due to a catering confusion, no coach class lunch meals had been put on board. Instead, only breakfasts had been packed, which meant there would be individual packs of cereal and a banana for all passengers, which they would have to eat with plastic knives and forks, because there were, unfortunately, no spoons, which may have been a good thing, because pretty soon there wasn't any milk for the cereal either.

It was a hell-flight, and Fat Charlie was sleeping through it.

In Fat Charlie's dream he was in a huge hall, and he was wearing a morning suit. Next to him was Rosie, wearing a white wedding dress, and on the other side of her on the dais was Rosie's mother, who was, a little jarringly, also wearing a wedding dress, although this one was covered with dust and with cobwebs. Far away, at the horizon, which was the distant edge of the hall, there were people firing guns and waving white flags.

It's just the people at Table H, said Rosie's mother. Don't pay them no attention.

Fat Charlie turned to Rosie. She smiled at him with her soft sweet smile, then she licked her lips.

Cake, said Rosie, in his dream.

This was the signal for an orchestra to begin to play. It was a New Orleans jazz band, playing a funeral march.

The people at Table B, who were not people but cartoon mice and rats and barnyard animals, human-size, and celebrating – began to sing songs from Disney cartoons. Fat Charlie knew that they wanted him to join in with them. Even asleep he could feel himself panicking at the simple idea of having to sing in public, his limbs becoming numb, his lips prickling.

I can't sing with you, he told them, desperate for an excuse. I have to cut this cake.

At this, the hall fell into silence. And in the silence, a chef entered, wheeling a little trolley with something on it. The chef wore Grahame Coats's face, and on the trolley was an extravagant white wedding cake: an ornate, many-tiered confection. A tiny bride and tiny groom perched precariously on the topmost tier of the cake, like two people trying to keep their balance on top of a sugar-frosted Chrysler Building.

The chef's assistant was a police officer. She was holding a pair of handcuffs. The chef wheeled the cake up on to the dais.

Now, *said Rosie to Fat Charlie, in his dream.* Cut the cake.

Rosie's mother reached under the table, and produced a long wooden-handled knife – almost a machete – with a rusty blade. She passed it to Rosie, who reached for Fat Charlie's right hand and placed it over her own, and, together, they pressed the rusty knife into the thick white icing on the topmost tier of the cake, pushed it in between the groom and the bride. The cake resisted the blade at first, and Fat Charlie pressed harder, putting all his weight on the knife. He felt the cake beginning to give. He pushed harder.

The blade sliced through the topmost tier of the wedding cake. It slipped and sliced down the cake, through every layer and tier, and as it did so, the cake opened . . .

In his dream, Fat Charlie supposed that the cake was filled with black beads, with beads of black glass or of polished jet, and then, as they tumbled out of the cake, he realised that the beads had legs, each bead had eight clever legs, and they came out of the inside of the cake like a black wave. The spiders surged forward and covered the white tablecloth; they covered Rosie's mother and Rosie herself, turning their white dresses black as ebony; then, as if controlled by some vast and malignant intelligence, they flowed, in their hundreds, towards Fat Charlie. He turned to run, but his legs were trapped in some kind of rubbery tanglefoot, and he tumbled to the floor.

Now they were upon him, their tiny legs crawling over his bare skin, and he tried to get up but he was drowning in spiders.

Fat Charlie wanted to scream, but his mouth was filled with spiders. They covered his eyes, and his world went dark . . .

Fat Charlie opened his eyes and saw nothing but blackness, and he screamed and he screamed and he screamed. Then he realised the lights were off, and the window-shades were drawn, because people were watching the film.

It was already a flight from hell. Fat Charlie had just made it a little worse for everyone else.

He stood up, and tried to get out to the aisle, tripping over people as he went past, then, when he was almost at the gangway, straightening up and banging the overhead locker with his forehead, which knocked open the locker door and tumbled someone's hand-luggage down on to his head.

People nearby, the ones who were watching, laughed. It was an elegant piece of slapstick, and it cheered them all up no end.

Chapter Seven

In Which Fat Charlie Goes a Long Way

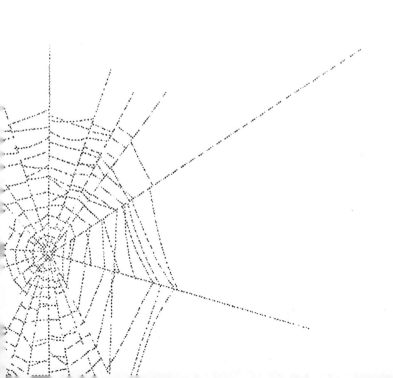

The immigration officer squinted at Fat Charlie's American passport as if she were disappointed he was not a foreign national of the kind she could simply stop coming into the country, then, with a sigh, she waved him through.

He wondered what he was going to do once he got through Customs. Rent a car, he supposed. And eat.

He got off the tram and walked through the security barrier, out into the wide shopping concourse of Orlando airport, and was nowhere nearly as surprised as he should have been to see Mrs Higgler standing there, scanning the faces of the arrivals, her enormous mug of coffee clutched in her hand. They saw each other at more or less the same moment, and she headed towards him.

'You hungry?' she asked him.

He nodded.

'Well,' she said, 'I hope you like turkey.'

* * *

Fat Charlie wondered if Mrs Higgler's maroon station wagon was the same car he remembered her driving when he was a boy. He suspected that it was. It must have been new once, that stood to reason. Everything was new once, after all. The seats were cracked and flaking leather, the dashboard was a dusty wooden veneer.

A brown-paper shopping bag sat between them, on the seat.

There was no cup-holder in Mrs Higgler's ancient car, and she clamped the jumbo mug of coffee between her thighs as she drove. The car appeared to pre-date air conditioning, and she drove with the windows down. Fat Charlie did not mind. After the damp chill of England, the Florida heat was welcome. Mrs Higgler headed south, towards the toll-road. She talked as she drove: she talked about the last hurricane, and about how she took her nephew Benjamin to Sea World and to Walt Disney World and how none of the tourist resorts were what they once were, about building codes, the price of gas, exactly what she had said to the doctor who had suggested a hip replacement, why tourists kept feeding 'gators, and why newcomers built houses on the beaches and were always surprised when the beach or the house went away or the 'gators ate their dogs. Fat Charlie let it all wash over him. It was just talk.

Mrs Higgler slowed down and took the ticket that would take her down the toll road. She stopped talking. She seemed to be thinking.

'So,' she said. 'You met your brother.'

'You know,' said Fat Charlie, 'you could have warned me.'

'I did warn you that he is a god.'

'You didn't mention that he was a complete and utter pain in the arse, though.'

Mrs Higgler sniffed. She took a swig of coffee from her mug.

'Is there anywhere we can stop and get a bite to eat?' asked Fat Charlie. 'They only had cereal and bananas on the plane. No spoons. And they ran out of milk before they got to my row. They said they were sorry and gave us all food vouchers to make up for it.'

Mrs Higgler shook her head.

'I could have used my voucher to get a hamburger in the airport.'

'I tell you already,' said Mrs Higgler. 'Louella Dunwiddy been cooking you a turkey. How do you think she feels if we get there and you fill up already at McDonald's and you ain't got no appetite. Eh?'

'But I'm *star*ving. And it's over two hours away.'

'Not,' she said firmly, 'the way I drive.'

And with that she put her foot down. Every now and then, as the maroon station wagon shuddered down the freeway, Fat Charlie would close his eyes tightly, while at the same time pushing his own left foot down on an imaginary brake pedal. It was exhausting work.

In significantly less than two hours they reached the tollway exit, and got on to a local highway. They drove towards the city. They drove past the Barnes and Noble and the Office Depot. They went past the seven-figure houses with security gates. They went down the older residential streets, which Fat Charlie remembered as being much better cared for when he was a boy. They went past the West Indian takeaway, and the restaurant with the Jamaican flag in the windows, with handwritten signs pushing the oxtail and rice specials and the homemade ginger beer and the curry chicken.

Fat Charlie's mouth watered; his stomach made a noise.

A lurch and a bounce. Now the houses were older, and this time everything was familiar.

The pink plastic flamingos were still striking attitudes in Mrs Dunwiddy's front yard, although the sun had faded them almost white over the years. There was a mirrored gazing ball as well, and when Fat Charlie spotted it he was, only for a moment, as scared as he had ever been of anything.

'How bad is it, with Spider?' asked Mrs Higgler, as they walked up to Mrs Dunwiddy's front door.

'Put it this way,' said Fat Charlie. 'I think he's sleeping with my fiancée. Which is rather more than I ever did.'

'Ah,' said Mrs Higgler. 'Tch.' And she rang the doorbell.

* * *

It was sort of like *Macbeth*, thought Fat Charlie, an hour later; in fact, if the witches in Macbeth had been four little old ladies, and if instead of stirring cauldrons and intoning dread incantations they had just welcomed Macbeth in and fed him turkey, and rice and peas spread out on white china plates on a red-and-white-patterned plastic tablecloth, not to mention sweet potato pudding and spicy cabbage, and encouraged him to take second helpings, and thirds, and then, when Macbeth had declaimed that nay, he was stuffed nigh unto bursting and on his oath could truly eat no more, the witches had pressed upon him their own special island rice pudding and a large slice of Mrs Bustamonte's famous pineapple upside-down cake, it would have been exactly like *Macbeth*.

'So,' said Mrs Dunwiddy, scratching a crumb of pineapple upside-down cake from the corner of her mouth, 'I understand your brother come to see you.'

'Yes. I talked to a spider. I suppose it was my own fault. I never expected anything to happen.'

A chorus of *tut*s and *tsk*s and *tch*s ran around the table as Mrs Higgler and Mrs Dunwiddy and Mrs Bustamonte and Miss Noles clicked their tongues and shook their heads. 'He always used to say you were the stupid one,' said Miss Noles. 'Your father, that is. I never believed him.'

'Well, how was I to know?' Fat Charlie protested. 'It's not as if my parents ever said to me, "By the way son, you have a brother you don't know about. Invite him into your life and he'll have you investigated by the police, he'll sleep with your fiancée, he'll not just move into your home but bring an entire extra house into your spare room. And he'll brainwash you and make you go to films and spend all night trying to get home and—"' He stopped. It was the way they were looking at him.

A sigh went around the table. It went from Mrs Higgler to Miss Noles to Mrs Bustamonte to Mrs Dunwiddy. It was extremely unsettling and quite spooky, but Mrs Bustamonte belched and ruined the effect.

'So what do you want?' asked Mrs Dunwiddy. 'Say what you want.'

Fat Charlie thought about what he wanted, in Mrs Dunwiddy's little dining room. Outside, the daylight was fading into a gentle twilight.

'He's made my life a misery,' said Fat Charlie. 'I want you to make him go away. Just go away. Can you do that?'

The three younger women said nothing. They simply looked at Mrs Dunwiddy.

'We can't actually make him go away,' said Mrs Dunwiddy. 'We already . . .' and she stopped herself, and said, 'Well, we done all we can about that, you see.'

It is to Fat Charlie's credit that he did not, as, deep down he might have wished to, burst into tears, or wail, or collapse in on himself like a problematic soufflé. He simply nodded. 'Well, then,' he said. 'Sorry to have bothered you all. Thank you for the dinner.'

'We can't make him go away,' said Mrs Dunwiddy, her old brown eyes almost black behind her pebble-thick spectacles. 'But we can send you to somebody who can.'

* * *

It was early evening in Florida, which meant that in London it was the dead of night. In Rosie's big bed, where Fat Charlie had never been, Spider shivered.

Rosie pressed close to him, skin to skin. 'Charles,' she said, 'are you all right?' She could feel the goose pimples bumping the skin of his arms.

'I'm fine,' said Spider. 'Sudden creepy feeling.'

'Somebody walking over your grave,' said Rosie.

He pulled her close then, and he kissed her.

And Daisy was sitting in the small common room of the house in Hendon, wearing a bright green nightdress and fluffy, vivid pink carpet slippers. She was sitting in front of a computer screen, shaking her head and clicking the mouse.

'You going to be much longer?' asked Carol. 'You know, there's a whole computer unit that's meant to be doing that. Not you.'

Daisy made a noise. It was not a yes-noise and it was not a no-noise. It was an I-know-somebody-just-said-something-to-me-and-if-I-make-a-noise-maybe-they'll-go-away sort of noise.

Carol had heard that noise before.

'Oy,' she said. 'Big bum. Are you going to be much longer? I want to do my blog.'

Daisy processed the words. Two of them sank in. 'Are you saying I've got a big bum?'

'No,' said Carol. 'I'm saying that it's getting late, and I want to do me blog. I'm going to have him shagging a supermodel in the loo of an unidentified London nightspot.'

Daisy sighed. 'All right,' she said. 'It's just fishy, that's all.'

'What's fishy?'

'Embezzlement. I think. Right, I've logged out. It's all yours. You know you can get into trouble for impersonating a member of the royal family.'

'Bog off.'

Carol blogged as a member of the British royal family, young, male and out of control. There had been arguments in the press about whether or not she was the real thing, many of them pointing to things that she wrote that could only have been known to an actual member of the British royal family, or to someone who read the glossy gossip magazines.

Daisy got up from the computer, still pondering the financial affairs of the Grahame Coats Agency.

While fast asleep in his bedroom, in a large but certainly not ostentatious house in Purley, Grahame Coats slept. If there was any justice in the world, he would have moaned and sweated in his sleep, tortured by nightmares, the furies of his conscience lashing him with scorpions. Thus it pains me to admit that Grahame Coats slept like a well-fed milk-scented baby, and he dreamed of nothing at all.

Somewhere in Grahame Coats's house, a grandfather clock chimed politely, twelve times. In London, it was midnight. In Florida it was seven in the evening.

Either way, it was the witching hour.

***

Mrs Dunwiddy removed the plasticated red-and-white-check tablecloth, and put it away.

She said, 'Who's got the black candles?'

Miss Noles said, 'I got the candles.' She had a shopping bag at her feet, and she rummaged about in it, producing four candles.

They were mostly black. One of them was tall and undecorated. The other three were in the shape of a cartoon black-and-yellow penguin, with the wick coming out of his head. 'It was all they got,' she said apologetically. 'And I had to go to three stores until I found anything.'

Mrs Dunwiddy said nothing, but she shook her head. She arranged the four candles at the four ends of the table, taking the single non-penguin at the head of the table, where she sat. Each of the candles sat on a plastic picnic plate. Mrs Dunwiddy took a large box of kosher salt, and she opened the spout and poured salt crystals on the table, in a pile. Then she glared at the salt, and pushed at it with a withered forefinger, prodding it into heaps and whorls.

Miss Noles came back from the kitchen with a large glass bowl, which she placed at the centre of the table. She unscrewed the top from a bottle of sherry, and poured a generous helping of sherry into the bowl.

'Now,' said Mrs Dunwiddy, 'the devil-grass, the St John the Conqueror root, and the love-lies-bleeding.'

Mrs Bustamonte rummaged in her shopping bag and took out a small glass jar. 'It's mixed herbs,' she explained. 'I thought it would be all right.'

'Mixed herbs!' said Mrs Dunwiddy. 'Mixed herbs!'

'Will that be a problem?' said Mrs Bustamonte. 'It's what I always use when the recipe says basil this or oregano that. I can't be doin' with it. You ask me, it's all mixed herbs.'

Mrs Dunwiddy sighed. 'Pour it in,' she said.

Half a bottle of mixed herbs was poured into the sherry. The dried leaves floated on the top of the liquid.

'Now,' said Mrs Dunwiddy, 'the four earths. I hope,' she said, choosing her words with care, 'that no one here going to tell me that they could not get the four earths, and now we have to make do with a pebble, a dead jellyfish, a refrigerator magnet and a bar of soap.'

'I got the earths,' said Mrs Higgler. She produced the brown paper bag, and pulled from it four zip-lock bags each containing what looked like sand, or dried clay, each of a different colour. She emptied each bag at one of the four corners of the table.

'Glad somebody is payin' attention,' said Mrs Dunwiddy.

Miss Noles lit the candles, pointing out as she did so how easily the penguins lit, and how cute and funny they were.

Mrs Bustamonte poured out a glass of leftover sherry for each of the four women.

'Don't I get a glass?' asked Fat Charlie, but he didn't really want one. He didn't like sherry.

'No,' said Mrs Dunwiddy, firmly, 'you don't. You'll need your wits about you.' She reached into her purse and took out a small golden-coloured pill-case.

Mrs Higgler turned off the lights.

The five of them sat around the table in the candlelight.

'Now what?' asked Fat Charlie. 'Shall we all join hands and contact the living?'

'We do not,' whispered Mrs Dunwiddy. 'And I do not want to hear another word out of you.'

'Sorry,' said Fat Charlie, then wished he hadn't said it.

'Listen,' said Mrs Dunwiddy. 'You will go where they may help you. Even so, give away nothing you own, and make no promises. You understand? If you have to give somebody something, then make sure you get something of equal value in return. Yes?'

Fat Charlie nearly said 'yes', but he caught himself in time and simply nodded.

'It is good.' And with that, Mrs Dunwiddy began to hum tunelessly, in her old old voice, which quavered and faltered.

Miss Noles also began to hum, rather more melodically. Her voice was higher, and stronger.

Mrs Bustamonte did not hum. She hissed instead, an intermittent, snake-like hissing, which seemed to find the rhythm of the humming and weave through it and beneath it.

Mrs Higgler started up, and she did not hum and she did not hiss. She buzzed, like a fly against a window, making a vibrating noise with her tongue and her teeth as odd and as unlikely as if she had a handful of angry bees in her mouth, buzzing against her teeth, trying to get out.

Fat Charlie wondered if he should join in, but he had no idea what sort of thing he ought to do if he did, so he concentrated on sitting there and trying not to be weirded out by all the noises.

Mrs Higgler threw a pinch of red earth into the bowl of sherry and mixed herbs. Mrs Bustamonte threw in a pinch of the yellow earth. Miss Noles threw in the brown earth, while Mrs Dunwiddy leaned over, painstakingly slowly, and dropped in a lump of black mud.

Mrs Dunwiddy took a sip of her sherry. Then, with arthritic fingers fumbling and pushing, she took something from the pill-case, and she dropped it into the candle flame. For a moment the room smelled of lemons, and then it simply smelled as if something was burning.

Miss Noles began to drum on the tabletop. She did not stop humming. The candle flames flickered, dancing huge shadows across the walls. Mrs Higgler began to tap on the tabletop as well, her fingers knocking out a different beat to Miss Noles, faster, more percussive, the two drum-beats twining to form a new rhythm.

In Fat Charlie's mind all the sounds began to blend into one strange sound: the humming and the hissing and the buzzing and the drums. He was starting to feel light-headed. Everything was funny. Everything was unlikely. In the noises of the women he could hear the sound of wildlife in the forest, hear the crackling of enormous fires. His fingers felt stretched and rubbery, his feet were an immensely long way away.

It seemed then that he was somewhere above them, somewhere above everything, and that beneath him there were five people around a table. Then one of the women at the table gestured and dropped something into the bowl in the middle of the table, and it flared up so brightly that Fat Charlie was momentarily blinded. He shut his eyes, which, he found, did no good at all. Even with his eyes closed, everything was much too bright for comfort.

He rubbed his eyes against the daylight. He looked around.

A sheer rock face skyscrapered up behind him, the side of a mountain. Ahead of him was a sheer drop: cliffs, going down. He walked to the cliff-edge and, warily, looked over. He saw some white things, and he thought they were sheep until he realised that they were clouds; large white fluffy clouds, a very long way below him. And then, beneath the clouds, there was nothing: he could see the blue sky, and it seemed that if he kept looking he could see the blackness of space, and beyond that nothing but the chill twinkling of stars.

He took a step back from the cliff-edge.

Then he turned and walked back towards the mountains, which rose up and up, so high that he could not see the tops of them, so high that he found himself convinced that they were falling on him, that they would tumble down and bury him for ever. He forced himself to look down again, to keep his eyes on the ground, and in so doing, he noticed holes in the rock face, near ground level, which looked like entrances to natural caves.

The place between the mountainside and the cliffs, on which he was standing, was, he guessed, less than quarter of a mile wide: a boulder-strewn sandy path dotted with patches of greenery and with, here and there, a dusty brown tree. The path seemed to follow the mountainside until it faded into a distant haze.

Someone is watching me, thought Fat Charlie. 'Hello?' he called, lifting his head back. 'Hello, is anybody there?'

The man who stepped out of the nearest cave mouth was much darker of skin than Fat Charlie, darker even than Spider, but his long hair was a tawny yellow and it framed his face like a mane. He wore a ragged yellow lion-skin around his waist, with a lion's tail hanging down from it behind, and the tail swished a fly from his shoulders.

The man blinked his golden eyes.

'Who are you?' he rumbled. 'And on whose authority do you walk in this place?'

'I'm Fat Charlie Nancy,' said Fat Charlie. 'Anansi the Spider was my father.'

The massive head nodded. 'And why do you come here, Compé Anansi's child?'

They were alone on the rocks, as far as Fat Charlie knew, yet it felt as if there were many people listening, many voices saying nothing, many ears twitching. Fat Charlie spoke loudly, so that anyone listening could hear. 'My brother. He is ruining my life. I don't have the power to make him leave.'

'So you seek our help?' asked the lion.

'Yes.'

'And this brother. He is, like you, of Anansi's blood?'

'He's not like me at all,' said Fat Charlie. 'He's one of you people.'

A fluid golden movement; the man-lion bounded down lightly, lazily, from the cave mouth, over the grey rocks, covering fifty yards in moments. Now he stood beside Fat Charlie. His tail swished impatiently.

His arms folded, he looked down at Fat Charlie and said, 'Why do you not deal with this matter yourself?'

Fat Charlie's mouth had dried. His throat felt extremely dusty. The creature facing him, taller than any man, did not smell like a man. The tips of his canine teeth rested on his lower lips.

'Can't,' squeaked Fat Charlie.

From the mouth of the next cave along, an immense man leaned out. His skin was a brownish grey, and he had rumpled, wrinkled skin, and round round legs. 'If you and your brother quarrel,' he said, 'then you must ask your father to judge between you. Submit to the will of the head of the family. That is the law.' He threw his head back, and made a noise then, in the back of his nose and in his throat, a powerful trumpeting noise, and Fat Charlie knew he was looking at Elephant.

Fat Charlie swallowed. 'My father is dead,' he said, and now his voice was clear again, cleaner and louder than he expected. It echoed from the cliff-wall, bounced back at him from a hundred cave mouths, a hundred jutting outcrops of rock. Dead *dead* dead *dead* dead, said the echo. 'That's why I came here.'

Lion said, 'I have no love for Anansi the Spider. Once, long ago, he tied me to a log, and had a donkey drag me through the dust, to the seat of Mawu who made all things.' He growled at the memory, and Fat Charlie wanted to be somewhere else.

'Walk on,' said Lion. 'There may be someone here who will help you, but it is not I.'

Elephant said, 'Nor I. Your father tricked me and ate my belly fat. He told me he was making me some shoes to wear, and he cooked me, and he laughed as he filled his stomach. I do not forget.'

Fat Charlie walked on.

In the next cave mouth along stood a man wearing a natty green suit and a sharp hat with a snake-skin band around it. He wore snake-skin boots and a snake-skin belt. He hissed as Fat Charlie came past. 'Walk on, Anansi's boy,' Snake said, his voice a dry rattle. 'Your whole damn family nothing but trouble. I ain't gettin' mixed up in your messes.'

The woman in the next cave mouth was very beautiful, and her eyes were black oil-drops, and her whiskers were snowy-white against her skin. She had two rows of breasts down her chest.

'I knew your father,' she said. 'Long time back. Hoo-ee.' She shook her head, in memory, and Fat Charlie felt like he had just read a private letter. She blew Fat Charlie a kiss, but shook her head when he made to approach closer.

He walked on. A dead tree stuck up from the ground before him like an assemblage of old grey bones. The shadows were getting longer now, as the sun was slowly descending in the endless sky, past where the cliffs cragged down into the end of the world; the eye of the sun was a monstrous golden-orange ball, and all the little white clouds beneath it were burnished with gold and with purple.

The Assyrian came down like a wolf on the fold, thought Fat Charlie, the line of the poem surfacing from some long-forgotten English lesson. *And his cohorts were gleaming in purple and gold.* He tried to remember what a cohort was, and failed. Probably, he decided, it was some kind of chariot.

Something moved, close to his elbow, and he realised that what he had thought was a brown rock, beneath the dead tree, was a man, sandy-coloured, his back spotted like a leopard's. His hair was very long and very black, and when he smiled his teeth were a big cat's teeth. He only smiled briefly, and it was a smile without warmth or humour or friendship in it. He said, 'I am Tiger. Your father, he injured me in a hundred ways and he insulted me in a thousand ways. Tiger does not forget.'

'I'm sorry,' said Fat Charlie.

'I'll walk along with you,' said Tiger. 'For a short while. You say that Anansi is dead?'

'Yes.'

'Well. Well, well. He played me for a fool so many times. Once, everything was mine – the stories, the stars, everything. He stole it all away from me. Maybe now he is dead people will stop telling those damn stories of his. Laughing at me.'

'I'm sure they will,' said Fat Charlie. 'I've never laughed at you.'

Eyes the colour of polished emeralds flashed in the man's face. 'Blood is blood,' was all he said. 'Anansi's bloodline is Anansi.'

'I am not my father,' said Fat Charlie.

Tiger bared his teeth. They were very sharp. 'You don't go around making people laugh at things,' explained Tiger. 'It's a big, serious world out there; nothing to laugh about. Not ever. You must teach the children to fear, teach them to tremble. Teach them to be cruel. Teach them to be the danger in the dark. Hide in the shadows, then pounce or spring or leap or drop, and always kill. You know what the true meaning of life is?'

'Um,' said Fat Charlie. 'Is it love one another?'

'The meaning of life is the hot blood of your prey on your tongue, the meat that rends beneath your teeth, the corpse of your enemy left in the sun for the carrion-eaters to finish. That is what life is. I am Tiger, and I am stronger than Anansi ever was, bigger, more dangerous, more powerful, crueller, wiser . . .'

Fat Charlie did not want to be in that place, talking to Tiger. It was not that Tiger was mad; it was that he was so earnest in his convictions, and that all his convictions were uniformly unpleasant. Also, he reminded Fat Charlie of someone, and while he could not have told you who, he knew it was someone he disliked. 'Will you help me get rid of my brother?'

Tiger coughed, as if he had a feather, or perhaps a whole blackbird, stuck in his throat.

'Would you like me to get you some water?' asked Fat Charlie.

Tiger eyed Fat Charlie with suspicion. 'Last time Anansi offered me water, I wound up trying to eat the moon out of a pond, and I drowned.'

'I was just trying to help.'

'That was what *he* said.' Tiger leaned in to Fat Charlie, stared him in the eye. Close-up, he did not look even faintly human – his nose was too flat, his eyes were positioned differently, and he smelled like a cage at the zoo. His voice was a rumbling growl.

'This is how you help me, Anansi's child. You and all your blood.
You keep well away from me. Understand? If you want to keep
the meat on those bones.' He licked his lips then, with a tongue
the red of fresh-killed flesh, and longer than any human tongue
had ever been.

Fat Charlie backed away, certain that if he turned, if he ran, he
would feel Tiger's teeth in his neck. There was nothing remotely
human about the creature now: it was the size of a real tiger. It
was every big cat that had turned man-eater, every tiger that had
broken a human's neck like a house-cat dispatching a mouse. So
he stared at Tiger as he edged backwards, and soon enough the
creature padded back to its dead tree, and stretched out on the
rocks, and vanished into the patchy shadows, only the impatient
swish of its tail betraying its position.

'Don't you worry yourself about him,' said a woman, from a
cave mouth. 'Come here.'

Fat Charlie could not decide if she was attractive or
monstrously ugly. He walked towards her.

'He come on all high-and-so-mighty, but he's a-scairt of his own
shadow. And he's scairter of your daddy's shadow. He got no
strength in his jaws.'

There was something doglike about her face. No, not
doglike . . .

'Now, me,' she continued, as he reached her, 'me, I crush the
bone. That's where the good stuff is hid. That's where the
sweetest meats are hid, and nobody knows it but me.'

'I'm looking for someone to help me to get rid of my brother.'

The woman threw back her head and laughed, a wild bray of a
laugh, loud, long and insane, and Fat Charlie knew her then.

'You won't find anyone here to help you,' she said. 'They all
suffered, when they went up against your father. Tiger hates you
and your kind more than anyone has ever hated anything, but
even he won't do anything while your father's out there in the
world. Listen: walk this path. You ask me, and I got a stone of
prophecy behind my eye, you won't find nobody to help you till
you find an empty cave. Go in. Talk to whoever you find there.
Understand me?'

'I think I do.'

She laughed. It was not a good laugh. 'You want to stop with me for a while first? I'm an education. You know what they say – nothing leaner, meaner, or obscener than Hyena.'

Fat Charlie shook his head, and kept walking, past the caves that line the rocky walls at the end of the world. As he passed the darkness of each cave, he would glance inside. There were people of all shapes and all sizes, tiny people and tall people, men and women. And as he passed, and as they moved in and out of the shadows, he would see flanks or scales, horns or claws.

Sometimes he scared them as he passed, and they would retreat into the back of the cave. Others would come forward, stare aggressively or curiously.

Something tumbled through the air from the rocks above a cave mouth, and landed beside Fat Charlie. 'Hello,' it said breathlessly.

'Hello,' said Fat Charlie.

The new one was excitable and hairy. Its arms and legs seemed all *wrong*. Fat Charlie tried to place it. The other animal-people were animals, yes, and people too, and there was nothing strange or contradictory about this – the animalness and the humanness combined like the stripes on a zebra to make something *other*. This one, however, seemed both human and almost-human, and the oddness of it made Fat Charlie's teeth hurt. Then he got it.

'Monkey,' he said. 'You're Monkey.'

'Got a peach?' said Monkey. 'Got a mango? Got a fig?'

''Fraid not,' said Fat Charlie.

'Give me something to eat,' said Monkey. 'I'll be your friend.'

Mrs Dunwiddy had warned him about this. *Give nothing away*, he thought. *Make no promises.*

'I'm not giving you anything, I'm afraid.'

'Who are you?' asked Monkey. 'What are you? You seem like half a thing. Are you from here or from there?'

'Anansi was my father,' said Fat Charlie. 'I'm looking for someone to help me deal with my brother, to make him go away.'

'Might get Anansi mad,' said Monkey. 'Very bad idea that. Get Anansi mad, you never in any more stories.'

'Anansi's dead,' said Fat Charlie.

'Dead there,' said Monkey. 'Maybe. But dead here? That's another stump of grubs entirely.'

'You mean, he could be here?' Fat Charlie looked up at the mountainside more warily: the idea that he might, in one of the cave mouths, find his father creaking back and forwards in a rocking chair, fedora hat pushed back on his head, sipping from a can of brown ale and stifling a yawn with his lemon-yellow gloves, was troubling indeed.

'Who? What?'

'Do you think he's here?'

'Who?'

'My father.'

'Your father?'

'Anansi.'

Monkey leaped to the top of a rock in terror, then he pressed himself against the rock, his gaze flicking from side to side, as if keeping an eye out for sudden tornadoes. 'Anansi? He's here?'

'I was asking you that,' said Fat Charlie.

Monkey swung suddenly, so he was hanging upside down from his feet, his upside-down face staring straight into Fat Charlie's. 'I go back to the world sometimes,' he said. 'They say, Monkey, wise Monkey, come, come. Come eat the peaches we have for you. And the nuts. And the grubs. And the figs.'

'Is my father here?' asked Fat Charlie, patiently.

'He doesn't have a cave,' said Monkey. 'I would know if he had a cave. I think. Maybe he had a cave and I forgot. If you gave me a peach, I would remember better.'

'I don't have anything on me,' said Fat Charlie.

'No peaches?'

'Nothing, I'm afraid.'

Monkey swung himself up to the top of his rock and he was gone.

Fat Charlie continued along the rocky path. The sun had sunk until it was level with the path, and it burned a deep orange. It shone its old light straight into the caves, and showed each cave to be inhabited. That must be Rhinoceros, grey of skin, staring out short-sightedly; there, the colour of a rotten log in shallow water, was Crocodile, his eyes as black as glass.

There was a rattle behind him, of stone scuttering against

stone, and Fat Charlie turned with a jerk. Monkey stared up at him, his knuckles brushing the path.

'I really haven't got any fruit,' said Fat Charlie. 'Or I'd give you some.'

Monkey said, 'Felt sorry for you. Maybe you should go home. This is a bad bad bad bad *bad* idea. Yes?'

'No,' said Fat Charlie.

'Ah,' said Monkey. 'Right. Right right right right *right*.' He stopped moving, then a sudden burst of loping speed, and he bounded past Fat Charlie, and stopped in front of a cave some little distance away.

'Not to go in there,' he called. 'Bad place.' He pointed to the cave opening.

'Why not?' asked Fat Charlie. 'Who's in there?'

'Nobody's in there,' said Monkey, triumphantly. 'So it's not the one you want, is it?'

'Yes,' said Fat Charlie. 'It is.'

Monkey chittered and bounced, but Fat Charlie walked past him, and clambered up the rocks until he reached the mouth of the empty cave, as the crimson sun fell below the cliffs at the end of the world.

Walking the path along the edge of the mountains at the beginning of the world (it's only the mountains at the end of the world if you're coming from the other direction) reality seemed strange and strained. These mountains and their caves are made from the stuff of the oldest stories (this was long before human-people, of course; whatever made you imagine that people were the first things to tell stories?) and stepping off the path, into the cave, Fat Charlie felt as if he were walking into someone else's reality entirely. The cave was deep; its floor was splashed white with bird-droppings. There were feathers on the cave floor too, and, here and there, like a desiccated and abandoned feather duster, was the corpse of a bird, flattened and dried.

At the back of the cave, nothing but darkness.

Fat Charlie called, 'Hello?' and the echo of his voice came back to him from the interior of the cave. *Hello hello hello hello*. He kept walking. Now the darkness in the cave seemed almost palpable, as if something thin and dark had been laid over his eyes. He walked slowly, a step at a time, his arms outstretched.

Something moved.

'Hello?'

His eyes were learning to use what little light there was, and he could make something out. *It's nothing. Rags and feathers, that's all.* Another step, and the wind stirred the feathers and flapped the rags on the floor of the cave.

Something fluttered about him, fluttered *through* him, beating the air with the clatter of a pigeon's wings.

Swirling. Dust stung his eyes and his face, and he blinked in the cold wind, and took a step back as it rose up before him, a storm of dust and rags and feathers. Then the wind was gone, and where the feathers had been blowing was a human figure, which reached out a hand and beckoned to Fat Charlie.

He would have stepped back, but it reached out and took him by the sleeve. Its touch was light and dry, and it pulled him towards it . . .

He took one step forward into the cave –

– and was standing in the open air, on a treeless, copper-coloured plain, beneath a sky the colour of sour milk.

Different creatures have different eyes. Human eyes (unlike, say, a cat's eyes, or an octopus's) are only made to see one version of reality at a time. Fat Charlie saw one thing with his eyes, and he saw something else with his mind, and in the gulf between the two things, madness waited. He could feel a wild panic welling up inside him, and he took a deep breath and held it in while his heart thudded against his ribcage. He forced himself to believe his eyes, not his mind.

So while he knew that he was seeing a bird, mad-eyed, ragged-feathered, bigger than any eagle, taller than an ostrich, its beak the cruel tearing weapon of a raptor, its feathers the colour of slate overlaid with an oilslick sheen, making a dark rainbow of purples and greens, he really only knew that for an instant, somewhere in the very back of his mind. What he saw with his eyes was a woman with raven-black hair, standing where the idea of a bird had been. She was neither young nor old, and she stared at him with a face that might have been carved from obsidian in ancient times, when the world was young.

She watched him, and she did not move. Clouds roiled across the sour-milk sky.

'I'm Charlie,' said Fat Charlie. 'Charlie Nancy. Some people, well, most people, call me Fat Charlie. You can too. If you like.'

No response.

'Anansi was my father.'

Still nothing. Not a quiver; not a breath.

'I want you to help me make my brother go away.'

She tilted her head at this. Enough to show that she was listening, enough to show that she was alive.

'I can't do it on my own. He's got magic powers and stuff. I spoke to a spider, and the next thing you know, my brother turns up. Now I can't make him go away.'

Her voice, when she spoke, was as rough and as deep as a crow's. 'What do you wish me to do about it?'

'Help me?' he suggested.

She appeared to be thinking.

Later, Fat Charlie tried, and failed, to remember what she had been wearing. Sometimes he thought it must have been a cloak of feathers; at other times he believed it must have been rags of some kind, or perhaps a tattered raincoat, of the kind she wore when he saw her in Piccadilly, later, when it had all started to go bad. She was not naked, though: of that he was nearly certain. He would have remembered if she had been naked, wouldn't he?

'Help you,' she echoed.

'Help me get rid of him.'

She nodded. 'You wish me to help you get rid of Anansi's bloodline.'

'I just want him to go away and leave me alone. I don't want you to hurt him or anything.'

'Then promise me Anansi's bloodline for my own.'

Fat Charlie stood on the vast coppery plain, which was somehow, he knew, inside the cave in the mountains at the end of the world, and was, in its turn, in some sense, inside Mrs Dunwiddy's violet-scented front room, and he tried to make sense of what she was asking for.

'I can't give things away. And I can't make promises.'

'You want him to go,' she said. 'Say it. My time is precious.' She folded her arms, stared at him with mad eyes. 'I am not scared of Anansi.'

He remembered Mrs Dunwiddy's voice. 'Um,' said Fat Charlie. 'I mustn't make promises. And I have to ask for something of equal value. I mean, it has to be a trade.'

The Bird Woman looked displeased, but she nodded. 'Then I shall give you something of equal value in trade. I give my word.' She put her hand over his hand, as if she was giving him something, then squeezed his hand closed. 'Now say it.'

'I give you Anansi's bloodline,' Fat Charlie said.

'It is good,' said a voice, and at that she went, quite literally, to pieces.

Where a woman had been standing, there was now a flock of birds, which were flying, as if startled by a gunshot, all in different directions. Now the sky filled with birds, more birds than Fat Charlie had ever imagined, brown birds and black, wheeling and crossing and flowing like a cloud of black smoke vaster than the mind could hold, like a cloud of midges as big as the world.

'You'll make him go away, now?' called Fat Charlie, shouting the words into the darkening milky sky. The birds slipped and slid in the air. Each moved only a fraction, and they kept flying, but suddenly Fat Charlie was staring up at a face in the sky, a face made of swirling birds. It was very big.

It said his name in the screams and caws and calls of a thousand, thousand, thousand birds, and lips the size of tower blocks formed the words in the sky.

Then the face dissolved into madness and chaos as the birds that made it flew down from that pale sky, flew straight towards him. He covered his face with his hands, trying to protect himself.

The pain in his cheek was harsh and sudden. For an instant he believed that one of the birds must have gashed him, torn at his cheek with its beak or talons. Then he saw where he was.

'Don't hit me again!' he said. 'It's all right. You don't have to hit me!'

On the table, the penguins were guttering low; their heads and shoulders were gone, and now the flames were burning in the shapeless black and yellow blobs that had once been their bellies, their feet in frozen pools of blackish candlewax. There were three old women staring at him.

Miss Noles threw the contents of a glass of water into his face. 'You didn't have to do that either,' he said. 'I'm here, aren't I?'

Mrs Dunwiddy came into the room. She was holding a small brown glass bottle triumphantly. 'Smelling salts,' she announced. 'I know I got some somewhere. I buy these in, oh, 'sixty-seven, 'sixty-eight. I don't know if they still any good.' She peered at Fat Charlie, then scowled. 'He wake up. Who did wake him up?'

'He wasn't breathing,' said Mrs Bustamonte. 'So I give him a slap.'

'And I pour water on him,' said Miss Noles, 'which help bring him around the rest of the way.'

'I don't need smelling salts,' said Fat Charlie. 'I'm already wet and in pain.' But, with elderly hands, Mrs Dunwiddy had removed the cap from the bottle, and she was pushing it under his nose. He breathed in as he moved back, and inhaled a wave of ammonia. His eyes watered, and he felt as if he had been punched in the nose. Water dripped down his face.

'There,' said Mrs Dunwiddy. 'Feeling better now?'

'What time is it?' asked Fat Charlie.

'It's almost five in the morning,' said Mrs Higgler. She took a swig of coffee from her gigantic mug. 'We all worried about you. You better tell us what happened.'

Fat Charlie tried to remember. It was not that it had evaporated, as dreams do, more as if the experience of the last few hours had happened to somebody else, someone who was not him, and he had to contact that person by some hitherto unpractised form of telepathy. It was all a jumble in his mind, the technicolor Ozness of the other place dissolving back into the sepia tones of reality. 'There were caves. I asked for help. There were lots of animals there. Animals who were people. None of them wanted to help. They were all scared of my daddy. Then one of them said she would help me.'

'She?' said Mrs Bustamonte.

'Some of them were men, and some of them were women,' said Fat Charlie. 'This one was a woman.'

'Do you know what she was? Crocodile? Hyena? Mouse?'

He shrugged. 'I might have remembered before people started hitting me and pouring water on me. And putting things in my nose. It drives stuff out of your head.'

Mrs Dunwiddy said, 'Do you remember what I tell you? Not giving anything away? Only trade?'

'Yes,' he said, vaguely proud of himself. 'Yes. There was a monkey who wanted me to give him things, and I said no. Look, I think I need a drink.'

Mrs Bustamonte took a glass of something from the table. 'We thought maybe you need a drink. So we put the sherry through the strainer. There may be a few mixed herbs in there, but nothin' big.'

His hands were fists in his lap. He opened his right hand to take the glass from the old woman. Then he stopped, and he stared.

'What?' asked Mrs Dunwiddy. 'What is it?'

In the palm of his hand, black and crushed out of shape, and wet with sweat, Fat Charlie was holding a feather. He remembered, then. He remembered all of it.

'It was the Bird Woman,' he said.

* * *

Grey dawn was breaking as Fat Charlie climbed into the passenger seat of Mrs Higgler's station wagon.

'You sleepy?' she asked him.

'Not really. I just feel weird.'

'Where do you want me to take you? My place? Your dad's house? A motel?'

'I don't know.'

She put the car into gear and lurched out into the road.

'Where are we going?'

She did not answer. She slurped some coffee from her megamug. Then she said. 'Maybe what we do tonight is for the best and maybe it ain't. Sometimes family things, they best left for families to fix. You and your brother. You're too similar. I guess that is why you fight.'

'I take it this is some obscure West Indian usage of the word "similar" which means "nothing at all alike"?'

'Don't you start going all British on me. I know what I'm sayin'. You and him, you both cut from the same cloth. I remember your father sayin' to me, Callyanne, my boys, they stupider than— You know, it don't matter what he actually said, but the point is, he said it about both of you.' A thought struck her. 'Hey. When you go to the place where the old gods are, you see your father in that place?'

'I don't think so. I'd remember.'

She nodded, and said nothing, as she drove.

She parked the car, and they got out.

It was chilly in the Florida dawn. The Garden of Rest looked like something from a movie: there was a low ground mist which threw everything into soft focus. Mrs Higgler opened the small gate, and they walked through the cemetery.

Where there had been only fresh earth filling his father's grave, now there was turf, and at the head of the grave was a metal plaque with a metal vase built into it, and in the vase a single yellow silk rose.

'Lord have mercy on the sinner in this grave,' said Mrs Higgler, with feeling. 'Amen, amen, amen.'

They had an audience: the two red-headed cranes, which Fat Charlie had observed on his previous visit, strutted towards them, heads bobbing, like two aristocratic prison visitors.

'Shoo!' said Mrs Higgler. The birds started at her, incuriously, and did not leave.

One of them ducked its head down into the grass, came up again with a lizard struggling in its beak. A gulp and a shake, and the lizard was a bulge in the bird's neck.

The dawn chorus was beginning: grackles and orioles and mockingbirds were singing in the day in the wilderness beyond the Garden of Rest. 'It'll be good to be home again,' said Fat Charlie. 'With any luck she'll have made him leave by the time I get there. Then everything will be all right. I can sort everything out with Rosie.' A mood of gentle optimism welled up within him. It was going to be a good day.

* * *

In the old stories, Anansi lives just like you do or I do, in his house. He is greedy, of course, and lustful, and tricky, and full of lies. And he is good-hearted, and lucky, and sometimes even honest. Sometimes he is good, sometimes he is bad. He is never evil. Mostly, you are on Anansi's side. This is because Anansi owns all the stories. Mawu gave him the stories, back in the dawn days, took them from Tiger and gave them to Anansi, and he spins the web of them so beautifully.

In the stories, Anansi is a spider, but he is also a man. It is not hard to keep two things in your head at the same time. Even a child could do it.

Anansi's stories are told by grandmothers and by aunts in the West Coast of Africa and across the Caribbean, and all over the world. The stories have made it into books for children: big old smiling Anansi playing his merry tricks upon the world. Trouble is, grandmothers and aunts and writers of books for children tend to leave things out. There are stories that aren't appropriate for little children any more.

This is a story you won't find in the nursery tales. I call it,

ANANSI AND BIRD

Anansi did not like Bird, because when Bird was hungry she ate many things, and one of the things that Bird ate was spiders, and Bird, she was always hungry.

They used to be friends, but they were friends no longer.

One day Anansi was walking, and he saw a hole in the ground, and that gave him an idea. He puts wood in the bottom of the hole, and he makes a fire, and he puts a cookpot in the hole and drops in roots and herbs. Then he starts running around the pot, running and dancing and calling and shouting, going, I feel good. I feel *soooo* good. Oh boy, all my aches and pains be gone and I never felt so good in my whole damn life!

Bird hears the commotion. Bird flies down from the skies to see what all the fuss is about. She goes, What you singing about? Why you carrying on like a madman, Anansi?

Anansi sings, I had a pain in my neck, but now it's gone. I had a pain in my belly, but not any longer. I had creaks in my joints, but now I'm supple as a young palm tree, I'm smooth as Snake the morning after he sheds his skin. I'm powerful happy, and now I shall be perfect, for I know the secret, and nobody else does.

What secret? asks Bird.

My secret, says Anansi. Everyone's going to give me their favourite things, their most precious things, just to learn my secret. *Whoo! Whee!* I do feel good!

Bird hops a little closer, and she puts her head on one side. Then she asks, Can I learn your secret?

Anansi looks at Bird with suspicion on his face, and he moves to stand in front of the pot in the hole, bubbling away.

I don't think so, Anansi says. May not be enough to go around. Don't bother yourself about it.

Bird says, Now, Anansi, I know we haven't always been friends. But I'll tell you what. You share your secret with me, and I promise you no bird will never eat no spider ever again. We'll be friends until the end of time.

Anansi scratches his chin, and he shakes his head. It's a mighty big secret, he says, making people young and spry and lusty and free from all pain.

Bird, she preens. Bird, she says, Oh, Anansi, I'm sure you know that I have always found you a particularly handsome figure of a man. Why don't we lie by the side of the road for a little while, and I'm sure I can make you forget all your reservations about telling me your secret.

So they lie by the side of the road, and they get to canoodling and laughing and getting all silly, and once Anansi has had what he wants Bird says, Now, Anansi, what about your secret?

Anansi says, Well, I wasn't going to tell anyone. But I'll tell you. It's a herbal bath, in this hole in the ground. Watch, I'll drop in these leaves, and these roots. Now, anyone who goes into the bath they going to live for ever, feeling no pain. I had the bath, and now I'm frisky as a young goat. But I don't think I should let anyone else use the bath.

Bird, she looks down at the bubbling water, and quick as anything she slips down into the pot.

It's awful hot, Anansi, she says.

It's got to be hot for the herbs to do their good things, says

Anansi. Then he takes the lid of the pot and he covers the pot with it. It's a heavy lid, and Anansi, he puts a rock on top of it, to weigh it down more.

Bam! Bem! Bom! comes the knocking from inside the cookpot.

If I let you out now, calls Anansi, all the good work of the bubbling bath will be undone. You just relax in there and feel yourself getting healthier.

But maybe Bird did not hear him, or believe him, because the knocking and the pushing kept on coming from inside the pot, for a while longer. And then it stopped.

That evening Anansi and his family had the most delicious Bird soup, with boiled Bird. They did not go hungry again for many days.

Since that time, birds eat spiders every chance they get, and spiders and birds aren't never going to be friends.

There's another version of the story where they talk Anansi into the cookpot too. The stories are all Anansi's, but he doesn't always come out ahead.

Chapter Eight

In Which a Pot of Coffee Comes in Particularly Useful

If anything was making Spider go away, Spider didn't know about it. On the contrary, Spider was having an excellent time being Fat Charlie. He was having such a good time being Fat Charlie he began to wonder why he hadn't been Fat Charlie before. It was more fun than a barrelful of monkeys.*

The bit of being Fat Charlie that Spider liked best was Rosie.

Until now Spider had regarded women as more or less interchangeable. You didn't give them a real name, or an address that would work for longer than a week, of course, or anything more than a disposable mobile number. Women were fun, and decorative, and terrific accessories, but there would always be more of them; like bowls of goulash coming along a conveyor belt, when you were done with one, you simply picked up the next, and spooned in your sour cream.

---

*Several years earlier Spider had actually been tremendously disappointed by a barrelful of monkeys. It had done nothing he had considered particularly entertaining, apart from emit interesting noises, and eventually, once the noises had stopped and the monkeys were no longer doing anything at all – except possibly on an organic level – had needed to be disposed of in the dead of night.

But Rosie . . .

Rosie was different.

He couldn't have told you how she was different. He had tried, and failed. Partly it was how he felt when he was with her: as if, seeing himself in her eyes, he became a wholly better person. That was part of it.

Spider liked knowing that Rosie knew where to find him. It made him feel comfortable. He delighted in the pillowy curves of her, the way she meant nothing but good to the world, the way she smiled. There was really nothing at all wrong with Rosie, apart from having to spend time away from her, and of course, he was beginning to discover, the little matter of Rosie's mother. On this particular evening, while Fat Charlie was in an airport, four thousand miles away, in the process of being bumped up to first class, Spider was in Rosie's mother's flat in Wimpole Street, and he was learning about her the hard way.

Spider was used to being able to push reality around a little, just a little but that was always enough. You just had to show reality who was boss, that was all. Having said that, he had never met anyone who inhabited her own reality quite so firmly as Rosie's mother.

'Who's this?' she asked, suspiciously, as they walked in.

'I'm Fat Charlie Nancy,' said Spider.

'Why is he saying that?' asked Rosie's mother. 'Who is he?'

'I'm Fat Charlie Nancy, your future son-in-law, and you really like me,' said Spider, with utter conviction.

Rosie's mother swayed and blinked and stared at him. 'You may be Fat Charlie,' she said, uncertainly, 'but I don't like you.'

'Well,' said Spider, 'you should. I am remarkably likeable. Few people have ever been as likeable as I am. There is, frankly, no end to my likeability. People gather together in public assemblies to discuss how much they like me. I have several awards, and a medal from a small country in South America which pays tribute both to how much I am liked and my general all-round wonderfulness. I don't have it on me, of course. I keep my medals in my sock drawer.'

Rosie's mother sniffed. She did not know what was going on, but whatever it was, she did not like it. Until now, she felt that she had got the measure of Fat Charlie. She might, she admitted to herself, have mishandled things a little in the beginning: it was quite possible that Rosie would not have attached herself to Fat Charlie with such enthusiasm if, following the first meeting of her mother and Fat Charlie, her mother had not expressed her opinion quite so vociferously. He was a loser, Rosie's mother had said, for she could smell fear like a shark scenting blood across the bay. But she had failed to persuade Rosie to dump him, and now her main strategy involved assuming control of the wedding plans, making Fat Charlie as miserable as possible, and contemplating the national divorce statistics with a certain grim satisfaction.

Something different was now happening, and she did not like it. Fat Charlie was no longer a large vulnerable person. This new, sharp creature confused her.

Spider, for his part, was having to work.

Most people do not notice other people. Rosie's mother did. She noticed everything. Now, she sipped her hot water from a bone china cup. She knew that she had just lost a skirmish, even if she could not have told you how, or what the battle was about. So she moved her next assault to higher ground.

'Charles, dear,' she said, 'tell me about your cousin Daisy. I worry that your family is under-represented. Would you like her to be given a larger role in the wedding party?'

'Who?'

'Daisy,' said Rosie's mother, sweetly. 'The young lady I met at your house the other morning, wandering around in her scanties. If she *was* your cousin, of course.'

'Mother! If Charlie says she was his cousin . . .'

'Let him talk for himself, Rosie,' said her mother, and she took another sip of hot water.

'Right,' said Spider. 'Daisy,' said Spider.

He cast his mind back to the night of wine, women and song: he had brought the prettiest and funniest of the women back to the flat with them, after telling her that it was her idea, and then had needed her help in getting the semi-conscious bulk of Fat Charlie up the stairs. Having already enjoyed the attentions of several of the other women during the course of the evening, he had brought the little funny one back with him rather as one might set aside an after-dinner mint, but he had found, on getting home and putting a cleaned-up Fat Charlie to bed, that he was no longer hungry. That one.

'Sweet little cousin Daisy,' he continued, without a pause. 'I am certain that she would love to be involved in the wedding, should she be in the country. Alas, she's a courier. Always travelling. One day she's here, the next, she's dropping off a confidential document in Murmansk.'

'You don't have her address? Or her phone number?'

'We can look for her together, you and I,' agreed Spider. 'Zooming around the world. She comes, she goes.'

'Then,' said Rosie's mother, much as Alexander the Great might have ordered the sacking and pillaging of a little Persian village, 'the next time she is in the country, you must invite her over. I thought she was such a pretty little thing, and I am sure that Rosie would just love to meet her.'

'Yes,' said Spider. 'I must. I really must.'

* * *

Each person who ever was or is or will be has a song. It isn't a song that anybody else wrote. It has its own melody, it has its own words. Very few people get to sing their own song. Most of us fear that we cannot do it justice with our voices, or that our words are too foolish or too honest, or too odd. So people live their songs instead.

Take Daisy, for example. Her song, which had been somewhere in the back of her head for most of her life, had a reassuring marching sort of beat, and words that were about protecting the weak, and it had a chorus that began 'Evildoers beware!' and was thus much too silly ever to be sung out loud. She would hum it to herself sometimes, though, in the shower, during the soapy bits.

And that is, more or less, everything you need to know about Daisy. The rest is details.

Daisy's father was born in Hong Kong. Her mother came from Ethiopia, of a family of wealthy carpet exporters: they owned a house in Addis Ababa, and another house and lands outside Nazret. Daisy's parents met at Cambridge – he was studying computing before that was something that was seen as being a sensible career path, and she was devouring molecular chemistry and international law. They were two young people who were equally studious, naturally shy, and generally ill-at-ease. They were both homesick, but for very different things; however, they both played chess, and they met on a Wednesday afternoon, at the chess club. They were, as novices, encouraged to play together, and during their first game Daisy's mother beat Daisy's father with ease.

Daisy's father was nettled by this, enough that he shyly asked for a rematch on the following Wednesday, and on every successive Wednesday after that (excluding vacations and public holidays) for the next two years.

Their social interaction increased as their social skills and her spoken English improved. Together, they held hands as part of a human chain and protested the arrival of large trucks loaded with missiles. Together, although as part of a much larger party, they travelled to Barcelona in order to protest the unstoppable flood of international capitalism, and to register stern protests at corporate hegemonies. This was also the time they got to experience officially squirted tear gas, and Mr Day's wrist was sprained as he was being pushed out of the way by the Spanish police.

And then, one Wednesday, at the beginning of their third year at Cambridge, Daisy's father beat Daisy's mother at chess. He was made so happy by this, so elated and triumphant that, buoyed and emboldened by his conquest, he proposed marriage; and Daisy's mother, who had been, deep down, afraid that as soon as he won a game he would lose interest in her, said yes, of course.

They stayed in England, and remained in academia, and they had one daughter, whom they called Daisy because at the time they owned (and, to Daisy's later amusement, actually rode) a tandem – a bicycle built for two. They moved from university to university across Britain: he taught computer sciences while his wife wrote books that nobody wanted to read about international corporate hegemonies, and books that they did want to read about chess, its strategies and its history, and thus in a good year she would make more money than he did, which was never very much. Their involvement in politics waned as they grew older, and as they approached middle age they had become a happy couple with no interests beyond each other, chess, Daisy, and the reconstruction and debugging of forgotten operating systems.

Neither of them understood Daisy, not even a little.

They blamed themselves for not having nipped her fascination with the police force in the bud when it first began to manifest, more or less at the same time that she began talking. Daisy would point out police cars in the same excited way that other little girls might point out ponies. Her seventh birthday party was held in fancy dress, to allow her to wear her junior policewoman's costume, and there are still photographs in a box in her parents' attic of her face suffused with a seven-year-old's perfect joy at the sight of her birthday cake – seven candles ringing a flashing blue light.

Daisy was a diligent, cheerful, intelligent teenager, who made both her parents happy when she went to the University of London to study law and computing. Her father had dreams of her becoming a lecturer in law; her mother nurtured dreams of her daughter taking silk, perhaps even becoming a judge and then using the law to crush corporate hegemonies whenever they appeared. And then Daisy went and ruined everything by taking the entry exams and joining the police force. The police welcomed her with open arms: on the one hand there were directives on the need to improve the diversity of the force, while on the other computer crime and computer-related fraud was on the increase. They needed Daisy. Frankly, they needed a whole string of Daisies.

At this point, four years on, it would be fair to say that a career in the police force had failed to live up to Daisy's expectations. It was not, as her parents had warned her repeatedly, that the police force was an institutionally racist and sexist monolith that would crush her individuality into something soul-destroying and uniform, that would make her as much a part of the canteen culture as instant coffee. No, the frustrating part of it was getting other coppers to understand that she was a copper too. She had come to the conclusion that, for most coppers, police work was something you did to protect Middle England from scary people of the wrong social background, who were probably out to steal their mobile phones. From where Daisy stood it was about something else. Daisy knew that a kid in his den in Germany could send out a virus that would shut down a hospital, cause more damage than a bomb. Daisy was of the opinion that the real bad guys these days understood FTP sites and high-level encryption and disposable pre-paid mobile phones. She was not sure that the good guys did.

She took a sip of coffee from a plastic cup, and made a face; while she had been scanning through screen after screen, her coffee had gone cold.

She had gone through all the information that Grahame Coats had given her. There was certainly a prima-facie case for thinking that something was wrong – if nothing else there was a cheque for two thousand pounds that Charles Nancy had apparently written to himself, the previous week.

Except. Except something did not feel right.

She walked down the corridor, knocked on the super-intendent's door.

'Come!'

Camberwell had smoked a pipe at his desk for thirty years, until the building had instituted a no-smoking policy. Now he made do with a lump of Plasticine, which he balled and squashed and kneaded and prodded. As a man with a pipe in his mouth, he had been placid, good-natured and, as far as those beneath him were concerned, the salt of the earth. As a man with a lump of Plasticine in his hand, he was uniformly irritable and short-tempered. On a good day he made it as far as tetchy.

'Yes?'

'The Grahame Coats Agency case.'

'Mm?'

'I'm not sure about it.'

'Not sure about it? What on earth is there not to be sure about?'

'Well, I think maybe I should take myself off the case.'

He did not look impressed. He stared at her. Down on the desk, unwatched, his fingers were kneading the blue Plasticine into the shape of a meerschaum. 'Because?'

'I've met the suspect socially.'

'And? You've been on holiday with him? You're godmother to his kids? What?'

'No. I met him once. I stayed overnight at his house.'

'So are you saying you and he did the nasty?' A deep sigh, in which world-weariness, irritation and a craving for half an ounce of Condor ready-rubbed mingled in equal parts.

'No, sir. Nothing like that. I just slept there.'

'And that's your total involvement with him?'

'Yes, sir.'

He crushed the Plasticine pipe back into a shapeless blob. 'You realise you're wasting my time?'

'Yes, sir. Sorry, sir.'

'Do whatever you have to do. Don't bother me.'

* * *

Maeve Livingstone rode the lift up to the fifth floor alone, the slow jerky journey giving her plenty of time to rehearse in her head what she would say to Grahame Coats when she got there.

She was carrying a slim brown briefcase, which had belonged to Morris: a peculiarly masculine object. She wore a white blouse, and a blue denim skirt, and over it, a grey coat. She had very long legs and extremely pale skin, and hair which remained, with only minimal chemical assistance, quite as blonde as it had been when Morris Livingstone had married her, twenty years earlier.

Maeve had loved Morris very much. When he died, she did not delete him from her mobile phone, not even after she had cancelled his service and returned his phone. Her nephew had taken the photo of Morris that was on her phone, and she did not want to lose that. She wished she could phone Morris now, ask his advice.

She had told the speakerphone who she was, to be buzzed in downstairs, and when she walked into reception Grahame Coats was already waiting for her.

'How de do, how de do, good lady?' he said.

'We need to talk privately, Grahame,' said Maeve. 'Now.'

Grahame Coats smirked; oddly enough, many of his favourite fantasies began with Maeve saying something fairly similar, before she went on to utter such statements as, 'I need you, Grahame, right now', and, 'Oh, Grahame, I've been such a bad bad bad bad girl who needs to be taught some discipline', and, on rare occasions, 'Grahame, you are too much for one woman, so let me introduce you to my identical naked twin sister, Maeve II.'

They went into his office.

Maeve, slightly disappointingly as far as Grahame Coats was concerned, said nothing about needing it right here, right now. She did not take off her coat. Instead she opened her briefcase and took out a sheaf of papers, which she placed upon the desk.

'Grahame, at my bank manager's suggestion, I had your figures and statements for the last decade independently audited. From back when Morris was still alive. You can look at them if you like. The numbers don't work. None of them. I thought I'd talk to you about it before I called in the police. In Morris's memory, I felt I owed you that.'

'You do indeed,' agreed Grahame Coats, smooth as a snake in a butter churn. 'Indeed you do.'

'Well?' Maeve Livingstone raised one perfect eyebrow. Her expression was not reassuring. Grahame Coats liked her better in his imagination.

'I'm afraid we've had a rogue employee at the Grahame Coats Agency for quite a while, Maeve. I actually called in the police myself, last week, when I realised that something was amiss. The long arm of the law is already investigating. Due to the illustrious nature of several of the clients of the Grahame Coats agency – yourself among them – the police are keeping this as quiet as possible, and who can blame them?' She did not seem as mollified as he had hoped. He tried another tack. 'They have high hopes of recovering much, if not all of the money.'

Maeve nodded. Grahame Coats relaxed, but only a little.

'Can I ask which employee?'

'Charles Nancy. I have to say I trusted him implicitly. It came as quite a shock.'

'Oh. He's sweet.'

'Appearances,' pointed out Grahame Coats, 'can be deceptive.'

She smiled then, and a very sweet smile it was. 'It won't wash, Grahame. This has been going on for yonks. Since long before Charles Nancy started here. Probably since before my time. Morris absolutely trusted you, and you stole from him. And now you're trying to tell me that you're hoping to frame one of your employees – or blame one of your confederates – well, it won't wash.'

'No,' said Grahame Coats, contritely. 'Sorry.'

She picked up the sheaf of papers. 'Out of interest,' she said, 'how much do you think you got from Morris and me over the years? I make it about three million quid.'

'Ah.' He was not smiling at all, now. It was certainly more than that, but still. 'That sounds about right.'

They looked at each other, and Grahame Coats calculated, furiously. He needed to buy time. That was what he needed. 'What if,' he said, 'what if I were to repay it, in full, in cash, now. With interest. Let's say, fifty per cent of the amount in question.'

'You're offering me four and a half million pounds? In cash?'

Grahame Coats smiled at her, in exactly the same way that striking cobras tend not to. 'Absatively. If you go to the police, then I will deny everything, and hire excellent lawyers. In a worst-case scenario, after an extremely lengthy trial, during which I shall be forced to blacken Morris's good name in every way I possibly can, I will be sentenced at most to ten to twelve years in prison. I might actually serve five years, with good behaviour – and I should be a model prisoner. Given the general overcrowding of the prison services, I'd serve most of my sentence in an open prison, or even on day release. I don't see this as being too problematic. On the flipside, I can guarantee that, if you go to the police, you will never get a penny of Morris's money. The alternative is to keep your mouth shut, get all the money you need, and more, while I buy myself a little time to . . . to do the decent thing. If you see what I mean.'

Maeve thought about it. 'I *would* like to see you rot in prison,' she said. And then she sighed, and nodded. 'All right,' she said. 'I take the money. I never have to see or deal with you again. All future royalty cheques come directly to me.'

'Absatively. The safe is over here,' he told her.

There was a bookcase on the far wall, on which were uniform leatherbound editions of Dickens, Thackeray, Trollope and Austen, all unread. He fumbled with a book, and the bookcase slipped to one side, revealing a door behind it, painted to match the wall.

Maeve wondered if it would have a combination, but no, there was just a small keyhole, which Grahame Coats unlocked with a large brass key. The door swung open.

He reached in and turned on the light. It was a narrow room, lined with rather amateurishly fixed shelves. At the far end was a small, fireproof filing cabinet.

'You can take it in cash, or in jewellery, or in a combination of the two,' he said, bluntly. 'I'd advise the latter. Lots of nice antique gold back there. Very portable.'

He unlocked several strongboxes, and displayed the contents. Rings and chains and lockets glittered and gleamed and shone.

Maeve's mouth opened. 'Take a look,' he told her, and she squeezed past him. It was a treasure cave.

She pulled out a golden locket on a chain, held it up, stared at it in wonder. 'This is gorgeous,' she said. 'It must be worth—' and she broke off. In the polished gold of the locket she saw something moving behind her, and she turned, which meant that the hammer did not hit her squarely on the back of the head, as Grahame Coats had intended, but instead glanced off the side of her cheek.

'You little shit!' she said, and she kicked him. Maeve had good legs and a powerful kick, but she and her attacker were at close quarters.

Maeve's foot connected with his shin, and she reached for the hammer he was holding. Grahame Coats smashed out with it; this time it connected, and Maeve stumbled to one side. Her eyes seemed to unfocus. He hit her again, squarely on the top of the head, and again, and again, and she went down.

Grahame Coats wished that he had a gun. A nice, sensible handgun. With a silencer, like in the films. Honestly, if it had ever occurred to him that he would need to kill someone in his office he would have been much better prepared for it. He might even have laid in a supply of poison. That would have been wise. No need for any of this nonsense.

There was blood and blonde hair adhering to the end of the hammer. He put it down with distaste, and, stepping around the woman on the floor, he grabbed the safe-deposit boxes containing the jewellery. He tipped them out on to his desk, and returned them to the safe, where he removed an attaché case, containing bundles of hundred-dollar bills and of five-hundred euro notes, and a small black velvet bag half full of unset diamonds. He removed some files from the filing cabinet. And, last but, as he would have pointed out, by no means least, he took out from the secret room a small leather vanity case, containing two wallets and two passports.

Then he pushed the heavy door closed, and locked it, and swung the bookcase back into position.

He stood there, panting somewhat, and caught his breath.

All in all, he decided, he was rather proud of himself. Good job, Grahame. Good man. Good show. He had improvised with the materials at hand, and come out ahead: bluffed and been bold and creative – ready, as the poet said, to risk it all on a turn of pitch and toss. He had risked, and he had won. He was the pitcher. He was the tosser. One day, on his tropical paradise, he would write his memoirs, and people would learn how he had bested a dangerous woman. Although, he thought, it might be better if she had actually been holding a gun.

Probably, he realised, on reflection, she *had* pulled a gun on him. He was fairly sure he had seen her reach for it. He had been extremely fortunate that the hammer had been there, that he had a toolkit in the room for moments of necessary DIY, or he would not have been able to act in self-defence with it so swiftly or so effectively.

Only now did it occur to him to lock the main door to his office.

There was, he noticed, blood on his shirt and on his hand, and on the sole of one shoe. He took off his shirt, and wiped down his shoe with it. Then he dropped the shirt into the bin beneath his desk. He surprised himself by putting his hand to his mouth and licking the gobbet of blood off it, like a cat, with his red tongue.

And then he yawned. He took Maeve's papers from the desk,

ran them through the shredder. She had a second set of documents in her briefcase, and he shredded them as well. He reshredded the shreddings.

He had a closet in the corner of his office, with a suit hanging in it, and spare shirts, socks, underpants and so on. You never knew when you would need to head to a first night from the office, after all. Be prepared.

He dressed, with care.

There was a small suitcase with wheels in it in the closet too, of the kind that is meant to be placed in overhead lockers, and he put things into it, moving them around to make room.

He called reception. 'Annie,' he said. 'Would you pop out and get me a sandwich? Not from Prêt, no. I thought the new place in Brewer Street? I'm just wrapping up with Mrs Livingstone. I may actually wind up taking her out for a spot of real lunch, but best to be prepared.'

He spent several minutes on the computer, running the kind of disk-cleaning program that takes your data, over-writes it with random ones and zeroes, then grinds it up extremely small before finally depositing it at the bottom of the Thames wearing concrete overshoes. Then he walked down the hall, pulling his wheeled suitcase behind him.

He put his head around one office door. 'Popping out for a bit,' he said. 'I'll be back in about three, if anyone asks.'

Annie was gone from reception, which, he thought, was a good thing. People would assume that Maeve Livingstone had already left the agency, just as they would expect Grahame Coats to return at any time. By the time they started looking for him, he would be a long way away.

He descended in the lift. This was all happening early, he thought. He would not turn fifty for more than a year. But the exit mechanisms were already in place. He needed simply to think of it as a golden handshake, or perhaps a golden parachute.

And then, pulling the wheelie suitcase behind him, he walked out of the front door into the sunny Aldwych morning, and out of the Grahame Coats Agency for ever.

* * *

Spider had slept peacefully in his own enormous bed, in his place in Fat Charlie's spare room. He had begun to wonder, in a vague sort of way, whether Fat Charlie had gone for good, and had resolved to investigate the matter the next time that he could in any way be bothered to do so, unless something more interesting distracted him or he forgot.

He had slept late, and was now on his way to meet Rosie for lunch. He would pick her up at her flat, and they would go somewhere good. It was a beautiful day in early autumn, and Spider's happiness was infectious. This was because Spider was, give or take a little, a god. When you're a god, your emotions are contagious – other people can catch them. When people stood near Spider on a day that he was this happy, their worlds would seem a little brighter. If he hummed a song, other people around him would start humming, in key, like something from a musical. Of course, if he yawned, a hundred people nearby would yawn, and when he was miserable it spread like a damp river-mist, making the world even gloomier for everyone caught up in it. It wasn't anything he did; it was something that he *was*.

Right now, the only thing casting a damper on his happiness was that he had resolved to tell Rosie the truth.

Spider was not terribly good at telling the truth. He regarded truth as fundamentally malleable, more or less a matter of opinion, and Spider was able to muster some pretty impressive opinions when he had to.

Being an imposter was not the problem. He liked being an imposter. He was good at it. It fitted in with his plans, which were fairly simple and could until now have been summarised more or less as: a) go somewhere, b) enjoy yourself and c) leave before you get bored. And it was now, he knew deep down, definitely time to leave. The world was his lobster, his bib was round his neck, and he had a pot of melted butter and an array of grotesque but effective lobster-eating implements and devices at the ready.

Only . . .

Only he didn't want to go.

He was having second thoughts about all this, something Spider found fairly disconcerting. Normally he didn't even have first thoughts about things. Life without thinking had been perfectly pleasant – instinct, impulse and an obscene amount of luck had served him quite well up to now. But even miracles can only take you so far. Spider walked down the street, and people smiled at him.

He had agreed with Rosie that he would meet her at her flat, so he was pleasantly surprised to see her standing at the end of the road, waiting for him. He felt a pang of something that was still not entirely guilt, and waved.

'Rosie? Hey!'

She came towards him, along the pavement, and he began to grin. They would sort things out. Everything would work out for the best. Everything would be fine. 'You look like a million dollars,' he told her. 'Maybe two million. What are you hungry for?'

Rosie smiled, and shrugged.

They were passing a Greek restaurant. 'Is Greek OK?' She nodded. They walked down some steps, and went inside. It was dark, and empty, having only just opened, and the proprietor pointed them towards a nook, or possibly a cranny, towards the rear.

They sat opposite each other, at a table just big enough for two. Spider said, 'There's something that I wanted to talk to you about.' She said nothing. 'It's not bad,' he went on. 'Well, it's not good. But. Well. It's something you ought to know.'

The proprietor asked them if they were ready to order anything. 'Coffee,' said Spider, and Rosie nodded her agreement. 'Two coffees,' said Spider. 'And if you can give us, um, five minutes? I need a little privacy here.'

The proprietor withdrew.

Rosie looked at Spider enquiringly.

He took a deep breath. 'Right. OK. Let me just say this, because it isn't easy and I don't know that I can . . . right. OK. Look, I'm not Fat Charlie. I know you think I am, but I'm not. I'm his brother, Spider. You think I'm him because we sort of look alike.'

She did not say anything.

'Well, I don't really look like him. But. Y'know, none of this really comes easy to me. Uh. I can't stop thinking about you. So I mean, I know you're engaged to my brother, but I'm sort of asking if you, well, if you'd think about maybe dumping him and possibly going out with me.'

A pot of coffee arrived, on a small silver tray, with two cups.

'Greek coffee,' said the proprietor, who had brought it.

'Yes. Thanks. I *did* ask for a couple of minutes . . .'

'Is very hot,' said the proprietor. 'Very hot coffee. Strong. Greek. Not Turkish.'

'That's great. Listen, if you don't mind – five minutes. Please?'

The proprietor shrugged and walked away.

'You probably hate me,' said Spider. 'If I was you I'd probably hate me too. But I mean this. More than I've ever meant anything in my life.' She was just looking at him, without expression, and he said, 'Please. Just say something. Anything.'

Her lips moved, as if she were trying to find the right words to say.

Spider waited.

Her mouth opened.

His first thought was that she was eating something, because the thing he saw between her teeth was brown, and was certainly not a tongue. Then it moved its head and its eyes, little black-bead eyes, stared at him. Rosie opened her mouth impossibly wide and the birds came out.

Spider said, 'Rosie?' and then the air was filled with beaks and feathers and claws. One after the other, birds poured out from her throat, each accompanied by a tiny coughing-choking noise, in a stream directed at him.

He threw up an arm to protect his eyes, and something hurt his wrist. He flailed out, and something flew at his face, heading for his eyes. He jerked his head backwards, and the beak punctured his cheek.

A moment of nightmare clarity: there was still a woman sitting opposite him. What he could no longer understand was how he could ever have mistaken her for Rosie. She was older than Rosie for a start, her blue-black hair streaked here and there with silver. Her skin was not the warm brown of Rosie's skin but black as flint. She was wearing a ragged ochre raincoat. And she grinned and opened her mouth wide once more, and now inside her mouth he could see the cruel beaks and crazy eyes of seagulls . . .

Spider did not stop to think. He acted. He grabbed the handle of the coffee-pot, swept it up in one hand, while with the other he pulled off the lid; then he jerked the pot towards the woman in the seat opposite him. The contents of the pot, scalding hot black coffee, went all over her.

She hissed in pain.

Birds crashed and flapped through the air of the cellar restaurant, but now there was nobody sitting opposite him, and the birds flew without direction, flapping into walls wildly.

The proprietor said, 'Sir? Are you hurt? I am sorry. They must have come in from the street.'

'I'm fine,' said Spider.

'Your face is bleeding,' said the man. He handed Spider a napkin, and Spider pressed it against his cheek. The cut stung.

Spider offered to help the man get the birds out. He opened the door to the street, but now the place was as empty of birds as it had been before his arrival.

Spider pulled out a five-pound note. 'Here,' he said. 'For the coffee. I've got to go.'

The proprietor nodded, gratefully. 'Keep the napkin.'

Spider stopped and thought. 'When I came in,' he asked, 'was there a woman with me?'

The proprietor looked puzzled – possibly even scared, Spider could not be sure. 'I do not remember,' he said, as if dazed. 'If you had been alone, I would not have seated you back there. But I do not know.'

Spider went back out into the street. The day was still bright, but the sunlight no longer seemed reassuring. He looked around. He saw a pigeon, shuffling and pecking at an abandoned ice-cream cone; a sparrow on a windowledge; and high above, a flash of white in the sunlight, its wings extended, a seagull circled.

Chapter Nine

In Which Fat Charlie Answers the Door and Spider Encounters Flamingos

Fat Charlie's luck was changing. He could feel it. The plane on which he was returning home had been oversold, and he had found himself bumped up to first class. The meal was excellent. Halfway across the Atlantic, a flight attendant came over to inform him that he had won a complimentary box of chocolates, and presented it to him. He put it in his overhead locker, and ordered a Drambuie on ice.

He would get home. He would sort everything out with Grahame Coats – after all, if there was one thing that Fat Charlie was certain of, it was the honesty of his own accounting. He would make everything good with Rosie. Everything was going to be just great.

He wondered if Spider would already be gone when he got home, or whether he would get the satisfaction of throwing him out. He hoped it would be the latter. Fat Charlie wanted to see his brother apologise, possibly even grovel. He started to imagine the things that he was going to say.

'Get out!' said Fat Charlie, 'And take your sunshine, your Jacuzzi and your bedroom with you!'

'Sorry?' said the flight attendant.

'Talking,' said Fat Charlie. 'To myself. Just um.'

But even the embarrassment he felt at this wasn't really that bad. He didn't even hope the plane would crash and end his mortification. Life was definitely looking up.

He opened the little kit of useful amenities he had been given, and put on his eye-shade, and pushed his seat back as far as it would go, which was most of the way. He thought about Rosie, although the Rosie in his mind kept shifting, morphing into someone smaller, who wasn't really wearing much of anything. Fat Charlie guiltily imagined her dressed, and was mortified when he realised that she seemed to be wearing a police uniform. He felt terrible about this, he told himself, but it didn't seem to make much of an impression. He ought to feel ashamed of himself. He ought to . . .

Fat Charlie shifted in his seat, and emitted one, small, satisfied snore.

He was still in an excellent mood when he landed at Heathrow. He took the Heathrow Express into Paddington, and was pleased to note that in his brief absence from England the sun had decided to come out. *Every little thing*, he told himself, *is going to be all right*.

The only odd note, which added a flavour of wrongness to the morning, occurred halfway through the train journey. He was staring out of the window, wishing he had bought a newspaper at Heathrow. The train was passing an expanse of green – a school playing field, perhaps – when the sky seemed, momentarily, to darken, and, with a hiss of brakes, the train stopped at a signal.

That did not disturb Fat Charlie. It was England in the autumn: the sun was, by definition, something that only happened when it wasn't cloudy or raining. But there was a figure standing on the edge of the green, by a stand of trees.

At first glance, he thought it was a scarecrow.

That was foolish. It could not have been a scarecrow. Scarecrows are found in fields, not on football pitches. Scarecrows certainly aren't left on the edge of the woodland. Anyway, if it was a scarecrow it was doing a very poor job.

There were crows everywhere, after all, big black ones.

And then it moved.

It was too far away to be anything more than a shape, a slight figure in a tattered brown raincoat. Still, Fat Charlie knew it. He knew that if he had been close enough, he would have seen a face chipped from obsidian, and raven-black hair, and eyes that held madness.

Then the train jerked, and began to move, and in moments the woman in the brown raincoat was out of sight.

Fat Charlie felt uncomfortable. He had practically convinced himself by now that what had happened, what he *thought* had happened, in Mrs Dunwiddy's front room, had been some form of hallucination, a high-octane dream, true on some level but not a real thing. Not something that had happened; rather, it was symbolic of a greater truth. He could not have gone to a real place, nor struck a real bargain, could he?

It was only a metaphor, after all.

He did not ask himself why he was now so certain that everything would soon begin to improve. There was reality, and there was *reality*, and some things were more real than others.

Faster and faster, the train rattled him further into London.

* * *

Spider was almost home from the Greek restaurant, napkin pushed against his cheek, when someone touched him on the shoulder.

'Charles?' said Rosie.

Spider jumped, or at least, he jerked and made a startled noise.

'Charles? Are you all right? What happened to your cheek?'

He stared at her. 'Are you you?' he asked.

'What?'

'Are you Rosie?'

'What kind of a question is that? Of course I'm Rosie. What did you do to your cheek?'

He pressed the napkin against his cheek. 'I cut it,' he said.

'Let me see.' She took his hand away from his cheek. The centre of the white napkin was stained crimson, as if he had bled into it, but his cheek was whole and untouched. 'There's nothing there.'

'Oh.'

'Charles? Are you all right?'

'Yes,' he said. 'I am. Unless I'm not. I think we should go back to my place. I think I'll be safer there.'

'We were going to have lunch,' said Rosie, in the tone of voice of one who worries that she'll only understand what's actually going on when a TV presenter leaps out and reveals the hidden cameras.

'Yes,' said Spider. 'I know. I think someone just tried to kill me, though. And she pretended she was you.'

'Nobody's trying to kill you,' said Rosie, failing to sound like she wasn't humouring him.

'Even if nobody's trying to kill me, can we skip lunch and go back to my place? I've got food there.'

'Of course.'

Rosie followed him down the road, wondering when Fat Charlie had lost all that weight. He looked good, she thought. He looked really good. They walked into Maxwell Gardens, in silence.

He said, 'Look at that.'

'What?'

He showed her. The fresh bloodstain had vanished from the napkin. It was now perfectly white.

'Is it a magic trick?'

'If it is, I didn't do it,' he said. 'For once.' He dropped the napkin into a bin. As he did so, a taxi pulled up in front of Fat Charlie's house, and Fat Charlie got out, rumpled and blinking and carrying a white plastic bag.

Rosie looked at Fat Charlie. She looked at Spider. She looked back at Fat Charlie, who had opened the bag and pulled out an enormous box of chocolates.

'They're for you,' he said.

Rosie took the chocolates and said, 'Thank you.' There were two men and they looked and sounded completely different, and she still could not work out which one of them was her fiancé. 'I'm going mad, aren't I?' she said, her voice taut. It was easier, now she knew what was wrong.

The thinner of the two Fat Charlies, the one with the earring, put his hand on her shoulder. 'You need to go home,' he said. 'Then you need a nap. When you wake up, you'll have forgotten all about this.'

Well, she thought, *that makes life easier. It's better with a plan.* She walked back to her flat with a spring in her step, carrying her box of chocolates.

'What did you do?' asked Fat Charlie. 'She just seemed to turn off.'

Spider shrugged. 'I didn't want to upset her,' he said.

'Why didn't you tell her the truth?'

'It didn't seem appropriate.'

'Like you'd know what was appropriate?'

Spider touched the front door and it opened.

'I have keys, you know,' said Fat Charlie. 'It's *my* front door.'

They walked into the hallway, walked up the stairs.

'Where have you been?' asked Spider.

'Nowhere. Out,' said Fat Charlie, as if he were a teenager.

'I was attacked by birds in the restaurant this morning. Do you know anything about that? You do, don't you?'

'Not really. Maybe. It's just time for you to leave, that's all.'

'Don't start anything,' said Spider.

'Me? *Me* start anything? I think I've been a model of restraint. You came into my life. You got my boss upset, and got the police on to me. You, you've been kissing my girlfriend. You screwed up my life.'

'Hey,' said Spider. 'You ask me, you've done a great job of screwing up your life on your own.'

Fat Charlie clenched his fist, swung back, and hit Spider in the jaw, like they do on the movies. Spider staggered back, more surprised than hurt. He put his hand to his lip, then looked down at the blood on his hand. 'You hit me,' he said.

'I can do it again,' said Fat Charlie, who wasn't sure that he could. His hand hurt.

Spider said, 'Yeah?' and launched himself at Fat Charlie, pummelling him with his fists, and Fat Charlie went over, his arm around Spider's waist, pulling Spider down with him.

They rolled up and down the hallway floor, hitting and flailing at each other. Fat Charlie half expected Spider to launch some kind of magical counterattack or to be supernaturally strong, but the two of them seemed fairly evenly matched. Both of them fought unscientifically, like boys – like brothers – and as they fought, Fat Charlie thought he remembered doing this once before, a long, long time ago. Spider was smarter and faster, but if Fat Charlie could just get on top of him, and get Spider's hands out of the way . . .

Fat Charlie grabbed for Spider's right hand, twisted it behind Spider's back, then sat on his brother's chest, putting all his weight on him.

'Give in?' he asked.

'No.' Spider wriggled and twisted, but Fat Charlie was solidly in position, sitting on Spider's chest.

'I want you to promise,' said Fat Charlie, 'to get out of my life, and to leave me and Rosie alone for ever.'

At this, Spider bucked, angrily, and Fat Charlie was dislodged. He landed, sprawled, on the kitchen floor. 'Look,' said Spider. 'I *told* you.'

There was a banging on the door downstairs, an imperious knocking of the kind that indicated someone needed to come in rather urgently. Fat Charlie glared at Spider, and Spider scowled at Fat Charlie, and slowly they got to their feet.

'Shall I answer it?' said Spider.

'No,' said Fat Charlie. 'It's *my* bloody house. And *I'm* going to bloody answer my *own* front door, thank you very much.'

'Whatever.'

Fat Charlie edged towards the stairs. Then he turned round. 'Once I've dealt with this,' he said, 'I'm dealing with you. Pack your stuff. You are on your way out.' He walked downstairs, tucking himself in, brushing the dust off, and generally trying to make it look as if he hadn't been brawling on the floor.

He opened the door. There were two large uniformed policemen, and one, smaller rather more exotic policewoman in extremely plain clothes.

'Charles Nancy?' said Daisy. She looked at him as if he was a stranger, her eyes expressionless.

'Glumph,' said Fat Charlie.

'Mr Nancy,' she said, 'you are under arrest. You have the right—'

Fat Charlie turned back to the interior of the house. 'Bastard!' he shouted up the stairs. 'Bastard bastard bastarding bastardy *bastard*!'

Daisy tapped him on the arm. 'Do you want to come quietly?' she asked, quietly. 'Only if you don't, we can subdue you first. I wouldn't recommend it, though. They're very enthusiastic subduers.'

'I'll come quietly,' said Fat Charlie.

'That's good,' said Daisy. She walked Fat Charlie outside and locked him into the back of a black police van.

The police searched the flat. The rooms were empty of life. At the end of the hall was a little spare bedroom, containing several boxes of books and toy cars. They poked around in there, but they didn't find anything interesting.

* * *

Spider lay on the couch in his bedroom, and sulked. He had gone to his room when Fat Charlie went off to answer the door. He needed to be on his own. He didn't do confrontations terribly well. When it got to that point was normally when he went away, and right now Spider knew it was time to go, but he still didn't want to leave.

He wasn't sure that sending Rosie home was the right thing to have done.

What he wanted to do – and Spider was driven entirely by *wants*, never by *oughts* or *shoulds* – was to tell Rosie that he wanted her – *he*, Spider. That he wasn't Fat Charlie. That he was something quite different. And that, in itself, wasn't the problem. He could simply have said to her, with enough conviction, 'I'm actually Spider, Fat Charlie's brother, and you're completely OK with this. It doesn't bother you,' and the universe would have pushed Rosie just a little, and she would have accepted it, just as she'd gone home earlier. She'd be fine with it. She would not have minded it, not at all.

Except, he knew, somewhere deep inside, she would.

Human beings do not like being pushed about by gods. They may seem to, on the surface, but somewhere on the inside, underneath it all, they sense it and they resent it. They know. Spider could tell her to be happy about the situation, and she would be happy, but it would be as real as painting a smile on her face – a smile that she would truly believe, in every way that mattered, was her own. In the short term (and until now Spider had only ever thought in the short term) none of this would be important, but in the long term it could only lead to problems. He didn't want some kind of seething, furious creature, someone who, though she hated him way down deep, was perfectly placid and doll-like and normal on the surface. He wanted Rosie.

And that wouldn't be Rosie, would it?

Spider stared out of the window, at the glorious waterfall and the tropical sky beyond it, and Spider began to wonder when Fat Charlie would come knocking on his door. Something had happened this morning in the restaurant, and he was certain that his brother knew more about it than he was saying.

After a while, he got bored with waiting, and wandered back into Fat Charlie's flat. There was nobody there. The place was a mess – it looked like it had been turned upside down by trained professionals. Spider decided that, in all probability, Fat Charlie had messed the place up himself, to indicate how upset he was that Spider had beaten him in their fight.

He looked out of the window. There was a police car parked outside, beside a black police van. As he watched, they drove away.

He made himself some toast, and he buttered it and ate it. Then he walked through the flat, carefully ensuring that all the curtains were closed.

The doorbell rang. Spider closed the last of the curtains, then he walked downstairs.

He opened the door and Rosie looked at him. She still seemed a little dazed. He looked at her. 'Well? Aren't you going to invite me in?'

'Of course. Come in.'

She walked up the stairs. 'What happened here? It looks like an earthquake hit.'

'Yeah?'

'Why are you just sitting in the dark?' She went to open the curtains.

'Don't do that! Just keep them closed.'

'What are you scared of?' asked Rosie.

Spider looked out of the window. 'Birds,' he said, eventually.

'But birds are our friends,' said Rosie, as if addressing a small child.

'Birds,' Spider said, 'are the last of the dinosaurs. Tiny velociraptors with wings. Devouring defenseless wiggly things and, and nuts, and fish, and, and other birds. They get the early worms. And have you ever watched a chicken eat? They may look innocent, but birds are, well, they're vicious.'

'There was a thing on the news the other day,' said Rosie, 'about a bird who saved a man's life.'

'That doesn't change the fact that—'

'It was a raven, or a crow. One of those big black ones. The man was lying on the lawn in his home in California, reading a magazine, and he hears this cawing and cawing, and it's a raven, trying to attract his attention. So he gets up and goes over to the tree it's perched on, and down beneath it is a mountain lion, that had been getting all ready to pounce on him. So he went inside. If that raven hadn't warned him, he would have been lion-food.'

'I don't think that's usual raven behaviour,' said Spider. 'But whether one raven once saved someone's life or not, it doesn't change anything. Birds are still out to get me.'

'Right,' said Rosie, trying to sound as if she wasn't humouring him. 'Birds are out to get you.'

'Yes.'

'And this is because . . . ?'

'Um.'

'There must be a reason. You can't tell me the great plurality of birds has just decided to treat you as an enormous early worm for no particular reason.'

He said, 'I don't think you'd believe me,' and he meant it.

'Charlie. You've always been really honest. I mean, I've trusted you. If you tell me something, I'll do my best to believe it. I'll try *really* hard. I love you and I believe in you. So why don't you let me find out if I believe you or not?'

Spider thought about this. Then he reached out for her hand, and he squeezed it.

'I think I ought to show you something,' he said.

He led her to the end of the corridor. They stopped outside the door to Fat Charlie's spare room. 'There's something in here,' he said. 'I think it'll explain it a bit better than I can.'

'You're a superhero,' she said, 'and this is where you keep the batpoles?'

'No.'

'Is it something kinky? You like to dress up in a twinset and pearls and call yourself Dora?'

'No.'

'It's not . . . a model trainset, is it?'

Spider pushed open the door to Fat Charlie's spare room, and at the same time he opened the door to his bedroom. The picture windows at the end of the room showed a waterfall, which crashed down into a jungle pool far below. The sky through the windows was bluer than sapphires.

Rosie made a small noise.

She turned round, walked back down the hall, into the kitchen, and looked out of the window at the grey London sky, doughy and unwelcoming. She came back. 'I don't understand,' she said. 'Charlie? What's happening?'

'I'm not Charlie,' said Spider. 'Look at me. *Really* look at me. I don't even look like him.'

She made no pretence of humouring him any longer. Her eyes were wide and scared.

'I'm his brother,' said Spider. 'I've screwed everything up. Everything. And I think probably the best thing I can do is just get out of all your lives and go away.'

'So where's Fat – where's Charlie?'

'I don't know. We were having a fight. He went off to answer the door, and I went off to my room, and he didn't come back.'

'He didn't come back? And you didn't even *try* to find out what had happened to him?'

'Er. He might have been taken away by the police,' said Spider. 'It's just an idea. I have no proof or anything.'

'What's your name?' she demanded.

'Spider.'

Rosie repeated it. 'Spider.' Outside the window, above the spray of the waterfall, she could see a flock of flamingos in the air, the sunlight blurring their wings in pink and white. They were stately and uncountable, and it was one of the most beautiful things Rosie had ever seen. She looked back at Spider, and looking at him, she could not understand how she had ever believed that this man was Fat Charlie. Where Fat Charlie was easygoing, open and uncomfortable, this man was like a steel rod bent back and ready to snap. 'You really aren't him, are you?'

'I told you I wasn't.'

'So. So who did I. Who have I. Who was it – who did I sleep with?'

'That would be me,' said Spider.

'I thought so,' said Rosie. She slapped him, as hard as she could, across his face. He could feel his lip start bleeding once more.

'I guess I deserved that,' he said.

'Of course you deserved it.' She paused. Then she said, 'Did Fat Charlie know about this? About you? That you were going out with me?'

'Well, yes. But he—'

'You are both sick,' she said. 'Sick, sick evil men. I hope you rot in Hell.'

She took one last puzzled glance around the enormous bedroom, and then out of the bedroom window at the jungle trees and the huge waterfall and the flock of flamingos, and walked away down the hall.

Spider sat down on the floor, with a thin trickle of blood coming from his lower lip, feeling stupid. He heard the front door slam. He walked over to the hot tub, and dipped the end of a fluffy towel into the hot water. Then he wrung it out and put it on his mouth. 'I don't need any of this,' said Spider. He said it aloud; it's easier to lie to yourself when you say things out loud. 'I didn't need any of you people a week ago and I don't need you now. I don't care. I'm done.'

The flamingos hit the window-glass like feathery, pink cannonballs, and the glass shattered, fragments of window flying across the room, scattering themselves and embedding themselves in the walls, the floor, the bed. The air was filled with plummeting pale-pink bodies, a confusion of huge pink wings and curved black beaks. The roar of a waterfall exploded into the room.

Spider pushed back against the wall. There were flamingos between him and the door, hundreds of them: five-foot-tall birds, all legs and neck. He got to his feet, and took several steps through a minefield of angry pink birds, each of them glowering at him through mad pink eyes. From a distance, they might have been beautiful. One of them snapped at Spider's hand. It didn't break the skin, but it hurt.

Spider's bedroom was a large room, but it was rapidly filling with crash-landing flamingos. And there was a dark cloud in the blue sky above the waterfall, that appeared to be another flock on its way.

They were pecking at him, and clawing at him, and buffeting him with their wings, and he knew that that was not actually the problem. The problem would be being suffocated under a fluffy pink blanket of feathers, with birds attached. It would be an astonishingly undignified way to go, crushed by birds, and not even particularly intelligent birds.

Think, he told himself. *They're flamingos. Bird-brains. You're Spider.*

So? he thought back at himself, irritated. *Tell me something I don't know.*

The flamingos on the ground were mobbing him. The ones in the air were diving towards him. He pulled his jacket over his head, and then the airborne flamingos began hitting him. It was like having someone firing chickens at you. He staggered and went down. *Well, trick them, stupid.*

Spider pushed himself to his feet, and waded through the sea of wings and beaks, until he reached the window, now an open jaw of jagged glass.

'Stupid birds,' he said, cheerfully. He pulled himself up on to the windowledge.

Flamingos are not famed for their cutting intelligence, nor for their problem-solving abilities: confronted with a twist of wire, and a bottle with something edible in it, a crow might try to make a tool out of the wire in order to get at the contents of the bottle. A flamingo, on the other hand, would try and eat the wire, if it looked like a shrimp, or possibly even if it didn't, just in case it was a new kind of shrimp. So if there was something slightly *smoky* and insubstantial about the man who stood on the windowledge insulting them, the flamingos failed to perceive it. They glared at him with the crazed pink eyes of killer rabbits, and they rushed towards him.

The man dived from the window, down into the spray of the waterfall, and a thousand flamingos launched themselves into the air after him, many of them, given the run-up a flamingo needs to get properly airborne, tumbling like stones.

Soon the bedroom contained only injured or dead flamingos: the ones who had broken the windows, the ones who had crashed into the walls, the ones who had been crushed beneath other flamingos. Those of the birds who were still alive watched the bedroom door open, apparently by itself, and close again, but, being flamingos, they thought very little of it.

Spider stood in the corridor of Fat Charlie's flat and tried to catch his breath. He concentrated on letting the bedroom stop existing, which was something that he hated to do, mostly because he was incredibly proud of his sound system, and also because it was where he kept his stuff.

You can always get more stuff, though.

If you're Spider, all you really have to do is ask.

* * *

Rosie's mother was not a woman given to gloating loudly, so when Rosie broke down in tears on the Chippendale sofa her mother refrained from whooping, from singing or from doing a small victory dance and then shimmying around the room. A careful observer, however, might have noticed a glint of triumph in her eyes.

She gave Rosie a large glass of vitaminised water with an ice-cube in it, and listened to her daughter's tearful litany of heartbreak and deception. By the end of it, the glint of triumph had been replaced with a look of confusion, and her head was starting to spin.

'So Fat Charlie wasn't really Fat Charlie?' said Rosie's mother.

'No. Well, yes. Fat Charlie *is* Fat Charlie, but for the last week I've been seeing his brother.'

'They are twins?'

'No. I don't even think they look alike. I don't know. I'm so confused.'

'So which one of them did you break up with?'

Rosie blew her nose. 'I broke up with Spider. That's Fat Charlie's brother.'

'But you weren't engaged to him.'

'No, but I thought I was. I thought he was Fat Charlie.'

'So you broke up with Fat Charlie as well?'

'Sort of. I just haven't told him yet.'

'Did he, did he know about this, this brother thing? Was it some kind of evil kinky conspiracy they did to my poor girl?'

'I don't think so. But it doesn't matter. I can't marry him.'

'No,' agreed her mother. 'You certainly cannot. Not one bit.' Inside, in her head, she did a victory jig, and set off a large but tasteful celebratory display of fireworks. 'We can find you a good boy. Don't you worry. That Fat Charlie. He was always up to no good. I knew it the first moment I saw him. He ate my wax fruit. I knew he was trouble. Where is he now?'

'I'm not sure. Spider said he might have been taken away by the police,' said Rosie.

'*Hah!*' said her mother, who increased the fireworks in her head to New Year's Eve at Disneyland proportions, and mentally sacrificed a dozen flawless black bulls for good measure. Aloud, all she said was, 'Probably in prison, if you ask me. Best place for him. I always said that was where that young man would end up.'

Rosie began to cry, if anything even harder than before. She pulled out another wodge of paper tissues and blew her nose with an extreme honk. She swallowed bravely. Then she cried some more. Her mother patted the back of Rosie's hand as reassuringly as she knew how. 'Of course you can't marry him,' she said. 'You can't marry a convict. But if he's in prison you can easily break off the engagement.' A spectre of a smile haunted the corners of her lips as she said, 'I could call on him for you. Or go there on a visitors' day and tell him he's a lousy crook and you never want to see him again. We could get a restraining order, as well,' she added helpfully.

'Th-that's not why I can't marry Fat Charlie,' said Rosie.

'No?' asked her mother, raising one perfectly pencilled eyebrow.

'No,' said Rosie. 'I can't marry Fat Charlie because I'm not in love with him.'

'Of course you aren't. I always knew that. It was a girlish infatuation, but now you see the true—'

'I'm in love,' continued Rosie, as if her mother had not spoken, 'with Spider. His brother.' The expression that made its way across her mother's face then was a cloud of wasps arriving at a picnic. 'It's OK,' said Rosie. 'I'm not going to marry him, either. I've told him I never want to see him again.'

Rosie's mother pursed her lips. 'Well,' she said, 'I can't pretend I understand any of this, but I can't say it's bad news either.' The gears in her head shifted and the cogs interlocked in new and interesting ways: ratchets ratcheted and springs resprung. 'You know,' she said, 'what would be the best thing for you right now? Have you thought about taking a little holiday? I'm happy to pay for it, all the money I'm saving on the wedding after all . . .'

That may have been the wrong thing to say. Rosie began to sob into her tissues once again. Her mother went on, 'Anyway, it would be my treat. I know you've got holiday time you haven't used at work. And you said things were quiet right now. At a time like this, a girl needs to get away from everything and simply relax.'

Rosie wondered whether she'd misjudged her mother all these years. She sniffed and swallowed and said, 'That would be nice.'

'Then it's settled,' said her mother. 'I shall come with you, to take care of my baby.' In her head, underneath the grand finale of the fireworks display, she added, *And to make sure that my baby only meets the right sort of man.*

'Where are we going?' asked Rosie.

'We're going to go,' said her mother, 'on a cruise.'

* * *

Fat Charlie was not handcuffed. That was good. Everything else was bad, but at least he wasn't in handcuffs. Life had become a confused blur, filled with too-sharp details: the duty sergeant scratching his nose and signing him in – 'Cell six is free' – through a green door and then the smell of the cells, a low-level stench he had never before encountered but which was immediately and horribly familiar, a pervasive fug of yesterday's vomit and disinfectant and smoke and stale blankets and unflushed toilets and despair. It was the smell of things at the bottom, and that was where Fat Charlie seemed to have ended up.

'When you need to flush the lavvy,' said the policeman accompanying him down the corridor, 'you press the button in your cell. One of us'll be by, sooner or later, to pull the chain for you. Stops you trying to flush away the evidence.'

'Evidence of what?'

'Leave it out, sunshine.'

Fat Charlie sighed. He'd been flushing away his own bodily waste products since he'd been old enough to take a certain pride in the activity, and the loss of that, more than the loss of his liberty, told him that everything had changed.

'It's your first time,' said the policeman.

'Sorry.'

'Drugs?' said the policeman.

'No, thank you,' said Fat Charlie.

'Is that what you're in for?'

'I don't know what I'm in for,' said Fat Charlie. 'I'm innocent.'

'White-collar crime, eh?' said the policeman, and he shook his head. 'I'll tell you something the blue-collar boys know without being told. The easier you make it on us, the easier we make it on you. You white-collar people. Always standing up for your rights. You just make it harder on yourselves.'

He opened the door to cell six. 'Home, sweet home,' he said.

The cell-stench was worse inside the room, which had been painted in the kind of speckled paint that resists graffiti, and which contained only a shelf-like bed, low to the ground, and a lidless toilet in the corner.

Fat Charlie put the blanket he'd been issued down on the bed.

'Right,' said the policeman. 'Well. Make yourself at home. And if you get bored, please don't block the toilet with your blanket.'

'Why would I do that?'

'I often wonder that myself,' said the policeman. 'Why indeed? Perhaps it breaks the monotony. I shouldn't know. Being a law-abiding sort with a police pension waiting for me, I've never actually had to spend much time in the cells.'

'You know, I didn't do it,' said Fat Charlie. 'Whatever it was.'

'That's good,' said the policeman.

'Excuse me,' said Fat Charlie. 'Do I get anything to read?'

'Does this look like a lending library to you?'

'No.'

'When I was a young copper, bloke asked me for a book, I went and found him the book I'd been reading. J. T. Edson, it was, or maybe Louis L'Amour. He only went and blocked up his toilet with it, didn't he? Won't catch me doing that again in a hurry.'

Then he went out, and locked the door, with Fat Charlie on the inside and himself on the outside.

* * *

The oddest thing, thought Grahame Coats, who was not given to self-inspection, was how normal, and chipper, and generally good he felt.

The captain told them to fasten their safety belts, and mentioned that they would be landing soon on Saint Andrews. Saint Andrews was a small Caribbean island which, on declaring independence in 1962, had elected to demonstrate its freedom from colonial rule in a number of ways, including the creation of its own judiciary and a singular lack of extradition treaties with the rest of the world.

The plane landed. Grahame Coats got off and walked across the sunny tarmac dragging his wheeled bag behind him. He produced the appropriate passport – Basil Finnegan's – and had it stamped, collected the rest of his luggage from the carousel, and walked out through an unattended customs hall, into the tiny airport and from there into the glorious sunshine. He wore a T-shirt and shorts and sandals and looked like a British Holidaymaker Abroad.

His groundskeeper was waiting for him outside the airport, and Grahame Coats sat himself in the back of the black Mercedes and said, 'Home, please.' On the road out of Williamstown, the road to his clifftop estate, he stared out at the island with a satisfied and proprietorial smile on his face.

It occurred to him that before he left England he had left a woman for dead. He wondered if she was still alive; he rather doubted it. It did not bother him to have killed. It felt instead, immensely satisfying, like something he had needed to do to feel complete. He wondered if he would ever get to do it again.

He wondered if it would be soon.

Chapter Ten

In Which Fat Charlie Sees the World, and Maeve Livingstone Is Dissatisfied

Fat Charlie sat on the blanket on the metal bed and waited for something to happen, but it didn't. What felt like several months passed, extremely slowly. He tried to go to sleep but he couldn't remember how.

He banged on the door.

Someone shouted 'Shut up!' but he couldn't tell whether it was an officer or a fellow inmate.

He walked around the cell for what, at a conservative estimate, he felt must have been two or three years. Then he sat down and let eternity wash over him. Daylight was visible through the thick glass block at the top of the wall that did duty as a window, by all appearances the same daylight that had been visible when the door was locked behind him that morning.

Fat Charlie tried to remember what people did in prison to pass the time, but all he could come up with was keeping secret diaries and hiding things in their bottoms. He had nothing to write on, and felt that a definite measure of how well one was getting on in life was not having to hide things in one's bottom.

Nothing happened. Nothing continued to happen. More

Nothing. The Return of Nothing. Son of Nothing. Nothing Rides Again. Nothing and Abbott and Costello meet the Wolfman . . .

When the door was unlocked, Fat Charlie nearly cheered.

'Right. Exercise yard. You can have a cigarette if you need one.'

'I don't smoke.'

'Filthy habit anyway.'

The exercise yard was an open space in the middle of the police station, surrounded by walls on all sides and topped by wire mesh, which Fat Charlie walked around while deciding that, if there was one thing he didn't like being in, it was police custody. Fat Charlie had had no real liking for the police, but, until now, he had still managed to cling to a fundamental trust in the natural order of things, a conviction that there was some kind of power – a Victorian might have thought of it as Providence – that ensured that the guilty would be punished, while the innocent would be set free. This faith had collapsed in the face of recent events, and had been replaced by the suspicion that he would spend the rest of his life pleading his innocence to a variety of implacable judges and tormenters, many of whom would look like Daisy, and that he would in all probability wake up in cell six the following morning to find that he had been transformed into an enormous cockroach. He had definitely been transported to the kind of maleficent universe that transformed people into cockroaches . . .

Something dropped out of the sky above him, on to the wire mesh. Fat Charlie looked up. A blackbird stared down at him, with lofty disinterest. There was more fluttering, and the blackbird was joined by several sparrows, and by something that Fat Charlie thought was probably a thrush.

They stared at him, he stared back at them.

More birds came.

It would have been hard for Fat Charlie to say exactly when the accumulation of birds on the wire mesh moved from interesting to terrifying. It was somewhere in the first hundred or so, anyway. And it was in the way they didn't coo, or caw, or trill, or sing. They simply landed on the wire and they watched him.

'Go away,' said Fat Charlie.

As one bird, they didn't. Instead, they spoke. They said his name.

Fat Charlie went over to the door in the corner. He banged on it. He said, 'Excuse me,' a few times, and then he started shouting 'Help!'

A clunk. The door was opened, and a heavy-lidded member of Her Majesty's constabulary said, 'This had better be good.'

Fat Charlie pointed upwards. He didn't say anything. He didn't need to. The constabular mouth dropped open peculiarly wide, and it hung there slackly. Fat Charlie's mother would have told the man to shut his mouth or something would fly into it.

The mesh sagged under the weight of thousands of birds. Tiny avian eyes stared down, unblinkingly.

'Christ on a bike,' said the policeman, and he ushered Fat Charlie back into the cell-block without saying another word.

* * *

Maeve Livingstone was in pain. She was sprawled on the floor. She woke, and her hair and face were wet and warm, and then she slept, and when next she woke her hair and face were sticky and cold. She dreamed and woke and dreamed again, woke enough to be conscious of the hurt at the back of her head, and then, because it was easier to sleep, and because when she slept it did not hurt, she allowed sleep to embrace her like a comfortable blanket.

In her dreams she was walking through a television studio, looking for Morris. Occasionally she would catch glimpses of him on the monitors. He always looked concerned. She tried to find her way out, but all ways led her back to the studio floor.

I'm so cold, she thought, and knew that she was awake once more. The pain, though, had subsided. All things considered, thought Maeve, she felt pretty good.

There was something she was upset about, but she was not entirely sure what it was. Perhaps it had been another part of her dream.

It was dark, wherever she was. It seemed to be some kind of broom closet, and she put out her arms to avoid bumping into anything in the darkness. She took a few nervous steps with her arms outstretched and her eyes closed, then she opened her eyes. Now she was in a room she knew. It was an office.

Grahame Coats's office.

She remembered then. The just-awake grogginess was still there – she wasn't yet thinking clearly, knew she wouldn't be properly all there until she had had her morning cup of coffee – but still, it came to her: Grahame Coats's perfidiousness, his treachery, his criminality, his . . .

. . . *why*, she thought, *he assaulted me. He hit me.* And then she thought, *The police. I should call the police.*

She reached down for the phone on the table and picked it up, or tried to, but the phone seemed very heavy, or slippery, or both, and she was unable to grasp it properly. It felt wrong for her fingers.

I must be weaker than I thought, Maeve decided. *I had better ask them to send a doctor as well.*

In the pocket of her jacket was a small silver phone which played 'Greensleeves' when it rang. She was relieved to find the phone still there, and that she had no problems at all in holding it. She dialled the emergency services. As she waited for someone to answer she wondered why they still called it 'dialling' when there weren't dials on telephones, not since she was much younger, and then after the phones with dials came the Trimphones with buttons on them and a particularly annoying ring. She had, as a teenager, had a boyfriend who could and continually did imitate the *breep* of a Trimphone, an ability that was, Maeve decided, looking back, his only real achievement. She wondered what had happened to him. She wondered how a man who could imitate a Trimphone coped in a world in which telephones could and did sound like *anything* . . .

'We apologise for the delay in placing your call,' said a mechanical voice. 'Please hold the line.'

Meave felt oddly calm, as if nothing bad could ever happen to her again.

A man's voice came on the line. 'Hello?' it said. It sounded extremely efficient.

'I need the police,' said Maeve.

'You do not need the police,' said the voice. 'All crimes will be dealt with by the appropriate and inevitable authorities.'

'You know,' said Maeve, 'I think I may have dialled the wrong number.'

'Likewise,' said the voice, 'all numbers are, ultimately, correct. They are simply numbers, and cannot thus be right or wrong.'

'That's all very well for you to say,' said Maeve. 'But I *do* need to speak to the police. I may also need an ambulance. And I have obviously called a wrong number.' She ended the call. Perhaps, she thought, 999 didn't work from a mobile. She pulled up her onscreen address book and called her sister's number. The phone rang once, and a now-familiar voice said, 'Let me clarify: I am not saying that you dialled a wrong number on purpose. What I trust that I am saying, is that all numbers are by their nature correct. Well, except for *pi*, of course. I can't be doing with *pi*. Gives me a headache just thinking about it, going on and on and on and on and on . . .'

Maeve pressed the red button and ended the call. She dialled her bank manager.

The voice that answered said, 'But here am I, wittering on about the correctness of numbers, and you're undoubtedly thinking that there's a time and a place for everything . . .'

Click. Called her best friend.

'. . . and right now what we should be discussing is your ultimate disposition. I'm afraid traffic is extremely heavy this afternoon, so if you wouldn't mind waiting where you are for a little while, you will be collected . . .' It was a reassuring voice, the voice of a radio vicar in the process of telling you his thought for the day.

If Maeve had not felt so placid, she would have panicked then. Instead, she pondered. Seeing that her phone had been – what would they call it, *hacked*? – then she would simply have to go down to the street and find a police officer and make a formal complaint. Nothing happened when Maeve pressed the button for the lift, so she walked down the stairs, thinking that there was probably never a police officer about when you wanted one anyway, they were always zooming about in those cars, the ones that went *neenorneenor*. The police, Maeve thought, should be strolling around in pairs telling people the time, or waiting at the bottom of drainpipes as burglars with bags of swag over their shoulder make their descent . . .

At the very bottom of the stairs, in the hallway, were two police officers, a man and a woman. They were out of uniform, but they were police all right. There was no mistaking them. The man was stout and red-faced, the woman was small and dark, and might, in other circumstances, have been extremely pretty. 'We know she came this far,' the woman was saying. 'The receptionist remembered her coming in, just before lunchtime. When she got back from lunch, they'd both gone.'

'You think they ran off together?' asked the stout man.

'Um, excuse me,' said Maeve Livingstone, politely.

'It's possible. There's got to be some kind of simple explanation. The disappearance of Grahame Coats. The disappearance of Maeve Livingstone. At least we've got Nancy in custody.'

'We certainly did *not* run off together,' said Maeve, but they ignored her.

The two police officers got into the lift and slammed the doors behind them. Maeve watched them judder up and away, towards the top floor.

She was still holding her mobile phone. It vibrated in her hand now, and then began to play 'Greensleeves'. She glanced down at it. Morris's photograph filled the screen. Nervously, she answered the phone. 'Yes?'

''Ullo, love. How's tricks?'

She said, 'Fine, thank you.' Then she said, 'Morris?' And then, 'No, it's not fine. It's all awful, actually.'

'Aye,' said Morris. 'I thought it might be. Still, nothing that can be done about that now. Time to move on.'

'Morris? *Where* are you calling from?'

'It's a bit complicated,' he said. 'I mean, I'm not actually on the phone. Just really wanted to help you along.'

'Grahame Coats,' she said. 'He was a crook.'

'Yes, love,' said Morris. 'But it's time to let all that go. Put it behind you.'

'He hit me on the back of the head,' she told him. 'And he's been stealing our money.'

'It's only material things, love,' said Morris, reassuringly. 'Now you're beyond the vale . . .'

'Morris,' said Maeve. 'That pestilent little worm attempted to murder your wife. I *do* think you should try to show a little more concern.'

'Don't be like that, love. I'm just trying to explain . . .'

'I have to tell you, Morris, that if you're going to take that kind of attitude, I'll simply deal with this myself. I'm certainly not going to forget about it. It's all right for you, you're dead. You don't have to worry about these things.'

'You're dead too, love.'

'That is *quite* beside the point,' she said. Then, 'I'm what?' And then, before he could say anything, Maeve said, 'Morris, I said that he *attempted* to murder me. Not that he succeeded.'

'Erm,' the late Morris Livingstone sounded lost for words. 'Maeve. Love. I know this may come as a bit of a shock to you, but the truth of the matter is that—'

The telephone made a 'plibble' noise, and the image of an empty battery appeared on the screen.

'I'm afraid I didn't get that, Morris,' she told him. 'I think the telephone battery is going.'

'You don't have a phone battery,' he told her. 'You don't have a phone. All is illusion. I keep trying to tell you, you've now transcended the vale of oojamaflip, and now you're becoming, oh heck, it's like worms and butterflies, love. You know.'

'Caterpillars,' said Maeve. 'I think you mean caterpillars and butterflies.'

'Er, that sounds right,' said Morris's voice, over the telephone. 'Caterpillars. That was what I meant. So what do worms turn into, then?'

'They don't turn into anything, Morris,' said Maeve, a little testily. 'They're just worms.' The silver phone emitted a small noise, like an electronic burp, showed the picture of an empty battery again, and turned itself off.

Maeve closed it and put it back into her pocket. She walked over to the nearest wall and, experimentally, pushed a finger against it. The wall felt clammy and gelatinous to the touch. She exerted a little more pressure, and her whole hand went into it. Then it went through it.

'Oh dear,' she said, and felt herself, not for the first time in her existence, wishing that she had listened to Morris, who after all, she admitted to herself, by now probably knew rather more about being dead than she did. *Ah well*, she thought. Being dead was probably just like everything else in life: you pick some of it up as you go along, and you just make up the rest.

She walked out the front door, and found herself coming through the wall at the back of the hall, into the building. She tried again, with the same result. Then she walked into the travel agency that occupied the bottom floor of the building, and tried pushing through the wall on the west of the building.

She went through it, and came out in the front hall again, entering from the east. It was like being in a TV set and trying to walk off the screen. Topographically speaking, the office building seemed to have become her universe.

She went back upstairs to see what the detectives were doing. They were staring at the desk, at the debris that Grahame Coats had left when he was packing.

'You know,' said Maeve helpfully, 'I'm in a room behind the bookcase. I'm in there.'

They ignored her.

The woman crouched down and rummaged in the bin. 'Bingo,' she said, and pulled out a man's white shirt, spattered with dried blood. She placed it into a plastic bag. The stout man pulled out his mobile phone.

'I want Forensic down here,' he said.

***

Fat Charlie now found himself viewing his cell as a refuge rather than as a prison. Cells were deep inside the building, for a start, far from the haunts of even the most adventurous birds. And his brother was nowhere to be seen. He no longer minded that nothing ever happened in cell six. Nothing was infinitely preferable to most of the somethings he found himself coming up with. Even a world populated exclusively with castles and cockroaches and people named K was preferable to a world filled with malignant birds that whispered his name in chorus.

The door opened.

'Don't you knock?' asked Fat Charlie.

'No,' said the policeman. 'We don't, actually. Your solicitor's finally here.'

'Mr Merryman?' said Fat Charlie, and then he stopped. Leonard Merryman was a rotund gentleman with small gold spectacles, and the man behind the cop most definitely wasn't.

'Everything's fine,' said the man who wasn't his solicitor. 'You can leave us here.'

'Buzz when you're done,' said the policeman, and he closed the door.

Spider took Fat Charlie by the hand. He said, 'I'm busting you out of here.'

'But I don't want to be busted out of here. I didn't *do* anything.'

'Good reason for getting out.'

'But if I leave then I *will* have done something. I'll be an escaped prisoner.'

'You're not a prisoner,' said Spider, cheerfully. 'You've not been charged with anything yet. You're just helping them with their inquiries. Look, are you hungry?'

'A bit.'

'What do you want? Tea? Coffee? Hot chocolate?'

Hot chocolate sounded extremely good to Fat Charlie. 'I'd love a hot chocolate,' he said.

'Right,' said Spider. He grabbed Fat Charlie's hand, and said, 'Close your eyes.'

'Why?'

'It makes it easier.'

Fat Charlie closed his eyes, although he was not certain what it would make easier. The world stretched and squeezed and Fat Charlie was certain that he was going to be sick. Then the inside of his mind settled down and he felt a warm breeze touch his face.

He opened his eyes.

They were in the open air, in a large market square, somewhere that looked extremely un-English.

'Where is this?'

'I think it's called Skopsie. Town in Italy or somewhere. I started coming here years ago. They do amazing hot chocolate here. Best I've ever had.'

They sat down at a small wooden table. It was painted fire-engine red. A waiter approached and said something to them in a language that didn't sound like Italian to Fat Charlie. Spider said, '*Dos Chocolatos*, dude,' and the man nodded and went away.

'Right,' said Fat Charlie. 'You've got me into even deeper trouble. Now they'll probably have to do a manhunt or something. It'll be in the papers.'

'What are they going to do?' asked Spider, with a smile. 'Send you to gaol?'

'Oh please.'

The hot chocolate arrived, and the waiter poured it into small cups. It was roughly the same temperature as molten lava, was halfway between a chocolate soup and a chocolate custard, and it smelled astonishingly good.

Spider said, 'Look, we've made rather a mess of this whole family reunion business, haven't we?'

'*We*'ve made rather a mess of it?' Fat Charlie managed outrage extremely well. '*I* wasn't the one who stole my fiancée. *I* wasn't the one who got me sacked from work. *I* wasn't the one who got me arrested—'

'No,' said Spider. 'But you were the one who brought the birds into it, weren't you?'

Fat Charlie took a very small initial sip of his hot chocolate. 'Ow. I think I've just burned my mouth.' He looked at his brother and saw his own expression staring back at him: worried, tired, frightened. 'Yes, I was the one who brought the birds into it. So what do we do now?'

Spider said, 'They do a really nice sort of noodly-stew thing here, by the way.'

'Are you sure we're in Italy?'

'Not really.'

'Can I ask you a question?'

Spider nodded.

Fat Charlie tried to think of the best way to put it. 'The bird thing. Where they all turn up and pretend they've escaped from an Alfred Hitchcock film. Do you think it's something that only happens in England?'

'Why?'

'Because I think those pigeons have noticed us.' He pointed to the far end of the square.

The pigeons were not doing the things that pigeons usually do. They were not pecking at sandwich crusts or bobbing along with their heads down hunting for tourist-dropped food. They were standing quite still, and they were staring. A clatter of wings and they were joined by another hundred birds, most of them landing on the statue of a fat man wearing an enormous hat that dominated the centre of the square. Fat Charlie looked at the pigeons, and the pigeons looked back at him. 'So what's the worst that could happen?' he asked Spider, in an undertone. 'They crap all over us?'

'I don't know. But I expect they can do worse than that. Finish your hot chocolate.'

'But it's *hot*.'

'And we'll need a couple of bottles of water, won't we? *Garçon?*'

A low susurrus of wings; the clack of more arriving birds; and beneath it all, low, burbling secretive coos.

The waiter brought them bottles of water. Spider, who was, Fat Charlie observed, now wearing his black and red leather jacket once more, put them into his pockets.

'They're only pigeons,' said Fat Charlie, but even as he said it, he knew the words were inadequate. They were not just pigeons. They were an army. The statue of the fat man had almost vanished from view beneath the grey and purple feathers.

'I think I preferred birds before they thought about ganging up on us.'

Spider said, 'And they're everywhere.' Then he grabbed Fat Charlie's hand. 'Close your eyes.'

The birds rose as one bird, then. Fat Charlie closed his eyes.

The pigeons came down like the wolf on the fold . . .

There was silence, and distance, and Fat Charlie thought, *I'm in an oven*. He opened his eyes and realised that it was true: an oven with red dunes that receded into the distance until they faded into a sky the colour of mother-of-pearl.

'Desert,' said Spider. 'Seemed like a good idea. Bird-free zone. Somewhere to finish a conversation. Here.' He handed Fat Charlie a bottle of water.

'Thanks.'

'So. Would you like to tell me where the birds come from?'

Fat Charlie said, 'There's this place. I went there. There were lots of animal-people there. They, um. They all knew Dad. One of them was a woman, a sort of bird woman.'

Spider looked at him. ' "There's this place"? That's not exactly very helpful.'

'There's a mountainside with caves in it. And then there are these cliffs, and they go down into nothing. It's like the end of the world.'

'It's the beginning of the world,' corrected Spider. 'I've heard of the caves. A girl I knew once told me all about them. Never been there, though. So you met the Bird Woman, and . . . ?'

'She offered to make you go away. And, um. Well, I took her up on it.'

'That,' said Spider, with a movie-star smile, 'was really stupid.'

'I didn't tell her to *hurt* you.'

'What did you think she was going to do to get rid of me? Write me a stiff letter?'

'I don't know. I didn't think. I was upset.'

'Great. Well, if she has her way, you'll be upset and I'll be dead. You could have simply asked me to leave, you know.'

'I did!'

'Er. What did I say?'

'That you liked it in my house and you weren't going anywhere.'

Spider drank some of the water. 'So what *exactly* did you say to her?'

Fat Charlie tried to remember. Now he thought about it, it seemed an odd sort of thing to say. 'Just that I was going to give her Anansi's bloodline,' he said, reluctantly.

'You what?'

'It was what she asked me to say.'

Spider looked incredulous. 'But that's not just me. That's both of us.'

Fat Charlie's mouth was suddenly very dry. He hoped it was the desert air, and sipped his bottled water.

'Hang on. Why the desert?' asked Fat Charlie.

'No birds. Remember?'

'So what are those?' He pointed. At first they looked tiny, and then you realised that they were simply very high: they were circling, and wobbling on the wing.

'Vultures,' said Spider. 'They don't attack living things.'

'Right. And pigeons are scared of people,' said Fat Charlie. The dots in the sky circled lower, and the birds appeared to grow as they descended.

Spider said, 'Point taken.' Then, 'Shit.'

They weren't alone. Someone was watching them on a distant dune. A casual observer might have mistaken the figure for a scarecrow.

Fat Charlie shouted, 'Go away!' His voice was swallowed by the sand. 'I take it all back. We don't have a deal! Leave us alone!'

A flutter of overcoat on the hot wind, and the dune was now deserted.

Fat Charlie said, 'She went away. Who would have thought it was going to be that simple?'

Spider touched his shoulder, and pointed. Now the woman in the brown overcoat was standing on the nearest ridge of sand, so close that Fat Charlie could see the glassy blacks of her eyes.

The vultures were raggedy black shadows, and then they landed: their naked mauve necks and scalps – featherless because that's so much easier when you're putting your head into rotting carcasses – extended as they stared short-sightedly at the brothers, as if wondering whether to wait until the two men died or if they should do something to hurry the process along.

Spider said, 'What else was there in the deal?'

'Um?'

'Was there anything else? Did she give you something to seal the bargain? Sometimes things like this involve a trade.'

The vultures were edging forward, a step at a time, closing their ranks, tightening the circle. There were more black slashes in the sky, growing and wobbling towards them. Spider's hand closed around Fat Charlie's hand.

'Close your eyes.'

The cold hit Fat Charlie like a punch to the gut. He took a deep breath and felt like someone had iced his lungs. He coughed and coughed, while the wind howled like a great beast.

He opened his eyes. 'Can I ask where we are this time?'

'Antarctica,' said Spider. He zipped up the front of his leather jacket, and did not seem to mind the cold. 'It's a bit chilly, I'm afraid.'

'Don't you have any middle gears? Straight from desert to ice field.'

'No birds here,' said Spider.

'Wouldn't it be easier just to go and sit inside a building that's nice and bird free? We could have lunch.'

Spider said, 'Right. Now you're complaining, just because it's a little bit nippy.'

'It's *not* a little bit nippy. It's fifty below. And anyway, *look*.'

Fat Charlie pointed at the sky. A pale squiggle, like a miniature letter m chalked on to the sky, hung unmoving in the cold air. 'Albatross,' he said.

'Frigate,' said Spider.

'Pardon?'

'It's not an albatross. It's a frigate. He probably hasn't even noticed us.'

'Possibly not,' admitted Fat Charlie. 'But *they* have.'

Spider turned, and said something else that sounded a lot like 'frigate'. There may not have been a million penguins waddling and slipping and bellysliding towards the brothers, but it certainly looked that way. As a general rule, the only things properly terrified by the approach of penguins tend to be smallish fish, but when the numbers get large enough . . .

Fat Charlie reached out without being told, and he held Spider's hand. He closed his eyes.

When he opened them, he was somewhere warmer, although opening his eyes made no difference to what he saw. Everything was the colour of night. 'Have I gone blind?'

'We're in a disused coal mine,' said Spider. 'I saw a photo of this place in a magazine a few years back. Unless there are flocks of sightless finches who have evolved to take advantage of the darkness and eat coal-chips, we're probably fine.'

'That's a joke isn't it? About the sightless finches?'

'More or less.'

Fat Charlie sighed, and the sigh echoed through the underground cavern. 'You know,' he said, 'if you'd just gone away, if you'd left my house when I asked you to, we'd not be in this mess.'

'That isn't very helpful.'

'It wasn't meant to be. God knows how I'm going to explain all this to Rosie.'

Spider cleared his throat. 'I don't think you'll have to worry about that.'

'Because . . . ?'

'She's broken up with us.'

There was a long silence. Then Fat Charlie said, 'Of course she has.'

'I made a kind of a sort of a mess of that part of things.' Spider sounded uncomfortable.

'But what if I explain it to her? I mean, if I tell her that I wasn't you, that you were pretending to be me—'

'I already did. That was when she decided she didn't want to see either of us ever again.'

'Me as well?'

''Fraid so.'

'Look,' said Spider's voice in the darkness. 'I really never meant to make . . . Well, when I came to see you, all I wanted to do was say hello. Not to. Um. I've pretty much completely cocked this all up, haven't I?'

'Are you trying to say sorry?'

Silence. Then, 'I guess. Maybe.'

More silence. Fat Charlie's said, 'Well, then I'm really sorry I called the Bird Woman to get rid of you.' Not seeing Spider while they were talking made it easier, somehow.

'Yeah. Thanks. I just wish I knew how to get rid of her.'

'*A feather!*' said Fat Charlie.

'No, you've lost me.'

'You asked if she gave me anything to seal the deal. She did. She gave me a feather.'

'Where is it?'

Fat Charlie tried to remember. 'I'm not sure. I had it when I woke up in Mrs Dunwiddy's front room. I didn't have it when I got on the plane. I suppose that Mrs Dunwiddy must still have it.'

The silence that met this was long and dark and unbroken. Fat Charlie began to worry that Spider had gone away, that he had been left abandoned in the darkness under the world. Eventually, he said 'Are you still there?

'Still here.'

'That's a relief. If you abandoned me down here I don't know how I'd get out.'

'Don't tempt me.'

More silence.

Fat Charlie said, 'What country are we in?'

'Poland, I think. Like I said, I saw a picture of it. Only they had the lights on in the photo.'

'You need to see photos of places to go to them?'

'I need to know where they are.'

It was astounding, thought Fat Charlie, how truly quiet it was in the mine. The place had its own special silence. He started to wonder about silences. Was the silence of the grave different in kind to the silence of, say, outer space?

Spider said, 'I remember Mrs Dunwiddy. She smells of violets.' People have said, 'All hope has fled. We're going to die,' with more enthusiasm.

'That's her,' said Fat Charlie. 'Small, old as the hills. Thick glasses. I suppose we'll just have to go and get the feather from her. Then we'll give it back to the Bird Woman. She'll call off this nightmare.' Fat Charlie finished the last of the bottled water, carried here from the little square somewhere that wasn't Italy. He screwed the top back on to the bottle, and put the empty bottle down into the darkness, wondering if it was littering if no one was ever going to see it. 'So let's hold hands and go and see Mrs Dunwiddy.'

Spider made a noise. The noise was not cocky. It was unsettled and unsure. In the darkness Fat Charlie imagined Spider deflating, like a bullfrog or a week-old balloon. Fat Charlie had wanted to see Spider taken down a peg; he had not wanted to hear him make a noise like a terrified six-year-old. 'Hang on. You're scared of Mrs Dunwiddy?'

'I . . . I can't go near her.'

'Well, if it's any consolation I was scared of her too when I was a kid, and then I met her again at the funeral and she wasn't that bad. Not really. She's just an old lady.' In his mind she lit the black candles once more, and sprinkled the herbs into the bowl. 'Maybe a bit spooky. But you'll be OK when you see her.'

'She made me go away,' said Spider. 'I didn't want to go. But I broke this ball in her garden. Big glass thing, like a giant Christmas tree ornament.'

'I did that too. She was pissed.'

'I know.' The voice from the dark was small and worried and confused. 'It was the same time. That was when it all started.'

'Well. Look. It's not the end of the world. You take me to Florida, I can go and get the feather back from Mrs Dunwiddy. I'm not scared. You can stay away.'

'I can't do that. I can't go to where she is.'

'So, what are you trying to say? She's taken out some kind of magical restraining order?'

'More or less. Yes.' Then Spider said, 'I miss Rosie. I'm sorry about. You know.'

Fat Charlie thought about Rosie. He found it peculiarly hard to remember her face. He thought about not having Rosie's mother as his mother-in-law; about the two silhouettes on the curtains in his bedroom window. He said, 'Don't feel bad about it. Well, you can feel bad about it if you want, because you behaved like a complete bastard. But maybe it was all for the best.' There was a twinge in the general region of Fat Charlie's heart, but he knew that he was speaking the truth. It's easier to say true things in the dark.

Spider said, 'You know what doesn't make sense here?'

'Everything?'

'No. Only one thing. I don't understand why the Bird Woman got involved. It doesn't make sense.'

'Dad pissed her off—'

'Dad pissed *everybody* off. She's wrong, though. And if she wanted to kill us, why doesn't she just try to do it?'

'I gave her our bloodline.'

'So you said. No, something else is going on, and I don't get it.'
Silence. Then Spider said, 'Hold my hand.'

'Do I need to close my eyes?'

'May as well.'

'Where are we going? The moon?'

'I'm going to take you somewhere safe,' said Spider.

'Oh good,' said Fat Charlie. 'I like safe. Where?'

But then, without even opening his eyes, Fat Charlie knew. The
smell was a dead giveaway: unwashed bodies and unflushed
toilets, disinfectant, old blankets and apathy.

'I bet I would have been just as safe in a luxury hotel room,' he
said aloud, but there was nobody there to hear him. He sat down
on the shelf-like bed of cell six, and wrapped the thin blanket
around his shoulders. He might have been there for ever.

Half an hour later, someone came and led him to the inter-
rogation room.

**

'Hello,' said Daisy, with a smile. 'Would you like a cup of tea?'

'You might as well not bother,' said Fat Charlie. 'I've seen
the telly. I know how it goes. This is that whole good-cop
bad-cop thing, isn't it? You'll give me a cup of tea and some Jaffa
cakes, then some big hard-bitten bastard with a hair-trigger
temper comes in and shouts at me and pours the tea away and
starts eating my Jaffa cakes and then you stop him from
physically attacking me, and make him give me my tea and Jaffa
cakes back, and in my gratitude I tell you everything you want to
know.'

'We could skip all that,' said Daisy, 'and you could just tell us
what we want to know. Anyway, we don't have any Jaffa cakes.'

'I told you everything I know,' said Fat Charlie. 'Everything.
Grahame Coats gave me a cheque for two grand and told me to
take two weeks off. He said he was pleased I'd brought some
irregularities to his attention. Then he asked for my password and
waved me goodbye. End of story.'

'And you still say you don't know anything about the
disappearance of Maeve Livingstone?'

'I don't think I ever actually met her properly. Maybe once when she came through the office. We talked on the phone a few times. She'd want to talk to Grahame Coats. I'd have to tell her the cheque was in the post.'

'Was it?'

'I don't know. I thought it was. Look, you can't believe I had anything to do with her disappearance.'

'No,' she said, cheerfully. 'I don't.'

'Because I honestly don't know what could have – you what?'

'I don't think you had anything to do with Maeve Livingstone's disappearance. I also don't believe that you had anything to do with the financial irregularities being perpetrated at the Grahame Coats Agency, although someone seems to have worked very hard to make it look like you did. But it's pretty obvious that the weird accounting practices and the steady syphoning off of money predates your arrival. You've only been there two years.'

'About that,' said Fat Charlie. He realised that his jaw was open. He closed it

Daisy said, 'Look, I know that cops in books and movies are mostly idiots, especially if it's the kind of book with a crime-fighting pensioner or a hard-arsed private eye in it. And I'm really sorry that we don't have any Jaffa cakes. But we're not all completely stupid.'

'I didn't say you were,' said Fat Charlie.

'No,' she said. 'But you were thinking it. You're free to go. With an apology if you'd like one.'

'Where did she, um, disappear?' asked Fat Charlie.

'Mrs Livingstone? Well, the last time anyone saw her, she was accompanying Grahame Coats into his office.'

'Ah.'

'I meant it about the cup of tea. Would you like one?'

'Yes. Very much. Um. I suppose your people already checked out the secret room in his office. The one behind the bookcase?'

It is to Daisy's credit that all she said, perfectly calmly, was, 'I don't believe they did.'

'I don't think we were supposed to know about it,' said Fat Charlie, 'but I went in once, and the bookshelf was pushed back, and he was inside. I went away again,' he added. 'I wasn't spying on him or anything.'

Daisy said, 'We can pick up some Jaffa cakes on the way.'

* * *

Fat Charlie wasn't certain that he liked freedom. There was too much open air involved.

'Are you OK?' asked Daisy.

'I'm fine.'

'You seem a bit twitchy.'

'I suppose I am. You'll think this is silly, but I'm a bit. Well, I have a thing about birds.'

'What, a phobia?'

'Sort of.'

'Well, that's the common term for an irrational fear of birds.'

'What do they call a rational fear of birds, then?' He nibbled the Jaffa cake.

There was silence. Daisy said, 'Well, anyway, there aren't any birds in this car.'

She parked the car on the double yellow lines outside the Grahame Coats Agency offices and they went inside together.

* * *

Rosie lay in the sun by the pool on the aft deck of a Korean cruise ship* with a magazine over her head and her mother beside her, trying to remember why she had ever thought a holiday with her mother would be a good idea.

There were no English newspapers on the cruise ship, and Rosie did not miss them. She missed everything else, though. In her mind the cruise was a form of floating purgatory, made bearable only by the islands they visited every day or so. The

*The ship had been the *Sunny Archipelago* until an attack of gastric flu had made international news. A cheap attempt to rebrand it without changing the ship's initials done by the chairman of the board, who did not speak English as well as he believed he did, had left the cruise ship rejoicing in the name of the *Squeak Attack*.

other passengers would go ashore and shop, or parasail, or go for rum-sodden trips on floating pirate ships. Rosie, on the other hand, would walk, and talk to people.

She would see people in pain, see people who looked hungry or miserable, and she wanted to help. Everything seemed very fixable to Rosie. It just needed someone to fix it.

* * *

Maeve Livingstone had expected death to be a number of things, but *irritating* had never been one of them. Still, she was irritated. She was tired of being walked through, tired of being ignored and, most of all, tired of not being able to leave the offices in the Aldwych.

'I mean, if I *have* to haunt anywhere,' she said to the receptionist, 'why can't I haunt Somerset House, over the road? Lovely buildings, excellent view over the Thames, several architecturally impressive features. Some very nice little restaurants as well. Even if you don't need to eat any longer, it'd be good for people-watching.'

Annie the receptionist, whose job since the vanishment of Grahame Coats had been to answer the phone in a bored voice and say, 'I'm afraid I don't know' to pretty much any question she was asked, and who, when she was not performing this function, would phone her friends and discuss the mystery in hushed but excitable tones, did not reply to this, as she had not replied to anything Maeve had said to her.

The monotony was broken by the arrival of Fat Charlie Nancy accompanied by the female police officer.

Maeve had always rather liked Fat Charlie, even when his function had been to assure her that a cheque would soon be in the mail, but now she saw things she had never seen before: there were shadows that fluttered about him, always keeping their distance: bad things coming. He looked like a man on the run from something, and it worried her.

She followed them into Grahame Coats's office, and was delighted to see Fat Charlie head straight over to the bookshelf at the back of the room.

'So where's the secret panel?' asked Daisy.

'It's not a panel. It was a door. Behind the bookshelf over here. I don't know. Maybe there's a secret catch or something.'

Daisy looked at the bookshelf. 'Did Grahame Coats ever write an autobiography?' she asked Fat Charlie.

'Not that I've ever heard about.'

She pushed on the leatherbound copy of *My Life by Grahame Coats*. It clicked, and the bookshelf swung away from the wall, revealing a locked door behind it.

'We'll need a locksmith,' she said. 'And I don't really think we need you here any longer, Mr Nancy.'

'Right,' said Fat Charlie. 'Well,' he said, 'it's been, um. Interesting.'

And then he said, 'I don't suppose you'd like. To get some food. With me. One day?'

'Dim sum,' she said. 'Sunday lunchtime. We'll go Dutch. You'll need to be there when they open the doors at eleven-thirty, or we'll have to queue for ages.' She scribbled down the address of a restaurant, and handed it to Fat Charlie. 'Watch out for birds on the way home,' she said.

'I will,' he said. 'See you Sunday.'

* * *

The locksmith unfolded a black cloth wallet, and took out several slim pieces of metal.

'Honestly,' he said, 'you'd think they'd learn. It's not like good locks are expensive. I mean, you look at that door, lovely piece of work. Solid that is. Take you half a day to get through it with a blow torch. And then they let the whole thing down with a lock that a five-year-old could open with a spoon-handle . . . There we go . . . Easy as falling off the wagon.'

He pulled on the door. The door opened and they saw the thing on the floor.

'Well, for goodness' sake,' said Maeve Livingstone. 'That's not *me*.' She thought she'd have more affection for her body, but she didn't; it reminded her of a dead animal at the side of the road.

Soon enough the room was filled with people. Maeve, who had

never had much patience for detective dramas, was quickly bored, only taking an interest in what was happening when she felt herself being pulled, unarguably, downstairs and out the front door, as the human remains were taken away in a discreet blue plastic bag.

'This is more like it,' said Maeve Livingstone.

She was out.

At least she was out of the office in the Aldwych.

Obviously, she knew, there were rules. There had to be rules. It's just that she wasn't very sure what they were.

She found herself wishing she'd been more religious in life, but she'd never been able to manage it: as a small girl, she had been unable to envision a God who disliked anyone enough to sentence them to an eternity of torture in Hell, mostly for not believing in Him properly, and as she grew up her childhood doubts had solidified into a rocky certainty that Life, from birth to grave, was all there was and that everything else was imaginary. It had been a good belief, and it had allowed her to cope, but now it was being severely tested.

Honestly, she wasn't sure that even a life spent attending the right sort of church would have prepared her for this. Maeve was rapidly coming to the conclusion that in a well-organised world, Death should be like the kind of all-expenses-included luxury vacation where they give you a folder at the start filled with tickets, discount vouchers, schedules, and several phone numbers to ring if you get into trouble.

She didn't walk. She didn't fly. She moved like the wind, like a cold autumn wind that made people shiver as she passed, that stirred the fallen leaves on the pavements.

She went where she always went first, when she came to London, to Selfridges, the department store in Oxford Street. Maeve had worked in the cosmetic department of Selfridges when she was much younger, between dancing jobs, and she had always made a point of going back whenever she could, and buying expensive make-up, just as she had promised herself she would in the old days.

She haunted the make-up department until she was bored, then took a look around home furnishings. She wasn't ever going to get another dining-room table, but really, there wasn't any harm in looking . . .

Then she drifted through the Selfridges home entertainment department, surrounded by television screens of all sizes. Some of the screens were showing the news. The volume was off on each set, but the picture that filled each screen was Grahame Coats. The dislike rose burning hot within her, like molten lava. The picture changed and now she was looking at herself – a clip of her at Morris's side. She recognised it as the 'Give me a fiver and I'll snog you rotten' sketch from *Morris Livingstone, I Presume.*

She wished she could figure out a way to recharge her phone. Even if the only person she could find was the irritating voice that had sounded like a vicar, she thought, she would even have spoken to him. But mostly she just wanted to talk to Morris. He'd know what to do. This time, she thought, she'd let him talk. This time, she'd listen.

'Maeve?'

Morris's face was looking out at her from a hundred television screens. She thought for a heartbeat that she was imagining it, then that it was part of the news, but he looked at her with concern, and said her name again, and she knew it was him.

'Morris . . . ?'

He smiled his famous smile, and every face on every screen focused on her. 'Hullo, love. I was wondering what was taking you so long. Well, it's time for you to come on over.'

'Over?'

'To the other side. Move beyond the vale. Or possibly the veil. Anyway, that.' And he held out a hundred hands from a hundred screens.

She knew that all she needed to do was reach out and take his hand. She surprised herself by saying, 'No, Morris. I don't think so.'

A hundred identical faces looked perplexed. 'Maeve, love. You need to put the flesh behind you.'

'Well, obviously, dear. And I will. I promise I will. As soon as I'm ready.'

'Maeve, you're dead. How much more ready can you be?'

She sighed. 'I've still got a few things to sort out at this end.'

'For instance?'

Maeve pulled herself up to her full height. 'Well,' she said. 'I was planning on finding that Grahame Coats creature and then doing . . . well, whatever it is that ghosts do. I could haunt him or something.'

Morris sounded slightly incredulous. 'You want to haunt Grahame Coats? Whatever for?'

'Because,' she said, 'I'm not done here.' She set her mouth into a line and raised her chin.

Morris Livingstone looked at her from a hundred television screens at the same time, and he shook his head, in a mixture of admiration and exasperation. He had married her because she was her own woman, and had loved her for that reason, but he wished he could, just for once, persuade her of something. Instead, he said, 'Well, I'm not going anywhere, pet. Let us know when you're ready.'

And then he began to fade.

'Morris. Do you have any idea how I go about finding him?' she asked. But the image of her husband had vanished completely, and now the televisions were showing the weather.

* * *

Fat Charlie met Daisy for Sunday dim sum, in a dimly lit restaurant in London's tiny Chinatown.

'You look nice,' he said.

'Thank you,' she said. 'I feel miserable. I've been taken off the Grahame Coats case. It's now a full-scale murder investigation. I reckon I was probably lucky to have been with it as long as I was.'

'Well,' he said brightly, 'if you hadn't been part of it you would never have had the fun of arresting me.'

'There is that.' She had the grace to look slightly rueful.

'Are there any leads?'

'Even if there were,' she said, 'I couldn't possibly tell you about them.' A small cart was trundled over to their table, and Daisy selected several dishes from it. 'There's a theory that he threw himself off the side of a Channel Ferry. That was the last purchase on one of his credit cards – a day-ticket to Dieppe.'

'Do you think that's likely?'

She picked a dumpling up from her plate with her chopsticks, popped it into her mouth.

'No,' she said. 'My guess is that he's gone somewhere with no extradition treaty. Probably Brazil. Killing Maeve Livingstone might have been a spur-of-the-moment thing, but everything else was so meticulous. He had a system in place. Money went into client accounts. Grahame took his fifteen per cent off the top and standing orders ensured that a whole lot more came off the bottom. Lot of foreign cheques never even made it into the client accounts in the first place. What's remarkable is how long he had kept it up.'

Fat Charlie chewed a rice ball with somethng sweet inside it. He said, 'I think you know where he is.'

Daisy stopped chewing her dumpling.

'It was something about the way you said he'd gone to Brazil. Like you know he wasn't there.'

'That would be police business,' she said. 'And I'm afraid I cannot possibly comment. How's your brother?'

'I don't know. I think he's gone. His room wasn't there when I got home.'

'His room?'

'His stuff. He'd taken his stuff. And no sign of him since.' Fat Charlie sipped his jasmine tea. 'I hope he's all right.'

'You think he wouldn't be?'

'Well, he's got the same phobia that I have.'

'The birds thing. Right.' Daisy nodded sympathetically. 'And how's the fiancée, and the future mother-in-law?'

'Um. I don't think either description is, um, currently operative.'

'Ah.'

'They've gone away.'

'Was this because of the arrest?'

'Not as far as I know.'

She looked across at him like a sympathetic pixie. 'I'm sorry.'

'Well,' he said. 'Right now I don't have a job, I don't have a love life, and – thanks mostly to your efforts – the neighbours are now all convinced I'm a yardie hit man. Some of them have started crossing the road to avoid me. On the other hand, my newsagent wants me to make sure the bloke who knocked up his daughter is taught a lesson.'

'What did you tell him?'

'The truth. I don't think he believed me, though. He gave me a free bag of cheese and onion crisps and a pack of Polo mints, and told me there would be more where that came from once I'd done the job.'

'It'll blow over.'

Fat Charlie sighed. 'It's mortifying.'

'Still,' she said. 'It's not as if it's the end of the world.'

They split the bill, and the waiter gave them two fortune cookies with their change.

'What does yours say?' asked Fat Charlie.

' "Persistence will pay off",' she read. 'What about yours?'

'It's the same as yours,' he said. 'Good old persistence.' He crumpled up the fortune into a pea-size ball, and dropped it into his pocket. He walked her down to Leicester Square tube station.

'Looks like it's your lucky day,' said Daisy.

'How do you mean?'

'No birds around,' she said.

As she said it, Fat Charlie realised it was true. There were no pigeons, no starlings. Not even any sparrows.

'But there are *always* birds in Leicester Square.'

'Not today,' she said. 'Maybe they're busy.'

They stopped at the tube, and for one foolish moment Fat Charlie thought that she was going to kiss him goodbye. She didn't. She just smiled and said, 'Bless', and he half-waved at her, an uncertain hand-movement that might have been a wave and could as easily have been an involuntary gesture, and then she was down the stairs and out of sight.

Fat Charlie walked back across Leicester Square, heading for Piccadilly Circus.

He pulled out the fortune cookie slip from his pocket and uncrumpled it. 'Meet you by Eros,' it said, and next to that was a hasty little drawing of something that looked like large asterisk, and might, conceivably, have been a spider.

He scanned the skies and the buildings as he walked, but there were no birds, and that was strange because there were always birds in London. There were always birds everywhere.

Spider was sitting beneath the statue, reading the *News of the World*. He looked up as Fat Charlie approached.

'It's not actually Eros, you know,' said Fat Charlie. 'It's the statue of Christian Charity.'

'So why is it naked and holding a bow and arrow? That doesn't seem a particularly charitable or Christian thing to do.'

'I'm just telling you what I read,' said Fat Charlie. 'Where have you been? I was worried about you.'

'I'm all right. I've just been avoiding birds, trying to get my head around all this.'

'You've noticed there aren't any birds around today?' said Fat Charlie.

'I've noticed. I don't really know what to make of it. But I've been thinking. And you know,' said Spider, 'there's something wrong with this whole thing.'

'Everything, for a start,' said Fat Charlie.

'No. I mean there's something wrong with the Bird Woman trying to hurt us.'

'Yup. It's wrong. It's a very, very bad thing to do. Do you want to tell her, or shall I?'

'Not wrong like that. Wrong like – well, think about it. I mean, despite the Hitchcock film, birds aren't the best thing to hurt someone with. They may be death-on-wings for insects but they really aren't very good at attacking people. Millions of years of learning that, on the whole, people will probably eat you first. Their first instinct is to leave us alone.'

'Not all of them,' said Fat Charlie. 'Not vultures. Or ravens. But they only turn up on the battlefield, when the fighting's done. Waiting for you to die.'

'What?'

'I said, except for vultures and ravens. I didn't mean anything . . .'

'No.' Spider concentrated. 'No, it's gone. You made me think of something, and I almost had it. Look, have you got hold of Mrs Dunwiddy yet?'

'I phoned Mrs Higgler, but there isn't any answer.'

'Well, go and talk to them.'

'It's all very well for you to say that, but I'm skint. Broke. Cleaned out. I can't keep flying back and forwards across the Atlantic. I don't even have a job any longer. I'm—'

Spider reached into his black and scarlet jacket and pulled out a wallet. He took out a sheaf of notes in an assortment of currencies, pushed them into Fat Charlie's hand. 'Here. This should be enough to get you there and back. Just get the feather.'

Fat Charlie said, 'Listen. Has it occurred to you that maybe Dad isn't dead after all?'

'What?'

'Well, I was thinking. Maybe all this was one of his jokes. It feels like the kind of thing he'd do, doesn't it?'

Spider said, 'I don't know. Could be.'

Fat Charlie said, 'I'm sure it is. That's the first thing I'm going to do. I'm going to head down to his grave and—'

But he said nothing else, because that was when the birds came. They were city birds: sparrows and starlings, pigeons and crows, thousands upon thousands of them, and they wove and wound as they flew like a tapestry, forming a wall of birds coming towards Fat Charlie and Spider down Regent Street. A feathered phalanx huge as the side of a skyscraper, perfectly flat, perfectly impossible, all of it in motion weaving and fluttering and swooping; Fat Charlie saw it, but it would not fit inside his mind, slipping and twisting and thinning the whole time inside his head. He looked up at it and tried to make sense of what he was seeing.

Spider jerked at Fat Charlie's elbow. He shouted, 'Run!'

Fat Charlie turned to run. Spider was methodically folding his newspaper, putting it down on the bin.

'You run too!'

'It doesn't want *you*. Not yet,' said Spider, and he grinned. It was a grin that had, in its time, persuaded more people than you can imagine to do things they did not want to do; and Fat Charlie really wanted to run. 'Get the feather. Get Dad too, if you think he's still around. Just *go*.'

Fat Charlie went.

The wall of birds swirled and transformed, became a

whirlwind of birds, heading for the statue of Eros and the man beneath it. Fat Charlie ran into a doorway and watched as the base of the dark tornado slammed into Spider. Fat Charlie imagined he could hear his brother screaming over the deafening whirr of wings. Maybe he could.

And then the birds dispersed and the street was empty. The wind teased a handful of feathers along the grey pavement.

Fat Charlie stood there and felt sick. If any of the passers-by had noticed what had happened, they had not reacted. Somehow, he was certain that no one had seen it but him.

There was a woman standing beneath the statue, near where his brother had been. Her ragged brown coat flapped in the wind. Fat Charlie walked back to her. 'Look,' he said, 'when I said to make him go away, I meant just to get him out of my life. Not do whatever it is you've done to him.'

She looked into his face and said nothing. There is a madness in the eyes of some birds of prey, a ferocity that can be perfectly intimidating. Fat Charlie tried not to be intimidated by it. 'I made a mistake,' he said. 'I'm willing to pay for it. Take me instead. Bring him back.'

She continued to stare. Then she said, 'Do not doubt your turn shall come, Compé Anansi's child. In time.'

'Why do you want him?'

'I don't want him,' she told him. 'Why would I want him? I had an obligation to another. Now I shall deliver him, and then my obligation shall be done.'

The newspaper fluttered, and Fat Charlie was alone.

Chapter Eleven

In Which Rosie Learns to Say No to Strangers and Fat Charlie Acquires a Lime

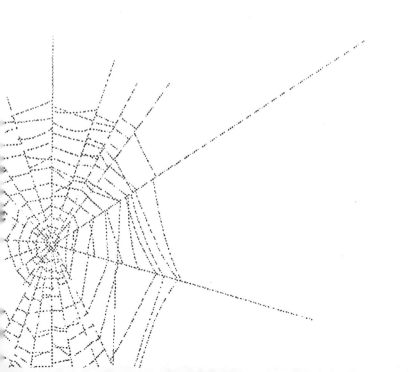

Fat Charlie looked down at his father's grave. 'Are you in there?' he said aloud. 'If you are, come out. I need to talk to you.'

He walked over to the floral grave marker and looked down. He was not certain what he was expecting – a hand to push up through the soil, perhaps, punching up and grabbing his leg – but nothing of the kind seemed to be about to happen.

He had been so certain.

Fat Charlie walked back through the Garden of Rest feeling stupid, like a game show contestant who had just made the mistake of betting his million dollars on the Mississippi being a longer river than the Amazon. He should have known. His father was as dead as roadkill, and he had wasted Spider's money on a wild-goose chase. By the windmills of Babyland he sat down and wept, and the mouldering toys seemed even sadder and lonelier than he remembered.

She was waiting for him in the parking lot, leaning against her car, smoking a cigarette. She looked uncomfortable.

'Hello, Mrs Bustamonte,' said Fat Charlie.

She took one final drag on the cigarette, then dropped it to the asphalt, and ground it out beneath the sole of her flat shoe. She was wearing black. She looked tired. 'Hello, Charles.'

'I think if I'd expected to see anyone here, it would be Mrs Higgler. Or Mrs Dunwiddy.'

'Callyanne's gone away. Mrs Dunwiddy sent me. She wants to see you.'

It's like the mafia, thought Fat Charlie. *A post-menopausal mafia.* 'She's going to make me an offer I can't refuse?'

'I doubt it. She is not very well.'

'Oh.'

He climbed into his rental, followed Mrs Bustamonte's Camry along the Florida streets. He had been so certain about his father. Certain he'd find him alive. Sure that he'd help . . .

They parked outside Mrs Dunwiddy's house. Fat Charlie looked at the front yard, at the faded plastic flamingos and the gnomes and the red mirrored gazing ball, like the one he had broken when he was a boy, sitting on a small concrete plinth like an enormous Christmas tree ornament. He walked over to the ball and saw himself, distorted, staring back from it.

'What's it for?' he said.

'It's not for anything. She liked it.'

Inside the house the smell of violets hung thick and cloying. Fat Charlie's Great Aunt Alanna had kept a tube of parma violet candies in her handbag, and, even as a chunky kid with a sweet tooth, Fat Charlie would eat them only if there wasn't anything else. This house smelled like those sweets had tasted. Fat Charlie hadn't thought of parma violets in twenty years. He wondered if they still made them. He wondered why anyone had ever made them in the first place . . .

'She's at the end of the hall,' said Mrs Bustamonte, and she stopped, and she pointed. Fat Charlie went into Mrs Dunwiddy's bedroom.

It was not a big bed, but Mrs Dunwiddy lay in it like an oversized doll. She wore her glasses, and above them something that Fat Charlie realised was the first nightcap he had ever seen, a yellowing tea-cosy-like affair, trimmed in lace. She was propped up on a mountain of pillows, her mouth open, and she was snoring gently as he walked in.

He coughed.

Mrs Dunwiddy jerked her head up, opened her eyes and stared at him. She pointed her finger to the nightstand beside the bed, and Fat Charlie picked up the glass of water sitting there and passed it to her. She took it with both hands, like a squirrel holding a nut, and she took a long sip before handing it back to him.

'My mouth get all dry,' she said. 'You know how old I am?'

'Um.' There was, he decided, no right answer. 'No.'

'Hunnert and four.'

'That's amazing. You're in such good shape. I mean, that's quite marvellous—'

'Shut up, Fat Charlie.'

'Sorry.'

'Don't say sorry like that neither, like a dog that get tell off for messin' on the kitchen floor. Hold your head up. Look the world in the eye. You hear me?'

'Yes. Sorry. I mean, just yes.'

She sighed. 'They want to take me to the hospital. I tell them, when you get to be hunnert and four, you earn the right to die in your own bed. I make babies in this bed long time back, and I birth babies in this bed, and damned if I going to die anywhere else. And another thing . . .' She stopped talking, closed her eyes and took a slow, deep breath. Just as Fat Charlie was convinced she had fallen asleep, her eyes opened and she said, 'Fat Charlie, if someone ever ask if you want to live to be hunnert and four, say no. Everything hurt. Everything. I hurt in places nobody ain't discover yet.'

'I'll bear that in mind.'

'None of your back talk.'

Fat Charlie looked at the little woman in her white wooden bed. 'Shall I say sorry?' he asked.

Mrs Dunwiddy looked away, guiltily. 'I do you wrong,' she said. 'Long time ago, I do you wrong.'

'I know,' said Fat Charlie.

Mrs Dunwiddy might have been dying, but she still shot Fat

Charlie the kind of look that would have sent children under the age of five screaming for their mothers. 'What you mean, you know?'

Fat Charlie said, 'I figured it out. Probably not all of it, but some of it. I'm not stupid.'

She examined him coldly through the thick glass of her spectacles, then she said, 'No. You not. True thing, that.'

She held out a gnarled hand. 'Give me the water back. That's better.' She sipped her water, dabbing at it with a small, purple tongue. 'Is a good thing you're here today. Tomorrow the whole house be fill with grievin' grandchildren and great-grandchildren, all of them tryin' to make me to die in the hospital, makin' up to me so I give them things. They don't know me. I outlive all my own children. Every one of them.'

Fat Charlie said, 'Are you going to talk about the bad turn you did to me?'

'You should never have break my garden mirror ball.'

'I'm sure I shouldn't.'

He remembered it, in the way you remember things from childhood, part memory, part memory of the memory: following the tennis ball into Mrs Dunwiddy's yard, and once he was there, experimentally picking up her mirrored ball to see his face in it, distorted and huge, feeling it tumble to the stone path, watching it smash into a thousand tiny shards of glass. He remembered the strong old fingers that grabbed him by the ear and dragged him out of her yard and into her house . . .

'You sent Spider away,' he said. 'Didn't you?'

Her jaw was set like a mechanical bulldog's. She nodded. 'I did a banishment,' she said. 'Didn't mean for it to go so. Everybody know a little magic back in those days. We didn't have all them kinda DVDs and cell phones and microwaves, but still, we know a lot regardless. I only wanted to teach you a lesson. You were so full of yourself, all mischief and back talk and vinegar. So I pull Spider out of you, to teach you a lesson.'

Fat Charlie heard the words, but they made no sense. 'You pulled him out?'

'I break him off from you. All the tricksiness. All the wickedness. All the devilry. All that.' She sighed. 'My mistake.

Nobody tell me that if you do magic around a, around people like your daddy's bloodline, it magnify everything. Everything get bigger.' Another sip of the water. 'Your mother never believe it. Not really. But that Spider, he worse than you. Your father never say nothing about it until I make Spider go away. Even then, all he tell me is if you can't fix it you not no son of his.'

He wanted to argue with her, to tell her how this was nonsense, that Spider was not a part of him, no more than he, Fat Charlie, was part of the sea or of the darkness. Instead, he said, 'Where's the feather?'

'What feather you talking about?'

'When I came back from that place. The place with the cliffs and the caves. I was holding a feather. What did you do with it?'

'I don't remember,' she said. 'I'm an old woman. I'm a hunnert and four.'

Fat Charlie said, 'Where is it?'

'I forget.'

'Please tell me.'

'I ain't got it.'

'Who does?'

'Callyanne.'

'Mrs Higgler?'

She leaned in, confidentially. 'The other two, they're just girls. They're flighty.'

'I called Mrs Higgler before I came out. I stopped at her house before I went to the cemetery. Mrs Bustamonte says she's gone away.'

Mrs Dunwiddy swayed gently from side to side in the bed, as if she were rocking herself to sleep. She said, 'I not going to be here for much longer. I stop eating solid food after you leave the last time. I done. Only water. Some women say they love your father, but I know him long long before them. Back when I had my looks, he would take me dancing. He come pick me up and whirl me around. He was an old man even then, but he always make a girl feel special. You don't feel . . .' She stopped, took another sip of water. Her hands were shaking. Fat Charlie took the empty glass from her. 'Hunnert and four,' she said. 'And never in my bed in the daytime except for confinements. And now I finish.'

'I'm sure you'll reach a hundred and five,' said Fat Charlie, uneasily.

'Don't you say that!' she said. She looked alarmed. *'Don't!* Your family do enough trouble already. Don't you go making things happen.'

'I'm not like my dad,' said Fat Charlie. 'I'm not magic. Spider got all that side of the family, remember?'

She did not appear to be listening. She said, 'When we would go dancing, way before the Second World War, your daddy would talk to the bandleader, and plenty times they call him up to sing with them. All the people laugh and cheer. Is so he make things happen. Singing.'

'Where is Mrs Higgler?'

'Gone home.'

'Her house is empty. Her car isn't there.'

'Gone home.'

'Er . . . you mean she's dead?'

The old woman on the white sheets wheezed and gasped for breath. She seemed unable to speak any longer. She motioned to him.

Fat Charlie said, 'Shall I get help?'

She nodded, and continued to gasp and choke and wheeze as he went out to find Mrs Bustamonte. She was sitting in the kitchen, watching Oprah on a very small countertop television. 'She wants you,' he said.

Mrs Bustamonte went out. She came back holding the empty water jug. 'What do you say to set her off like that?'

'Was she having an attack or something?'

Mrs Bustamonte gave him a look. 'No, Charles. She was laughing at you. She say you make her feel good.'

'Oh. She said Mrs Higgler had gone home. I asked if she meant she was dead.'

Mrs Bustamonte smiled, then. 'Saint Andrews,' she said. 'Callyanne's gone to Saint Andrews.' She refilled the jug in the sink.

Fat Charlie said, 'When all this started I thought that it was me against Spider, and you four were on my side. And now Spider's been taken, and it's me against the four of you.'

She turned off the water, and gazed at him sullenly.

'I don't believe anyone any more,' said Fat Charlie. 'Mrs Dunwiddy's probably faking being ill. Probably as soon as I leave here she'll be out of bed and doing the charleston around her bedroom.'

'She not eating. She say it makes her feel bad inside. Won't take a thing to fill her belly. Just water.'

'Where in Saint Andrews is she?' asked Fat Charlie.

'Just go,' said Mrs Bustamonte. 'Your family, you done enough harm here.'

Fat Charlie looked as if he was about to say something, and then he didn't, and he left without another word.

Mrs Bustamonte took the jug of water in to Mrs Dunwiddy, who lay quiet in the bed.

'Nancy's son hates us,' said Mrs Bustamonte. 'What you tell him anyhow?'

Mrs Dunwiddy said nothing. Mrs Bustamonte listened, and when she was sure that the older woman was still breathing, she took off Mrs Dunwiddy's thick spectacles, and put them down by the bed, then pulled up the sheet to cover Mrs Dunwiddy's shoulders.

After that, she simply waited for the end.

* * *

Fat Charlie drove off, not entirely certain where he was going. He had crossed the Atlantic for the third time in two weeks, and the money that Spider had given him was almost tapped out. He was alone in the car, and being alone, he hummed.

He passed a clutch of Jamaican restaurants when he noticed a sign in a storefront window: 'CUT PRICE TO THE ISLANDS'. He pulled up and went inside.

'We at A-One travel are here to serve all your travel needs,' said the travel agent, in the hushed and apologetic tone of voice doctors normally reserve for telling people that the limb in question is going to have to come off.

'Er. Yeah. Thanks. Er. What's the cheapest way to get out to Saint Andrews?'

'Will you be going on vacation?'

'Not really. I just want to go out for a day. Maybe two days.'

'Leaving when?'

'This afternoon.'

'You are, I take it, joshing with me.'

'Not at all.'

A computer screen was gazed at, lugubriously. A keyboard was tapped. 'It doesn't look like there's anything out there for less than 1200 dollars.'

'Oh.' Fat Charlie slumped.

More keyboard clicking. The man sniffed. 'That can't be right.' Then he said, 'Hold on.' A phone call, 'Is this rate still valid?' He jotted down some figures on a scratch pad. He looked up at Fat Charlie. 'If you could go out for a week, and stay at the Dolphin Hotel, I could get you a week's vacation for five hundred dollars, with your meals at the hotel thrown in. The flight will only cost you airport tax.'

Fat Charlie blinked. 'Is there a catch?'

'It's an island tourism promotion. Something to do with the music festival. I didn't think it was still going on. But then, you know what they say. You get what you pay for. And if you want to eat anywhere else it will cost you.'

Fat Charlie gave the man five crumpled hundred-dollar bills.

* * *

Daisy was starting to feel like the kind of cop you only ever see in movies: tough, hard-bitten, and perfectly ready to buck the system; the kind of cop who wants to know whether or not you feel lucky, or if you're interested in making his day, and particularly the kind of cop who says, 'I'm getting too old for this shit'. She was twenty-six years old, and she wanted to tell people she was too old for this shit. She was quite aware of how ridiculous this was, thank you very much.

At this moment, she was standing in Camberwell's office and saying, 'Yes, sir. Saint Andrew's.'

'Went there on my holidays some years back, with the former Mrs Camberwell. Very pleasant place. Rum cake.'

'That sounds like the place, sir. The closed-circuit footage from Gatwick is definitely him. Travelling under the name of Bronstein. Roger Bronstein flies to Miami, changes planes, and takes a connection to Saint Andrews.'

'You're sure it's him?'

'Sure.'

'Well,' said Camberwell. 'That buggers us good and proper, doesn't it? No extradition treaty.'

'There must be *something* we can do.'

'Mm. We can freeze his remaining accounts and grab his assets, and we will, and that'll be as much use to us as a water-soluble umbrella, because he'll have lots of cash sitting in places we can't find it or touch it.'

Daisy said, 'But that's *cheating*.'

He looked up at her as if he wasn't certain exactly what he was looking at. 'It's not a playground game of tag. If they kept the rules, they'd be on our side. If he comes back, then we arrest him.' He squashed a little Plasticine man into a Plasticine ball and began to mash it out into a flat sheet, pinching it between finger and thumb. 'In the old days,' he said, 'they could claim sanctuary in a church. If you stayed in the church the law couldn't touch you. Even if you killed a man. Of course, it limited your social life. Right.'

He looked at her as if he expected her to leave now. She said, 'He killed Maeve Livingstone. He's been cheating his clients blind for years.'

'And?'

'We should be bringing him to justice.'

'Don't let it get to you,' he said.

Daisy thought, *I'm getting too old for this shit*. She kept her mouth shut, and the words simply went round and round inside her head.

'Don't let it get to you,' he repeated. He folded the Plasticine sheet into a rough cube, then squeezed it viciously between finger and thumb. 'I don't let any of it get to me. Think of it as if you were a traffic warden. Grahame Coats is just a car that parked on the double yellow lines, but drove off before you were able to give him a ticket. Yes?'

'Sure,' said Daisy. 'Of course. Sorry.'

'Right,' he said.

She went back to her desk, went to the police internal website and examined her options for several hours. Finally, she went home. Carol was sitting in front of *Coronation Street*, eating a microwavable chicken korma.

'I'm taking a break,' said Daisy. 'I'm going on holiday.'

'You don't have any holiday time left,' pointed out Carol, reasonably.

'Too bad,' said Daisy. 'I'm too old for this shit.'

'Oh. Where are you going?'

'I'm going to catch a crook,' said Daisy.

* * *

Fat Charlie liked Caribbeair. They might have been an international airline, but they felt like a local bus company. The flight attendant called him 'darlin'' and told him jus' to sit anywhere that struck his fancy.

He stretched out across three seats, and went to sleep. In Fat Charlie's dream he was walking beneath copper skies and the world was silent and still. He was walking towards a bird vaster than cities, its eyes aflame, its beak agape, and Fat Charlie walked into the beak and down the creature's throat.

Then, in the way of dreams, he was in a room, its walls covered with soft feathers and with eyes, round like the eyes of owls, which did not blink.

Spider was in the centre of the room, his legs and arms extended. He was held up by chains made of bone, like the bones of a chicken's neck, and they ran from each corner of the room, and held him tightly, like a fly in a web.

Oh, said Spider. *It's you.*

Yes, said Fat Charlie in his dream.

The bone-chains pulled and tugged at Spider's flesh, and Fat Charlie could see the pain in his face.

Well, said Fat Charlie. *I suppose it could be worse.*

I don't think this is it, said his brother. *I think she has plans for me. Plans for us. I just don't know what they are.*

They're only birds, said Fat Charlie. *How bad could it be?*
Ever heard of Prometheus?
Er . . .
Gave fire to man. Was punished by the gods by being chained to a rock. Every day an eagle would come down and tear out his liver.
Didn't he ever run out of liver?
He grew a new one every day. It's a god thing.
There was a pause. The two brothers stared at each other.
I'll sort it out, said Fat Charlie. *I'll fix it.*
Just like you fixed the rest of your life, I suppose? Spider grinned, without mirth.
I'm sorry.
No. I'm sorry. Spider sighed. *So look, have you got a plan?*
A plan?
I'll take that as a no. Just do whatever you have to do. Get me out of here.
Are you in Hell?
I don't know where I am. If it's anywhere, this is the Hell of Birds. You have to get me out.
How?
You're Dad's son, aren't you? You're my brother. Come up with something. Just get me out of here.
Fat Charlie woke, shivering. The flight attendant brought him coffee, and he drank it gratefully. He was awake, now, and he had no desire to go back to sleep, so he read the Caribbeair magazine and learned many useful things about Saint Andrews.

He learned that Saint Andrews is not the smallest of the Caribbean Islands, but it tends to be one of the ones that people forget about, when they make lists. It was discovered by the Spanish around 1500, an uninhabited volcanic hill teeming with animal-life, not to mention a multiplicity of plants. It was said that anything that you planted on Saint Andrews would grow.

It belonged to the Spanish, and then to British, then to the Dutch, then to the British again, and then, for a short while after it was made independent in 1962, it belonged to Major F. E. Garrett, who took over the government, broke off diplomatic relations with all other countries except Albania and the Congo, and ruled the country with a rod of iron until his unfortunate death from falling out of bed several years later. He fell out of bed hard enough to break a number of bones, despite the presence in his bedroom of an entire squad of soldiers, who testified that they had all tried, but failed, to break Major Garrett's fall; and despite their best efforts he was dead by the time that he arrived in the island's sole hospital. Since then, Saint Andrews had been ruled by a beneficent and elected local government, and was everybody's friend.

It had miles of sandy beaches and an extremely small rainforest in the centre of the island; it had bananas and sugar cane, a banking system that encouraged foreign investment and off-shore corporate banking, and no extradition treaties with anybody at all, except possibly the Congo and Albania.

If Saint Andrews was known for anything, it was for its cuisine: the inhabitants claimed to have been jerking chickens before the Jamaicans, currying goats before the Trinidadians, frying flying fish before the Bajans.

There were two towns on Saint Andrews – Williamstown, on the southeast side of the island, and Newcastle, on the north. There were street markets in which anything that grew on the island could be bought, and several supermarkets, in which the same foodstuffs could be bought for twice the price. One day Saint Andrews would get a real international airport.

It was a matter of opinion whether the deep harbour of Williamstown was a good thing or not. It was indisputable that the deep harbour brought the cruise ships, though, floating islands filled with people, who were changing the economy and nature of Saint Andrews as they were changing the economy of many Caribbean islands. At high season there would be up to half a dozen cruise ships in Williamstown Bay, and thousands of people waiting to disembark, to stretch their legs, to buy things. And the people of Saint Andrews grumbled, but they welcomed the visitors ashore, they sold them things, they fed them until they could eat no more and then they sent them back to their ships . . .

The Caribbeair plane landed with a bump that made Fat Charlie drop his magazine. He put it back into the seat pocket in front of him, walked down the steps and across the tarmac.

It was late afternoon.

Fat Charlie took a taxi from the airport to his hotel. During the taxi ride, he learned a number of things that had not been mentioned in the Caribbeair magazine.

For example, he learned that music, real music, proper music, was country-and-western music. On Saint Andrews, even the rastas knew it. Johnny Cash? He was a god. Willie Nelson? A demi-god.

He learned that there was no reason ever to leave Saint Andrews. The taxi driver himself had seen no reason ever to leave Saint Andrews, and he had given it much thought. The island had a cave, and a mountain, and a rainforest. Hotels? It had twenty. Restaurants? Several dozen. It contained a city, three towns and a scattering of villages. Food? Everything grew here. Oranges. Bananas. Nutmegs. It even, the taxi driver said, had limes.

Fat Charlie said 'No!' at this, mostly in order to feel like he was taking part in the conversation, but the driver appeared to take it as a challenge to his honesty. He slammed on the taxi's brakes, sending the car slewing over to the side of the road, got out of the car, reached over a fence, pulled something from a tree and walked back to the car.

'Look at this!' he said. 'Nobody ever tell you that I is a liar. What it is?'

'A lime?' said Fat Charlie.

'Exactly.'

The taxi driver lurched the car back into the road. He told Fat Charlie that the Dolphin was an excellent hotel. Did Fat Charlie have family on the island? Did he know anyone here?

'Actually,' said Fat Charlie, 'I'm here looking for someone. For a woman.'

The taxi driver thought this was a splendid idea, since Saint Andrews was a perfect place to come if you were looking for a woman. This was, he elaborated, because the women of Saint Andrews were curvier than the women of Jamaica, and less likely to give you grief and heartbreak than the Trinis. In addition, they were more beautiful than the women of Dominica, and they were better cooks than you would find anywhere on Earth.

If Fat Charlie was looking for a woman, he had come to the right place.

'It's not just any woman. It's a specific woman,' said Fat Charlie.

The taxi driver told Fat Charlie that this was his lucky day, for the taxi driver prided himself on knowing everyone on the Island. If you spend your life somewhere, he said, you can do that. He was willing to bet that Fat Charlie did not know by sight all the people in England, and Fat Charlie admitted that this was in fact the case.

'She's a friend of the family,' said Fat Charlie. 'Her name is Mrs Higgler. Callyanne Higgler. You heard of her?'

The taxi driver was quiet for a while. He seemed to be thinking. Then he said that, no, he hadn't ever heard of her. The taxi pulled up in front of the Dolphin Hotel, and Fat Charlie paid him.

Fat Charlie went inside. There was a young woman on reception. He showed her his passport, and the reservation number. He put the lime down on the reservation desk.

'Do you have any luggage?'

'No,' said Fat Charlie, apologetically.

'Nothing?'

'Nothing. Just this lime.'

He filled out several forms, and she gave him a key and directions to his room.

Fat Charlie was in the bath when a knock came on the door. He wrapped a towel around his midriff. It was the bellman. 'You left your lime in reception,' he said, and handed it to Fat Charlie.

'Thanks,' said Fat Charlie. He went back to his bath. Afterward, he went to bed, and dreamed uncomfortable dreams.

***

In his house on the clifftop, Grahame Coats was also having the strangest dreams, dark and unwelcome, if not actually unpleasant. He could not remember them properly when he woke, but he would open his eyes the next morning with a vague impression that he had spent the night stalking smaller creatures through the long grass, dispatching them with a blow of his paw, rending their bodies with his teeth.

In his dreams, his teeth were weapons of destruction.

He woke from the dreams feeling disturbed, with the day slightly charged.

And, each morning, a new day would begin and here, only a week away from his old life, Grahame Coats was already experiencing the frustration of the fugitive. He had a swimming pool, true, and cocoa trees and grapefruit and nutmeg trees; he had a full wine cellar and an empty meat cellar and a media centre. He had satellite television, a large DVD collection, not to mention art, thousands of dollars worth of art, all over the walls. He had a cook, who came in each day and cooked his meals, a housekeeper and a groundskeeper (a married couple who came in for a few hours each day). The food was excellent, the climate was, if you liked warm sunny days, perfect, and none of these things made Grahame Coats as happy as he felt was his due.

He had not shaved since leaving England, which had not yet endowed him with a beard, merely given him a thin covering of the kind of facial hair that makes men look shifty. His eyes sat in panda-dark sockets, and the bags beneath his eyes were so dark as to appear to be bruises.

He swam in the pool once each day, in the morning, but otherwise avoided the sun; he had not, he told himself, amassed an ill-gotten fortune to lose it to skin cancer. Or to anything else at all.

He thought about London too much. In London, each of his favourite restaurants had a maître d' who called him by name and ensured he left happy. In London there were people who owed him favours, and there was never any difficulty in getting first-night tickets, and for that matter in London there were theatres to have first nights in. He had always thought he would make a fine exile; he was starting to suspect that he had been wrong.

Needing someone to blame, he came to the conclusion that the entire affair was Maeve Livingstone's fault. She had led him on. She had attempted to rob him. She was a vixen, a minx, and a hussy. She had deserved everything she had coming to her. She had gotten off easily. Should he be interviewed on television, he could already hear the bruised innocence in his voice as he explained that he had been defending his property and his honour from a dangerous madwoman. Frankly, it was some kind of miracle that he'd made it out of that office alive . . .

And he had liked being Grahame Coats. He was now, as always while he was on the island, Basil Finnegan, and it irked him. He didn't feel like a Basil. His Basilhood had been hard-won – the original Basil had died as an infant, and had a birthdate close to Grahame's own. One copy of the birth certificate, along with a letter from an imaginary clergyman, later, and Grahame possessed a passport and an identity. He had kept the identity alive – Basil had a solid credit history, Basil travelled to exotic places, Basil had bought a luxury house on Saint Andrews without ever seeing it. But in Grahame's mind, Basil had been working for him, and now the servant had become the master. Basil Finnegan had eaten him alive.

'If I stay here,' said Grahame Coats, 'I shall go mad.'

'What you say?' asked the housekeeper, duster in hand, leaning in at the bedroom door.

'Nothing,' said Grahame Coats.

'Sound like you say if you stay in you go mad. You ought to go for a walk. Walking good for you.'

Grahame Coats did not go for walks; he had people to do that for him. But, he thought, perhaps Basil Finnegan went for walks. He put on a broad-brimmed hat, and exchanged his sandals for walking shoes. He took his mobile phone, instructed the groundskeeper to come and get him when he called, and set out from the house on the cliff-edge, heading towards the nearest town.

It is a small world. You do not have to live in it particularly long to learn that for yourself. There is a theory that, in the whole world, there are only five hundred real people (the cast, as it were. All the rest of the people in the world, the theory suggests, are extras), and what is more, they all know each other. And it's true, or true as far as it goes. In reality the world is made of thousands upon thousands of groups of about five hundred people, all of whom will spend their lives bumping into each other, trying to avoid each other, and discovering each other in the same unlikely teashop in Vancouver. There is an unavoidability to this process. It's not even coincidence. It's just the way the world works, with no regard for individuals or for propriety.

So it was that Grahame Coats walked into a small café on the road to Williamstown, in order to purchase a soft drink, and to have somewhere to sit while he called his gardener to tell him that he should come and pick him up.

He ordered a Fanta and sat down at a table. The place was practically empty: two women, one young, one older, sat in the far corner, drinking coffee and writing postcards.

Grahame Coats gazed out, across the road, at the beach. It was paradise, he thought. And it might behove him to get more deeply involved with local politics – perhaps as a sponsor of the arts. He had already made several substantial donations to the island's police force, and it might even become necessary to make sure that . . .

A voice from behind him, thrilled and tentative, said, 'Mr Coats?' and his heart lurched. The younger of the women sat down beside him. She had the warmest smile.

'Fancy running into you here,' she said. 'You on your holidays too?'

'Something like that.' He had no idea who this woman was.

'You remember me, don't you? Rosie Noah. I used to go out with Fat, with Charlie Nancy. Yes?'

'Hello. Rosie. Yes, of course.'

'I'm on a cruise, with my mum. She's still writing postcards home.'

Grahame Coats glanced back over his shoulder, to the back of the little café, and something resembling a South American mummy in a floral dress glared back at him.

'Honestly,' continued Rosie, 'I'm not really a cruise sort of person. Ten days of going from island to island. It's nice to see a familiar face, isn't it?'

'Absatively,' said Grahame Coats. 'Should I take it that you and our Charles are no longer, well, an item?'

'Yes,' she said. 'I suppose you should. I mean, we're not.'

Grahame Coats smiled sympathetically on the outside. He picked up his Fanta and walked, with Rosie, to the table in the corner. Rosie's mother radiated ill will just as an old iron radiator can radiate chill into a room, but Grahame Coats was perfectly charming and entirely helpful, and he agreed with her on every point. It was indeed appalling what the cruise companies thought they could get away with these days; it was disgusting how sloppy the administration of the cruise ship had been allowed to get; it was shocking how little there was to do in the islands; and it was, in every respect, outrageous what passengers were expected to put up with: ten days without a bathtub, with only the tiniest of shower facilities. Shocking.

Rosie's mother told him about the several quite impressive enmities she had managed to cultivate with certain American passengers whose main crime, as Grahame Coats understood it, was to overload their plates in the buffet line of the *Squeak Attack*, and to sunbathe in the spot by the aft deck pool that Rosie's mother had decided, on the first day out, was undisputedly hers.

Grahame Coats nodded, and made sympathetic noises as the vitriol dripped over him, *tch*ing and agreeing and clucking, until Rosie's mother was prepared to overlook her dislike both of strangers and people connected in some way to Fat Charlie, and she talked, and she talked, and she talked. Grahame Coats was barely listening. Grahame Coats pondered.

It would be unfortunate, Grahame Coats was thinking, if someone was to return to London at this precise point in time and inform the authorities that Grahame Coats had been encountered in Saint Andrews. It was inevitable that he would be noticed one day, but still, the inevitable could, perhaps, be postponed.

'Let me,' said Grahame Coats, 'suggest a solution to at least one of your problems. A little way up the road I have a holiday house. Rather a nice house, I like to think. And if there's one thing I have a surplus of, it's baths. Would you care to come back and indulge yourselves?'

'No, thanks,' said Rosie. Had she agreed, it is to be expected that her mother would have pointed out that they were due back at the Williamstown Port for pick-up later that afternoon, and would then have chided Rosie for accepting such invitations from virtual strangers. But Rosie said no.

'That is extremely kind of you,' said Rosie's mother. 'We would be delighted.'

The gardener pulled up outside soon after, in a black Mercedes, and Grahame Coats opened the back door for Rosie and her mother. He assured them he would absatively have them back in the harbour well before the last boat back to their ship.

'Where to, Mr Finnegan?' asked the gardener.

'Home,' he said.

'Mr Finnegan?' asked Rosie.

'It's an old family name,' said Grahame Coats, and he was sure it was. Somebody's family anyway. He closed the back door, and went around to the front.

* * *

Maeve Livingtone was lost. It had started out so well: she had wanted to be at home, in Pontefract, and there was a shimmer and a tremendous wind, and in one ectoplasmic gusting, she was home. She wandered around the house for one last time, then went out into the autumn day. She wanted to see her sister in Rye, and before she could think, there she was there in the garden at Rye, watching her sister walking her springer spaniel.

It had seemed so easy.

That was the point she had decided that she wanted to see Grahame Coats, and that was where it had all gone wrong. She was, momentarily, back in the office in the Aldwych, and then in an empty house in Purley, which she remembered from a small dinner party Grahame Coats had hosted a decade back, and then . . .

Then she was lost. And everywhere she tried to go only made matters worse.

She had no idea where she was now. It seemed to be some kind of garden.

A brief downpour of rain drenched the place and left her untouched. Now the ground was steaming, and she knew she wasn't in England. It was starting to get dark.

She sat down on the ground, and she started to sniffle.

Honestly, she told herself. *Maeve Livingstone. Pull yourself together.* But the sniffling just got worse.

'You want a tissue?' asked someone.

Maeve looked up. An elderly gentleman with a green hat and a pencil-thin moustache was offering her a tissue.

She nodded. Then she said, 'It's probably not any use, though. I won't be able to touch it.'

He smiled sympathetically and passed her the tissue. It didn't fall through her fingers, so she blew her nose with it, and dabbed at her eyes. 'Thank you. Sorry about that. It all got a bit much.'

'It happens,' said the man. He looked her up and down, appraisingly. 'What are you? A duppy?'

'No,' she said. 'I don't think so . . . What's a duppy?'

'A ghost,' he said. With his pencil moustache, he reminded her of Cab Calloway, perhaps, or Don Ameche, one of those stars who aged but never stopped being stars. Whoever the old man was, he was still a star.

'Oh. Right. Yes, I'm one of them. Um. You?'

'More or less,' he said. 'I'm dead, anyway.'

'Oh. Would you mind if I asked where I was?'

'We're in Florida.' he told her. 'In the buryin' ground. It's good you caught me,' he added. 'I was going for a walk. You want to come along?'

'Shouldn't you be in a grave?' she asked, hesitantly.

'I was bored,' he told her. 'I thought I could do with a walk. And maybe a spot of fishin'.'

She hesitated, then nodded. It was nice to have someone to talk to.

'You want to hear a story?' asked the old man.

'Not really,' she admitted.

He helped her to her feet, and they walked out of the Garden of Rest.

'Fair enough. Then I'll keep it short. Not go on too long. You know, I can tell one of these stories so it lasts for weeks. It's all in the details – what you put in, what you don't. I mean, you leave out the weather and what people are wearing, you can skip half the story. I once told a story—'

'Look,' she said, 'if you're going to tell a story, then just tell it to me, all right?' It was bad enough walking along the side of the road, in the gathering dusk. She reminded herself that she wasn't going to be hit by a passing car, but it did nothing to make her feel more at ease.

The old man started to talk, in a gentle sing-song. 'When I say Tiger,' he said, 'you got to understand it's not just the stripy cat, the India one. It's just what people call big cats – the pumas and the bobcats and the jaguars and all of them. You got that?'

'Certainly.'

'Good. So . . . a long time ago,' he began, 'Tiger had the stories. All the stories there ever were was Tiger stories, all the songs were Tiger songs, and I'd say that all the jokes were Tiger jokes, but there weren't no jokes told back in the Tiger days. In Tiger stories all that matters is how strong your teeth are, how you hunt and how you kill. Ain't no gentleness in Tiger stories, no tricksiness, and no peace.'

Maeve tried to imagine what kind of stories a big cat might tell. 'So they were violent?'

'Sometimes. But mostly what they was, was bad. When all the stories and the songs were Tiger's, that was a bad time for everyone. People take on the shapes of the songs and the stories that surround them, especially if they don't have their own song. And in Tiger times all the songs were dark. They began in tears, and they'd end in blood, and they were the only stories that the people of this world knew.

'Then Anansi comes along. Now, I guess you know all about Anansi—'

'I don't think so,' said Maeve.

'Well, if I started to tell you how clever and how handsome and how charming and how cunning Anansi was, I could start today and not finish until next Thursday,' began the old man.

'Then don't,' said Maeve. 'We'll take it as said. And what did this Anansi do?'

'Well, Anansi won the stories – won them? No. He *earned* them. He took them from Tiger, and made it so Tiger couldn't enter the real world no more. Not in the flesh. The stories people told became Anansi stories. This was, what, ten, fifteen thousand years back.

'Now, Anansi stories, they have wit and trickery and wisdom. So, all over the world, all of the people, they aren't just thinking of hunting and being hunted any more. Now they're starting to *think* their way out of problems – sometimes thinking their way into worse problems. They still need to keep their bellies full, but now they're trying to figure out how to do it without working – and *that's* the point where people start using their heads. Some people think the first tools were weapons, but that's all upside down. First of all, people figure out the tools. It's the crutch before the club, every time. Because now people are telling Anansi stories, and they're starting to think about how to get kissed, how to get something for nothing by being smarter or funnier. That's when they start to make the world.'

'It's just a folk story,' she said. 'People made up the stories in the first place.'

'Does that change things?' asked the old man. 'Maybe Anansi's just some guy from a story, made up back in Africa in the dawn days of the world by some boy with blackfly on his leg, pushing his crutch in the dirt, making up some goofy story about a man made of tar. Does that change anything? People respond to the stories. They tell them themselves. The stories spread, and as people tell them, the stories change the tellers. Because now the folk who never had any thought in their head but how to run from lions and keep far enough away from rivers that the crocodiles don't get an easy meal, now they're starting to dream about a whole new place to live. The world may be the same, but the wallpaper's changed. Yes? People still have the same story, the one where they get born and they do stuff and they die, but now the story means something different to what it meant before.'

'You're telling me that before the Anansi stories the world was savage and bad?'

'Yeah. Pretty much.'

She digested this. 'Well,' she said cheerily, 'it's certainly a good thing that the stories are now Anansi's.'

The old man nodded.

And then she said, 'Doesn't Tiger want them back?'

He nodded. 'He's wanted them back for ten thousand years.'

'But he won't get them, will he?'

The old man said nothing. He stared into the distance. Then he shrugged. 'Be a bad thing if he did.'

'What about Anansi?'

'Anansi's dead,' said the old man. 'And there ain't a lot a duppy can do.'

'As a duppy myself,' she said, 'I resent that.'

'Well,' said the old man, 'duppies can't touch the living. Remember?'

She pondered this a moment. 'So what can I touch?' she asked.

The look that flickered across his elderly face was both wily and wicked. 'I guess,' he said, 'you could touch me.'

'I'll have you know,' she told him, mock-offended, 'that I'm a married woman.'

His smile only grew wider. It was a sweet smile now, and a gentle one, as heartwarming as it was dangerous. 'Generally speaking, that kind of contract terminates in a *till death us do part.*'

Maeve was unimpressed.

'Thing is,' he told her, 'you're an immaterial girl. You can touch immaterial things. Like me. I mean, if you want, we could go dancing. There's a place just down the street here. Won't nobody notice a couple of duppies on their dance floor.'

Maeve thought about it. It had been a long time since she had gone dancing. 'Are you a good dancer?' she asked.

'I've never had any complaints,' said the old man.

'I want to find a man – a living man – called Grahame Coats,' she said. 'Can you help me find him?'

'I can certainly steer you in the right direction,' he said. 'So, are you dancing?'

A smile crept about the edges of her lips. 'You asking?' she said.

* * *

The chains that had kept Spider captive fell away. The pain, which had been searing and continuous, like a bad toothache that occupied his entire body, began to pass.

Spider took a step forward.

In front of him was what appeared to be a rip in the sky, and he moved towards it.

Ahead of him he could see an island. He could see a small

mountain in the centre of the island. He could see a pure blue sky, and swaying palm trees, a white gull high in the sky. But even as he saw it the world seemed to be receding. It was as if he was looking at it through the wrong end of a telescope. It shrank and slipped from him, and the more he ran towards it the further away it seemed to get.

The island was a reflection in a puddle of water, and then it was nothing at all.

He was in a cave. The edges of things were crisp – crisper and sharper than anywhere that Spider had ever been before. This was a different kind of place.

She was standing in the mouth of the cave, between him and the open air. He knew her. She had stared into his face in a Greek restaurant in South London, and birds had come from her mouth.

'You know,' said Spider, 'I have to say, you've got the strangest ideas about hospitality. You come to my world, I'd make you dinner, open a bottle of wine, put on some soft music, give you an evening you would never forget.'

Her face was impassive; carved from black rock it was. The wind tugged at the edges of her old brown coat. She spoke then, her voice high and lonely as the call of a distant gull.

'I took you,' she said. 'Now, you will call him.'

'Call him? Call who?'

'You will bleat,' she said. 'You will whimper. Your fear will excite him.'

'Spider does not bleat,' he said. He was not certain this was true.

Eyes as black and as shiny as chips of obsidian stared back into his. They were eyes like black holes, letting nothing out, not even information.

'If you kill me,' said Spider, 'my curse will be upon you.' He wondered if he actually had a curse. He probably did; and if he didn't, he was sure that he could fake it.

'It will not be I that kills you,' she said. She raised her hand, and it was not a hand but a raptor's talon. She raked her talon down his face, down his chest, her cruel claws sinking into his flesh, tearing his skin.

It did not hurt, although Spider knew that it would hurt soon enough.

Beads of blood crimsoned his chest and dripped down his face. His eyes stung. His blood touched his lips. He could taste it and smell the iron scent of it.

'Now,' she said in the cries of distant birds. 'Now your death begins.'

Spider said, 'We're both reasonable entities. Let me present you with a perhaps rather more feasible alternative scenario that might conceivably have benefits for both of us.' He said it with an easy smile. He said it convincingly.

'You talk too much,' she said, and shook her head. 'No more talking.'

Then she reached into his mouth with her sharp talons, and with one wrenching movement she tore out his tongue.

'There,' she said. And then she seemed to take pity on him, for she touched Spider's face in a way that was almost kindly, and she said, 'Sleep.'

He slept.

* * *

Rosie's mother, now bathed, reappeared refreshed, invigorated and positively glowing.

'Before I give you both a ride into Williamstown, can I give you a hasty guided tour of the house?' asked Grahame Coats.

'We do have to get back to the ship, thanks all the same,' said Rosie, who had not been able to convince herself that she wanted a bath in Grahame Coats's house.

Her mother checked her watch. 'We have ninety minutes,' she said. 'It won't take more than fifteen minutes to get back to the harbour. Don't be ungracious, Rosie. We would love to see your house.'

So Grahame Coats showed them the sitting room, the study, the library, the television room, the dining room, the kitchen and the swimming pool. He opened a door beneath the kitchen stairs that looked as if it would lead to a broom cupboard, and walked his guests down the wooden steps into the rock-walled wine cellar.

He showed them the wine, most of which had come with the house when he had bought it. He walked them to the far end of the wine cellar, to the bare room that had, back in the days before refrigeration, been a meat-storage locker. It was always chilly in the meat locker, where heavy chains came down from the ceiling, the empty hooks on the ends showing where once whole carcasses had hung long before. Grahame Coats held the heavy iron door open politely while both the women walked inside.

'You know,' he said, helpfully, 'I've just realised. The light switch is back where we came in. Hold on.' And then he slammed the door behind the women, and he rammed closed the bolts.

He picked out a dusty-looking bottle of 1995 Chablis Premier Cru from a wine rack.

He went upstairs with a swing in his step, and let his three employees know that he would be giving them the week off.

It seemed to him, as he walked up the stairs to his study, as if something were padding soundlessly behind him, but when he turned there was nothing there. Oddly, he found this comforting. He found a corkscrew, opened the bottle and poured himself a pale glass of wine. He drank it and, although he had never previously had much time for red wines, he found himself wishing that what he was drinking was richer and darker. *It should be*, he thought, *the colour of blood*.

As he finished his second glass of Chablis, he realised that he had been blaming the wrong person for his plight. Maeve Livingstone was, he saw it now, merely a dupe. No, the person to blame, obviously and undeniably, was Fat Charlie. Without his meddling, without his criminal trespass into Grahame Coats's office computer systems, Grahame Coats wouldn't be here, an exile, like a blond Napoleon on a perfect, sunny Elba. He wouldn't be in the unfortunate predicament of having two women imprisoned in his meat locker. *If Fat Charlie was here*, he thought, *I would tear out his throat with my teeth*, and the thought shocked him even as it excited him. You didn't want to screw with Grahame Coats.

Evening came, and Grahame Coats watched the *Squeak Attack* from his window as it drifted past his house on the cliff and off into the sunset. He wondered how long it would take them to notice that two passengers were missing. He even waved.

Chapter Twelve

In Which Fat Charlie Does Several Things for the First Time

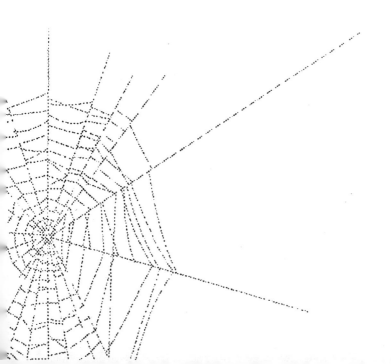

The Dolphin Hotel had a concierge. He was young and bespectacled, and he was reading a paperback novel with a rose and a gun on the cover.

'I'm trying to find someone,' said Fat Charlie. 'On the island.'

'Who?'

'A lady named Callyanne Higgler. She's here from Florida. She's an old friend of my family.'

The young man closed his book thoughtfully, then he looked at Fat Charlie through narrowed eyes. When people do this in paperback books it gives an immediate impression of dangerous alertness, but in reality it just made the young man look like he was trying not to fall asleep. He said, 'Are you the man with the lime?'

'What?'

'The man with the lime?'

'Yes, I suppose I am.'

'Lemme see it, nuh?'

'My lime?'

The young man nodded, gravely.

'No, you can't. It's back in my room.'

'But you *are* the man with the lime?'

'Can you help me find Mrs Higgler? Are there any Higglers on the island? Do you have a phone book I could look at? I was hoping for a phone book in my bedroom.'

'It's a kinda common name, you know?' said the young man. 'The phone book not going to help.'

'How common could it be?'

'Well,' said the young man, 'for example, I'm Benjamin Higgler. She over there, on reception, she name Amerila Higgler.'

'Oh. Right. Lots of Higglers on the island. I see.'

'She on the island for the music festival?'

'What?'

'It going on all this week.' He handed Fat Charlie a leaflet, informing him that Willie Nelson (cancelled) would be headlining the Saint Andrews Music Festival.

'Why'd he cancel?'

'Same reason Garth Brooks cancel. Nobody tell them it was happening in the first place.'

'I don't think she's going to the music festival. I really need to track her down. She's got something I'm looking for. Look, if you were me, how would you go about looking for her?'

Benjamin Higgler reached into a desk drawer and pulled out a map of the island. 'We're here, just south of Williamstown . . .' he began, making a felt-pen mark on the paper. From there, he began marking out a plan of campaign for Fat Charlie: he divided the island into segments that could easily be covered in a day by a man on a bicycle, marked out each rum-shop and café with small crosses. He put a circle beside each tourist attraction.

Then he rented Fat Charlie a bicycle.

Fat Charlie pedalled off to the south.

There were information conduits on Saint Andrews that Fat Charlie, who, on some level believed that coconut palms and cellular telephones ought to be mutually exclusive, had not expected. It did not seem to make any difference who he talked to: old men playing draughts in the shade; women with breasts like watermelons and buttocks like armchairs and laughter like mockingbirds; a sensible young lady in the tourist office; a bearded rasta with a Jamaica-coloured knit cap and what appeared to be a woollen miniskirt: they all had the same response.

'You the one with the lime?'

'I suppose so.'

'Show us your lime.'

'It's back at the hotel. Look, I'm trying to find Callyanne Higgler. She's about sixty. American. Big mug of coffee in her hand.'

'Never heard of her.'

Bicycling around the island, Fat Charlie soon discovered, had its dangers. The chief mode of transportation on the island was the minibus: unlicensed, unsafe, always overfilled, the minibuses hurtled around the island tooting and squealing their brakes, slamming around corners on two wheels whilst relying on the weight of their passengers to ensure they never tipped over. Fat Charlie would have been killed a dozen times on his first morning out were it not for the low thud of drum and bass being played over each bus's sound system: he could feel them in the pit of his stomach even before he heard their engines, and he had plenty of time to wheel the bicycle over to the side of the road.

While none of the people he spoke to were exactly what you could call helpful, they were still all extremely friendly. Fat Charlie stopped several times on his day's expedition to the south and refilled his water bottle: he stopped at cafés and at private houses. Everyone was so pleased to see him, even if they didn't know anything about Mrs Higgler. He got back to the Dolphin Hotel in time for dinner.

On the following day he went north. On his way back to Williamstown, in the late afternoon, he stopped on a clifftop, dismounted and walked his bike down to the entry gate of a luxurious house that sat on its own, overlooking the bay. He pressed the speakerphone button, said hello, but no one replied. A large black car sat in the driveway. Fat Charlie wondered if perhaps the place was deserted, but a curtain twitched in an upper room.

He pressed the button again. 'Hullo,' he said. 'Just wanted to see if I could fill my water bottle here.'

There was no reply. Perhaps he had only imagined that there was someone at the window. He seemed extremely prone to imagining things here: he started to fancy that he was being watched, not by someone in the house, but by someone or something in the bushes that bordered the road. 'Sorry to have bothered you,' he said into the speaker, and clambered back on to his bike. It was downhill from here all the way to Williamstown. He was sure that he'd pass a café or two on the way, or another house, a friendly one.

He was on his way down the road – the cliffs had become a steepish hill down to the sea – when a black car came up behind him, and accelerated forward with a roar. Too late, Fat Charlie realised that the driver had not seen him, for there was a long scrape of car against the bike's handlebar, and Fat Charlie found himself tumbling, with the bike, down the hill. The black car drove on.

Fat Charlie picked himself up halfway down the hill. 'That could have been nasty,' he said aloud. The handlebars were twisted. He hauled his bike back up the hill and on to the road. A low bass rumble alerted him to the approach of a minibus, and he waved it down.

'Can I put my bike in the back?'

'No room,' said the driver, but he produced several bungee cords from beneath his seat, and used them to fasten the bike on to the roof of the bus. Then he grinned. 'You must be the Englishman with the lime.'

'I don't have it on me. It's back at the hotel.'

Fat Charlie squeezed on to the bus, where the booming bass resolved itself, extremely improbably, into Deep Purple's 'Smoke on the Water'. Fat Charlie squeezed in next to a large woman with a chicken on her lap. Behind them two white girls chattered about the parties they had attended the previous night and the shortcomings of the temporary boyfriends they had accumulated during their holiday.

Fat Charlie noticed the black car – a Mercedes – as it came back up the road. It had a long scratch along one side. He felt guilty, hoped his bike hadn't scraped the paintwork too badly. The windows were tinted so dark that the car might have been driving itself . . .

Then one of the white girls tapped Fat Charlie on the shoulder and asked him if he knew of any good parties on the island that night, and when he said he didn't, started telling him about one that she'd been to in a cave two nights before, where there was a swimming pool and a sound system and lights and everyfink, and so Fat Charlie completely failed to notice that the black Mercedes was now following the minibus into Williamstown, and that it only went on its way once Fat Charlie had retrieved his bike from the roof of the minibus ('next time, you should bring the lime') and carried the bike into the hotel lobby.

Only then did the car return to the house on the clifftop.

Benjamin the concierge examined the bike and told Fat Charlie not to worry, and they'd have it all fixed and good as new by tomorrow.

Fat Charlie went back to his hotel room, the colour of underwater, where his lime sat, like a small green Buddha, on the countertop.

'You're no help,' he told the lime. This was unfair. It was only a lime; there was nothing special about it at all. It was doing the best it could.

***

Stories are webs, interconnected, strand to strand, and you follow each story to the centre, because the centre is the end. Each person is a strand of story.

Daisy, for example.

Daisy could not have lasted as long as she had in the police force without having a sensible side to her nature, which was mostly all anybody saw. She respected laws, and she respected rules. She understood that many of these rules are perfectly arbitrary – decisions about where one could park, for example, or what hours shops were permitted to open – but that even these rules helped the big picture. They kept society safe. They kept things secure.

Her flatmate, Carol, thought she'd gone mad.

'You can't just leave and say you're going on holiday. It doesn't work like that. You're not on a TV cop show, you know. You can't just zoom all over the world to follow up a lead.'

'Well, then, in that case I'm not,' Daisy had retorted, untruthfully. 'I'm really just going on holiday.'

She said it so convincingly that the sensible cop who lived at the back of her head was shocked into silence, and then began to explain to her exactly what she was doing wrong, beginning with pointing out that she was about to go off on an entirely unauthorised leave – tantamount, muttered the sensible cop, to neglect of duty – and moving on from there.

It explained it on the way to the airport, and all across the Atlantic. It pointed out that even if she managed to avoid a permanent black mark in her personal files, let alone being thrown out of the police force altogether, even if she did find Grahame Coats, there was nothing she could do once she found him. Her Majesty's Constabulary look unkindly on kidnapping foreign criminals, let alone arresting them, and she rather doubted she would be able to persuade him to return to the UK willingly.

It was only when Daisy got off the little plane from Jamaica and tasted the air – earthy, spicy, wet, almost sweet – of Saint Andrews, that the sensible cop stopped pointing out the sheer ill-considered madness of what she was doing. That was because it was drowned out by another voice. 'Evildoers beware!' it sang. 'Beware! Take care! Evildoers everywhere!' and Daisy was marching to its beat. Grahame Coats had killed a woman in his office in the Aldwych, and he had walked out of there scot-free. He had done it practically under Daisy's nose.

She shook her head, collected her bag, brightly informed the immigration officer that she was here on her holidays, and went out to the taxi rank.

'I want a hotel that's not too expensive, but isn't icky, please,' she said to the driver.

'I got just the place for you, darlin',' he said. 'Hop in.'

* * *

Spider opened his eyes and discovered that he was staked out, face down. His arms were tied to a large stake, pounded into the earth in front of him. He could not move his legs, or twist his neck enough to see behind him, but he was willing to bet that they were similarly hobbled. The movement, as he tried to lift himself out of the dirt, to look behind him, caused his scratches to burn.

He opened his mouth, and dark blood drooled on to the dust, wetting it.

He heard a sound and twisted his head as much as he could. A white woman was looking down at him curiously.

'Are you all right? Silly question. Just look at the state of you. I suppose you're another duppy. Do I have that right?'

Spider thought about it. He didn't think he was a duppy. He shook his head.

'If you are, it's nothing to be ashamed of. Apparently, I'm a duppy myself. I hadn't heard the term before, but I met a delightful old gentleman on the way here who told me all about it. Let me see if I can be of any assistance.'

She crouched down next to him, reached out to help loosen his bonds.

Her hand slipped through him. He could feel her fingers, like strands of fog, brushing his skin.

'I'm afraid I don't seem able actually to touch you,' she said. 'Still, that means that you're not dead yet. So cheer up.'

Spider hoped this odd ghost-woman would go away soon. He couldn't think straight.

'Anyway, once I had everything sorted out, I resolved to remain walking the Earth until I take vengeance on my killer. I explained it to Morris – he was on a television screen in Selfridges – and he said he rather thought I was missing the entire point of having moved beyond the flesh, but I ask you, if they expect me to turn the other cheek they have several other thinks coming. Anyway, there are a number of precedents. And I'm sure I can do a Banquo-at-the-feast thing, given the opportunity. Do you talk?'

Spider shook his head, and blood dripped from his forehead into his eyes. It stung. Spider wondered how long it would take him to grow a new tongue. Prometheus had managed to grow a new liver on a daily basis, and Spider was pretty sure that a liver had to be a lot more work than a tongue. Livers did chemical reactions – bilirubin, urea, enzymes, all that. They broke down alcohol, and that had to be a lot of work on its own. All tongues did was talk. Well, that and lick, of course . . .

'I can't keep yattering on,' said the yellow-haired ghost lady. 'I've got a long way to go, I think.' She began to walk away, and she faded as she walked. Spider raised his head and watched her slip from one reality to another, like a photograph fading in the sunlight. He tried to call her back, but all the noises he could make were muffled, incoherent. Tongueless.

Somewhere in the distance, he heard the cry of a bird.

Spider tested his bonds. They held.

He found himself thinking, once again, of Rosie's story of the raven who saved the man from the mountain lion. It itched in his head, worse than the claw-tracks on his face and chest. *Concentrate.* The man lay on the ground, reading or sunbathing. The raven cawed in the tree. There was a big cat in the undergrowth . . .

And then the story reshaped itself, and he had it. Nothing had changed. It was all a matter of how you looked at the ingredients.

What if, he thought, the bird wasn't calling to warn the man that there was a big cat stalking him? What if it was calling to tell the mountain lion that there was a man on the ground – dead, or asleep or dying. That all the big cat had to do was finish the man off. And then the raven would feast on what it left . . .

Spider opened his mouth to moan, and blood ran from his mouth and puddled on the powdery clay.

Reality thinned. Time passed, in that place.

Spider, tongueless and furious, raised his head and twisted it to look at the ghost birds that flew around him, screaming.

He wondered where he was. This was not the bird-woman's copper-coloured universe, nor her cave, but neither was it the place he had previously tended to think of as the real world. It was closer to the real world, though, close enough that he could almost taste it, or would have tasted it if he could taste anything in his mouth but the iron tang of the blood, close enough that, if he were not staked out on the ground, he could have touched it.

If he had not been perfectly certain of his own sanity, certain to a degree that normally is only found in people who have concluded that they're definitely Julius Caesar and have been sent to save the world, he might have thought that he was going mad. First he saw a blonde woman who claimed to be a duppy, and now he heard voices. Well, he heard one voice anyway. Rosie's.

She was saying, 'I dunno. I thought it would be a holiday, but seeing those kids, without anything, it breaks your heart. There's so much they need.' And then, while Spider was trying to assess the significance of this, she said, 'I wonder how much longer she's going to be in the bath. Good thing you've got plenty of hot water here.'

Spider wondered if Rosie's words were meant to be important, whether they held the key to escaping from his predicament. He doubted it. Still, he listened harder, wondering whether the wind would carry any more words between the worlds. Apart from the crash of the waves on breakers behind and far below him, he heard nothing, only silence. But a specific kind of silence. There are, as Fat Charlie once suspected, many kinds of silences. Graves have their own silence, space has its silence, mountaintops have theirs. This was a hunting silence. It was a stalking silence. In this silence something moved on velvet-soft pads, with muscles like steel springs coiled beneath soft fur: something the colour of shadows in the long grass; something that would ensure that you heard nothing it did not wish you to hear. It was a silence that was moving from side to side in front of him, slowly and relentlessly, and with every arc it was getting closer.

Spider heard that in the silence, and the hairs on the back of his neck stiffened. He spat blood on to the dust by his face, and he waited.

***

In his house on the clifftop, Grahame Coats paced back and forth. He walked from his bedroom to the study, then down the stairs to the kitchen and back up to the library and from there back to his bedroom again. He was angry with himself: how could he have been so stupid as to assume that Rosie's visit was a coincidence?

He had realised it when the buzzer had sounded, and he had looked into the closed circuit TV screen at Fat Charlie's inane face. There was no mistaking it. *It was a conspiracy.*

He had imitated the action of a tiger, and climbed into the car, certain of an easy hit-and-run: if they found a mangled bicycle rider, people would blame it on a minibus. Unfortunately, he had not counted on Fat Charlie cycling so close to the road's drop-off: Grahame Coats had been unwilling to push his car any closer to the edge of the road, and now he was regretting it. No, Fat Charlie had sent in the women in the meat locker, they were his spies. They had infiltrated Grahame Coats's house. He was lucky that he had tumbled their scheme. He had known there was something *wrong* about them.

As he thought of the women, he realised that he had not fed them yet. He ought to give them something to eat. And a bucket. They would probably need a bucket after twenty-four hours. Nobody could say that he was an animal.

He had bought a handgun in Williamstown, the previous week. You could buy guns pretty easily on Saint Andrews, it was that sort of island. Most people didn't bother with buying guns, though, it was that sort of island too. He took the gun from his bedside drawer and went down to the kitchen. He took a plastic bucket from under the sink, tossed several tomatoes, a raw yam, a half-eaten lump of Cheddar cheese and a carton of orange juice into it. Then, pleased with himself for thinking of it, he fetched a toilet roll.

He went down to the wine cellar. There was no noise from inside the meat locker.

'I've got a gun,' he said. 'And I'm not afraid to use it. I'm going to open the door now. Please go over to the far wall, turn around and put your hands against it. I've brought food. Co-operate and you will both be released unharmed. Co-operate and nobody gets hurt. That means,' he said, delighted to find himself able to deploy an entire battalion of clichés hitherto off limits, 'no funny business.'

He turned on the lights inside the room, then pulled the bolts. The walls of the room were rock and brick. Rusting chains hung from hooks in the ceiling.

They were against the far wall. Rosie looked at the rock. Her mother stared over her shoulder at him like a trapped rat, furious and filled with hate.

Grahame Coats put down the bucket; he did not put down the gun. 'Lovely grub,' he said. 'And, better late than never, a bucket. I see you've been using the corner. There's toilet paper, too. Don't ever say I didn't do anything for you.'

'You're going to kill us,' said Rosie. 'Aren't you?'

'Don't antagonise him, you stupid girl,' spat her mother. Then, assuming a smile of sorts, she said, 'We're grateful for the food.'

'Of course I'm not going to kill you,' said Grahame Coats. It was only as he heard the words coming out of his mouth that he admitted to himself that, yes, of course he was going to have to kill them. What other option did he have? 'You didn't tell me that Fat Charlie sent you here.'

Rosie said, 'We came on a cruise ship. This evening we're meant to be in Barbados for the fish fry. Fat Charlie's in England. I don't even think he knows where we've gone. I didn't tell him.'

'It doesn't matter what you say,' said Grahame Coats. 'I've got the gun.'

He pushed the door closed and bolted it. Through the door he could hear Rosie's mother saying, 'The animal. Why didn't you ask him about the animal?'

'Because you're just imagining it, Mum. I keep telling you. There isn't an animal in here. Anyway, he's nuts. He'd probably just agree with you. He probably sees invisible tigers himself.'

Stung by this, Grahame Coats turned off their lights. He pulled out a bottle of red wine and went upstairs, slamming the cellar door behind him.

In the darkness beneath the house, Rosie broke the lump of cheese into four bits and ate one as slowly as she could.

'What did he mean about Fat Charlie?' she asked her mother, after the cheese had dissolved in her mouth.

'Your bloody Fat Charlie. I don't want to know about Fat Charlie,' said her mother. 'He's the reason that we're down here.'

'No, we're here because that Coats man is a total nutjob. A nutter with a gun. It's not Fat Charlie's fault.' She had tried not to let herself think about Fat Charlie, because thinking about Fat

Charlie meant that she inevitably found herself thinking about Spider . . .

'It's back,' said her mother. 'The animal is back. I heard it. I can smell it.'

'Yes, Mum,' said Rosie. She sat on the concrete floor of the meat cellar and thought about Spider. She missed him. When Grahame Coats saw reason and let them go, she'd try to locate Spider, she decided. Find out if there was room for a new beginning. She knew it was only a silly daydream, but it was a good dream, and it comforted her.

She wondered if Grahame Coats would kill them tomorrow.

* * *

A candle flame's thickness away, Spider was staked out for the beast.

It was late afternoon, and the sun was low behind him.

Spider was pushing at something with his nose and lips: it had been dry earth, before his spit and blood had soaked into it. Now it was a ball of mud, a rough marble of reddish clay. He had pushed it into a shape that was more or less spherical. Now he flicked at it, getting his nose underneath it and then jerking his head up. Nothing happened, as nothing had happened the previous how-many times. Twenty? A hundred? He wasn't keeping count. He simply kept on. He pushed his face further into the dirt, pushed his nose further under the ball of clay, jerked his head up and forward . . .

Nothing happened. Nothing was going to happen.

He needed another approach.

He closed his lips on the ball, closed them around it. He breathed in through his nose, as deeply as he could. Then he expelled the air through his mouth. The ball popped from his lips, with a pop like a champagne cork, and landed about eighteen inches away.

Now he twisted his right hand. It was bound at the wrist, with the rope pulling it tightly towards the stake. He pulled the hand back, bent it round. His fingers reached for the lump of bloody mud, and they fell short.

It was so near . . .

Spider took another deep breath, but choked on the dry dust, and began to cough. He tried again, twisting his head over to one side to fill his lungs. Then he rolled over and began to blow, in the direction of the ball, forcing the air from his lungs as hard as he could.

The clay ball rolled – less than an inch, but it was enough. He stretched, and now he was holding the clay in his fingers. He began to pinch the clay between finger and thumb, then turning it and doing it again. Eight times.

He repeated the process once more, this time squeezing the pinched clay a little tighter. One of the pinches fell off on to the dirt, but the others held. He had something in his hand that looked like a small ball with seven points coming out of it, like a child's model of the sun.

He looked at it with pride: given the circumstances, he felt as proud of it as anything a child has ever brought home from school.

The word, that would be the hardest part. Making a spider, or something quite like it, from blood and spit and clay, that was easy. Gods, even minor mischief gods like Spider, know how to do that. But the final part of Making was going to prove the hardest. You need a word to give something life. You need to name it.

He opened his mouth. 'Hrrurrrurrr,' he said, with his tongueless mouth.

Nothing happened.

He tried again. 'Hrrurrurr!' The clay sat, a dead lump in his hand.

His face fell back into the dirt. He was exhausted. Every movement tore the scabs on his face and chest. They oozed and burned and – worse – itched. *Think!* he told himself. There had to be a way of doing this . . . To talk without his tongue . . .

His lips still had a layer of clay on them. He sucked at them, moistening as well as he could, without a tongue.

He took a deep breath, and let it push through his lips, controlling it as best he could, saying it with such certainty that not even the universe could argue with him: he described the thing on his hand, and he said his own name, which was the best magic he knew: '*hhssspphhhrrriiivver*'.

And on his hand, where the lump of bloody mud had been, sat a fat spider, the colour of red clay, with seven spindly legs.

Help me, thought Spider. *Get help.*

The spider stared at him, its eyes gleaming in the sunlight. Then it dropped from his hand to the earth, and it proceeded to make its lopsided way into the grass, its gait wobbly and uneven.

Spider watched it until it was out of sight. Then he lowered his head into the dirt, and he closed his eyes.

The wind changed then, and he smelled the ammoniac scent of male cat on the air. It had marked its territory . . .

High in the air, Spider could hear birds caw in triumph.

* * *

Fat Charlie's stomach growled. If he had had any superfluous money he would have gone somewhere for dinner, just to get away from his hotel, but he was, as near as dammit, now quite broke, and evening meals were included in the cost of the room, so as soon as it turned seven, he went down to the restaurant.

The maitre d' had a glorious smile, and she told him that they would open the restaurant in just a few more minutes. They had to give the band time to finish setting up. Then she looked at him. Fat Charlie was beginning to know that look.

'Are you . . . ?' she began.

'Yes,' he said. 'I've even got it with me.' He took the lime out of his pocket and showed it to her.

'Very nice,' she said. 'That's definitely a lime you've got there. I was going to say, are you going to want the *à la carte* menu or would you rather do the buffet?'

'Buffet,' said Fat Charlie. The buffet was free. He stood in the hall outside the restaurant holding his lime.

'Just wait a moment,' said the maître d'.

A small woman came down the corridor from behind Fat Charlie. She smiled at the maître d' and said, 'Is the restaurant open yet? I'm completely starved.'

There was a final *thrum-thung-thdum* from the bass guitar and a *plunk* from the electric piano. The band put down their instruments and waved at the maître d'. 'It's open,' she said. 'Come in.'

The small woman stared at Fat Charlie with an expression of wary surprise. 'Hello, Fat Charlie,' she said. 'What's the lime for?'

'It's a long story.'

'Well,' said Daisy. 'We've got the whole of dinnertime ahead of us. Why don't you tell me all about it?'

* * *

Rosie wondered whether madness could be contagious. In the blind darkness beneath the house on the cliff, she had felt something brush past her. Something soft and lithe. Something huge. Something that growled, softly, as it circled them.

'Did you hear that too?' she said.

'Of course I heard it, you stupid girl,' said her mother. Then she said, 'Is there any orange juice left?'

Rosie fumbled in the darkness for the juice carton, passed it to her mother. She heard the sound of drinking, then her mother said, 'The animal will not be the one that kills us. *He* will.'

'Grahame Coats. Yes.'

'He's a bad man. There is something riding him, like a horse, but he would be a bad horse, and he is a bad man.'

Rosie reached out and held her mother's bony hand in her own. She didn't say anything. There wasn't anything much to say.

'You know,' said her mother, after a while, 'I'm very proud of you. You were a good daughter.'

'Oh,' said Rosie. The idea of not being a disappointment to her mother was a new one, and something about which she was not sure how she felt.

'Maybe you should have married Fat Charlie,' said her mother. 'Then we wouldn't be here.'

'No,' said Rosie. 'I should never have married Fat Charlie. I don't love Fat Charlie. So you weren't entirely wrong.'

They heard a door slam upstairs.

'He's gone out,' said Rosie. 'Quick. While he's out. Dig a tunnel.' First she began to giggle, and then she began to cry.

* * *

Fat Charlie was trying to understand what Daisy was doing on the island. Daisy was trying, equally as hard, to understand what Fat Charlie was doing on the island. Neither of them was having much success. A singer, in a long red slinky dress, who was too good for a little hotel restaurant's Friday Night Fun, was up on the little dais at the end of the room singing 'I've Got You Under My Skin'.

Daisy said, 'You're looking for the lady who lived next door when you were a little boy, because she may be able to help you find your brother.'

'I was given a feather. If she's still got it, I may be able to exchange it for my brother. It's worth a try.'

She blinked, slowly, thoughtfully, entirely unimpressed, and picked at her salad.

Fat Charlie said, 'Well, you're here because you think that Grahame Coats came here after he killed Maeve Livingstone. But you're not here as a cop. You just powered in under your own steam on the off chance that he's here. And if he is here, there's absolutely nothing you can do about it.'

Daisy licked a fleck of tomato seed from the corner of her lips, and looked uncomfortable. 'I'm not here as a police officer,' she said. 'I'm here as a tourist.'

'But you just walked off the job and came here after him. They could probably send you to prison for that, or something.'

'Then,' she said, drily, 'it's a good thing that Saint Andrews doesn't have any extradition treaties, isn't it?'

Under his breath Fat Charlie said 'Oh God.'

The reason Fat Charlie said 'Oh God' was because the singer had left the stage and was now starting to walk around the restaurant with a radio microphone. Right now, she was asking two German tourists where they were from.

'Why would he come *here*?' asked Fat Charlie.

'Confidential banking. Cheap property. No extradition treaties. Maybe he really likes citrus fruit.'

'I spent two years terrified of that man,' said Fat Charlie. 'I'm going to get some more of that fish-and-green-banana thing. You coming?'

'I'm fine,' said Daisy. 'I want to leave room for dessert.'

Fat Charlie walked over to the buffet, going the long way around to avoid catching the singer's eye. She was very beautiful, and her red sequined dress caught the light and glittered as she moved. She was better than the band. He wished she'd go back on to the little stage and keep singing her standards – he had enjoyed her 'Night and Day' and a peculiarly soulful 'Spoonful of Sugar' – and stop interacting with the diners. Or at least, stop talking to people on his side of the room.

He piled his plate high with more of the things he had liked the first time. The thing about bicycling around the island, he thought, was that it gave you an appetite.

When he returned to his table, Grahame Coats, with something vaguely beardish growing on the lower part of his face, was sitting next to Daisy, and he was grinning like a weasel on speed. 'Fat Charlie,' said Grahame Coats, and he chuckled, uncomfortably. 'It's amazing, isn't it? I come looking for you here, for a little tête-à-tête, and what do I find as a bonus? This glamourous little police officer. Please, sit down over there and try not to make a scene.'

Fat Charlie stood like a waxwork.

'Sit down,' repeated Grahame Coats. 'I have a gun pressed against Miss Day's stomach.'

Daisy looked at Fat Charlie imploringly, and she nodded. Her hands were on the tablecloth, pressed flat.

Fat Charlie sat down.

'Hands where I can see them. Spread them on the table, just like hers.'

Fat Charlie obeyed.

Grahame Coats sniffed. 'I always knew you were an undercover cop, Nancy,' he said. 'An *agent provocateur*, eh? You come into my offices, set me up, steal me blind.'

'I never—' said Fat Charlie, but he saw the look in Grahame Coats's eyes, and he shut up.

'You thought you were so clever,' said Grahame Coats. 'You all thought I'd fall for it. That was why you sent the other two in, wasn't it? The two at the house? Did you think I'd believe they were really from the cruise ship? You have to get up pretty early in the morning to put one over on me, you know. Who else have you told? Who else knows?'

Daisy said, 'I'm not entirely sure what you're talking about, Grahame.'

The singer was finishing 'Some of These Days': her voice was bluesy and rich, and it twined around them all like a velvet scarf.

> *'Some of these days*
> *You're gonna miss me, honey*
> *Some of these days*
> *You're gonna feel so lonely*
> *You'll miss my huggin'*
> *You'll miss my kissin'* . . .'

'You're going to pay the bill,' said Grahame. 'Then I'll escort you and the young lady out to the car. And we'll go back to my place, for a proper talk. Any funny business, and I shoot you both. *Capisce?*'

Fat Charlie *capisced*. He also *capisced* who had been driving the black Mercedes that afternoon, and just how close he had already come to death that day. He was beginning to *capisce* how utterly cracked Grahame Coats was and how little chance Daisy and he had of getting out of this alive.

The singer finished her song. The other people scattered around the restaurant clapped. Fat Charlie kept his hands palms down on the table. He stared past Graham Coats at the singer, and, with the eye that Grahame Coats could not see, he winked at her. She was tired of people avoiding her eyes; Fat Charlie's wink was extremely welcome.

Daisy said, 'Grahame, obviously I came here because of you, but Charlie's just—' She stopped and made the kind of expression you make when someone pushes a gun barrel deeper into your stomach.

Grahame Coats said, 'Listen to me. For the purposes of the innocent bystanders here assembled, we're all good friends. I'm going to put the gun into my pocket, but it will still be pointing at you. We're going to get up. We're going to my car. And I will—'

He stopped. A woman with a red spangly dress and a

microphone was heading for their table, with an enormous smile
on her face. She was making for Fat Charlie. She said, into her
microphone, 'What's your name, darlin'?' She put the microphone
into Fat Charlie's face.

'Charlie Nancy,' said Fat Charlie. His voice caught and wavered.

'And where you from, Charlie?'

'England. Me and my friends. We're all from England.'

'And what do you do, Charlie?'

Everything slowed. It was like diving off a cliff into the ocean.
It was the only way out. He took a deep breath and said it 'I'm
between jobs,' he started. 'But I'm really a singer. I sing. Just like
you.'

'Like me? What kind of things you sing?'

Fat Charlie swallowed. 'What have you got?'

She turned to the other people at Fat Charlie's table. 'Do you
think we could get him to sing for us?' she asked, gesturing with
her microphone.

'Er. Don't think so. No. Absatively out of the question,' said
Grahame Coats. Daisy shrugged, her hands flat on the table.

The woman in the red dress turned to the rest of the room.
'What do we think?' she asked them.

There was a rustle of clapping from the diners at the other
tables, and more enthusiastic applause from the serving staff. The
barman called out, 'Sing us something!'

The singer leaned in to Fat Charlie, covered the mike and said,
'Better make it something the boys know.'

Fat Charlie said, 'Do they know "Under the Boardwalk"?' and
she nodded, announced it, and gave him the microphone.

The band began to play. The singer led Fat Charlie up to the
little stage, his heart beating wildly in his chest.

Fat Charlie began to sing, and the audience began to listen.

All he had wanted was to buy himself some time, but he felt
comfortable. No one was throwing things. He seemed to have
plenty of room in his head to think in. He was aware of everyone
in the room: the tourists and the serving staff, and the people over
at the bar. He could see everything: he could see the barman
measuring out a cocktail, and the old woman in the rear of the
room filling a large plastic mug with coffee. He was still terrified,

still angry, but he took all the terror and the anger and he put it into the song, and let it all become a song about lazing and loving. As he sang, he thought.

What would Spider do? thought Fat Charlie. *What would my dad do?*

He sang. In his song he told them all exactly what he planned to do under the boardwalk, and it mostly involved making love.

The singer in the red dress was smiling, and snapping her fingers, and shimmying her body to the music. She leaned into the keyboard player's microphone and began to harmonise.

I'm actually singing in front of an audience, thought Fat Charlie. *Bugger me.*

He kept his eyes on Grahame Coats.

As he entered the last chorus, he began to clap his hands above his head, and soon the whole room was clapping along with him, diners and waiters and chefs, everyone except Grahame Coats, whose hands were beneath the tablecloth, and Daisy, whose hands were flat on the table. Daisy was looking at him as if he was not simply barking mad, but had picked an extremely odd moment to discover his inner Drifters.

The audience clapped, and Fat Charlie smiled and he sang, and as he sang he knew, without any shadow of a doubt, that everything was going to be all right. They were going to be just fine, him and Spider and Daisy and Rosie too, wherever she was, they'd be OK. He knew what he was going to do: it was foolish and unlikely and the act of an idiot, but it would work. And as the last notes of the song faded away, he said, 'There's a young lady at the table I was sitting at. Her name's Daisy Day. She's from England too. Daisy, can you wave at everyone?'

Daisy gave him a sick look, but she raised a hand from the table, and she waved.

'There's something I wanted to say to Daisy. She doesn't know I'm going to say this.' *If this doesn't work*, whispered a voice at the back of his head, *she's dead. You know that?* 'But let's hope she says yes. Daisy? Will you marry me?'

The room was quiet. Fat Charlie stared at Daisy, willing her to understand, to play along.

Daisy nodded.

The diners applauded. *This* was a floor show. The singer, the maître d' and several of the waitresses descended on the table, hauled Daisy to her feet and pulled her over to the middle of the floor. They pulled her over to Fat Charlie, and, as the band played 'I Just Called to Say I Love You' he put his arm around her.

'You got a ring for her?' asked the singer.

He put his hand into his pocket. 'Here,' he said to Daisy. 'This is for you.' He put his arms around her and kissed her. If anyone is going to get shot, he thought, it will be now. Then the kiss was over, and people were shaking his hand and hugging him – one man, in town, he said, for the music festival, insisted on giving Fat Charlie his card – and now Daisy was holding the lime he had given her with a very strange expression on her face; and when he looked back to the table they had been sitting at, Grahame Coats was gone.

Chapter Thirteen

Which Proves to Be Unlucky for Some

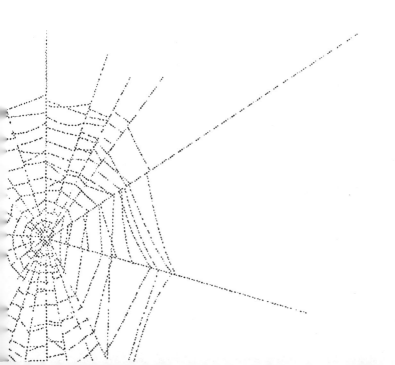

The birds were excited, now. They were cawing and crying and chattering in the treetops. *It's coming,* thought Spider, and he cursed. He was spent, and done. There was nothing left in him. Nothing but fatigue, nothing but exhaustion.

He thought about lying on the ground and being devoured. Overall, he decided, it was a lousy way to go. He wasn't even certain that he'd be able to regrow a liver, while he was pretty sure that whatever was stalking him had no plans to stop at just the liver anyway.

He began to wrench at the stake. He counted to three, and then, as best as he could and as much as he could, jerked both of his arms towards him so they'd tense the rope and pull the stake, then he counted to three and did it again.

It had about as much effect as if he was to try to pull a mountain across a road. One two three . . . *tug.* And *again.* And *again.*

He wondered if the beast would come soon.

One two three . . . *tug.* One two three . . . *tug.*

Somewhere, someone was singing, he could hear it. And the song made Spider smile. He found himself wishing that he still had a tongue: he'd stick it out at the tiger when it finally made its appearance. The thought gave him strength.

One two three . . . *tug.*

And the stake gave and shifted in his hands.

One more pull and the stake came out of the ground, slick as a sword sliding out of a stone.

He pulled the ropes towards him, and held the stake in his hands. It was about three feet long. One end had been sharpened, to go into the ground. He pushed it out of the loops of rope with numb hands. Ropes dangled uselessly from his wrists. He hefted the stake in his right hand. It would do. And he knew then that he was being watched: that it had been watching him for some time now, like a cat watching a mousehole.

It came to him in silence, or nearly, insinuating its way towards him like a shadow moving across the day. The only movement that caught the eye was its tail, which swished impatiently. Otherwise, it might have been a statue, or a mound of sand that looked, due to a trick of the light, like a monstrous beast, for its coat was a sandy colour, its unblinking eyes the green of the midwinter sea. Its face was the wide cruel face of a panther. In the islands they called any big cat Tiger, and this was every big cat there had ever been – bigger, meaner, more dangerous.

Spider's ankles were still hobbled, and he could barely walk. Pins and needles pricked his hands and his feet. He hopped from one foot to another and tried to look as if he was doing it on purpose, some kind of dance of intimidation, and not because standing hurt.

He wanted to crouch and untie his ankles, but he did not dare take his eyes off the beast.

The stake was heavy, and thick, but was too short to be a spear, too clumsy and large to be anything else. Spider held it by the narrower end, where it had been sharpened, and he looked away, out to sea, intentionally not looking at the place the animal was, relying on his peripheral vision for information.

What had she said? *You will bleat. You will whimper. Your fear will excite him.*

Spider began to whimper. Then he bleated, like an injured goat, lost and plump and alone.

A flash of sandy-coloured motion, barely enough time to register teeth and claws as they blurred towards him. Spider swung the stake like a baseball bat, as hard as he could, feeling it connect with a satisfying thunk across the beast's nose.

Tiger stopped, stared at him as if unable to believe its eyes, then made a noise in the back of its throat, a querulous growl, and it walked, stiff-legged, back in the direction it had come, toward the scrub, as if it had a prior appointment that it wished it could get out of. It glared back at Spider resentfully, over its shoulder, a beast in pain; gave him the look of an animal who would be returning.

Spider watched it go.

Then he sat down, and untangled and untied his ankles.

He walked, a little unsteadily, along the cliff-edge, following it gently downhill. Soon a stream crossed his path, running off the cliff-edge in a sparkling waterfall. Spider went down on his knees, cupped his hands together, and began to drink the cool water.

Then he began to collect rocks. Good, fist-sized rocks. He stacked them together, like snowballs.

* * *

'You've hardly eaten anything,' said Rosie.

'*You* eat. Keep your strength up,' said her mother. 'I had a little of that cheese. It was enough.'

It was cold in the meat cellar, and it was dark. Not the kind of dark your eyes get used to, either. There was no light. Rosie had walked the perimeter of the cellar, her fingers trailing against the whitewash and rock and crumbling brick, looking for something that would help, finding nothing.

'You used to eat,' said Rosie. 'Back when Dad was alive.'

'Your father,' said her mother, 'used to eat, too. And see where it got him? A heart attack, aged forty-one. What kind of world is that?'

'But he loved his food.'

'He loved everything,' said her mother bitterly. 'He loved food, he loved people, he loved his daughter. He loved cooking. He loved me. What did it get him? Just an early grave. You mustn't go loving things like that. I've told you.'

'Yes,' said Rosie. 'I suppose you have.'

She walked towards the sound of her mother's voice, hand in front of her face to stop it banging into one of the metal chains that hung in the middle of the room. She found her mother's bony shoulder, put an arm around her.

'I'm not scared,' said Rosie, in the darkness.

'You're crazy, then,' said her mother.

Rosie let go of her mother, moved back into the middle of the room. There was a sudden creaking noise. Dust and powdered plaster fell from the ceiling.

'Rosie? What are you doing?' asked Rosie's mother.

'Swinging on the chain.'

'You be careful. If that chain gives way, you'll be on the floor with a broken head before you can say Jack Robinson.' There was no answer from her daughter. Mrs Noah said, 'I told you. You're crazy.'

'No,' said Rosie. 'I'm not. I'm just not scared any more.'

Above them, in the house, the front door slammed.

'Bluebeard's home,' said Rosie's mother.

'I know. I heard,' said Rosie. 'I'm still not scared.'

* * *

People kept clapping Fat Charlie on the back, and buying him drinks with umbrellas in them; in addition to which, he had now collected five business cards from people in the music world, on the island for the festival.

All around the room, people were smiling at him. He had an arm round Daisy: he could feel her trembling. She put her lips to his ear. 'You're a complete loony, you know that?'

'It worked, didn't it?'

She looked at him. 'You're full of surprises.'

'Come on,' he said. 'We're not done yet.'

He made for the maître d'. 'Excuse me . . . There was a lady.

While I was singing. She came in, refilled her coffee mug from the pot back there, by the bar. Where did she go?'

The maître d' blinked and shrugged. She said, 'I don't know . . .'

'Yes, you do,' said Fat Charlie. He felt certain, and smart. Soon enough, he knew, he would feel like himself again, but he had sung a song to an audience, and he had enjoyed it. He had done it to save Daisy's life, and his own, and he had succeeded in doing both these things. 'Let's talk out there.' It was the song. While he had been singing, everything had become perfectly clear. It was still clear. He headed for the hallway, and Daisy and the maître d' followed.

'What's your name?' he asked the maître d'.

'I'm Clarissa.'

'Hello, Clarissa. What's your last name?'

Daisy said, 'Charlie, shouldn't we call the police?'

'In a minute. Clarissa what?'

'Higgler.'

'And what's your relationship to Benjamin? The concierge?'

'He's my brother.'

'And how exactly are you two related to Mrs Higgler. To Callyanne Higgler?'

'They're my neice and nephew, Fat Charlie,' said Mrs Higgler, from the doorway. 'Now, I think you better listen to your fiancée, and talk to the police. Don't you?'

* * *

Spider was sitting by the stream on the clifftop, with his back to the cliff and a heap of throwing stones in front of him, when a man came loping out of the long grass. The man was naked, save for a pelt of sandy fur around his waist, behind which a tail hung down; he wore a necklace of teeth, sharp and white and pointed; his hair was long and black. He walked casually towards Spider, as if he were merely out for an early morning constitutional, and Spider's appearance there was a pleasant surprise.

Spider picked up a rock the size of a grapefruit, hefted it in his hand.

'Heya, Anansi's child,' said the stranger. 'I was just passing, and

I noticed you, and wondered if there was anything I could do to help.' His nose looked crooked and bruised.

Spider shook his head. He missed his tongue.

'Seeing you there, I find myself thinking, poor Anansi's child, he must be so hungry.' The stranger smiled too widely. 'Here. I've got food enough to share with you.' He had a sack over his shoulder, and now he opened the sack, and reached his right hand into it, producing a freshly killed black-tailed lamb. He held it by the neck. Its head lolled. 'Your father and I ate together on many an occasion. Is there any reason that you and I cannot do likewise? You can make the fire and I will clean the lamb and make a spit to turn it. Can you not taste it already?'

Spider was so hungry he was light-headed. Had he still been in possession of his tongue, perhaps he would have said 'yes', confident of his ability to talk himself out of trouble; but he had no tongue. He picked up a second rock in his left hand.

'So let us feast and be friends; and let there be no more misunderstandings,' said the stranger.

And the vulture and the raven will clean my bones, thought Spider.

The stranger took another step toward Spider, who decided that this was his cue to throw the first rock. He had a good eye and an excellent arm, and the rock struck where he had intended it to strike, on the stranger's right arm; he dropped the lamb. The next rock hit the stranger on the side of the head – Spider had been aiming for a spot just between the too-widely set eyes, but the man had moved.

The stranger ran, then, a bounding run, with his tail straight out behind him. Sometimes he looked like a man when he ran, and sometimes he looked like a beast.

When he was gone, Spider walked to the place he had been, to retrieve the black-tailed lamb. It was moving, when he reached it, and for a heartbeat he imagined that it was still alive, but then he saw that the flesh was creeping with maggots. It stank, and the stench of the corpse helped Spider forget how hungry he was, for a little while.

He carried it at arm's length to the cliff-edge, and threw it down into the sea. Then he washed his hands in the stream.

He did not know how long he had been in this place. Time was stretched and squashed here. The sun was lowering on the horizon.

After the sun has set, and before the moon has risen, thought Spider. *That is when the beast will be back.*

* * *

The implacably cheerful representative of the Saint Andrews police force sat in the hotel front office with Daisy and Fat Charlie, and listened to everything each of them had to say with a placid, but unimpressed smile on his wide face. Sometimes he would reach up a finger and scratch his moustache.

They told the police officer that a fugitive from justice called Grahame Coats had come in to them while they were eating dinner, and threatened Daisy with a gun. Which, they were also forced to admit, nobody but Daisy had actually seen. Then Fat Charlie told him about the incident with the black Mercedes and the bicycle, earlier that afternoon, and no, he hadn't actually seen who was driving the car. But he knew where it came from. He told the officer about the house on the clifftop.

The man touched his pepper-and-salt moustache, thoughtfully. 'Indeed, there is a house where you describe. However, it does not belong to your man Coats. Far from it. You are describing the house of Basil Finnegan, an extremely respectable man. For many years, Mr Finnegan has had a healthy interest in law and order. He has given money to schools, but more important, he contributed a healthy sum toward the construction of the new police station.'

'He put a gun to my stomach,' said Daisy. 'He told me that unless we came with him, he'd shoot.'

'If this was Mr Finnegan, little lady,' said the police office, 'I'm sure that there is a perfectly simple explanation.' He opened his briefcase, produced a thick sheaf of papers. 'I'll tell you what. You think about the matter. Sleep on it. If, in the morning, you are convinced that it was more than high spirits, you simply have to fill in this form, and drop off all three copies at the police station. Ask for the new police station, at the back of the city square. Everyone knows where it is.'

He shook both of their hands and went on his way.

'You should have told him you were a cop too,' said Fat Charlie. 'He might have taken you more seriously.'

'I don't think it would have done any good,' she said. 'Anyone who calls you 'little lady' has already excluded you from the set of people worth listening to.'

They walked out into the hotel reception.

'Where did she go?' asked Fat Charlie.

Benjamin Higgler said, 'Aunt Callyanne? She's waiting for you in the conference room.'

* * *

'There,' said Rosie. 'I knew I could do it, if I just kept swinging.'

'He'll kill you.'

'He's going to kill us anyway.'

'It won't work.'

'Mum, have you got a better idea?'

'He'll see you.'

'Mum, will you please stop being so negative? If you've got any suggestions that would help, please say them. Otherwise just don't bother. OK?'

Silence.

Then, 'I could show him my bum.'

'What?'

'You heard me.'

'Er. Instead of?'

'In addition to.'

Silence. Then Rosie said, 'Well, it couldn't hurt.'

* * *

'Hello, Mrs Higgler,' said Fat Charlie. 'I want the feather back.'

'What make you think I got your feather?' she asked, arms folded across her vast bosom.

'Mrs Dunwiddy told me.'

Mrs Higgler seemed surprised by this, for the first time. 'Louella did tell you I got the feather?'

'She said you had the feather.'

'I keeping it safe.' Mrs Higgler gestured towards Daisy with her mug of coffee. 'You can't expect me to start talkin' in front of her. I don't know her.'

'This is Daisy. You can say anything to her you'd say to me.'

'She's your fiancée,' said Mrs Higgler. 'I heard.'

Fat Charlie could feel his cheeks starting to burn. 'She's not my— We aren't actually. I had to say something to get her away from the man with the gun. It seemed the simplest thing.'

Mrs Higgler looked at him. Behind her thick spectacles, her eyes began to twinkle. 'I know that,' she said. 'It was during your song. In front of an audience.' She shook her head, in the way that old people like to do when pondering the foolishness of the young. She opened her black purse, took out an envelope, passed it to Fat Charlie. 'I promised Louella I keep it safe.'

Fat Charlie took out the feather from the envelope, half crushed from where he had been holding it tightly the night of the séance. 'OK,' he said. 'Feather. Excellent. Now,' he said to Mrs Higgler, 'what exactly do I do with it?'

'You don't know?'

Fat Charlie's mother had told him, when he was young, to count to ten before he lost his temper. He counted, silently and unhurriedly, to ten, whereupon he lost his temper. 'Of course I don't know what to do with it, you stupid old woman! In the last two weeks I've been arrested, I've lost my fiancée and my job, I've watched my semi-imaginary brother get eaten by a wall of birds in Piccadilly Circus, I've flown back and forth across the Atlantic like some kind of lunatic transatlantic pingpong ball, and today I got up in front of an audience and I, and I *sang* because my psycho ex-boss had a gun barrel against the stomach of the girl I'm having dinner with. All I'm trying to do is sort out the mess my life has turned into since *you* suggested I might want to talk to my brother. So, no. No, I don't know what to do with this bloody feather. Burn it? Chop it up and eat it? Build a nest with it? Hold it out in front of me and jump out of the window?'

Mrs Higgins looked sullen. 'You have to ask Louella Dunwiddy.'

'I'm not sure that I can. She wasn't looking very well the last time I saw her. And we don't have much time.'

Daisy said, 'Great. You got your feather back. Now, can we please talk about Grahame Coats?'

'It's not only a feather. It's the feather I swapped for my brother.'

'So swap it back, and let's get on with things. We've got to do something.'

'It's not as simple as that,' said Fat Charlie. Then he stopped, and thought about what he had said and what she had said. He looked at Daisy admiringly. 'God, you're smart,' he said.

'I try,' she said. 'What did I say?'

They didn't have four old ladies, but they had Mrs Higgler, Benjamin, and Daisy. Dinner was almost finished, so Clarissa, the maître d', seemed perfectly happy to come and join them. They didn't have earths of four different colours, but there was white sand from the beach behind the hotel and black dirt from the flowerbed in front of it, red mud at the side of the hotel, multicoloured sand in test tubes in the gift shop. The candles they borrowed from the poolside bar were small and white, not tall and black. Mrs Higgler assured them that she could find all the herbs they actually needed on the island, but Fat Charlie had Clarissa borrow a pouch of bouquet garni from the kitchen.

'I think it's all a matter of confidence,' Fat Charlie explained. 'The most important thing isn't the details. It's the magical atmosphere.'

The magical atmosphere in this case was not enhanced by Benjamin Higgler's tendency to look around the table and burst into explosive giggles, nor by Daisy's continually pointing out that the whole procedure was extremely silly.

Mrs Higgler sprinkled the bouquet garni into a bowl of left-over white wine.

Mrs Higgler began to hum. She raised her hands in encouragement, and the others began to hum along with her, like drunken bees. Fat Charlie waited for something to happen.

Nothing did.

'Fat Charlie,' said Mrs Higgler. 'You hum too.'

Fat Charlie swallowed. There's nothing to be scared of, he told himself: he had sung in front of a roomful of people; he had proposed marriage in front of an audience to a woman he barely knew. Humming would be a doddle.

He found the note that Mrs Higgler was humming, and he let it vibrate in his throat . . .

He held his feather. He concentrated and he hummed.

Benjamin stopped giggling. His eyes widened. There was an expression of alarm on his face, and Fat Charlie was going to stop humming to find out what was troubling him, but the hum was inside him now, and the candles were flickering . . .

'Look at him!' said Benjamin. 'He's—'

– and Fat Charlie would have wondered what exactly he was, but it was too late to wonder.

Mists parted.

Fat Charlie was walking along a bridge, a long white footbridge across an expanse of grey water. A little way ahead of him, in the middle of the bridge, a man sat on a small wooden chair. The man was fishing. A green fedora hat covered his eyes. He appeared to be dozing, and he did not stir as Fat Charlie approached.

Fat Charlie recognised the man. He rested his hand on the man's shoulder.

'You know,' he said, 'I knew you were faking it. I didn't think you were really dead.'

The man in the chair did not move, but he smiled. 'Shows how much you know,' said Anansi. 'I'm dead as they come.' He stretched luxuriantly, pulled a little black cheroot from behind his ear, and lit it with a match. 'Yup. I'm dead. Figure I'll stay dead for a lickle while. If you don't die now and again, people start takin' you for granted.'

Fat Charlie said, 'But.'

Anansi touched his finger to his lips for silence. He picked up his fishing rod and began to wind the reel. He pointed to a small net. Fat Charlie picked it up, and held it out as his father lowered a silver fish, long and wriggling, into it. Anansi took the hook from the fish's mouth, then dropped the fish into a white pail. 'There,' he said. 'That's tonight's dinner taken care of.'

For the first time it registered with Fat Charlie that it had been dark night when he had sat down at the table with Daisy and the Higglers, but that while the sun was low wherever he was now, it had not set.

His father folded up the chair, and gave Fat Charlie the chair and the bucket to carry. They began to walk along the bridge. 'You know,' said Mr Nancy, 'I always thought that if you ever came to talk to me, I'd tell you all manner of things. But you seem to be doing pretty good on your own. So what brings you here?'

'I'm not sure. I was trying to find the Bird Woman. I want to give her back her feather.'

'You shouldn't have been messin' about with people like that,' said his father, blithely. 'No good ever comes from it. She's a mess of resentments, that one. But she's a coward.'

'It was Spider—' said Fat Charlie.

'Your own fault. Letting that old busybody send half of you away.'

'I was only a kid. Why didn't you *do* anything?'

Anansi pushed the hat back on his head. 'Ol' Dunwiddy couldn't do anything to you you didn't let her do,' he said. 'You're *my* son, after all.'

Fat Charlie thought about this. Then he said. 'But why didn't you *tell* me?'

'You're doing OK. You're figurin' it all out by yourself. You figured out the songs, didn't you?'

Fat Charlie felt clumsier and fatter and even more of a disappointment to his father, but he didn't simply say 'No'. Instead he said, 'What do you think?'

'I think you're gettin' there. The important thing about songs is that they're just like stories. They don't mean a damn unless there's people listenin' to them.'

They were approaching the end of the bridge. Fat Charlie knew, without being told, that this was the last chance they'd ever have to talk. There were so many things he needed to find out, so many things he wanted to know. He said, 'Dad. When I was a kid. Why did you humiliate me?'

The old man's brow creased. 'Humiliate you? I loved you.'

'You got me to go to school dressed as President Taft. You call that love?'

There was a high-pitched yelp of something that might have been laughter from the old man, then he sucked on his cheroot. The smoke drifted from his lips like a ghostly speech balloon. 'Your mother had something to say about that,' he said. Then he said, 'We don't have long, Charlie. You want to spend the time we got left fighting?'

Fat Charlie shook his head. 'Guess not.'

They had reached the end of the bridge. 'Now,' said his father. 'When you see your brother. I want you to give him something from me.'

'What?'

His father reached up a hand, pulled Fat Charlie's head down. Then he kissed him, gently, on the forehead. 'That,' he said.

Fat Charlie straightened up. His father was looking up at him with an expression that, if he had seen it on anyone else's face, he would have thought of as pride. 'Let me see the feather,' said his father.

Fat Charlie reached into his pocket. The feather was there, looking even more crumpled and dilapidated than it looked before.

His father made a *tch* noise, and held the feather up to the light. 'This is a beautiful feather,' said his father. 'You don't want it to get all manky. She won't take it back if it's messed up.' Mr Nancy ran his hand over the feather, and it was perfect. He frowned at it, 'Now, you'll just get it messed up again.' He breathed on his fingernails, polished them against his jacket. Then he seemed to have arrived at a decision. He removed his fedora, slipped the feather into the hatband. 'Here. You could do with a natty hat anyway.' He put the hat on to Fat Charlie's head. 'It suits you,' he said.

Fat Charlie sighed. 'Dad. I don't wear hats. It'll look stupid. I'll look a complete tit. Why do you always try to embarrass me?'

In the fading light, the old man looked at his son. 'You think I'd lie to you? Son, all you need to wear a hat is attitude. And you got that. You think I'd tell you you looked good if you didn't? You look real sharp. You don't believe me?'

Fat Charlie said, 'Not really.'

'Look,' said his father. He pointed over the side of the bridge. The water beneath them was still and smooth as a mirror, and the man looking up at him from the water looked real sharp in his new green hat.

Fat Charlie looked up to tell his father that maybe he had been wrong, but the old man was gone.

He stepped off the bridge into the dusk.

* * *

'Right. I want to know exactly where he is. Where did he go? What have you done to him?'

'I didn't do anything. Lord, child,' said Mrs Higgler. 'This never happened the last time.'

'It looked like he was beamed up to the mothership,' said Benjamin. 'Cool. Real-life special effects.'

'I want you to bring him back,' said Daisy, fiercely. 'I want him back *now*.'

'I don't even know where he is,' said Mrs Higgler. 'And I didn't send him there. He do that himself.'

'Anyway,' said Clarissa. 'What if he's off doing what he's doing and we make him come back? We could ruin it all.'

'Exactly,' said Benjamin. 'Like beaming the landing party back, halfway through their mission.'

Daisy thought about this, and was irritated to realise that it made sense – as much as anything made sense these days, anyway.

'If nothing else is happening,' said Clarissa, 'I ought to go back to the restaurant. Make sure everything's all right.'

Mrs Higgler sipped her coffee. 'Nothin' happenin' here,' she agreed.

Daisy slammed her hand down on the table. 'Excuse me. We've got a killer out there. And now Fat Charlie's beamed up to the mastership.'

'Mothership,' said Benjamin.

Mrs Higgler blinked. 'OK,' she said. 'We should do something. What do you suggest?'

'I don't know,' said Daisy. 'Kill time, I suppose.' She picked up the copy of the *Williamstown Courier* that Mrs Higgler had been reading, and began to flip through it.

The story about the missing tourists, the women who hadn't gone back to their cruise ship, was a column on page three. *The two at the house*, said Grahame Coats in her head. *Did you think I'd believe they were from the ship?*

At the end of the day, Daisy was a cop.

'Get me the phone,' she said.

'Who are you calling?'

'I think we'll start with the Minister of Tourism and the Chief of Police, and we'll go on from there.'

* * *

The crimson sun was shrinking on the horizon. Spider, had he not been Spider, would have despaired. On the island, in that place, there was a clean line between day and night, and Spider watched the last red crumb of sun being swallowed by the sea. He had his stones, and the two stakes.

He wished he had fire.

He wondered when the moon would be up. When the moon rose, he might have a chance.

The sun set – the final smudge of red sank into the dark sea, and it was night.

'Anansi's child,' said a voice from out of the darkness. 'Soon enough, I shall feed. You will not know I am there until you feel my breath on the back of your head. I stood above you, while you were staked out for me, and I could have crunched through your neck then and there, but I thought better of it. Killing you in your sleep would have brought me no pleasure. I want to feel you die. I want you to know why I have taken your life.'

Spider threw a rock towards where he thought the voice was coming from, and heard it crash harmlessly into the undergrowth.

'You have fingers,' said the voice, 'but I have claws sharper than knives. You have your two legs, but I have four legs that will never tire, that can run ten times as fast as you ever will and keep on running. Your teeth can eat meat, if it has been made soft and tasteless by the fire, for you have little monkey-teeth, good for chewing soft fruit and crawling bugs; but I have teeth that rend and tear the living flesh from the bones, and I can swallow it while the lifeblood still fountains into the sky.'

And then Spider made a noise. It was a noise that could be

made without a tongue, without even opening his lips. It was a
meh noise, of amused disdain. *You may be all these things, Tiger,*
it seemed to say, *but so what? All the stories there ever were are
Anansi's. Nobody tells Tiger stories.*

There was a roar from the darkness, a roar of fury and
frustration.

Spider began to hum the tune of the 'Tiger Rag'. It's an old song,
good for teasing tigers with: 'Hold that tiger,' it goes. 'Where's that
tiger?'

When the voice came next from the darkness, it was nearer.

'I have your woman, Anansi's child. When I am done with you,
I shall tear her flesh. Her meat will taste sweeter than yours.'

Spider made the *hmph!* noise people make when they know
they're being lied to.

'Her name is Rosie.'

Spider made an involuntary noise then.

In the darkness, someone laughed. 'And as for eyes,' it said,
'you have eyes that see the obvious, in broad daylight, if you are
lucky, whereas my people have eyes that can see the hairs prickle
on your arms as I talk to you, see the terror on your face, and see
that in the night time. Fear me, Anansi's child, and if you have
any final prayers to say, say them now.'

Spider had no prayers, but he had rocks, and he could throw
them. Perhaps he might get lucky, and a rock might do some
damage in the darkness. Spider knew that it would be a miracle
if it did, but he had spent his entire life relying on miracles.

He reached for another rock.

Something brushed the back of his hand.

Hello, said the little clay spider, in his mind.

Hi, thought Spider. *Look, I'm a bit busy here, trying not to be
eaten, so if you don't mind keeping out of the way for a while . . .*

But I brought them, thought the spider. *Like you asked.*

Like I asked?

*You told me to go for help. I brought them back with me. They
followed my webstrand. There are no spiders in this creation, so I
slipped back and webbed from there to here and from here to there
again. I brought the warriors. I brought the brave.*

'A penny for your thoughts,' said the big cat voice in the

darkness. And then it said, with a certain refined amusement, 'What's the matter? Cat got your tongue?'

A single spider is silent. They cultivate silence. Even the ones that do make noises will normally remain as still as they can, waiting. So much of what spiders do is waiting.

The night was slowly filled with a gentle rustling.

Spider thought his gratitude and pride at the little seven-legged spider he had made from his blood and spittle and from the earth. The spider scuttled from the back of his hand up to his shoulder.

Spider could not see them, but he knew they were all there: the great spiders and the small spiders, venomous spiders and biting spiders: huge hairy spiders and elegant chitinous spiders. Their eyes took whatever light they could find, but they saw through their legs and their feet, constructing vibrations into a virtual image of the world about them.

They were an army.

Tiger spoke again from the darkness. 'When you are dead, Anansi's child – when all of your bloodline is dead – then the stories will be mine. Once again, people will tell Tiger stories. They will gather together and praise my cunning and my strength, my cruelty and my joy. Every story will be mine. Every song will be mine. The world will be as it once was again: a hard place. A dark place.'

Spider listened to the rustle of his army.

He was sitting at the cliff-edge for a reason. While it gave him nowhere to retreat to, it meant that Tiger could not charge, he could only creep.

Spider started to laugh.

'What are you laughing at, Anansi's child? Have you lost your reason?'

At that, Spider laughed longer and louder.

There was a yowl from the darkness. Tiger had met Spider's army.

Spider venom comes in many forms. It can often take a long while to discover the full effects of the bite. Naturalists have pondered this for years: there are even spiders whose bite can cause the place bitten to rot and to die, sometimes more than a year after it was bitten. As to why spiders do this, the answer is simple. It's because spiders think this is funny, and they don't want you ever to forget them.

Black widow bites on Tiger's bruised nose, tarantula bites on his ears: in moments his sensitive places burned and throbbed, swelled and itched. Tiger did not know what was happening: all he knew was the burning and the pain and the sudden fear.

Spider laughed, longer and louder, and listened to the sound of a huge animal bolting into the undergrowth, roaring in agony and in fright.

Then he sat and he waited. Tiger would be back, he had no doubt. It was not over yet.

Spider took the seven-legged spider from his shoulder, and stroked it, running his fingers back and forth across its broad back.

A little way down the hill something glowed with a cold green luminescence, and it flickered, like the lights of a tiny city, flashing on and off into the night. It was coming towards him.

The flickering resolved itself into a hundred thousand fireflies. Silhouetted and illuminated in the centre of the firefly-light was a dark figure, man-shaped. It was walking steadily up the hill.

Spider raised a rock, mentally readied his spider-troops for one more attack. And then he stopped. There was something familiar about the figure in the firefly-light; it wore a green fedora.

* * *

Grahame Coats was most of the way through a half-bottle of rum he had found in the kitchen. He had opened the rum because he had no desire to go down into the wine cellar, and because he imagined it would get him drunk faster than wine would. Unfortunately, it didn't. It did not seem to be doing much of anything, let alone providing the emotional off-switch he felt he needed. He walked around the house with a bottle in one hand and a half-full glass in the other, and sometimes he took a swig from one, and sometimes from the other. He caught sight of his reflection in the mirror, hangdog and sweaty. 'Cheer up,' he said aloud. 'Might never happen. Cloud silver lining. Life rain mus' fall. Too many cooks. 'S an ill wind.' The rum was pretty much gone.

He went back into the kitchen. He opened several cupboards before he noticed a bottle of sherry, towards the back. Grahame picked it up and cradled it gratefully, as if it were a very small old friend who had just returned after years at sea.

He unscrewed the top of the bottle. It was a sweet cooking sherry, but he drank it down like lemonade.

There were other things Graham Coats had noticed, while looking for alcohol in the kitchen. There were, for example, knives. Some of them were very sharp. In a drawer, there was even a small stainless-steel hacksaw. Grahame Coats approved. It would be the very simple solution to the problem in the basement.

'*Habeas corpus*,' he said. 'Or *habeas delicti*. One of those. If there is no body, then there was no crime. *Ergo. Quod erat demonstrandum.*'

He took his gun out of his jacket pocket, put it on the kitchen table. He arranged the knives around it in a pattern, like the spokes of a wheel. 'Well,' he said, in the same tones he had once used to use to persuade innocent boy bands that it was time to sign their contract with him and to say hello to fame if not actually fortune, 'no time like the present.'

He pushed three kitchen knives blade down through his belt, placed the hacksaw in his jacket pocket, and then, gun in hand, he went down the cellar stairs. He turned on the lights, blinked at the wine bottles on their side, each in their rack, each covered with a thin layer of dust, and then he was standing beside the iron meat-locker door.

'Right,' he shouted. 'You'll be pleased to hear that I'm not going to hurt you. I'll be letting you both go now. All a bit of a mistake. Still, no hard feelings. No use crying over spilt. Stand by the far wall. Assume the position. No funny stuff.'

It was, he reflected, as he pulled back the bolts, almost comforting how many clichés already exist for people holding guns. It made Grahame Coats feel like one of a brotherhood: Bogart stood beside him, and Cagney, and all the people who shout at each other on *COPS*.

He turned the light on and pulled open the door. Rosie's mother stood against the far wall, with her back to him. As he came in, she flipped up her skirt and waggled an astonishingly bony brown bottom.

His jaw dropped open. That was when Rosie slammed down a length of rusty chain on to Grahame Coat's wrist, sending the gun flying across the room.

With the enthusiasm and accuracy of a much younger woman, Rosie's mother kicked Grahame Coats in the groin, and as he clutched his crotch and doubled up, making noises pitched at a level that only dogs and bats could hear, Rosie and her mother stumbled out of the meat locker.

They pushed the door closed and Rosie pushed shut one of the bolts. They hugged.

They were still in the wine cellar when all the lights went off.

'It's just the fuses,' said Rosie, to reassure her mother. She was not certain that she believed it, but she had no other explanation.

'You should have locked both bolts,' said her mother. And then, 'Ow,' as she stubbed her toe on something, and cursed.

'On the bright side,' said Rosie, '*he* can't see in the dark either. Just hold my hand. I think the stairs are up this way.'

Grahame Coats was down on all fours on the concrete floor of the meat cellar, in the darkness when the lights went out. There was something hot dripping down his leg. He thought for one uncomfortable moment that he had wet himself, before he understood that the blade of one of the knives he had pushed into his belt had cut deeply into the top of his leg.

He stopped moving and lay on the floor. He decided that he had been very sensible to have drunk so much: it was practically an anaesthetic. He decided to go to sleep.

He was not alone in the meat locker. There was someone in there with him. Something that moved on four legs.

Somebody growled, 'Get up.'

'Can't get up. I'm hurt. Want to go to bed.'

'You're a pitiful little creature and you destroy everything you touch. Now get up.'

'Would love to,' said Grahame Coats in the reasonable tones of a drunk. 'Can't. Just going to lie on the floor for a bit. Anyway. She bolted the door. I heard her.'

He heard a scraping from the other side of the door, as if a bolt was slowly being released.

'The door is open. Now: if you stay here, you'll die.' An impatient rustling; the swish of a tail; a roar, half-muffled in the back of a throat. 'Give me your hand and your allegiance. Invite me inside you.'

'I don't underst—'

'Give me your hand, or bleed to death.'

In the black of the meat cellar, Grahame Coats put out his hand. Someone – something – took it, and held it, reassuringly. 'Now, are you willing to invite me in?'

A moment of cold sobriety touched Grahame Coats then. He had already gone too far. Nothing he did would make matters worse, after all.

'Absatively,' whispered Grahame Coats, and as he said it he began to change. He could see through the darkness easy as daylight. He thought, but only for a moment, that he saw something beside him, bigger than a man, with sharp, sharp teeth. And then it was gone, and Grahame Coats felt wonderful. The blood no longer spurted from his leg.

He could see clearly in the darkness. He pulled the knives from his belt, dropped them on to the floor. He pulled off his shoes, too. There was a gun on the ground, but he left it there. Tools were for apes and crows and weaklings. He was no ape.

He was a hunter.

He pulled himself up on to his hands and his knees, and then he padded, four-footed, out into the wine-cellar.

He could see the women. They had found the steps up to the house, and they were edging up them blindly, hand in hand in the darkness.

One of them was old and stringy. The other was young and tender. The mouth salivated in something that was partly Grahame Coats.

* * *

Fat Charlie left the bridge, with his father's green fedora pushed back on his head, and he walked into the dusk. He walked up the rocky beach, slipping on the rocks, splashing into pools. Then he trod on something that moved. A stumble, and he stepped off it.

It rose into the air, and it kept rising. Whatever it was, it was enormous: he thought at first that it was the size of an elephant, but it grew bigger still.

Light, thought Fat Charlie. He sang aloud, and all the lightning bugs, the fireflies of that place, clustered around him, flickering off and on with their cold green luminescence, and in their light he could make out two eyes, bigger than dinner plates, staring down at him from a supercilious reptilian face.

He stared back. 'Evening,' he said, cheerfully.

A voice from the creature, smooth as buttered oil. 'He-llo,' it said. 'Ding-dong. You look remarkably like dinner.'

'I'm Charlie Nancy,' said Charlie Nancy. 'Who are you?'

'I am Dragon,' said the dragon. 'And I shall devour you in one slow mouthful, little man in a hat.'

Charlie blinked. *What would my father do?* he wondered. *What would Spider have done?* He had absolutely no idea. *Come on. After all, Spider's sort of a part of me. I can do whatever he can do.*

'Er. You're bored with talking to me now, and you're going to let me pass unhindered,' he told the dragon, with as much conviction as he was able to muster.

'Gosh. Good try. But I'm afraid I'm not,' said the dragon, enthusiastically. 'Actually, I'm going to eat you.'

'You aren't scared of limes, are you?' asked Charlie, before remembering that he'd given the lime to Daisy.

The creature laughed, scornfully. 'I,' it said, 'am frightened of nothing.'

'Nothing?'

'Nothing,' it said.

Charlie said, 'Are you *extremely* frightened of nothing?'

'Absolutely terrified of it,' admitted the Dragon.

'You know,' said Charlie, 'I have nothing in my pockets. Would you like to see it?'

'No,' said the Dragon, uncomfortably, 'I most definitely would not.'

There was a flapping of wings like sails, and Charlie was alone on the beach. 'That,' he said, 'was much too easy.'

He kept on walking. He made up a song for his walk. Charlie had always wanted to make up songs, but he never did, mostly because of the conviction that if he ever had written a song, someone would have asked him to sing it, and that would not have been a good thing, much as death by hanging would not be a good thing. Now, he cared less and less, and he sang his song to the fireflies, who followed him up the hillside. It was a song about meeting the Bird Woman and finding his brother. He hoped the fireflies were enjoying it: their light seemed to be pulsing and flickering in time with the tune.

The Bird Woman was waiting for him at the top of the hill.

Charlie took off his hat. He pulled the feather from the hatband. 'Here. This is yours, I believe.'

She made no move to take it.

'Our deal's over,' said Charlie. 'I brought your feather. I want my brother. You took him. I want him back. Anansi's bloodline was not mine to give.'

'And if I no longer have your brother?'

It was hard to tell, in the firefly light, but Charlie did not believe that her lips had moved. Her words surrounded him, however, in the cries of nightjars, and in the owls' shrieks and hoots.

'I want my brother back,' he told her. 'I want him whole and in one piece and uninjured. And I want him now. Or whatever went on between you and my father over the years was just the prelude. You know. The overture.'

Charlie had never threatened anyone before. He had no idea how he would carry out his threats – but he had no doubt that he would indeed carry them out.

'I had him,' she said, in the bittern's distant boom. 'But I left him, tongueless, in Tiger's world. I could not hurt your father's line. Tiger could, once he found his courage.'

A hush. The night-frogs and the night-birds were perfectly silent. She stared at him impassively, her face almost part of the shadows. Her hand went into the pocket of her coat. 'Give me the feather,' she said.

Charlie put it into her hand.

He felt lighter, then, as if she had taken more from him than just an old feather . . .

Then she placed something into his hand: something cold and damp. It felt like a lump of meat, and Charlie had to quell the urge to fling it away.

'Return it to him,' she said, in the voice of the night. 'He has no quarrel with me, now.'

'How do I get to Tiger's world.'

'How did you get here?' she asked, sounding almost amused, and the night was complete, and Charlie was alone on the hill.

He opened his hand and looked at the lump of meat that sat there, floppy and ridged. It looked like a tongue, and he knew whose tongue it had to be.

He put the fedora back on his head, and he thought, *Put my thinking cap on*, and as he thought it, it didn't seem so funny. The green fedora was not a thinking cap: but it was the kind of hat that would be worn by someone who not only thought but also came to conclusions of an important and vital kind.

He imagined the worlds as a web: it blazed in his mind, connecting him to everyone he knew. The strand that connected him to Spider was strong and bright, and it burned with a cold light, like a lightning bug or a star.

Spider had been a part of him, once. He held on to this knowledge, let the web fill his mind. And in his hand was his brother's tongue: that had been part of Spider until very recently, and it wished devoutly to be part of him again. Living things remember.

The wild light of the web burned about him. All Charlie needed to do was follow it . . .

He followed it, and the fireflies clustered around and travelled with him.

'Hey,' he said. 'It's me.'

Spider made a small, terrible noise.

In the glimmer of firefly light, Spider looked awful: he looked hunted and he looked hurt. There were scabs on his face and chest.

'I think this is probably yours,' said Charlie.

Spider took the tongue from his brother, with an exaggerated *thank you* gesture, placed it into his mouth, pushed it in and held it down. Charlie watched and waited as the tongue took root. Soon, Spider seemed satisfied – he moved his mouth experimentally, pushing the tongue to one side and then to the other, as if he were preparing to shave off a moustache, opening his mouth widely and waggling his tongue about. He closed his mouth and stood up.

Finally, in a voice that was still a little wobbly around the edges, he said, 'Nice hat.'

* * *

Rosie made it to the top of the steps first, and she pushed open the wine-cellar door. She stumbled into the house. She waited for her mother, then she slammed and bolted the cellar door behind her. The power was out up here as well, but the moon was high and nearly full, and, after the darkness, the pallid moonlight coming through the kitchen windows might as well have been floodlighting.

Boys and girls come out to play, thought Rosie. *The moon does shine as bright as day . . .*

'Phone the police,' said her mother.

'Where's the phone?'

'How the hell should I know where the phone is? He's still down there.'

'Right,' said Rosie, wondering whether she should find a phone to call the police, or just get out of the house, but before she had reached a decision, it was too late.

There was a bang so loud it hurt her ears, and the door to the cellar crashed open.

The shadow came out of the cellar.

It was real. She knew it was real. She was looking at it. But it was impossible: it was the shadow of a great cat, shaggy and huge. Strangely, though, when the moonlight touched it, the shadow seemed *darker*. Rosie could not see its eyes, but she knew it was looking at her, and that it was hungry.

It was going to kill her. This was where it would end.

Her mother said, 'It wants you, Rosie.'

'I know.'

Rosie picked up the nearest large object, a wooden block that had once held knives, and she threw it at the shadow as hard as she could, and then, without waiting to see if it made contact, she moved as fast as she could out of the kitchen, into the hallway. She knew where the front door was . . .

Something dark, something four-footed, moved faster: it bounded over her head, landed almost silently in front of her.

Rosie backed up against the wall. Her mouth was dry.

The beast was between them and the front door, and it was padding slowly back towards Rosie, as if it had all the time in the world.

Her mother ran out of the kitchen then, then ran past Rosie – tottered down the moonlit corridor towards the great shadow, her arms flailing. With her thin fists she punched the thing in the ribs. There was a pause, as if the world was holding its breath, and then it turned on her. A blur of motion and Rosie's mother was down on the ground, while the shadow shook her like a dog with a rag doll between its teeth.

The doorbell rang.

Rosie wanted to call for help, but instead she found she was screaming, loudly and insistently. Rosie, when confronted with an unexpected spider in a bathtub, was capable of screaming like a B-movie actress on her first encounter with a man in a rubber suit. Now she was in a dark house containing a shadowy tiger and a potential serial killer, and one, perhaps both, of those entities, had just attacked her mother. Her head thought of a couple of courses of action (the gun: the gun was down in the cellar. She ought to go down and get the gun. Or the door – she could try to get past her mother and the shadow and unlock the front door) but her lungs and her mouth would only scream.

Something banged at the front door. *They're trying to break in,* she thought. *They won't get through that door. It's solid.*

Her mother lay on the floor in a patch of moonlight, and the shadow crouched above her, and it threw back its head and it roared, a deep rattling roar of fear and challenge and possession.

I'm hallucinating, thought Rosie with a wild certainty. *I've been*

*locked up in a cellar for two days and now I'm hallucinating. There
is no tiger.*

By the same token, she was certain that there was no pale
woman in the moonlight, even though she could see her walking
down the corridor, a woman with blonde hair, and the long, long
legs and narrow hips of a dancer. The woman stopped when she
reached the shadow of the tiger. She said, 'Hello, Grahame.'

The shadow-beast lifted its massive head and growled.

'Don't think you can hide from me in that silly animal costume,'
said the woman. She did not look pleased.

Rosie realised that she could see the window through the
woman's upper body, and she backed up until she was pressing
hard against the wall.

The beast growled again, this time a little more uncertainly.

The woman said, 'I don't believe in ghosts, Grahame. I spent
my life, my whole life, not believing in ghosts. And then I met
you. You let Morris's career run aground. You steal from us. You
murder me. And finally, to add insult to injury, you force me to
believe in ghosts.'

The shadowy big-cat-shape was whimpering now, and backing
down the hall.

'Don't think you can avoid me like that, you useless little
man. You can pretend to be a tiger all you like. You aren't a
tiger. You're a rat. No, that's an insult to a noble and numerous
species of rodent. You're less than a rat. You're a gerbil. You're a
stoat.'

Rosie ran down the hall. She ran past the shadow-beast, past
her fallen mother. She ran *through* the pale woman, and it felt like
she was passing through fog. She reached the front door, and
began feeling for the bolts.

In her head or in the world Rosie could hear an argument.

Someone was saying, *Pay no attention to her, idiot. She can't
touch you. It's just a duppy. She's barely real. Get the girl! Stop the
girl!*

And someone else was replying, *You certainly do have a valid
point here. But I'm not convinced that you've taken all the
circumstances into account, vis-à-vis, well, discretion, um, better
part of valour, if you follow me . . .*

I *lead*. You *follow*.

But . . .

'What I want to know,' said the pale woman, 'is just how ghostly you currently are. I mean, I can't touch people. I can't really even touch things. I *can* touch ghosts.'

The pale woman aimed a serious kick at the beast's face. The shadow-cat hissed and took a step back, and the foot missed it by less than an inch.

The next kick connected, and the beast yowled. Another kick, hard against the place the cat's shadowy nose would be, and the beast made the noise of a cat being shampooed, a lonely wail of horror and outrage, of shame and defeat.

The corridor was filled with the sound of a dead woman laughing, a laugh of exultation and delight. 'Stoat,' said the pale woman's voice, again. 'Grahame Stoat.'

A cold wind blew through the house.

Rosie pulled the last of the bolts, and she turned the lock. The front door fell open. There were the beams of flashlights, blinding-bright. People. Cars. A woman's voice said, 'It's one of the missing tourists.' And then she said, 'My God.'

Rosie turned.

In the flashlight's beam Rosie could see her mother, crumpled on the tiled floor, and, beside her, shoeless and unconscious and unmistakably human, Grahame Coats. There was a red liquid splashed all around them, like crimson paint, and Rosie found herself, for a breath, unable to work out what it was.

A woman was talking to her. She was saying, 'You're Rosie Noah. My name's Daisy. Let's find somewhere for you to sit down. Would you like to sit down?'

Someone must have found the fuse box, for at that moment the lights went on all over the house.

A large man in a police uniform was bent over the bodies. He looked up and said, 'It is definitely Mr Finnegan. He is not breathing.'

Rosie said, 'Yes, please. I would like to sit down very much.'

* * *

Charlie sat beside Spider on the edge of the cliff, in the moonlight, his legs dangling over the side.

'You know,' he said, 'you used to be a part of me. When we were kids.'

Spider put his head on one side. 'Really?'

'I think so.'

'Well, that would explain a few things.' He held out his hand: a seven-legged clay spider sat on the back of his fingers, tasting the air. 'So what now? Are you going to take me back or something?'

Charlie's brow crinkled. 'I think you've turned out better than you would have done if you were part of me. And you've had a lot more fun.'

Spider said, 'Rosie. Tiger knows about Rosie. We have to do something.'

'Of course we do,' said Charlie. It was like book-keeping, he thought: you put entries in one column, deduct them from another, and if you've done it correctly, everything should come out right at the bottom of the page. He took his brother's hand.

They stood up, and took a step forward, off the cliff –

– and everything was bright –

A cold wind blew between the worlds.

Charlie said, 'You're not the magical bit of me, you know.'

'I'm not?' Spider took another step. Stars were falling now by the dozen, streaking their way across the dark sky. Someone, somewhere, was playing high sweet music on a flute.

Another step, and now distant sirens were blaring. 'No,' said Charlie. 'You're not. Mrs Dunwiddy thought you were, I think. She split us apart, but she never really understood what she was doing. We're more like two halves of a starfish. You grew up into a whole person. And so,' he said, realising it was true as he said it, 'did I.'

They stood on the cliff-edge in the dawn. An ambulance was on its way up the hill, lights flashing, and another, behind that. They parked by the side of the road, beside a cluster of police cars.

Daisy seemed to be telling everyone what to do.

'Not much that we can do here. Not now,' said Charlie. 'Come on.' The last of the fireflies left him, and blinked its way to sleep.

They rode the first minibus of the morning back to Williamstown.

***

Maeve Livingstone sat upstairs in the library of Grahame Coats's house, surrounded by Grahame Coats's art and books and DVDs, and she stared out of the window. Down below the island's emergency services were putting Rosie and her mother into one ambulance, Grahame Coats into another.

She had, she reflected, really enjoyed kicking the beast-thing that Grahame Coats had become. It was the most profoundly satisfying thing she had done since she had been killed – although if she were to be honest with herself, she would have to admit that dancing with Mr Nancy came in an extremely close second. He had been remarkably spry, and nimble on his feet.

She was tired.

'Maeve?'

'Morris?' She looked around her, but the room was empty.

'I wouldn't want to disturb you, if you were still busy, pet.'

'That's very sweet of you,' she said. 'But I think I'm done.'

The walls of the library were beginning to fade. They were losing colour and form. The world behind the walls was starting to show, and in its light she saw a small figure in a smart suit waiting for her.

Her hand crept into his. She said, 'Where are we going now, Morris?'

He told her.

'Oh. Well, that will be a pleasant change,' she said. 'I've always wanted to go there.'

And, hand in hand, they went.

Chapter Fourteen

Which Comes to
Several Conclusions

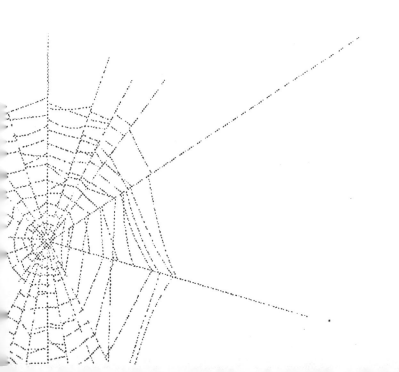

Charlie woke to a banging on a door. Disorientated, he looked around: he was in a hotel room, and various unlikely events clustered inside his head like moths around a naked bulb, and while he tried to make sense of them he let his feet get up and walk him to the hotel-room door. He blinked at the diagram on the back of the door, which told him where to go in case of fire, trying to remember the events of the previous night. Then he unlocked the door and pulled it open.

Daisy looked up at him. She said, 'Were you asleep in that hat?'

Charlie put his hand up and felt his head. There was definitely a hat on it. 'Yes,' he said. 'I think I must have been.'

'Bless,' she said. 'Well, at least you took your shoes off. You know you missed all the excitement, last night?'

'I did?'

'Brush your teeth,' she said helpfully. 'And change your shirt. Yes, you did. While you were . . .' and then she hesitated. It seemed quite improbable, on reflection, that he really had vanished in the middle of a séance. These things did not happen.

Not in the real world. 'While you weren't there. I got the police chief to go up to Grahame Coats's house. He had those tourists.'

'Tourists . . . ?'

'It was what he said at dinner, something about us sending the two people in, the two at the house. It was your fiancée and her mother. He'd locked them up in his basement.'

'Are they OK?'

'They're both in the hospital.'

'Oh.'

'Her mum's in rough shape. I think your fiancée will be OK.'

'Will you stop calling her that? She's not my fiancée. She ended the engagement.'

'Yes. But you didn't, did you?'

'She's not in love with me,' said Charlie. 'Now, I'm going to brush my teeth and change my shirt, and I need a certain amount of privacy.'

'You should shower too,' she said. 'And that hat smells like a cigar.'

'It's a family heirloom,' he told her, and he went into the bathroom and locked the door behind him.

* * *

The hospital was a ten-minute walk from the hotel, and Spider was sitting in the waiting room, holding a dog-eared copy of *Entertainment Weekly* magazine as if he were actually reading it.

Charlie tapped him on the shoulder, and Spider jumped. He looked up warily and then, seeing his brother, he relaxed, but not much. 'They said I had to wait out here,' Spider said. 'Because I'm not a relation or anything.'

Charlie boggled. 'Well, why didn't you just *tell* them you were a relative? Or a doctor?'

Spider looked uncomfortable. 'Well, it's easy to do that stuff if you don't *care*. If it doesn't matter if I go in or I don't, it's easy to go in. But now it matters, and I'd hate to get in the way or do something wrong, and I mean, what if I tried and they said no, and then . . . what are you grinning about?'

'Nothing really,' said Charlie. 'It just all sounds a bit familiar.

Come on. Let's go and find Rosie. You know,' he said to Daisy, as they set off down a random corridor, 'there are two ways to walk through a hospital. Either you look like you belong there – here you go, Spider. White coat on back of door, just your size. Put it on – or you should look so out of place that no one will complain that you're there. They'll just leave it for someone else to sort out.' He began to hum.

'What's that song?' asked Daisy.

'It's called "Yellow Bird",' said Spider.

Charlie pushed his hat back on his head, and they walked into Rosie's hospital room.

Rosie was sitting up in bed, reading a magazine and looking worried. When she saw the three of them come in, she looked more worried. She looked from Spider to Charlie and back again.

'You're both a long way from home,' was all she said.

'We all are,' said Charlie. 'Now, you've met Spider. This is Daisy. She's in the police.'

'I'm not sure that I am any more,' said Daisy. 'I'm probably in all kinds of hot water.'

'You're the one who was there last night? The one who got the island police to come up to the house?' Rosie stopped. She said, 'Any word on Grahame Coats?'

'He's in intensive care, just like your mum.'

'Well, if she comes to before he does,' said Rosie, 'I expect she'll kill him.' Then she said, 'They won't talk to me about my mum's condition. They just say that it's very serious, and they'll tell me as soon as there's anything to tell.' She looked at Charlie with clear eyes. 'She's not as bad as you think she is, really. Not when you get time to know her. We had a lot of time to talk, locked up in the dark. She's all right.'

She blew her nose. Then she said, 'They don't think she's going to make it. They haven't directly said that to me, but they sort of said it in a not-saying it sort of way. It's funny. I thought she'd live through anything.'

Charlie said, 'Me too. I figured even if there was a nuclear war, it would still leave radioactive cockroaches and your mum.'

Daisy stepped on his foot. She said, 'Do they know anything more about what hurt her?'

'I told them,' said Rosie. 'There was some kind of animal in the house. Maybe it was just Grahame Coats. I mean it sort of was him, but it was sort of someone else. She distracted it from me, and it went for her . . .' She had explained it all as best she could to the island police that morning. She had decided not to talk about the blonde ghost-woman. Sometimes minds snap under pressure, and she thought it best if people did not know that hers had.

Rosie broke off. She was staring at Spider as if she had only just remembered who he was. She said, 'I still hate you, you know.' Spider said nothing, but a miserable expression crept across his face, and he no longer looked like a doctor: now he looked like a man who had borrowed a white coat from behind a door and was worried that someone would notice. A dreamlike tone came into her voice. 'Only,' she said, 'only when I was in the dark, I thought that you were helping me. That you were keeping the animal away. What happened to your face? It's all scratched.'

'It was an animal,' said Spider.

'You know,' she said, 'now I see you both at once, you don't look anything alike at all.'

'I'm the good-looking one,' said Charlie, and Daisy's foot pressed down on his toes for the second time.

'Bless,' said Daisy, quietly. And then, slightly louder, 'Charlie? There's something we need to talk about outside. Now.'

They went out into the hospital corridor, leaving Spider inside.

'What?' said Charlie.

'What what?' said Daisy.

'What have we got to talk about?'

'Nothing.'

'Then why are we out here? You heard her. She hates him. We shouldn't have left them alone together. She's probably killed him by now.

Daisy looked up at him with the kind of expression that Jesus might have given someone who had just explained that he was probably allergic to bread and fishes, so could He possibly do him a quick chicken salad: there was pity in that expression, along with almost infinite compassion.

She touched a finger to her lips and pulled him back towards the door. He looked back into the hospital room: Rosie did not appear to be killing Spider. Quite the opposite, if anything. 'Oh,' said Charlie.

They were kissing. Put like that, and you could be forgiven for presuming that this was a normal kiss, all lips and skin and possibly even a little tongue. You'd miss how he smiled, how his eyes glowed. And then, after the kiss was done, how he stood, like a man who had just discovered the art of standing and had figured out how to do it better than anyone else who would ever come along.

Charlie turned his attention back to the corridor, to find Daisy in conversation with several doctors and the police officer they had encountered the previous evening.

'Well, we always had him figured as a bad man,' the police officer was saying to Daisy. 'I mean, frankly, you only get this kind of behaviour from foreigners. The local people, they simply wouldn't do that kind of thing.'

'Obviously not,' said Daisy.

'Very. Very grateful,' said the police chief, patting her shoulder in a way that set Daisy's teeth on edge. 'This little lady saved that woman's life,' he told Charlie, giving his shoulder a patronising pat for good measure, before setting off, with the doctors, down the corridor.

'So what's happening?' asked Charlie.

'Well, Grahame Coats is dead,' she said. 'More or less. And they don't hold out any hope for Rosie's mum, either.'

'I see,' said Charlie. He thought about this. Then he finished thinking, and came to a decision. Said, 'Would you mind if I just chatted to my brother for a bit? I think he and I need to talk.'

'I'm going back to the hotel anyway. I'm going to check my e-mail. Probably going to have to say sorry on the phone a lot. Find out if I still have a career.'

'But you're a hero, aren't you?'

'I don't think that's what anyone was paying me for,' she said, a little wanly. 'Come and find me at the hotel when you're done.'

Spider and Charlie walked down the Williamstown high street in the morning sun.

'You know, that really is a good hat,' said Spider.

'You really think so?'

'Yeah. Can I try it on?'

Charlie gave Spider the green fedora. Spider put it on, looked at his reflection in a shop window. He made a face, and gave Charlie the hat back. 'Well,' he said, disappointed, 'it looks good on you, anyway.'

Charlie pushed his fedora back on to his head. Some hats can only be worn if you're willing to be jaunty, to set them at an angle and to walk beneath them with a spring in your stride, as if you're only a step away from dancing. They demand a lot of you. This hat was one of those, and Charlie was up to it. He said, 'Rosie's mum is dying.'

'Yeah.'

'I really, *really* never liked her.'

'I didn't know her as well as you did. But given time, I'm sure I would have really, really disliked her too.'

Charlie said, 'We have to try and save her life, don't we?' He said it without enthusiasm, like someone pointing out it was time to visit the dentist.

'I don't think we can do things like that.'

'Dad did something like it for Mum. He got her better, for a while.'

'But that was him. I don't know how we'd do that.'

Charlie said, 'The place at the end of the world. With the caves.'

'Beginning of the world, not the end. What about it?'

'Can we just get there? Without all that candles and herbs malarkey?'

Spider was quiet. Then he nodded, 'I think so.'

They turned together, turned in a direction that wasn't usually there, and they walked away from the Williamstown high street.

Now the sun was rising, and Charlie and Spider walked across a beach littered with skulls. They were not proper human skulls, and they covered the beach like yellow pebbles. Charlie avoided them, where he could, while Spider crunched his way through them. At the end of the beach they took a left turn that was left to absolutely everything, and the mountains at the beginning of the world towered above them and the cliffs fell away below.

Charlie remembered the last time he was here, and it seemed

like a thousand years ago. 'Where is everyone?' he said aloud, and his voice echoed against the rocks and came back to him. He said, loudly, 'Hello?'

And then they were there, watching him. All of them. They seemed grander, now, less human, more animal, *wilder*. He realised that he had seen them as people last time because he had expected to meet people. But they were not people. Arrayed on the rocks above them were Lion and Elephant, Crocodile and Python, Rabbit and Scorpion, and the rest of them, hundreds of them, and they stared at him with eyes unsmiling: animals he recognised; animals that no one living would be able to identify. All the animals that have ever been in stories. All the animals that people have dreamed of, worshipped or placated.

Charlie saw all of them.

It's one thing, he thought, *singing for your life, in a room filled with diners, on the spur-of-the-moment, with a gun barrel in the ribs of the girl you . . .*

That you . . .

Oh.

Well, thought Charlie, *I can worry about that later.*

Right now he badly wanted either to breathe into a brown paper bag, or to vanish.

'There must be hundreds of them,' said Spider, and there was awe in his voice.

There was a flurry in the air, on a nearby rock, which resolved itself into the Bird Woman. She folded her arms and stared at them.

'Whatever it is you're going to do,' Spider said, 'you'd better do it soon. They aren't going to wait around for ever.'

Charlie's mouth was dry. 'Right.'

Spider said, 'So. Um. What exactly do we do now?'

'We sing to them,' said Charlie, simply.

'What?'

'It's how we fix things. I figured it out. We just sing it all, you and I.'

'I don't understand. Sing *what*?'

Charlie said, 'The *song*. You sing the song, you fix things.' Now he sounded desperate. 'The *song*.'

Spider's eyes were like puddles, after the rain, and Charlie saw things in them he had not seen before: affection, perhaps, and confusion, and, mostly, apology. 'I don't know what you're talking about.'

Lion watched them from the side of a boulder. Monkey looked at them from the top of a tree. And Tiger . . .

Charlie saw Tiger. It was walking gingerly towards them, on four feet. Its face was swollen and bruised, but there was a glint in its eyes, and it looked as if it would be more than happy to even the score.

Charlie opened his mouth. A small croaking noise came out, as if Charlie had recently swallowed a particularly nervous frog. 'It's no use,' he whispered to Spider. 'This was a stupid idea, wasn't it?

'Yup.'

'Do you think we can just go away again?' Charlie's nervous glance swept the mountainside and the caves, took in each of the hundreds of totem creatures from before the dawn of time. There was one he had not seen the last time he had looked: a small man, with lemon-yellow gloves, and a pencil-thin moustache, and no fedora hat to cover his thinning hair.

The old man winked when he caught Charlie's gaze.

It wasn't much, but it was enough.

Charlie filled his lungs, and he began to sing. 'I am Charlie,' he sang. 'I am Anansi's son. Listen as I sing my song. Listen to my life.'

He sang them the song of a boy who was half a god, and who was broken into two by an old woman with a grudge. He sang of his father, and he sang of his mother.

He sang of names and words, of the building blocks beneath the real, the worlds that make worlds, the truths beneath the way things are; he sang of appropriate ends and just conclusions for those who would have hurt him and his.

He sang the world.

It was a good song, and it was his song. Sometimes it had words, and sometimes it didn't have any words at all.

As he sang, all the creatures listening began to clap and to stamp and to hum along; Charlie felt like he was the conduit for a great song that took in all of them. He sang of birds, of the magic of looking up and seeing them in flight, of the sheen of the sun on a wingfeather in the morning.

The totem creatures were dancing now, the dances of their kind. The Bird Woman danced the wheeling dance of birds, fanning her tailfeathers, tossing back her beak.

There was only one creature on the mountainside who did not dance.

Tiger lashed his tail. He was not clapping or singing or dancing. His face was bruised purple, and his body was covered in welts and in bite-marks. He had padded down the rocks, a step at a time, until he was close to Charlie. 'The songs aren't yours,' he growled.

Charlie looked at him, and sang about Tiger, and about Grahame Coats, and those who would prey upon the innocent. He turned: Spider was looking up at him with admiration.

Tiger roared in anger, and Charlie took the roar and wound his song around it. Then he did the roar himself, just like Tiger had done it. Well, the roar began just as Tiger's roar had, but then Charlie changed it, so it became a really goofy sort of roar, and all the creatures watching from the rocks started to laugh. They couldn't help it. Charlie did the goofy roar again. Like any impersonation, like any perfect caricature, it had the effect of making what it made fun of intrinsically ridiculous. No one would ever hear Tiger roar again without hearing Charlie's roar underneath it. 'Goofy sort of a roar,' they'd say.

Tiger turned his back on Charlie. He loped through the crowd, roaring as he ran, which only made the crowd laugh the harder; and Tiger angrily retreated back into his cave.

Spider gestured with his hands; a curt movement.

There was a rumble, and the mouth of Tiger's cave collapsed in a small rockslide. Spider looked satisfied. Charlie kept singing.

He sang the song of Rosie Noah, and the song of Rosie's mother: he sang a long life for Mrs Noah and all the happiness that she deserved.

He sang of his life, all of their lives, and in his song he saw the pattern of their lives as a web that a fly had blundered into, and with his song he wrapped the fly, made certain it would not escape, and he repaired the web with new strands.

And now the song was coming to its natural end.

Charlie realised, with no little surprise, that he enjoyed singing to other people, and he knew, at that moment, that this was what he would spend the rest of his life doing. He would sing: not big, magical songs that made worlds or recreated existence. Just small songs, that would make people happy for a breath, make them move, make them, for a little while, forget their problems. And he knew that there would always be the fear before performing, the stage-fright, that would never go away, but he also understood that it would be like jumping into a swimming pool – only uncomfortably chill for a few seconds – and then the discomfort would pass and it would be good . . .

Never *this* good. Never this good again. But good enough.

And then he was done. Charlie hung his head. The creatures on the clifftop let the last notes die away, stopped stamping, stopped clapping, stopped dancing. Charlie took off his father's green fedora and fanned his face with it.

Under his breath, Spider said, 'That was amazing.'

'You could have done it too,' said Charlie.

'I don't think so. What was happening at the end? I felt you doing *something*, but I couldn't really tell what it was.'

'I fixed things,' said Charlie. 'For us. I think. I'm not really sure . . .' And he wasn't. Now the song was over, the content of the song was unravelling like a dream in the morning.

He pointed to the cave mouth that was blocked by rocks. 'Did you do that?'

'Yeah,' said Spider. 'Seemed the least I could do. Tiger will dig his way out eventually, though. I wish I'd done something worse than just shut the door on him, to be honest.'

'Not to worry,' said Charlie. 'I did. Something much worse.'

He watched the animals disperse. His father was nowhere to be seen, which did not surprise him. 'Come on,' he said. 'We ought to be getting back.'

* * *

Spider went back to see Rosie at visiting time. He was carrying a large box of chocolates, the largest that the hospital gift shop sold.

'For you,' he said.

'Thanks.'

'They told me,' she said, 'that they think my mum's going to pull through. Apparently she opened her eyes and asked for porridge. The doctor said it's a miracle.'

'Yup. Your mother asking for food. Certainly sounds like a miracle to me.'

She swatted his arm with her hand, then left her hand resting on his arm.

'You know,' she said, after a while, 'you're going to think this is silly of me. But when I was in the dark, with Mum, I thought that you were helping me. I felt like you were keeping the beast at bay. That if you hadn't've done what you were doing, he would have killed us.'

'Um. I probably helped.'

'Really?'

'I don't know. I think so. I was in trouble as well, and I thought about you.'

'Were you in very big trouble?'

'Enormous. Yes.'

'Will you pour me a glass of water, please?'

He did. She said, 'Spider, what do you *do*?'

'Do?'

'For a job.'

'Whatever I feel like doing.'

'I think,' she said, 'I may stay here, for a bit. The nurses have been telling me how much they need teachers here on the island. I'd like to see that I was making a difference.'

'That might be fun.'

'And what would you do, if I did?'

'Oh. Well, if you were here, I'm sure I could find something to keep me busy.'

Their fingers twined, tight as a ship's knot.

'Do you think we can make this work?' she asked.

'I think so,' said Spider, soberly. 'And if I get bored with you, I'll just go away and do something else. So not to worry.'

'Oh,' said Rosie, 'I'm not worried.' And she wasn't. There was steel in her voice, beneath the softness. You could tell where her mother got it from.

* * *

Charlie found Daisy on a deck chair out on the beach. He thought she was asleep in the sun. When his shadow touched her, she said, 'Hello, Charlie.' She didn't open her eyes.

'How did you know it was me?'

'Your hat smells like a cigar. Are you going to be getting rid of it soon?'

'No,' said Charlie. 'I told you. Family heirloom. I plan to wear it till I die, then leave it to my children. So. Do you still have a job with the police force?'

'Sort of,' she said. 'My boss said that it's been decided I was suffering from nervous exhaustion brought on by overwork, and I'm on sick leave until I feel well enough to come back.'

'Ah. And when will that be?'

'Not sure,' she said. 'Can you pass the suntan oil?'

He had a box in his pocket. He took it out and put it on the arm of the deck chair. 'In a minute. Er.' He paused. 'You know,' he said, 'we've already done the big embarrassing one of these at gunpoint.' He opened the box. 'But this is for you, from me. Well, Rosie returned it to me. And we can swap it for one you like. Pick out a different one. Probably it won't even fit. But it's yours. If you want it. And um. Me.'

She reached into the box and took out the engagement ring.

'Hmph. All right,' she said. 'As long as you're not just doing it to get the lime back.'

* * *

Tiger prowled. His tail lashed irritably from side to side, as he paced back and forth across the mouth of his cave. His eyes burned like emerald torches in the shadows.

'Whole world and everything used to be mine,' said Tiger. 'Moon and stars and sun and stories. I owned them all.'

'I feel it incumbent on me to point out,' said a small voice from the back of the cave, 'that you said that already.'

Tiger paused in his pacing; he turned then, and insinuated himself into the back of his cave, rippling as he walked, like a fur rug over hydraulic springs. He padded back until he came to the carcass of an ox and he said, in a quiet voice, 'I *beg* your pardon.'

There was a scrabbling from inside the carcass. The tip of a nose protruded from the ribcage. 'Actually,' it said, 'I was, so to speak, agreeing with you. That was what I was doing.'

Little white hands pulled a thin strip of dried meat from between two ribs, revealing a small animal the colour of dirty snow. It might have been an albino mongoose, or perhaps some particularly shifty kind of weasel in its winter coat. It had a scavenger's eyes.

'Whole world and everything used to be mine. Moon and stars and sun and stories. I owned them all,' said Tiger. Then he said, 'Would have been mine again.'

Tiger stared down at the little beast. Then, without warning, one huge paw descended, smashing the ribcage, breaking the carcass into foul-smelling fragments, pinning the little animal to the floor; it wriggled and writhed but it could not escape.

'You are here,' said Tiger, his huge head nose to nose with the pale animal's tiny head, 'you are here under my sufferance. Do you understand that? Because the next time you say something irritating, I shall bite your head off.'

'Mmmph,' said the weaselly thing.

'You wouldn't like it if I bit off your head, would you?'

'*Nngk*,' said the smaller animal. Its eyes were a pale blue, two chips of ice, and they glinted as it twisted uncomfortably beneath the weight of the huge paw.

'So will you promise me that you will behave, and you will be quiet?' rumbled Tiger. He lifted his paw a little to allow the beast to speak.

'Indeedy,' said the small white thing, extremely politely. Then, with one stoat-like movement, it twisted and sank its sharp little teeth into Tiger's paw. Tiger bellowed in pain, whipped the paw back, sending the little animal flying through the air. It struck the rock ceiling, bounced over to a ledge and from there it darted, like a dirty white streak, to the very back of the cave, where the ceiling got low and close to the floor, and where there were many hiding places for a small animal, places a larger animal could not go.

Tiger padded as far back into the cave as it could easily walk. 'You think I can't wait?' he asked. 'You have to come out sooner or later. I'm not going anywhere.' Tiger lay down. He closed his eyes and soon began to make fairly convincing snoring noises.

After about half an hour of snoring from Tiger, the pale animal crept out from the rocks, and slipped from shadow to shadow, making for a large bone that still had plenty of good meat on it, if you didn't mind a certain rankness, and it didn't. Still, to get to the bone, it would have to pass Tiger. It lurked in the shadows, then it ventured out on little silent feet.

As it passed the sleeping Tiger, a forepaw shot out, and a claw slammed down on the creature's tail, pinning it down. Another paw held the little creature behind the neck. The great cat opened its eyes. 'Frankly,' it said, 'we appear to be stuck with each other. So all I'm asking is that you make an effort. We can both make an effort. I rather doubt that we'll ever be friends, but perhaps we could learn to tolerate each other.'

'I take your point,' said the small ferrety thing. 'Needs must, as they say, when the Devil drives.'

'That's an example of what I'm saying,' said Tiger. 'You just have to learn when to keep your mouth shut.'

'It's an ill wind,' said the little animal, 'that blows nobody any good.'

'Now you're irritating me again,' said Tiger. 'I'm trying to tell you. Don't irritate me, and I won't bite off your head.'

'You keep using the phrase "bite my head off". Now, when you say "bite my head off", I take it I can assume that this is actually some kind of metaphorical statement, implying that you'll shout at me, perhaps rather angrily?'

'Bite your head off. Then crunch it. Then chew it. Then swallow it,' said Tiger. 'Neither of us can leave until Anansi's child forgets we're here. The way that bastard seems to have arranged things, even if I kill you in the morning you'll be reincarnated back in this blasted cave by the end of the afternoon. So don't irritate me.'

'Ah well. Another day . . .' said the small white animal.

'If you say "another dollar",' said Tiger, 'I will be irritated, and there will be serious consequences. Don't. Say anything. Irritating. Do you understand?'

There was a brief silence in the cave at the end of the world. It was broken by a small, weaselly voice, saying 'Absatively.'

It started to say, 'Oww!' but the noise was suddenly and effectively silenced.

And then there was nothing in that place but the sound of crunching.

* * *

The thing they don't tell you about coffins in the literature, because frankly it's not much of a selling point to the people who are buying them, is just how comfortable they are.

Mr Nancy was extremely satisfied with his coffin. Now that all the excitement was over, he'd gone back to his coffin, and was comfortably dozing. Every once in a while he would wake and remember where he was, then he'd roll over and go back to sleep.

The grave, as has been pointed out, is a fine place, not to mention a private one, and this is an excellent place to get a little down time. Six feet down, best kind there is. Another twenty years or so, he thought, and he would have to think about getting up.

He opened one eye when the funeral started.

He could hear them up above him: Callyanne Higgler and the Bustamonte woman and the other one, the thin one, not to mention a small horde of grandchildren, great-grandchildren and great-great-grandchildren, all of them sighing and wailing and crying their eyes out for the late Mrs Dunwiddy.

Mr Nancy thought about pushing one hand up through the turf and grabbing Callyanne Higgler's ankle. It was something he'd wanted to do ever since he saw *Carrie* at a drive-in, thirty years earlier, but now the opportunity presented itself, he found himself able to resist the temptation. Honestly, he couldn't be bothered. She'd only scream and have a heart attack and die, and then the damn Garden of Rest would get even more crowded than it already was.

Too much like hard work, anyway. There were good dreams to be dreamed, in the world beneath the soil. *Twenty years*, he thought. *Maybe twenty-five.* By that time, he might even have grandchildren. It's always interesting to see how the grandchildren turn out.

He could hear Callyanne Higgler wailing and carrying on up above him. Then she stopped her sobbing long enough to announce, 'Still. It's not as if she don't have a good life and a long one. That woman's a hundred and three years old when she passes from us.'

'Hunnert and four!' said an irritated voice from under the ground beside him.

Mr Nancy reached one insubstantial arm out and tapped the new coffin sharply on the side. 'Keep it down, there, woman,' he barked. 'Some of us is tryin' to sleep.'

                        * * *

Rosie had made it clear to Spider that she expected him to get a steady job, the kind that involved getting up in the morning and going somewhere.

So one morning the day before Rosie was to be discharged from the hospital, Spider got up early and went down to the town library. He logged on to the library computer, sauntered on to the internet and, very carefully, cleared out all Grahame Coats's remaining bank accounts, the ones that the police forces of several continents had so far failed to find. He arranged for the stud farm in Argentina to be sold. He bought a small, off-the-peg company, endowed it with the money, and applied for charitable status. He sent off an e-mail, in the name of Roger Bronstein, hiring a lawyer to administer the foundation's business, and suggested that the lawyer might wish to seek out Miss Rosie Noah, late of London, currently of Saint Andrews, and hire her to Do Good.

Rosie was hired. Her first task was to find office space.

Following this, Spider spent four full days walking (and, at nights, sleeping on) the beach that circled most of the island, tasting the food in each of the dining establishments he encountered along the way until he came to Dawson's Fish Shack. He tried the fried flying fish, the boiled green figs, the grilled chicken and the coconut pie, then he went back into the kitchen and found the chef, who was also the owner, and offered him money enough for partnership and cooking lessons.

Dawson's Fish Shack is now a restaurant, and Mr Dawson has retired. Sometimes Spider's out front and sometimes he's back in the kitchen: you go down there and look for him, you'll see him. The food is the best on the island. He's fatter than he used to be, though not as fat as he'll wind up if he keeps tasting everything he cooks.

Not that Rosie minds.

She does some teaching, and some helping out, and a lot of Doing Good, and if she ever misses London she never lets it show. Rosie's mother, on the other hand, misses London continually and vocally, but takes any suggestion that she might want to return there as an attempt to part her from her as-yet-unborn (and, for that matter, unconceived) grandchildren.

Nothing would give this author greater pleasure than to be able to assure you that, following her return from the valley of the shadow of death, Rosie's mother became a new person, a jolly woman with a kind word for everyone, that her new-found appetite for food was only matched by her appetite for life and all it had to offer. Alas, respect for the truth compels perfect honesty and the truth is that when she came out of hospital Rosie's mother was still herself, just as suspicious and uncharitable as ever, although significantly more frail, and now given to sleeping with the light on.

She announced that she would be selling her flat in London and would move to wherever in the world Spider and Rosie were, to be near her grandchildren; and, as time went on, she would drop pointed comments about the lack of grandchildren, the quantity and motility of Spider's spermatozoa, the frequency and positions of Spider and Rosie's sexual relations and the relative cheapness and ease of *in vitro* fertilisation, to the point where Spider seriously began to think about not going to bed with Rosie any more, just to spite Rosie's mother. He thought about this for about eleven seconds one afternoon, while Rosie's mother was handing them photocopies of an article from a magazine that she had found which suggested that Rosie should stand on her head for half an hour after sex; and he mentioned these thoughts to

Rosie that night, and she laughed, and told him that her mother wasn't allowed in their bedroom anyway, and that she wasn't going to be standing on her head after making love for anybody.

Mrs Noah has a flat in Williamstown, near Spider and Rosie's house, and twice a week one of Callyanne Higgler's many nieces looks in on her, does the vacuuming, dusts the glass fruit (the wax fruit melted in the island heat), and makes a little food and leaves it in the fridge, and sometimes Rosie's mum eats it and sometimes she doesn't.

* * *

Charlie's a singer these days. He's lost a lot of the softness. He's a lean man, now, with a trademark fedora hat. He has lots of different fedoras, in different colours; his favourite one is green.

Charlie has a son. His name is Marcus: he is four and a half, and possesses that deep gravity and seriousness that only small children and mountain gorillas have ever been able to master.

Nobody ever calls Charlie 'Fat Charlie' any more, and honestly, sometimes he misses it.

It was early in the morning in the summer, and it was already light. There was already noise coming from the room next door. Charlie let Daisy sleep. He climbed out of bed quietly, grabbed a T-shirt and shorts, and went through the door, to see his son naked on the floor playing with a small wooden train set. Together they pulled on their T-shirts and shorts and flip-flops, and Charlie put on a hat, and they walked down to the beach.

'Daddy?' said the boy. His jaw was set, and he seemed to be pondering something.

'Yes, Marcus?'

'Who was the shortest president?'

'You mean in height?'

'No. In, in days. Who was the shortest?'

'Harrison. He caught pneumonia during his inauguration and died. He was president for forty-something days, and he spent most of his time in office dying.'

'Oh. Well, who was the longest then?'

'Franklin Delano Roosevelt. He served three full terms. Died in office during his fourth. We'll take off our shoes here.'

They placed their shoes on a rock, carried on walking down towards the waves, their toes digging into the damp sand.

'How do you know so much about presidents?'

'Because my father thought it would do me good to find out about them, when I was a kid.'

'Oh.'

They waded out into the water, making for a boulder, one that could only be seen at low tide. After a while, Charlie picked the boy up and let him ride on his shoulders.

'Daddy?'

'Yes, Marcus.'

'P'choona says you're famous.'

'And who's Petunia?'

'At playgroup. She says her mom has all your CDs. She says she loves your singing.'

'Ah.'

'*Are* you famous?'

'Not really. A little bit.' He put Marcus down on the top of the boulder, then he clambered up it himself. 'OK. Ready to sing?'

'Yes.'

'What do you want to sing?'

'My favourite song.'

'I don't know if she'll like that one.'

'She will.' Marcus had the certainty of walls, of mountains.

'OK. One, two, three . . .'

They sang 'Yellow Bird' together, which was Marcus's favourite song that week, and then they sang 'Zombie Jamboree', which was his second favourite, and 'She'll Be Coming Round the Mountain', which was his third favourite. Marcus, whose eyes were better than Charlie's, spotted her as they were finishing 'She'll Be Coming Round the Mountain' and he began to wave.

'There she is, Daddy.'

'Are you sure?'

The morning haze blurred the sea and sky together into a pale whiteness, and Charlie squinted at the horizon. 'I don't see anything.'

'She's gone under the water. She'll be here soon.'

There was a splash, and she surfaced immediately below them; with a reach and a flip and a wiggle she was sitting on the rock beside them, her silvery tail dangling down into the Atlantic, flicking beads of water up on to her scales. She had long, orange-red hair.

They all sang together now, the man and the boy and the mermaid. They sang 'The Lady Is a Tramp' and 'Yellow Submarine' and then Marcus taught the mermaid the words to *The Flintstones* theme song.

'He reminds me of you,' she said to Charlie, 'when you were a little boy.'

'You knew me then?'

She smiled. 'You and your father used to walk down the beach, back then. Your father,' she said. 'He was quite some gentleman.' She sighed. Mermaids sigh better than anyone. Then she said, 'You should go back now. The tide's coming in.' She pushed her long hair back, and jack-knifed into the ocean. She raised her head above the waves, touched her fingertips to her lips, and blew Marcus a kiss before vanishing under the water.

Charlie put his son on to his shoulders and he waded through the sea, back to the beach, where his son slipped down from his shoulders on to the sand. He took off his old fedora hat and placed it on his son's head. It was much too big for the boy, but it still made him smile.

'Hey,' said Charlie, 'you want to see something?'

'OK. But I want breakfast. I want pancakes. No, I want oatmeal. No, I want pancakes.'

'Watch this.' Charlie began to do a sand-dance in his bare feet, soft-shoe shuffling through the sand.

'I can do that,' said Marcus.

'Really?'

'Watch me, Daddy.' He could, too.

Together the man and the boy danced their way back up the sand to the house, singing a wordless song that they made up as they went along, and which lingered in the air even after they had gone in for breakfast.

Acknowledgments

To begin with, an enormous bunch of flowers to Nalo Hopkinson, who kept a helpful eye on the Caribbean dialogue and not only told me what I needed to fix but suggested ways to fix it; and also to Lenworth Henry, who was there on the day I made it all up, and whose voice I heard in the back of my head when I was writing it (which is why I was delighted to hear that he would be narrating the audio book).

As with my last adult novel, *American Gods*, I was given two boltholes while I was writing this novel. I started writing it in Tori's spare house in Ireland, and I finished it there as well. She is a most gracious hostess and was this novel's shoe consultant. At one point in the middle, hurricanes permitting, I worked in Jonathan and Jane's spare house in Florida. It's a good thing to have friends with more houses than they have bodies, especially if they're happy to share. Most of the rest of the time I wrote in the local coffee house, and drank cup after cup of terrible tea in a rather pathetic demonstration of hope over experience.

Roger Forsdick and Graeme Baker gave up their time to answer my questions about the police, and fraud, and extradition treaties, while Roger also showed me around the cells, fed me dinner and looked over the finished manuscript. I'm very grateful.

Sharon Stiteler kept an eye on the book to make sure the birds passed muster and she answered my birding questions. Pam Noles was the first person to read any of the book, and her responses kept me going. There was a small host of other people who lent me their eyes and minds and opinions, including Olga Nunes, Colin Greenland, Giorgia Grilli, Anne Bobby, Peter Straub, John M. Ford, Anne Murphy and Paul Kinkaid, Bill Stiteler and Dan and Michael Johnson. Errors of fact or of opinion are mine, not theirs.

Thanks also go to Ellie Wylie; Thea Gilmore; The Ladies of

Lakeside; to Miss Holly Gaiman who turned up to help whenever she decided I needed a sensible daughter around; to the Petes of Hill House Publications; to Michael Morrison, Lisa Gallagher, Jack Womack and Julia Bannon; and to Dave McKean.

Jennifer Brehl, my editor at Morrow, was the person who persuaded me that the story I told her over lunch that day really would make a good novel, at a time when I really wasn't sure what the next novel was going to be, and she sat patiently when I phoned her up one night and read her the first third of the book. For these things alone she should be sainted. Jane Morpeth at Headline is the kind of editor writers hope to get if they're very good and eat all their vegetables. Merrilee Heifetz at Writers House, with the assistance of Ginger Clark, and, in the UK, Dorie Simmonds are my literary agents. I'm lucky to have them all on my side, and I know just how lucky I am.

Jon Levin keeps the world of movies running for me. My assistant Lorraine helped keep me writing and made really good cups of tea.

I don't think I could have written Fat Charlie without having had both an excellent but embarrassing father and wonderful but embarrassed children. Hurrah for families.

And a final thank you to something that didn't exist when I wrote *American Gods*: to the readers of the journal at www.neil gaiman.com, who were always there whenever I needed to know anything, and who, between them all, as far as I can tell, know everything there is to be known.

Neil Gaiman, June 2005